THE FARRINGFORD CADENZA

Other books by Robert D. Sutherland

Language and Lewis Carroll

Sticklewort and Feverfew
A novel (with 74 pencil illustrations by the author);
received the **Friends of American Writers**
1981 Juvenile Book Merit Award for author/illustrator

THE FARRINGFORD CADENZA
is a work in the tradition of the following:

THE EIGER SANCTION
THE HOLCROFT COVENANT
THE DA VINCI CODE
THE SCARLATTI INHERITANCE
THE EUSTACE DIAMONDS
THE WAPSHOT CHRONICLE
THE BOURNE IDENTITY
THE CHANCELLOR MANUSCRIPT
THE IPCRESS FILE
THE MUSGRAVE RITUAL
THE MATARESE CIRCLE
THE DAIN CURSE
THE BRASHER DOUBLOON
THE SOTWEED FACTOR
THE LAZARUS VENDETTA
THE CASSANDRA COMPACT
THE DISNEY VERSION
and
THE PETER PRINCIPLE

If you enjoy **THE FARRINGFORD CADENZA**,
you'd probably like other N. F. Trntl mysteries also:

THE ESHOBI TRUNCTURE
THE SNODGRASS STYCHMODIUM
THE HALLERELLI PÚCERON

THE FARRINGFORD CADENZA

A Novel

by

Robert D. Sutherland

The PIKESTAFF PRESS

Library of Congress Control Number: 2006933874

ISBN: 978-0-936044-08-8

Published by

The PIKESTAFF PRESS
P.O. BOX 127
Normal, Illinois 61761

e-mail: staff@pikestaffpress.com

Cover: *design,* © Robert D. Sutherland 2007;
electronic pre-press, Carl Burton

Printed on permanent/durable acid-free paper
and bound in the United States of America.

The Farringford Cadenza is dedicated with thanks to the memory of two remarkable, gifted friends: J. W. Rivers *and* Will Leinicke

I also wish to thank the following:

City of Baltimore Department of Parks & Monuments, Mike and Mary Jane Brunt, Terry and Sue Cain, Jolene Eatherly, Eileen FitzGerald, Manon Getsi, Matt Haller, Charles Harris, Robert Hathway, Dorothy Kennett, members of the Killinger family: Bill, Joleen, Ed, and Libby Killinger Chavez; Monty Python, J. D. Scrimgeour, James R. Scrimgeour, Ellen and Ralph Smith, David Staniford, members of the Sutherland family: Allan, Bhavani, David, Jennifer, Marilyn; Tom Tcheng, Arnold Tracy, Drake Zimmerman, The English Department at Illinois State University, and the many writers (too numerous to list) both present and departed whom I've read, enjoyed, admired, and learned from over many years and whose works have helped to establish the themes and conventions of mystery, intrigue, and suspense fiction upon which infinite variations can be composed and played.

PROLOGUE

I

October 18, 1947

As the train slows to a crawl for its scheduled stop at Bristow, Pennsylvania, its cars glide like dark coffins past the lights spaced evenly on poles along the station platform. Eight coaches back from the locomotive, the window of a particular sleeping compartment presents a blank and staring eye to the lights as they tick rhythmically past. Each, in its turn, briefly illuminates the table just inside the window—the highball glasses and overflowing ashtray—the formal dress-suit, with tailed coat, hanging on the wall—the rumpled bed—the body on the bed.

When the train has chuffed to a halt with a rumbling shudder and hissing of steam, a light-pole stands directly opposite the window. Should anyone look in—that porter, say, trundling past with his baggage cart—he'd see, starkly displayed among the tangled bedclothes, a man of middle-age—lean, angular, face-up and stretched full-length in striped pajamas. Left arm bent across the chest; right flung far aside to hang in space. Dark chestnut hair just slightly streaked with gray. Face like putty, gone to sag; backward tilted, mouth agape; eyes slitted upward with a jellied stare.

A closer look: the pajama shirt is wrongly buttoned, the trousers twisted awkwardly askew and backside front.

Three cars forward—bundled in a heavy coat and carrying two suitcases—a passenger descends from the train, maneuvers past three men waiting to board, deftly evades the porter, and strides quickly into the station. The waiting room clock reads 3:17.

Passengers aboard, steam shrouds the platform, and with a slight jolt that rocks the body's head upon the pillow, the train begins to move. Slowly at first, then ever more quickly, the compartment flickers bright and dark as lights flash past the window. A water tower; sheds; the open country. And, settled into coursing speed, trailing a smoke-plume over its long cortege of somber cars, the engine churns eastward through the Pennsylvania hills, bearing the body, in darkness total, across the night.

2

II

From *The New York Post-Inquirer* (October 18, 1947):

BULLETIN
Charles Philip Farringford, noted American composer and concert pianist, died late last night
while traveling from Cleveland,
Ohio to his home in New York.
He had just concluded a successful concert tour of three cities
in which he performed his recently completed but as yet unpublished Fifth Piano Concerto.
He was 46. An obituary will
follow in the morning edition.

From *The New York Daily Chronicle* (October 20, 1947):

FARRINGFORD CADENZA MISSING!
The manuscript of the cadenza of Charles Philip
Farringford's Fifth Piano Concerto, which disappeared at the time of his death two days ago, has
not been recovered. The cadenza is a six-minute
piano solo in the concerto's fourth movement.

Farringford, one of America's foremost composers and concert pianists, died on a train while
returning to New York from a tour in which he
performed his recently completed Fifth Concerto
in St. Louis, Chicago, and Cleveland. Presumably
he had the cadenza manuscript with him when he
boarded the train in Cleveland, for he intended
to deliver it to his publishers upon reaching New
York.

Although Farringford's death is ascribed to
natural causes and no foul play is suspected, when
the train bearing his body arrived at Pennsylvania
Station, neither his luggage nor the cadenza was
found. Despite an intensive search by railroad au-

thorities and police in New York and Cleveland, no trace of the cadenza has been discovered. Farringford's publisher, Norton Lunner, president of the firm Lunner & Dinch, has offered a reward for information leading to the manuscript's recovery. In a press conference today, he said that the cadenza is "the capstone of the concerto, and—by all accounts from those who heard it performed in the three concerts—probably some of the finest piano music that Farringford wrote." The firm intends to publish the Fifth Concerto as originally planned. If the cadenza is not recovered, a blank will be left in the score at the spot where it should occur. "We must do everything in our power to find the manuscript," Lunner said. "Loss of the cadenza would be one of the greatest tragedies in the history of music."

From "Knowing the Score" by Chesney Fleischauer in **Music, Maestro!** *Magazine* (May 19, 1948):

Of special note to the musical world is the publication this week of the long-awaited *Fifth Piano Concerto* of Charles Philip Farringford. Lunner & Dinch, the firm which has had exclusive rights to publish Farringford's works since 1934, has provided the world in this, the composer's final composition, not only a modern masterpiece, but what well may prove to be Farringford's crowning achievement. I do not speak lightly. My faithful readers well know my loathing of hyperbole, my caution in bestowing praise. They know how stringent my standards are, how discriminating my taste. Be advised, then, that having studied the score in pre-publication copy, I can promise that you will be astounded, overwhelmed, utterly enthralled when you hear this concerto performed by Rubinstein, Brailowsky, Lipatti, Serkin, or Myra Hess.

Unfortunately, the cadenza which Farringford wrote to be performed in the fourth movement, the manuscript of which disappeared at the time of his death last October, has alas! not been recovered and is thus of necessity omitted in the present version. A bitter loss! In the face of such exquisite beauty as the concerto embodies, the cadenza's absence gaps like a missing tooth in an otherwise dazzling smile. We can only hope that the cadenza will subsequently come to light to be included in a future edition.

Immediately prior to his untimely death, when Farringford performed the concerto for audiences in three midwestern cities, the solo and orchestral parts were available in galley proofs. But the cadenza existed only in a single manuscript which Farringford kept with him for revising prior to publication. All those lucky ones who heard Farringford perform the cadenza testify uniformly that the experience was unlike anything they had encountered previously—indescribably exalting and unutterably sublime. I myself have interviewed thirty-eight of these fortunate individuals, and all of them—*without exception*—assert that hearing Farringford play the cadenza was one of the climactic moments of their lives. Some refuse to say more than this; they simply smile and maddeningly denote the nature of the experience "a private matter." Others, less reticent, try to be forthcoming but find language simply not adequate to describe the quality of the experience. Twenty-two assured me that hearing the cadenza was a watershed event that marked a turning point in their lives. Obviously, those privileged few—how many altogether?—1,000? 1,500? 3,000?—have shared an event that already has acquired legendary—yes, even mythic stature; they are uniquely fortunate in knowing the cadenza, and Farringford's playing of it, if only in their collective memories.

How can the rest of us not envy them? We can only wonder, speculate, and grieve our loss. Oh, such a *bitter* pill! While Farringford was performing for those midland audiences—in St. Louis, *Chicago*, *CLEVELAND!*— I—*I* was visiting cousins in Philadelphia!

III

February 28, 1981   (Saturday)

The dozen people emerging from the side door of Symphony Hall did not linger on the sidewalk for long goodbyes. The five-hour board meeting had been irksome, rancorous, filled with invective and circular debate. The delicatessen food catered in at six was of such poor quality that eating it only increased their tension. Cocooned in the over-heated conference room, they were unaware that a major front had moved into the city; and thus, at eight, when they finally adjourned and escaped to the street, the cold met them like a fist. There was a rush to their waiting cars, a slamming of doors, a settling back in warm interiors.

While Morgan Latimer sank gratefully into the cushions, Victor Zyzynski slid open the glass panel behind the front seat and said, "To the Club, Marco." The driver nodded and eased the limousine into the flow of traffic.

Zyzynski took a large cigar from a platinum case, nipped its end with a miniature gold guillotine fished from his vest pocket, lit up, and inhaled deeply. With a grunt of fatigue, he too leaned back against the cushions. He was immensely fat, his face broad as a rump roast, with plump puffy jowls and a triple chin. "Thank God these meetings only come three times a year!" he muttered. "Today's was a waste of everybody's time."

Without opening his eyes, Morgan Latimer smoothed his white mustache and nodded tiredly. "Maybe we're just getting too old to find pleasure in it, Victor."

Zyzynski snorted a billow of blue smoke. "Speak for yourself. The problem with the board is lack of will and vision. How to cure an ailing orchestra? Get a new Musical Director. Fire Mitchell. But rather than face it head on, they go round and round, avoiding the obvious, preferring to pussyfoot, and find excuses, and sit on their thumbs. I could take pleasure in the process if it weren't for all the inaction." Morgan did seem unusually done-in tonight, his face pale and shrunken above his fur collar. With his dry skin stretched taut over pointed cheekbones, and the bridge of his nose arched razor-thin, he looked as fragile as a Dresden teacup.

"Well, you're only sixty-five," said Latimer. "I'm eighty-two come June, and *I'm* too old for it. This will be my last term on the board. I'm tired of hassling budgets, drumming up subscriptions, farting around with the damn unions. But I agree we should dump Mitchell." He shook his head and managed a wry smile. "Six years ago, I thought you were wrong when you voted against hiring him. But you were right. You saw farther than any of us, Victor."

Zyzynski triumphantly exhaled another cloud of smoke. "His contract's up for renewal after this season. If I made a motion not to rehire him, would it carry?"

Latimer yawned. "Hard to say. I'd vote for it. I think Kennedy would. And maybe Mrs. Sternberg."

The car angled in to the curb. Zyzynski slid back the panel. "Wait in the garage, Marco. I'll call down when I want to leave. And tell Mr. Latimer's driver that we're here."

Marco nodded. The two men left the car and hurried through plate-glass doors into a thickly-carpeted lobby, oak-paneled and hung round with portraits in ponderous gilt frames. The elevator operator was a white-haired man in a maroon uniform with decorous gold buttons. "Good evening, gentlemen. Shall I take you to the sauna?"

Latimer shook his head. "Not tonight, Selden. Please take us to the fourth floor lounge."

As the elevator rose, Latimer pursued his train of thought, fatigue giving his voice a querulous edge: "Look at the programming we've had this season. Nothing but nineteenth century crap. Niedermann for guest conductor!—what else but Beethoven? Aaronson with the Brahms Violin Concerto—futzy old chestnut! Rena Fracetti-Mousse pummeling Puccini! And coming up in two weeks, Piano Night, with Miss Rosamond Foxe doing her thing with Rachmaninoff's Second."

"Farringford's Second," Zyzynski said.

"My point is," said Latimer, "that it's no wonder we're not gaining subscribers. Truthfully now, does any of that turn you on?"

Though Zyzynski would never have admitted it to Latimer (or anyone else), he was turned on very much indeed by Rosamond Foxe. Not only by her playing of Farringford (and the other composers she interpreted so brilliantly—Rachmaninoff, Prokofiev, Ravel, Bartok, Beach), but by her arms, ears, legs, breasts, teeth, hips, thighs, and lustrous raven hair. Her smoky-topaz eyes danced with intelligence and good humor. Her smile (he'd observed it close-up on several occasions) would have closed the Stock Exchange in the thick of business. Just watching her cross the stage to the piano was enough to set his pulse jumping. His opera-glasses, fixed unwavering, brought Zyzynski intense private joy in the deft flight of her fingers, the gleam of saliva as she moistened her lips, the sinewy, smooth muscularity of her wrists. During the five years since she'd won the International Farringford Competition at age twenty-one, he'd followed her career with intense, almost proprietary zeal.

"It's not all nineteenth century crap," he said to Latimer. "*Foxe* plays lots of twentieth-century stuff."

But Latimer wasn't listening. "And what's scheduled for next season? More of the same. Hirschfeld on the cello; Albert Nicodemus as guest conductor—*if* we can get him (and I hope we can't!); Neeta Blessingham on the clarinet with (good Lord!) the Mozart concerto. Poop poop a doop. The only bright spot is Piano Night with Peter Shipley Abbott."

Abbott! *Pompous little turd*, thought Zyzynski. They stepped from the elevator onto a rich burgundy carpet; and, after leaving their overcoats in an adjacent cloakroom, sank exhaustedly into deep leather chairs. A balding man in maroon and gold materialized beside them. "Good evening, gentlemen. Would you like something from the bar?"

"Thank you, Meadows," said Latimer. "A brandy and water, please."

"The usual," said Zyzynski, still thinking of Rosamond Foxe. "And something to eat: a club sandwich, I think—with lots of mayonnaise—and a large lobster salad."

Meadows nodded. "Brandy and water; whiskey sour. I'll bring a table with the food. Have you gentlemen seen today's editions?" He wheeled up a display rack containing various newspapers.

"Thank you," said Latimer. "No, we've been in a daylong meeting. Had the end of the world come, I'm afraid we would've missed it."

Meadows smiled dutifully—"Very amusing, sir."—and went to fill their orders.

Zyzynski opened his paper to the financial section. Latimer unfolded his in his lap and glanced idly at the front page. Then, with a sharp gasp, he snatched the paper closer to his eyes. "Oh my God, Victor! Look at this!" He rattled the page in Zyzynski's face. "They've found the Farringford Cadenza!"

Zyzynski batted the paper away and followed Latimer's trembling finger. The story was centered at the bottom:

FARRINGFORD CADENZA FOUND!

BALTIMORE (AP)—The manuscript containing the cadenza of Charles Philip Farringford's Fifth Piano Concerto, assumed lost or destroyed since its disappearance thirty-four years ago, has been discovered in a Baltimore secondhand shop.

Announcing the discovery at a press conference late yesterday afternoon, Dr. Theodore Pettigrew, Professor of Music History at the Hastings Institute, claimed the recovery of the cadenza to be a musical event of the first importance.

"Farringford's Fifth Concerto is regarded as one of the greatest piano works of the 20th century," he said. "The missing six-minute cadenza for solo piano which occurs in the fourth movement has long had legendary status as the most moving and brilliant music that Farringford wrote. Discovery of the cadenza in Farringford's autograph manuscript restores to music-lovers everywhere one of the finest piano compositions ever written," Pettigrew said.

The cadenza had never been published or recorded. It was publicly performed by the composer on three occasions in 1947, immediately before his death, at age 46, on a train en route from Cleveland to New York. Though it is assumed that he was in possession of the cadenza at the time of his death, no trace of the manuscript, or of his luggage, was found.

After an intensive search failed to disclose the whereabouts of the manuscript, the Fifth Concerto was published in 1948 by Lunner & Dinch, Inc. of New York, in an edition that left a blank spot in the score where the cadenza would have been featured.

An extremely popular concerto, Farringford's Fifth is frequently heard in concert. Performers have been forced to improvise their own cadenzas to fill the gap left in the published version. "Now improvisation will no longer be required," said Dr. Pettigrew.

After studying the manuscript, he plans to hand it over to Lunner & Dinch for publication. "Since Farringford was going to deliver the cadenza to them when he reached New York," Pettigrew said, "it's only fitting that they should be the firm to publish it." But first he plans to make a detailed study of the score. "It's a rare privilege," he said, "to be the first scholar to examine the manuscript of what, by all accounts, may be Farringford's finest piano writing."

Pettigrew himself was not one of those who heard the cadenza performed. He said that he counts that as one of the great disappointments of his life. "But now it will be available for everyone. It's a priceless find," he said.

The cadenza was discovered yesterday afternoon by Stephanie Simms, a student of Dr. Pettigrew's at the Hastings Institute. She found it by accident in the bottom of an old piano bench in a secondhand store whose owner prefers the shop not be identified. Miss Simms said, "I knew the manuscript was that of a lengthy piano composition, and I gave it to Dr. Pettigrew thinking that he might find it interesting. I had no idea that it was so important and valuable."

Silas Dinch, publisher of the Fifth Concerto, said when contacted, "We're amazed and delighted. A new edition of the concerto will be published at the earliest opportunity."

When he looked up, Zyzynski was startled to see Latimer hunched forward, eyes wide, staring blankly into space. "So it finally turned up," Zyzynski said, knocking ash from his cigar. "I remember Farringford's death, and the fuss the press kicked up over his missing cadenza. I was thirty-one at the time—in Costa Rica, concluding my takeover of Amalgamated Fruit."

No response. Zyzynski reached out and poked Latimer's arm. "What's wrong? Aren't you feeling well?"

The vague, unfocused eyes turned toward him; and slowly, as though he didn't trust the steadiness of his voice, Latimer whispered "I heard Farringford play the cadenza at the Cleveland concert." He gave each word equal emphasis, letting each pass his lips only reluctantly, as though it were a precious talisman, the token of a memory too sacred to trust to normal speech. "The—very—last—performance." Zyzynski stared at him through a cloud of smoke. Latimer had lapsed into silence, his eyes closed, a faint smile playing about his lips. Zyzynski grew impatient.

"It must have been impressive," he said drily.

"It was—sublime," said Latimer. And this time as he spoke, his eyes seemed to ignite with an inner flame. "Oh, Victor, I can't begin to tell you how beautiful the music was! I—oh, it was just absolutely—I—I'd never, ever experienced anything like it." He shook his head. "And never again. Oh, it's hopeless. Hopeless. You just can't imagine—"

"No," said Zyzynski. "I can't." He'd never seen Latimer so staggered, so off-base, so out of control. He didn't like it at all.

Meadows returned, wheeling a table containing the drinks and Zyzynski's food. Zyzynski began crunching the potato chips that accompanied the club sandwich. Latimer seized his brandy and downed it in one gulp. Then, gripping the glass in both hands to stop their trembling, he continued in a shaky voice:

"I was forty-eight. Just been made a full partner in the firm. After the performance, my wife and I left the concert hall in a daze and wandered for—oh, it must have been three hours. Seeing nothing. Not talking. Oblivious to where we were and where we went. Alive only to the cadenza. Reliving it. Hearing it again, playing over and over in our heads." He paused, as though mustering his strength, and took a deep breath. "Even now I can sometimes remember it—not often, and only just a little. Not the music itself, but what it was like to have heard the music. I dream about it sometimes. There I am in the dark concert hall, Bertha beside me—Farringford up on the lighted stage—the audience hushed and stunned. But then I wake up, and it's gone, and all I have is the memory of the dream—the music just a ghost of the ghost of an echo. Glorious!"

Zyzynski frowned. This was not the Latimer he knew. Where was the hard-headed stock-broker, the rock-ribbed Goldwater Republican who could be upset only by something the magnitude of October 1929 or the revelations of Watergate? He found this unwonted display irritating in the extreme, and faintly disgusting. "You make it sound like a religious experience," he snapped, his mouth full of lobster salad. "Or something sexual."

"Well, yes," said Latimer. "I think it *was*. Both of those. You know I'm not a religious man, Victor—and I wasn't then. But what I experienced that night made me *want* to be. And as for the other, yes: it *was* sexual. The entire audience was feeling it—a kind of orgasmic sharing. Do you know what I mean?"

"No," said Zyzynski.

Latimer shook his head sadly. "No, of course you couldn't, since you didn't experience it. Six minutes, Victor. Six endless minutes at the peak! And that night, when we got back to the ho-tel—" he paused for a moment, considering, then plunged ahead "—well,—and this is in confidence, you understand—I've never told anyone else—before that night, I hadn't been able to make love to my wife for over eight years. It wasn't her fault; I'd been having—uh—performance problems. But, Victor, *that* night, after hearing the cadenza, there was no problem at all!"

Zyzynski gagged on the lobster, set down his fork, and took a long swig of his drink. He shifted uneasily in the chair and wiped his mouth.

"And then, the next day," Latimer continued, not noticing Zyzynski's discomfort, "the news came that Farringford was dead, and the cadenza missing! Oh, it was awful!" The memory brought a tremor into his voice which he had to struggle to control. "And after that," he concluded hastily, "I wasn't able to perform for a year and a half."

Darkly flushed, Zyzynski's face had swelled to the tautness of an overripe plum. He squirmed around in his seat to face away from Latimer and wheezed out a strangled guffaw: "No lead in the pencil, huh?"

"That's right," said Latimer. "And when that dark period passed, I could make love only on those rare occasions when the memory of the cadenza was very strong. Just remembering that night in Cleveland would make it possible!" From the corner of his eye Zyzynski could see, beneath the thin pale skin on the back of the old man's hand, the blue veins bulging urgently.

Latimer suddenly chugged down his chaser and leaped out of his chair. "I'm sorry, Victor. I can't stay sitting any longer. I've got to get home and share the good news with Bertha." Humming softly, eyes shining, mustache abristle, he straightened his tie. "And I'll have to call Silas Dinch and congratulate him on recovering the cadenza."

"I didn't know you knew him," said Zyzynski.

"Since he was a schoolboy. I used to play golf with his father." He threw back his head and burst out with a great laugh. "I just can't believe that I'll get to hear it again!"

"Lucky you," Zyzynski growled acidly. Without taking his eyes from Latimer's radiant face, he viciously stubbed out his cigar. "*I* was not one of the fortunate few."

"Well, now you'll have your chance," said Latimer. "Of course, nothing will ever match Farringford's performance of it. And that's a pity. But the *music* will be available for *everyone's* enjoyment!" He smiled and pointed. "Why, Victor, you're as excited as I am. You've put out your cigar in your whiskey sour!"

He crossed the room with a bouncing gait, playfully punched the waiter's arm in passing, and said with a wink: "Meadows, be a good fellow and meet me in the cloakroom with two bottles of our very best champagne!"

Zyzynski glared after him, his dark eyebrows gathered into a ferocious thunderhead. No, Zyzynski had *not* been one of the fortunate few. He sat for a moment staring at his ruined drink, then—gnawing angrily at his lower lip—carefully spread out the paper and began re-reading the news from Baltimore—slowly, word by word.

Chapter 1

March 1, 1981   (Sunday)

Rapping a second time with the heavy knocker, Trntl asked, "Are you sure this is the right house?"

"It's the right address," said Felix, huddled deep into his over-coat against the wind from Central Park. "And it's just six, so we're on time." He'd planned to spend the evening with friends in SoHo, not freeze his butt on the stoop of a prospective client who, refusing to discuss his business on the phone, had said only that the skills of a *very* private investigator were required on "an extremely sensitive matter"; that N. F. Trntl Associates had been highly recommended. Could they come?

The office rent said, yes they could. And here they were, on a Sunday night, facing the solid door of a tall brownstone in the East 80's.

As Trntl was about to knock again, the door abruptly opened; and a large man having in silhouette the appearance of a pear-shaped dufflebag stood peering at them through gold wire-rims. He saw before him a tallish woman of 36 or -7 with glasses, short blond hair, a mouth too small, a nose far too large, and steady green eyes. Beside her, a bearded man of medium height with a red stocking cap pulled over his ears. After a moment's hesitation, he fixed on the beard: "N. F. Trntl?"

"No, I'm Felix McKay, an Associate. *This* is N. F. Trntl."

She extended her hand. "Mr. Dinch?"

"No, he's inside with the others. I'm Anton Farringford." He grasped her hand warmly, holding it longer and more snugly than she found comfortable. "I apologize for assuming that you were Mr. McKay—that is, that he was N. F. Trntl. I—well, I guess I was expecting you to be a *man*."

"That happens frequently," said Trntl, withdrawing her hand with some difficulty. "The price I pay for using my initials in what's generally assumed to be a male profession. But who, after all, would want to hire a private investigator named Nasturtia Fanny Trntl?"

He smiled uneasily. "Um. Yes, I see what you mean. A professional necessity. Now, in my line of work—investment banking—names don't matter so much. My father named me Anton—for either Rubinstein or Bruckner. I'm not sure which. Though I don't much care for it, the name hasn't affected my work at all." Yes, her nose was too large by half; and if only she'd use darker lip rouge, and more of it, she could turn that prim little prune into a ripely luscious plum. "Nasturtia's a name I've not encountered before," he continued. "But to tell the truth, I've always liked Fanny. I had an aunt in Poughkeepsie—"

Felix coughed and began scraping his shoes loudly on the stoop. Farringford pulled up short. "Of course! You must be getting cold. Come in, please. The others are waiting in the parlor." He bustled them in, hung up their coats, and led them to a closed door that was on the hallway's right as they entered. Trntl judged him to be fifty-five. Possibly fairly good-looking in his youth, before everything had settled, his face had gone so puffy and his hair so thin. Gleaming on the back of his head, a perfectly round bald spot, surrounded by a staunch last stand of chestnut going gray. Striped bowtie, slightly askew. Shapeless gray business suit, shiny in the seat. That he was a banker surprised her; had she seen him passing on the street, she'd have pegged him as a not-very-successful insurance salesman.

High-ceilinged and stuffy-hot, the parlor was crammed with bric-a-brac and maroon plush-nappy furniture from the 1930's. Heavy drapes shrouded the tall windows facing the street. On the left wall as they entered, a log fire blazed beneath a carved white-marble mantelpiece. The five people clustered about the hearth turned their eyes with one accord to study the visitors. Just like prairie dogs, or a stand of meerkats, Trntl thought.

Weighting his words pointedly, Anton Farringford said: "This is N. F. Trntl and her associate, Mr. Felix McKay."

A small man came quickly from the fireplace and shook their hands. "I'm Silas Dinch, president of the music publishers, Lunner & Dinch." Above tobacco-stained teeth his ginger mustache squirmed like a caterpillar. "I called this morning on the recommendation of Henry Gittings, who was amazed last November at how quickly you found his missing daughter and recovered his wife's stolen pearls."

"We try for speedy resolution," said Trntl. (And pray for good luck, she added silently. As with the pearls. When—through her hairdresser—they'd tracked the daughter down and cornered her on the Staten Island Ferry, there was no way they could've known that in her purse she'd be carrying the pawn ticket.)

"Henry didn't tell me you were a woman, however," said Dinch.

"He may not have known it. Mr. McKay and Torvald Grimsson worked on the Gittings case."

"Well, no matter." An impatient wave of dismissal. "Can Mr. McKay or Mr. Grimsson leave for Baltimore tonight?"

"No," said Felix. "I'm scheduled to give a deposition tomorrow. And Mr. Grimsson's in Albany." He eyed the tumbler of whiskey Dinch was clutching and wished he had one, too.

"But we've got to get someone to Baltimore tonight! The Farringford Cadenza's been stolen, and we've got to get it back!"

Ah, thought Trntl. Farringford. Of course. And Dinch on the TV news yesterday, gloating about the manuscript's discovery.

Anton Farringford raised a restraining palm. "Silas, they should meet the others before we go on." And before Dinch could reply, Anton had placed his hand on Trntl's elbow and guided her to an elderly woman sitting by the fire. "This is my mother, Mrs. Charles Philip Farringford. Mother, N. F. Trntl and Mr. McKay."

Mrs. Farringford offered her hand. "Pleased to meet you. You'll pardon me if I don't get up." She patted a cane leaning against her chair. "I turned my ankle on the curb last week, and still feel some pain." Her voice was strong and resonant. Trntl guessed her age at seventy-five, though her makeup was so skillfully applied that in dimmer light she probably could've passed for sixty. But here, in the unflattering glare of an adjacent floorlamp, a network of tiny wrinkles radiated from the corners of her eyes across her high cheekbones to web her lips and chin. Her eyes were alert beneath half-lowered lids. Her thin lips, stretched in a frozen ritual smile, exposed only the edges of her upper teeth. A woman used to having her own way, Trntl decided.

"And I'm pleased to meet *you*, Mr. McKay," Mrs. Farringford added, touching his fingers, her smile thawing to show her upper teeth entire. "Your beard becomes you." She took a cigarette from a silver box on the table beside her, tapped it smartly on the lid, and held it shoulder-high while an elegantly-dressed, much younger man leaned forward from behind to light it. "Thank you, Peter," she said, and deeply inhaled. Unfiltered Turkish ovals, Trntl noted.

But already Anton was squeezing her arm and steering her toward a very old man who was leaning against the mantelpiece and swirling a brandy snifter. "This is Morgan Latimer, a friend of Mr. Dinch. He was present at Father's last concert—the only one of us who's ever heard the cadenza played."

Trntl thought Latimer looked extremely ill. Deepset eyes, sunken cheeks, and papery yellow skin gave him the aspect of an ancient mummy; and she took his small blue-veined hand cautiously, fearing that too vigorous a shake might disintegrate him into flying tatters and scrolls of dust. But his grip was surprisingly strong.

"If you accept our commission," he said, "and succeed in recovering the cadenza, you'll be doing all mankind—the *entire world*, Miss Trntl—a service of incalculable value for which future generations will bless your name. It simply *can't* be lost to us again! I can't begin to describe for you what's at stake." His voice faltered. He drew a shuddering breath and gulped his brandy. Taken aback by his vehemence, by the feverish glint in his eyes and the droplet of foamy spittle clinging to his chin, Trntl found herself speechless, able only to smile vacantly and nod agreement.

"And here," said Anton, giving her elbow another squeeze, "two of our dearest friends, both concert pianists—Peter Shipley Abbott and Rosamond Foxe."

Abbott, who'd lighted Mrs. Farringford's cigarette, was in his forties, square-jawed and deeply tanned (sun-lamp, thought Trntl); simply but expensively dressed in a navy suit with a pearl stickpin in his sky-blue tie—so impeccably and fastidiously groomed that Felix had an immediate urge to muss him up. Arms behind his back, Abbott bowed stiffly from the waist. "I'm delighted to meet you both. Begging your pardon, but I never shake hands." He smiled gravely. "I was six when Charles Farringford died. As a student I found that his works spoke to me as no other composer's did. Consequently, I've devoted my career, in large measure, to understanding, performing, and promoting his music. When I heard the cadenza had been discovered, I was so excited I couldn't sleep. Finally, after thirty-four years, we would know Farringford's last musical thoughts!—would understand why the cadenza was accorded such praise by those who heard it in 1947!"

"Hearing it," said Latimer, "was to have been alive."

Even Felix, whose taste ran more to jazz and bluegrass than to classical piano, knew Abbott's reputation as a Farringford specialist—like Arthur Rubinstein's for interpreting Chopin. And though his record collection held only a few classical titles, he did own Abbott's recording of Farringford's Fifth Concerto—and played it often.

But now Felix was focused on Rosamond Foxe. She was the sort of woman he encountered in his very best dreams. Everything about her was the right size, the right shape, and in the right place. It was as though, in forming Rosamond, Nature had made up for all her past mistakes. Rosamond's smile alone was enough to lift his feet right off the floor. And when she spoke, her voice vibrant with emotion—"We'll do whatever's in our power to help you get the cadenza back"—the lilt of her soft Virginia Tidewater wafted Felix, balloonwise, to bump against the ceiling.

"We're very fond of Rosamond," said Anton, placing his hand on the young woman's shoulder and giving her an affectionate squeeze.

Mrs. Farringford stomped the floor with her cane. "Let's get on with it, Anton. There's a train to catch."

"Right," said Anton, clearing his throat. He indicated where Trntl and Felix should sit. "My sister Clara should be arriving any moment. She's a concert flutist who teaches at the Chadwick Conservatory in Boston, and she's taking a train down to be present at this meeting. Now, Silas, we're ready to begin."

Silas Dinch spoke from the sideboard where he was refilling his whiskey glass. "Two days ago, a music student found the manuscript of Farringford's cadenza in an old piano bench in a Baltimore junkshop. She gave it to a Professor Theodore Pettigrew, who teaches at the Hastings Institute. Late that afternoon Pettigrew called a press conference to announce the cadenza's discovery.

"We at Lunner & Dinch were astonished when we were contacted by the press. Since Charles had intended for us to publish it along with the rest of the Fifth Concerto, we regard the cadenza as rightfully ours. We immediately called Pettigrew to assert our claim before any of our competitors could weasel in to get it for themselves.

"Pettigrew agreed that we should have the cadenza. We made him promise to ignore any approaches made by other publishers.

He said he only wanted time to study the cadenza before turning it over to us, to write an article or something, as the first musicologist to see it.

"We said we were sending Ray Tuttle, one of our vice-presidents, down to inspect the manuscript and scheduled an appointment at Pettigrew's house for nine the next morning—that is to say, *this* morning. We directed Pettigrew to inform the media that he was turning the manuscript over to us. We told him that such an announcement would make his life easier, since he wouldn't be hounded by our competitors. As a double safeguard, we issued our own announcement here and called the Baltimore media as well. They interviewed Pettigrew, and this extended story hit the news last night.

"Late yesterday afternoon, Ray went to Baltimore and checked into a hotel. He wasn't able to meet Pettigrew yesterday evening because the professor had promised to see his son perform in a high school play." Dinch sighed in discouragement and took a sip. "Sometime after midnight the professor's house was burglarized, and when Tuttle arrived this morning at nine, he learned the cadenza had been stolen. Lunner & Dinch, the Farringford family, and Mr. Latimer wish to hire your firm to recover it."

"Was anything else taken in the burglary?" asked Trntl.

"Apparently not, though Pettigrew was a little vague about that. You can ask him yourself when you get to Baltimore."

"Were the police called in to investigate the burglary?" asked Felix.

"Oh yes. Pettigrew was injured in the break-in and treated at the hospital. There was no way he could avoid talking to the police. And the press learned about *that,* too—so of course the theft of the cadenza was all over the television news tonight!" He finished his drink and shook his head angrily. "So now the whole world knows that *we* don't have the cadenza. Not only is Lunner & Dinch publicly humiliated, but all of our competitors will feel free to go on fishing expeditions. Unless, of course, one of them has the manuscript already."

"And the police—?" said Trntl.

"Handling it as a routine burglary. Which means we can't expect *them* to get it back."

The two pianists had been whispering together. Abbott suddenly asked, "Mr. Dinch, didn't Pettigrew make photocopies of the manuscript? That's the first thing he should've done."

"No, he didn't. It's the first thing you or I would've done—but not Pettigrew. He said it didn't *occur* to him."

"Jesus!" said Abbott, slapping his brow.

"And of course," continued Dinch, "when we found he hadn't, we expressly told him not to. We didn't want any extra copies floating about. Ray Tuttle would make copies when he got there."

Trntl asked, "In your first call, did you offer Pettigrew any money for the cadenza?"

Dinch was shocked. "No, it didn't seem appropriate under the circumstances, and Pettigrew never suggested it. He saw it as our rightful property."

"Could someone else have offered to buy it from him?" asked Trntl.

"Certainly. Our chief competitors would pay a great deal to get their hands on it."

Rosamond Foxe said, "Isn't it possible that the burglary was staged to cover up a sale that's already happened?"

"That's a good point," Felix told her; and, turning to Dinch: "And beyond *that* as a possibility, what proof do you have that Pettigrew actually *did* possess the cadenza? Only he and this student claim to have seen the manuscript. Couldn't the discovery be a hoax, and the burglary a fabrication to hide the fact?"

Dinch shook his head impatiently. "In view of the press conference and hospital treatment? No, I think Pettigrew's being injured indicates that he had the cadenza, and that the break-in really did occur. Ray said he was bruised, his head bandaged."

"All right," said Felix, looking up from his yellow note pad, "assuming that Pettigrew's telling the truth, do either you or he have any idea who might have stolen the cadenza, or why?" On a page separate from his notes he'd sketched a likeness of Rosamond's face, accentuating the eyes.

Dinch sighed resignedly and phrased his answer as though explaining a simple math problem to a slow third grader. "Pettigrew doesn't. He's completely baffled. But since nothing but the manuscript seems to have been stolen, it's obvious the bastards knew exactly what they were after, and where to find it. Now, who would have that knowledge and be willing to stoop to burglary and assault to get it? Obviously someone who didn't want *us* to publish the cadenza; who knew, after reading the news accounts, that they had to act quickly before Pettigrew turned it over to us."

"Okay, *who?*" said Felix.

"Who? Why, one of our competitors, of course! Most likely, Humboldt-Hartmann Gesellschaft of Hamburg, for years our chief rival in obtaining exclusive rights to the works of twentieth-century composers. They've got agents everywhere. If not Humboldt-Hartmann, then, I suppose, either L'Enfant Devereux of Paris, B. F. Cleavenger & Sons of Los Angeles, or Cameron Stewart of Edinburgh. And there are others."

"But now that the fact of the theft is public knowledge," Trntl said, "wouldn't it be extremely awkward for any of them to publish the cadenza?"

Dinch gave a loud snort. "Immediately, perhaps. But in several years they could publish it, claiming they'd obtained it from a third party."

"Is it possible," said Felix, "that it isn't one of your competitors at all—but someone who wants to hold the cadenza for ransom?"

"I've thought of that," said Dinch. "But a whole day has gone by, and no one has contacted us."

"Well, then," said Felix, "the thief may be planning to hold an auction and sell it to the highest bidder."

At this, Dinch staggered where he stood. Latimer said, "Silas, don't worry about the money. If we have to buy it back, we'll pay whatever it takes."

The door to the hallway opened, and a tall middle-aged woman came into the room. "Sorry I'm late. We were delayed by the track having to be cleared this side of Bridgeport."

"Well, at least you made it," Anton smiled. "You know Mr. Dinch, I think—and Peter and Rosamond. This is Morgan Latimer, who actually heard Father play the cadenza in Cleveland. And N. F. Trntl, and Felix McKay, private investigators." And to them he said, "My sister Clara—" (for Schumann, no doubt, thought Trntl) "—down from Boston, where she's organizing a music festival."

"Celebrating Arthur Foote," said Clara. "Anton called me at noon to tell me about this meeting, and I barely had time to catch the train." She went to the sideboard; and while she poured and sipped a glass of sherry, Anton gave her a summary of the discussion so far. Trntl studied her with interest, for she'd admired her flute-playing for many years, had heard her in live performance four seasons ago in Philadelphia, and had purchased all three of her recordings.

In her late forties, Clara Farringford had quick observant eyes behind gold-rimmed glasses, and her mother's thin lips and prominent cheekbones. Her chestnut hair was darker than Anton's, and her face considerably leaner. An easy straight-backed posture gave her an air of relaxed tranquility. Trntl could imagine her standing firm in the blast of a hurricane, fluting a Handel gigue without missing a note.

Though Dinch seemed impatient to continue, Trntl wasn't to be hurried. "Going back a bit," she said, "—since Lunner & Dinch has already published the Fifth Concerto, couldn't you sue for infringement of copyright if one of your competitors *did* try to publish the cadenza at some future time?"

Dinch shook his head. "Our legal staff says it's not clear that *anyone* holds the rights to the cadenza. Not Lunner & Dinch, not even the Farringford family. After its having been lost for thirty-four years, legally it doesn't matter whether it was Charles's wish and intention that we should publish the cadenza along with the concerto. Our contract with Charles in 1946 only stipulated the Fifth Concerto. There was no specific mention of the cadenza as a separate piece of music. I suppose a case could be made that it's technically a part of Charles's estate—but even that isn't clear. We don't know why it was missing, or what disposition Charles might have privately made of it before he died. Had he canceled it from the score? Destroyed it? Not likely, but possible. We don't even have proof that it was with him on the train. Had he given the manuscript to someone? Who's to say?"

"Didn't Farringford own the copyright on the concerto?" Felix asked.

"No. In the contract, as always, we purchased it from him outright. It's ours. Since 1934 we'd always owned the copyrights on his works."

"I'd have thought your copyright on the concerto would have covered the cadenza, too," said Trntl.

Dinch was becoming testy. "No, apparently it doesn't. The year after Charles died, we published the entire concerto, copyrighted per contract, leaving a blank spot in the score where the cadenza should have come. But since Charles's cadenza was not part of that publication, *its* copyright never has been claimed or registered. When we renewed the concerto's copyright in 1976, we assumed the cadenza was gone forever. Our legal staff feels that the cadenza has the status of a separate piece of music, independent of the concerto; that whoever publishes it will have sole rights to it under the new copyright law.

"As for ownership of the manuscript, if, after thirty-four years, it turns up in a junkshop, it's unattached and abandoned property: finders keepers. I suppose we could sue if someone published it, but there's no guarantee that we'd win." The whiskey was beginning to slur his speech, and his face had become suffused with a ruddy flush. He took a step backwards, tilted his head to one side and gave the impression, while staring at her, of trying to focus his eyes. "But all that is really beside the point, Miss Trntl. The point is, that if someone else brings out the cadenza, the music will be available to the public, and Lunner & Dinch will be denied first publication *and* copyright."

"Thanks for the clarification," said Trntl. "Now: even if one of your competitors did steal the manuscript from Professor Pettigrew—or comes into possession of it in some other way—wouldn't it be silly to publish the cadenza by itself, detached from the rest of the concerto?"

Dinch set down his empty glass and drew himself up to full height, his mustache pooching outward like a bottle brush. "You still don't seem to understand the importance of the Farringford Cadenza," he said, articulating his words very carefully. "Its publication will be the musical event of the century. All pianists will want a copy. There will be guaranteed sales to generations of piano students. All the major concert artists will want to record the concerto exhibiting *their* playing of Farringford's cadenza." He ran a hand through his hair distractedly. "Oh God, it's awful to conceive! They'd buy the concerto from us, and the cadenza from Humboldt-Hartmann!"

"Or whoever," said Felix, jotting on his pad. "And if *you* had possession of the cadenza—?"

"We'd bring out a new edition of the complete concerto, and register it under the current copyright law."

"Giving *you* exclusive rights and guaranteed sales to concert artists and generations of piano students."

Dinch smiled at him for having finally understood.

Mrs. Farringford said crisply: "I think you will find, Silas, that under the new copyright law, any rights not specifically relinquished to another party are owned by the creator of the work— or his heirs until fifty years after his death. That will take us to 1997. Sixteen more years, Silas. When the cadenza is recovered, the family's attorneys will see to it that all rights are retained by the Charles Philip Farringford Estate—not to be sold or bargained away. *We* will own the rights, and *we* will determine how the cadenza will be used." She leaned forward and stubbed her cigarette into an onyx ashtray. "It *is* important that the cadenza be published with the rest of the concerto in a new edition," she continued briskly. "But to achieve this will require a new contract, Silas, and the negotiation of a new royalty schedule. It's conceivable that the cadenza might be licensed, or leased, for use in a print-run of so-many copies, the license subsequently to be re-negotiated or assigned elsewhere. Charles was never a good businessman. When he died, he wasn't even insured! and with a thirteen-year-old daughter, and a son not yet through college."

Yep, thought Trntl, a woman used to having her way. More than a shot fired across his bow, this was a broadside that left Dinch heeled to starboard, awash and foundering. Struggling mightily to suppress a grin, Felix caught the laughing eyes of Rosamond Foxe upon him; their gaze met, locked, and both of them smiled together.

Dinch was maneuvering to regain control of the situation. He turned to Trntl and said "We'll pay your firm handsomely when you deliver the cadenza to us."

"The firm's standard rate is two hundred dollars a day plus expenses," said Trntl.

"That seems rather steep," said Dinch.

"We're very good," said Trntl. "There are four people, rent's high, and we have to make a living."

"At that daily rate, I'd think it would be to your advantage to take as long as possible."

"On the contrary, Mr. Dinch. It's to our advantage to resolve our cases as quickly and efficiently as we can." She stood up, and Felix followed suit. "I think we've taken enough of each other's time. Best of luck with your problem. Good night."

Chapter 2

"Oh no, please!" Clara Farringford blocked their path to the door. "We desperately need your help. We'll gladly pay whatever it takes."

Latimer wheezed from the mantel: "For God's sake, Silas. Two hundred a day plus expenses! I'll pay it myself."

Clara frowned. "You shouldn't have to do that. It's the family's responsibility, and Mr. Dinch's."

Latimer gave her a weary smile. "My dear, if it enables us to recover the cadenza, I'll consider it my legacy to the world."

"That's very generous of you," said Dinch. He knew that Latimer was worth at least three and a half million. He also knew how little the Farringford family had—and how little prospect of more.

Mrs. Farringford was thinking along the same lines. She turned to Latimer while reaching for another cigarette. "Although Lunner & Dinch has been generous over the years, and Charles's other works have enjoyed steady and continuous sales, life has not been easy. It's very kind of you to take such an interest in the matter. Will you have another brandy?"

"No more brandy, thanks. 'Take' an interest, Mrs. Farringford? I *have* an interest. I want to hear the cadenza again before I die."

She nodded and held her cigarette shoulder-high to be lighted. "I trust that we'll all get what we want," she said. "Thank you, Peter. Clara, I wonder if you'd pour me a drink, too. Scotch on the rocks."

"It's ten till seven," Dinch said to Trntl. "Will you accept the assignment? If so, you'll have to catch a train to Baltimore tonight."

Trntl and Felix exchanged a glance, and Trntl said, "We accept. We'll keep you posted on developments and will give you a strict accounting of expenses. But on your end, you'll have to let us pursue the investigation in our own way and in accord with our best judgment. Is that agreed?" A unified murmur of assent. "Now, to work efficiently, we need as many facts as we can get. I'd like more information about the cadenza's first disappearance thirty-four years ago."

With a startled riveting of gaze and puzzled frown, Anton Farringford said, "What bearing could that possibly have on the present matter?"

Trntl said, "It's surprising what can sometimes be learned from events that have no apparent connection."

"I don't see how anything can be gained from it," Dinch said irritably. "But it's simply told. It was Charles's custom to test out his major compositions with orchestras and audiences prior to official publication. For his St. Louis, Chicago, and Cleveland performances of the Fifth Concerto, the orchestral parts and all of the piano score except the cadenza were available in galley proof. The cadenza existed only in his single manuscript copy, for he was still making final revisions. After the last concert, when he boarded his train, he had the cadenza with him—or at least we think he did. When the train reached New York, he was found dead in his sleeping compartment, dressed in his pajamas. The clothes he'd worn for the concert were still in the compartment, but his alligator suitcase was gone, and there was no trace of the cadenza manuscript. We assume it vanished with the suitcase."

"Was there any sign of foul play?" asked Trntl. "Or evidence that anyone had been in the compartment with him?"

Dinch paused, his mouth half-open, for a full ten seconds; then, obviously uncomfortable, he said "The inquest established that he died of natural causes. There was no sign of foul play. There were a lot of cigarette butts in the ashtray—and Charles didn't smoke. Also, two one-way tickets to New York were found in the compartment."

"Charles was murdered," Mrs. Farringford said quietly. "I'm convinced of it. Murdered and robbed."

"Now, Mother," Clara said softly, "you know the autopsy showed that Father died of a coronary thrombosis."

Mrs. Farringford's eyes, fixed on the fire, were as blank as nailheads. "I've never for one minute believed it was a natural death. Someone was in that compartment with him, and that person killed him and took the suitcase."

"Do you think the person who took the suitcase was intending to steal the cadenza?" Trntl asked. "Or do you think it was a routine theft that carried off the cadenza by accident?" Good grief! she thought. When is a theft 'routine'?

Mrs. Farringford closed her eyes. "How would I know what the killer intended? Probably the latter. What value would the cadenza have to anybody? If someone did want it for itself, why would it turn up in a junkshop after all these years?"

Dinch cleared his throat loudly, wanting to get on with it. "The train was thoroughly searched, of course, and my father and Mr. Lunner offered a reward—no questions asked—for the return of the manuscript. No one came forward. There was never any explanation for there being two tickets in the compartment.

"Charles's death shocked the musical world. Many prominent composers and musicians came to his large public funeral here in New York. And the mayor, and several ambassadors from foreign countries. Even a representative of the President of the United States."

"Toscanini was there," Anton said, "and Myra Hess. I was twenty and remember it like yesterday. The Manhattan Chamber Orchestra performed Father's *Elegy for Strings*, and Susanna Jacobi played the adagio from his Ninth Piano Sonata."

"For several months," Dinch continued, "the Cleveland and New York police, the railway company, and various private detectives conducted intensive searches and investigations—but no trace was ever found of suitcase or cadenza. After the concerto was published in 1948, performers had to improvise when they came to the blank spot in the fourth movement. Some, like Abbott here, composed their own substitute cadenzas—and Abbott's became so popular we published it in 1968 for use by other performers."

Abbott ducked his head demurely. "Kind of you to mention it. Of course I'm glad that others find it useful. But I'm not a composer, and my cadenza was never intended to serve as more than a stopgap until Farringford's came to light."

"Did Mr. Farringford normally have anyone accompany him on concert tours?" Trntl asked.

From Mrs. Farringford: "No! Charles always traveled alone. He insisted on it." She swirled her Scotch angrily. "That's why there's something so very peculiar about this trip—why I'm convinced he was murdered." She took a deep drag on her cigarette. "You must realize, Miss Trntl, that you're stirring up very painful memories."

"Yes, is it really necessary to pursue this?" Abbott asked. "Isn't the important thing to plan how to get the cadenza back?" He placed his hand on Mrs. Farringford's shoulder in a reassuring gesture of comfort, which she acknowledged by reaching up and gently patting his hand.

"I'm sorry," said Trntl. "I didn't mean to reopen old wounds."
To Dinch: "Thank you for giving me the details."

He said, "Your train leaves in forty minutes. You should
reach Baltimore around twelve-thirty. We've reserved a room at
the Cavendish Hotel in the name of Lunner & Dinch. Professor
Pettigrew is expecting to meet with you at his home the first thing
in the morning—nine sharp." He lifted a thick leather briefcase
from the coffee table and handed it to her. "This contains a variety
of documents. Dossiers on Humboldt-Hartmann Gesellschaft and
our other competitors. Photocopies of original music manuscripts
in Charles Farringford's autograph so that you can recognize the
cadenza and verify its authenticity. Addresses and telephone numbers to call day or night when you discover something or need information from us. Letters of introduction written by me. And a
cashier's check to cover initial expenses."

Trntl asked, "What procedure do we follow if we find the manuscript or learn who has it?"

"If you find it, get it to our offices at once. Or, if that's not possible for some reason, send it here to the Farringford family. If you
discover where it is but can't obtain it, call me and we'll go from
there."

She tucked the briefcase under her arm, acknowledged the
group's murmured well-wishes, and, with Felix following, started
for the door. Anton Farringford hurried after them: "Here, let me
see you out." He followed them into the hall and carefully latched
the parlor door behind him. Handing them their coats, he whispered, "I'd like a word with you. Out on the steps."

In the cold? thought Felix. He caught Trntl's eye; she shrugged;
he sighed resignedly.

The street was empty of passing cars when they gathered on
the stoop. The wind was no less cutting than before, but seemed
colder by far after the over-heated house. Once the front door was
closed behind them, Anton began speaking rapidly: "Your bringing
up the circumstances of Father's death was most awkward. But of
course you couldn't have known. Mother finds the subject bitterly
painful, even after all these years, and we all respect her feelings
by never speaking of it. Nevertheless, I think you have a right to
know the details; I've read enough detective fiction to know that
sometimes the past does throw light on present difficulties." His
speech became ever more rapid as he talked. (Either he's afraid
of being interrupted, Trntl thought, or else he's finding it colder

on the steps than he'd anticipated.) "As you saw, my mother is convinced that Father was murdered. This is something she's led herself to believe over the years even though there's not one shred of evidence to support the notion. The autopsy showed that Father died of a heart attack. But she clings to the belief because it surrounds his death with an intriguing veil of mystery, leaving open a variety of possibilities—a necessity, for it enables her to ignore the harsh mundane fact that when Father died, he was entertaining a woman in that compartment. She's conveniently forgotten that when they found him, his pajama pants had been put on backwards." Noting their quizzical stares, he added hastily: "Well, have you ever tried to dress a corpse?" They hadn't, but they grasped the difficulty. "And those cigarette butts in the ashtray all showed traces of lipstick. This was common knowledge at the time. Mother simply chose not to acknowledge the obvious implications. And I understand her refusal to admit that Father was playing around. How could she easily face the fact that he found her unappealing? How else accept all those concert tours he took without her? While she deeply reveres his memory, she *is* angry that he didn't leave her well provided for—no life insurance, no investments, no will. His business affairs were a shambles—missing records, unpaid bills, a delinquent income tax return. That's the main reason she wanted me to go into banking. And I must say that the family finances *have* been on a better footing these last twenty-five years."

Largely to stop the flow of words, Trntl said, "And, in the disappearance of the suitcase, she's seen robbery as a motive for the murder."

"That's right. Now, the disappearance of the suitcase does present a problem. But I have a theory about what happened."

"Do tell us," said Felix, stamping his feet to revive his numbing toes.

"I do have to catch a train—" said Trntl.

"It'll only take a moment." Anton lowered his voice confidentially. "Just between us, my father had quite an eye for the ladies. Though the public never knew it—for he was very careful—he was, well, let's face it: an avid womanizer. I recall one time, when I was nineteen—the year before he died—I accidentally interrupted him with one of his piano students in the back parlor where he gave lessons. A beautiful girl, about twenty, with honey gold hair and luscious great—well, one thing I can say for him: Father had excellent taste. They were on the couch. When he looked up and saw me in the doorway, he blushed mightily and said—without breaking his rhythm, mind you—'Not one word to your mother, do you hear?' And of course I never betrayed his confidence. Mother never did learn about his women—and Clara didn't, either."

"And your theory about the disappearance of the suitcase?" Felix prompted him.

"Oh, it's very simple. After the Cleveland concert, Father picked up some woman to share his trip to New York. A—well, you know—a paid professional. And unfortunately he died during the night. She panicked; and not wanting to be with the body when it arrived at Penn Station, she simply grabbed his suitcase for whatever it might contain that she could sell, and got off at the next stop."

"Just a simple theft, then," said Felix. "No specific desire to steal the cadenza. No foreign plot to get at military secrets your father had encoded in the score."

Anton laughed. "Oh no, no. Father wasn't at all political. No, I expect the woman didn't even know that the cadenza was in the suitcase, or what it was when she found it. For her, it was just a business transaction that went sour."

"But both tickets found in the compartment were one-way to New York," said Trntl. "Why would a—a paid professional living in Cleveland want a one-way ticket to New York? Wouldn't a round-trip ticket make more sense?"

"I've wondered about that, too," said Anton. "I assume Father was simply giving a lift to a working woman who wanted to go to New York."

"It's a plausible theory, Mr. Farringford," said Felix. "Thanks for sharing it with us. We won't breathe it to a soul."

Behind Anton, the door popped open, and Peter Shipley Abbott stepped out in a fur overcoat and matching hat. Seeing them huddled on the stoop, his eyes widened in surprise. "Oh, here you are, Anton. I hope I'm not interrupting anything." He stood smiling, framed by the doorway, carefully pulling on his fur-lined leather gloves.

"Oh no, no. Certainly not, Peter. Nothing to interrupt. Just saying goodbye, wishing them luck."

"I've never met Professor Pettigrew," said Abbott. "But I'm acquainted with some of his scholarship. A mediocre musicologist, I'm afraid. He's written one or two articles on the early quartets of Beethoven, and a very shallow book on Chopin's influence on later composers. I think he's also written on the Gossbeck-Linenweber Feud. Definitely a lightweight. And, if I'm not mistaken, he's announced that he's working on a systematic study of the piano works of Brahms." Abbott appeared to be ready to say a great deal more—in fact, to go on indefinitely.

"Well, I'm off to meet him," said Trntl, edging down the steps. Abbott followed her.

"If I can be of any help to you," he said, "any at all, in any way, please let me know. Here's my card, with my unlisted home telephone number."

Trntl and Felix reached the sidewalk. Abbott turned to Anton Farringford. "Thanks for inviting me to this meeting. Keep me posted on developments—and if Dinch thinks I can be of use, let me know. Now I must leave; I have a recording session in the morning."

"We appreciate your concern," Anton replied, moving backward into the lighted hallway. "You're such a comfort to Mother."

Abbott waited until the door closed, then hurried down the steps and caught up with Felix and Trntl, who were halfway to their car. "I'm actually going in the other direction," he said breathlessly. "But I did want to say one thing before you got away. I wasn't free to say it during the meeting because—well, it's a sensitive issue. Regarding who may have stolen the cadenza from Professor Pettigrew, I'm obligated to say that I don't agree with Silas Dinch that it was one of his competitors in the publishing business. He's firmly convinced of it, I'm afraid. But honestly I can't see Humboldt-Hartmann or any of the others actually committing burglary to prevent Lunner & Dinch from obtaining it."

"Do you have other ideas?" asked Trntl. She found Abbott altogether irritating: his archness, self-centeredness, and precious mannerisms; his scrupulous tailoring and sunlamp tan; his haughty New England prep school intonation which, as a man of forty, he should have long ago outgrown. Even his nasty fur-lined gloves.

"Two possibilities come to mind," said Abbott. "First, that some concert pianist arranged to have it stolen so that he can be the first to perform or record the Fifth Concerto with the Farringford Cadenza in place—steal a march on everybody else, make a big splash, with guaranteed record sales and all the rest."

"I'm not sure I find that very plausible," said Trntl. "The burglary's being publicized would make possession of the cadenza just as awkward for a performer as it would for a publisher. Any professional pianist who would come up with such a scheme and not foresee the consequences would have to be either demented or stupid. Don't you agree? If your theory's correct, and the thieving pianist is sane, I'd expect him to make a photocopy of the score to practice with, then return the original to Lunner & Dinch for publication. He could still make his splash by having a performance or a recording session within a week of the cadenza's being published. Now, should this be the case, I'd expect the cadenza to turn up shortly, and our services won't be needed. Do you have any candidates in mind who would be so desperate or mad as to steal the cadenza from Pettigrew?"

"Well, no," said Abbott, "not off the top of my head. Almost any pianist would want to be the first to perform the Farringford Cadenza. I know that Rosamond Foxe was counting on being the first to record it; Dinch had promised her a copy of the score prior to publication to make this possible. Such a coup would certainly boost her career. I, on the other hand, have been given the privilege of being the first to present it in live performance. It's the family's wish, and of course I'm grateful for their faith that I can do it justice."

"You said you had two theories," Felix said impatiently. They had been gradually moving down the block and were now standing beside the car.

"Well—as you suggested—maybe there wasn't a burglary at all. But *not* because the cadenza wasn't actually found. Maybe the Simms girl did find it, and Professor Pettigrew *still has it*."

"Why, then, would he announce it stolen?" asked Trntl, opening the passenger door.

"After announcing at the press conference that he was giving it to Lunner & Dinch, he may have changed his mind, and decided to keep it for himself—"

"Or to sell it to the highest bidder," said Felix.

Abbott pondered this for a moment with a rather blank expression. "At any rate," he resumed, "it's possible he fabricated the burglary as an excuse for not giving the cadenza up. You're right; there's no proof that it was actually stolen."

"Nor any proof that it was actually ever *found*," Felix reminded him. "What if Pettigrew realized—after the press conference—that what he had wasn't the Farringford Cadenza at all? He'd have to find some way of avoiding the professional embarrassment of making a stupid blunder. You've implied that his reputation as a musicologist is fairly shaky."

"Now, *that's* an interesting possibility," said Abbott.

"We have to be going," Trntl said, getting into the car. "I have exactly twenty-eight minutes to catch the train. Thanks for sharing your theories with us; I'll keep them in mind when talking to Pettigrew."

"The best of luck!" Abbott said to her as Felix got behind the wheel. "And by the way, Toscanini didn't come to Farringford's funeral. Nor Myra Hess. Anton's memory of it has gotten muddled, and he likes to dramatize things. He has a pretty dull life, juggling figures year in, year out." They left him standing on the curb.

As they drove, Trntl said, "I'll give you a call after I've talked to Pettigrew. If I have to stay in Baltimore beyond tomorrow night, I'll want Carol to pack a bag for me and zip it down on the Metroliner. I'll make a list of the things I'll need."

Luckily, traffic was fairly thin, and Felix made excellent time. He said, "I've had my fill of theories. Those folks do like to talk! Chatter, chatter. Like a bunch of squirrels."

Trntl nodded. "A strange gathering of people. But you have to admit that Rosamond Foxe makes a good impression."

Felix glanced at her sharply. She was smiling at him. "Oh, come on, Trntl. Was it that obvious?"

"For those who have eyes to see," said Trntl, "it takes only half an eye."

"Now you've got me embarrassed," he groaned. "I thought I wasn't being obvious at all."

"There are some things not easy for a man to hide," said Trntl. "Anyway, she was flattered and amused. And, I suspect, more than mildly interested in you. I saw the glance the two of you exchanged. If you want to follow it up, you should send her the sketch you made. It's quite good."

They lapsed into silence as they approached the station. Then Trntl suddenly said, "I agree with you: far too many theories. We need facts, and there are precious few so far. WATCH OUT FOR THAT CAB! I had a couple of questions I wanted to ask Dinch, but things were getting so tense I felt it wasn't advisable." She sighed. "You know, hearing all these speculations about who might have stolen the cadenza—if there *is* a cadenza, and if it *was* stolen—and what their motives might or might not have been has turned my brain to mush."

"Yeah," said Felix. "I've stopped speculating. I want a hot toddy and a good night's sleep. Here we are, with six minutes to spare."

They pulled up to the curb, and Trntl opened her door. "I can think of one other reason why somebody might steal the cadenza."

"What's that?"

"Why, to get it *back!*" She hopped out of the car and started off at a run.

Felix was glad he wasn't going to Baltimore. The night was still young. He headed south toward SoHo.

Normally, Latimer liked the sauna. It was a place of anonymity and refuge where, defenses down, he could sit relaxed, unhinge his mind, and swing out into sweet oblivion, allowing the burden of his Wall Street worries to slough off and dissipate into the soothing steam. Tonight, however, having just come from the meeting with Dinch, the Farringfords, and their detectives, whiplashed into profound despondency by the emotional shocks of the last two days, he found the steam-room threatening. Standing at the threshold, peering into the dim clouds of mist, he felt suddenly queasy, as though the doorway were the hatch of an airplane, and that to step through it would be to plunge into a swirling gray thunderhead for a plummeting, sightless drop.

If he hadn't agreed to meet Zyzynski here at ten, he'd have turned back and hurried straight to his room, where the steward had delivered him a bottle of choice cognac.

But Victor was expecting him. Cautiously he entered the steam, creeping his rubber-soled sandals across the smooth tiled floor. Without his glasses, he could see only a general, billowing grayness clotted now and then with darker shapes where, on benches lining the walls, men muttered quietly together in clumps of two or three or, more often, huddled solitary and silent. Still, the room was not crowded, and a moment's groping along one wall brought him to his usual place. He carefully spread his towel on the bench, lowered himself gingerly, and leaned back, hands cupped on bony knees. Once settled, he was glad of the moist heat. The meeting at the Farringford house had exhausted him. Trntl and McKay had impressed him favorably; but he despaired of their recovering the cadenza.

He fervently hoped that a ransom demand would come: *that* could be dealt with, cleanly, in unmarked bills. But if the manuscript should be *destroyed!* or should vanish forever into a selfish collector's private vault! or be *scattered!* He'd been squirrel-caging all day long—treadmilling round and round in a dither of anguish: and always, when he reached this point, involuntary spasms locked his jaw on the left-hand side and caused his head to wobble. The long ride home to Connecticut had simply been unthinkable; so, after arriving at the Club for his appointment, he'd called his wife to say that he was staying over—and, as always, Bertha understood.

He'd been seated only five minutes when a huge shape emerged from the fog to loom before him like the hull of a freighter or a suddenly-surfaced kraken.

"Well, how did the meeting go?" Zyzynski asked. "Has Dinch received a ransom demand yet?"

"Ah!—Victor. No, so far he's heard nothing. We spent most of the meeting trying to figure out who might've stolen the cadenza." Latimer reached down to massage his hairless calves.

Zyzynski plopped his massive buttocks onto the bench beside him and leaned closer, rivulets of sweat trickling over the folds of his chest and the great slick watermelon of his belly. "Did you come to any conclusions?"

"No, just empty speculations. Today has been a living hell!—1947 all over again. Last night, sheer ecstasy knowing the cadenza was found! That we'd get to hear it again! Thirty-four years, Victor, since we'd known even a *tenth* of last night's happiness. It was as though Bertha and I were nineteen again—on an all-night jouncing hayride! We got to sleep at dawn.

"Then, this morning, the shock of the theft. I nearly fainted when Dinch told me. Vomited my breakfast. Couldn't eat lunch. Felt sick all afternoon. Tonight I can't even face going home." He began rubbing his flaccid thighs.

"Sorry I played a part in ruining your day," said Zyzynski. "When I rang you this morning asking if you'd call Dinch to inquire when he anticipated publishing the cadenza, I had no idea he'd have such bad news."

"He'd learned about it just after nine," said Latimer. "I'm sorry it took me so long to call you back; I just couldn't function for an hour or so."

"Well, when you did call, you got me all curious about tonight's meeting. I'm certainly not accustomed to ten p.m. saunas, but I do want a report."

Latimer sighed wearily. "Dinch was there, and the entire Farringford family. And—I was surprised at this—Peter Shipley Abbott and Rosamond Foxe."

A metallic taste filled Zyzynski's mouth. "Abbott and Foxe?" Behind his thigh, his hand clenched into a fist, and the nails dug into his palm.

"They're friends of the family. I assume Mrs. Farringford or the son invited them."

"Did they come together?" His breathing had tightened, but he managed to hold his voice steady, and keep his tone casual.

"No. Abbott got there first, Foxe about ten minutes later. Why do you ask?"

"No reason in particular. Idle curiosity. Let's go on. You say there's been no ransom demand."

"Not yet. Dinch is sure that one of his competitors in publishing stole the cadenza. If that's true, there won't be a ransom demand. But I think he's wrong. None of his competitors would risk the scandal of publishing a stolen cadenza. I think it was stolen for money, and that there'll be a ransom demand shortly. Or perhaps word that it'll be sold to the highest bidder. Either way, we've got to pay whatever's required." He folded his arms and leaned back dejectedly against the wall. "We also decided to hire a private investigator to recover it if possible."

Zyzynski gave a start of surprise. "A detective?"

"We felt we had to do something. Delay is dangerous. The Baltimore police are treating the burglary as a common theft—which is *not* what we need."

"Who's the detective you've hired?"

"A woman—N. F. Trntl—"

"Eh?" said Zyzynski.

"Trntl. T-r-n-t-l. Her firm was highly recommended by one of Dinch's friends."

"Located in Baltimore?"

"No, here in New York. Dinch says the firm's been in operation for six years. I was impressed with Trntl. She seems very quick. She left for Baltimore tonight and will talk to that idiot Pettigrew tomorrow morning."

"How much is this Trntl charging for her services?"

"Two hundred a day plus expenses."

Zyzynski snorted. "And you think you'll get decent results for *that?* Penny-ante operator! And I'll bet *you're* footing the entire bill, aren't you, Morgan?"

"Half of it. Lunner & Dinch is in for the other half. The Farringfords aren't very well off. The widow's living on royalties and what her son and daughter give her. He's an accountant of some sort at Swinfurth Lightfoot, and she's a concert flutist—fairly well-known, though not a Rampal or Steegmuller."

"Clara Farringford," said Zyzynski. "I've heard her play." He sat silent for a moment, then said wryly, "I'm betting this Trntl will bleed you on expenses. Fancy restaurant meals. Champagne. How long's she staying in Baltimore?"

"As long as the investigation takes. Her job is to recover the cadenza. If there's a ransom demand, or it turns up in the hands of one of Dinch's competitors, her job's finished."

Zyzynski shook his head. "It sounds to me like you've given her a blank check. You surprise me, Morgan; I thought you were more sensible than that. I'll bet she'll be staying in one of the most expensive hotels."

"No, Lunner & Dinch put her up at the Cavendish." Latimer's tone had acquired a defensive edge. "In a moderately priced single room. We'll expect a rigorous accounting of her expenses, Victor, you may be sure."

Zyzynski stood up and wrapped a huge towel around his middle. "I hope she earns her money and finds the cadenza. In short order. But if she doesn't, and a ransom demand comes through, let me know. I'd like to contribute to a fund if you're forced to buy the cadenza back from the thieves. But anonymously. I want no publicity."

Latimer squinted up at him, smiling his surprise. "Why, Victor, that's fine of you. May I tell Dinch that you've offered to help?"

Zyzynski shook his head. "No, I want to remain anonymous."

Latimer's voice was trembling with emotion. "And you've not *heard* the cadenza!"

"But I know what it means to you," Zyzynski said. "And if we do recover it, I'll get to hear it too. I'm very fond of Farringford's Fifth—I want to hear that cadenza in the context where it belongs. I'm prepared to do whatever it takes to get the chance."

Latimer said, "Are you leaving already? Don't you want a rubdown and a drink?"

"Just a shower," said Zyzynski. "I've got to do some paperwork for the merger negotiations. Give Bertha my regards." And with that, he heaved off and disappeared into the fog.

Chapter 3

March 2 (Monday)

When she'd parked her rented car in front of Professor Pettigrew's house, Trntl sat for a moment observing the scene of the crime. Set well back from the street in a quiet residential neighborhood, the house was a modest red brick from the 1920's. Dark yew bushes flanked the porch; the windows were small-paned casements trimmed in white. A flagstone walk curved up to the front door past a circular flower bed. White picket fences separated the yard from those on either side. Not much cover to screen burglars from observant eyes in the adjacent houses, Trntl decided; she'd ask if the neighbors had seen anything unusual the night of the break-in.

Nine o'clock. She hurried up the front walk and rang the bell.

After a lengthy pause, the door was opened by a plump gray-haired woman wearing a knee-length apron over a house dress. About fifty, she was square-shouldered, square-faced, and heavily jowled, her jaw line buried in a sheath of flesh folds like collars of melted candle wax. Her small tight mouth seemed chiseled into place; her pale brown eyes were as uncompromisingly direct as twin drill bits. She reminded Trntl of an iguana. Expressionless, she continually wiped her hands on a white kitchen towel while Trntl introduced herself and stated her business.

"He's expecting you." She stepped back to let Trntl enter. "I'm *Mrs.* Pettigrew." She took Trntl's coat and impaled it on a hook fastened to the wall. "He's back there in the study." She led Trntl down the hall to a doorway opposite the stairs. "Theodore, the person from Lunner & Dinch is here."

He filled the doorway, loose-jointed and heavy-footed, with a protruding potbelly, a large melon head, and a wad of matted sandy hair. His glasses sat askew on his face, the left ear piece missing, the left lens crazed with a starburst fracture. A fresh red scab straddled the bridge of his nose, and a gauze pad was taped high on the left side of his forehead, just below the hairline.

He shook Trntl's hand and ushered her into a smallish room lined with bookshelves on three sides and well-lighted by casement windows on the fourth. One of the panes was covered with a piece of heavy cardboard. Trntl gave him Dinch's letter of introduction, and Pettigrew motioned her to a chair. Mrs. Pettigrew, with the towel draped over her shoulder, leaned against the wall just inside the doorway and watched unblinking.

"Mr. Dinch says that I'm to answer whatever questions you have regarding the theft." His right eye, greatly magnified by the lens, bulged like a chameleon's; his left was masked by the center of the starburst. "Needless to say, Miss Trntl—it *is* Miss, I take it? I see no wedding band—I'm devastated that the cadenza was stolen while in my possession. I feel like a sentry asleep at his post, a steward who's betrayed his trust and let the pigs into the garden. I'm doubly responsible because my press conference precipitated the theft." Deep from the diaphragm, his voice was self-consciously well-modulated, as though he knew he played his cello well, and took great pride in his performance. A professor's voice, thought Trntl, used to the fifty-minute hour. Or an actor's.

She said, "My firm has been asked to recover the cadenza. What information can you provide?"

He encompassed the room with a sweep of his arm. "You see the mess the study's in. I'm just getting things organized. The burglars tore the place apart. Books pulled from the shelves, papers scattered everywhere. Desk drawers strewn about. Pictures ripped down—"

"You must've had the cadenza well-hidden," said Trntl.

"No, that's the odd part." He eased himself down into a swivel chair behind the desk. "It was lying in plain sight here on the desk, and the burglars got it the first time. No, the trashing of the room took place during the second break-in."

Trntl jolted to attention. "There were *two* break-ins?"

"Well, three, actually. All on the same night. It was during the second that I got hit on the head." He tenderly touched his bandage with a pale finger. "Four stitches were required to close the gash. It was during the third break-in, while we were at the hospital, that the upstairs was searched."

"We knew of only one break-in," said Trntl. At least that's all she'd been told about. "Let's start at the beginning and get things in sequence. Explain just how the cadenza was discovered, then recount the events leading up to and surrounding the theft." She positioned a note pad on her knee.

Pettigrew selected a pipe from a walnut rack and began slowly packing it with tobacco. "I presume you understand the importance of the Farringford Cadenza. What its discovery means for the history of music."

"I'm certainly beginning to," said Trntl. She hoped he wasn't settling in for a lecture.

"For thirty-four years it was one of those baffling and wistful losses that occur in all disciplines—and finding it became the dream of every music historian, the kind of fantasy one has in graduate school on the threshold of one's career—and then again, later, as one's career grinds on, and the years creep by, and one finds that fame and achievement have not come to one in the measure that one had hoped." He paused here for a long space to light his pipe. It took him three wooden matches to accomplish it.

"And here I must make a distinction," he continued. "The Farringford Cadenza wasn't like some of the vanished music we learn of only through lists of titles, notebook jottings, or hearsay mention—items whose nature and qualities aren't really known. No, hundreds of people had actually heard Farringford perform it on three occasions. I wasn't one of the lucky ones, and this is a great sadness to me. But over the years I've met perhaps twenty of those people, and invariably their having heard it comes up in the course of conversation. And—astoundingly—they all have comparable, even similar memories of the experience! First they get thoughtful and misty-eyed, then flushed with excitement. But language fails them when they try to describe the music. In 1967, I met a woman who'd heard both the St. Louis and Chicago performances: she'd followed Farringford north just to hear it a second time!"

"Twice blest," said Trntl. "But I'd like to know how the cadenza came to be discovered after so many years."

Pettigrew nodded and relit his pipe. "Four days ago, one of my students, Miss Stephanie Simms, was browsing in a second-hand shop downtown—Finegold's Flea-Market. She has a habit of frequenting such places—hunting old phonograph records and sheet music. Incidentally, she's found some early Scott Joplin and some very interesting Edison cylinders—" He caught his wife's eye over Trntl's shoulder and did a quick turn—"Well, she saw this old piano bench—no piano with it, you understand—but clearly the sort of bench that would've gone with a very fine instrument. She opened it to see if any sheet music was inside, found it empty, and was about to close the lid when she noticed a split in the bottom panel and what appeared to be music manuscript showing through the crack. She pried the panel loose and found a lengthy piano score—twelve pages on thinnish flexible paper, yellow with age—written small with a careful pen. Since there were almost no cross-outs, she knew it had to be a clean, or near-final, copy. She couldn't identify the score; but, thinking I'd be interested in it, bought it for two dollars. I reimbursed her, of course."

He leaned back in his chair, eye suddenly alight, voice trembling with emotion. "When she showed it to me early Friday afternoon, I immediately guessed what it was. I'd seen Farringford's penmanship on numerous occasions. Though the piece was not titled, it was a work for solo piano obviously complete and whole. It had thematic elements of the fourth movement of the Fifth Concerto, and—for the clincher—at the bottom of the last page, a tiny monogram signature: 'C.P.F.'!"

Trntl smiled, taking notes, and said "Go on."

"Well, you can imagine how excited we were. The dream come true! I immediately called a press conference to announce our discovery to the world. Here—" he reached into a drawer "—I have an extra clipping from the Baltimore *Sun* so you can read what I said. Keep it for reference; I have more." She took it and glanced over it while he relit his pipe.

The article was similar to what she'd seen in the New York paper, with only a few additional details of local interest, and more about Pettigrew's career and relationship to the Hastings Institute. She folded the clipping into her pad. Pettigrew seemed to be slipping into a reverie. "And then—?" she prompted.

He shook out the match flame with a flourish and dropped the stick into the heaped ashtray. "On Saturday, as the news spread around the world, I received telegrams of congratulation from scholars everywhere—England, France, Rochester, Princeton, Indonesia, Germany, Rome! A great moment, Miss Trntl! The kind of thing that happens just once in a lifetime to a lucky few!" He blew a smoke ring, remembering. "But then—" His pause caused her to look up at him. His mouth had dropped open, lower lip pendulous and slack, saliva glistening on his yellow teeth. His eye had gone dead, as though someone had flipped a switch. "Then came the burglary, and everything turned to shit. And I have only *myself* to blame! Fool, fool, fool—" He began beating the right side of his forehead, rocking back and forth.

Trntl pushed on. "In your press conference, you characterized the cadenza as extremely valuable, a 'priceless find'. I assume you feel it was that statement that brought about the theft?"

"Why else would someone steal it?"

"I don't know," said Trntl. "Its assumed value is the most obvious motive. Still, there may be others. Go on with your story. Did anything odd or suspicious occur on the day of the press conference, or the day after, which might have led one to think the cadenza might be in jeopardy?" God, thought Trntl, I'm beginning to talk like he does.

"No," he answered after a moment's thought. "As I said, telegrams were arriving. And Mr. Dinch called, asserting his claim to the manuscript. We reached an agreement, and I informed the press so that it could be reported in Saturday's news. We arranged for Mr. Tuttle to inspect the manuscript early Sunday morning. I told them I wanted time to make a preliminary examination of the score. It seemed only fitting that I should have the chance to write an article about it."

Trntl nodded. "And neither you nor Miss Simms made photocopies of the manuscript?"

"No—and I've cursed myself ever since. But don't you see? I had the thing itself—was working with it all day Saturday. It never *dawned* on me to photocopy it."

"*I* would have made a copy," said Mrs. Pettigrew from the doorway.

He barely glanced at her. "When Mr. Dinch called, he asked me the same question. I said no, and he ordered me *not* to make photocopies on pain of a possible lawsuit. So of course I didn't."

"Let's get to the break-ins," said Trntl.

He gave a deep sigh. "That evening—Saturday—my wife and I had to attend the performance of a high-school play. Our son Robbie had the role of Jack in *The Importance of Being Earnest*. I left the cadenza on my desk in plain sight. We had an early supper and left for the school about seven-thirty. We got home around eleven—Robbie had gone to a cast party and wouldn't be home till late—and I told Irma I wanted to work on the cadenza for awhile before going to bed. When I came into the study and turned on the light, I saw that the manuscript was gone." The horror of the moment repossessed him, and Trntl doodled patiently until he recovered himself.

"Desk top bare. Broken window, glass on the floor. And whoever it was had knocked down a hanging flower pot when he crawled into the room."

"Did you find anything missing besides the cadenza?" Trntl asked.

"Only a few other music manuscripts that had been on the desk: copies I was making in ink of certain of Brahms's piano compositions. I'm at work on a book analyzing his bridgework." Her cocked eyebrow made him quickly translate: "His transitional passages. I've always felt that insufficient attention—"

"Please describe these other manuscripts that were taken. Just their physical appearance."

"Well, they were in a neat stack—about ten sheets upon which I'd transcribed in my own hand portions of Brahms's capriccios, intermezzos, and rhapsodies for solo piano." He smiled, a shade defensively. "It may seem odd to you that I was copying them by hand. But I was trying to replicate for myself what Brahms must have gone through as he wrote out his scores. By doing the same physical labor, I think I can gain a clearer understanding of his music. Those papers represent hours of work for me—but I can't see why anyone else would want them."

"Had you written the titles of the works on your copies?"

"Not *Brahms's* titles; just my own code numbers to identify the pieces."

"And they were on the desk alongside Farringford's manuscript?"

"Yes, and that was about all. My pens, of course; a bottle of ink; my pipe rack. Those wound up on the floor. The published editions of Brahms's works that I was copying from were on the end table beside the desk, and *they* weren't touched."

Trntl nodded. "Since the burglary took place before you got home at eleven, is there a possibility that your neighbors on this side of the house might have seen something suspicious?"

"No, the Nelsons have been gone for nearly a week. They went to Detroit to see their new grand-daughter—"

"Grandson," said Mrs. Pettigrew.

"Did you call the police when you discovered the burglary?" Trntl asked.

"Not immediately." Defensive again, and apologetic, he began to fidget. "First I searched to see if the cadenza was anywhere in the room—on the floor, under the desk, in the wastebasket—"

"*I* called the police," said Mrs. Pettigrew. "Face it, Theodore, you were in a panic. Incoherent. Hysterical. Beating yourself and pounding on the wall."

Pettigrew flushed, compressed his lips, and carefully set his pipe on the heap of matches in the ashtray. "One patrolman came—in his own sweet time, I might add—and took our statements; said we should come down to headquarters in the morning."

"What time was this?" asked Trntl.

"About midnight. Isn't that right, Irma? He was here only fifteen or twenty minutes. I couldn't make him understand the importance of the cadenza, the seriousness of the theft. I thought he was very casual about investigating."

"Then what? You said there was a second break-in."

"Yes, and a third. After the patrolman left, Irma insisted that we go up to bed—"

"There was nothing more we could do," said Mrs. Pettigrew. "And I had to be up early for a hairdresser's appointment."

"So we went upstairs," Pettigrew continued. "But I couldn't sleep. I kept going over in my mind what I should've done differently. Worried sick at what I'd tell Mr. Tuttle when he came at nine o'clock." He took off his glasses, and, holding them by the single bow, began polishing the good lens with his handkerchief. "Much later—it must have been two-thirty or three—I heard noises downstairs. A kind of random bumping and scuffling, now and then a soft thud. At first I assumed it was Robbie just home from the cast party. Possibly a little tipsy, you know how these parties are, maybe getting himself a late snack in the kitchen. But when the noises continued, I thought I'd better get up and investigate. Irma was sleeping soundly, and I didn't wake her. I tiptoed out into the hall and down the stairs. The noises were coming from the study, and occasional beams of light shone under the door. When I saw this, I'm afraid I did something very foolish, Miss Trntl. But you must understand my state of mind, that my judgment wasn't functioning very well. I flung open the door and charged into the room."

"It wasn't very prudent," Trntl agreed.

"It was stupid," said Mrs. Pettigrew.

"The room was dark," he went on quickly. "I had a brief glimpse of two flashlight beams, then someone grabbed me from behind, pinning my arms, and something hit me on the head. When I came to, Robbie had just come home, and he and Irma took me to the hospital emergency room."

"Here by the door," said Mrs. Pettigrew, "you can see where he bled on the carpet." Trntl observed the small brown spot on the rug. "The next morning the police told us not to touch anything till they'd finished their investigation; so by last night, when I was finally able to clean it, some of the stain had set."

Trntl turned back to the professor. "You said the study was ransacked during the second break-in. Was anything taken this time?"

"When I put the room to rights, nothing seemed to be missing. But in the third break-in, fifty-seven dollars was taken from our bedroom."

"Tell me about the third break-in."

"The hospital wanted to hold me for observation, but I refused; and, after talking to the police, the three of us came home about five in the morning. We'd left some of the house lights on when we left, but the house was dark when we pulled into the driveway. While we were gone, somebody had come in through the study window and systematically gone through the house room by room—evidently in a great hurry."

"Flour and salt were strewn all over the kitchen," Mrs. Pettigrew said bitterly. "Things were pulled from the cupboards, and a plate of cold chicken was missing from the refrigerator."

"Robbie's room was the least upset," the professor went on. "Drawers pulled out, socks and underwear thrown about, school papers scattered on the floor. It was *our* bedroom and the bookshelves in the upstairs hall that got the full treatment."

"They went through the clothes closets and the dresser. All our personal things," said Mrs. Pettigrew.

"Irma's little writing desk was lying on its side, the wood splintered as though someone had kicked it."

"And fifty-seven dollars was taken?" asked Trntl.

"Yes, and my grandfather's gold pocket watch which was on the bureau."

"Did you call the police?"

"Right away. They sent out a couple of detectives about eight o'clock. They poked around and made notes of what was stolen.

But *they* couldn't seem to grasp the importance of the Farringford Cadenza, either—kept calling it 'the music'. They couldn't understand why anyone would want to steal it. They thought it strange the burglars hadn't taken my tape deck and electric typewriter."

Trntl looked up from her notes. "Since, in the first break-in, nothing was taken except Farringford's manuscript—"

"And my copies of Brahms's works," he reminded her.

"—it's clear the burglars were after the cadenza."

"But they *got* it. Why come back and ransack the study?"

"Why, indeed," said Trntl. "And you say nothing was taken in the second burglary?"

"Right. But maybe only because I surprised them in the act. I think they came back later to finish the job while we were at the hospital."

"Do you have any specific reason for assuming the first two break-ins, or the second and third, or—for that matter—all three were the work of the same burglars?" asked Trntl.

"Surely you're not suggesting three separate sets of burglars!" he cried.

"It's possible," said Trntl. "Three would be highly disturbing. Two sets is more likely. Both after the cadenza. The first burglars accomplished their objective. Since the second set of burglars began their search in the study, I assume they came through the same window the first burglars did. If they were at all professional, they'd have noticed the broken window and known that somebody had been there ahead of them."

He was staring at her open-mouthed. "But they wouldn't have had any way of knowing the first group had taken the cadenza."

"Right. For all they knew, it might be locked in a wall safe or stashed upstairs."

"But what about the fifty-seven dollars and my grandfather's watch?"

"What about the typewriter and tape deck they *didn't* take? I think the money and watch were either an attempt to obscure the true object of the search, or else a little bonus on the side. Like the cold chicken. Now, please recount the events of the day following the burglaries. You stopped with the visit of the police detectives."

He gathered his thoughts and said hesitantly, "After the police left, I thought I'd lie down until Mr. Tuttle arrived. You don't know how I dreaded seeing him—"

"Tell her about the reporter," said Mrs. Pettigrew.

"Oh yes, I forgot. Not five minutes after the police left, a newspaper reporter came to interview me. He said he was assigned the police beat, and had seen the report of last night's break-in—that would have been the first burglary, I assume. He recognized my name from the press conference, and suspected that something was up, though the police report was scanty on details. A bright young man. He asked me point blank if the cadenza had been stolen. I said yes it had, and told him about all three burglaries and showed him the cut on my head. He was very friendly and left after ten minutes."

Pettigrew took off his glasses and wearily rubbed his eyes. "Then I lay down for a few minutes, and at nine sharp Mr. Tuttle arrived. When I told him the cadenza was gone, he immediately phoned Mr. Dinch in New York. They told me not to talk to any reporters, since the best hope of getting the cadenza back was not to advertise its theft. When I heard that, I was sorry that I'd spoken to the young man that morning; and I felt obliged to make a clean breast of it, and told them that the story was already out. They were very angry with me. And with good reason."

"Anybody would have done the same," Trntl said. "Then what?"

"Mr. Tuttle left, and I went back to bed. But about an hour later the phone started ringing—reporters and TV people wanting to know about the cadenza. We stopped answering the phone. So they began arriving at the house, gathering on the front lawn—"

"Trampling my flower beds," said Mrs. Pettigrew.

"—and I had to go out onto the front porch and tell them all what had happened. It was three in the afternoon before I could get to sleep."

Trntl sat silent for a minute, assembling and fitting together what she'd heard. Things were far from clear, and she fought her urge to launch freewheeling speculations. Premature, premature. "Tell me about that first reporter," she said. "The one who came just after the police left. Can you describe him?"

Mrs. Pettigrew answered. "He was tall, about six feet two. Young—27 or 28. Clean-cut, with short blond hair, a small blond mustache. Pleasant-looking and very polite. He was wearing a brown overcoat and a neat, narrow-brimmed hat. He didn't remove his coat, but under it I could see that he was wearing a dark suit and tie."

"Did he show a press card or any other identification?" asked Trntl. "What paper was he working for?"

"He flashed a card," said the professor. "I assumed he was working for the *Sun*."

"Had you seen him before? Was he at your initial press conference?"

"*I* never saw him before," said Mrs. Pettigrew.

"What sorts of questions did he ask? Please be specific."

"Well, he asked if the cadenza had been stolen, and I said yes. And he asked me if I had any idea who might have taken it. And I said I had no idea—unless it might've been Mr. Finegold of the Flea-Market, angry at having sold for a measly two dollars what he later learned from the papers was a priceless treasure."

"If it *had* been Finegold, that would account for only the first break-in," said Trntl. "Still, it's a possibility." Not a good one, she thought. How could Finegold easily dispose of the cadenza once word of the theft got out? Still, talking to him might be useful. He might remember where and how he'd acquired the false-bottomed piano bench; and *that* might suggest how the manuscript had come to be hidden there. And even—as a very long shot—who might have stolen it from Pettigrew.

"I invited Mr. Finegold to the first press conference," Pettigrew continued. "But he was very unfriendly, refusing to come and insisting that his name not be mentioned in the news accounts of the discovery. I suppose he didn't want the world to see him as a fool."

"I don't find that strange," said Trntl.

"I thought it was a little odd at the time," Pettigrew went on. "It would have been free publicity for his shop. So when I was casting about for suspects, he immediately came to mind—and I said as much. The reporter took down his name."

"Why are you so interested in this reporter?" Mrs. Pettigrew snapped.

Trntl faced her. "I think it's possible he wasn't a reporter at all, but one of the second set of burglars trying to find out whether the earlier thieves had managed to steal the cadenza."

Professor Pettigrew swayed sideways in his chair. "Then he might have been the man who hit me!" His face had gone toadstool white. He fumbled about in one of the desk drawers, pulled out a half-pint of bourbon, uncapped it with a shaking hand, and took a long swallow.

"On the other hand," said Trntl, "he may have been a reporter."

"He didn't look like a burglar," said Pettigrew, wiping his mouth. Seemingly exhausted, he had sagged into his chair, eyes closed, head weaving back and forth.

"Between your talk with Tuttle and my arrival has anything occurred which struck you as odd or suspicious?"

"No, but I've pretty much secluded myself. I'm on leave from the Institute, so I don't have to go in to teach."

"Stephanie Simms came over yesterday afternoon," his wife reminded him sharply. "You told *her* about the theft of the cadenza."

He jerked himself erect and glared at her. "Well, she had a right to know!"

"You called her over to tell her."

"I wasn't going to go to the office with my wound and broken glasses."

"You could have told her on the telephone."

"That's not the kind of thing you tell someone on the telephone! I knew it would be a major shock. And I needed to get her opinion as to who might have taken it."

"*And* some moist-eyed sympathy, and a chance for Little Miss Pattycake to hold your hand. And, more to the point, for you to hold hers!"

"Irma—!"

"You must think I'm pretty stupid." She viciously snapped her towel, and Trntl saw a puff of flour gust past her head. "I know all about that three-day convention you went to in New Haven. She's not welcome in this house, Theodore!"

Pettigrew scowled at her, his right cheek twitching.

"How did Miss Simms take the news?" Trntl asked.

Pettigrew looked at her blankly for a moment, then loudly stammered out: "She was devastated, of course. *She* knows the importance of the cadenza. And she was anguished that her discovery had put me into such physical danger."

"Did she have any idea who might've taken it?"

"No, but she agreed that Finegold was a possibility."

"I'd better talk to her," said Trntl. "May I have her address, please?"

"717 North Charles," said Mrs. Pettigrew. "Apartment 3. You'll find her charming."

"Thank you. Here's my number at the Cavendish Hotel. Call if anything else occurs to you that might be of help. It probably would be best if you didn't tell anyone about my presence in Baltimore. If I have further questions, I'll call you. Thanks for your time and cooperation. If you don't mind, I'd like to look around outside before I leave."

As Trntl moved past his wife and through the doorway, Pettigrew slumped in his chair like a half-empty sack of fertilizer. Her last glimpse of him as Mrs. Pettigrew began marching her down the hall was of one pale hand inverting the bottle of bourbon and a scrawny adam's apple leaping in quick convulsive gulps.

Chapter 4

Having combed his beard and poured a second cup of coffee, Felix McKay was finally ready to riffle through the morning's mail. As usual, mostly junk and bills.

Carol Brown, another of the Associates, looked over his shoulder. "Not much of interest."

"A brochure from a stationery outfit that thinks we're an advertising agency having our tenth anniversary. And a check from P. K. Jenkins for services rendered."

She nipped the check from his fingers like a heron striking a fish. "Well, hurrah for old P. K. It's about time." She went to her desk and made quick jottings in a ledger. As business manager, Carol was responsible for keeping the firm afloat—a nervy and precarious balancing act, for income was erratic and spotty at best, outgo as steady as runoff down a drain. Her success was due in part to her organizing and planning skills; in part to her undergraduate major in Economics; in part to her tendency to look on the darkest side of things, which enabled her to anticipate disasters before they occurred and take evasive action.

Five-foot-three and slimly built, she prided herself on keeping fit, working out three or four times a week at Smalley's Gym. She used very little make-up, wore her nails short and her hair long—it too being a source of pride: black, glossy, and shoulder-length, mostly straight, but with an odd wave, almost a cowlick, high on the left side.

Following her husband's death on the New Jersey Turnpike seven years ago, Carol had worked as an editorial assistant at a glossy fashion magazine—her job basically trouble-shooting in order to make her bosses appear more competent than they actually were. In late summer of 1974, while working out at the gym, she'd met Trntl, who was restless and increasingly bored working as an investigator for an insurance company which seemed to think it had more than its rightful share of fraudulent claims. They'd clicked, and after four months of lunches and going to movies, they decided, over beer and pizza on New Year's Day, to pool their resources—the remnant of Howard Brown's life insurance and Trntl's hoarded savings—and launch N. F. Trntl Associates, Private Investigators.

Today, still single by choice, Carol shared her skylighted Brooklyn apartment with three cats and a jungle of exotic plants. In her free time at home, her favorite activity was reading: Margaret Mead's writings, all that she could find of Katherine Anne Porter's, much of Thoreau, and certain novels of Sinclair Lewis. During the last year she'd been systematically progressing through the works of George Orwell.

Trntl, too, lived alone. After weathering two divorces by age twenty-eight and having dated, in the last six years, a policeman, a psychologist, a postal clerk, and a sculptor—with none of the relationships proving capable of long-term endurance—she'd begun to suspect that she was setting her standards too high. As an explanation, this conclusion was more comfortable than admitting that she might be hard to get along with, or not even very likable. When, at unguarded moments, such prickly thoughts invaded her consciousness, she quickly buried them with cream cheese or sweated them out at the gym.

What she *was* able to admit was her need to be in control—of her circumstances, her self, her decisions, her actions. This she'd learned from living with her first husband, who'd been something of a control-person himself. And from her second, who was so ineffectual at making decisions that, whenever she deferred to him, she found herself ensnared by a tangle of financial and emotional crises which left her exhausted. Occasionally, when in a reflective mood (usually after a couple of beers), she was able to acknowledge that perhaps, in the last analysis, it was her need for asserting personal autonomy, and the zealous guarding of her turf, that prevented her relationships from setting roots.

Her need to be in control had certainly made her impatient with her bosses at the insurance company. She'd found their orders and demands increasingly irritating, and she'd come to resent bitterly having to expend her life energy to save (and make) them money. Being a private investigator allowed her to be her own boss. And she knew that she was a good investigator. *Very* good. Experienced, quick, efficient, cool. Observant. Not easily conned. Skilled in reading people's motivations, discerning hidden interests, detecting falsehood, ferreting out the truth. And her colleagues were good investigators, too. The firm could boast a remarkable string of successes. Unfortunately, their commissions brought them barely enough money to stay afloat. But, for Trntl, the satisfaction of a successfully concluded case—particularly one that entailed intellectual challenge, keen analysis, and puzzles to be solved—was not the money it earned but the proof it provided (to her and to the world at large) that she did indeed possess a superior mind. Her need for this proof was the residue of constantly being reminded of her late father's keen disappointment in having, as his only child, a daughter instead of a son. Death had silenced his ridicule, but his ghost still taunted her.

And as part of the residue, she had long ago determined that what there was in her life she *could* control, she damn well *would* control. All things considered, she was content to be living alone.

Her modest fifth-floor one-bedroom flat had bright prints of French Impressionists on the walls, a perpetual clutter of books and phonograph records on the floor, sporadic invasions of cockroaches, and an unobstructed view of at least twelve stories of a blank-faced office building across the street. Much of the living room was taken up by a quilting frame, which Trntl had inherited from her mother along with her mother's addiction to fabric. She found that designing and piecing quilt-tops was a constructive way to preserve her sanity in the face of the insurance company's paranoia; and, besides, she liked presenting quilts and wall-hangings to her nieces and nephews, who—much to her gratification—seemed to like getting them. Most of her bedroom was taken up by stockpiled and color-grouped fabrics, stacked on every flat surface except the bed.

She kept only one cat—an arrogant chocolate-point Siamese which slept at the foot of her bed and drooled a bit when scratched behind the ears.

Felix, at thirty-two, was one year younger than Carol, three younger than Trntl. Before coming to work for the firm a little over two years ago, he'd been teaching high school chemistry in Racine, Wisconsin, supplementing his meager income by playing clarinet in a '40's-style dance band. Not surprisingly, his wife felt neglected by his many nights away from home; and this opened the door for the broad shoulders, blond crewcut, and flattened nose of a strapping high-school coach-turned-principal who had plenty of time to keep her occupied. The crash had come on a cold December night when his wife quietly announced, "I'm leaving you, Felix, for a better man—a stud with a future who's *never* played the clarinet." Worse yet, the stud was Felix's boss, whom Felix had frequently characterized as "an orangutan in a brown suit and red bowtie who doesn't know Bach from Benny Goodman." When the dust had settled, Felix had simply quit teaching, grown his beard, and come East to seek his fortune. At N. F. Trntl Associates, he was the expert on matters medical and chemical—as well as chief legwork investigator. He enjoyed this life far more than teaching; and though he hadn't yet found his fortune, he still played the clarinet.

"I wonder what Trntl's learned in Baltimore," Carol said, as she put away the ledger.

"She was to call in at eleven." He glanced at his watch. "Ten minutes late. Well, I hope she's learned *something*. Having no specifics of any sort, last night's meeting with the clients was a riot of woolly speculation and wild surmise."

"It sounds like an odd group. You gave me the impression that Mr. Dinch is a man obsessed."

"He's a businessman," said Felix. "Money's his motivation. His main concern in recovering the cadenza is the sales he'll make on a new edition of the concerto. If he's obsessed, it's with the fear that one of his competitors will get it first."

"And the Farringford family?"

"They want the cadenza published to complete the Fifth Concerto, to restore what may well be Father's finest achievement. They also want the royalties that would come from a new edition. Charles didn't leave the family in good financial shape, and Mrs. Farringford's had some lean years."

"She doesn't live in a cheap neighborhood," said Carol.

"Her 'lean' may not be yours and mine," smiled Felix. "But seriously, I don't think the family's all that flush. Her furniture dates from before World War II—and looks it. The son Anton's in banking, but he looks anything but prosperous. Clara teaches flute at some school in the Boston area. She's had a modest concert career and made some recordings, seems far more sensible and level-headed than Anton.

"Anton apparently admires his father intensely, with a kind of hero-worship, and envies his success with women. Wants the cadenza published as a memorial, or tribute to his daddy's great-ness. Clara seems more interested in its musical importance—Father's final legacy, and so on. Now, Mrs. Farringford's position is more complex. She thinks Charles was murdered back in 1947, and the cadenza stolen by the killer. I wonder if, for her, publishing the cadenza wouldn't be a kind of vindication, or poetic justice, or retribution upon the person she thinks killed him. A settling of accounts which would not only pay back the killer, but dispel the shadows of the old crime and exorcise the ghost of scandal."

Carol gave a low whistle. "All that? It sounds very romantic, Felix."

"Only guesswork," said Felix. "But Mrs. Farringford's been brooding for over thirty years. Now, I suspect *she's* something of a romantic—but also a tough old bird who's been through and survived a lot."

"Okay," Carol said with a grin. "And the others?"

"Morgan Latimer's an old old man who was a friend of Dinch's father. He's got piles of money, sits on the board of the Metropolitan Symphony, establishes scholarships, and looks very ill—well, worse than very ill. More like something resurrected from a crypt. He actually heard Farringford play the cadenza in Cleveland, and he's willing to pay any ransom that's required to get it back. I think his motive is altruistic. Wants the world to have this music which gave him so much pleasure. I don't sense anything selfish in his concern." Again he glanced at his watch. "The two pianists seem altruistic also. They want the concerto complete, the cadenza in the repertoire."

"Earlier you didn't sound greatly impressed with Peter Shipley Abbott."

"He tries hard to be a self-important prig," said Felix. "Snob, stuffed-shirt, dandy—take your pick; they all apply. But he's also one of the best classical pianists we've got, so whatcha gonna do?"

"I've got his recording of the Fifth Concerto," said Carol. "It's marvelous."

"With the cadenza he wrote to substitute for Farringford's?" said Felix.

"Sure. But don't most performers use it?"

"Yes, I guess they do. Anyway, Dinch promised Abbott that he will be the first to perform Farringford's cadenza in public. Whereas Rosamond Foxe has been promised the first recording."

"You seemed to like her somewhat better than Abbott," Carol interjected with a sly smile.

"She was fine."

"Nice boobs?"

"Cynic! As a matter of fact, yes—but she has other points in her favor—"

"You're saying she's not a stuffed-shirt?" said Carol.

"Let's say she isn't a prig or a self-centered snob. She's performing with the Metropolitan Symphony on the twelfth; you can come with me and see for yourself."

"I just might do that."

The door whipped open, and Torvald Grimsson, the third Associate, bustled in, big as a grizzly in his rough tweed greatcoat and woolly astrakhan. "It's getting colder out," he announced, dropping a large battered briefcase onto his desk. "Albany was downright warm when I left last night." He shrugged his coat off and hung it on the back of the door. Then, still wearing his hat, he seated himself and began pulling papers from the briefcase—the results of his morning's work.

He'd joined the Associates four years ago, having left an unrewarding job as legal secretary in a stodgy Minnesota law firm that specialized in probate, divorce, child custody, and trusts. Just short of a law degree himself, he'd concluded that he had no desire to practice law. Trntl's ad in *The Paralegal Review* had immediately caught his eye: "WANTED: A person with legal expertise for confidential investigative work promising adventure and personal growth." He'd called long-distance from his employer's office and arranged to send his résumé. And, on a bright May morning, he'd appeared on Trntl's threshold: a broad, rectangular giant (six feet four in his socks) with lumberjack shoulders, freckled hands as large as catcher's mitts, chicory blue eyes in constant motion behind thick lenses, and a long narrow skull capped with a tangled thatch of wheat-straw hair. In one hand, he'd carried a huge suitcase; in his pocket, a cashier's check for six thousand dollars—the sum of his worldly goods. All he'd said was, "Torvald. I'm here." Trntl had pointed to the corner desk; and there, four years later, he still was.

A black belt in karate, Torvald was skilled in research techniques, legal protocols, chess, and general strategizing. He rarely dealt with clients or other contacts outside the office, preferring to let Felix and Trntl do the street work. He spent most of his time in libraries, news morgues, public registries, and courthouse fossil beds—or else at his desk typing with machinegun regularity his sixty-three words a minute. He was responsible for managing the firm's files, and had created an elaborate system of indexed and cross-referenced folders, tape cassettes, and news clippings that occupied one entire wall. In August he was scheduled to marry Rachel Weintraub, a buyer in women's wear at Macy's and heiress to a delicatessen on Lexington Avenue.

"Did you find the things I wanted?" Felix asked him.

"Most of them, and some other things, too." He handed Felix a stack of crisp photocopies. "News stories dealing with Farringford's death and the initial disappearance of the cadenza. Items kept showing up till December, and then there was another wave the next year when the concerto was published." He gave Felix another stack. "Biographies of Charles and Clara Farringford, Peter Shipley Abbott, and Rosamond Foxe culled from various *Who's Who*'s and musicians' directories. And here"—two more stacks— "a complete discography of Foxe's recordings, along with her address and phone number in Hempstead; and—finally—notes on the legal hassles attending the settlement of Farringford's estate. He left things in a mess, as you learned last night, and the creditors swarmed in like gulls at low tide. Mrs. Farringford came out of it with the clothes on her back, but that's about all—and only because she had some shrewd attorneys. Charles seems to have been an irresponsible dolt in managing his finances, and the Mrs. has every right to be pissed with him."

The telephone rang, and Felix answered: "N. F. Trntl Associates."

Trntl's voice: "Good morning, Felix. I'm calling from my hotel with the first progress report. Turn on the tape recorder."

"Good morning yourself," said Felix. "Dinch has already called to see if you've learned anything." He switched on the recorder.

"I left my magic wand in New York with my toothbrush," said Trntl. "Yes, I've learned some things—but it's not clear yet how they all relate. Maybe you folks can figure it out. Ready?" She summarized what she'd learned from talking to Professor Pettigrew.

Felix read her back an abstract: "Three break-ins—probably by two groups of burglars, both after the cadenza. One early, two late on the same night. The first burglars got the cadenza along with some Brahms manuscripts in Pettigrew's hand. The second group trashed the study and sent Pettigrew to the hospital, then probably came back and went through the rest of the house."

"Good," said Trntl. "I also observed some tension between the Professor and Mrs. Pettigrew regarding Stephanie Simms. Mrs. Pettigrew is self-absorbed, trivial, conventional, and drab. The kind of person who'd wear white gloves while visiting to see if you'd dusted the tops of picture frames. She's observant, however, and remembers details far better than he."

"And you think the second group sent a man in the guise of a reporter to learn from Pettigrew whether the first burglars got the cadenza."

"Right. And Pettigrew told him yes, and gave him the name of the shop where the cadenza was discovered. I'll say more about that in a minute. This first: when I examined the ground outside the broken window, there wasn't much to see. The police had trampled everything quite thoroughly. I did find a partial print of what seemed to be a gym shoe, and, about seven feet from the window, a tiny roach that appeared to have been tossed away."

"The end of a joint?"

"You've got it. And I doubt if the police were smoking. It was a recent discard; the paper was damp but still firm."

"Not much help, though. Might have been the son's."

"True," said Trntl, "but worth logging in. Now here's the interesting part. I went to see the owner of the shop where the cadenza was found—a Nathan Finegold. I didn't think it very likely that he'd done the burglary to get back a valuable item he'd practically given away; but I wanted to learn what he knew about that piano bench the cadenza was found in. When I got there at ten-thirty, the shop was closed and the lights out—which seemed strange on a weekday. Finegold lives upstairs above the shop, with a separate stairway opening onto the street. I went up to see if he was home."

The narrow stairs led up to a dark hallway that ran the depth of the building, front to back. Several closed doors lined the right-hand wall. The second one down from the head of the stairs was labeled 'FINEGOLD' on a small name-plate. Trntl knocked briskly. She heard a faint scuffling from behind the door, and then a live silence.

She knocked again, more authoritatively. This time, after some urgent soft mutterings, there was a loud click as the bolt was drawn back. The door slowly opened the space of an inch, and a single frightened eye peered out over a slack guard chain. "What do you want?" A woman's voice, breathless with fear.

Afterwards, Trntl decided that she began badly. She should have chirped, with a bright smile, "Hello! I'm with the Consumer Bureau" or something similar. But not being a naturally devious person, she'd said straight out: "I'm here to see Nathan Finegold about the Farringford Cadenza." The *wrong* thing to say.

Inside, a rapid scuffling. A man's hoarse whisper: "Lock the door!"

The door slammed shut; the bolt shot home. Trntl was glad she didn't have her toe in the crack. She knocked again. "Mr. Finegold, I'm a private investigator—not the police. Please talk to me—" Thumps and scrapings. Something was being pushed in front of the door. "Mr. Finegold, do you hear me?"

At the far end of the hall, a door flew open. And with the speed of a clay pigeon flung from a trap, a man darted out, turned, and clattered down a back stairway. Trntl charged after him; and as she ran, it flashed on her that maybe he *had* stolen the cadenza. Hurtling a good clip when she reached the end of the passage, she stiff-armed the wall to bound sideways down the stairs. A dim-lit, narrow flight leading to the back of the shop. Dark storeroom piled with crates and boxes, bald mannequins, floor lamps, bird cages, pots and pans. Flinging herself through a curtained doorway into the salesroom, she saw the man leaping through counters and tables toward a cash register near the front window. She followed, shouting "Wait! I just want to talk!" He fumbled at a drawer beneath the cash register, then turned at bay, shakily holding a pistol in his left hand.

"Stop right there!" he shouted. "I have a gun!"

She ducked behind a table heaped with old fruit jars, magneto telephones, and stand-up picture frames. "I *don't* have a gun, Mr. Finegold. And I'm not with the police, if that's what you're worried about. I'm a private investigator, and I only want to ask you some questions."

"Then come out with your hands up," he cried, crouching down behind the cash register.

She thought this over for a bit; then, raising only her hands above the table top so he could see them empty, she said, "I just want to ask you about the piano bench where the Farringford Cadenza was found."

"I don't have the cadenza!" he shouted. "And I don't know where it is."

The terror in his voice inclined her to believe him. But *why* the terror? "Did someone think you'd stolen it from Professor Pettigrew's house?" she asked.

"Why should I steal it? It's nothing to me. Nothing! And you're the fourth to come asking about it. Yesterday the others, and I told them no, I didn't have it, and they beat me up. They broke my arm!"

With her hands still raised, Trntl slowly came out from behind the table. Using the cash register as a shield, Nathan Finegold continued to point the gun at her. He was a small man, thin and bald; his right arm, bent at the elbow, was encased in a plaster cast and suspended by a sling. His left eye was blackened and puffed nearly shut.

"Why did they think you'd stolen the cadenza from Pettigrew's house?" Trntl asked.

"How should I know? I'm an honest man, not a thief. I never saw the music after I sold it to the girl. Now you get out of here. How do I know you're not with them?"

"I don't know who they are," Trntl said. "I'm a private investigator hired by Lunner & Dinch, who were planning to publish the music. They sent me to Baltimore to find who stole it from Professor Pettigrew."

"Then why come here?" he shouted. "It wasn't me!" And the gun barrel jumped scarily.

"No, no," said Trntl. "No one's accusing you. Can you describe the men who came here and beat you up?"

"I want no more trouble," said Finegold. "Start for the door. I'll let you out. Don't ever come back. I have the right to refuse anyone."

"Won't you at least describe the men who broke your arm?"

"Get moving. Now!" The pistol jerked twice toward the door.

Trntl started for the front of the shop. "If they think you stole the cadenza or know where it is," she said evenly, "you've already got trouble. There were two break-ins at Pettigrew's house. The first burglary got the cadenza. The guys who beat you up were the second group. They think you got there first."

"Nope. No more. You want I should call the cops?" He came from behind the cash register, gestured with the gun barrel. "You, unlock the door."

She did as she was told. First the deadbolt, then the key. "Was one of the men blond, clean-cut, with a small mustache?"

"Out!" he said.

"Dammit," said Trntl, turning in the doorway, "answer me one question—just one! Where did you get the piano bench?"

The muzzle did not waver. But Finegold frowned. "What do you mean?"

"The bench where the cadenza was found. Where did you get it?"

"I don't remember. It was a long time ago. An auction lot. From somewhere in Pennsylvania, maybe. Why do you want to know?"

"That," said Trntl with a nasty smile, "is *my* business." *And she was out on the sidewalk, hearing the door slam and lock behind her.*

"Interesting," said Felix, when Trntl had finished reporting her encounter with Finegold. "Do you think the bully-boys decided he wasn't responsible for the first burglary?"

"I suspect so. But they had to break his arm before they were convinced."

"That makes them seem desperate to know who *did* get the cadenza."

"Yes, and it makes me think they were clutching at straws. But the question remains for them and us: who has the cadenza now? I have an appointment with Stephanie Simms at two o'clock. Would it be possible for Carol to come down on the Metroliner with some clothes and toilet articles—oh yes, and a tape recorder? All I've got is what I'm wearing, and I don't know how long I'm going to be here. Carol should plan to stay awhile."

Felix looked over his shoulder. "Carol, Trntl wants you to go to Baltimore, take her some clothes and a tape recorder. Are you free to go and stay?"

"Sure," Carol said. "I've got her key; I'll pack her bag, see my neighbor about watering the plants and feeding the cats, and be there late this afternoon."

"She's on her way," Felix said into the phone. "Is there anything we can do for you here?"

"If something occurs to me, I'll let you know."

"We'll expect a call from you the same time tomorrow," said Felix. "What should we tell Dinch the next time he calls?"

"Tell him there were two burglaries, and that the first one got the cadenza. Let him chew on that awhile. If he can get beyond thinking his competitors did it, he might come up with other possibilities."

She hung up, and Felix turned to the others. "It gets stranger all the time."

"Let's hear the tape," said Carol.

They listened carefully; and when the tape was finished, Torvald Grimsson nodded gravely. "Trntl observes well, and seems to have made some likely inferences. But it's been two days since the cadenza was stolen. If ransom was the motive, or selling it, wouldn't Lunner & Dinch have been contacted by now?"

"You'd think so," said Felix.

"Since they haven't, isn't there a strong possibility that money might *not* be the motive for the burglars who got it?"

"But where does that leave us?" asked Carol. "Back with Lunner & Dinch's competitors?"

"Not necessarily." From his briefcase Torvald removed a brown paper bag and prepared to eat his lunch. Bagels from Lexington Avenue, lox, cream cheese, a monstrous pickle. A large slab of halvah. "Felix, didn't Trntl once suggest to you that it might've been stolen by somebody who wanted it *back*? Somebody who had it once, lost it somehow, and decided to repossess it after Pettigrew's press conference."

"Sorry," said Carol. "That seems unlikely to me. Why would someone want an unpublished cadenza all to himself?"

Torvald shrugged. "Maybe the person thought it was rightfully his—or *hers*, as the case might be. Remember the lipstick on the cigarette butts in the train compartment. Or maybe he's just a dog-in-the-manger who doesn't want anyone else, or the public, to have it."

"A collector?" said Felix.

"Possibly. Or someone who simply doesn't want it published at all—by anybody."

"Or both," said Carol. "But if that person was involved in the original disappearance in 1947, thirty-four years is a long time to wait for it to resurface. He'd be getting a bit old to break into the professor's house through a window."

Torvald shook his head. "The person trying to repossess it might not have been involved in the first disappearance. Or the manuscript might not have been out of the person's hands for all of the thirty-four years." He paused in his munching for a drink of water. "I found the news accounts of Farringford's death quite interesting. No mention of the lipsticked cigarettes. The Cleveland reviewer knocked himself out praising the performance. I even found the advertisements that Dinch's father ran trying to get the cadenza back, no questions asked. And Farringford's funeral: lots of important folks got their names listed. About two-thirds of them are dead now."

"Was Toscanini there?" Felix inquired.

"I didn't see his name. Why do you ask?"

"Anton Farringford says yes, Abbott says no."

Again Torvald shrugged. "If he was, the papers didn't mention him. You can read about it yourself; the accounts of the funeral are in those photocopies I gave you."

"It's not important," said Felix. "Anton may not be remembering rightly. Thirty-four years is a long time."

"It depends," Torvald said, "on which end you start from."

Felix poured another cup of coffee. Carol said thoughtfully, "There are a few other items in Trntl's report that interest me. And they might have a bearing on motive for theft." She filched a chunk of Torvald's halvah. "First, why did the thieves take both the cadenza and Pettigrew's manuscript of the Brahms works? Did they want them all? Or was it an accident, a mistake in the dark? Or being in too much of a hurry to notice?"

"Or too high on pot to make distinctions?" Felix added.

"Assuming it was the first burglars who were doing the smoking," said Torvald.

"Any of those are possible reasons why both Farringford and Brahms were taken," Carol continued. "But it could have been simple ignorance. People who weren't able to tell the difference—who thought *all* the manuscripts were Farringford's. Or maybe so unsure of themselves they just took the whole batch to be on the safe side."

"Or someone who didn't know much about music at all," said Felix. "But that hypothesis doesn't square with Torvald's notion of someone trying to repossess the cadenza who thought it was rightfully his. *That* person would recognize it when he saw it."

"Unless that person had simply hired a musically-ignorant flunky to do the burglary," said Carol. "An aged party from 1947 too old to crawl through a window himself. Look, we know this for sure: it wasn't a random theft. Someone broke in specifically to steal the Farringford manuscript. Nothing else was taken in that first break-in except the Brahms manuscripts that were on the desk with it. If money isn't the motive—ransom or sale—and if this person wasn't trying simply to get it back for himself or someone else—what *is* the motive?"

"To prevent its being published," said Felix.

"To put it in a private collection," said Torvald.

"Or simply to humiliate or injure Professor Pettigrew," said Carol. "Finding the cadenza was the biggest thing ever to happen to him. It brought recognition, fame, press conferences. Wouldn't taking all that away be a way of crushing the man?"

"An old enemy?" said Felix. "A rival scholar? A disgruntled student? Maybe the theft is only a prank or a vicious joke."

"The second and third break-ins weren't just a prank," said Carol.

"But Pettigrew's students are musicians," said Torvald. "And rival scholars would know the difference between Farringford and Brahms. Wouldn't that undercut the ignorance argument? That's enough halvah, Carol."

"Not necessarily," said Felix. "It might have been a dumb student. And grudge might provide a motive for wanting revenge on Pettigrew. Don't forget the roach. If it was a student, he might have been doping up for hours before making the break-in."

"Theories," muttered Torvald. "I'm going to do my income tax."

Chapter 5

Stephanie Simms lived just off Mt. Vernon Place, at the northern edge of downtown Baltimore, in an old, once-elegant rowhouse divided long ago into a gaggle of small apartments. The house was located only two blocks from the Hastings Institute and one block north of the towering column of the Washington Monument. Along with its sisters and an imposing old church, it faced a narrow park that divided Charles Street into a boulevard. This park instersected at right angles two larger parks that divided Monument Street on either side of the memorial column. In summertime, the benches, statues, trees, and shrubs of the parks would no doubt have lent to Mt. Vernon Place a semblance of its former grace. But today, as Trntl observed the parks March-desolate, with only hints of green to temper the midwinter brown, with trash and old leaves heaped beneath the benches, and vistas fuzzed gray with naked twigs, their bleakness merely underscored how shabby the neighborhood had become.

In the vestibule at the top of the white marble steps, Trntl scanned the mailboxes for Stephanie's name. Three flights up. She pushed the button beside the nameplate, and was immediately buzzed through the inner door into the downstairs hallway. High-ceilinged and poorly lit, and darkened further by maroon and chalk-blue wallpaper in a vaguely floral pattern, the hall tunneled away toward the back of the house like the entrance to a mine. The staircase on Trntl's left, though steep and narrow, had been designed with a sense of style: beside it climbed a superbly molded hardwood bannister that curved gracefully with a half-twist at each landing. And everywhere, the faint musty odor of advanced age, dry rot, carpets leaked on, and over-heated pipes.

Stephanie's apartment was near the head of the staircase. She answered the door at once, as though she'd been listening behind the panels to Trntl's footsteps ascending the stairs. "You're right on time," she said, when Trntl had introduced herself. "Come in. Let me take your coat."

She was twenty-three or four, slightly plump, with long eyelashes and fluffy blond hair caught up with pink ribbon into a ponytail. She reminded Trntl of a doll she'd once had that opened and closed its eyes, drank water from a bottle, and wet its pants. When you pulled a string protruding from its belly, it always squeaked "I-love-you."

Stephanie was wearing flat-heeled shoes, dark blue slacks, and a pale orange sweater—self-consciously tight to show off her breasts. She used makeup well—turquoise eye shadow, cheek blush (no winter pallor there, just the proper rosy glow), bright carmine lipstick. In high school, Trntl guessed, she'd been a cheer-leader—or, at the very least, a member of the pompon squad.

Her apartment was a single large room, high-ceilinged, with one narrow window that opened onto an areaway between her building and the one adjacent. From a large plaster rosette in the center of the ceiling hung a spidery chandelier with multiple lightbulbs, each peeking from its scalloped shade of frosted glass (morning glories? tulips?). In an alcove near the window, a kitch-enette. On the right wall upon entering, a closet and a bathroom no bigger than a closet. Against the left hand wall, a sofa that opened into a bed.

Despite her practiced ease at living in mess, Trntl found the room claustrophobic with its ill-organized clutter. Books and magazines piled knee-deep. Old phonograph records tumbled into cardboard boxes. Stacks of sheet music. A windup Victrola. Two tennis racquets. A plaster bust of Beethoven glaring into the closet with the traditional grumpy frown (for all the world, Trntl thought, like a bulldog with hemorrhoids). Remnants of a sparse lunch on the drop-leaf table. A pile of unwashed dishes in the sink. "Please sit down," Stephanie said, indicating the sofa-bed. "Now, what can I do for you?"

She wore a polite smile, but her eyes were guarded and anx-ious, spoiling the gee-whiz peaches-innocent effect of her care-fully-applied makeup. She held her body rigid, elbows close in to her sides, as though she feared that, left to themselves, her move-ments might be spasmodic and twitchy.

"As I said on the phone, my firm's been hired by Lunner & Dinch and the Farringford family to recover the cadenza. When I spoke to Professor Pettigrew this morning, he said he'd already discussed the theft with you." Stephanie seemed to become even more nervous as Trntl spoke. Intrigued by this, but preferring to have her at ease, Trntl began on neutral turf: "I understand you discovered the cadenza in a secondhand shop."

Stephanie sat stiffly on the edge of a wooden chair, her hands tightly gripping her knees. "Yes, that's right. Hidden in an old piano bench—"

"So I understand. What sort of bench was it? Or rather, what sort of piano would the bench have belonged to?"

"Oh, it had been a very good bench at one time. The sort that would've gone with a very expensive piano."

"Not the sort of piano you'd find in a typical home? not an old upright or spinet?"

"Oh no. I've seen such benches with older concert grands."

"Was it the professional type with padded top and a knob for raising and lowering—"

"No, just a rectangular bench with a hinged lid. Pretty beat up, though—scratched and scarred."

"When you bought the manuscript from Mr. Finegold, did he seem to be particularly interested in it? Or curious as to where you'd found it?"

"No, he just glanced at it and said 'Two dollars'. He seemed pretty ignorant about music—held it upside down while he looked at it. And besides, he was busy with another customer who was pricing a couple of chamber pots."

"Have you heard from him since you bought the cadenza?"

"No, and I haven't been back to the shop. I did invite him to our press conference, but he refused to come and insisted that his name not be given to the reporters."

"Did you think that was odd?"

"Not at the time. Ted—Professor Pettigrew thinks it's strange: it would have been free publicity for Mr. Finegold."

"I understand the manuscript was hidden in a false bottom in the bench."

She seemed to be relaxing a little, breathing more deeply. "That's right. I saw it through a crack and pried up the bottom to get it out."

Trntl decided to leave the neutral turf. "You're aware that there were three break-ins at Professor Pettigrew's house on the night the cadenza was stolen. Whoever was responsible for the first burglary got the cadenza. Those involved in the second and third, who attacked Pettigrew and sent him to the hospital, were after the cadenza too."

Stephanie's grip had so tightened on her knees that her knuckles flared white. Her face, too, had blanched, and—except for her wide watchful eyes—had become as immobile as an ivory mask. "My job is to get the cadenza back," Trntl continued, "no questions asked. Do you know who took it?"

For a long moment, Stephanie seemed to have stopped breathing altogether. Then suddenly her face crumpled, her hand flew to her mouth, and she gave a strangled sob—prelude to a torrent of tears.

Trntl snatched a Kleenex from a box at the end of the sofa and handed it to her. Between heavy sobs and great gulps of air, Stephanie gasped: "Oh Miss Trntl! Can I trust you? I've got to talk to someone!" She blew her nose loudly. Trntl handed her the whole box of tissues. "I told you why I'm here," she said soothingly. "My only interest is in recovering the cadenza."

"You won't go to the police?"

"I'm a *private* investigator. If you have something you want to say, please do so. It won't go any farther."

"I've *got* to trust someone. I'm just *sick* at what's happened, and I can't keep it all to myself anymore!" Her sobs were subsiding into hiccups. Trntl settled back and waited patiently. Finally, Stephanie blurted: "I know who has the cadenza, Miss Trntl!"

Trntl smiled encouragingly but said nothing.

"It's a friend of mine—Morris Waite. He broke into Professor Pettigrew's study and took it off the desk." She blew her nose again, and, with red-rimmed eyes, gazed at Trntl with mingled fear and hope—much like a young child who, having confessed to cutting holes in Mother's favorite tablecloth, doesn't know whether to expect punishment for the offense, or praise for being truthful.

Trntl wasn't Mother, however, and was not the least bit interested in either punishment or praise. "Does he still have it?"

"He had it yesterday when he told me about the break-in."

"Why did he take it?"

"Oh, it's all so stupid!" Stephanie cried. "So childish! He took it because he was angry at Professor Pettigrew and wanted to get back at him. Last year, when Morris was a student at the Hastings Institute, he plagiarized a paper he had to turn in for Ted's course in European Romanticism—and Ted accused him of dishonesty and had him expelled from the Institute. Morris has been working as a restaurant cook ever since."

"I take it you and Morris are *close* friends?" Trntl asked.

"Well, yes, you could say that. We go places and do things together. Yes, I guess we're close. When he was a student we saw each other every day, and now it's only two or three times a week. I guess you could say we used to be closer than we are now." "Come now, Miss Simms. Are you telling me that his stealing the cadenza was simply a matter of getting revenge on Pettigrew for having him expelled? That's *all?*" Trntl laced her tone with weighty skepticism, and the implied incredulity pulled the rest of it out.

"Well, no," Stephanie replied, "there's more to it than that. Morris is a very jealous person. In many ways he's still an adolescent. He misunderstood the friendship I have with Professor Pettigrew. He thought we were seeing too much of each other, that there was something going on between us. Just because I did well in Ted's classes, and admire him so much, and played tennis with him all last summer, Morris thought that Ted was cutting him out, that we were having an affair!" (Silly Morris, thought Trntl; and silly Mrs. Pettigrew, who would agree with him.) "So when the Farringford Cadenza was discovered, and Ted was getting so much attention after the press conference, Morris decided that stealing the cadenza would be the best way to hurt him."

"Did Morris tell you this?" Trntl asked.

"Yes, but only after he got frightened."

"Frightened?"

"Yes, when I told him about the second burglary. He hadn't known about it, and it came as a big shock to him."

"Perhaps you'd better start at the beginning," said Trntl.

Stephanie fumbled a cigarette from a pack beside her and lit it shakily. Trntl seized the opportunity to light one of her own. "The first I heard about the theft was yesterday morning when Ted— Professor Pettigrew called me to his house and told me. He said the publishers didn't want him telling anyone about the theft, but that he thought I had a right to know. He told me there had been three break-ins, that the cadenza had been taken during the first, and that he'd been attacked during the second. He showed me his stitches. It was an awful wound, Miss Trntl!

"Well, I was just beside myself. When I saw Morris that afternoon, I told him everything. I had no idea he was the thief. He got real scared when he heard about the second break-in. I asked why, and then he swore me to secrecy and confessed that he'd taken the cadenza. You can't imagine how dumbfounded I was! I had no idea Morris hated Professor Pettigrew so much, or that he assumed Ted and I were having an affair. Weren't Morris and

I still going out—at least twice a week? And I reminded him that Professor Pettigrew is a married man, for goodness sakes!"

Trntl blew a smoke ring. "If no one knew that Morris had taken the cadenza, why was he scared when he heard about the second break-in?"

"He's afraid he'll be blamed for it if he tries to give the cadenza back. Morris realizes he did a foolish thing, Miss Trntl. He said he wasn't thinking straight the night he broke into the house. He knows how important the cadenza is. He's a musician himself, and was studying music history. He wants it published, and he knows that if anything happens to it while it's in his possession—if it's damaged or destroyed—I'd never forgive him. He'd thought about mailing it back to Ted so that he wouldn't be connected with the break-ins, but he thinks the cadenza's too valuable to trust to the mails. I offered to take it and give it back for him, but he said No, that would involve me in the burglary. How could I explain finding it *twice*? Questions would be raised that would lead back to him, and he'd be charged with burglary and assault. He knows he can't keep the cadenza—and he doesn't want to—but he doesn't know how to go about giving it back. And while he works it out, I've got to keep silent to protect him. It's been driving me crazy!" She began sniffling again.

"Frankly," said Trntl, "it doesn't sound like he's thinking straight yet. Does he understand the full significance of the second break-in?"

"He knows it means someone else wants the cadenza. That frightens him, too."

"It should," Trntl said gravely. "Whoever they are, they play rough. Besides attacking Pettigrew, they beat up Mr. Finegold and broke his arm."

Stephanie's eyes popped wide. "Mr. Finegold? When did this happen?"

"Yesterday morning. They thought *he* might've been the first burglar, that he might have the manuscript."

Stephanie gasped. "Does that mean Morris is in danger?"

"Only if they find out he's got the cadenza. Has he told anyone else besides you?"

Her eyes grew wider still. "I asked him that. He said that before he talked to me, he'd told just one other person—another cook he works with at the restaurant—Tony Scaevola. Morris and I have double-dated with him and his girlfriend Tammy several times.

Morris said that sometime around midnight, after he'd stashed the cadenza in his apartment, he went over to Tony's place and had some drinks and bragged about what he'd done to get even with Professor Pettigrew. He explained the whole thing to Tony, showed him a clipping of the press conference and everything. He said Tony laughed a lot and said it was a great revenge." She paused. "Telling Tony won't put Morris in any danger, will it?"

"Hard to say," said Trntl. "But the longer Morris keeps the manuscript, the more danger he's in. Do you think he'd give it to me? I'd deliver it to Lunner & Dinch and never reveal where I got it."

Stephanie said, "I think he'd give it to you—and be glad to be rid of it. Particularly if I told him he should."

"Could you call him now and arrange a time?"

Aflutter with relief, Stephanie leaped up and rushed to the phone, as pumped as if the team had made a touchdown. "He should be home now—maybe sleeping," she said, dialing the number. Trntl lit another cigarette and puffed impatiently while the phone rang repeatedly and Stephanie became ever more agitated. "He must be gone," Stephanie said, finally hanging up the receiver. "Maybe he was called back in to work." Her lower lip was trembling.

Trntl stumped out her cigarette, shrugged into her coat, and pulled on her gloves. "We'd better go over to his place," she said, trying not to sound too urgent. "Wait for him if he's not there. You'll want your gloves; it's cold out."

Stephanie nodded and silently got her coat and earmuffs. They hurried to Trntl's car and drove to Morris's address on Gobel Street. On the way, Stephanie chattered continuously, and Trntl learned much about Morris: that he was a very nice person and fun to be with, though he probably did too much marijuana (Stephanie had urged him to smoke less dope, and besides, it gave him a paranoid reaction)—that he played the dulcimer, pretty well, too, and someday wanted to compose music and write a novel and travel to Europe and get a master's degree in musicology and have an unsightly mole removed from his right shoulder and get back to sharing an apartment with Stephanie again sometime. "And we go to recitals and concerts," she said, finally running out of steam. "Morris always has such unusual insights into the music. And we go to Patapsco Park to picnic and walk in the woods, and up the Washington Monument, and out to Fort McHenry and down to the harbor, oh, we do lots of things. I've been wanting Morris to learn to play tennis, but he says he's not interested." She pointed. "Turn here. He lives in the middle of the next block."

Trntl was listening with only half an ear—being far more interested in the gray Oldsmobile Cutlass she'd been observing in the rear-view mirror ever since they'd left Stephanie's apartment. It had faithfully followed them turn by turn, maintaining a distance of one to two blocks. She was so intent on watching it she nearly missed the turn onto Gobel Street.

"That's his house up there," Stephanie said. "The one with the flagpole."

Sure enough, the Cutlass turned after them onto Gobel. "Quick!" said Stephanie. "There's a parking place. Grab it, they're hard to find." Trntl braked, reversed, and angled in parallel to the curb. She was intending to sit behind the wheel until the Cutlass passed them; but as she killed the engine, she saw in the mirror that it had turned off Gobel onto a side street before it reached the second block.

Stephanie was already out of the car and dashing up the sidewalk. Trntl pulled the ignition key and hurried after her. "Now," she said to herself, "assuming they were tailing us, who were they following—Stephanie, or me?"

Morris's apartment was in a tall, narrow building of aged red brick with carved stone lintels above the windows. The entry was lined with white marble that had yellowed with hard use and decades of grime. "Fourth floor," said Stephanie, leading the way. The stairs were extremely steep and narrow, covered with threadbare carpet for the first two flights, and dimly lit with wall sconces containing small, tapered, low-wattage bulbs that succeeded quite well in simulating orange candle flames.

The two of them were out of breath when they reached the fourth floor. Stephanie led Trntl down a dark corridor lined with garbage cans and stopped at a paneled door painted chocolate brown. There was no answer to her frantic knocking.

Reaching past her, Trntl tried the knob with her gloved hand. The door swung open. As they entered, Trntl scanned a quick inventory. A rather stark room. Little furniture. No window curtains to prevent the afternoon sun from streaming in. European tour posters on the walls—Vienna, Paris, London, Rome. Bare hardwood floor. A single bed, unmade and rumpled, pulled out at an angle from the wall. A hot plate in one corner. Above it, a small wall-cupboard with canned goods, a bottle of vinegar, and an open box of soda crackers. In the center of the room, a small table littered with empty beer cans. Beside it, a chair lying on its side. By the head of the bed, a pair of greasy gym shoes. On the floor at the foot of the bed, the remains of a dulcimer crushed flat by what Trntl guessed were the repeated stampings of a very large foot.

"Morris?" Stephanie called.

"Where does he keep the cadenza?" Trntl asked, the smashed dulcimer and toppled chair giving her voice new urgency.

"He told me he'd locked it in his music case and hidden it with his dope," said Stephanie. "There's a stash hole in the wall behind his bed."

Sure enough, there where the bed had been pulled away from the wall, the wainscoting of vertical wooden boards had been wrenched from the plaster to expose a dark recess. It was empty.

"No cadenza here," Trntl announced. "No marijuana, either."

Stephanie peered into the hole. "The cadenza was in a locked brown leather briefcase."

"We'll search," Trntl said. "Stephanie, see if you can find the cadenza anywhere in this room. Check everything—mattress, books, drawers, behind the posters. It might not be in the briefcase anymore. At least you've seen the manuscript, and will be able to recognize it. But don't take off your gloves, and don't disturb anything. Is that the bathroom? I'll look in there."

Through a narrow doorway, the bathroom was a long closet with just enough space for a sink, tub, and toilet to be lined up in series on the opposing wall. The bright sunlight slanted through the single window at the end opposite the stool. As she entered, Trntl noted that the bare bulb above the sink was lit.

Behind a plastic shower curtain, the bathtub, two-thirds filled with scummy water, contained the mostly submerged body of a naked man.

Precisely what Trntl had hoped not to find. Although not a complete surprise, nonetheless still a shock to the system. "Can you describe Morris?" Trntl asked casually into the other room.

"He's tall, with blue eyes," Stephanie answered, her voice muffled by the bathroom wall, "with longish blond hair and a kind of scraggly beard. He's not very muscular—but he would be if he'd learn to play tennis. Oh, and he has a little bluebird tattoo."

The body lay on its back, its swollen face just below the surface of the water. The face was framed by a tangled weblike mass of darkish hair and beard. With the lids half-closed, it was hard to tell the color of the eyes. On the right shoulder was a large dark mole, and high on the left thigh adjacent to the groin, a small tattoo. A little bluebird with spread wings, waterlogged and not going anywhere.

Trntl reached out and gently nudged the right shoulder; the body shifted away in the water. No blood. No apparent wounds. Severe abrasions on both knees. Blue jeans and underwear tossed into a soggy heap beside the toilet. A pair of scuffed leather shoes. Evidence of a considerable amount of water drying on the floor around the tub.

Trntl opened the medicine chest, scanned the aspirin tablets, toothbrush, and dental floss, closed the door, observed that the cabinet was securely bolted to the wall. Removed the top of the water closet, looked in: no stash, no cadenza. Studied the ceiling, the light fixture, the window frame, the molding where the walls joined the ceiling, the vinyl floor. No wainscoting, just painted plaster. She turned and went back to the bedroom.

From the kitchen area, Stephanie said, "There's no sign of the cadenza. I've gone through the cupboards, even the cracker box, and—since you said search everything—even his bag of dirty laundry."

"It wasn't in the bathroom, either," said Trntl.

"Someone must've come in and taken it from his stash hole. Morris would never leave the boards pulled away like that. And his dulcimer's lying smashed on the floor!"

"We'd better go," said Trntl, guiding Stephanie into the hall. She carefully closed the door behind them, noting as she did that there was no sign of forced entry: no jimmy marks, the lock intact. Then she followed Stephanie down the stairs.

"I don't know where Morris could be," Stephanie said on the second flight down. "He wasn't scheduled to work today. On his days off he's usually home at this time. And who got into his apartment? Do you suppose it was those people who hurt Mr. Finegold?"

"Possibly," said Trntl. *Probably*, she thought—and they were playing *very* rough. She felt fairly confident in reconstructing what had happened. Since the light was still on in the sun-washed bathroom, Morris had been killed at night. He'd probably been clothed, possibly just home from work; since his jeans and shorts were wet and at some distance from the tub, he'd been drowned while wearing them. It would take at least two intruders to force him down onto his knees and hold his head under water till he told them where the cadenza was hidden—and then to drown him. Once he was dead, they'd placed his clothes by the toilet to make it look as though he'd undressed himself and drowned while taking a bath. But the toppled chair and crushed dulcimer suggested a struggle. Since the room had not been further disrupted to signify a thoroughgoing search, Morris had probably told them where the stash-hole was behind the bed. But it hadn't saved him.

"Of course, Morris himself may have taken the cadenza out of the hiding place and gone off with it," Stephanie said. "He might've known that someone was coming for it and wanted to escape." Trntl let her continue to clutch at her straws. Her own thoughts were concerned with who had the cadenza now. Pettigrew's attackers? Most likely. But who were they? The polite young man with the blond mustache and his friends (however many there were)? Agents of Humboldt-Hartmann Gesellschaft? Or Cameron Stewart, Ltd.? B. F. Cleavenger & Sons? L'Enfant Devereux? The dossiers Dinch had given her asserted that his competitors would stop at nothing. But if the killers were agents of one of the competitors, how did they learn that Morris had the cadenza? He'd said he'd told no one except Stephanie and his friend Tony the cook. Well, then: Tony?

At the street, Trntl made a quick decision. "Where did you say Morris works?"

"Hanrahan's. On Charles Street."

"An Irish place?"

"Well, more Italian, I guess. Pizza, spaghetti, lasagna, stuff like that. It's very expensive."

"Maybe we should go there and see what this friend of his might know."

"Tony Scaevola. He's the owner's nephew. That's a good idea. Maybe Morris was called back to work tonight, and we'll find him there, too."

"And if not, they might know where he is," said Trntl. "I'd like to get a look at Tony. If anyone asks about me, just say I'm your Aunt Fanny."

As they drove back to Charles, Trntl noticed that the Olds Cutlass was still in her rear-view mirror. She said nothing, not wishing to upset Stephanie further. Later, she wished that she had.

When they arrived at Hanrahan's, the parking lot was nearly full of very pricey cars. Happy hour folks. Trntl pulled in between a Rolls-Royce and a Ferrari, and observed casually: "Quite a clientele. The place doesn't look like much on the outside. They must have good lasagna."

"Gee, I don't know," said Stephanie. "I've never eaten here."

It was a fairly old building which had undergone a modernizing facelift of stone veneer and silvery weathered wood. Adjacent to the plate glass doors were elegant stone planters filled with some type of creeping evergreen. Passing through the doors was like entering a cave: windowless walls painted black, dim indirect lighting, and a thick black carpet. A single candle in a tall ruby chimney graced each of the small, intimate tables that receded into the darkness; an endless succession of red glowings. (There has to be a mirror on the far wall, Trntl thought. The building isn't big enough to have so many tables.) A blond hostess approached them.

"Is Morris Waite working tonight?" Stephanie asked her.

"Morris? No, this is his night off."

"What about Tony Scaevola?"

"He's in the kitchen."

"Could we see him, please?" Trntl asked.

The hostess hesitated briefly. "I suppose so. Just a minute."

She moved back through the tables toward the bar. "I'll ask him if he knows where Morris is," Stephanie said. "He might know something we don't."

"Yes, he might," said Trntl, straining to see into the kitchen through the small glass panel set in the swinging door. Even as she peered, the door swung open, and a stocky man with glossy black hair pushed through and strode toward them. At close range, he looked them over, unsmiling and precise. "It's irregular to have people asking to see the kitchen help. What's the nature of your business?"

"We just want to ask Tony Scaevola a question," said Stephanie, "—about Morris Waite."

The briefest flicker of a shadow darkened his eyes. "Neither Morris Waite nor Tony Scaevola is working tonight. If you'd care to leave a message—?" His voice trailed off, and he watched them.

"No, I don't think we want to do that," said Trntl. "You're the manager, I take it? What's your name in case we want to call in a message later?"

"Yes, I'm the manager, Angelo Torelli. I'm here every evening."

Trntl tugged at Stephanie's elbow and moved her toward the door. Angelo Torelli stared at their backs as they hurried into the parking lot.

"Nothing more to be gained here," said Trntl, as they got into the car. "I'm going to take you home. I advise you to say nothing about Morris's stealing the cadenza—to *anyone*. And don't tell anybody we were at his apartment this afternoon. Keep your door locked and don't open it for strangers. Don't try to contact Morris. He's in very deep waters, and if you try to find him, you may be in danger yourself."

Stephanie arrived at her apartment house ashen and perplexed, confused and jittery, and once again on the verge of tears. Trntl waited until she'd unlocked the outer door and disappeared inside. Then she drove to a public telephone booth and called an anonymous tip to the police that a body would be found four flights up at a certain address on Gobel Street.

Preoccupied with sorting out the events of the day, she got into the car, lit a cigarette, and started back to the hotel. She was not too preoccupied to watch the rear-view mirror. Yes, there it was: no doubt about it now. The Cutlass was following *her*.

Chapter 6

When Trntl got back to the hotel at 5:20, she found a space on the second level of the parking garage and hurried down to the lobby. Carol Brown was waiting for her on a couch opposite the registration desk. "Am I glad to see you!" Trntl exclaimed, throwing herself onto the cushions beside her. "How long have you been here?"

"About forty-five minutes. When I found you weren't in, I decided to sit here and get a feel for the place. I finished reading *The Wall Street Journal* and met a couple of extremely friendly men: a lonely claims adjuster from Wichita, and a nice older fellow with a red toupee and a cabin cruiser who wanted to take me out for an evening on Chesapeake Bay."

"I hope you're not going with him," said Trntl. "I need you here."

"No, I told him I had a prior engagement."

"I'm glad neither of them was a sales rep for Humboldt-Hartmann Gesellschaft," said Trntl. "*That* would have made my day."

"I brought your toothbrush and assorted clothes," said Carol, patting the suitcase beside her. "Also the small tape recorder." She was studying Trntl's face quizzically. "You seem tense. What's happened?"

"All hell's broken loose. I thought I almost had my hands on the cadenza, but it got away again. And there's been a murder."

"A *murder?* The ante's going up. Sounds like you need a drink."

"You're right. Let's go up to my room, ditch the suitcase, and get some supper. We've got a lot to discuss tonight." They went to the elevator; and on their way to the sixth floor, Trntl began recounting the events of the afternoon.

They ate in the hotel restaurant, Trntl still keyed up and talking nonstop through her pre-dinner martini. By the time their meals were served, she'd smoked four cigarettes and relaxed a little; halfway through their crab cakes and white wine, she finally ran down.

Carol said, "I'm surprised you didn't tell Stephanie that Morris is dead."

"I was afraid she'd get hysterical," said Trntl. "And we'd have had to call the police, and wait around, and answer questions— and I thought we'd better get on with *our* investigation before the trail got any colder."

"Well, you called the cops anonymously," said Carol. "It'll be in tomorrow's news. How will Stephanie take it?"

"I tried to warn her that she's in potential danger herself. I don't know what she'll do when she learns about Morris. Possibly go to Pettigrew and tell him everything. Possibly call me—she knows I'm at the Cavendish. But tonight I didn't want her underfoot. I need to get your thoughts on what's been happening."

"Hmmm," said Carol. "First, it seems to me that your analysis is valid. Morris's death is either related to the cadenza, or it's not. If it is, he was probably killed either by the people who savaged Finegold or else Tony Scaevola and his friends. If the former, we don't know how they learned that Morris had the manuscript. If the latter, we don't know Tony's motive."

"Money," said Trntl. "He'll either try to sell it, or hold it for ransom. Morris showed him the clipping of the press conference, where Pettigrew told all the world it's priceless."

"So Tony gets to set the price," Carol mused. "Now, on the other hand, if Morris's death *isn't* related to the cadenza, why was he killed? And where's the cadenza now?"

"Drugs," said Trntl. "He may have been a dealer, for all we know. A deal may have gone sour, or his suppliers may have felt he was holding out on them. It's entirely possible that someone killed him to steal his stash. The hole was empty, after all."

"Then why would the cadenza be gone?"

"Morris told Stephanie that he kept the manuscript locked in his leather briefcase. If the briefcase was in the stash hole, whoever killed him might've taken it too, assuming it contained drugs or money."

"Oh gad," said Carol. "And after they get the briefcase open and see that it isn't drugs—"

"Exactly. The cadenza may wind up in a Dumpster somewhere, or blowing in the wind."

"So we should hope it *was* Tony," Carol said wryly.

"Well, that would give us a place to start," said Trntl. "But there's nothing to indicate that Tony *was* involved. When Stephanie and I went to Hanrahan's to talk to him, things got a little fishy. The hostess said he was in the kitchen; Torelli said he wasn't. But fishy doesn't prove a thing."

Carol decided on chocolate mousse for dessert, and Trntl chose caramel custard.

"Getting back to the drug angle," Carol said, when the waiter had left, "there's no proof that whoever killed Morris and emptied the stash got the cadenza; it might not have been in the hole. Morris may have hidden it somewhere else or given it to someone for safekeeping. It may still be hidden."

"So who killed Morris? Tony and friends? the burglars who injured Pettigrew (and maybe Finegold)? somebody with a drug connection?"

Carol shook her head. "The murder just confuses things. Let's stick with the cadenza. We know that the burglars responsible for the second and third break-ins—and maybe for breaking Finegold's arm—want the cadenza badly. Why? Try another motive besides money."

Trntl finished her coffee and lit another cigarette. "A competing publisher might want to upstage Lunner & Dinch and publish the cadenza first. Or, if that's not possible, considering the legal problems, at least to keep Lunner & Dinch from publishing it. That certainly would be Dinch's view." She picked up the bill and started away from the table.

"My God," said Carol. "Burglary, black bag jobs. You make it sound like industrial espionage. Here, Trntl, you've forgotten your cigarettes, as usual." She handed her the pack. "Surely music publishing isn't in the same league as real estate development, electronics, aeronautics, plastics and pharmaceuticals!"

"You haven't read the dossiers Dinch gave me on his competitors," Trntl said darkly. "They're up in the room; you'll see."

The door locked, and a bottle of Scotch and a bucket of ice on the table beside them, they sprawled on the double bed and prepared to go systematically through the folders Dinch had provided. "Dinch was very thorough," Trntl said, as Carol filled their glasses. "See: first the letters of introduction—to the Director of the Hastings Institute, the police, the news editor of the *Sun* and 'Whom it may concern'. Then a tape cassette of Farringford's Fifth

Concerto played by Rosamond Foxe. But he forgot to give me a tape recorder to play it on."

"We've got one now," said Carol. "Do you want to play it?"

"Later, maybe," said Trntl. "Then there's the retainer check which we'll cash tomorrow. And these photocopies of music manuscripts in Farringford's hand." She laid these documents aside and took up six fat manila folders. "And now to the meat of the matter. Are you ready? Dossiers on Dinch's chief competitors: Humboldt-Hartmann Gesellschaft; B. F. Cleavenger & Sons; Cameron Stewart, Ltd.; L'Enfant Devereux; Franzen-Van Eyck of Rotterdam; and Winifred House, Inc. He says in his cover letter, 'The first four have shown themselves to be especially aggressive and utterly unscrupulous in their efforts to acquire the works of living and recently dead composers. These files were compiled with great care over a period of many years. I include them so that you may see how viciously these firms operate, what they're capable of, and what you'll be up against.'"

"My God," said Carol, "they're huge! Humboldt-Hartmann is an inch thick."

Trntl continued reading the letter: "'To give you an idea of their tactics: in 1932, B. F. Cleavenger acquired the rights to all of Abner Solheim's works by cultivating and subsequently marrying Solheim's widow. In 1949, Cameron Stewart stole the rights to Archibald Ingraham's last three symphonies by bribing the executor of Ingraham's estate—an unprincipled brother-in-law.'"

Carol asked, "Wouldn't that be 'buying' rather than 'stealing'?"

"The worst is yet to come," said Trntl. "'For many years, L'Enfant Devereux has engaged in the unfair business practice of giving money grants and loans to struggling composers in exchange for their works—an extortion they call *patronage* and *commissions*.'"

"Why, that's *awful*," said Carol.

"And," continued Trntl, "he accuses Humboldt-Hartmann of blackmail: 'For example, they obtained the rights to Pandofsky's works by threatening to tell his wife about his numerous adulterous affairs and his six illegitimate children. They got Rundelmann's quartets by threatening to publicly expose his sexual interest in young boys.'"

"Ah, that's closer to the marrow!" said Carol. "But what makes a child 'illegitimate'?"

"*I* don't know; it's Dinch's word, not mine. He goes on to say, 'Humboldt-Hartmann's intelligence network is the largest—but the other five have spies and agents everywhere—including infiltrators in each other's home offices and sales departments. They have their people on the editorial staffs of major music magazines and on the judging panels of awards-competitions. They've secretly bankrolled critics and reviewers to guarantee that their composers will get favorable notices and their competitors' composers won't. As a case in point, Luella Campbell Knightley of *Music, Maestro! Magazine* (see Cleavenger file, p. 13) is invariably present at Cleavenger's private cocktail parties; but she has refused to come to ours on *ethical grounds.*'"

"Maybe Cleavenger has better booze," said Carol.

"And note this," said Trntl: "'In each file, a red star marks those operatives who seem to me the most likely to be involved in the theft of the Farringford Cadenza. Familiarize yourself with their physical characteristics and habits, and study their photographs so that you'll recognize them if you encounter them. They're capable of adopting clever disguises. Employ the utmost discretion in your inquiries; if any of these firms learn that you're working for us, you may be sure that you'll be under constant surveillance at the very least.' He concludes by saying that in our communications with his office, it would be wise to assume that our telephone is bugged, and to conduct ourselves accordingly."

"Well, well," said Carol. "And somebody *is* following you in a gray Cutlass." She stifled a small yawn. "What does he mean by 'under surveillance *at the very least*', do you suppose?"

"It does give one pause," said Trntl. "Particularly in view of Finegold's broken arm and Morris's last bath."

"Maybe we'd better look at those photographs," said Carol.

Together they opened the Humboldt-Hartmann folder. Trntl removed a stack of seven single-spaced typewritten pages. "What's that?" asked Carol.

"A profile of the company and a historical sketch of its operations and activities. Concise summary for the period 1905 to 1947; exceedingly detailed from 1947 to the present."

"And this?" Twelve pages stapled into a separate bundle.

"Financial information. Balance sheets, tax statements, royalty payments, payroll, the terms of particular composers' contracts."

"How the hell did Dinch obtain all *that*?" Carol gasped.

"Lunner & Dinch has spies and agents everywhere," said Trntl. "Here are some key items." She scanned the sheets. "HHG had a moratorium on publishing Jewish composers in the 1930's; but, beginning in 1949, made a concerted effort to enlist them. In 1954, one of Lunner & Dinch's most prolific and profitable composers, Rebecca Steinmetz, was lured away when HHG convinced her that L & D was cheating her on royalties. In 1956, just as Lunner & Dinch came forth with an offer for Quincy Forrester's Woodwind Quintet, HHG intercepted him as he arrived in Salzburg, whisked him away to an Alpine hunting lodge ('kidnapped him' is Dinch's term), and flattered him into signing a contract with them. In 1969, when L & D was making a secret bid to Oliver Pritchett's 80-year-old widow for the rights to his unpublished works, the offer was leaked by Lunner's personal secretary, enabling HHG to top their bid and purchase the works."

"Do you suppose HHG has a comparable file on L & D?" Carol asked.

"The question does rise unbidden to the mind," said Trntl.

They'd arrived at the personal data sheets. The first photograph marked with a red star was that of Rudolph Geisler, born 1936, Stuttgart. A nondescript blondish man with horn-rimmed glasses, receding hairline, and a small goatee. "He's currently Assistant Vice-President for Marketing, U. S. Office (New York)," said Trntl. "His father was a member of the Nazi Party and Deputy Minister of Cultural Affairs, killed in the Dresden fire-bombing. Rudolph has an American wife and three daughters."

Carol pointed to a piece of paper taped to a card. "And this is a sample of his handwriting, I suppose." It was a torn half-sheet of what appeared to be an inter-office memorandum—mustard-stained and crumpled, as though it had been plucked from a wastebasket.

"His hobbies are listed," said Trntl. "Gardening, jogging—and get this, Carol: hunting with bow and arrows."

Carol gave a little whistle.

The next starred photo—dated 1978—was of a woman in her late 20's or early 30's. Snapped on the street, it caught her in smiling profile entering a taxi. "Ilse Sturm," Carol read, "née Adler, born 1948, in Bonn. Current position: Assistant Editor, Keyboard Division, home-office Hamburg. Smokes small cigars, changes hair-color frequently, has a small brown mole under her right eye. Known to have numerous contacts with music critics and reviewers in both Europe and America. Served as a judge in the Larsen-Pitts Competition in 1976—the winner that year being Inez Olson, one of HHG's regulars. Husband killed in a Swiss cable car accident in 1975."

"Do you think you'd recognize her across a crowded room?" Trntl asked.

"Possibly," said Carol, "But I'd hate to be in a position where my life depended on it."

"Probably would help if she was smoking one of her cigars," said Trntl.

The third photo was a distance shot, fuzzy and blurred, of a group of people sitting at a banquet table. The star was placed above a man who might possibly have been dark-haired and of medium build, who might or might not have been wearing a beard. "Horace Alonzo H. Neville, Jr.," Carol read. "Born 1952, Cooksville, Pennsylvania. Currently Assistant Sales Director, Western States Division, San Francisco. Well, Trntl, he's far enough away you don't have to worry about him."

"Dreamer," said Trntl.

"Says he was formerly an HHG undercover agent at B. F. Cleavenger in Los Angeles, but was unmasked and fired."

"Go on," said Trntl.

"Neville's unmarried. 'Hobbies: boys and young men, aged 16 to 25. Current boyfriend (1980): R. J. "Bubba" Simpkins, lifeguard at the Achilles Club, San Francisco.' It says he was the chief operative in HHG's obtaining Rundelmann's quartets, and in scotching the agreement Lunner & Dinch was negotiating with Maximilian Poore in 1980."

"It gets better," said Trntl.

"'Extremely dangerous. In December, 1976, he caused LD #8 (who was assigned to him) to fall and break his leg on a flight of stairs at the "Boy Howdy!" bar in Chicago; and, in May 1977, he arranged the arrest, for indecent exposure, of LD #13 by an undercover vice cop at the "Man Alive!" bar in Seattle.'"

"Nice guy," said Trntl, lying back on the bed, one arm over her eyes. "It goes on that way through all six folders. A, for example, has a luxurious villa on the Côte d'Azur for week-long orgies; B writes a biased column for Journal X—under a pseudonym; C has a severe alcohol problem; D enjoys a twist of lemon in her vodka tonic. And the photographs! Just flip through them."

Carol did. Page after page of formal portraits, and candid shots of people coming out of doorways or crossing streets, standing in reception lines or descending stairs, posing in groups or wandering in crowds—the named individuals identified by neatly penned arrows and tiny red stars—chatting on park benches, buying chestnuts from street vendors, sitting in parked cars, eating pizza, walking with their children at the zoo, and—in one arresting picture—riding on a carousel, staring directly into the camera, open-mouthed with shock.

Carol closed the folders and stacked them on the floor beside the bed. Trntl yawned, and placed her glasses on the bedside table. "That gray Cutlass following me—? Maybe it's LD #16 checking to make sure I'm doing my job."

Carol started for the bathroom to brush her teeth. "I wouldn't count on it," she said.

Chapter 7

March 3   (Tuesday)

Trntl was doing leg-lifts in the center of the floor when Carol breezed in with the morning paper. "Well, Morris made page three."

Cranking up on one elbow, Trntl took the paper, flattened it on the carpet, and turned to the story. One column inch: Morris Waite discovered drowned in his bathtub; foul play suspected; police investigating. "I wonder if Stephanie has read this," Trntl said. "I'll call her later today and see how she's doing." She jack-knifed to her feet and rummaged in the closet for street clothes. "Breakfast first, and then to work. I want to know more about Tony's uncle, the owner of Hanrahan's. That means the public library, maybe the courthouse. We need to pay another visit to Mr. Finegold; maybe you'll have better luck than I did. If the store's open, go in as a customer and get him talking about his broken arm. If the store's closed, go upstairs to his apartment and talk there."

"And if he *won't* talk?"

"Then we cudgel our brains about what to do next," said Trntl. "But now, let's eat."

Before they set out on their separate missions, Trntl decided to phone Professor Pettigrew to ask if he could recall having talked to anyone else after the break-ins besides herself, Stephanie, the man with the blond mustache, and the pack of reporters who'd converged on his lawn. And particularly to inquire if he'd mentioned the name of Morris Waite to anyone at all. "A long shot," she said, not expecting much from the call, "but it's gotta be done."

She got even less than she expected. Mrs. Pettigrew answered on the first ring.

"This is N. F. Trntl. Is Professor Pettigrew in?"

"He's not in, and he won't be taking any more calls, so you needn't try ever again."

"Mrs. Pettigrew, I've been hired by Lunner & Dinch—"

"Dinch is a foul-mouthed, pushy, disgusting toad!"—a shriek in Trntl's ear. "He called this morning and accused Theodore of still having the cadenza! Yes! of keeping it for himself and announcing the theft as a hoax! After he called, Theodore was taken ill and actually lost his breakfast on the living room couch!"

"I had no idea Mr. Dinch would be calling you—"

"We've had nothing but trouble since that music was found! Reporters, calls from everywhere, break-ins, and now accusations! I wish we'd never seen that miserable music! And if that's not bad enough, Dinch has even set spies on us! I know there's someone watching our house."

"Maybe it's the police," Trntl said, not believing it for a minute.

"It's not the police," said Mrs. Pettigrew. "We want nothing more to do with Dinch—or you. Or reporters. We're finished. We're going to my sister's in Omaha." She hung up with a loud click.

With a sigh, Trntl replaced the receiver and reported the conversation to Carol, who raised her eyebrows and said "Interesting."

"I was afraid Dinch would interfere with our investigation," said Trntl.

"Well, we know two things from that call. First, Dinch is cracking under the strain. Second, there's been no ransom demand as yet."

"It's only been one day since Morris gave it up," said Trntl. "I'd welcome a ransom demand. Then we'd know the cadenza's not lost or destroyed." She put on her coat. "Let's go, and meet back here for lunch at eleven."

At ten-twenty, while Trntl is studying documents at the courthouse and Carol is leaving Finegold's Flea-Market, Victor Zyzynski crosses the lobby of the Cavendish Hotel, enters the elevator, and viciously punches the button for the ninth floor.

As the car rises, he opens his overcoat, letting his belly expand, takes cigar case from suitcoat pocket, and selects a large Havana. It's fortunate that he's alone in the elevator; for had there been other passengers, they'd have shrunk back against the walls, cowed by his thunderous brows, his downturned mouth tight as a zipper, his unblinking basilisk stare.

Zyzynski is not happy to be in Baltimore. Having to leave the merger negotiations to fly down for a personal inquiry into the whereabouts of the Farringford Cadenza is vastly more than an irritation. It's a bitter admission, acute as a kidney stone, that someone, somehow, has managed to get ahead of him. *Snick!* The blade of the gold guillotine flashes down to lop off the end of his fat cigar.

In the ninth floor hallway he pauses a moment to get his bearings, then moves quickly to Room 917. He knocks loudly: three—two—three. The door is opened by a tall young man, blond, with a blond mustache. Neither speaks. Zyzynski removes his hat and coat and flings them onto the bed. The young man moves to the center of the room and stands waiting at a tense parade rest. Zyzynski seats himself ponderously in a chair at the foot of the bed, crosses his legs by hefting his right ankle onto his left knee. Then, puffing his cigar, leans back and stares at the young man for a full thirty seconds. Stretched tight across his vest, the guillotine's gold chain gleams in the sunlight streaming through the window. Finally, with a jet of thick blue smoke, he says: "Not an impressive performance, Chip. You men don't usually disappoint me."

So that's the form it will take. "No, sir, not a good performance," says Chip. He braces himself for what he knows will be coming next.

"I find it hard to understand," Zyzynski continues, flinging his words like darts, "that the three of you—normally so cool, so efficient and skilled, so careful, so *practiced*—could bungle something so simple as an entry at Pettigrew's house."

As he talks, ever more rapidly, his voice becomes louder, higher in pitch. He jabs the cigar at Chip like an accusing finger. "You, who've penetrated the most sophisticated electronic security systems in the world! to whom attack dogs and armed guards have never been an obstacle! who snatched the Charles IX Coronation Cup right before the eyes of three hundred guests at the Investiture Ceremony! who lifted all twelve tons of *The Temptation of Saint Anthony* right off the flatcar as it arrived at the Vatican! who made off with all four hundred square feet of *The Death of Caligula*!—" (Twenty by twenty, recalls Chip, with an inward smirk of justifiable pride.) "—who extracted the Komiroff Sapphire from its Deep Vault in the Moscow Kremlin despite the best defenses of the KGB!" He gives a snort of contempt. "And I thought you were experts! Marco—ten years in the circus with The

Flying Gruschenkos! Jerry—with his Special Forces training and five and a half years in Southeast Asia! And you—you, with your Princeton degree! It's just incredible!" Cigar ashes shower onto the rug. Chip blinks rapidly and swallows hard.

"Now," Zyzynski says in a calmer tone, "what the hell went wrong?"

Chip knows the worst is over and visibly eases his rigid stance. "When you ordered us to come down, we took the jet and got here just after midnight. Mr. Meggs had two rental cars waiting for us as you ordered, and we made our preparations. Drove in and reached Pettigrew's house just before two o'clock." The next part is difficult for Chip, and he can't hide the note of defensiveness that creeps in: "We got there just as soon as we could. But when we saw the cardboard taped over the broken window, we knew that somebody else had got there first." Too late he realizes he's said the wrong thing: he sees Zyzynski's face flush darkly, the cigar twitch upright to stand quivering in his fist. Never, never does one suggest to Zyzynski that anyone else could ever be "first". Chip tries to cover it by plunging ahead: "It was clearly an amateur job. We immediately knew they were after the cadenza, too. But we went in and searched; couldn't find it anywhere. Then, at that point, I guess we kind of freaked out and began tearing the place apart." He gestures helplessly. He doesn't say that all three of them had been pushed past panic into gibbering despair at the thought of Zyzynski's wrath. "It was the realization that someone else had gotten there f—before *we* did, you understand—and an *amateur!*—that blew our cool."

Zyzynski shakes his head in disgust. "Not well handled at all." He puffs on his cigar for a moment and then inquires acidly, "Was it absolutely necessary to attack Pettigrew?"

"He surprised us, and we didn't want him to get a good look at us." Chip hopes this answer will satisfy Zyzynski; he has almost convinced himself that it's the whole truth. But deep down he knows that, in their rage, and fear, and pent-up frustration, it had been a great pleasure to bash the old fart.

"If you hadn't been banging around, he wouldn't have come down to surprise you."

"You're right, Chief." Chip hangs his head.

"However," Zyzynski adds grudgingly. "I congratulate you on your presence of mind to pose as a reporter the next day to determine if the earlier burglar actually *did* get the cadenza. That's the kind of professionalism I'd come to expect of you." He tugs reflectively at his lower lip while Chip waits nervously, with increasing discomfort: when Zyzynski had knocked, Chip had been on his way to the toilet.

Zyzynski notes but chooses to disregard his discomfort. "And when you reported to me that the cadenza had been stolen, you followed my orders with admirable dispatch in notifying the press that the theft had occurred. Nonetheless—" and here the cigar starts jabbing again "—I think your visit to Finegold was unnecessary, and ill-advised in that you exposed your presence and gained nothing in return."

Chip offers up a feeble defense. "It was the only lead we had. And we did learn that *he* hadn't stolen the cadenza." In their report they hadn't mentioned Marco's breaking of Finegold's arm. "We pretended to be reporters to get into his apartment, and I don't think he'll ever be able to identify us." Nor had they told Zyzynski of their warning Finegold that if he went to the police, they'd be back for his wife. But clearly, Chip would be the first to admit, it wasn't their usual smooth operation. All three of them are embarrassed by it and agree that the less Zyzynski knows of the particulars, the better.

Zyzynski gives another snort. "It was highly unlikely that Finegold had stolen it. There are far bigger fish in these waters." With a wave of his hand he silences anything else Chip might have been planning to say. "What I find hard to understand," he continues, his voice once again edged with contempt, "is that you haven't found the cadenza in three days of searching. We've got to have closure on this, Chip. Every day that passes increases the possibility of the cadenza getting away."

"It's the most frustrating baffle we've ever dealt with," Chip admits. "There just aren't any leads."

"What about Trntl?"

"Marco's following her now, and Jerry's down on the sixth floor bugging her phone."

"You haven't bugged her phone *yet?*" Zyzynski sputters in dismay. "Why's it taken so long? And why don't you have a room closer to hers?"

"When you called us after your talk with Latimer, we hurried right over to the Cavendish to get a room. But there's some sort of sales convention going on, and the ninth floor was the best we could do. We've got our eye on the room across the hall from hers, waiting till it opens up. As for bugging her phone, we didn't bring the equipment with us when we left New York. We had Mr. Meggs send it by courier, and it arrived last night."

"What's Trntl learning in her investigation?

"She saw Pettigrew yesterday morning. And in the afternoon, that Simms girl who found the cadenza. Trntl probably doesn't know any more than we do at this point." For a number of reasons, Chip thinks it prudent not to mention Trntl's visit to Finegold.

"But you don't *know* she doesn't know any more than you do, *do* you?" Zyzynski grunts. "You haven't bugged her *phone!*" He gives a resigned sigh. "Keep following her, listen to all her phone conversations. She may learn something that'll give you a lead."

With that, Zyzynski lapses into silence. Chip takes it as a dismissal and hurries to the bathroom.

Zyzynski relit his cigar, puffed twice, and watched contemplatively as the smoke spiraled lazily toward the ceiling. It should have been so simple: a quick hop down, a lightning raid on the unsuspecting professor, and wham! the Farringford Cadenza his and his alone. Nothing at all for Lunner & Dinch, so uppity smug with their fatuous "prior claim". Nothing at all for Morgan Latimer: the doddering old husk had already *had* his pleasure. And nothing—nothing *at all*—for shitface Abbott, who would *never* get to play the cadenza, and—because Zyzynski's possession of it was the ultimate trump—would *never* get Rosamond Foxe!

But "simple" had become an unwinding chain of disasters. Who *was* this Mysterious Other who'd twitched away the prize and fixed asses' ears on Marco, Jerry, and Chip? Could it be *another Collector?*—some unguessed rival who'd squirrel the cadenza forever out of reach into some secret, inaccessible cache? He squirmed in his chair and began gnawing at his knuckles. An amateur burglary, Chip had called it. A kid's job! That was the final humiliation—and it lashed him like a red-hot whip.

For Zyzynski could never admit to failure or acknowledge personal defeat; could never bear to be surpassed or thwarted. Always to succeed, to prevail, and always, always to be *first*—these were the compass and goad that governed his actions. His relentless single-mindedness of purpose had its roots in history.

Until he was twenty-one, the spelling of his name had been 'Zzzyzzzynski' (a vile joke perpetrated by a xenophobic immigration officer who added the four extra z's while writing the name of Victor's grandfather on official documents). For three generations the spelling had persisted until Victor, at age 21, had legally changed it to its present form. But by then the damage had been done. And in view of his needs and temperament, by assigning him the name (no matter whether it began with three Z's or only one), Fate had played Victor a filthy trick.

For, as the world organizes things, from his earliest school days, his name had always placed him last. Last in roll-call, and alphabetical seating. Last in thought, consideration, and esteem. Never did his teachers invert the order to start with Z. In Victor's world, the end of the alphabet was always the end of the line. How he'd hated the A's and B's and C's who never had to wait till last: the Aarslofs, Ackermans, and Ashbrooks, the Bennetts, Borglums, and Browns, the Chases, Craddocks, and Coles who were first to go to the toilet. First to get the teacher's handouts—graham crackers, crayons, exams. First into the cafeteria; first to get tickets to games and shows, first to board the field-trip buses (and grab the best seats).

As a child, he'd withdrawn into himself and cried at the unfairness of it: the full bladder, the picked-over food, the broken crayons. The teachers' jokes: "Where's Victor? Oh, *there* he is—at the end of the line!"; "Children, don't be greedy, or there won't be any cookies left for Victor!"; "If you don't behave, you'll have to go to the end of the line—and be with Victor!" And the other kids laughing at him, despising him, calling him "Tail"—a hated name that followed him through high school.

Early fat—and ever fatter—ungainly, awkward, ugly to behold, he'd watched the Andersons and Arbuthnots, the Barlows and Bells, Cliffords and Creightons—even the Wooleys and Wyatts—get the girls. Having no athletic ability, he avoided sports and watched the others get the glory. With only modest academic skills, he did not compete in schoolwork. An only child, he'd had to nurse his many injuries alone.

But as he suffered through childhood into adolescence and early manhood, tears gave way to anger, and anger to bone-deep bitterness and a granite resolve. Though he would always come at the butt-end of the alphabet, like some trivial codicil or unimportant afterthought, he would nonetheless gain such success in business and finance that he would be universally acknowledged as Number One. First in wealth. First in power. First in the nightmares of commercial rivals. His financial daring was matched only by his ruthlessness in crushing opponents. By age 45, with lizard cunning and pile-driver persistence, he had accomplished his aim.

He began his ascent at twenty, in 1936, when the death of his parents in a ferryboat sinking enabled him to sell the family's hardware business to obtain a capital base. He invested some of this in parcels of underpriced real estate prime for development when the Depression ended, and the rest in financing the invention and manufacture of electronic devices that would prove indispensable to the government in the coming War. To be First, he *had* to be in on the ground floor, ahead of the game; had to sense the drift of things before others did, had to possess the courage and will to shape opportunities that would catapult him into the future. Since he'd arrived too late to be Number One in railroads, steel, motion pictures, oil, or automobiles, he had to look ahead, to anticipate where the world would be in thirty years and plan for *that*, all the while absorbing or annihilating his rivals.

From land speculation and innovative electronics in the late 1930's, he advanced to munitions, military aircraft, bombsights and radar in World War II, profiting hugely from fat government contracts. During and after the War, he expanded into petrochemicals, plastics, synthetic fibers, and housing construction. In the '50s, he added pharmaceuticals, micro-circuitry, and nuclear energy; in the '60s and '70s, computers, aerospace research, global communications, laser technology, and biogenetic engineering. Now, at 65, with his personal net worth estimated by *Wealth* magazine at sixty-three billion dollars, he stood master of a vast global empire which pursued its own foreign policy and flew its own flag—a tangled network of nested corporations, secret holding companies, clandestine political arrangements, and private financial pipelines.

Zyzynski controlled banks, publishing conglomerates, broadcasting networks, countless blocks of office buildings and other prime real estate in the world's major cities, plantations in Guatemala, farms in Colombia, fisheries in Japan, the votes of twenty-seven U.S. Senators and seventy Representatives (give or take five or six, depending on electoral flukes), the governments of at least seven small nations, and the economies of at least a dozen more, both large and small. Prominently displayed in each of his managers' offices—whether at AAA#1 Petrochemicals or Arch-Apex Electronics, Top of the Line Beefburgers, or First and Foremost Business Machines—was a framed motto drawn from the Gospel of Mark: "THE LAST SHALL BE FIRST, AND THE FIRST SHALL BE LAST." Employees called it "the guiding principle".

Zyzynski. Strong men blanched at the mention of his name. Rivals quaked. Politicians everywhere bent themselves to please.

Hobbies? Only building his Collection. And this he pursued with the same relentless singlemindedness he employed in making money. As a young man he'd begun with first editions, determined to build the greatest collection the world had ever seen. But this quickly palled. However rare, most of the books existed in more than a single copy. Knowing that an item was not unique in its class blunted the point of his pleasure. Likewise with coins, postage stamps, and anything else that had been created in multiples. What, after all, did it signify to have one more Roman sarcophagus (no matter how fine), or one of several similar Stradivari violins? yet another Tiffany lamp shade, or one of Monet's endless pools of water lilies? He came to desire only that which enjoyed the undisputed status of first in its class—or, better yet, uniquely constituted a class unto itself. There was only one Hope Diamond, after all; one Shroud of Turin; one *Mona Lisa*; one Blarney Stone; one Liberty Bell.

Thus, year by year, unknown to anyone but Zyzynski and his various Black Baggers, the vaults at his homes in Zurich, London, Lake Forest, Phoenix, Santa Barbara, Nice, and St. Croix received into their private silence the very finest expressions of the human spirit. The choicest examples of supreme craftsmanship, the most stirring of mankind's imaginative flights, the most precious symbols of national and ethnic pride.

From castles they came, and modern fortresses; from cathedrals, museums, and National Trusts. Acquisitioned by operatives skilled in electronics, demolition, and disguise, who gained their access by parachute and submarine, descending from skylights, tunneling underground, and burrowing through walls. Who variously presented themselves as security guards, police, librarians, construction workers, firefighters, priests, plumbers, soldiers, electricians, art-restorers, government officials, pilgrims, and tourists. Some of the acquisitions made international headlines; some were known only to the robbed and their insurance carriers; still others only to curators and boards of directors who quickly substituted replicas for the originals and kept their silence.

Toward the bottom of his want-list were some items that Zyzynski grudgingly admitted were probably beyond his reach. These—such as the Declaration of Independence, the Colossi of Memnon, the Kamakura Buddha, and Da Vinci's *Last Supper*— were too well-guarded, bulky, or otherwise inaccessible for his technology and personnel resources. He took sour consolation in knowing that no other collector could obtain them either. But he kept them on the list, and now and then would spend a pleasur-able hour in working out elaborate schemes by which they might be acquisitioned.

But the Farringford Cadenza wasn't one of these. After its dis-covery, it *had* been accessible. Acquiring it should have been as easy as taking pencils from a blind beggar. Zyzynski clenched his teeth in a spasm of fury. *Who* had been there ahead of him? If one of Dinch's competitors, the music would be published before he, Zyzynski, could prevent it—and that would ruin everything. If a freelance hustler with money as his aim, there might still be a chance to be the first to buy it. But if it was a hustler, how could Zyzynski be sure that photocopies didn't already exist? And of course if it had been stolen by another *collector* . . . A breath-stop-ping pain began a rhythmic beating in his temple, a ball-peen ham-mer striking ping, ping, inside his skull, on a single fixed point no bigger than a match head. Zyzynski pressed his thumb against the throbbing. As far as Marco, Jerry, and Chip knew (and would ever know), the object of Zyzynski's interest was the *manuscript*—one more unique artifact to add to his collection. But the manuscript was just notes on paper, a vehicle, a conveyance that served to provide access to what he *really* desired. No, his ultimate objec-tive wasn't the manuscript: it was *the music itself*.

Since that night at the Club when Morgan Latimer had learned of the cadenza's discovery, Zyzynski had been haunted to sleepless-ness by the old man's seraphic joy, the miraculous restoration of his youthful bounce. Gall and brimstone! Just the *memory* of the music had empowered Latimer to rise and stand; had put wings to his heels and rushed him home to enjoy an all-night hayride with his wife!

Since he was twenty-two, Zyzynski hadn't been able to rise and stand. For forty-three long years he'd been accursed with intense desire and no means whatsoever to fulfill it. Oh, he'd tried. He'd bought the company of some of the world's most desirable and beautiful women; but their company was the limit of what he could enjoy. These affairs died quickly of his humiliation; of his awareness that they saw him—Zyzynski!—as an impotent pretender, a limp noodle, a rich man yet a pauper. Of his certainty that they were laughing about him behind his back. It drove him nearly to a frenzy to know they regarded him as weak, unmanly, ridiculous, and—since utterly incapable of performing—a grotesque and ludicrous joke.

To bring his powers back, he'd tried everything his imagination could devise. Steam baths, red pepper soaks, massage and meditation, creative acupuncture, oysters and champagne, powdered rhinoceros horn, bee stings, hypnosis, vinegar enemas, pornography and electric shocks, megadoses of Vitamin E, testosterone, tiger gall, injections of sheep-liver cells, alfalfa and buckwheat honey, cold showers, and ginseng tea. Even charms and spells from around the world administered by assorted high-priced quacks. Nothing could make his lily blossom.

But there was Latimer, dashing off as spunky as a teen. All right, then. The cadenza would be Zyzynski's Grand Elixir! His key to open the magic door. Ah yes. And *his alone.*

The telephone jarred him from his reverie. Chip emerged from the bathroom to answer the call. "It's Marco," he told Zyzynski. "Trntl's leaving the courthouse. He'll follow her."

Zyzynski gave a grunt. "Maybe *she'll* turn something up. *You* certainly haven't. My God, what if she finds the cadenza and gets it back to Lunner & Dinch before you can stop her? Keep her away from mailboxes."

Quick taps on the door: three—two—three. Chip released the chain, and a tall scarecrow in work coveralls sidled through the doorway two steps into the room—but stopped abruptly when he saw Zyzynski.

"Hello, Jerry," Zyzynski said coldly. "I've already told Chip how displeased I am at the progress you men *aren't* making."

Jerry had spent three days rehearsing what he would say in response to Zyzynski's wrath. "We've done what we could," he answered. His nose was long and pointed like a wolfhound's; a thin white scar angled down the left side of his face from ear to corner of mouth. When he spoke, he didn't move his upper lip—a habit he'd acquired with considerable practice, from observing colonels in Vietnam and watching generals giving press conferences on TV.

"Done what you could," Zyzynski intoned with heavy irony. "That's precious little, that I can see. Whatever you do in the future, avoid getting the police involved. I don't have any contacts on the Baltimore force."

"I don't think we have to worry about the police," Jerry said, stretching his lower lip into a broad smile.

"Chip says you've been bugging Trntl's phone. It took you long enough to get around to it."

"We had to order the bug from Central Supply," said Jerry. "It's the very latest model." He went to the telephone and flipped a switch on a small black box beside it. "Any time she gets or makes a call, a red light will flash on this box, and we can tune in on the conversation, which will automatically be recorded on the attached tape recorder."

The pain in Zyzynski's head was slowly abating. "We've got to initiate some action. It's hell to be so passive and not be *doing*. We can't sit here and follow Trntl's lead." Again he relit his cigar. "I've done some thinking. My idea of informing the press of the cadenza's theft from Pettigrew was a shrewd move. Public knowledge closes down options for whoever stole it, and for the people who want it—such as Lunner & Dinch's competitors—who can't risk scandal. And it narrows the channels through which the cadenza could be sold for profit." The cigar tasted terrible. He stubbed it out and lit another one. "Silence regarding the theft would increase everybody's flexibility to maneuver in the dark. Publicity reduces everybody's flexibility but ours." He fished in an inner coat pocket and brought forth a small address book, which he tossed to Chip. "Call Mr. Meggs and have him contact all my dealers—Van Voort, Kropotkin, Siefkis—Huyck in Amsterdam, Fouchet in Paris, Patel in Calcutta—Chou in Hong Kong, and McKillop in Sydney. I want them all informed that Client 1-Primus-Triple-A is in the market for 'recently discovered' piano compositions in original holograph manuscript, and that they're to let him know immediately if any such item comes to their attention. They'll know what we're after." Chip nodded and made rapid jottings on a pad. "Then, to cover all bases—assuming that the cadenza hasn't left Baltimore—take out a post office box in the name of Aakers and place a classified ad in the *Sun* to run for two weeks: 'WANTED—Musicologist seeks original piano compositions in composer's autograph: works of Bartok, Prokofiev, Rachmaninoff, and Farringford. Transactions confidential. Top dollar paid.' Have them write to the post office box."

He closed his eyes and leaned back in the chair. There, that was more like it: the rapidfire decision-making that was the terror of boardrooms the world over. His headache was nearly gone. It helped to be doing something aggressive and tangible. He felt as though he'd been stranded on the freeway with a plane to catch while continuous streams of traffic passed him by.

Chapter 8

When Trntl got back to the hotel at ten till eleven, Carol was sitting on her couch in the lobby reading *The Wall Street Journal*. Beside her was a large brown paper bag. "How did you fare with Finegold?" Trntl asked.

"Pretty well. But I'm starved. We just have time for lunch before calling our report to Felix." She expertly folded the newspaper into a narrow swatch, tucked it under her arm, grabbed up her package, and led the way to the coffee shop.

"I learned a few things," Trntl said. "The courthouse was more helpful than the library. And I tried several times to call Stephanie Simms, but never got an answer. If I don't get her on the next try, I'm going to her apartment. If she isn't in, I'll leave a note."

"Was your shadow with you?"

"Yeah, for part of the time at least. The same gray Cutlass. But he's clever; never would let me get a look at him up close, and I tried some tricky maneuvers. If he followed me on foot, he's good, 'cause I never saw anybody on my tail."

They found a table and ordered sandwiches and coffee. "Now tell me what you accomplished," said Trntl.

"I half expected to find the Flea-Market closed and the Finegolds gone on a sudden vacation. But no, the shop was open, and there were two other customers when I arrived. I had a nice talk with Finegold and bought this piece of cobalt glass—" she pulled a dark blue bowl from the paper sack and displayed it happily "—it's Pilchard, 1936, and I had to pay forty dollars for it."

"Oof," said Trntl. "Dinch will explode if it appears on the expense account."

"We'll have to be shrewd," said Carol. "Well, at any rate, here's what happened—"

When Carol entered the shop, Mr. Finegold was at the cash register concluding a sale. She wandered back among the crowded tables and china cabinets, browsing for something to buy. She wanted no repetition of the panic Trntl had caused on the earlier visit. She was a little staggered at the variety of things for sale. A complete set of Dickens in stamped leather bindings caught her eye; a carved wooden bootjack; a bronze funerary urn. And the usual sets of dinnerware in pale pink Depression Glass, stacks of 78-rpm phonograph records, large family portraits in elaborate frames, antique medicine bottles (some of them none too clean), ancient toasters, flatirons, serving spoons. An old piano bench— probably *the* bench—looking much the worse for wear. She was drawn to the shelf of cobalt glass; and there was a Pilchard bowl for $40. Not a bad price at all. She carried it to the rear of the store where Mr. Finegold was arranging sun helmets and visored caps on a mahogany hall-tree.

"Are you the proprietor?" she asked. "I'd like to buy this bowl."

"Yes, I'm Finegold. Ah, the Pilchard 1936! You've made a good choice. Many things I don't know; cobalt glass I do. I assume you saw the set of water glasses?"

"Yes, and they're very handsome. But this bowl is special."

"I agree," he said with a smile. "Would you mind bringing it up to the front? I have only one hand for carrying, as you see." He pointed to the cast and sling which immobilized his right arm.

"Oh dear!" said Carol. "Did you have an accident? I hope it wasn't hoodlums or thugs who beat you up. People just aren't safe anymore. The law-abiding citizen is more and more victimized by the lawless. It *was* an accident, wasn't it?" She paused, her expression one of intense concern.

"Well, no," he said in a lowered voice, glancing nervously toward the front of the shop. "As a matter of fact, it was thugs who broke my arm. They came to my apartment upstairs and attacked me and threatened my wife."

"Why, that's terrible!" Carol said. "Were they trying to rob you?"

"No, they didn't want money. They wanted me to tell them about a piece of music that was discovered here in the shop and was later stolen from a professor over at the Hastings Institute. They thought *I'd* stolen it! But of course I hadn't."

"How awful!" said Carol, shaking her head in dismay. She set the bowl on the counter and opened her purse. "Did they break your arm to punish you for stealing the music?"

"No, no. Because they thought I knew where it was. *They* wanted the music."

"But if you didn't steal it, how could you *know* where it was?"

"That's what I told them. But they didn't believe me."

"Why did they want it? Did the music belong to them?"

"I don't know why they wanted it." He punched the amount of her purchase into the cash register, and she gave him the money in cash. "They were vicious men. They said if I went to the police, they'd come back and break my wife's legs."

"Monsters!" said Carol. "It's just terrible what these young kids do these days!"

"Oh, they weren't kids," said Mr. Finegold, putting the bowl into a paper bag. "Grown men. Three of them. A team of thugs."

"They must not have looked like criminals," said Carol, taking the bag. "Or else you wouldn't have been caught off guard."

"No, they said they were reporters who wanted to talk to me about the discovery. When I said I didn't want to talk about it, they barged in, locked my wife in a closet, and beat me up."

"Horrible!" she said. "So there was nothing unusual or suspicious in their appearance?"

"Nothing. One was nice-looking—tall, with a tie and a little hat. He had a blond mustache—not bushy, trimmed. And one of the others—the one who questioned me—was skinny with a scar on his face all the way down on the left side, ear to mouth. It was the third man—big shoulders like an ox—who broke my arm. And yes," he added, eyes frightened, remembering, "the man with the mustache called him Marco. He said, 'Hey, Marco, don't get *too* rough, okay?' But my arm was already broken by then."

Another customer had approached the cash register, and Finegold turned to serve her. "Well, thank you," said Carol. "It was nice talking to you. I'm so glad I came in today and found this bowl."

"A good choice," said Finegold. "You don't see Pilchard very often. A pleasure to serve you. Please come again."

Carol finished her story as the sandwiches arrived. "Remarkable," said Trntl. "And you didn't have to bring up the Farringford Cadenza at all."

"That's right," said Carol. "He did it for me."

While Carol and Trntl were having their lunch, three miles away, in a small modern office building, a family crisis was about to erupt. The building was in all ways modest, with clean, simple lines, walls of unadorned red brick, and plate-glass windows backed by Venetian blinds. Near the front door, in a neat plot of landscaped lawn, a tall flagpole flew the Stars and Stripes. At a discreet distance from the pole, a simple sign of brick and stainless-steel read: CIMACORP.

The eruption was about to occur on the building's third floor, in an office at the rear of a three-room suite entered by a glass door marked SCAEVOLA DEVELOPMENT. Here, Giuseppe Scaevola (known as "Lefty" to his friends) was working himself down from an incandescent to merely a cold fury.

He was staring out the window past the flag, which was whipping in a stiff breeze, to the crowded parking lot of a large supermarket across the street. (He would have preferred a golf course to look at; but the land was his, zoned commercial, and the revenue gained by building and leasing the store to a major chain had more than compensated him for the loss of view.) A short man, lean and muscular, bald, but with fluffy gray hair on his powerful arms, Lefty Scaevola might well have qualified for Grandpa of the Year—except for the chill of his hooded black eyes, blank and bottomless as cigarette holes burnt into a corkboard.

The walls of his office were covered with framed testimonials to forty years of business acumen and public service. Citations and commendations from civic organizations and commercial groups. Plaques commemorating his leadership on governmental boards and planning commissions. Photographs of Lefty posing with City and State officials, two Maryland Governors, three U. S. Senators, and various judges (local and Federal). On his desk, a fold-out picture of his wife and children, taken twelve years ago. An elegant pen-set in an alabaster base presented by Howard County's Waste Management Association. A small pedestal holding a baseball autographed by all of the Baltimore Orioles. An Italian letter-opener, dagger-shaped. And the morning *Sun.*

Bristling with impatience, he turned from the window. The digital clock read 11:14. Muttering, he crossed to a small refrigerator in the corner and poured himself a glass of grapefruit juice. He'd drunk half, when the intercom beeped: "Mr. Scaevola, three people to see you: Mr. Torelli, Mr. Speranza, and your nephew Tony."

"Send them in." He slugged down the remaining juice and went to stand behind the desk facing the door.

Angelo Torelli, his dark square face blank as a skillet, and Giovanni Speranza, broad and solid as a granite double-tombstone, advanced only a few feet into the room, then took positions on either side of the doorway. The young man between them was left standing alone in the center of the office facing the desk.

Tony Scaevola was of moderate height, thin and high-shouldered, with a prominent nose and neatly coiffed black curls. Pale and sullen, he was palpably nervous; for though he was striving mightily to present an appearance of nonchalance and sophisticated cool, a fine dew of sweat beaded his forehead and glistened in droplets on his scrawny black mustache. Lefty Scaevola stared at him unsmiling for a long minute, studying the face so like his brother's, noting the sweat and the dark eyes moving restlessly, avoiding contact.

"I'm very angry with you, Tony." His tone was flat and matter-of-fact. "You been free-lancing. You know that's against the rules. Don't we pay you enough but you've got to go out on your own?"

Tony said nothing, knowing that it wasn't yet his time to speak. Lefty held up the newspaper. "Have you seen this, Tony? Here, on page three, this guy drowned who worked with you in the kitchen at Hanrahan's—a guy who's known to be your friend." He dropped the paper on the desk. "It won't be long till the police come round to check on his friends and the place he worked. That's no good for Hanrahan's or the Organization or the family."

He came from behind the desk and stood before Tony at slapping distance; Tony tightened up defiantly. "You got another problem besides free-lancing, Tony. You got loose lips. You like to brag about what you've done. That's very bad. You been telling folks you stole this Farringford Cadenza from the Morris guy. The guy who's dead! That's real stupid, Tony. You've put the whole Organization in a bad position. The trail leads right to you; and if it leads to you, it leads to us. What were you thinking of, Tony?"

He clamped his mouth and glared, waiting for an answer. The direct question caught Tony off guard, and he raced his thoughts before attempting a reply. He hadn't wanted Morris killed; but the silly jerk had refused to go along with the ransom plan. A business partnership, with a four-way split. Morris said he was going to give the cadenza *back*, for chrissakes! Wouldn't tell them where it was, so they had to make him. Bill just got carried away when he and Lonnie had Morris in the bathtub. It wasn't *Tony's* fault that Morris got dead.

And when *had* he bragged about taking the cadenza?—was it during the poker party?—somebody must've got word to Torelli. What the hell, there was no use denying his involvement. His answer was brief. "The cadenza's worth lots of money."

"Who was going to buy it?" Lefty asked.

"The publishers who want it so bad—Lunner & Dinch."

"So you were going to sell it to them. Break the rules, huh. Go it alone."

"It was a partnership—a three-way split."

"How much were you going to ask?"

Tony swallowed. "Fifty thousand."

Lefty Scaevola just stared at him.

"See, it's worth lotsa money," Tony said quickly.

"How'd you know they'd buy? You get an offer?"

"No. I called *them*. This morning. Said fifty thousand was what they'd have to pay—"

Lefty slapped him so hard that Tony nearly lost his balance.

"Stupid!" Lefty snorted. "My own brother's kid!" He took a deep breath and brought himself under control. "What did you tell them, Tony? How were they to deliver the money?"

Tony's eyes had become hard, hot, and dry. But he was frightened as well as angry. "I didn't say. I told them what the price was. They said they'd have to talk it over. I said I'd call back to get their answer and give them instructions then."

Lefty felt a wave of relief but kept his face impassive. "Why, Tony?" he asked. "Why free-lance?"

"I need the money," Tony said. "I got debts. You don't pay me enough as a cook at that lousy restaurant for me to meet my expenses."

"I know about your debts and expenses," Lefty said. "Your new sports car, that girl you live with and her charge accounts, the big color TV, the weekend poker games. You think you're a big man already? You're a little guy just learning the ropes. You're living beyond your means, Tony."

"Well, if you paid me more, I'd be okay!" Anger had the upper hand. In a surly tone he added: "Why do I have to be a cook at Hanrahan's? I want to be something bigger in the Organization. I thought you'd find something else for me."

"Tony, Tony, you know how it goes in the Organization. You start at the bottom and work your way up. Your father knew that.

He and I started as roustabouts in your grandpa's salvage yard at a dollar-fifty an hour. When I promised your father I'd take care of you, I expected you to work your way up. You got to learn the system from the ground floor and know how to be patient. How to follow the rules. Then you understand the Organization, and see how you fit in. But you got greedy and couldn't wait—no discipline, no loyalty to the greater good. You had to branch out on your own." The barest pause. "Why did you kill the guy, Tony?"

"I didn't kill him," Tony yelped. "I just wanted the music. It was the other two who put him in the tub."

"The other two, huh? A three-way split." Lefty gave Torelli a slight nod. "Who are they, Tony? your two-bit friends. Tell me their names and how to find them."

"But they're my *friends*," said Tony, in desperation. "I can't rat on 'em."

"They *know*, Tony. They know *you*, and that puts them too close to all of us."

"They're my friends—"

"They aren't family. How can you be sure they won't rat on *you*? With family, you *know*." He leaned back with one haunch on the corner of the desk, picked up the baseball and began rhythmically squeezing it with his left hand.

Tony began talking rapidly, fear now uppermost. "We wanted Morris to tell us where he'd hidden the music. He had to be persuaded. And then after he told us, and I went to get it, the others—well, I don't know just what happened—but Morris was dead."

"Did he think you were his friend?"

"Yeah. We did a lot of stuff together."

"That's my point, Tony." His hand completely hid the baseball. The rhythm never varied. Grip. Squeeze. The knuckles showing white. "Now, these other two. They're in this ransom thing with you, aren't they?"

"Yeah."

"Do they know it's fifty thousand?"

"No, they think I'm asking for ten."

Lefty was silent for a long time, staring at Tony as he shuffled on the carpet. Then in a conversational tone, he said: "You're family, Tony. That's special. I promised your father I'd take care of you. There's still a place in the Organization for you." Grip. Squeeze. "Don't spoil it, Tony. Don't throw away your future."

Tony's shoulders had slumped; in a thin, reedy voice he qua-vered, "You're asking me to rat—"

"They aren't family," Lefty said. He replaced the baseball on its pedestal and handed his nephew a pencil and pad of paper. "Now write down their names and addresses and how we can find them. Pool halls. Taverns." Tony scribbled dutifully while Lefty read along. Then Lefty took the pad and handed it to Angelo Torelli. "A wise decision, Tony. Now where's the music?"

"At my apartment, in a locked brown leather briefcase that belonged to Morris."

"Where in your apartment?"

"I left it under one of the seat cushions on the living room couch."

"A real safe place, Tony. Does your girlfriend know about it?"

Tony jerked as though he'd once again been slapped. "No! I swear she doesn't know anything about the music. I don't tell her nothing about what I'm doing, and she knows not to ask ques-tions."

"You say you called these publishers—what's their name?—Dunner & Lynch—about the ransom. How many times?"

"Just once. This morning."

"It's Lunner & Dinch," Torelli interjected quietly.

"Whatever," said Lefty. "One call, huh?"

"From a public phone booth."

"And they needed some time to decide if they want to pay. When were you to contact 'em again?"

"Tomorrow morning at nine."

"It's best that you leave town, Tony. I'm going to send you away for awhile—"

Tony lurched a step backward, his eyes wide. "Not to Philadelphia—!" Pleading, terrified.

Lefty shook his head. "No, not Philly. Things are a mess over there right now. No, I've made arrangements for you to go to your Uncle Vinnie in Newark. He'll have a job for you. You'll like New Jersey." He reached into a desk drawer, withdrew some bills and gave them to Tony. "Here's two hundred dollars you can use for clothes. You'll be staying at Uncle Vinnie's house, so rent's no problem." He turned to Giovanni Speranza. "Johnny, there's a company limo waiting in the car pool; you take Tony straight to it, and ride with him to make sure he gets to his Uncle Vinnie safe and sound. No phone calls or side trips, right?"

Speranza nodded. "I'll see he gets there. You want me to come right back?"

"Stay over a week. Keep Tony company."

"But what about Tammy?" Tony cried. "And my car?"

Lefty stood at the window, looking out, his hands clasped behind his back. "Tammy will stay here for now. We'll tell her you were called away to a new job. If things work out in Jersey, maybe we'll send her up later. And you won't be needing your little sports car. We'll take good care of it for you. Give me your keys. All of them." Tony tossed the keyring onto the desk. Lefty nodded, and Speranza stepped forward to stand at Tony's elbow.

"You be good, Tony. Do what your Uncle Vinnie says. And no more free-lancing, huh?" He continued to look out the window. Speranza gripped Tony's arm and took him from the office.

When the door had closed behind them, Torelli approached the desk. Lefty turned his head and gave him a somber nod of approval. "You did good, Angelo, keeping your ears open. I hope we nipped this thing off short. The police haven't been to Hanrahan's yet, but they'll be coming. Ditch Tony's time-card, and let the other employees know that he hasn't worked there for the past two weeks. Say he went to Wyoming on a fishing trip. Take his keys, go to his apartment, get that damned music and destroy it. Close the place up, put his car in storage at Benno's. Pack up the girl and put her in one of the apartments in the new McHenry Highrise—one without a telephone. Tell her that Tony's gone to Philadelphia to do a job for me. Don't let her talk to nobody. Give her plenty of whatever she needs—food, magazines, booze, pills. Have someone watch the mailbox at the old apartment, and whatever's delivered, bring it here to me." He waited until Torelli had finished jotting on the pad. "Find Tony's two friends, pick 'em up without attracting attention—use as many men as you need—and take 'em on a one-way trip out to the middle of Chesapeake Bay. Move fast. I want this thing settled by tonight."

"You want me to destroy the cadenza?" Torelli asked. "When we get it, wouldn't it be smart to go ahead and use it? Tony's got it all set up for us."

Lefty shook his head. "Not smart. I already rejected that. It's tied in with the killing that's already too close to us."

"But fifty thousand—"

"Peanuts, Angelo. It would make some interest payments, or buy a judge. We don't need the risk. Not now, not when we've got the Justice Department on our butts and the possibility of Federal indictments coming down any day. Destroy it."

"Okay," said Torelli. "Can I use your phone to call Benno and George?"

"Sure." But as Torelli reached for the phone on the desk, Lefty stopped his hand. "No, not that one. That's the FBI's line. Use this one." He unlocked a lower desk drawer and pulled it out to reveal a built-in box with several pushbuttons and a receiver. "This one's safe; it's got a special scrambler device manufactured by Arch-Apex Electronics—the latest thing." Torelli moved behind the desk and began studying the complex bank of buttons.

"Oh, something else," said Lefty, tapping on the window glass. "We need to put up a new flag. This old one's getting frayed around the edges."

Chapter 9

Carol glanced at her watch. "Eleven twenty-five. Time to call Felix." Trntl signed the lunch bill, and together they sauntered into the lobby, where Trntl popped into the gift shop to buy a pack of cigarettes. Carol was waiting for her by the elevators.

"You smoke too many of those things," she commented, as Trntl opened the pack. "Incidentally, there's a man standing near the telephones trying to look casual, but watching us in the wall mirror. Fairly short, dark hair, built like a stevedore, wearing a gray trenchcoat."

Turning slowly to drop the cellophane wrapper into the sand urn, Trntl studied the man Carol had indicated. His back was to them, and he appeared to be intently reading the hotel directory-of-events. In the large mirror on the wall before him, she could see their own reflections but only the top of his head.

Trntl said, "He was in the coffee shop yesterday when I had breakfast. He may simply be a guest at the hotel."

"Perhaps," said Carol. "But he was giving us his full attention. These elevators have indicators over the doors to show what floor the car's arrived at. Just for fun, let's ride up to eight and take the stairs down to six."

"Why not?" said Trntl.

In Room 917, Victor Zyzynski had just stretched out on the bed for a quick nap when the telephone rang. Chip snatched up the receiver.

"It's Marco, in the lobby. Trntl's finished her lunch. She and that woman who's staying with her have just gone up to the eighth floor."

"The eighth?" said Jerry. "Her room's on six."

Zyzynski opened one eye. "Who's this other woman?"

"We don't know," Jerry answered. "She arrived yesterday with a suitcase."

"Find out," said Zyzynski.

Chip continued listening to Marco for a long minute, then turned to the others. "He says that Trntl spent much of the morning at the library and the courthouse. He doesn't know what she was doing, but she took a long time doing it. Yesterday she spent much of the afternoon with Stephanie Simms, the girl who discovered the cadenza. They went to another apartment building and stayed inside a while, and then to a restaurant named Hanrahan's, where they didn't stay long enough to eat. Marco wonders if *we* shouldn't pay a visit to Stephanie Simms, too."

"We don't want Trntl to know we're tailing her," said Zyzynski. "How could the Simms girl possibly know who stole the cadenza? She didn't do it. She *gave* it to Pettigrew, for godsakes."

The little black box gave a beep, and the red light began flashing. "Trntl's using her phone!" Jerry cried. "Hang up, Chip. Our line has to be free for the bug to work!"

Chip said, "Hang up, Marco. By the way, the Chief's here. What? Okay." He turned to Zyzynski. "Marco wants to know what he should do now. Stay in the lobby, or come up here?"

"Tell him to get up here!" Zyzynski shouted. "And clear the line!"

As Marco hung up, Chip flipped the switch on the black box, and Trntl's voice came through to the listeners in Room 917: "— settle a score with Pettigrew. But he was murdered, Felix, and it looks as though the killers got the cadenza."

"Murdered!" said Felix. "That tightens the screw."

"Pettigrew's dead?" Zyzynski groaned, leaning his head against the wall. "You idiots! You must have hit him harder than you thought. Oh, hell!"

"He was drowned in his bathtub two nights ago," said Trntl. "I sent the police an anonymous tip on where they could find the body."

"Bathtub?" said Jerry. Zyzynski fell back on the bed.

"Do you think he was killed by the people responsible for the second break-in?" Felix asked. "The ones who questioned Finegold and broke his arm?"

"Broke his arm?" said Zyzynski. He rolled onto his side and stared at Jerry and Chip, who carefully kept their eyes fixed on the black box.

"I don't know," said Trntl. "It's possible. But how could they have learned that Morris was the thief? Their visit to Finegold on Sunday shows they didn't know about Morris. And Finegold didn't know that Morris had it, so *he* didn't tell them."

"Who the hell is Morris?" Zyzynski sputtered.

"There's another possibility I'm pursuing," said Trntl. "Have Torvald see what he can learn about the Scaevola family—s-c-a-e-v-o-l-a—and about Angelo Torelli, and the Scaevola Development Company, and CIMACORP—c-i-m-a-c-o-r-p. Baltimore folks. What are they into? What's their history? Stephanie didn't have much information about them. I've done a little digging here, but Torvald's better at it, and he'll discover more."

"Will do."

"Now what's your news?"

"Lunner & Dinch received a call this morning from someone who claims to have the cadenza. He wants fifty thousand for it."

"Ransom or sale?"

"Ransom. He said he'll destroy the manuscript if payment isn't made."

"What was Dinch's response?"

"That he'd have to think it over. The man will call back for his decision tomorrow morning at nine. Dinch called us immediately and asked me to come to a meeting tonight at Mrs. Farringford's, where they'll decide what to do."

"Take Torvald with you. If they pay the ransom and get the cadenza back, our work is finished. If they don't, the cadenza may or may not be destroyed. If it's not—and it's offered to another publisher, or in open sale to the highest bidder—we may have more work to do." She paused. "Does Dinch still think that Humboldt-Hartmann Gesellschaft, or one of those others, is behind the theft?"

"The ransom demand blew that out of the water. He doesn't know what to think now."

"He shouldn't forget that there were *two* burglaries," said Trntl. "And Mrs. Pettigrew is convinced that someone is watching their house."

Viciously chewing an unlit cigar, Zyzynski heaved himself up to sit on the edge of the bed. The situation was becoming more and more complicated. Altogether too complicated. Again, he had the sense that things were spinning out of control.

"Give us a call after the meeting at Mrs. Farringford's," Trntl said. "We'll be up late. By the way, it sounds as though you have a bad cold."

"I do. It came on yesterday and has been getting steadily worse. Thanks to Anton Farringford, who likes to hold long private conversations on his front steps. Hey, before I go, what sort of score was Stephanie's boyfriend trying to settle with Pettigrew?"

"Pettigrew had caused him to be expelled from the Institute, and Morris was jealous of Stephanie's relationship with the professor. He didn't intend any harm to come to the cadenza."

"Do you suppose he was killed trying to protect it?"

"That's a possibility. This ransom demand might suggest it. We need more information before we can say for sure. And speaking of Stephanie, I've tried to reach her all morning and got no answer. When I'm done talking to you, I'm going to give her one more call, and then I'm going to her apartment." They said goodbye and rang off.

Zyzynski sat frowning angrily at the black box. "It's a hell of a note," he growled, "that *our* telephone has to be clear before the bug works. It caused us almost to misidentify who'd been killed. Who manufactured the crappy thing anyway?"

Jerry grinned nervously. "*We* did, Chief. At Arch-Apex Electronics. Henderson designed it. It's the latest thing—top of the line."

"You'd think somebody was trying to sabotage us," Zyzynski snapped. "Have Mr. Meggs tell Henderson that he's got three weeks to do it over right, or he'll be back in the video games division." He tried to light his cigar, found it too mangled and soggy to draw, and threw it down in disgust. "So it was the boyfriend!" he said. "A kid's job!" He gave a wry laugh and selected another cigar, pleased that, in a sense, he hadn't been upstaged at all.

"Yeah, who'd a-guessed it," said Chip. "But somebody killed him. And that somebody has the cadenza."

There was a long silence while they all pondered the implications of that. Then Zyzynski pulled himself together and inquired acidly, "Why didn't you tell me that you'd broken Finegold's arm?"

His tone brought them both to stand at attention. "I didn't know it was broken," said Chip.

"Me neither," said Jerry. "There was nothing to show it. Marco had to be vigorous with him, since he wasn't telling us what we wanted to know."

Zyzynski hoisted himself off the bed and strode to the window. "And I'm *paying* for such incompetence!" He poured himself a glass of water from a pitcher. "It's bad enough you went there in the first place, revealing yourselves to no purpose. But it was stupid to hurt him so he'd remember you well! You say it was Marco who broke his arm?"

Chip and Jerry exchanged glances. "We know that *we* didn't," said Chip.

"I was hoping to get back to the merger negotiations," Zyzynski said. "But I see that I'll have to stay until Trntl gets a report on tonight's ransom discussion at the Farringford house. Then I'll know if I have to call Latimer or not. I'm not sure I can trust you to get the message to me straight."

There was a light knock on the door: three—two—three.

"Let him in," said Zyzynski. Jerry opened the door. A burly man in a gray trenchcoat stepped in quickly to face a blue cloud of cigar smoke. "Come in, Marco," Zyzynski said. "Take off your coat. Have a seat."

When she'd finished talking to Felix, Trntl gave Carol a summary of what he'd said. "The ransom demand probably isn't a hoax," she concluded. "We've got to assume that whoever made it really *does* have the cadenza and could possibly destroy it."

"Also," said Carol, "if the manuscript was taken from Morris's apartment at the time of his death, we have to assume that the demand came from Morris's killer—someone who knew that he had it, knew what it was, and knew enough to call Lunner & Dinch."

"And who was willing to kill for it," said Trntl. "Stephanie said that Morris had only told Tony Scaevola."

"As far as she *knew*," said Carol. "He might have told others."

Trntl nodded. "But we still have to consider the possibility that Morris was killed by the people who broke Finegold's arm—the folks who might or might not have been responsible for the second and third break-ins."

"If the ones responsible for the later break-ins are the killers," said Carol, "the ransom demand establishes that the motive for the later break-ins was *money*—not some other reason, such as preventing the cadenza from being published. And the ransom demand does seem to eliminate Dinch's competitors as suspects."

Trntl mashed her cigarette into an overflowing ashtray. "It took more than one person to drown Morris in his bathtub."

"Which suggests the possibility of Finegold's friends: the man with the mustache, the man with the scar, and Marco the ox."

Trntl crossed to the phone. "I'm going to try to reach Stephanie again." She dialed and listened for eight rings. "Nothing. I'm getting quite concerned. On the way to her apartment I want to photocopy these notes I made on the Scaevola family and get them in the mail to Torvald."

"There's a copy shop three blocks over," said Carol. "I'll come with you."

As they crossed the lobby, Trntl noted the gilt clock above the registration desk. "It's just noon; it's been a busy morning." Then, on a sudden impulse, she went to the desk and caught the clerk's attention. "Have there been any messages left for N. F. Trntl in Room 609?" He scanned the bank of pigeonholes on the wall behind him. "No, there haven't."

"Thanks." She rejoined Carol, and together they left by the revolving door.

Stephanie Simms had not read the morning paper. Thus, when her repeated calls to Morris's apartment between eight and nine weren't answered, she could only assume that he was still gone. But where? Trntl had said that he was in grave danger. Was he hiding, perhaps? In her anxiety she paced aimlessly about her room sipping from a cup of last night's coffee. Then she went to the phone again and dialed Hanrahan's, not sure whether anyone would be there at nine-fifteen—it wasn't a restaurant that served breakfast. But surprise, after several rings, she did raise the kitchen manager. No, he didn't know where Morris was; yesterday had been his day off—but he should be in at three this afternoon.

That made her feel a little better, but her brain was still abuzz with fears and speculations. However, she knew that pointless stewing would accomplish nothing, and she did have a paper to write for her seminar in the German Baroque. She took a quick shower, dressed in her brown slacks and the cream cashmere sweater Ted had given her for her birthday, and—with only a twinge of guilt at disregarding Trntl's order to stay in—hurried off to the library at the Hastings Institute.

But despite her best efforts, her worries kept nagging her. Though she sat in the library for over an hour, she found she couldn't concentrate: the words in the books wouldn't come into focus; her own words wouldn't come. Morris's disappearance, his silence, the fate of the cadenza continuously churned her thoughts.

His apartment had been burglarized. Had the cadenza been stolen? Had Morris taken it to a place of greater safety? She prayed that nothing had happened to Morris. For although he wasn't as exciting or mature or intellectually stimulating as Ted Pettigrew, Stephanie still had much affection for him—silly goofus, with his pot and dulcimer, his scratchy beard and funny ways and perky little bluebird. They'd always had good times together—listening to music, going to the zoo, climbing the endless flight of winding marble steps to the top of the Washington Monument, where they had a breathless view of all Baltimore spread out below them. That was their favorite. It was so cozy, so intimate, so romantic and shivery to be alone together between the curved brick walls, on the narrow corkscrew stairs! They might've been in a fairytale castle, never knowing what they'd discover next as they ascended through the tight blind curves. Until Morris got expelled from the Institute and became all sour with this jealousy thing against Ted, he'd always been able to make her laugh. And now, despite his long silences when they were together, his sad eyes watching her as she ate, or studied, or did her nails, she still found him fun to be with—a change of pace, for sure, from the earnestness of the Professor, who always, no matter how relaxed he got, worried about being fifty years old and "over the hill" as he called it, who fretted about his arthritic knee and the knowledge that he was facing a lot of expensive dental work. Morris wasn't worried about growing old, he didn't whine about life passing him by. She wished he wouldn't do so much dope, though. Not that she minded an occasional joint herself. But Morris did so *much*.

With a sigh, Stephanie acknowledged that she was getting nowhere with her paper. She went to the pay phone in the foyer and dialed Morris's number. No answer. She returned to the reading room, closed up and returned the books she'd been using, gathered her things, checked to see that she had her key to Morris's apartment, put on her coat and earmuffs, and caught the bus to Gobel Street.

When Stephanie arrived at Morris's apartment building at 11:30, she saw a police car parked outside and two officers talking in the vestibule. Her first thought: the police had somehow fingered Morris for the break-in at Ted's house. Had they already arrested him? Was that why he hadn't answered the phone? But if so, why were they still here? Maybe they were waiting for him to return! She stood for a moment undecided, not wanting to jeopardize Morris further by asking questions, and also not wanting to draw the officers' attention to herself. Maybe they were investigating the burglary of Morris's apartment. Had Trntl reported it? Had Morris? No, it wouldn't have been Morris. He had too much at stake.

She walked back toward the bus stop in extreme agitation. And it suddenly occurred to her that Tony Scaevola, as his closest male friend, might know where Morris was. In fact, if Morris was hiding out, it might very well be at Tony's. She fumbled in her purse for Tony's address (she'd only been there twice), hurried back a block, and succeeded in flagging down a cab.

It was a ten minute ride to Tony's apartment. Stephanie paid the driver and rang Tony's bell. "Who is it?" A woman's voice over the intercom.

"It's Stephanie Simms, Tammy. Can I come up?"

"Sure. Come on." The door buzzed, and Stephanie flung it open and hurried in. Tony's place was one flight up. Tammy was a very thin blonde with shoulder-length hair; dressed in T-shirt and blue jeans, she held a cigarette in one hand, a dust cloth in the other. "Been housecleaning," she said in a flat tone without warmth. "Hate it. Haven't seen you for awhile."

"No, I've—that is, Morris and I have been busy. I'm trying to find him now. I haven't seen him for a couple of days. Has he been around here? with Tony maybe?"

"No, I haven't seen Morris since Saturday night, when he and Tony went out for a beer. And Tony's not here either; they called him in to work. Come on in and sit down. Want a cuppa coffee?"

Stephanie said "Coffee would be fine." She moved four steps into the living room and stopped short. A brown leather briefcase lay on the glass-topped coffee table. "Where did this come from?" she cried.

"That? I found it under the sofa cushion when I was cleaning. I guess Tony must've put it there. I don't know why. I've never seen it before. And it's locked, so I don't know what's inside."

"It's Morris's music case," said Stephanie.

"Huh! I wonder why it was there." Tammy draped her dust cloth on the back of a chair. "I'll get your coffee." And she dragged off to the kitchen.

Stephanie seized the briefcase. On the flap, MORRIS WAITE was stamped in faded gold. She clutched it to her, engulfed by a nauseous wave of shock and panic.

"Do you take anything in your coffee?" Tammy called from the kitchen. Stephanie turned and ran through the door, down the stairs, into the street.

She had the cadenza at least. But what should she do with it? Of course! Call Trntl at the hotel. She trotted down the sidewalk for three blocks, hunting at each intersection for a phone booth. Finding none, she hailed a cab and had it take her to the Cavendish Hotel. Trntl was not in her room. She hurried back downstairs and stopped at the registration desk. Could she leave a message for the occupant of Room 609? Certainly. The clerk handed her note-paper, pen, envelope. With fingers so shaky and numb she could hardly hold the pen, she scrawled:

> I have the cadenza. It's locked in Morris's leather
> briefcase. It was at Tony Scaevola's apartment. I
> tried to find you and couldn't—so I'm taking it to
> Professor Pettigrew.
> Stephanie.

She sealed the envelope and handed it to the clerk. Then, clamping the briefcase under one arm and gripping its edge with the other hand, she rubberlegged out to the street, where the sunlight seemed far too bright, the noise of the traffic jarringly shrill. Had Morris left the cadenza at Tony's to keep it safe? Or—she approached this cautiously, like the brink of an abyss—had Tony been the one who stole it from Morris? If so, then where was Morris? She signaled a cab, climbed in, and gave the driver Ted Pettigrew's address.

As she'd brought the cup and saucer into the living room saying "It's only instant, but they *claim* it's coffee!", Tammy had stopped, looked about in puzzlement, seen that both Stephanie and the briefcase were gone, said "What the shit!", and gone back to the kitchen to pour the coffee down the sink, muttering, "She always *was* a ding-a-ling."

Then to the living room again, lighting a joint. The cleaning was almost done. One thing about Tony, he expected a clean house. She flipped on the color TV to her favorite soap opera, "Break of

Day", padded back to the kitchen to get a can of beer from the refrigerator, and seated herself in Tony's favorite chair to relax. Ten minutes into her show, she heard a key in the door. "Tony—?" she called. The door opened and Angelo Torelli entered, followed by two other men.

Torelli went straight to the couch and began throwing the seat cushions onto the floor.

"Hey, whatcha doin'?" Tammy cried, leaping up. Torelli turned and took a step toward her, which froze her in place. "Where's the briefcase?" he demanded.

"The briefcase? A woman was just here and took it away with her."

"A woman? Who?"

"Stephanie—uh, Simms, I think."

Torelli's face went gray. "How long ago?"

"Maybe twenty minutes. I don't know. I didn't time it."

"Here, Benno." Torelli tossed a set of keys to the taller of the two men. "These are for Tony's car; it's in the lot at Hanrahan's. Tammy, pack your bags. Just clothes and personal stuff. We're moving you to another apartment."

"Hey," she cried. "Where's Tony?"

"Mr. Scaevola sent him to Philadelphia on business. You'll hear from him. Now shut up and get packed." He punched off the TV. "George, get her into the bedroom, I've got to make a call." George hustled her out still protesting, and Torelli dialed a number. "This is Angelo. Get me the private line."

When the cab pulled up in front of Professor Pettigrew's house, Stephanie stumbled out, told the driver to wait, and ran up the walk. She'd simply deliver the cadenza without saying how she'd acquired it. Wouldn't mention Morris's involvement in the first break-in. Wouldn't explain how the manuscript came to be in Morris's briefcase. Nothing said, nothing proved. Since there was no key, Ted would have to break the lock to see what was inside. *He* could get the cadenza to Lunner & Dinch and redeem himself in their eyes. She just wanted out of it all. She knocked frantically at the door.

There was no answer at first, so she kept pounding away. At last the door was warily opened, and Mrs. Pettigrew peered out.

When she saw who was standing on the porch, her head recoiled, like a turtle's, into rumpled folds of flesh, and her neck visibly, puffily, swelled in girth. "Go away." Uttered with icy contempt.

"Is Professor Pettigrew in?" Stephanie asked breathlessly. "I have something to give him."

"He's gone," said Mrs. Pettigrew, stepping back to shut the door.

"Wait, wait! Please, he has to get this!" She thrust the briefcase past Mrs. Pettigrew onto the hallway floor. "It's the Farringford Cadenza!"

Mrs. Pettigrew slammed the door. Stephanie stood bewildered for a moment; then, suddenly feeling a stupendous rush of relief, turned and ran back to the waiting cab.

Inside, her back to the door, Mrs. Pettigrew held the briefcase and glared at it with loathing. "Hell thing!" she hissed at it. "It's you who've caused all our trouble! And here you are again, dumped on our doorstep by Little Miss Pattycake with her great big buttery eyes. Snot-faced bitch!" The name stamped on the flap had no associations for her. She held the briefcase in both hands, crushing and tugging, as though wrestling it into submission, or trying to kill it. "The fire's the place for you!" But Mrs. Pettigrew was not a fool. She understood the cadenza's importance, that it mustn't be destroyed. But she also was not going to let her husband have it.

"This is for New Haven," she smiled, "and all those afternoons of tennis. And for talking about her in front of my friends."

She carried the briefcase down the hall to her sewing room at the back of the house. As she passed the study, Theodore called out, "Irma, who was at the front door?"

"Nothing important," she answered. Ah, the very place:— her pattern drawer in the cabinet behind the sewing machine. "Nothing at all. Just a person who came to the wrong house."

When Stephanie arrived back at her apartment at 12:50, she was suffering an exhausted letdown. She paid the cabdriver and watched him glide away up Charles. Adjusting her earmuffs and pulling out her keys, she climbed the steps to her front door. As she paused in the vestibule to open her mailbox, two men in dark overcoats left a car parked three doors down and hurried along the sidewalk toward her.

Clutching her mail, she had just turned to unlock the inner door when she saw them coming. The manager from Hanrahan's was in the lead. "Miss Simms—" he shouted.

Terror thrummed her like an electric jolt. She turned the key, shoved open the door, and plunged through. It was a heavy door; and once she was in the hallway, she spun around and tried to force it shut. Through the glass she saw them crowding into the vestibule. She leaned all her weight against the door, but one of the men had thrust his leg into the crack, flexing it to block closure, twisting and working it spasmically against the jamb. She couldn't hold the door against their combined weight; so, calculating distance and the speed she'd need to cover it, she suddenly turned and bolted up the stairs. The men spilled into the hallway behind her and came thudding up in hot pursuit.

At the first landing, she hurled a pot of dusty plastic ferns down the steps behind her and managed to gain a six-foot lead. Pell-mell up the second flight, apartment-key ready in her right hand, mail clutched in her left, she sprinted to her door. It took three seconds to fit the key into the lock, turn the knob, throw herself into her apartment, and slam the door. She was fumbling with the guard-chain when they arrived on the other side; they hit the panels shoulder-first, and the door burst inward. Stephanie spun backwards, stumbling over boxes of records and stacks of books. Angelo Torelli closed the door. Stephanie scrambled into the kitchenette, seized a butcher knife, and turned at bay. The other man whipped out a pistol fitted with a silencer.

Torelli came slowly toward her through the clutter. "Where's the briefcase?"

Stephanie brandished the knife and began to scream.

Pfsst! Pfsst! the pistol farted, and down she went.

Chapter 10

Shortly after twelve-thirty, having buzzed Stephanie's apartment and received no response, Carol and Trntl had walked back to their hotel. While passing the Hastings Institute, they'd stopped in to see if they could find Stephanie there. It was a rather daunting place. Lots of closed doors. Great expanses of polished marble. Antique musical instruments behind glass. A very large library with tiers of books stretching upward for three stories, the stacks framed by a glorious array of carved and polished wood, effusively molded plaster, and gilded ornamental grillwork. "Great heavens," said Trntl.

Many students were about; and in a commons area where food was served, Trntl scanned the crowded tables for Stephanie. Finally she approached a woman who was holding a violin case and reading notices posted on a bulletin board. "Excuse me, do you know Stephanie Simms?"

The woman looked her over coolly. "Yes, I do. Why do you ask?"

"I need to find her. Have you seen her today?"

"She was studying in the library this morning," the woman said. "But I haven't seen her since."

"Thanks." They gave it up and went back to the street. "I should have told her about the Cutlass," Trntl said, "but I figured it was following *me*."

"You *warned* her to stay in."

"Yeah, but since I didn't tell her about finding Morris, she had no reason to think I wasn't just being overly cautious. My not telling her may have caused her to do something foolish."

"Maybe so," said Carol. "But you can't be sure anything's happened to her. And blaming yourself does no good at all. If she's in personal danger, there's no way for you to protect her unless you stay with her round the clock, or bring her along wherever you go."

"Still and all, I should have told her about Morris," said Trntl.

When they entered the lobby, the desk clerk flagged them down. "Miss Trntl, a message was left for you shortly after you spoke to me. Room 609. Yes, here it is." He handed her the plain white envelope. "A young woman wrote it for you here at the desk."

On the back, the clerk's time-clock had stamped 12:18. "Damn, we just missed her." Trntl tore open the envelope, and she and Carol read the note together. "It's almost one-thirty," Trntl said. "We'd better call Pettigrew and see if she arrived with the cadenza."

They went to the bank of public telephones, and Trntl flipped to the number in her pocket notebook. On the seventh ring, Mrs. Pettigrew answered: "Yes?"

"This is N. F. Trntl. Is Professor Pettigrew in?"

Mrs. Pettigrew hung up.

"Dammit!" said Trntl. She called again, and this time the phone rang twelve times. She was prepared to let it ring a hundred.

Finally, Professor Pettigrew picked up the receiver: "Hello?"

Mrs. Pettigrew's voice snapped in the background: "Get off the line, Theodore. I'll handle this." Then, loudly, in Trntl's ear: "What do you want?"

"Mrs. Pettigrew—"

"I told you earlier, we won't talk to you anymore. We're done with you *and* Mr. Dinch."

"It's a matter of life and death!" Trntl said quickly. "Has Stephanie Simms been to your house today?"

"She has not. She's not welcome here."

"She left me a message that she'd found the cadenza and was taking it to the Professor. If she does come, please have her call me immediately at the Cavendish Hotel. You have my number. And please keep her there at your house till I can reach her—"

"She won't be getting in if she does come," said Mrs. Pettigrew.

"If the cadenza's in her possession, she's in extremely grave danger," said Trntl. "There's already been one murder—her boyfriend, Morris Waite—"

"Morris Waite?" A long pause. "Murdered, you say?"

"That's right. And because of the cadenza. Please have her call me when she arrives." Trntl hung up before Mrs. Pettigrew could refuse, and said to Carol: "She hasn't been there. I'm going to ask you to stay here and sit by our phone while I go back to Stephanie's apartment. Let's hope for the best."

Carol went to the elevator. Trntl hurried to the parking garage and charged her car into heavy traffic. There was no sign anywhere of the man in the trenchcoat.

It wasn't far to Mt. Vernon Place, but the driving was slow and tedious, and Trntl found herself fuming with impatience. Park to Centre Street, Centre to Charles, then north on Charles. Finally: the Hastings Institute. Dead ahead, the tall marble column of the Washington Monument. She veered around it, crossing Monument Street, the boulevard bare, deserted, and continued north on Charles. A parking place! She slammed out of the car. Up the steps. Stephanie's buzzer. No response. All right, the superintendent, manager, whatever. There: Jim Eggleston. *Buzzzzzzzzzz.*

"Yes?"—a gravelly voice on the intercom.

"Stephanie Simms, third floor. She doesn't answer, and I've reason to believe she may have met with foul play. I'm a detective. You can see my ID when you come to the door. I must ask that you accompany me up to Miss Simms's apartment to see if she's all right."

"Just a minute."

And one minute later he let Trntl in after studying her ID through the glass. As he led the way upstairs, he said with a distinctly worried tone, "I wondered if something might be wrong. When I got back from my dental appointment, I found a broken flowerpot here on the first flight. And Mrs. Gresham in second rear told me she heard noises, like running in the hall."

"We can hope nothing's wrong," said Trntl.

Approaching Stephanie's door, Trntl studied the jamb and lock. The frame had been splintered around the latch. Mr. Eggleston knocked on the panels, and the door swung inward of its own accord.

"Ohmi*lord!*" Eggleston groaned. Stephanie was lying in the kitchenette like a heap of old clothes. Trntl reached her in five strides, knelt and felt for a pulse. "She's dead. Shot. Don't touch anything in here. Get downstairs and call the police. Tell them there's been a homicide."

The superintendent stared down at the body open-mouthed, muscles twitching in his face. Then with a disbelieving shake of his head, he turned and went stumbling down the hall to the stairs, muttering "Ohmilord!—oh!—oh!" all the way.

Trntl looked at her watch. 1:42. She used her few moments alone to assess the situation. Stephanie had been shot twice. The body was still fairly warm. She lay crumpled on her left side in her overcoat and earmuffs. ("Either going out, or just come in," thought Trntl.) On the floor near Stephanie's right hand, a butcher knife. (To defend herself? But no blood on the blade.) Near her left hand, a scattering of unopened mail with canceled stamps. (Since the mailbox was in the vestibule: "Just come in," Trntl concluded.) But even if she'd been out and had just come in, she *hadn't*—according to Mrs. Pettigrew—reached the professor's house. Therefore, she must have come back to her apartment after writing the note at the hotel. To get the cadenza to take to Pettigrew's? If so, where was it now?

Either the killer had it, or it was still in the apartment. Quickly, with intense concentration, she moved her eyes about the room. The mess was much more chaotic than on her previous visit. Boxes were dumped over, their contents spilled onto the floor, drawers yanked open, books pulled off the shelves to lie heaped among the scattered sheet music and phonograph records.

Yet the disarray didn't look like the aftermath of a struggle. A search, rather—which indicated that the killer hadn't found the cadenza on Stephanie's body. Unless, of course, she'd had the cadenza with her all along, and the search had occurred *before* she returned. Had she surprised the killer during his search, then? Not likely; how would she have made it across the room to the kitchenette? And besides, the door had been broken in. She probably would've noticed that and not entered. In all likelihood, she had been followed to the room and killed prior to the search. Well, then, had the killer found the cadenza?

Possibly; but—since the search had been extensive and apparently hasty, possibly not. Was it still here? A brown leather briefcase, she'd said. Nothing of that sort in sight. So, if it wasn't at Pettigrew's, and it wasn't here, where *was* it?

She heard the superintendent coming up the stairs. Quickly she pulled on her gloves and stooped to examine the items of mail. Circulars, bills with windowed addresses and company letterheads, something official from the Treasury Department. Only three items that looked like personal letters: one postmarked Ohio, one California, one Baltimore. Ah. Canceled 10:26 p.m., the night before last. Return address, Gobel Street. Trntl scooped up this envelope and slipped it into her coat pocket just as Eggleston approached the door.

"The police are coming," he said, wheezing from the fast climb. "This is just terrible! She was such a nice girl! Who could have done it?"

"I'd give a great deal to know," said Trntl. She felt a great weariness, a crushing melancholy. Anger. And—despite what Carol had said—the stab of guilt. She and Eggleston made their way downstairs to the front hall to wait for the police. Descending, she felt as though her legs were weighted with 50-pound sacks of sand. When she got to the front hall, she sank into a chair and stared at the worn carpet beneath the chandelier. The fixture's small glass pendants cast oblique, watery shadows on the floor. "She was a good tenant," the super was saying. "Never no noise. Never any overnight guests. Who'd kill a nice girl like her?"

A squad car pulled up in front of the house. A uniformed patrolman came to the door and Eggleston let him in. Together they went upstairs. Another patrolman knocked on the glass; Trntl wedged the door open with a rubber doorstop. "What's happened here?" he asked.

"A homicide on the third floor," she answered. "A woman named Stephanie Simms—a music student at the Hastings Institute. The person who discovered the Farringford Cadenza."

"The what?"

"The Farringford Cadenza. A piece of music that's cost two people's lives."

"Two people? Upstairs?"

"No, the other was Morris Waite. Night before last on Gobel Street."

"Where's the—whadja call it?—the music?"

"Gone," said Trntl. "Gone, gone, gone."

It was six o'clock before Trntl was able to leave Stephanie's apartment building. She'd called Carol and told her the bad news, then sat in the downstairs hall and watched the medical examiner and photographers and laboratory people trooping up and down the stairs. She'd watched Stephanie's body taken out on a covered stretcher. Clearly, it was time to tell the police the whole story, sharing what she knew and her perceptions of what this knowledge implied. It was the least she could do to make some restitution for her responsibility in Stephanie's death.

When she'd identified herself to the Detectives Adcock and Price, she showed them her credentials, and let them read the letter of introduction which Dinch had addressed to "Chief of Police." Then she explained her role in attempting to recover the Farringford Cadenza and recounted the whole sequence of events as she understood them: the break-ins, Morris's desire for revenge, his telling Tony Scaevola of the theft; the beating of Finegold; Stephanie's discovery of the briefcase in Tony's apartment, her aborted plan to return the cadenza to Pettigrew. She finished with the ransom demand made that morning to Lunner & Dinch. The narrative took a long time. The detectives had many questions.

"In my opinion," she told them, "your investigation should certainly include Tony Scaevola, who works at Hanrahan's Restaurant, his uncle Giuseppe Scaevola, who owns the restaurant, Angelo Torelli, the manager, and somebody named Marco, who broke Mr. Finegold's arm."

Detective Adcock said, "Do you mean the Giuseppe Scaevola of the Development Company?—the man who received the Business Council Award and served on the Governor's Urban Renewal Commission?"

"That's the one," said Trntl. "I don't know if he has any part in this—but I think there's a distinct possibility that his nephew Tony may be involved in both murders."

Detective Price frowned. "Those are pretty serious accusations. Lefty Scaevola's a very important man."

"I'm not making accusations," said Trntl from the depths of fatigue, "I'm suggesting lines of inquiry. I grant that much of this is conjecture—guess-work, really—but it's consistent with the information I've been able to collect."

Adcock said, "Why the hell didn't you come talk to us earlier when you began to get these suspicions? To have information of the sort you claim to have and not share it with the police is downright criminal. You goddamned free-lancers futz around in matters you're not equipped to handle and screw things up for the professionals!"

"That may be," Trntl said wearily. "I'm not happy about the way things are going. But I'm telling you *now*—so do something about it." She stood up and buttoned her coat. "You know where to reach me—Cavendish Hotel, Room 609." She left the superintendent's apartment and turned up the stairs.

"Hey, where are you going?" Adcock demanded.

"I want to ask Mrs. Gresham one question. It relates to the cadenza."

"All right," he said grudgingly. "Go up with her, Price."

Drained of all energy, Trntl climbed to the second floor. Her anger, frustration, and emotional shock had left her neutralized and blank, like an erased tape. Detective Price followed her up in sullen silence, radiating an aura of dislike which Trntl simply chose to ignore.

Mrs. Gresham opened quickly in response to her knock and peered out eagerly—a wispy wren of a woman, short and frail, her eyes alert and sparkling. Her face was soft and wrinkled like a dried apricot; a spot of rouge blazed on each cheekbone. She wore a cheap but attractive wig with tight gray curls, a loose-fitting burgundy dress (perhaps her Sunday best, thought Trntl) which undoubtedly had fit her well at one time, but now hung baggily on her shrunken frame, and a glittering rhinestone brooch above her left breast. "Yes?" she beamed. "You want to ask me more questions?"

"Mrs. Gresham, I'm N. F. Trntl, a private investigator. I'm not with the police. Mr. Eggleston and I found Miss Simms's body this afternoon. I understand you've already given a statement to the police—"

"Yes, that's right." Mrs. Gresham looked up at Detective Price with a quick, self-important smile.

"—but I wonder if you could answer a question for *me*."

"I'll be happy to try. Anything to be of help. Stephanie was such a *nice* girl."

Trntl immediately noted the use of first name. A close friend, perhaps? "Mr. Eggleston said that you heard noises on the stairs and in the hall. Could you describe them for me? Were there voices? And about what time did you hear the commotion?"

"As I told the police, there was quite a thumping and clatter. It sounded like a group of people running up the stairs. But they turned and just went on up to the third floor. I didn't hear anybody talking. And then everything got quiet. I opened my door and looked out. But I can't really see the stairs from here. I remember it was shortly before one o'clock. I had my radio on, and the hour-long newscast I listen to at noon was almost over."

"Did you hear anybody coming down the stairs later?"

"No. I did think I heard a scream very faintly, from far away. But I wasn't sure—there are so many noises all the time—sirens, doors closing, refrigerators whirring—I didn't pay much attention."

Detective Price cleared his throat menacingly. Trntl quickly said, "Stephanie was the one who discovered the Farringford Cadenza, I suppose you know."

Mrs. Gresham nodded sadly. "Yes, she was so excited about that. And then, when it was stolen from Professor Pettigrew, she was just beside herself."

"Did she ever show it to you?"

"No, she took it to the professor as soon as she found it. She told me it was a very important piece of music."

"Thank you, Mrs. Gresham," Detective Price interjected. "You've been very helpful. Time to go," he told Trntl. And he had her by the elbow, tugging her away from the door.

"Yes, thank you very much, Mrs. Gresham," Trntl said.

"It's a citizen's duty," she responded with a proud smile. "And besides, Stephanie was a lovely girl. She came to talk to me, and she enjoyed listening to my Nelson Eddy records. You don't find many young people today who appreciate Nelson Eddy."

"I'm sure that's true," said Trntl. And to herself she muttered, We'll talk again, Mrs. Gresham.

But now she had to deal with Detective Price, who was tailgating her down the stairs. "You shouldn't be investigating murders, Miss Trntl; that's police work. You're not on your own turf here in Baltimore. *Leave it to us.* You don't want to be charged with interfering in a police investigation."

"I'm not trying to encroach on your territory," said Trntl. "I'm not trying to solve murders. I was hired to recover the Farringford Cadenza, and that's all I'm interested in. Believe me, nothing would make me happier than to accomplish that and get back to New York."

But of course that wasn't all she was interested in. She took Stephanie's death personally. Morris's was an abstraction, a chapter closed before she'd arrived. But her own actions implicated her in Stephanie's. And, however briefly, she'd gotten to *know*

Stephanie: self-centered, shallow, bumbling, naive—all of those—but well-intentioned, too, despite her self-delusions, her affair with Pettigrew, her manipulations of Morris for her own gratification. Stephanie had truly cared about Morris. She had cared for music. She had been committed to the cadenza's publication. And finally, she had trusted Trntl: she had revealed her secret knowledge of Morris's theft, had tried to reach Trntl at the hotel to give her the briefcase, had informed Trntl of her attempt to return the cadenza to Pettigrew.

When Trntl had expressed all of this to Carol over a quick and tasteless supper in the hotel coffee shop, her fatigue and depression were evident; Carol had never seen Trntl at so low an ebb.

"I understand something of what you're feeling," Carol said over coffee and Trntl's second brandy. "But you're not playing fair with yourself to accept the blame for Stephanie's death. You don't know what all happened to her today. You didn't tell her about Morris's death because you thought she'd panic, which would complicate your work. You did warn her of possible danger and urged her to lock herself in till you could contact her. And you tried repeatedly to reach her. There may be larger forces at work here than we're aware of, and it's possible that nothing you might have said or done could have saved her."

"I want to see her killer punished," said Trntl.

"Well, you told the police all you know," said Carol. "Let them do their job."

"I held back only one thing. I didn't tell them that I was the one who discovered Morris's body. I didn't see *that* to be necessary. It's easy enough for them to link up Morris and Tony through the Hanrahan's connection." She suddenly remembered the envelope she'd put in her coat pocket. "Oh, and there's something else I didn't tell them. Upstairs in my coat I have a letter Morris wrote to Stephanie which arrived shortly before she was killed. It was in a heap of unopened mail beside her body. Let's go look at it."

"Okay," said Carol. "I'll pay the bill." Trntl hurried out while Carol fished her billfold from her purse and extracted money for the waiter's tip. She placed the cash beside her plate and saw that once again Trntl had forgotten to take her pack of cigarettes. "She smokes too much," Carol said, "I should just leave 'em here." But of course she didn't; she picked up the pack and dropped it in her purse.

Wearing her gloves, Trntl took Morris's letter from her coat pocket, and with infinite patience, held the envelope over hot running water in the bathroom sink until she was able, with the blade of her Swiss Army knife, to lift the dampened flap. "Very neat," Carol said, from the bathroom doorway, preferring not to enter the humid room.

"This well may be evidence regarding her murder," Trntl said. "It might help to nail down a conviction. I don't want to be accused of tampering with it." She brought the envelope into the bedroom and carefully slid out the folded sheet of notepaper. Still wearing her gloves, she spread it flat on the bedside table. The letter was undated and brief:

> Dear Stef,
> After we talked and I was still deciding what to do, Tony started urging me to hold the cadenza for ransom and make Lunner and Dinch buy it back. At first I thought he was kidding. Then I realized he wasn't and I got nervous. To play it safe I pulled the cadenza from the other music and hid it. The key is in our Special Place—the "Key Hole", get it? I just cant give it back to that horses ass Pettigrew. You better get it and send it to the publisher. I dont know what's with Tony but I'm getting scared. Why aren't you ever at home when I phone?
>
> > I love you all ways,
> > Morris

"Well, it does turn the screw on Tony," Carol said, "but it doesn't prove Tony killed Morris. And there's nothing there that even suggests he might've killed Stephanie."

"It establishes that Tony wanted to hold the cadenza for ransom. This morning a demand was made, and we're assuming it was Morris's killer who made it."

"And that he had the cadenza in his possession when he made it. But Morris says he hid the cadenza; the letter seems to be telling Stephanie how to find it. How could the killer have gotten possession of it?"

"He might have forced Morris to reveal the hiding place," said Trntl.

"Let's look at it this way. At nine this morning, Dinch gets the ransom call, presumably from somebody who has the cadenza. At 12:18, in her note to you, Stephanie claims that *she* has the cadenza—"

"Which she said she found at Tony's apartment."

"Since she was familiar with its appearance, she'd certainly know whether what she had was the cadenza or not."

"Yeah, and at one o'clock, she's dead."

Carol changed her tack. "Okay, assuming that the guy who called Dinch had it at nine (it might or might not have been Tony), and assuming that Stephanie had it at 12:18, how did it get from him to her? Where *was* she all morning when you were trying to reach her?"

"I don't know where she was," Trntl said testily, "or how she got it."

"And where's the cadenza now? Evidently she never made it to Pettigrew's. You said it wasn't in her apartment—"

"No, I said I didn't see it there," said Trntl. "Someone had obviously searched the place. Probably her killer."

"Which doesn't mean her killer *found* it."

"I'm convinced," said Trntl, "that she'd just come in off the street when she was killed. Since Mrs. Pettigrew says that she never reached their house, then Stephanie either had the cadenza with her when she was killed, or had hidden it in the apartment, or had ditched it somewhere between the hotel and home. If she'd had it on her person, the killer wouldn't have been forced to search the apartment—assuming the search took place after the shooting. If the search occurred before she got home, and she had the cadenza with her, then maybe the killer *does* have it. But what I don't understand is why she would've come back home before going to Pettigrew's? It was a long distance out of her way. Carol, it doesn't add up."

"Would she have left the cadenza someplace else? It doesn't seem likely after what she said in her note to you. Unless something changed her mind. Frightened her, maybe, made her think she'd never get to Pettigrew's."

"Something else bothers me," said Trntl. "Morris was drowned, and the killers went to some trouble to make it look like an accident. Stephanie was shot twice and left lying where she fell. The killings don't have the same *feel* about them; they may not have been done by the same people."

"Well, why would she be killed unless it was to get the cadenza?" Carol asked.

"Maybe the killer thought she had it," said Trntl. "Also, there was a butcher knife beside her. She might've put up a fight and forced the killer to shoot."

"Well, if the killer is the same man who called Dinch, and he did get the cadenza back from Stephanie, then Dinch will get a second ransom demand at nine tomorrow morning. If no call comes through, it may mean that the killer didn't recover the cadenza, or that the killer isn't the man who called Dinch this morning."

"It'll be interesting to see if Dinch gets that call," Trntl agreed. "Let's move on." She flattened the letter on the table once again, and reread it. "What is this key Morris mentions? 'The key is in our Special Place—the "Key Hole", get it?' Does that make any sense to you?"

Carol thought for a bit. "Stephanie's note said that he'd locked the cadenza inside the briefcase. Maybe the key opens *that* lock. But the 'Special Place' couldn't be the hole in the wall where he stashed his dope and hid the briefcase—because if he locked the briefcase to keep the cadenza safe, he surely wouldn't have put the key into the stash hole *with* it. I can't tell if 'Special Place' and 'Key Hole' refer to the same thing or two different things."

Trntl gave a wry laugh. "It's a bizarre and cryptic message. His 'get it?' could imply either that he's making a joke and wants her to appreciate it, or else signaling that he's talking in some sort of code, and drawing her attention to the coded message."

"And what does he mean when he says 'I pulled the cadenza from the other music'?" Carol asked.

"He may be referring to Pettigrew's manuscript copies of Brahms' works which the professor claims were stolen along with the cadenza. In daylight when he wasn't stoned, Morris would have had enough musical knowledge to tell the difference between the two sets of manuscripts." Trntl lit a cigarette and rubbed her forehead tiredly. "There also was a lot of sheet music in his apartment. Maybe Morris had originally hidden the cadenza in the midst of it. Like Poe's purloined letter. And then, when he got really frightened, locked up the Farringford in his briefcase and stuck it in the wall."

"It probably doesn't matter," said Carol, "since in her note Stephanie claims to have the cadenza."

Trntl sighed. "Then maybe Morris's letter is a dead end. A piece of history outdistanced by events. As our friend Torvald would say, 'Nah, it's moot.' Still, it links the deaths of Morris and Stephanie and ties Tony Scaevola in with the extortion plot. The police should have it for their investigation."

"And how are you going to get it to them without revealing that you lifted it from the scene of the crime?" asked Carol.

"That's a problem," said Trntl. "Adcock and Price already think I've meddled too much." She seated herself and made a meticulous copy of Morris's letter, then double checked her text against his before sliding the original back into its envelope. "I won't reseal the envelope. The gum is dry on the flap, and we can always moisten it and paste it down. Having it open, but not torn open—as though it had never been sealed—may provide us flexibility when we give it to the police." She placed the envelope in her purse, peeled off her gloves, and went to take a shower. Carol sat pondering the copy of Morris's text.

Chapter 11

Lefty Scaevola lived in the suburban community of Grafton, a walled and exclusive enclave of gracefully curving streets, spacious lawns and gardens, handsome trees, and expensive houses. Designed to provide all the amenities of gracious living, it had its own golf and swimming club, communal tennis courts, bridle paths, and recreation center (with pool tables and video games), as well as reading and discussion groups, elected residents' council, and private security force. Lefty's house—of his own design and construction—was a large, rambling ranch-style red-brick Georgian with fanlight windows and white trim. Across the front stretched a broad veranda, with a stubby triangular pediment and six fluted white Corinthian columns. Since Lefty liked fine woods, the rooms of the house were variously paneled in oak, teak, walnut, pecan, and knotty pine. Since his wife Theresa liked gardening, the landscaped lot was subdivided into numerous flower beds separated by gravel paths. In the rear was a broad flagstone terrace surrounding a private swimming pool. In the center of the backyard stood a tall silver pole, flood-lit at night, which continuously flew the American flag.

Tonight Lefty was entertaining guests. A small, intimate dinner party for two State Senators and their wives, and Judge and Mrs. McPhee. At seven, Lefty's guests were enjoying their cocktails and hors d'oeuvres. Tonight the main course would be Lefty's favorite, Veal Scaloppine Scaevola, made by Theresa's own hands from Lefty's mother's recipe. Thin and trim at fifty-five, Theresa was an elegant hostess in chocolate moire taffeta, her performance smoothly perfect after thirty years' practice. Lefty's mother, seventy-eight, and frail since fracturing her hip three years ago, was sitting in her accustomed place by the fire, sipping, as usual, her favorite Marsala. An orchestral arrangement of Puccini's *Madama Butterfly* was softly playing as a background to the buzz of spirited conversation. It promised to be a delightful evening.

Why, then, should Lefty feel this nagging queasiness? Why should his mouth, every now and then, be filled with the residue of a sour belch? Why this hot coal lodged behind his sternum?

Torelli had reported that things were under control. Tony safely with his Uncle Vinnie in Newark; Tony's two friends in drums of cement at the bottom of Chesapeake Bay; Tammy on ice in the McHenry Highrise; the Simms girl silenced.

There'd been only two snags in what seemed to be a very smooth operation: Torelli hadn't been able to make the Simms girl's death appear to be an accident—which meant further police investigation (he *said* she'd attacked them with a butcher knife, and they'd really had no choice). And secondly, he hadn't recovered the Farringford Cadenza. This last was more irksome than threatening. For even if the music turned up, it couldn't easily be linked back to Tony and the family. Still, the failure was irritatingly untidy.

On the other hand, the sloppiness of the Simms matter did pose a potential hazard. Particularly since foul play was already assumed in the death of her boyfriend. Fortunately, George's gun was safely at the bottom of the Bay. *Damn* the sour stomach! He couldn't afford a flareup of his ulcer—not with the Federal Grand Jury preparing to hand down its indictments.

With a broad smile, he was listening to Judge McPhee extol the glories of his new Mercedes when he noticed his valet beckoning him urgently from the doorway that led to the front hall.

"Excuse me a moment," he said to the judge. "My man wants me." He walked casually to the hallway and followed the valet to the door of the TV room, far out of the hearing of his guests. "What is it?" he asked impatiently.

"Mr. Torelli is here to see you, sir. He's waiting in the sunroom. He says it's important."

"Damnation! We're just at the point of sitting down to eat." Puffing angrily on his pipe, Lefty strode past him down the hall. *Madama Butterfly* accompanied him to the back of the house and into the large sunroom whose floor-to-ceiling windows were heavily curtained against the night. There, in a dark overcoat, holding his hat in his hands, Angelo Torelli stood by the door that opened onto the terrace.

"All right, what is it?" Lefty snapped. "I've got important people in there. You know I don't want business coming to the house."

"I'm sorry," said Torelli. "It's something you should know. Something I didn't want to trust to the telephone—even the safe line. Our source at police headquarters says that your name, and

Tony's, and mine are being mentioned in connection with the drowning on Gobel Street and the death of Stephanie Simms today."

Lefty nearly bit through his pipestem. A wad of something hot and heavy gave a sluggish hop! and turned over in his stomach. "More," he demanded.

"It's all in the report of the Simms homicide that was turned in late this afternoon. A woman named N. F. Trntl—t-r-n-t-l—told the police to check for links between you, me, Tony, and the two deaths."

"Who the hell is N. F. Trntl?" Lefty cried in a hoarse whisper.

"She's a private detective from New York who was hired by Lunner & Dinch to find the cadenza. She discovered the Simms girl's body and is telling the cops that the two deaths are related through the music. Oh yeah, she also said that their investigation should include somebody named Marco."

"Marco? Marco who? Borghesi? Are you using him in this?"

"No. I don't know where she came up with that name."

"How the hell did she come up with *our* names?"

"I don't know. Maybe the same way that Simms knew to go to Tony's house to find the cadenza. This Trntl probably made a tie-in with the boyfriend's working with Tony at Hanrahan's. Or maybe Simms told her she found it in Tony's apartment." He stopped abruptly and pursed his lips in thought. "You know, I think maybe I've seen this Trntl. Yesterday afternoon some woman came into the restaurant with Stephanie Simms hunting for Morris Waite and wanting to talk to Tony. I said he wasn't working that night. She's a blondish woman—somewhere in her thirties—with glasses, a big nose, and a cheap cloth coat." He referred to a slip of paper. "Our source at police headquarters says she's staying at the Cavendish Hotel—Room 609."

Scaevola leaned over an ashtray and savagely knocked out his pipe bowl on the heel of his hand. "Another loose end, Angelo! There's too many of them." He blew through the pipe and stuffed it into his jacket pocket. "Jesus Christ!"—he quickly crossed himself—"Am I paying good money to feed a bunch of screw-ups?" He shook his finger in Torelli's face. "The Simms girl shoulda had an accident! You screwed that up bad, Angelo. There's too much coming loose. It's getting outa the box!" He forced himself calm, took a deep breath. Paused. Struck: "Are you a screw-up, Angelo?"

"I messed this one up," Torelli acknowledged nervously. "But I have a good track record. You've been good to me. It won't happen again."

"Well, it damn well better not. You have a chance to prove it. This Trntl woman has to be shut up fast before she talks to anybody else. Does *she* have the cadenza? Is that why you couldn't find it?"

"I asked about that," said Torelli. He'd gone white about the lips. "Our source says no. From the report, he says it looks as though she thinks *we* have it."

It took Lefty only a moment. "Okay, then, use the cadenza as bait. Make her come and get it. But no screw-ups, Angelo. I want her to disappear."

"No trace?"

"No trace."

Torelli nodded and went out the terrace door. Lefty locked it after him and started back to his guests. That goddam Tony! Couldn't wait his turn. Impatient. Greedy. Just like his father before him. Well, it would be a long time before Tony worked up from the bottom. In the front hall, he chewed down three antacid tablets. Damn stomach. And with veal scaloppine tonight. His mother's best recipe.

"Ah, there you are, Lefty," said Judge McPhee. "We've been waiting for you. Theresa says we should go in and sit down. And by the way, these little sausages are marvelous!"

"Glad you like them, Judge. My cousin Gino makes them up in Harrisburg. One of the family specialties. But wait till you've tried the veal!" He swallowed vigorously several times to force back the acid that was creeping up his throat; and—smiling broadly—with expansive gestures herded his guests into the dining room. He pressed one hand deeply into his belly. He knew he could count on Torelli. No trace. Not now. Not ever.

While Scaevola was having his dinner in Grafton, a different sort of gathering was taking place in Manhattan. Watching Silas Dinch fill his glass at the sideboard, Felix McKay was struck by a keen sense of déjà vu. Except for some fresh magazines on the coffee table, Mrs. Farringford's parlor was exactly as he'd seen it last; and, except for Clara, who'd been unable to leave her teaching duties in Boston, all the clients were present as before.

Leaning heavily on her cane before the fireplace, tonight Mrs. Farringford was wearing a floor-length dove-gray dress, her auburn hair pulled back severely in a bun. Anton Farringford—also suffering from a head cold (one much nastier than *his*, Felix was pleased to note)—was perched on the edge of the reading-table, now and again blowing his nose gingerly into a huge white handkerchief.

Peter Shipley Abbott, nattily outfitted in a vested tweed suit, was leaning against the mantelpiece as though posing for a photograph. Gold and garnet links glittered on the soft white cuffs of his broadcloth shirt.

Opposite Felix, relaxed and svelte in slacks and corduroy jacket, Rosamond Foxe nestled deep in an easy chair, her long legs crossed demurely at the ankles. Ah, fair Rosamond! In the firelight, it seemed to Felix that her face glowed with an inner radiance—gleaming mellow, like a Japanese lantern—against the night-dark of her hair: rose-pink mingled with honey-yellow flame.

By contrast, Morgan Latimer's chalky pallor and sunken cheeks gave the impression that he'd climbed off a slab to be present. His knobby fingers, continually twitching and fidgeting, plucked at the fabric of his trouser legs as though picking lint or trying vainly to find the end of a raveling thread.

Straight-backed beside Felix on the couch, his legal pad ready for notes, Torvald Grimsson sat knee to knee with Latimer, quietly chewing gum, moving his large jaws slowly from side to side, like a camel working its cud.

Drink in hand, Dinch stood with his back to the fire. "It was a man," he said, "calling from Baltimore. He said the cadenza will be destroyed if we don't pay fifty thousand dollars in used, unmarked twenty-dollar bills. A fairly young man, judging by the voice. I told him I'd have to consult with the rest of you before giving him an answer. He will call back at nine in the morning and give us instructions on delivering the money."

Anton blew his nose. "We can't let it be destroyed. Fifty thousud is a lot of buddy, but we *have* to pay. The fably will codtribute; it's dot fair that Ludder & Ditch carry the load alode."

"Where do you think the family will *get* the money?" said Mrs. Farringford. "We don't *have* any!"

Anton retreated into silence, staring at the floor and snuffling into his handkerchief.

"I suppose we don't have any choice," Dinch said bitterly. "They know how badly we want it—thanks to Pettigrew's damned press conference."

"The family won't have to pay anything," Morgan Latimer said quietly. "I'm willing to help. Also, Silas, there's another concerned party—who wants the cadenza published as much as I do, but who prefers to remain anonymous. He's prepared to make a substantial contribution. If we decide to pay the ransom, I'll contact him tomorrow."

Anton said, "I'b surprised they're askig so liddle." Then he added hastily: "Dot that I'd wat it to be *bore*. It's just sad they put such a low value od Father's work."

"So little?" Mrs. Farringford pivoted on her cane to glare at him. "You're talking nonsense, Anton. Fifty thousand dollars is a *hell* of a lot of money—more than your annual salary." Anton again pulled back into silence.

Felix lit a cigarette and winced as the smoke stung his raw throat. "Mr. Dinch, how likely is it they'd actually destroy the cadenza? If they did, they'd have no return whatever on a rather large investment. They've committed murder to get it."

"Murder?" cried Rosamond Foxe. Peter Shipley Abbott clamped his lips and went pale.

"Murder," said Felix. And he briefly summarized what Trntl had reported regarding Morris's initial theft of the cadenza from Pettigrew, and her finding his body in the bathtub. When he finished, the others sat for a long moment subdued and thoughtful. Latimer was the first to rally: "Well, that certainly puts a different light on things. I'm inclined to agree with Mr. McKay. The killers have too high a stake to destroy the cadenza."

"If you refused to pay," Felix continued, "they could simply offer to sell it to the highest bidder. I'm sure they're aware that other publishers would like to get it."

Dinch set his bourbon on the mantel and wiped his forehead with his coat sleeve. He'd wrestled with that possibility all afternoon.

"Still," said Abbott, "there's a chance they might destroy it. We can't afford to assume they won't."

"Does the name 'Scaevola' ring a bell with any of you?" Torvald asked suddenly.

"A music publisher?" said Dinch. "Scaevola—Scaevola. No, I don't know of one. Sounds Italian."

"There was a composer named Scaevola in the eighteenth century," said Abbott. "Antonio, I believe. Not very well known. He wrote some suites for harpsichord, two violin concerti, and a Mass."

"No matter," said Torvald. "It's a potential lead Trntl picked up in Baltimore. We'll pursue it."

"Which brings us back to the question of what *we're* going to do," said Dinch. "Fifty thousand is a lot of money. If they have nothing to gain by destroying the cadenza, how would they react if we simply told them we aren't going to pay that much? Do you think they'd lower their price, Mr. McKay?"

Felix shrugged. "How can I say? Trying to haggle them down would be to assume they don't know what the market might bear. Or to assume they feel they're stuck with a white elephant which they'd like to dump for *whatever* they can get—"

"Or to assume they don't have other avenues for disposing of it," Torvald interjected.

"—It would be to assume that they're bluffing about destroying it—a dangerous assumption—and to counter them with a bluff of your own."

Dinch, impatient, was almost dancing a jig. "Well, point blank then, do you think we should try to get them to reduce their demand?"

"I'd hesitate to advise that," Felix said. "Trntl and Associates doesn't want to do anything that might jeopardize the cadenza."

Dinch scowled thoughtfully and swirled his drink. Peter Shipley Abbott moved from the fireplace to stand behind Rosamond's chair. "Clearly there's a huge risk," he said. "Still, I'm inclined to agree with what Mr. McKay said a moment ago: that it's unlikely they'd destroy it and have nothing, when—by taking less—they'd at least have *something*."

"Excuse me, that's not what I said," Felix countered. "I said it's unlikely that they'd destroy it after committing murder to get it and thus gain no return on a rather heavy investment. I have no idea whether they'd settle for less than fifty thousand." God, his throat hurt; and now his nose was beginning to run. He sniffed wetly. Torvald shot him a glance and increased the space between them on the couch.

"I don't like it," said Rosamond. "It's too big a risk." Oh, that voice! Felix exulted; but the truth was, he felt so rotten tonight that her Tidewater couldn't raise so much as his toes.

"I dod't like it either," said Anton. "They bight destroy it out of *spite!*"

"Well," said Abbott, "if you *want* to pay the fifty thousand—"

"Of course we don't!" said Dinch. "It's—it's infuriating to pay a bunch of crooks for something that's rightfully ours."

"Pardon me," Torvald said. "For whatever it's worth, I think we're dealing with a bunch of amateurs—or at least with people who don't know much about the true value of what they have. While fifty thousand is a lot of money however you look at it, I think Mr. Farringford made a good point when he said that they were valuing the cadenza rather cheaply. If they were really knowledgeable and clever, they'd know they could ask much more than fifty thousand and get it somewhere. For example, if they asked half a million, perhaps the world's major music publishers would form a consortium and pool their money for a joint purchase—"

Dinch choked on his bourbon, and there ensued a prolonged coughing spell, during which Anton pounded him on the back. Finally, his coughing ended, he stared at Torvald with watery eyes, wheezing, while Torvald went on as though nothing had occurred to interrupt him: "But I don't think the thieves realize this. Since there's no market value established for the cadenza—it's not like a Rembrandt painting, where there might be a ball-park figure for starters—they don't really know what it might be worth to potential buyers. The low price they've put on it leads me to wonder if they know much about music, or even about Farringford's importance. Beyond Lunner & Dinch, who they learned about in the press conference, they have no idea of who might want to buy it. I suspect they're just testing the water. If you refused to pay the fifty thousand, they well *might* lower the price."

"Or throw it open to the highest bidder," said Dinch.

"Or destroy it," said Rosamond, shaking her head.

"My point is," Torvald concluded, "that, even though they've committed murder to get the cadenza, they're not big-time operators who specialize in this kind of thing. Opportunists, rather, who barely know what they're doing. Probably free-lancers, or only a mid-rank gang of hometown hoodlums."

"Just a Baltimore group?" Mrs. Farringford asked. "Not an international cabal?"

"That's my guess," said Torvald. Was her last question laced with irony? He found he couldn't decide. Already she was looking elsewhere, preoccupied. She crossed the room slowly, not relying much on her cane, and poured herself a formidable shot of Scotch. She carried herself erect, shoulders back, and from a distance looked younger than her years. Her drawn-back hair was not becoming, however; it threw her sharp cheekbones into high relief, accentuated her nose and the trowel-like point of her chin. Dinch joined her at the sideboard and refilled his glass. "Let's vote on what we should do," he said. "Who of us feels that we should refuse to pay the fifty thousand? Mrs. Farringford?"

"I'm not sure," she answered.

"Anton?"

With a nervous smile, Anton replied, "I'll wait till I hear what Peter has to say."

Dinch turned to the pianist. "Well?"

Abbott was frowning thoughtfully. "It's a terribly hard decision. But I think they're just bluffing about destroying the cadenza. I vote that we tell them the price is too high—say the cadenza just isn't worth fifty thousand—to us or to anyone else. Tell them we'll go ten thousand—but that's our last offer. They know it's worth *something*."

"Anton?"

With a great sigh of misgiving: "I'll cast by vote with Peter."

"What about you, Rosamond?"

"I just don't want anything to happen to the cadenza," she said. "But since I don't have more than three or four hundred dollars to contribute toward the ransom, I don't think I have any right to commit anyone else to a particular course of action. I think Mr. Grimsson is probably right when he suggests that the thieves don't really know what they're doing. You might be able to get away with calling their bluff. But I hate taking the risk."

"Mr. Latimer?"

"I say don't take chances. We should pay it all. And I've already said that the family won't have to put up any money. Or Miss Foxe. For me, further discussion is pointless. I'd personally pay ten times fifty thousand to get the cadenza published." A faint wave of shock rippled through the room; and sensing this, he said hurriedly: "I've heard the cadenza and know what it is. The rest of you don't."

Dinch turned back to Mrs. Farringford. "How do you vote?"

She took the time to light one of her Turkish ovals before answering. "Since Mr. Latimer feels so strongly, and has actually heard the music, I defer to his judgment. I vote we go the whole fifty thousand."

"I feel the same way," said Dinch, "though I hate like hell to give in to extortion."

He tallied their votes. "Three for paying the full ransom; two against; one abstention. Now we've got to call Clara." He went to the phone and dialed the number lying beside it on a card. His conversation with Clara Farringford was brief. "She says we shouldn't try to bluff," he said to the room. "She's willing to contribute five thousand of her own money to their full asking price."

"She doesn't have that much to spare!" said Mrs. Farringford, surprised.

"Nevertheless," Dinch said impatiently. He let Clara know their decision and hung up. "She's pleased," he announced. "And now we have our answer for the extortionist when he calls. Morgan, I want to express how grateful we are for your interest in the matter, and your generosity."

Latimer shook his head. "It has to be saved and given to the world."

Dinch turned to Felix and Torvald. "You'll inform Miss Trntl of our decision, I trust? If we recover the cadenza by paying the ransom, we of course will no longer require the services of your firm."

"Understood," said Felix. "But until the cadenza's in your hands, we'll remain on the case. Trntl's actively pursuing matters in Baltimore, and she may be able to find out who has it now."

With that, the meeting broke up. Moving fast, before he had time for second thoughts, Felix pulled an envelope from his inside coat pocket and handed it to Rosamond Foxe. "This is a sketch I made of you at the last meeting," he said quickly. "Trntl thought it was a good likeness and said I should give it to you. I'd be happy if you'd accept it as a token of my esteem."

She smiled, quickly opened the envelope, and spent a long minute studying the picture. "Why, it's very good," she said. "Thank you very much."

"Um," said Abbott looking at the drawing over her shoulder. "Have you had art training, Mr. McKay?"

Felix was blushing with pleasure and relief. "No, it's just intuitive, I guess. Eye and hand. No training." Rosamond was putting the envelope carefully into her handbag.

"Self-taught, then," said Abbott. "You certainly do have a flair."

"I appreciate your giving me the picture," Rosamond said to Felix. "I will treasure it." She reached out and gently pressed his hand.

And then everybody left in pairs: Abbott and Foxe; Dinch and Latimer; Felix and Torvald. Anton stayed to talk with his mother before going back to his apartment in Queens.

As they drove back to the office, Felix, still exhilarated by his exchange with Rosamond, felt the urge to burst out singing. To avoid the embarrassment of doing this, he asked Torvald, "Well, what did you think of them?"

Working the sugar out of a fresh piece of gum, Torvald did a quick memory scan. "They're pretty much what you'd led me to expect. Certainly that Foxe woman is everything you claimed. I found I had to keep my mind on something else—uh, you know what I mean."

"It helps to have a head cold," said Felix.

Torvald nodded. "I looked at Latimer. That helped a lot. Now, Abbott seems very much taken with himself, like a cock pheasant displaying his plumage. But I don't think he's after any hens. Not even Rosamond Foxe. No, he'd be happiest with a full-length mirror where he could admire himself preening. Dinch is deeply agitated, as though his honor's been besmirched—"

"His face has broken out in a rash since I saw him last," said Felix.

"I was wondering about that," said Torvald. "Unsightly to say the least. Anyway, he appears to feel violated, as though the cadenza had been stolen from *him*—he sees it as a personal loss. But he's delighted that Latimer's willing to foot the bill. Latimer's interesting. I don't recall ever seeing anyone quite like him; a strange mixture of desperation and zeal, with hardly enough energy left to handle either. Now, Mrs. Farringford—can you imagine being married to a tough old kestrel like her for thirty years? She doesn't seem to hold Anton in very high regard, and she's obviously centered on money."

Felix smiled. "If, as Anton claims, old Charles Philip was inclined to stray, it's not too hard to understand. We'll call our report to Trntl; then, for me, it's home to a hot toddy and a good night's sleep."

"For me," said Torvald, "it's chess with Papa Weintraub. Rachel and her Mom are going to an uncle in Brooklyn, but I'll get some good kraut and a dandy corned beef sandwich."

Swirling ice in a fresh glass of whiskey, Mrs. Farringford stood at the sideboard regarding her son with stunned disbelief. Anton had just told her that, because of his own financial difficulties, he'd no longer be able to provide her the $500 allowance he'd been giving her each month for the last five years (and the equivalent amount, relative to his salary, for the seventeen years before that). $160 was all he could afford for March.

When she'd recovered from her initial shock, she exploded—first in a silent paroxysm that showered him with Scotch and shards of ice, then with white hot indignation, altogether like a spew of magma.

"Financial difficulties!" she shrieked. "*I'm* the one with financial difficulties! You've got a good job, making forty-six thousand a year. I have nothing—nothing! The roof over my head, this moth-eaten furniture, the pitiful trickle from my father's estate. And the roof leaks—go up and see for yourself! A great brown stain on the ceiling of the old nursery. The plumbing's shot. The carpet looks like it's from a fleabag hotel. I've survived—barely—by scrimping and cutting corners, no thanks to your father. When he died, it was like he'd run out on me, leaving me with two teenage kids to raise, and a mountain of debts! I don't ask much from you, Anton. Five hundred a month. With that, and what Clara can provide, I manage. I manage by saving coupons for grocery sales, by eating lean, not going to plays or restaurants, wearing old clothes, letting things go to pot. And I've sacrificed for you, Anton. I've given everything I could. I saw you through your accounting degree. Clara through her music lessons and the conservatory. You owe me, Anton. So what's this crap about your having financial difficulties?"

Slumped on the couch, almost unable to breathe for his nasal congestion, Anton would not meet her ferocious glare. His head felt as though it were stuffed with cottage cheese. "I've had setbacks—"

"Hah! You're not a gambler," she said. "What do you mean, 'setbacks'? You haven't lost your job, have you?"

He shook his head—a mistake: his nose began to run. He blew loudly into the handkerchief.

"Bad investments? Is that it, Anton?"

"That's it," he said quickly. "A big loss."

She thumped her cane on the floor. "No more sense than your father! Why the *hell* do you insist on having that expensive apartment out in Queens? You never should have rented it. You should have stayed here; there's plenty of room for both of us, your old room is still up there waiting for you. Just think of the money you'd save! Why, this house is even close to your work. You could get rid of your car and save that expense too."

"It's dot possible," Anton said. (Besides, he'd already sold his car.)

"Nonsense. There's nothing keeping you in Queens." (True, he thought wryly; the problem, Mother, is what *I'm* keeping in Queens.) She began moving restlessly back and forth beside the couch. "You're not married, you're getting on in years—yes you are, Anton, you'll be fifty-four in August! Your place is here with me, in the family home."

He'd been working up the courage to suggest that she sell the house and move into a small, furnished apartment; but at that statement, his resolve wilted. Family home, indeed! For him, the rooms were crowded with foul memories: the continuous nattering, the badgerings, the snide undercuttings and vicious quarrels. Mother—always demanding, criticizing; Father retreating to his studio, slamming the door. Clara as a child locking herself in her room to escape it all; himself, hiding down cellar with his girlie magazines.

There were some good memories: his father taking little—then not so little—Anton aside in whispered confidence: "Now don't tell your mother—", and Anton entering into the game with excited and secret delight; later, the loyal camaraderie, the intricate conspiracies concocted with his father against the common enemy, Anton covering up and running interference, helping his dad find ways to compose without interruption, to sneak an afternoon off or an evening out; devising ready excuses for his unexplained absences, providing a friendly eye to spot the lipstick on his collar. But the good memories did not, could not outweigh the bad.

Abruptly, Anton stood up, went to the table, and quickly wrote out a check. He handed it to his mother and opened the door to the hallway.

"It's for only a hundred and sixty dollars—" Mrs. Farringford cried.

"That's right," Anton said.

She saw that she'd lost the battle. Anton was putting on his hat and coat.

"What will I do?" she asked. "How can I live?"

"Wad am *I* to do?" he shouted back. He started for the outer door.

"I suppose I could sell your father's piano," she said loudly.

He stopped in mid-stride, then planted his foot, and turned around slowly. "Don't *ever* say that again!" he whispered, his right hand, at shoulder height, clenched in a shaking fist. His intensity made her quail. She took a step backward. "The piano's about all your father left us," she said, trying to cover her fright. "We won't even get any money for the cadenza after Dinch gets his hands on it."

"Royalties," said Anton.

"Royalties!" she wailed, as though in pain. "The lucky ones are the thieves who are holding it for ransom! *They'll* get fifty thousand!"

He spun around, flung open the door, marched out, and slammed it behind him. Halfway down the steps, he laughed harshly: She was right. The thieves were the lucky ones. Goddam! Fifty thousand, paid by Morgan Latimer, who'd never miss it. The bastards had really cut themselves a trick. Guaranteed payment. As good as money in the bank.

He hailed a cab, and all the way to the station replayed the conversation in his head. Paying off the driver, he began to laugh again. Now that his anger had subsided, he felt damn good. How he'd dreaded this confrontation, his mother's razor tongue! But by God, he'd faced her down. He really *had*. And now, with that problem solved, his others appeared more manageable. He bought himself a candy bar and took the train to Queens.

Chapter 12

In Room 609, the telephone rang. Trntl picked up the receiver.

In Room 917, the red light flashed on Jerry's black box. "She's making a call," Chip said, flipping the switch. Jerry and Marco took up positions on either side with note pads. In his shirtsleeves, Victor Zyzynski turned expectantly from the window where, in a haze of cigar smoke, he'd been brooding over the lights of the city.

"Torvald. Hello, Trntl. Felix doesn't feel well enough to talk and wants to go home to bed."

"Well, tell him to hang around a minute," said Trntl. "I've got some news he needs to hear. First, what happened at the meeting?"

"They agreed to pay the fifty thousand and will so inform the guy when he calls tomorrow. Basically, they're all afraid if they don't, the cadenza will be destroyed. And if it's not, Dinch is afraid his competitors will get it."

"Thank God they've decided to pay!" Zyzynski crowed, puffing triumphantly.

"And Morgan Latimer will pick up most of the tab; though he did say there's an anonymous donor who would want to help, and he'll get in touch with him tomorrow."

Oh crap, Zyzynski thought. No evading it. Well, he'd be back in New York before morning, but it would be Latimer's problem to get through to him at the merger negotiations. What would be a plausible amount to contribute? Ten thousand? Probably enough. A "one-fifth share"! If paying ransom was the only way to get the cadenza back within reach, it was fine with him if Latimer paid the bulk of it.

"Are you done?" said Trntl. "Okay, a lot's happened here since we talked to Felix at 11:30. Stephanie Simms was murdered sometime around one o'clock. At 12:18 she wrote me a note saying that she had the cadenza—"

Torvald gave a whistle of surprise. "Two murders now! How did she get possession of the cadenza?"

"I knew we shoulda paid the Simms girl a visit!" Marco whispered to Chip.

"Don't know," said Trntl. "Evidently it was at Tony Scaevola's apartment. She said she was going to take it to Pettigrew's, but she never got there. She was shot in her apartment shortly after she wrote me the note and before she left for the professor's house. There's a good possibility her killer has the cadenza now. But then again, maybe not. She may have hidden it or passed it to someone else."

"What about the guy that made the ransom demand this morning?" asked Torvald.

"He may be the killer. But on the other hand, he may not."

"I see," said Torvald.

"We're extremely curious as to whether Dinch will get the scheduled ransom call at nine tomorrow."

"Dinch made it clear that if he does get the cadenza, he's eager to terminate our services. I'm sure he's already dreading your expense account. But I told him we stay on the case till the clients have the cadenza in hand."

"Good. I mailed you some stuff today—the information on Scaevola & Company that I was able to ferret out this morning. Did you get a chance to do any research?"

"Well, it so happens I had nothing down for this afternoon, so I spent it grubbing for worms. Want a report?"

"Sure. Let me turn on the tape recorder."

"I found out quite a bit, but there's some stuff you'll have to get for me down there. I'll study what you've sent, then tell you what you still need to look for. Here's what I've got.

"The Scaevola family controls CIMACORP, which is an umbrella for several development and construction companies that do residential, commercial, and public works projects. There's also a lumberyard, nursery and landscaping business, a salvage yard, and three restaurants. It's basically a Baltimore operation, but it owns tracts of land as far away as Annapolis and Harrisburg. It holds a 60% share of three similar outfits in New Jersey which have the same range of activities—in Atlantic City, Newark, and Paterson. Now, that's just the above-board operations. I talked to Gretchen in Annapolis, Herb in Newark, and Joel in Trenton, and there seems to be a range of undercover activities too—prostitution, gambling, pornography, drugs, bribery, kickbacks, et cetera. They've evaded several attempts by the Justice Department to nail them; but scuttlebutt has it that new Federal indictments are pending which will result in convictions.

"The business was founded by three brothers who immigrated from Sicily in 1913, opened a salvage yard in Baltimore in 1917, and a chain of saloons and fun parlors in 1926. The Baltimore branch is currently headed by Giuseppe, who's 60 years old—the oldest of four brothers, three of whom are living. Tony's father—Dominic—died sixteen years ago in a warehouse fire. Giuseppe has two sons of his own. One manages a construction company in Toledo, and the other is a lieutenant-colonel in the Air Force. Now what do you have?" There was a faint click as he turned on his tape recorder.

"The Scaevola family owns a great deal of land in the Baltimore area," Trntl said. "The Development Company has constructed and leased two shopping malls, built nine residential subdivisions, seven supermarkets, three public parking lots, and a drainage ditch. They've been highly successful in bidding for street and highway construction in the region. Various Scaevolas (cousins, in-laws)—many with other names—have aided the restoration of downtown Baltimore by buying old rundown rowhouses from the city for one dollar each and renovating them for eventual rental or resale. Giuseppe has served on the board of the Maryland Initiative for Economic Enhancement, The Governor's Urban Renewal Commission, the County Retail Development Board, the Chamber of Commerce Executive Committee, the Anne Arundel Citizens' Community Improvement League, and the Clean-Up-Baltimore Task Force Against Pornography. He has cousins on the Planning Commission and the Zoning Board."

Zyzynski had listened to all of this with intense interest; when it was over, he gave a relieved chuckle and blew a jet of smoke at the telephone: this guy Scaevola was in the game, all right—but only as a nickel and dime player.

"With his fingers in all those pies," Torvald said, "do you really think Giuseppe would be involved in holding up Lunner & Dinch for fifty thousand dollars?"

"Fifty thou would buy a lot of rundown rowhouses," Trntl said with a laugh, "Even some votes. But no, I doubt if someone who's into pornography and gambling, who builds public sewers and shopping malls, would commit two murders in order to have a manuscript to ransom for peanuts. I think his nephew Tony is going it alone. At this point, I feel sure he killed both Morris and

Stephanie, and is the caller who's shaking Dinch down. I've told the police I suspect his involvement in both murders."

"And you think he has the cadenza back again?"

"I don't know. I'm afraid so."

"At least you've tipped off the police," said Torvald. "Maybe they'll get him for the murders and recover the cadenza themselves."

"Uh oh," said Zyzynski. "We don't want the police to get it. Marco, is this Tony Scaevola's address in the directory?" "How do you spell it?" Marco asked. Chip flipped back through his notes of the 11:30 conversation, found Trntl's spelling, and passed it over to him.

"I don't know how vigorously the police will follow up the leads I gave them," Trntl said. "They made it quite clear they don't want me mucking around in their murder investigation. As far as I know, Tony Scaevola isn't aware that I know about his involvement. When you give Dinch your next report, use discretion in deciding what to tell him."

"Right. Discretion it is. We'll be waiting for your call tomorrow at eleven-thirty."

The red light winked out. "Well!" Zyzynski said, putting on his suitcoat. "I've got to fly back to New York. Call me a report tomorrow at three. Use the Arrow-A Line; and if I'm not available, put your call through to Mr. Meggs." He put on his topcoat and gray homburg. "Was Tony Scaevola in the directory, Marco?"

"Yep," said Marco. "Should we pay him a visit?"

"In this case, by all means. Be very careful. We have both the police and his uncle Giuseppe to reckon with, and I don't want to be bothered by either of them getting in our way." He left, briskly closing the door behind him.

They all relaxed. Jerry and Marco took off their shoes. Chip broke out the bottle and glasses. "The sales convention ends tonight," said Chip. "And that guy from Delaware will be moving out of the room directly across the hall from Trntl's. Marco, get down to the front desk and reserve that room so we can move in right after checkout. Use the Aarslof credit card. Tell them you want that specific room for sentimental reasons—like you spent your honeymoon there, or something."

Marco gave a squeaky little laugh. "That's rich, Chip. You're a card."

"We'll keep this room, too," said Jerry. "It's got a great view. The nice thing about having another room across the hall from Trntl is that we can watch through that little peephole-bubble in the door to see when she goes in or out."

Jerry was a man of action, and the inactivity of the last three days was driving him nuts. While Marco had been following Trntl, Jerry had been tailing her girlfriend; but she hadn't done much— gone to Finegold's, yes, but all she'd done there was buy a blue bowl. Most of the rest of the time, she'd just stayed in the hotel.

But now there was promise of action in the black bagging of Tony Scaevola! Tony sounded like one heavy dude: wasted two people to get the cadenza, and had his uncle's organization to back him up. More like it! As he poured a glass of tomato juice, his lower lip was doing a smile.

Anton Farringford's apartment was not the sort of place he'd dreamed of as a young accountant starting out on what had proved to be a very bumpy road. It was a small unit in a very large building—living room, bedroom, kitchenette, bath—surrounded above, below, and on three sides by countless similar units. But anything was better than living in his mother's house, trapped in his little upstairs room with no friends of any sort allowed above the second floor, no music after 10 p.m., and Mother everywhere, snooping, prying, waiting in the parlor to see what time he came in at night (ready to sally forth to confront him in the hall with having no respect for her person, her health, her peace of mind);—with oatmeal for breakfast every morning and chicken suppers twice a week (God how he hated chicken!), Mother's grisly bridge parties twice a month, her constant harping about money and how badly off Father had left her. He despised the continual economizing— her saving of aluminum foil and string, empty boxes and plastic bags; scanning newspapers for bargain sales, snipping coupons, soaking off uncanceled stamps to use a second time. (Yet she always found money to have her hair and nails done, to buy cosmetics and booze and her Turkish cigarettes.)

He recalled her rage and his acute embarrassment when—in his fifteenth year—she'd discovered his girlie magazines, and a year or so later the package of condoms he'd secreted beneath his mattress. Clara was the lucky one, escaping to Boston and a distant career at age nineteen. He'd had to stay until he was twenty-six, and then he'd simply fled. Free at last from the probing eye, the hostile scrutiny of his women friends, the perpetual litany of woe, the petty bickering, the never-ending diatribes against Father. Over the years he'd lived in a series of cheap apartments, edging farther and farther from the East 80's, until now, at 54, he'd gotten as far as Queens.

From his window he could see three cemeteries and a park. And even with neighbors above, below, right, left, and behind, he still felt a modicum of privacy (his mother had never been to this apartment!)—it was a place of refuge, a haven of retreat from the routine hurly-burly of Swinfurth Lightfoot Bank and Trust, where he held a most responsible position as Chief Accountant in the Trust Division.

The apartment enabled him to express himself, to be "his own boss" as he liked to put it; to wear his checkered bathrobe all Sunday long, or his purple Bermuda shorts, or nothing at all if he chose (his mother would have stood for none of this); to entertain guests, to shun oatmeal and save no string, to keep his condoms where they belonged—in his top drawer, ready to hand for frequent use.

He still had to keep his girlie magazines out of sight, however; for Twila Bidwell, his lover for the last three years, was a jealous woman who brooked no competition even from the soft-lighted glossy models who posed for airbrushed photographs.

Two months past her thirtieth birthday, Twila was a salesclerk at a discount shoestore; blond, shapely, slim; she was true to Anton in her fashion, and liked her bread nicely buttered. She resented bitterly the monthly allowance he gave his mother; for after that was creamed off, the remainder of their combined paychecks was never sufficient to cover expenses.

For all its small size, the apartment was a marvel of comfort and convenience: new furniture in both rooms, a new large-screen color TV, new stereo (though they had to keep the volume down to appease the neighbors), new microwave oven, new refrigerator, and electrically-powered can-opener, carving-knife, and toothbrushes. In addition, there was a new Dodge for Twila, and a large amount of expensive computer equipment for Anton.

The bedroom closet and dresser drawers were filled with Twila's clothes, the vanity with Twila's beauty aids, restoratives, and scents. A lovely rosewood box overflowed with Twila's hoard of jewelry. She liked elegant night spots and restaurants; enjoyed dressing up and doing the town; loved lobster, steak, champagne, and lush desserts. In the corner of the living room was a fancy bar, upholstered in padded leather (with four rotating stools), and a well-stocked liquor cabinet which, in the last year, Anton had made more and more use of.

For in addition to pleasing his lady, Anton also liked to play the horses: and over the last two years, he'd sustained a staggering series of losses. He'd managed to stay afloat and keep her pleased only by skillfully juggling six credit cards and discreetly embezzling funds from a number of Swinfurth Lightfoot's trust accounts. As Chief Accountant, he had privileged information and access to records, the confidence of his employers, the wherewithal to find chinks, crevices, and crannies in financial structures, the skill to tinker unobtrusively and cover his tracks, and the intelligence not to take too much from any one place.

In the space of five years, he'd managed to siphon off forty-eight thousand dollars from various accounts—all of which had been spent on personal maintenance, on the horses, on various women he'd supported comfortably, and—in the last three years—on Twila Bidwell. Initially, he'd planned to take only a little for short-term needs and to faithfully pay it back (with the addition of the same interest that would've accrued had the funds been left in place); brief loans, so to speak, from large trusts that wouldn't miss a hundred here, two hundred there. But obligations mounted, the horses wouldn't cooperate, Mother demanded her checks, and the various women—Brenda, Michelle, Tonya, Sandy, and now Twila—expected large compensations for "spending my youth" (Tonya's phrase—but they all felt it) with a man old enough to be their father, balding, slope-shouldered, baggy in the seat. He knew this; and in his desperation to keep the women attracted and attentive, he found himself spending more and more to shore things up.

Managing his "loans" was his biggest worry. In each of his apartments during the last five years one corner of the living room had been reserved for his ledgers, calculators, notebooks, reference works, and—recently—the latest in home computers. Of course he kept strict accounts of his "borrowing", and of the growth the funds would have sustained if they'd been left in place; but after two years or so, he'd ceased agonizing about paying back the "loans"—though the hope kept dimly flickering that someday he would, with all of the accrued "interest" that had been lost. He knew that when his luck improved at the races, he'd be able to make full restitution.

Twila knew nothing of these "loans"; and while she was aware that he played the horses, he never let her know how much he lost. She'd have seen it as a waste of their resources rather than a high-risk investment for their mutual benefit. And of course his mother knew nothing at all of the horses (or the women).

Tonight's confrontation with his mother had been occasioned by the harsh fact that three weeks ago, his elaborate structure had suddenly been threatened with collapse. Swinfurth Lightfoot was aware that something was amiss in several major trust accounts. There'd been emergency staff meetings of the Trust Division, the Department Heads, and the firm's Executive Committee. (Anton had been required to compile a detailed report summarizing the work of the internal auditors.) Now a special team of external auditors was being called in. There would be a rigorous investigation. Anton saw that his intricate subterranean labyrinth was about to be stripped open and flooded with light. In all likelihood, for him it would mean exposure, prosecution, conviction, loss of license. *Prison.* "We have to police ourselves," the President had stated. "Keep our stables clean. We can't afford loss of public confidence, or the taint of Federal suspicion. The auditors will have complete access to our operations, and carte blanche to do whatever's needed to get the matter solved. They'll be working with you, Farringford, and we know you'll cooperate with them fully."

The auditors would arrive in nine days. For the last three weeks Anton had been frantically retracing his routes to erase his tracks. Yet how could he be sure? He'd been too many places over too long a period. Though his records were precise and well-kept, he knew he'd overlooked something, had gotten dangerously, perhaps fatally, cocky with the ease of raiding the accounts.

He'd liquidated some of his own assets in an attempt at reimbursement; had sold his car (much to Twila's dismay), his golf clubs (he never used them anyway), borrowed against his life insurance, auctioned off a drawing by Winslow Homer that had belonged to his father. He'd stopped playing the horses, had borrowed three hundred dollars from Clara (all she could spare), and—as of tonight—reduced his mother's allowance. He couldn't sell the computer stuff—he needed it for his panicky adjustments.

All in all, he'd been able to scrape together a sum just short of seven thousand dollars, which he'd carefully fed back into the plundered accounts. Yet no matter how precise and thorough he was in covering his trail, he was plagued by nightmares that he'd done a sloppy, half-ass job which would convict him. And what of the Internal Revenue? their interest in his five years' undeclared income? Five years of tax fraud—the final blow. Oh Jesus, he felt the rope around his neck, the trap beneath his feet!

One more crisis was not what he needed; but that's what he walked into when, miserable with his head cold but still elated from his victorious bout with Mother, he entered his apartment. Twila Bidwell, in her silk bathrobe and fuzzy pink slippers, was waiting with a question: "Anton, where are my credit cards?"

Without looking at her, he hung up his overcoat. "Aren't they in your purse?"

"No, they're not in my purse!" Her stance was aggressive, elbows out, legs wide apart, feet planted firmly on the shag carpet. "I've got to have them. There's a new spring coat I want to buy tomorrow at Joliot's."

"You have plenty of coats." He sneezed, then blew his nose loudly into the soggy handkerchief.

"Did you take my credit cards?" It was as much a threat as a question. Her voice, rising in pitch, was approaching a shriek.

He seated himself at his work table, pressed his lips together, and tried to focus on a stack of computer printouts.

She took three steps closer. "I said, *Did you take my credit cards?*" This time it was a shout, strident and challenging.

He twisted around, glowering. "Yes! You're spedding too buch buddy! I said things were getting tight, and you wouldn't listen."

"Tight! That's what *you* are!" She flung the telephone directory onto the floor "It's been over three weeks since we've been to any decent place to eat! We never go anywhere anymore. You sit in your corner fiddling with your computer crap, and don't ever think about me or *my* needs!"

He sneezed, hauled out his handkerchief, and sneezed again. "Big project," he gasped. "Lots to do."

"Your work means more to you than I do. You can sit here and rot if you want. I'm going out!"

He leaped up, flushed and quivering. "It's ten o'clock! What do you mean you're going out? Where are you going?"

She tossed her head. "That's none of your business, chum."

"It is *so* my business!" he shouted. He slammed the table with his fist. "You walk out that door and you won't be welcome back!"

"Hah! That's a laugh! What makes you think I want to come back!" She started toward the bedroom.

"You'll be back!" he sneered. "You need me!"

She laughed at him over her shoulder. "Don't kid yourself, old man. I don't need to have your fat clammy hands fumbling at me. Smell your onion breath. Listen to you puff and grunt! You're disgusting, Anton. You need *me*—don't you forget it!" She snapped her fingers at him.

And it was as though something had burst in his head. He lurched out of the chair, a froth of saliva on his lips. "Bitch!" he screamed. "Whore!" He grabbed up the stack of computer printouts and flung them at her—a long accordion-pleated streamer fanning across the room.

She flailed at the papers. "Wimp! Faggot!"

"Slut!" he screamed.

"Scum-ball!"

"Sleaze-bag!"

"Mama's boy!"

With a roar, Anton ran to the wall and pounded his fist against it seven times as fast and hard as he could. Immediately, someone in the neighboring apartment thudded *his* fist on the other side of the wall. A man's voice, muffled and angry: "Pipe down in there! Keep it to yourselves, or we'll call the cops!"

With a sob, Anton leaned his head against the cracked plaster, gasping and heaving, and nursed his bruised, aching hand. "I think I've broken it," he moaned.

Twila stood in the bedroom doorway looking first at the printouts scattered about the floor, then regarding him thoughtfully. She gathered her robe about her, waded to him through the strewn paper, and gently touched his shoulder, "Gee, honey, you really *are* strung out."

He nodded slowly, but wouldn't look at her.

"The money really *is* important to you, isn't it?" She paused, then went on in a soothing tone: "I don't have to have that coat. It was a pretty one, just my style, and you would've liked the way it looked on me. But pooh, it's just a coat. Hey, are you all right, honey?"

He hadn't moved from the wall. "I'm okay." He wiped his nose with his good hand. "I've just been under a lot of strain. I'm sorry I shouted at you. I don't know what came over me."

She caressed his shoulder reassuringly. "I'm sorry too. We've been through a lot together, honey. We can't let little flare-ups like this upset our relationship." She moved closer, pressing her body against his back, and ran her fingers through his thinning hair.

"You're right," he said. "I've been neglecting you. It's just this goddam work."

"You work so hard, Anton. All the time. You wear yourself out, and that's no good." She turned him around and gave him her best smile. "You need a break. It's getting you down. Hey, listen, why don't you *take* a break? It'd surprise you how much better you'd feel. We'll go out to some little place—quiet and dark—with a little music, maybe—have a coupla drinks. Come back relaxed. Things will go better then. Whatcha say?"

He sighed deeply and nodded. "It might be a good thing to do. This is a dead end, for sure."

"We've got to take time for ourselves," she whispered, giving him a little squeeze where he most liked to be squeezed. "Okay, it's a deal. I'll just go slip into some decent clothes, and we'll go out and enjoy ourselves, huh? Won't be a minute." She gave him a kiss on the cheek and moved quickly into the bedroom. "We have to trust each other, don't we?" she called. "Without trust, there's no relationship, is there?"

"Right," he said, surveying the littered room.

"I trust you, Anton. I always have. And I hope you trust me. I want you to."

"I trust you." He got down on his knees to gather up the print-outs. His headache was much worse now.

In three minutes she'd returned dressed in a plaid wool skirt and cashmere sweater that gave the illusion her bust measured 40 instead of 38. With her came wafting the scent of Anton's favorite perfume. "I'm ready, honey. How do I look?" She posed for him, shoulders back, hand on hip, one foot turned out just so.

"You look fine, Twila." He reached out and hugged her close, savoring the softness of the cashmere, giddy with her scent. Humming softly, he nuzzled her neck below the ear.

"Oh, honey!" she laughed. "You'll muss me. There'll be plenty of time for that later. Now go get your coat, and let's have fun!"

By morning, she knew, she'd have her credit cards back.

x x x

Tony Scaevola's apartment received two visits that night. The first, about ten-thirty, was made by Trntl and Carol; the second, about two a.m., by Marco, Jerry, and Chip. Both groups found the apartment dark, letters uncollected in the mailbox. "Well, at least we've seen where he lives," said Trntl. "Now let's go to Hanrahan's for a drink."

Marco and Chip did more. While Jerry stood watch on the street, they scaled a wall, climbed a fire escape, and, from a small balcony outside Tony's apartment, gained entry and looked the place over. Using only flashlights they made a thorough but tidy search for the cadenza, and in the process discovered food in the kitchen cabinets, toilet articles in the bathroom medicine chest, a half-empty box of chocolates beside the telephone. In the living room they carefully studied Tony's picture in a high school year-book, then neatly sliced it out to take away for future reference. In the desk they found Tony's checkbook, a bundle of canceled checks (they took one of these in order to have his signature), a 9 millimeter Smith & Wesson (loaded), a penciled copy of Morris Waite's work schedule, and a birthday card ("Happy 23rd") from Aunt Maria.

"How do you figure it?" said Chip.

"Where's the lady's underthings?" asked Marco. "There's still some of her stuff in the bathroom—but no cosmetics. Some of her shoes and summer clothes in the closet—but lots of empty hangers. Her winter things are gone. *His* clothes all seem to be here."

"Maybe she's a part-timer," said Chip.

"Nope," said Marco. "Too many lipstick-stained cigarette butts in the trash. She's the smoker here. There's an unopened carton of cigarettes in the pantry. Potted plants all over the place, still moist from watering. Women's magazines under the coffee table, movie star gossip, letters addressed to Tammy O'Rourke. I'd say she left in a big hurry."

"But Tony's stuff is still here: clothes, electric shaver, checkbook. He hasn't moved out."

"So it seems. Can you think of anyplace we haven't looked?"

Chip surveyed the living room, stepped into the kitchen, shone his flashlight around, did the same in the bedroom and bath. "Mattress, laundry hamper, water closet, cupboards, freezer, refrigerator, dish washer, lighting fixtures, sofa cushions. Under the rug, behind the pictures—jeez! these are terrible pictures, aren't they?—no, I can't think of anywhere else."

"Me neither. Let's get out of here."

On the way back to the hotel, the three of them drew straws, and Jerry was designated to stake out Tony's apartment to see when he returned.

The parking lot at Hanrahan's was crowded. New Cadillacs and Continentals, four BMW's, a customized Mercedes, a Rolls-Royce, two Corvettes, and a vintage Bentley. "Some company," said Carol.

"Luck of the Irish," said Trntl. "I'm hoping there won't be a cover charge."

There wasn't a cover charge; and when they told the hostess they only wanted drinks, she steered them away from the dining room and led them to a small table near the rear wall of the piano-bar/lounge. Carol ordered a Daiquiri; Trntl, black-label Johnnie Walker on the rocks.

"It's certainly dark in here," Carol remarked. "I'm glad we're *not* eating."

Except for a small bullet spotlight on the woman pianist (who was singing a bluesy torch song) and some pale indirect illumination over the bar (reflected eerily in the inverted glasses racked over the bartender's head), lighting was provided only by the solitary candles standing in ruby chimneys on each table. There were many tables, at nearly all of which dark figures loomed and huddled. But, from across the room, even those figures near the bullet-spot were indistinct. Occasionally there would be the momentary gleam of a gold cufflink or watchband, the glitter of a jeweled ring or pendant, a half-seen profile or dull red swatch of reflected light limning the underside of a chin. But beyond that, the matte black walls and ceiling and thick sable carpet swallowed what light there was. Unlike the restaurant, here there were no mirrors.

"It's evidently not a place where people come to be seen," said Trntl.

"Or for people who are scared of the dark," said Carol.

Their drinks arrived, priced at six dollars each.

"Six dollars!" Carol whispered, as the waitress left.

"Well, there isn't a cover charge," said Trntl. "Look, this is research. I got a receipt; it goes on Dinch's expense account."

Carol sampled her Daiquiri. "Glad to hear it. I'd hate to have paid for this drink myself."

Trntl's complaint was of a different order: it was Scotch all right, but it wasn't the Johnnie Walker Black she'd ordered. "Do you suppose they're trying to tell us something? Maybe we aren't dressed right."

"Maybe two women is an unusual combination here," said Carol. "Do you suppose the people at those other tables are looking at us askance?"

"No, they can't see us any better than we can see them. I think this is a conspiracy between the waitress and the bartender."

"Hanrahan is probably spinning in his grave like a yo-yo," said Carol.

"No, he's still here," said Trntl. "Back in the kitchen, standing firm in the deep-freeze."

Having finished their drinks, and feeling that they'd acquired a good sense of Hanrahan's ambience, they made their way out to the reception area. "I'm going to try it once more," said Trntl. "This is a different hostess from the one Stephanie and I talked to yesterday."

The hostess saw them and came forward with two menus. "May I seat you now?"

"Thank you, no," said Trntl. "I wonder, though, if you could do me a favor. I understand Tony Scaevola works in the kitchen. I'm his Aunt Fanny from Atlantic City, in town for just a few hours, and I'd like to say hello to him. I wonder if I might see him for just one minute?"

The hostess stared at her perhaps more sharply than she realized, and then her eyes went cool. "I'm sorry," she said, "Tony Scaevola no longer works here."

"Dear me, I didn't know," said Trntl. "How long has he been gone?"

"He hasn't worked for two weeks," said the hostess. "He's in Wyoming on a camping trip."

"Well, I'm sorry I missed him," said Trntl. "Thanks so much for your trouble." She smiled and, with Carol in tow, made a leisurely exit. Outside, Trntl said, "We know he was working here yesterday. Why did they push it back two weeks?"

"Sounds like someone's covering for him," Carol suggested.

"Or for themselves," said Trntl.

Trntl was brushing her teeth when a sudden idea clicked into focus. She spun around and leaned out of the bathroom: "Carol! I think I've got it!"

Carol had already gone to bed and was halfway through the third chapter of Orwell's *The Road to Wigan Pier*. "Um?" she said, marking her place with a finger.

"When I first saw Stephanie, and she told me that Morris had stolen the cadenza, she already knew that Morris had hidden it in the stash-hole in his apartment. If he'd already told her that when he confessed to the theft, then why did he need to send her a letter telling her where he'd hidden it? Unless—"

"He'd subsequently put it somewhere else," said Carol. She grinned. "A very 'Special Place'."

Chapter 13

March 4   (Wednesday)

The morning paper's front page announced Stephanie's death with a banner headline: FINDER OF FARRINGFORD CADENZA SLAIN. The account of her shooting was rather lurid, and much was made of the fact that Morris Waite, drowned two nights before, had been her boyfriend. The article recounted once again Stephanie's finding of the cadenza, and its theft from Professor Pettigrew's home. "Special to the *Sun*," said Carol, "but the wire services have it too, so all the world knows what's happening in Baltimore."

"Unfortunately, my name gets mentioned too," said Trntl, "along with Mr. Eggleston's. And of course I'm identified as a private detective hired by Lunner & Dinch and the Farringford family to recover the cadenza. Now, I don't need publicity like that."

"Reporters will be showing up to interview you," said Carol.

"I'm at the no comment stage. You probably should stay here by the phone in case Felix or Torvald should call to say whether Dinch got his second ransom demand this morning. I'm going to the library to do some more checking on Scaevola. I'll be back by eleven."

But she didn't get back until twelve-thirty: and when she entered the room, Carol said, "You look awful—like spinach that should've been reduced for quick sale three weeks ago."

"I assume you mean 'wilted'?"

"Well, I really intended *more* than that," said Carol. "The library must've worked you over."

"Oh, I was done at the library by ten-twenty." Trntl kicked off her shoes and lay back on the bed. "I've also been to the courthouse, the grave of Edgar Allan Poe, the B & O Transportation Museum, and the zoo."

"Well, well, I hope you found what you were looking for."

"I learned some new things about the Scaevolas and their business interests. But my biggest adventure was ditching the man in the gray trenchcoat."

"The man we saw watching us in the lobby."

"The very same. He followed me all morning. He's pretty good at it; but once I got a good look at him, I kept seeing him everywhere. I managed to give him a run for his money. There he was, playing hide-and-seek in the library, and later lurking about the courthouse to see which office I went into. He wasn't threatening, never got close, and was certainly trying to stay out of sight. When I was done with the research, I decided to see just how tenacious he was. I went to see Poe. Yep, there Trenchcoat was, watching me through the churchyard fence. And then I went to the Transportation Museum and we spent quite a long time looking at trains. Then to the zoo, where I had a jolly time feeding the goats. But, when the game had gone on long enough, and he knew that I knew he was tailing me, I decided to ditch him. It was simpler than I expected. I drove out of Druid Hill Park to the northeast and lost him in three minutes flat in a tangle of narrow, hilly residential streets so confusing that I just about lost *myself*. He may still be there, for all I know."

"Who do you think he is?" asked Carol.

"Dunno. He's driving a rental car, which suggests he's from out of town. I managed to walk past and look in when it was parked at the zoo, and saw that he had a notebook and a Baltimore map on the front seat."

"Okay, an out-of-towner. *Why* is he following you?"

"It's the same car that followed Stephanie and me. Therefore he's been watching me for three days—maybe ever since I got here. I don't think he's one of Dinch's operatives making sure I'm on the job. And I don't think he's the person who shot Stephanie. He might be an agent of one of Dinch's competitors thinking I can lead him to the cadenza. But, before this morning's paper spilled everything, who-all knew I was here pursuing the cadenza? Only our clients, the Pettigrews, and the police. If the competitors *do* have spies in the offices of Lunner & Dinch, then maybe Trenchcoat is an agent of B. F. Cleavenger or Cameron Stewart, Ltd."

"Oh, come on, Trntl—"

"You've seen Dinch's dossiers. No, I don't know what to think. I'll go through those photographs tonight and see if I can spot him."

"Incidentally," said Carol, "you had three calls from reporters this morning, and some TV hustler who wants to interview you on a local talk show with call-in questions from the audience."

"What did you tell them?"

"I told the reporters you weren't available; I told the TV person—Sukey Somebody—that your standard fee is a thousand dollars an hour for talk-show appearances. She lost interest in a hurry."

"Too bad," said Trntl. "I'd have done it for that." She reached for the telephone. "Well, Torvald hasn't called, so it's time we call him."

In Room 917, the red light flashed. Jerry, just back from his morning vigil at Tony's apartment, gave a whistle: "Hey, Chip, she's making a call." Chip left his crossword puzzle and came to listen. As they bent over the black box, the door opened, and Marco entered, his trenchcoat spattered with grease.

"Hello, Torvald. I hope your day has gone better than mine."

"Fairly routine," he replied. "Felix is home in bed with his cold. I've been doing Carol's work, his, and mine. The biggest news at this end is that Dinch did *not* get a ransom call this morning. He's very upset. He's afraid that the cadenza's been destroyed, or that his competitors have moved in."

"The Chief will want to know this immediately," said Jerry.

"If a ransom call does come through, I'll let you know at once," Torvald said. "I got the stuff you sent me in the mail. You did good."

"I got some more today. Is the tape recorder on?" And she summarized for him what she'd learned: dates of certain real estate transactions, lists of directors of various subsidiary corporations, accounts of several key news items from back issues of the *Sun*.

"Great," he said, "that fills in some blanks. Now if you can get the following information, we'll have a nice composite profile for our permanent records." He told her what to look for. "Anything else to report?"

"Since I've been here I've been followed by a grubby little fellow in a trenchcoat. He's not a local; drives a rental car with a map of Baltimore in it. He sticks like a burr; today we've done the tourist bit—railroad museum, Poe's grave, the works. After the zoo, I ditched him."

Chip shook his head. "Ditched you, Marco?"

Marco said nothing, but angrily popped the top of a can of soda he'd bought at the vending machine on his way to the room. 'A grubby little fellow'!—he, Marco of the barrel chest and massive arms, the Death-Defying Leap, two and a half aerial somersaults, ten years' trapeze and high-wire work with The Flying Gruschenkos!

"Any idea who he might be?" Torvald asked. "Or why he tags along?"

"I'm not sure. He isn't hostile. Maybe one of Dinch's people, or an agent of one of the competitors."

"Take care," said Torvald. A sound bit of advice with which to end their conversation.

Chip went back to his crossword puzzle. "I'm surprised she gave you the slip, Marco."

Marco scowled into his soda. "When she left the park, she drove lickety-split into a maze of crazy up-and-down streets. I wasn't prepared. She'd just spent twenty minutes feeding the goats in the Children's Zoo, for crissakes."

"Now that she's identified you," said Chip, "somebody else had better follow her. Jerry, what about you? One of us could take over watching Tony Scaevola's apartment."

"Okay by me," Jerry said. "There's certainly not much happening at Tony's. The apartment's still empty. About ten o'clock an older man with gray hair came by and collected the newspaper and Tony's mail. He had to have Tony's key to open the mailbox."

"Well then, maybe there's not much point in having somebody there," said Chip. "Tony and the cadenza are clearly somewhere else."

"We could follow the guy that picks up the mail," said Marco.

"Are you willing?" asked Chip.

"Sure, since I'm through with Trntl. Shit, Jerry, you'll see what it's like. Two hours in the library for crissakes. And every time she'd leave her table and go to the stacks, I'd have to go too, for fear she wouldn't come back. And the train museum! You'll see. She likes broad open spaces where you can't find any cover, or else narrow twisty little places where she's always out of sight. She doubles back a lot, so you really have to scramble. And if she takes you to the zoo, be real careful leaving the park."

"I'll manage," said Jerry. "It'll probably take some disguises. Let's see what we've got."

He hauled the brown suitcase from under Chip's bed and opened it. Wigs, false mustaches and beards, eyeglasses in various styles, appliqué tattoos, bottles of latex, tubes and jars of theatrical makeup, bundles of identification and business cards. "Actually," he muttered, a little disappointed, "we didn't expect to need disguises on this trip. Except for my workman's coveralls, I don't have much at all. That's the secret, Marco. Now that she's on her guard, I won't give her the chance of seeing me look the same way twice."

"You'd better take the blue car," said Chip. "And we can rent others if we have to."

Jerry was still examining the contents of the suitcase. "I really enjoyed being a Lieutenant-General," he said wistfully, "when we got the Esterházy Chalice out of Fort Clephard."

Chip said, "My favorite was acquiring the Tears of St. Ursula, when we got the chance to be two nuns and a cardinal-archbishop."

Jerry closed the suitcase. "This routine stuff we've got is pretty skimpy. I'll have to put some thought to it. May do a little shopping."

"It's very frustrating," said Carol, "to have so little in this case by way of concrete fact. Almost everything is guesswork and assumption." They were having a quick lunch in the hotel coffee shop before starting an afternoon of interviews. "We assume, for example, that Tony Scaevola stole the cadenza from Morris and made the first ransom call to Dinch. But if it's true, as Stephanie claimed, that *she* had the cadenza at noon, then she must've gotten it away from him at his apartment. If he's the one who killed her, it's clear he didn't recover the cadenza—or else Dinch would have received the second ransom call this morning."

"The ransom attempt seems to have aborted," said Trntl. "Which suggests either that someone else other than the initial ransomer now has the cadenza, or that Stephanie, instead of taking it to Pettigrew, changed her mind—for whatever reason—and hid it, or left it for safekeeping with a trusted friend. I think we can assume that if the killer *did* get the manuscript from Stephanie, the killer isn't Tony Scaevola. If *that's* the case, then I'm not sure what the killer's motive is for wanting the cadenza. Not holding it for ransom, evidently. Anyway, we've got to proceed on the assumption that the killer—whoever it was—*didn't* get the cadenza. Anything else, and we're stymied." She signed her room number on the lunch bill. "I'll drop you at the Hastings Institute to talk to teachers and other students. I'll see Eggleston, Mrs. Gresham, and Professor Pettigrew."

Mr. Eggleston was glad to see her. He opened the front door at once and led her into his apartment off the front hall. The living room was overcrowded with furniture, the walls covered with framed steel engravings. A large console radio took up the center of one wall, and near this, hanging from a tall wrought-iron stand, was a domed cage containing a blue and yellow parrot. The parrot quizzically took note of her when she entered, then opened its curved beak on a bunched gray-purple tongue, and leered at her with a white-rimmed eye.

Eggleston seated Trntl on the sofa. "Have you seen the morning paper?" he asked excitedly, pointing to the coffee table and the spread front page.

"Yes, I have."

"Right there on page one!" he said. "Your name and mine. Oh, but this sad business won't do our apartments any good. Not any good at all."

"Bad boy!" said the parrot.

"That there's Rossetti," said Eggleston. "He's almost as old as I am."

Trntl smiled wanly. "I'm sorry the news story had so much detail in it. Have you been contacted by any reporters?"

"One came by this morning, and I've had calls from Philadelphia, Washington, and London."

"London," said Trntl.

"They all wanted to know more, and I told 'em all I could. Oh yeah, and Sukey Caltrop—she's one of our local TV folks—wants to interview me on her talk show!"

"And answer call-in questions from the audience," said Trntl.

"That's right."

"What did you tell her?"

"That I'd think it over and get back to her."

"She called me, too," said Trntl. "I feel it would be a sensationalist exploitation of Stephanie's death—turning it into a media event. I don't want to be a part of that."

"I hadn't thought of it that way," he said. "It does seem kinda disrespectful. Stephanie was a real nice person. Frankly, Miss Trntl, finding that poor girl was one of the worst shocks I've ever had. I didn't sleep hardly at all last night."

"A bad experience," Trntl agreed. "It's given me a hard time, too."

"Would you like a cuppa coffee?" he asked.

"No, thanks. But I would like to ask you some questions about Stephanie, if you don't mind. I know the police asked you a lot yesterday; but there are some additional ones that have occurred to me. You might be able to throw some useful light on who might have killed her."

"Anything I can do to bring the killers to justice. So, sure, ask your questions. There's still police upstairs; they don't want anybody up on third floor."

"Thanks for your cooperation, Mr. Eggleston. First: the outer door locks automatically and can only be opened by a key or by a tenant's releasing the lock with a buzzer. How do think the killer got in?"

"The police asked me that. Well, I checked the door pretty carefully: there's nothing wrong with the lock, and the glass isn't broken. My guess is that Stephanie—or even someone else in the building—buzzed them in when they rang."

"Could the killer have had his own key?"

Mr. Eggleston's mouth dropped, and he stared at her with a worried frown. "Well, I don't rightly see how. We're pretty careful with our keys."

"Could someone have made a duplicate?"

"There's a rule against it. I have duplicates, of course; but I counted 'em when I talked to the police, and there's just the right number."

"Could Stephanie have lost her key or given it to someone, do you suppose?"

"No, she had the outside door key on her. And they found her apartment key on the floor near the body."

"And you don't think it's likely that one of the other tenants may have opened the front door to let the killer in?"

"The police talked to everybody. Nobody buzzed the door open."

"So: either Stephanie buzzed the killer in, or he came in with her when she entered."

"One of those two," said Eggleston. "And since no one in the building remembers hearing a buzzer, I think the last is what happened, if you want to know the truth."

"Dork!" said the parrot.

"You shut up, Rossetti!" Eggleston shouted. Canted back on its perch with one foot against the bars of its cage, the parrot flexed its toes at him.

"That would imply the killer was a friend, or at least someone she thought she had no cause to fear."

He nodded. "Unless it was somebody who waylaid her in the vestibule after she'd unlocked the outer door and then forced his way in. We warn our tenants about getting ambushed by muggers. They're to have their keys out, get that door unlocked, and get through as fast as they can—especially after dark."

"This was broad daylight," said Trntl. "If it was an ambush, maybe there were witnesses on the street."

"The street's not crowded that time of day. The park's right in front; not many people using it in this cold weather. The houses on the other side of the park—they're kinda far away, and what with the trees and all, I don't know. It'd have to be the people in the front apartments who saw anything."

"It might be worth checking out. Could you give me the names of the managers of the buildings across the street?"

"I don't know 'em all. And besides, the police have already done it. They've interviewed everybody in those front apartments all up and down the block."

"I see. Did they turn up any witnesses?"

"I don't know. They didn't talk to me about it."

Trntl decided that it would be very awkward to go back to the same people, retracing the police's steps, and ask them the same questions over again. She gave a shrug of dismissal. "One further question, Mr. Eggleston. Did Stephanie have any close friends that you know of? People who visited her here? Or that she talked about?"

"As far as I could tell, she had only two visitors. A young guy with long hair and a beard used to come a lot, not so much lately.

He never stayed long, and it was always during the day. The other was an older man, kinda distinguished looking, with glasses and all. He only went upstairs twice that I know of, and he didn't stay long either. Most of the time he called for her wearing clothes like he was going to play tennis or go jogging or something. Do you think one of them might be the killer?"

"No," said Trntl. "The bearded man is dead. He's in the newspaper, too, under the name of Morris Waite." Eggleston half-turned to stare at the front page, his eyes wide with this new horror. "The other man was one of Stephanie's teachers at the Institute." Trntl rose from the sofa. "I'd like to speak to Mrs. Gresham," she said, edging toward the door. "I hope she's in."

"Oh, she's always in except to go to church on Sunday. Wouldn't you like to stay a few minutes longer? I'll put on a pot of coffee."

"No, thanks. I've got lots of ground to cover today. Thanks anyway." She opened the door and stepped into the hall. "I appreciate your help."

"Any time," he said, standing rather aimlessly in the center of the room. "I think I won't go on that TV program after all." Rossetti cocked his head to one side and shot Trntl a baleful glare.

Detective Adcock was coming down the stairs. "Well, Miss Trntl, returning to the scene of the crime?" His tone was distinctly unfriendly.

"Thanks for putting my name in the paper," she countered.

"I didn't do that. Price was the one the reporters interviewed. May I ask what you're doing here?"

"I'm trying to establish if Stephanie Simms had close friends in whom she might have confided, or with whom she might possibly have left the cadenza for safekeeping."

"Yesterday you were accusing Tony Scaevola of having taken it," said Adcock.

"That's still a possibility, of course," Trntl said. "But it's my responsibility to my clients to do everything in my power to find the manuscript. I have to pursue all possibilities."

"We've done some checking on Tony Scaevola. I'm not obligated to tell you anything about our investigation, but I'm going to share this with you. He seems not to be working at Hanrahan's as you claim. Hasn't worked there for two weeks. And he doesn't seem to be coming back to his apartment, either. He's supposed to be in Wyoming on a camping trip."

"Then you might find these interesting," said Trntl. She took from her purse the note Stephanie had written her, and the letter from Morris to Stephanie. "I was intending to stop by headquarters today and give you these. Stephanie received this letter from Morris; she left the note for me at the hotel desk shortly before she was killed. There's a date-and-time stamp on the back of the envelope."

He took them and read them carefully. "Where did you get this letter addressed to Stephanie Simms?" he asked.

"From Stephanie. She was extremely worried about Morris."

"I understand the basis for your suspicions about Tony," he said. "You're giving these to me as material evidence?"

"That's right. But I'd like a signed, dated receipt for them. And I have my own photocopies, of course."

"Of course." He took out his notebook, wrote out what she requested, and gave her the paper.

"Thank you," he said. "This is considerable help in our investigation. Why didn't you tell me about the notes yesterday?"

She said, "It slipped my mind in the shock of finding Stephanie dead."

Adcock said, "I see." He turned the postmarked envelope over. "Did this letter from Morris come through the mail with its envelope unsealed? The flap is intact. The gum is slightly disturbed. It looks almost as though the envelope's been steamed open. Do you suppose Miss Simms—"

"I only know that Stephanie claimed to have found Morris's briefcase at Tony's apartment," said Trntl. "I do not know how she opened her mail."

"Neither do I," said Adcock. "There was a quantity of unopened mail beside her body. As I'm sure you noticed."

"That's why I assume she was killed after returning from outside. Her earmuffs and coat suggest that the killer followed her in from the street when she entered."

Adcock slipped the note and letter into a plastic bag which he placed in his attache case.

"One other thing," Trntl said. "Tony Scaevola was working at Hanrahan's two days ago when Stephanie and I went there hunting for Morris. The hostess said that Morris wasn't there; but when Stephanie asked to see Tony, the hostess said he was in the kitchen, and took him the message. A minute later, Angelo Torelli came out and said that Tony wasn't working that evening."

"Maybe the hostess didn't know that Tony had quit work to go camping," said Adcock.

"Well, that's understandable," said Trntl, "since she knew he was in the kitchen." She brushed by him and started up the stairs. "And now I want to ask Mrs. Gresham about Stephanie's friends."

His tone was flat: "Stay in touch, Miss Trntl."

Chapter 14

Mrs. Gresham was surprised and pleased to find Trntl on her threshold. "Do come in," she said. "I've just started a pot of tea, and surely you'll have a cup." Today she was in a striped house dress and woolly slippers. "I do look a fright," she apologized, as Trntl sat on her ancient sofa. "Just took off my shoes an hour ago. Some reporters were here this morning, but I wasn't expecting anyone else to call today. Frankly, I've been so upset by Stephanie's death that I really haven't gotten myself together yet. Would you like some toast with your tea?"

"No thank you. The tea sounds very good, though."

"It's such a terrible thing," Mrs. Gresham continued, placing cups and saucers on a small tray. "She was such a sweet girl, so friendly. And she knew so much about music! She knew I liked Nelson Eddy, and she found some old 78's for me in secondhand shops. She was always on the lookout for things she thought I'd like." She began to cry over the tea things. "Excuse me,"—fetching a Kleenex from a box on the kitchen counter—"I'm going to miss her so."

Trntl glanced about the apartment while Mrs. Gresham recovered herself, noting the chairs with antimacassars on the backs, the Readers' Digest condensed books neatly arranged on a shelf, framed photographs, a portable record player, an embroidery hoop with a design newly started on stretched fabric, a wooden rack with needlework magazines, *Newsweek*, *National Geographic*, and *The Christian Missionary*.

"There, I'm better now." Mrs. Gresham set the tray on a low table before Trntl. "Would you like to hear one of the Nelson Eddy records that Stephanie found for me?"

"That would be very nice," said Trntl.

Mrs. Gresham hurried to the record player, selected a thick platter from a stack of 78's beside it, and carefully placed it on the turntable. "It's 'Stout-hearted Men' by Sigmund Romberg," she said, "one of my favorites." She sat beside Trntl and poured tea, while, with only a faint scratchiness as surface noise, Nelson Eddy's rich baritone filled the room.

"Isn't he wonderful?" said Mrs. Gresham, when the record was over, and the automatic changer had stopped the machine. "There's no one quite like him."

"A beautiful voice," said Trntl.

"It's a shame that the younger generation doesn't know him," Mrs. Gresham said with a sigh.

"Young people have their own," said Trntl. "And someday they'll be able to say the same about *their* favorites."

"I suppose so. Still, quality is quality; Stephanie was able to appreciate Nelson Eddy. She was a very sensitive girl."

"I imagine she had lots of close friends," Trntl said. "Incidentally, this tea is quite good."

"Thank you. The secret is a pinch of catnip I put in with the leaves. But no, I wouldn't say that Stephanie had lots of close friends. I didn't know most of the people she dealt with at the Institute, of course. But she never mentioned many people. Until about six months ago, her best friend was this boy Morris Waite who died several days ago." She shook her head in dismay. "The newspaper left the strong impression that his death and Stephanie's might be related."

"I'm afraid they are. In each case, the killer was trying to get possession of the Farringford Cadenza."

"Why, that's just awful!—that someone would take lives for a piece of *music!*"

"My job, as the paper stated, is to recover the cadenza for the Farringford family and the publisher of the Fifth Concerto. Stephanie informed me that she'd come across the cadenza after it had been stolen from Professor Pettigrew. She was planning to return it to the professor, but she never arrived at his house. While it's likely that her killer may have taken the manuscript from her, there's a remote possibility that—if Stephanie knew the killer was closing in—she may have given it to a friend for safekeeping. I'm trying to find out who those friends might be that she'd trust with it. So any leads you can give me would be very helpful."

"Well, she didn't give it to *me*," Mrs. Gresham said. "I've seen very little of her during the past week. Let me think. As I said, Morris Waite was her best friend up till about six months ago. She had a good friend Louisa—I forget her last name—who was a student at the Institute, but she went back to France. And lately she's been seeing a lot of Professor Pettigrew, who she said was helping her with her thesis. She respected him a lot—admired him, really.

He'd come by to play tennis with her—though he was actually old enough to be her father. I'm sure there was nothing unseemly in their relationship." She gazed searchingly at Trntl over the rim of her teacup; Trntl chose not to pursue the implied question.

"I very much appreciate your help. If anything else should occur to you, please contact me at the Cavendish Hotel, Room 609. I'll probably be there for a few more days at least."

She wrote out the information on a card and gave it to her. And while Trntl was finishing her tea, Mrs. Gresham rose and went to the record player. "Won't you listen to one more of Nelson Eddy's recordings? It's so nice to have someone to share them with—and now particularly when Stephanie—"

"Yes, I'd be happy to." She'd much rather be getting on to Professor Pettigrew's, but the 78's didn't take long to play.

Mrs. Gresham quickly selected another record and put it on the turntable. "This one's 'Short'nin' Bread'," she said, as she carefully slid "Stout-hearted Men" back into its slipcase. "Very much out of fashion nowadays, I suppose: 'Mammy's little baby loves short'nin' bread'—but very popular when he made the recording. And he does it so well."

And he did, Trntl had to agree.

When, after a long delay, Mrs. Pettigrew opened the door, Trntl was startled at the change wrought in the woman since her last visit. Gone were the hostility and arrogance, the gimlet stare and haughty contempt. In their place was naked fear. Peering through the crack of the barely opened door, she reminded Trntl of a frightened possum peeking from a hole. Her manner was subdued and furtive, her eyes continually darting here, there, over and past Trntl's shoulder, and up and down the street while Trntl explained why she'd come.

"I've got to see Professor Pettigrew immediately. It's a matter of the utmost importance."

Without a word, Mrs. Pettigrew opened the door wide enough for her to sidle through, then slammed it shut and chain-locked it. "Who is it, Irma? Who's there?" the professor called from the study.

Trntl announced herself as she rushed down the hall and entered the study with Mrs. Pettigrew trotting behind her. The professor was seated at his desk, the front page of the morning paper spread before him. He too had undergone a change: his face appeared to have aged ten years. His glasses had been repaired, and he was wearing a smaller bandage on his forehead. But his skin was milky white with a tawny cast, faintly mottled with bluish veins—rather like Stilton cheese, Trntl thought; the flesh hung loose on his cheeks and wattled under his chin.

"You've seen the paper?" he quavered. "It's vile, horrid! Stephanie shot to death. Morris drowned in his bathtub! And is it because of that wretched cadenza? *Why*, Miss Trntl? Who'd want it so desperately that he'd kill two young people to get it?"

Trntl seated herself across from him, and Mrs. Pettigrew took up her position beside the doorway. "Yes, it's because of the cadenza," Trntl said; and she recounted the whole story, from Morris's theft ("because he wanted to pay you back for having him expelled") to her discovery of Stephanie's body. She omitted mention of Tony Scaevola. "And about the time she was killed, she was intending to return the cadenza to you. I take it you've not had the cadenza returned through any means—personal delivery, messenger, the mails? It might come as a package, or locked in Morris's brown briefcase."

"No," he said. "Stephanie never came here the day she was killed. Did she, Irma?"

"No, that's right, she didn't," said Mrs. Pettigrew.

"It's possible she was preparing to come here when she was killed," said Trntl. "When she died, she was in her apartment wearing her overcoat and ear-muffs."

"Oh God," moaned the professor, taking off his glasses. He put his elbows on the desk and held his head in both hands. "I haven't seen the cadenza since it was lying here on the desk. We haven't received it in the mail, have we, Irma?"

"No," said Mrs. Pettigrew.

"There's a slim chance it still might come in the mail," said Trntl. "If it does, call me immediately at this number." She gave him one of her handwritten cards. "I'll come right out and get it, and deliver it personally to Lunner & Dinch." She turned to Mrs. Pettigrew. "Be extremely careful who you let into the house. I don't think you're in any danger as long as you don't have the cadenza. But should it arrive, consider yourself in extreme hazard until you get it to me or to Lunner & Dinch. Be constantly on guard."

"Do you think the killer is some sort of madman?" Pettigrew asked.

"No, I think money's at the bottom of it. Yesterday morning Dinch received a ransom demand; but that was before the time that Stephanie claimed to have recovered the manuscript. It's possible the killer *has* the cadenza now."

"And if he doesn't?" asked Mrs. Pettigrew.

"Then I'm sure he'll keep looking for it."

"It's likely the killer was the person responsible for the second and third break-ins!" Pettigrew cried, fumbling for his glasses. "Irma, he's already been in our house! Upstairs, downstairs, in our bedroom!"

Mrs. Pettigrew gave a strange gargling sound, and, white as bleached bone, fell back against the doorframe—then steadied herself and sank into a chair. The professor, staring abstractedly at his wife, asked Trntl in a hoarse voice: "When will this matter be settled? How long till we can breathe easy?"

"I don't know. I suppose, when the cadenza's heard from again."

The answer clearly didn't satisfy him. She went on with her agenda: "Perhaps you could answer a question of mine. On the off-chance that Stephanie might have given the manuscript to a friend for safekeeping, who might it be? It would have to be someone close and intimate that she could trust."

He took a long time to respond. "Stephanie was something of a loner. She didn't have many close friends. Let me think." He reached for his pipe and began packing it with tobacco. "There was Louisa Claudel, a student friend, but she went back to Paris four months ago. And Professor Markowitz—but they weren't intimate. Oh yes, a Mrs. Gresham, who lived in her apartment building—Stephanie spent some time with her. And Morris, of course." He paused again, lighting his pipe. "And that's about it. I can't think of anyone else she ever mentioned as a close friend."

"Well, thank you," said Trntl, rising to go. "You know how to reach me if anything else should come to mind—or if anything happens that I should know about."

Professor Pettigrew went with her down the hall. Mrs. Pettigrew sat slumped in her chair, her face sheened with a thin film of sweat. Her mind was galloping over the various horrors that Trntl had discussed so calmly. The wild ride took her to the back of the house, where, beneath a stack of dress patterns, a locked leather briefcase bearing the name MORRIS WAITE rested in her sewing-cabinet drawer.

When Professor Pettigrew returned to the study after seeing Trntl out, his wife had come to a decision. She waited until he'd seated himself at the desk and relighted his pipe, and then she walked around to the back of his chair and placed her hand on his shoulder. "It's been a terrible week, Theodore. It's as though the cadenza had a curse on it."

Pettigrew gave a shuddering sigh. "An apt way of putting it, Irma. And *I* curse the day it came into this house!"

She patted his shoulder gently. "We've not had a moment's peace." All that morning she'd had to fend off calls and visits from reporters who'd swarmed like vultures after Stephanie's death. She'd finally refused to answer the phone, and those that came to the door she'd met with a single statement: "We have nothing to say." One enterprising young woman had taken her picture as she stood blocking the doorway, an incident that had both infuriated and frightened her. But the photographer was already down the walk before she could protest.

Pettigrew stared sadly at the newspaper before him. "Our lives will never be the same, Irma."

"No," she agreed, "they won't."

"I respect Miss Trntl for coming to warn us; it was decent of her."

"She works for Dinch," Mrs. Pettigrew snapped, "a vicious, mean-spirited man. I'll never forgive him for treating you as he did: berating you, blaming you for losing the cadenza, accusing you of complicity in the theft, of perpetrating a hoax."

The memory caused the professor's eyes to smart. "He was just overwrought, Irma. He backed down from that position."

"But he never apologized. He's an unreasonable ass. It would serve him right if he *never* saw the cadenza!"

"Irma! He'd publish it for the whole world."

"I don't care. It's what I feel. I understand the cadenza's importance, Theodore. The world should have it. But *Dinch* shouldn't be the one to publish it." Her hand moved to the back of his neck and rested there caressingly.

"Lunner & Dinch has the best claim," he said. "No other reputable publisher would touch it under the circumstances."

She pursed her lips. "Publishers aside, who—after Dinch— would most want to have the cadenza?"

He thought for a moment. "The Farringford family, I suppose. They'd have the biggest personal stake."

"And are they in New York, too?"

"Dinch told me that the widow and the son Anton are living in New York, and I think the daughter Clara's in Boston. She's a flautist with a considerable reputation in her own right."

She began to massage the back of his neck. "Do you think Miss Trntl was exaggerating when she said that *we* might be in danger?"

"My God, Irma!" he cried. "Trntl isn't exaggerating. Look at the trail of blood! Stephanie. Morris. The attack on me. On Finegold. It's only if the killer already has the cadenza that we're not in danger. If he doesn't have it and for some reason comes to think we do—then we might have our throats cut in the dead of night!"

His vehemence made her shrink away. But, after a moment to recoup, she once again began massaging his neck, using both hands this time. He laid his pipe down, closed his eyes, and relaxed to the pressure of her soothing thumbs.

"It's all so insane, so terrifying!" she said. "Until the cadenza's whereabouts is known, we're to stay in the house and guard ourselves. Prisoners in our own home, Theodore!"

"It's probably the best course of action. Due caution, Irma. It probably won't be long till the police catch the killer."

"Well, if I'm to be a prisoner in my own home, I'm going to the library and get some of my kinds of books to read. Four or five novels; perhaps a biography. I'll go now, and be back in an hour or so."

"You're going out? Well, then, let me go with you. You shouldn't be out alone."

"I'll only be gone a little while, and be back in time to fix you a nice supper. Your favorite Swiss steak with mushroom gravy. I'll stop at the store on my way back from the library." She laid a finger on his lips as he started to speak. "No, Theodore, stay here and work on your book. Your sabbatical leave's almost over, and you still have a long way to go."

He sat back and folded the newspaper, placing it in the center of the desk. "It's been a long time since we had Swiss steak with mushroom gravy," he said. "But I just don't have the heart to work on my book. I can't concentrate, Irma. After all that's happened, a study of Brahms's bridgework doesn't seem very important."

"You mustn't think that!" She gently touched his cheek. "You've been working on it for over a year. It will be a fine book, an important book. You'll see; it'll be well-received and make a significant contribution! Please don't lose heart, Theodore. It's your most important scholarship to date, and the world will see that."

His eyes had become misty. "I didn't know you felt that way about the book," he said. "You've shown so little interest in my work over the years. I'm grateful to know your feelings."

"I've always been interested in your work, Theodore. I just don't have the technical knowledge to discuss it with you. But I've always believed in its importance."

He smiled up at her. "You inspire me, Irma. Perhaps I *will* work on the book. Try to collect my thoughts, focus in. But these distractions have made it so difficult."

"It'll help keep your mind off the stress we're living under," she said. "Which is why I want to get some good novels to lose myself in. I'll only be gone briefly, and then I'll get right to the kitchen. When I get back, show me that you're hard at work."

She patted the top of his head on his little bald spot and slipped the newspaper off the desk with the other hand. "Don't let me down," she smiled, moving to the door. "I'll just change clothes and get a shopping bag to carry the books. I'll keep the car doors locked while I drive."

She left him lighting his pipe with fresh vigor and went straight to the kitchen. She wadded up the newspaper and tossed it into the garbage pail, then hurried into the utility room, where she found a box just the right size. From a cupboard she took a quantity of brown wrapping paper and a roll of mailing tape. Then to the sewing room, where she pulled Morris's briefcase from the pattern drawer. With a ball-point pen she wrote on a piece of blank paper:

> This briefcase contains the Farringford Cadenza
> stolen in Baltimore. Do with it as you will.
> A friend.

She taped the paper to the briefcase, put the briefcase into the box, wrapped the box in brown paper, and taped it securely. She slid the package into her opaque plastic shopping bag, went upstairs briefly to put on a long-sleeved sweater, then came down and marched past the study door to the coat closet. "I'll see you later," she called. Her husband barely looked up from his papers: "Hurry back." And she was gone.

At the library, she looked up 'Farringford' in the New York City telephone directory, found Anton's address in Queens, and printed it on the outside of the package with her pen. Then she browsed for a bit, selected several books, and checked them out. Off to the post office, where she had the package weighed and stamped. She decided to send it first-class, its importance befitting the expense. And when it was gone, entrusted to the implacable efficiency of the US Mails, she heaved a great sigh of relief.

Away, foul thing! Do your bloody damage somewhere else! Morris she hadn't known; Stephanie she'd come to know too well. Not that she was happy that Stephanie had been killed: that was truly awful. But she wasn't the least bit sorry that Stephanie was gone. She'd had her fling in New Haven, her jolly tennis on long summer afternoons. Now Theodore was liberated, free to concentrate on his pointless, dreary scholarship. And she Irma would see to it that he wasn't distracted from it ever again. She was humming softly to herself as she turned the car toward the supermarket to get the beef and mushrooms: "Come To Me, Bend To Me"—a song from *Brigadoon*. And she already knew which novel in her shopping bag would be the first she'd read.

When Trntl returned to the hotel a little after four, she found Carol already in their room. And with her—primly elegant in a tailored tweed suit, mauve shirt with large gold cufflinks, and blue silk tie—Peter Shipley Abbott. (Oh hell, thought Trntl, what's *he* doing here?)

He'd been lounging in a chair, sleek as a cat, with one elbow on the writing table. As she stood gawking in the doorway, he lithely rose to greet her, and, casually slipping his right hand into his coat pocket, gave her a tight little bow. "Ah, Miss Trntl. Good to see you again. Mrs. Brown and I have been having a most interesting chat."

She hung up her coat in the closet. "What brings you to Baltimore?"

"I've been commissioned by Mr. Dinch to see what progress you've made in discovering the cadenza's whereabouts. I had some personal business here, and Silas said that since I was coming anyway, I should stop by and see you."

"If you've read today's paper," said Trntl, "it should be apparent that things have become considerably more complicated."

"Yes, I saw both the New York and Baltimore papers. The account of the murder of the Simms girl is shocking. Mr. Dinch finds all this publicity and sensationalism regarding the cadenza altogether deplorable. And I must say that I agree with him: the discovery of the cadenza should have been an occasion of universal rejoicing."

"If and when we recover the manuscript," Trntl said tiredly, "the publicity and sensationalism will probably increase sales." She stopped herself and backtracked. "I'm sorry. I shouldn't have said that. I'm very tired; been interviewing people all afternoon. I need a drink."

Abbott seemed prepared to let it pass. "I understand; you've surely been under a lot of strain. Mrs. Brown has filled me in on the other things that have happened."

Trntl shot Carol a searching look, and Carol responded with a slow, ironic wink. Trntl nodded acknowledgment; and, feeling relieved, dipped into the freshly filled ice bucket and poured herself a weak Scotch. "When did you leave New York?" she asked Abbott.

"This morning, as soon as it became clear that we weren't going to get a second call regarding the ransom. I took the Metroliner down and came straight to the hotel. I'm staying in Room 603."

"Oh," said Trntl, "just down the hall."

"My business here may take a couple of days—though I do have a concert in Philadelphia this weekend. Since I knew you were staying at the Cavendish and I wanted to see you, it seemed convenient to use this hotel." (The better to keep an eye on us, thought Trntl.) "Though I must say," he added with a tone of distaste, "the accommodations seem only mediocre at best. Adequate, but only barely."

"It's where Mr. Dinch put us up," said Trntl. "You were lucky to catch us. We've both been out conducting interviews. I take it Mr. Dinch hasn't received any further instructions this afternoon about paying the ransom?"

"When I arrived, I called him to see if anything had happened since I left the city. Not a word. He's getting quite concerned. While I was in his office, Clara Farringford called from Boston to inquire if there'd been a further ransom demand. She was horribly upset by the Simms girl's murder, and she's *certain* the cadenza's been destroyed."

Trntl swirled the ice in her drink. "As Carol undoubtedly told you, we don't know where the manuscript is at the moment, but there's no reason to assume it's been destroyed."

"I'm relieved to hear that." Abbott went to the bed, where his hat, overcoat, and leather gloves were lying. He drew a silver cigarette case from the coat pocket and lit up a Turkish oval. "Do you have some concrete basis for your belief? or is it only supposition?"

"No evidentiary proof," Trntl answered—in what Carol discerned was a faintly mocking tone—"but it seems unlikely that people who've gone to such lengths to obtain it would throw their investment away."

"I surmise you think it's still in Baltimore," he said. "Would you mind if a had a sip of your whiskey?"—indicating the bottle on the dresser. (I thought you'd never ask, Trntl sighed.)

"Help yourself. Yes, we think it's still in Baltimore."

Abbott went to the dresser and carefully unwrapped one of the hotel's plastic cups. "I never use ice." He filled the cup with Scotch. "And I don't usually drink Johnnie Walker Red Label—I'm sure it will be a treat." He returned to the writing table, arranged himself in the chair with precise deliberation (exactly as though he were building a nest, Trntl thought), and crossed his legs. Trntl decided to ignore him and gave Carol a report of her interviews with Eggleston, Adcock, Mrs. Gresham, and the Pettigrews. "No suggestions of other close friends with whom Stephanie might have left the manuscript," she concluded. "But the Pettigrews are warned to be on guard, and Adcock has the letters."

Carol nodded. "I didn't learn much at the Institute. I talked to several faculty members and a couple of students who knew Stephanie. No one could think of any close friends besides Morris and Pettigrew. One faculty member, a Professor Markowitz, who teaches theory, knew her fairly well—but only as a student she respected."

"I guess I didn't think we'd learn much," Trntl said. "To be on the safe side, I suppose we have to assume that the killers have the manuscript. But we're agreed, aren't we, that it appears that there are others besides the killers and ourselves who are after it?"

Carol nodded. "Some things have happened that can't be explained in any other way."

This exchange evoked an immediate response from Abbott. "Others besides the ransomers and ourselves?"

"At least one other group," said Trntl. "I don't know who they are or what they plan to do with the cadenza if they get it."

"That's very disturbing." Abbott set down his cup. "Dinch has learned that B. F. Cleavenger & Sons, in Los Angeles, are so extremely interested in the situation they've created a task force to monitor events."

Trntl, having read the Cleavenger dossier supplied by Dinch, accepted this at face value. But, more to the point: "Does Cleavenger have agents in Baltimore?"

"Dinch is sure of it. But he always assumes the worst. Oh! that reminds me: he said that he'd also learned that one of Cameron Stewart's New York sales managers has unaccountably disappeared."

"Maybe he's taking a spring vacation," said Trntl.

"Dinch thinks he's gone underground." Abbott shrugged, dismissing the subject, and returned to his drink.

The man in the gray trenchcoat? thought Trntl. The people who beat up Finegold? Scarface, Mustache, and Marco. She'd already gone through the photos in the dossiers and found no one who looked remotely like the man in the gray trenchcoat. More puzzling still, he no longer seemed to be following her. She hadn't seen him since losing him in the twisting streets north of Druid Hill Park. Maybe he *was* still there. If Dinch's competitors possessed the intelligence networks the dossiers claimed, then of course they'd have known of her role as private investigator long before this morning's news spelled everything out for folks who *didn't* have a network.

To top off her frustrations, even though Gray Trenchcoat was no longer in evidence, she still had the eerie sense that she was being followed. She'd never rejected the possibility that Dinch had sent his own agents down to see that she was doing her job. Like this man facing me in my own room, drinking my whiskey, she thought.

Carol asked, "Has Dinch learned whether any other publishers have created cadenza squads?"

"If so, he hasn't confided in me," said Abbott. He studied his fingernails, one eyebrow raised. "Naturally, I want Lunner & Dinch to be the ones to publish it. But—if I may speak frankly—despite my loyalty to Silas, my chief concern is that it be published by *someone*—just so it's made available to the world. *My* greatest fear's that it'll be destroyed."

186

The phone rang, startling them all.

Trntl switched on the tape recorder and answered "Hello" without giving her name.

A man's voice: "Who am I speaking to?"

"Who do you wish to speak to?"

A slight pause. "n—f—t—r—n—t—l."

Her best receptionist's voice: "Who's calling please?"

"A friend with important information about the Farringford Cadenza."

On the ninth floor, Chip, listening at the black box, winked at Marco.

Covering the mouthpiece, Trntl told Carol in a small whisper what was up and gave her the receiver.

"Hello," said Carol. "N. F. Trntl speaking. How can I help you?"

"Jesus Christ," said Marco, "she's changed her voice!"

"It's that other dame that's living with her," said Chip. "Shut up."

Carol's question seemed to have nonplused the caller. After another brief pause, he said: "No, lady, it's how I can help *you*. You want the Farringford Cadenza, right? Well, I know how you can get it."

"How?" said Carol.

"I'm not gonna talk about it over the phone. The man that's got it wants to get rid of it. There's been too much publicity. You meet me, and I'll see that you get it."

"How do I know you're on the level?"

"You gotta trust me. Look, you want the cadenza, dontcha? This'll be your only chance."

"All right. Where shall I meet you?"

"At eight-thirty tonight, take a cab to the corner of Fayette and Monroe. Come alone. If you bring anybody else, the deal's off. When you reach the corner, get ridda the cab. There's a pay phone in the middle of the block. Be there at nine sharp. When the phone rings, answer it, and you'll get more instructions then. If you aren't there to answer the call, the deal's off."

He hung up. Carol reversed the tape and replayed the whole conversation for Trntl and Abbott. "Good," Trntl nodded. "you got him to talk a lot, and we've got a good sample of his speech patterns. The voice doesn't sound disguised or muffled. Not Baltimorean: more like New York or New Jersey."

Abbott, fidgeting with excitement: "Is he serious? Will he give you the cadenza?"

"Hard to say," said Trntl. "If Stephanie's killer has it, I can't see him giving it up just because publicity has made it too hot to handle. If one of Dinch's competitors has it, I can see why they'd want to get rid of it. The call may be a hoax—occasioned by some nut finding my name in the paper and learning my purpose for being here, staying at a local hotel." (She didn't believe this.) "Or, it may be a trap." (Far more likely.)

"A trap?" It caught Abbott in mid-swallow, and he set his drink down hurriedly.

"Sure," said Trntl, "it's quite possible that somebody's finding me a pain in the ass."

"Are you going to meet this person?" Abbott asked. "It seems such a risk."

"It's my job," said Trntl. "I can't refuse to make an effort to recover the cadenza when an opportunity's offered." (Damn! With Abbott as a witness to the call, she had no choice in the matter. If she turned down the "offer" simply because it might be spurious, or a trap, Abbott would smugly report to Dinch that she hadn't done everything in her power to reclaim the cadenza.) "But I will take precautions," she added. "Carol, you should probably follow my cab in the car."

"I was going to insist on it," said Carol.

"I'm wondering if I should let Detective Adcock know about this new development. He might want to stake out the telephone booth and see what happens."

Carol nodded. "Though we've no proof that this caller is connected with the murders of Morris and Stephanie, I think you should call Adcock and tell him you've been contacted. Repeat what the caller said. Let Adcock decide if he wants to do anything."

"I don't want him interfering," said Trntl. "Still, it might gain me some brownie points if I have to work with him in the future."

Across the hall in the newly-acquired Room 610, Jerry had just sat down to enjoy his sackful of hamburgers and fries, when his phone rang. It was Chip, in 917, calling to report the message Trntl had just received. But Chip had said no more than three words when Marco shouted in the background: "Hang up! She's using her phone again!"—and Jerry's line went dead.

After a long delay, Detective Adcock came on the line. Trntl recounted her anonymous call, and Adcock said drily, "I'm glad you're staying in touch, Miss Trntl. Now, according to your theory of the Simms murder, it might be very dangerous for you to go out and meet this person. What do you intend to do?"

"I'm going. My job's to get the cadenza back. I'd be derelict and unprofessional if I didn't pursue a promising lead."

"Are you asking for police protection?"

"I don't feel it's my place to ask for police protection. I'm simply informing you of this new development and letting you know that I'll be at the corner of Fayette and Monroe at nine. I will say this: if the meeting should result in the cadenza's being turned over to me, I don't want the police interfering with the transaction."

"Miss Trntl, in view of the letters you gave us, I'm afraid the manuscript will have to be regarded as material evidence in a murder investigation."

She swore under her breath, thought rapidly. "I understand your position. I would ask that, if you *do* impound the manuscript, I be allowed to deliver photocopies of it to my clients."

"I'd have to think about that," said Adcock, "and consult with my superiors."

What a prick! she thought. He was clearly enjoying this.

"Well," she said, "I've told you what I'm going to do."

After a long pause, Adcock said, "I'm not free to come myself. I'll see if I can get Detective Price to be there in an unmarked car."

"Thanks," said Trntl. So much for brownie points.

"Now the cops are in on it," Chip said to Marco. "This could be the big one." He called Jerry in Room 610 and reported what they'd just heard.

"I'll take the blue car," Jerry said, "and be waiting at the corner when she arrives. You guys follow her cab in the brown car. If this is on the up and up, we deal ourselves into the game."

Chip said, "Synchronize watches. I have 5:07."

"In synch," said Jerry. "By the way, all Trntl did this afternoon was go to Stephanie's apartment house and to Professor Pettigrew's. Did you get the Chief's classified ad into the paper?"

"Should be in the morning edition."

"Wait—they're opening their door. Just a minute." Chip heard the receiver clunk onto a hard surface, and he doodled impatiently on his pad for forty-three seconds by his sweep second-hand. He could visualize Jerry peering through the bubble-peephole. Then Jerry was back. "There's some guy with them in a fur-collared coat and fur hat. I don't know where he came from. They're arguing about where to eat supper."

"Follow them. They'll probably come back here before Trntl has to meet the Man. But if they don't, let us know, and we'll link up with you at the phone booth."

Chip hung up and reported to Marco, who listened intently while cracking his knuckles. Black hair spiraled from his shirt cuffs to cover the backs of his beefy hands. "It's about time," Marco said when Chip had finished. "Some action at last. But now we got the cops to deal with—and maybe a whole organization, too. I think we should take some equipment." He turned and hauled a black satchel from the closet.

"And *we'd* better get some supper, too," said Chip. "We may be needing lots of energy."

Chapter 15

At the elevator, the argument was finally winding down. Abbott's voice had taken on a plaintive tone: "But when I come to Baltimore, I always eat at Haussner's."

"You can eat wherever you like," said Trntl. "*We're* eating in the hotel coffee shop."

"The *coffee shop?*" She'd thought that would frost him. Trntl and Carol had things to discuss, and one of the items was Abbott's presence in Baltimore.

But he threw a curve: "Look," he said quickly. "Don't worry about the expense account. *I'll* buy your dinners. You can be my guests at Haussner's."

"We couldn't allow you to do that," Carol responded, just as quickly. "We appreciate the offer, but—really—we have to maintain our professional independence." She wasn't sure what this last phrase meant (it just popped out), but the pianist took it as an adequate explanation. As the elevator arrived and the door slid open, he began pulling off his fur-lined gloves. "All right, then, all right," he said, with a martyr's resignation, "the coffee shop it will have to be. I presume they *do* have crabs?"

Reverently, with hands as gentle as a lover's, Victor Zyzynski placed on the turntable Farringford's Fifth Concerto as played by Rosamond Foxe. He cleaned the stylus with four strokes of a camel's hair brush and tapped the start button. While the trombones and kettledrums filled the room with their somber fanfare, he crossed to the marble-topped bar and made himself a whiskey sour.

The drums and brass quintet gave way to cellos and basses in a majestic rising series of deceptive cadences, this quickly followed by the same progressions echoed successively, in canon—and with ever-increasing tempo—by the bassoons, clarinets, oboes, and violins. Zyzynski stood transfixed, sipping his drink and beating time with two fingers. What a splendid opening! the harmonic irresolutions building, climbing to a frenzied climax. And—now!

the violins tremolo, for a moment of almost unbearable tension, followed by an exquisite melody in two parts, a dialogue between French horns and violas underscored by plucked strings in the cellos. Zyzynski closed his eyes and let the music take him.

The melody arched and soared, like a suspension bridge vaulting over smooth water, profound in its simplicity of line, but subtly contoured and textured with muted embellishments in harp and flute. Clarinets and violins took over the melody (with flutes in counterpoint), the pizzicato bass slyly syncopating into a mazurka rhythm; and then—almost unnoticeable at first—the piano began insinuating itself into the melodic line, threading an intricate embroidery through, among, around the notes of the main theme; initially as accompaniment, then gradually as full partner in the melodic development, finally vanquishing the violins to freely carry on its own duet with the clarinets—till, leaping solo over the syncopated bass, it asserted its own full statement of the theme.

Zyzynski dug his toes into the carpet. O Rosamond! your touch—so loving and sure. Definitive. Crisp. Your fingers, strong but infinitely gentle, authoritative—yet sensual—in caressing and stroking the keys!

He hurried to a deep leather chair positioned at a window overlooking Central Park. Far to the west beyond the park's dark expanse, the spangle of city lights stretched to the Hudson. The night sky retained one dim swash of the descended sun. He took a cigar from the humidor beside the chair, clipped the end, and lit it slowly, rotating the end one inch above the flame.

In just eight days—March 12, circled in his pocket calendar—Rosamond Foxe would be featured soloist with the Metropolitan Symphony. Playing Farringford's Second Concerto—the one glory in a program of dull orchestral stuff by Mozart, Mendelssohn, and Brahms. What joy to see Rosamond, flushed with success, bare-armed in her floor-length gown, dark hair shimmering beneath the spotlights, graciously queenlike, engulfed in applause!

He'd been eagerly looking forward to this night for a full year. While the Board of Directors was scheduling the current season, he'd been the one to suggest Foxe for Piano Night, and, with the help of Morgan Latimer and Mrs. Sternberg, had gathered enough votes to overwhelm the opposition who wanted Peter Shipley Abbott (who'd have to wait till *next* year, pompous toad). Rosamond's concert would bring the season to a close; and following the performance, a reception, with a celebratory buffet, would be held for her in the Gold Room on the top floor of Symphony Hall. There he would bask in her presence. Savoring her nearness. Hearing her voice. Smelling her scent. And finding a way, an opportunity, an excuse, to touch, if only for a moment,—oh ecstasy!—her warm and yielding flesh.

Bitterly he begrudged the presence of the other Directors, the invited patrons of the Symphony, the crowd of musical celebrities with their loathsome hangers-on. The evening ought to be his and hers alone. But, by God, *this* time he'd manage to get her off by herself—just the two of them together. This time he'd find a way.

He'd been physically close to her on seven occasions—always in these abominable social settings. Never had he gotten as close as he'd wanted: always there'd been crowds of people in the way— gushing well-wishers, fawning admirers, possessive critics, dense public officials, nasty autograph hounds. Once, in April 1979, at a formal banquet honoring the eightieth birthday of conductor Sir Samuel Poindexter, he'd been seated sufficiently close to her to smell her perfume.

But between him and Rosamond at the long table, the seating arrangement had placed a major obstacle: Peter Shipley Abbott. And asshole Abbott, pursuing his own lustful designs, had monopolized Rosamond throughout the meal. As Zyzynski's frustration mounted, he had to fight the urge to stab a fork into Abbott's thigh, or tip a bowl of hot turkey soup into his crotch. But, in this case, frustration was the mother of invention; and as the meal dragged on, he succeeded in adroitly maneuvering his salad bowl so as to soak Abbott's coat sleeve with cream garlic dressing.

On these seven occasions, he'd been near enough to observe the firm and pliant textures of Rosamond's skin, the dark peach-fuzz down on the backs of her arms; to revel in the fullness of her lips, her vivacious eyes, her laughter and melodious Richmond accent. On these occasions, standing near her, he'd fantasize grasping her in his arms and pulling her to him. And—yielding, melting into his embrace, closing her eyes and tilting back her head, full lips parted, moist and glistening—she'd whisper, "Oh, Victor! I've waited so long! Take me! I'm yours!" And finally, at long last, the man in him would rise and stand, and he Zyzynski would again prevail, proving yet again the maxim: The last shall be first—

A discreet cough behind his chair. "Excuse me, sir." It was Wilson, his valet. "The telephone: Mr. Meggs on the line. Will you take the call?"

Zyzynski hunched forward and cleared his throat. "Yes, of course. Always at home to Mr. Meggs."

Wilson plugged a telephone into the wall and went away. "This is Mr. Meggs." A flat, featureless voice. "I have a response to your dealers' query."

Zyzynski raised his eyebrows. "That didn't take long."

"It came as a message to Client 1-Primus-Triple-A from D. H. Van Voort, here in New York. I quote: 'Regarding your expression of interest in acquiring newly discovered manuscripts of piano music that have come onto the market: another client has contacted me expressing similar interest, saying that he will pay top dollar for the Farringford Cadenza should it become available. This client is reliable and of long standing, and I thought I should bring the matter to your attention. Should I be in a position to offer such an item, I would be painfully torn in my loyalties to two greatly esteemed and valued clients. Please advise.' End of quote."

Zyzynski groped for his whiskey sour. "This is very unusual. Van Voort doesn't mention his transactions or his clients to third parties. That's why he *has* clients. Is he doing this as a favor to me for having been a steady customer? Or is he actually in possession of the cadenza and trying to jack up the price for sale to the highest bidder? I want you to ask him directly, Mr. Meggs, whether he now has the cadenza. If he does, tell him that *I* will pay top dollar."

"Very well," said Mr. Meggs.

"And if he doesn't have the cadenza, but some other client has been making inquiries about it, I'm very interested to know who."

"Van Voort keeps all his client relationships in the strictest confidence," said Mr. Meggs.

"I know, I know. And I certainly wouldn't want it any other way." Zyzynski puffed thoughtfully at his cigar, and Mr. Meggs waited silently for him to continue. When he did, he chose his words with care: "Yet I would very much like to know who this other person is who wants the Farringford Cadenza—if not his identity, at least a notion of what his resources are, the degree of his determination to have it. It's competition, Mr. Meggs, and I always need to gauge the power of the opposition."

"I understand," said Mr. Meggs.

"It's possible that he's already actively pursuing the matter in Baltimore. That's a most disquieting thought." He took a sip of his drink, three puffs on the cigar. "Contact Van Voort again. Tell him that Client 1-Primus-Triple-A is sensitive to the unusual nature of the present situation. That I'm prepared to pay top dollar, but that I would appreciate meeting this other client—himself, not an agent—if it would be possible for Van Voort to arrange it. A private meeting, with anonymity assured, and the strictest security enforced. I'll expect his answer tomorrow night as to whether such a conference can be held."

"Strictest security," said Mr. Meggs. "Anonymity of both parties to be assured."

"You can also tell Van Voort that Client 1-Primus-Triple-A understands the ethical constraints he's working under, that I respect his professional integrity and reputation. But that I would be *very much obliged* if he could convince his other client that such a meeting would be to our mutual advantage."

"I'll report back tomorrow night," said Mr. Meggs.

Zyzynski hung up and brooded for the remainder of his cigar about the implications of this new development, trying to see if and how it fit in with what Marco, Jerry, and Chip had reported earlier in the evening.

Now there were two murders involving the cadenza. Trntl believed that Tony Scaevola had been holding it for ransom. But Dinch had not received a follow-up ransom call this morning. Tony's apartment was empty, the cadenza was not there, and Tony seemed to have vanished. Since Trntl had told the police about Tony, presumably *they* were after him, too. But the police must not, through some ghastly fluke, be the ones to recover the cadenza. If Tony didn't have it, who did?

What if someone else entirely—another Collector, say—had killed Simms and was now in possession of the cadenza? A thought so painful, so nauseating that he hurried on. Or a dealer, perhaps? Van Voort? The uncertainty, the enforced inactivity, the realization that things were out of his control were simply intolerable. He slugged back the rest of his drink and went to the bar for another.

The triple harp glissando alerted him to the beginning of the concerto's third movement. Five timpani strokes. A brief chorale for trumpets and horns. And then the tornado of dense piano chords played presto agitato that introduced the main theme. He leaned against the wall and once again closed his eyes. Ah, Rosamond! those fingers could perform the impossible! work miracles! return the dead to life!

X X X

When they'd finished eating, they returned to Trntl's room to make last-minute preparations for her meeting with the anonymous caller. No sooner had they entered when Peter Shipley Abbott declared: "I insist on coming along. My interest in the safe return of the cadenza is as great as yours—if not greater. And I would remind you that I am here as the representative of both Lunner & Dinch and the Farringford family." (Shit! shit! shit! thought Trntl.)

She said: "It's not usual for clients and their representatives to take part in actions they've hired detective agencies to do."

"This is a highly unusual circumstance," said Abbott. He was going to stand his ground, no doubt about it. What a drag.

"There may be danger," said Carol.

"I'm willing to risk it," Abbott said, arms akimbo, thumbs hooked into the pockets of his vest. "It's the least I can do."

"Danger aside," said Trntl, "has it occurred to you that you might simply be in the way?"

"Has it occurred to *you*," he rejoined hotly, "that if—through some horrid accident or wanton action on the part of the thieves— the manuscript should be damaged or destroyed, you'd want some reliable witness to give Dinch and the family a faithful account of what happened?"

This just about pushed her over the edge. It was only with the greatest exertion of will that she avoided cursing aloud. The stare she gave him caused him to moderate his tone: "I'm only offering you my services," he said, "to be of whatever material help I can. Assuming that you do obtain what purports to be the cadenza, I daresay that I'm one of the best qualified people anywhere to verify its authenticity. It's entirely possible that whoever has the real cadenza would try to put you off the scent by giving you a fake. I know the Fifth Concerto. I know Farringford's holograph, and his habits of composition and musical notation. I'd be able to tell in a moment if the manuscript was genuine, or if someone was trying to trick you."

Trntl was irritated that Abbott had thought of this while she herself hadn't. Trickery was a distinct possibility, particularly in view of the unexplained happenings that continued to percolate through and around the Tony Scaevola connection. For Trntl and Associates triumphantly to present Silas Dinch with a bogus cadenza would be a major embarrassment which the firm might not survive.

"You have a good point there," she told Abbott. He acknowledged her concession with a curt bob of his head and a little bow. Turning to Carol, she said, "Abbott can ride with you. Follow my cab at a suitable distance, and then, when we get to the phone booth, play it by ear. I'd better take my gun." She went to the suitcase, dug out her Smith & Wesson .38 Special, and placed it carefully in her leather handbag.

Abbott blanched but said nothing.

Carol remarked, "If I'd known we'd be getting into these kinds of activities, I'd have brought the binoculars and camera when I came down. All you wanted was a change of clothing, the tape recorder, and a toothbrush."

Turning her back on Abbott, Trntl said "It's hard to plan for all contingencies."

Chapter 16

At 8:53 the cab let Trntl off at the designated corner. She paid the driver and watched him leave. Looking back the way they'd come, she saw Carol and Abbott pull into a parking space a block away. Inside the phone booth, a young woman was talking animatedly. Standing near the door to indicate she wanted to use the phone, Trntl took the occasion of her wait to get the lay of the land. Only a few people on the sidewalk in this block and the next. A bag woman, scarf covering her head, huddled on a bench at the bus stop. Eating something—a sandwich? No sign of an unmarked police car containing Detective Price. "Well," she said, "so much for that."

Trntl's watch said one minute till nine. The woman in the booth seemed to have no intention of ending her conversation. With the edge of a quarter, Trntl tapped on the glass door.

At the rhythmic clinking, the woman turned to look at her, shooed her away with a swift hand gesture, then swiveled back and resumed talking. Nine o'clock. Trntl tapped again. The woman swung her head around and pushed the door open a crack: "Whatcha want?"

"Excuse me," Trntl said. "I'm expecting a call on that phone at nine."

The woman said "Listen, my man's havin' a crisis!", closed the door, and resumed talking.

Trntl paced nervously back and forth, glancing at her watch. Now the young woman was doing more listening than talking. 9:02. Trntl tapped the glass again. The woman frowned at her, then whipped the door open. Before she could speak, Trntl said: "Listen, *I'm* having a crisis! An important call was to come through two minutes ago."

The young woman glared at her in exasperation, and turned back to the phone. "Roosevelt, there's a lady here who needs to use the phone. Just don't let 'em in, honey, and I'll call ya right back." Roosevelt evidently had something else to say, and it was a moment more before the woman could hang up. Trntl said "Thanks" as the woman came out of the booth, and then had the satisfaction of hearing the phone ring. She stepped into the booth and lifted the receiver. The young woman stood impatiently just outside the door.

The New York/New Jersey voice said: "Who is this?"

"N. F. Trntl."

"I can see you. You can't see me. Did you come alone?"

"If you can see me, you can see that I'm alone."

"In a minute, another cab'll be along. It'll stop for you; get in and tell the driver to take you out Frederick to Woodington; have him turn north on Woodington to Euclid, then east on Euclid. There'll be a black Buick parked on Euclid, near the corner. Leave the cab and get into the Buick. The driver will take you to the cadenza."

The line went dead. Trntl left the booth, and the young woman went inside and shut the door. Trntl stood by the curb looking for a cab in the moderately heavy traffic. The old woman with the scarf, having finished her snack, had moved off with her shopping bag, and was turning the corner at the end of the block. A cab was coming slowly down the street. It angled in to the curb and stopped beside Trntl.

"Where to?" the driver asked.

"Out Frederick to Woodington; turn north on Woodington to Euclid."

She got into the back seat, and the cab pulled away. Through the rear window she saw Carol following at a considerable distance. Neither Trntl nor the driver spoke. Out of long habit she studied their route for landmarks that could be recalled, if necessary. When she arrived someplace, she liked to know how she'd gotten there.

Traffic was much heavier on Frederick. Carol had gained on them, but was still separated from the cab by five or six cars.

"Can't you get closer?" Abbott wailed. "One red light, and we'll lose her!"

"I can try," said Carol. "It *is* the only cab ahead of us, however." Abbott was squirming as though afflicted with boils. The cab was going a good clip and actually pulling away from them. They crossed a river. Passed a large cemetery on their right. "Oh, look out!" cried Abbott. A large van pulled out of a side street in front of them, and Carol stomped the brake. The truck started into a left turn, blocking their view of the street ahead.

From his vantage point three cars behind Carol's, Jerry could still see the cab when he edged to the extreme left of his lane. Steering with his left hand, and keeping tabs on Marco and Chip in the rearview mirror as they stayed about eight cars behind him (also hugging the left of the lane), he continually dipped into a plastic bag on the seat beside him to select and thoughtfully munch assorted jujubes. He liked the ones with lemon flavor best.

The cab turned right onto Woodington—so suddenly that Trntl was thrown against the door-handle. A short block, another right turn. The cab stopped with its engine running. "Okay," the driver said. "Get out."

"What's the fare?" Trntl asked.

"Taken care of," said the driver. "Get *out!*" He revved the motor.

As soon as she slammed the door, the cab moved away. Beside her, the rear door of a black Buick sedan swung open. "Get in," a man said from the back seat.

She tried to get a look at him, but the smoked windows made the interior very dark.

"N. F. Trntl?" he asked. "Hurry up, get in."

Glancing over her shoulder and seeing no sign of Carol, Trntl reluctantly bent down and edged onto the back seat. The man's voice wasn't the one she'd heard on the phone. He leaned across her and closed the door. A heavy-set thirty-or-so.

From Woodington, a car turned the corner onto Euclid; and Trntl, invisible behind the smoked glass, watched Carol and Abbott rush by in pursuit of the cab, which, having reached the end of the block, was now making another right turn—back toward Frederick.

"Let's go," the man said to the driver. The car pulled away from the curb just as Carol reached the end of the block and turned right to follow the cab.

"Where are we going?" Trntl asked.

"My job was to pick you up," the man said, "not to talk."

He was wearing a tan overcoat and brown hat. His square face, clean-shaven and deeply pocked with acne scars, was without expression. After scrutinizing her when she'd entered, he hadn't looked at her again.

Having turned onto Euclid from Woodington—furious at having lost the cab—Jerry saw smoked glass gleaming under the streetlight as a car turned at the far end of the block. With the instinct that had served him well in many tight situations, he decided to follow the Buick. By the time *he* reached the corner, Marco and Chip had turned onto Euclid behind him. All right then: hope for the best.

Trntl found the ride lengthy and tedious. Her silent companion sat with his hands folded in his lap, staring at the floor—a demeanor that discouraged any attempt at conversation. The driver, whose eyes she could see in the rearview mirror, only occasionally looked at her, and he too said nothing. So she sat staring out her window, not even noticing the street signs, craving a cigarette and clutching in her lap her leather handbag, heavy with the reassuring weight of the .38 Special.

At last the Buick turned into a driveway that led to a concrete parking apron crowded with cars. Before them, a large white building of concrete blocks: she could barely make out the words BODY WORK painted above the broad paneled door. As the car approached the building, this door slid upward, revealing darkness inside. When the Buick had passed in, the door slid shut behind it.

The car stopped, and the man in the tan coat said, "Here we are. Get out."

She stepped into a cavernous room dimly lighted with a single bare bulb at the far end. It seemed to be cluttered with automobile parts, hoses, stacks of tires. Several cars stood about in the shadows in various stages of disassembly. Beside the Buick and pointing in the same direction was a black 1976 Cadillac, also with smoked windows. The man in the tan coat opened its right rear door and said, "Get in." Their driver opened the front door and slid behind the wheel.

Dandy, she thought, climbing in. I should write a book on how not to be a private investigator. The man in the tan coat climbed in behind her and closed the door. It was very dark in the back seat, but Trntl immediately realized there was a third person with them. Something hard pressed into her side.

"N. F. Trntl," said the Third Party. "Glad you decided to come. But you shouldn't have told the police. It made our planning more difficult." It also was not the voice she'd heard on the phone. The engine started, and a door slid up opposite the one they'd entered by. The car moved forward through this rear doorway into a dimly lit alley. The light was sufficient to reveal what she already knew. The man beside her was Angelo Torelli, and the thing poking her in the side was a silencer affixed to the barrel of a very ugly revolver.

From a block away Jerry saw the Buick turn into the driveway of a large autobody shop. A sign near the edge of the property read BENNO'S BODY PARTS. He slowed, passed the garage as the overhead door was closing, turned right at the next corner, and stopped.

A moment later, Marco and Chip parked behind him. He got out and joined them.

"They're in that garage," he said, "in a black Buick."

"Helluva place to hide a cadenza," said Chip.

"What happened to the cab?" asked Marco.

Jerry shrugged. "When I turned onto Euclid, it was gone. But the Buick was pulling away. Must've been a quick switch." They'd done it themselves many a time.

Chip gave him a skeptical look. "Are you sure Trntl's in that car?"

"I didn't see her get in," Jerry said evasively. "But she has to be."

"Jeez," Chip groaned, "you mean we've been following that car across town and don't even know she's *in* it?"

"How often have my hunches been wrong?" Jerry snapped. "To get away as quick as it did, the cab would've had to go back south to Frederick. That wouldn't make sense if she was still in it. The Buick turned north."

"Let's get moving," said Marco. "The deal may be going down while we stand here jabbering."

"Okay," Jerry said. "You guys take the front. I'll go up this alley at the back. Got your radios?"

Marco and Chip hurried back to the corner. Jerry went to his car, took his .38 from the shopping bag lying on the front seat, and, clutching his radio, started for the mouth of the alley. He was halfway there when he heard a car engine start up, and then the crunching of gravel. He leaped into the shrubbery that lined the sidewalk and crouched down as a large black Cadillac, its lights off, nosed out of the alley and turned past him. At the intersection its headlights switched on, and it turned left to pass in front of the garage.

Jerry plunged from the bushes and worked the radio as he ran back to his car: "They came out the back and turned left on Shickel. I'm going to follow." He was behind the wheel when Marco answered: "We're inside. The place is dark, seems empty. We found the Buick, but no sign of Trntl." Jerry squealed a tight U-turn and rounded the corner. The Cadillac was two blocks away. "We're right behind you," said Marco. "Come on, Chip, quit dickin' around in there!"

Traffic was light. Jerry sat back, again steering with one hand while fishing in the bag of jujubes. Trntl had *better* be in that car. God help them all if she wasn't. After the boondoggle at Pettigrew's and the Finegold fiasco, the Chief would fry their asses if she actually got the cadenza and they weren't there to intercept. He swore out loud. This was the most frustrating assignment they'd ever tackled. In the past, they'd always known specifically—or at least in a general way—where their objective was located. The problems in those cases were of method and planning—devising ingenious ways of gaining access and snatching the prize and getting away. But with the cadenza floating in the never-never, *no* plan was possible, and precious little method.

Jerry liked the certainty of knowing what had to be done; the challenge of strategizing to create a chain of predictable events, which—once appropriate moves were made—would fire off automatically, in proper sequence, each one triggering the next, like dominoes going down in ripple drill to the bafflement and consternation of the Enemy. This assignment was like trying to play a chess game blindfolded: they didn't know where the pieces were on the board, or where the Enemy was, or what he was doing when he made his moves. Jerry turned to look in the seat beside him, fearing the worst. Yep. Damn! The lemon-flavored ones were all gone.

In the Cadillac, Trntl had assessed her situation realistically, sorted through the possible courses of action available to her, and computed her odds. Her conclusions weren't encouraging. She'd known that following up the anonymous phone call was risky. But she'd thought Carol and Detective Price were an adequate backup. Finding the police nowhere in evidence had been disturbing; but sitting in the Buick watching Carol and Abbott go zooming by in pursuit of the cab was like having the sudden knowledge that her parachute wasn't going to open.

To her right, the man in the tan overcoat, immobile as a rock. To her left, like a prosperous businessman in his gray hat, black overcoat, and white scarf, Angelo Torelli, half facing her, his gun barrel pointing directly at her spleen. The street was in poor repair; at every bump and jounce, the silencer poked her painfully in the lower ribs.

Torelli was regarding her intently, like a lizard watching a mealworm. "I thought so," he said with satisfaction, "you *are* the one who came to Hanrahan's with the Simms girl."

"I'm surprised you got a good look at me," said Trntl, "what with your keeping the restaurant so bloody dark. Since I'm sure you can afford electricity, it must be by design. Are you ashamed of the food you serve? Or of your customers?"

"Our customers *like* it dark," said Torelli.

"Maybe they're ashamed of *themselves*," said Trntl.

Torelli sneered contemptuously.

"You charge too much for your drinks, too," said Trntl. "Where did you find your bartender? Under a bridge?"

"If you don't like our restaurant," Torelli said softly, "you'll be happy to know you won't be coming back." His tone had acquired a slight edge; but after a pause, when he spoke next, it had reverted to a silky flatness: "You've been busy, Miss Trntl. You've been saying bad things about me behind my back. That was neither polite nor wise."

Trntl said, "Those who work the vineyard should have to eat the grapes."

This gave him long pause. Then he said, "The vineyard *you've* been working has produced a poor crop, Miss Trntl. You'll find the grapes very sour."

She didn't respond to this, so after a moment he continued: "You fell into our trap rather easily. It was a long shot, since we weren't sure you didn't have the cadenza already."

Her ears pricked up at this. "No, I don't have the cadenza," she said carefully. "I assumed that Stephanie's killer had it, since she had it in her possession when she was shot."

"As a matter of fact, she didn't," said Torelli.

"If I did have it," said Trntl, "I'd have been long gone from Baltimore by now." Her side was becoming quite sore where the gun kept poking it. "You say I fell into your trap easily," she went on. "You flatter yourself. If I supposed the people offering me the cadenza were Stephanie's killers, do you really think I'd come to meet them without taking—certain precautions?"

He smiled with half his mouth. "Informing the police, you mean. Well, I don't see they provided you much protection."

"Oh, heavens, one can't rely on the police alone. Calling them was only *one* of my precautions. Give my regards to Detective Adcock next time you see him."

Torelli curled his lip in contempt. "Adcock! That man has never learned where his advantage lies."

"Well, to Detective Price, then."

"You think you're pretty smart, don't you? Busy, busy. You have a big nose, Miss Trntl."

"So I've been told. And you, Mr. Torelli, have extremely bad breath. You really ought to see a dentist."

The silencer twitched and viciously gouged into her side. "You also have a big mouth," he hissed through clenched teeth. "The only thing that keeps me from shooting you now is that I don't want to stain the upholstery!"

"I didn't think it would be from concern for your silent partner sitting here beside me," she said. The man in the tan overcoat quickly turned his head and flung Torelli a sharp look.

After the space of fifty heartbeats (which Trntl had no trouble counting), Torelli leaned back, breathing heavily, and the pressure of the silencer abated. His face was a pale blur in the darkness.

"You're going for a boat ride on Chesapeake Bay," he said. "Have you ever been to the Eastern Shore, Miss Trntl?"

"No."

"Too bad. Because I'm afraid you'll never get there."

"Oh well," she said, "I probably won't get to Alaska, either."

While talking, Trntl had been observing their route as well as she could. She'd noted that they'd gone south on Hanover, crossed a sizable body of water on a long bridge, turned southeast on Potee, made a jog, and were now continuing east on Frankfurst. Her careful study of the map on her first night in town told her that they were in south Baltimore, heading straight for land's end at the broad mouth of the Patapsco River, which—further east— merged into the waters of the Bay.

On Frankfurst, they were passing through desolate, scrubby woodland; a gravel pit to the left, B & O freight yard to the right, a housing project. Then they turned onto a street named Chesapeake which took them into an industrial area with fenced-in tracts, oil storage tanks, a small residential area, factories. She could smell the nearby oil refinery; saw dimly in the darkness what appeared to be warehouses and truck depots. They drove through a wide gate in a chain-link fence toward a dark expanse of water dead ahead. Another turn, and they were in the parking lot of a large warehouse. To their left, a sign read CIMACORP.

The car stopped near the building in an ill-lighted area. To the driver, Torelli said, "Wait here, Benno. We won't be long." Then he and the man in the tan coat got out one at a time, each keeping a gun trained on Trntl. Torelli grabbed her arm and pulled her out of the car. "Up the steps," he ordered.

She climbed four concrete steps; and, going through a door into the warehouse, she managed surreptitiously to unclasp her handbag against the fold of her coat. But then, with the muzzle of the silencer against the back of her neck, she was hustled across the echoing floor toward a cargo port in the opposite wall. Through the opening she could see a wharf with a large motor launch moored beside it.

Inside, adjacent to this port, stood six large steel drums: a single bare bulb low on the wall cast their coffin-shaped shadows the length of the room. "Stand there," said Torelli, pointing to a drum slightly separated from the rest. In a tub beside it were several sacks of Double-A-1 Top-Dog Redi-Mix Cement. Suspended over the tub was a water hose with a tap spigot.

"Start mixing it," Torelli told the man in the tan overcoat. The man removed his coat and began tearing open the sacks and pouring cement into the tub. "We're going to put you in the drum, fill it with cement, and take you on a boat ride," said Torelli.

"To be dumped like toxic waste," said Trntl.

"That's right. You'll stay at the bottom a very long time."

"It sounds like something out of the 1920's," said Trntl. "Aren't you capable of updating your script?"

"Why change a method that's proved effective?" said Torelli. "Note the holes punched in the lid to let the air out."

"You think of everything. The cadenza must be awfully important to Giuseppe Scaevola for you to go to so much trouble."

"You do have a one-track mind," said Torelli. "Mr. Scaevola's not interested in the damn cadenza. It's nothing to him. If we'd been able to recover it from the Simms girl, my orders were to destroy it."

"I thought he wanted to hold it for ransom," she said. "With Tony the front man."

He gave a derisive snort. "You're the one who's behind the times. The ransom thing was Tony's own idea—going it alone. Our organization wants nothing to do with the cadenza."

"So where is it?" Trntl asked.

"*I* don't know," Torelli said. "And I don't *care*."

"So why are you taking me on this boat ride?"

"You know too much. And you talk too much about what you know. You drop names and make accusations. In fact, you're talking too much now." Over his shoulder: "Joe, how's the cement coming?"

"It's getting there." Mixing and stirring.

Outside, leaning against the Cadillac's front fender, and keeping a general lookout while smoking a cigarette, Benno didn't see the dark shadow creeping from the heaps of jumbled machinery on the opposite side of the car. A slim, silent figure, moving stealthily from one pool of shadow to the next until it was directly behind Benno across the car hood. In its hand it carried a billiard ball tied into the toe of a black, knee-length stocking. Holding tight to the sock's other end, and taking careful aim, the figure swung the billiard ball in a high arc over the hood—*thwack!* onto Benno's cranium, and Benno collapsed without a sound beside the front tire. Fishnet, stocking, it's all the same, thought Jerry, as he pulled the key from the ignition and released the catch of the hood.

While Marco and Chip sprinted from the shadows and started up the steps of the warehouse, Jerry removed the distributor cap and sent it skittering across the gravel into the water. Then, when the others had disappeared into the dark interior, he dashed around the corner of the building onto the wharf which he'd seen from the road.

As they moved toward the group by the cargo port, using as cover the crates and heavy machines that stood here and there about the room, Marco and Chip overheard the tail end of the exchange between Trntl and Torelli. They were within twenty feet of the tableau—but at some distance from each other—when the man stirring the cement announced: "It's ready to go."

"Then so is Miss Trntl," said Torelli. "Get into the drum," he told her, "and crouch down."

"Can't you let me have one last cigarette?" Trntl asked, reaching with her right hand toward her open handbag.

"You should've had it while we were waiting. Throw that purse in the drum—*now!*"

"*Police!*" Marco shouted, in a booming voice. "Drop the gun. Raise your hands. You're surrounded!"

From the other side of the room Chip shouted, "Don't anybody move! You're under arrest!"

Torelli and Joe spasmed and froze. Torelli dropped the revolver, and both raised their hands.

Marco darted forward, pistol aimed, scooped up Torelli's gun, moved quickly to Joe, patted him down, and pulled his gun from its holster. He then gave Joe a blow with the gun butt that toppled him face downward into the tub of wet cement.

Chip meanwhile had rushed up to Trntl. "Get out of here!" he hissed at her. "Fast!"

Pistol-whipping an unarmed man wasn't her notion of normal police procedure. But she wasn't about to dally while figuring it out. Gripping her bag, she ran to the doorway, down the steps and past the Cadillac, where she saw Benno lying on the gravel. With long strides she loped up the road to the gate and made for the street.

Jerry entered the warehouse from the wharf and joined the others. "You," Marco said, pointing his pistol at Torelli, "get into the drum."

Torelli gave a bleat of realization: "You're not the police!"

"Into the drum," said Marco. "Come on, hunker down, pull it in. Make small."

Torelli did as commanded. And once he was huddled in the drum, crouched into a jack-knifed fetal position, Marco slammed the lid on, hammered it tight with a rubber mallet, and methodically went round the rim, crimping down the flanges. "Huh," he said. "There's even holes punched to let the air out."

"And the water in," said Chip.

When the lid was secure, he tipped the drum over and stood it on its top. Jerry meanwhile had hauled down a blunt hook fastened to the end of a chain which ran through a pulley on the ceiling. Then he and Chip dragged Joe to his feet coated with wet cement all down his front, and stood him groggily beside the tub.

Jerry brought the hook over, unzipped Joe's pants, passed the hook behind the belt and out through the open fly, activated the pulley, hoisted him five feet off the floor.

Chip kicked the side of the steel drum and said to Torelli, "You told Trntl you'd take her to the cadenza. She's gone. You can give it to *us* instead. Where is it?"

The muffled voice was breathless and strained: "I don't have it. I never did. Tony had it, but it's gone."

"This is your last chance," Chip said. "Where is it? Who has it now?"

"I don't know where it is!"

"Don't believe you," said Chip. "Did the Simms girl have it?"

"No. We even searched her place. Nothing."

"Where's Tony?"

"I don't know."

"Sure you do," Chip said. "Time's up. Okay, boys, roll him out into the water."

Marco and Jerry tilted the drum onto its side and began rolling it toward the cargo port. "Just drop him off the end of the pier," said Chip.

"No, no!" Torelli screamed. "Tony's in Newark with his Uncle Vinnie!"

"With the cadenza?" Chip asked.

"No, the Simms girl had it!"

"You said she *didn't* have it."

"She didn't, she didn't! Not when we found her."

"And you killed her to get it."

"She pulled a knife on us. George doesn't like knives. But no,—you've got to believe me!—she *didn't* have the cadenza. I've never even seen it."

"Who are you working for?" Chip demanded.

Torelli was silent. Chip nodded, and Marco and Jerry began rolling the drum toward the pier.

"I work for Lefty Scaevola!" Torelli shrieked.

Again Chip nodded, and Marco and Jerry pulled the drum upright, upending it to stand on its lid, topside down. They saw that holes had been punched in the bottom, too.

Joe was groaning from his hook, "Let me down!"—his face becoming stiff with the drying concrete.

"Let's get out of here," said Jerry. "These guys are no help at all."

Benno was still unconscious, but breathing in shallow gasps. They took his gun and headed for their cars which were parked on the road beyond the fence.

Pacing herself by alternately running and walking, Trntl had come a considerable distance since leaving the warehouse. Her course was restricted because of the chain-link fences that lined both sides of the road. By the time she'd reached Chesapeake Avenue and proceeded along it for four minutes, she'd seen only two people—a night watchman silhouetted in the doorway of a distant guardhouse and a workman some three hundred yards away parking a forklift for the night.

A cloud cover had moved in, and the sky overhead was dusky red with the lights of Baltimore. The air was cold, but her running in the overcoat had drenched her with sweat. The combination chilled her through. Ah, the refinery odors. Chemical plants. As she walked and ran, she sorted through what she'd learned from talking to Torelli.

Scaevola's people had killed Stephanie, but the cadenza wasn't on her when they had. Scaevola didn't have the cadenza, didn't want the cadenza, would destroy it if he obtained it. It pleased her to get corroboration that it *had* been Tony who'd planned to hold it for ransom—a scheme which apparently had come to nothing. But always the insoluble remained: if Stephanie did have the cadenza at one time (but not when she was killed), and it didn't get to the Pettigrews, where the hell was it now?

And now she knew that Scaevola was trying to kill *her*, too. Torelli said she knew too much and talked too much. Well, she'd certainly named names to the police. And the police were clearly not to be trusted: since Torelli knew about her call to Adcock, there must be a leak—if not a pipeline—from the department. But Torelli had implied that Adcock was an honest cop. Someone else, then. Since this attempt to get her hadn't worked out, she had to assume that Scaevola would probably try again. Obviously, more precautions were needed. Finally, despite what they'd said, the people who'd rescued her in the warehouse were not the police. So who were they? how did they appear on the scene? and *why* did they rescue her? Were they a rival gang? Not likely. Agents of Silas Dinch? Maybe. Agents of one of his competitors? Perhaps.

She remembered that a small residential area lay ahead of her, with houses and taverns. When she got there, she'd find a phone and try to reach Carol, or at least call a cab. She heard the sound of a car approaching from behind and turned defensively. A blue Chevrolet she hadn't seen before. It slowed as it neared her. With one hand in her purse clutching the Special, she peered through and beyond the headlights and saw only one person inside.

The car pulled to a stop beside her. The driver was a slim elderly man with white hair, a bushy gray mustache, and tinted eyeglasses.

"Hey there," he called in a quavery voice. "I'm driving into the city. Can I give you a lift?"

She decided quickly. "That would be nice, I'd appreciate it. I'm headed there myself, and it's cold out here." Having first glanced behind the front seat, she got in.

"My name's Jolley," the old man said. "Here, let me move this sack of jujubes. Help yourself, if you want. There's lime and cherry and one pineapple left. But the lemon's all gone, I'm afraid."

"Thanks," she said, "don't mind if I do."

Chapter 17

When the blue Chevrolet had let her off at the front door of the hotel, Trntl asked at the desk if she'd received any messages, and then went straight to the public restroom just off the lobby. There, after relieving herself, she washed her face at the sink and studied her reflection in the mirror.

Nothing in her appearance even hinted that she'd come within a gnat's whisker of going to the bottom of the Bay. But now, alone, the crisis past, adrenalin no longer pumping into her system, she was exhausted, fluttery, weak. And very angry. Enraged at how ineffectual and helpless she'd felt when Torelli was ordering her to climb into the drum. How violated. How totally within his power and control. She felt she knew and understood, better than ever before, what women must feel when they've been raped.

She ran warm water over her cold hands. On the ride back to the city, she hadn't been able to stop her teeth from chattering. Never had she gotten into such a scrape, come so close to being killed. Once, caught in the middle of a domestic quarrel, she'd nearly been sliced by an angry wife assaulting her husband with a cleaver. On another occasion, she'd been standing some sixty feet away when a client's letter-bomb exploded. But in neither of these incidents had she been the *target*. Dealing with corporate thieves and insurance crooks, tracing youthful runaways and missing husbands, performing guard duties and standing stakeouts, doing documentary research into vital statistics, corporate holdings, deeds, titles, and newspaper files—the staple fare of her investigative work—none of these had ever brought her to the brink of annihilation.

And yet, she had to admit, the potential had always been there. The crazy business executive who, aware that the jig was up, would decide to take everybody with him. The errant husband who, for his own reasons, didn't *wish* to be found, and who would remove the finder as a threat to his peace of mind and future happiness. Or the guard duty that would turn out to be for real, terminating abruptly in a fusillade of bullets. Even the old newspaper story that would open the lid of buried secrets and bring a stalker from the shadows to un-disturb the past.

With a paper towel she dried her face and hands. She didn't like being a target. And she had to assume that she'd continue to be a target as long as she remained in Baltimore.

On the drive to the warehouse she'd kept up a good front, wisecracking, appearing unafraid. But even then, while having to think fast to parry Torelli's thrusts, she realized it was basically a performance, served up to mask (from Torelli *and* herself) how terrified she was. It was also an act of bravado, attempting to compensate, or atone, for what she all too clearly saw was her own stupidity in underestimating the unpredictable and trusting to a half-baked plan. She should never have gotten herself into such a position of helplessness. But she was not going to give Torelli the satisfaction of thinking he'd bested her and broken her spirit.

And the final irony: what the fuck did it signify that she'd had a gun in her handbag? Torelli's was already out and aimed. And she'd been neither foolhardy nor courageous enough to seize the risk, pull forth her .38, and trigger off a shootout. So, then, of what use *was* the gun beyond providing a reassuring presence, an empty promise of power, a cold comfort in the grip of fear? What use had it ever been? Oh, she'd occasionally taken the gun with her during investigations, but she'd never once had occasion to use it—except for practice on the firing range. Basically, it was just so much dead weight to lug around. And tonight, it had almost joined with the wet cement to take her more swiftly to the bottom.

The lenses of her glasses were so dirty she could hardly see through them. She held them under the water faucet and rubbed them with her thumb. That helped a little. Her hair could've doubled as a bird's nest. She tugged a comb through it several times, found that accomplished nothing, and gave up. Now that her shock and residual fear had abated, she felt only anger and leaden fatigue. Hoping that Carol was waiting upstairs, she left the restroom and headed for the elevators.

When she opened the door to her room, both Carol and Peter Shipley Abbott leaped up from where they'd been sitting beside the telephone. "Thank God you're safe!" Carol cried.

"Did you get the cadenza?" Abbott asked.

To Carol, Trntl said, "For the moment." To Abbott: "No, I didn't." She kicked off her shoes and began pouring herself a tall Scotch. "Have you called Torvald yet?"

"At ten o'clock," Carol said. "He's waiting at the office to hear more." She'd been blaming herself for having not given Trntl adequate backup, and now found herself driven to provide explanation: "We kept following the cab, thinking you were in it. But when it stopped on Frederick to pick up a fare, we knew something was wrong. We passed it, saw you weren't in it, and then circled back to Euclid. When we couldn't find you, we wandered around aimlessly for awhile, then came back here, hoping you'd call. We'd just about given you up."

"On your first pass," said Trntl, "I was sitting in a parked Buick watching you go by. Then I was transferred to another car, and taken south to a warehouse on the Patapsco River, where Angelo Torelli tried to kill me—"

"Torelli!" said Carol.

"The whole setup was simply a ruse to put me away," said Trntl. "On orders from Giuseppe Scaevola. They think I know too much about Tony's involvement in Morris's death, and are afraid of what I might tell the police. Somebody at the police department did pass on to them what I *had* said after Stephanie's death. I'm sure that Torelli was present when Stephanie was killed, though I'm not sure he's the person who shot her. They were hunting the cadenza to destroy it."

"Destroy it!" said Abbott. "And did they?"

"No, because they didn't find it on her. They want it gone because it ties Tony to Morris. And, we were right—Tony *was* the one holding it for ransom."

"So how did you get away from Torelli?" Carol asked.

"I was rescued," said Trntl. "By two guys who claimed to be police, but weren't. They had guns and did some sort of violence to the driver of Torelli's car. They must've followed us to the warehouse. I don't understand how they knew what was coming down. And it's not clear to me whether their object was to save my skin or to nail Torelli's. For awhile I thought they might be members of a rival gang—but that wouldn't explain why they followed us. I now think they were working for Lunner & Dinch, keeping me from harm; or else, agents of one of Dinch's competitors who see me as potentially valuable in helping *them*."

Abbott asked, "B. F. Cleavenger, perhaps? Members of the cadenza task force?"

"Why not?" And she picked up the telephone to give Torvald a report.

While Trntl was being returned to the hotel, Victor Zyzynski in New York was on the telephone with Mr. Meggs, who—surprisingly—had managed to contact D. H. Van Voort about Zyzynski's proposal. At first, Van Voort had been extremely hesitant to attempt arranging a meeting—however secure and anonymous—between two of his most valued clients. But Mr. Meggs had been unyielding and highly persuasive: Van Voort was made to realize that should he lose the business or goodwill of Client 1-Primus-Triple-A, he could not hope to stay financially afloat—and the dealer had quickly agreed to inquire if the other collector would consent to a meeting.

Within an hour Van Voort had called back to inform Mr. Meggs that, contrary to his expectations, the other client had been extremely interested in such a meeting. Since he too was currently in New York, would it be possible to have the meeting soon—tomorrow night, say? A private room could be provided for that purpose at Van Voort's Gallery and Auction House. Ten-thirty, then, the two collectors to be alone, face to face, with separate means of entry and exit. To preserve anonymity, it might be wise for both to wear masks. Van Voort would be happy to supply them. Would that be satisfactory?

"The meeting arrangements are satisfactory," Zyzynski said to Mr. Meggs, "but the idea of wearing a mask does not appeal. Van Voort's always had a baroque sensibility. This is clearly an opportunity for him to work out his frustrated romanticism. He'd have been happiest living in eighteenth-century Venice in perpetual carnival. I will not let him choose a mask for me. Stop by a novelty store, Mr. Meggs, and get me one of those latex masks that cover the entire head. Not a Frankenstein's Monster or King Kong, if you please, and nothing with fangs, pointed ears, or sparkle dust. I'll trust your judgment."

"I'll see what I can find," said Mr. Meggs.

"And I'll want a couple of men to go with me—just as a precaution. Willett and Strunk, I think."

"I'll arrange it," said Mr. Meggs.

Marco, Jerry, and Chip recorded Trntl's report to Torvald Grimsson and then took stock of their night's activities. Like Trntl, they were back to square one, no closer to the cadenza.

"She got herself in a helluva spot," said Marco. "What's she been doing to make those goons want to kill her?"

"They think she knows too much about the Simms murder," Chip replied. "But none of that concerns us. All we know is that Scaevola and Torelli don't have the cadenza, and that Trntl doesn't have it. It Scaevola gets it, he'll destroy it. So, he mustn't be allowed to get it. Trntl might possibly be the one to find it. If she does, we can't let her keep it."

Jerry looked up from cleaning his nails. "You've got to agree: it was fun *doing* something for a change. Just sitting around, or following Trntl, I feel like I'm gathering cobwebs. She never goes anyplace that's very interesting."

"Wait till she takes you to the zoo," said Marco.

Chip was pondering what to say in their nightly report. "Just how much should we tell the Chief?"

Jerry frowned. "About today? Not much. Just that Scaevola is out to kill Trntl and that he pretended to have the cadenza to bait her into a trap. We can tell him she escaped, but we'd better not mention the part we played. If he learns we've been messing in murder plots and mixing it up with the local hoods, he'll go right through the floor."

Chip threw up his hands in exasperation. "The Chief wants this manuscript as much as he's ever wanted anything. But here we sit. Our asses are on the line, and all we're able to do is hope that a female snoop can find it for us!" He began shredding paper from the pages of his notebook.

"You've been spending too much time in the room," Jerry said. "You need to get out more."

"Go to the train museum," said Marco. "Visit Poe."

Chip flung a shoe at him and dialed Zyzynski in New York.

After finishing her conversation with Torvald, Trntl—finally feeling the effects of the Scotch—stretched out on the bed. "Let's have some music, Carol."

"Okay. Here's our cassette of Farringford's Fifth as played by Rosamond Foxe." She slipped it into the tape recorder and punched the play button.

Sprawled in the easy chair with his legs extended before him, Peter Shipley Abbott had been sunk in a dank depression since hearing Trntl's report and learning that the cadenza was no closer than before. Well along on his third Scotch, he brightened up a bit at mention of the concerto. "A fine recording. If I may say so, the best versions of the Fifth are Rosamond's and mine."

"Dinch sent *this* one with us," said Trntl.

Abbott made a bridge of his fingers. "I do the second movement scherzo a little faster than she does. She uses a little more rubato in the third movement andante than I do. But it's a very creditable performance; these differences in interpretation are basically a matter of taste. Rosamond's a very gifted musician, and, with a little maturation, has a bright future before her."

"I have your recording with the Cleveland Philharmonic," said Carol.

"That's an early one," Abbott said, obviously pleased. "You must have it on the budget Zeno label. I've recorded the Fifth six times during my career."

"I have you with the Philadelphia Symphony *and* the Cleveland Philharmonic," said Trntl.

"I prefer the Philadelphia version," he said. "Sieberling wanted to bring out the brass at the end of the first movement, but I told him it would overshadow the piano, and of course he toned it down." He laughed triumphantly. "All conductors want to blare forth with the brass at that point. That *isn't* the way Farringford intended it. Oh, listen to this!" He raised a hand; they listened, and the music was glorious. "The writing here is just brilliant! God, what a genius Farringford was!"

Exhausted, emotionally drained, and more than a little drunk, they lounged about the room listening to the concerto. The profundity and brilliance of Farringford's concepts were given exquisite life by Rosamond's musicianship and technique. Finally, as the fourth movement built to the climactic solo passage called for in the score—the six-minute cadenza that was the cause of all their woes—Abbott cried out in a bleary voice: "And here: she's going to perform my cadenza. I was only twenty-one when I wrote it back in 1962—and though I'm sure it doesn't anywhere, in anywise, begin to approach Farringford's own, I flatter myself that it does do the concerto justice. Most of my colleagues have seen fit to incorporate it into their performances. I thought that Charles's six minutes was excessive, so I confined my cadenza to two and a half minutes, a more conventional length."

Rosamond launched into Abbott's cadenza; the writing was complex, her performance superb. While the substitute cadenza was true to the spirit of the concerto and of the fourth movement, it was essentially more of the same, translated into solo bravura passages which allowed the pianist to show off technical skills. It lacked the authoritative address which characterized the rest of the concerto; and if it was written in imitation of Farringford's style, it was an imitation of a Farringford nodding off to sleep. It lasted two minutes and thirty-six seconds by Trntl's watch.

"You must be very proud to have written that," Carol said.

"Oh," said Abbott with a decorous blush, "let's say that I'm pleased to have been *able* to write it. Clearly the structure of the concerto needs a cadenza there for balance; it would have been unthinkable to leave that section blank just because we don't have Farringford's original. Several people besides me have tried their hands at writing a cadenza. Mine seems to have become standard, for which I'm pleased. My homage to the composer, if you will. But of course it's Farringford's we want in that spot."

Farringford's, thought Trntl through her alcohol buzz: the "stunning", the "indescribably beautiful", the "exalting", mind-boggling six friggin' minutes which—by all accounts—constituted a turning point, a peak experience, a life-changing encounter for everyone who'd heard it. No, Abbott's was certainly not that.

"What else have you composed?" she asked.

This time he blushed in earnest. "Really, nothing at all. Oh, a few sketches for piano which have never been published. I'm not a composer. In this case, inspiration and a sense of duty somehow combined to lift me above myself. No, I'm basically a performer."

The tape ended, and Carol turned off the recorder. Trntl rose to brush her teeth. "Good night," she said to Abbott, who'd gathered up his coat and gloves and was now moving unsteadily toward the door. "We've had a long day. Tomorrow may be just as long."

He murmured his goodnights and went weaving down the hall. From the bathroom, Trntl said, "I'm glad we played the music; I really enjoyed it. Did he make it to his room? Okay, lock and chain the door. From this point on, we've got to be as watchful as the Secret Service during a Presidential walkabout."

When Felix had heard the tape of Trntl's report from Baltimore, his response was brief: "Well, she's in it up to her armpits."

"You've got the Phillips case to finish up," Torvald said. "I'm going down to join Trntl and Carol."

"You've heard Trntl's speculations," said Felix. "Who do you think saved her life?"

"Either somebody who wanted to foil Scaevola's plan, or somebody who specifically wanted to save Trntl. I incline to the second view."

"Approaching it from a different angle: *Why* did the rescuers want to keep Trntl alive? Answering that might suggest who they are."

"Agents of Lunner & Dinch," said Torvald, "protecting the boss's investment."

"No, I don't buy it," said Felix. "If Dinch has agents he can field, why did he hire us? I think whoever it was thinks Trntl can lead them to the cadenza."

Torvald opened a fresh box of chocolate covered cherries, selected one, and tossed it into his mouth. "Well, clearly there's at least two of them; and if we grant your hypothesis, it's a team that can't find the cadenza for itself."

"One of Dinch's competitors? Someone else we haven't learned about yet? A third party who'd like to hold it for ransom? A collector who wants it for himself? Somebody besides Scaevola who wants to destroy it?"

Torvald ate another cherry. "Why hasn't the manuscript surfaced again after that first ransom call? Is someone holding it? Is it simply misplaced?—or maybe hidden somewhere, waiting to turn up?"

"Holding," said Felix.

"Hidden," said Torvald, stifling a yawn. He put the box of chocolate cherries into his desk drawer, stretched, and shrugged into his coat. "I've got to get home, pack, and catch an early train. Are you staying here awhile?"

"Yeah, I slept most of the day. What work needs to be done?"

"A little of Carol's book-keeping I didn't get finished. And sorting through today's mail."

"I can do those things before I leave. In case you're interested, my cold's a lot better."

From the doorway Torvald said, "Maybe Anton Farringford's cold is better too."

"I hope not," said Felix.

Alone in the office, Felix opened Torvald's drawer and helped himself to a few more chocolate covered cherries than he would've taken had Torvald been present. Carol's book-keeping was meticulous and well-organized; entering the new receipts in the ledger took only a few minutes. When he'd done that, he turned to the stack of mail. There were the usual throwaways. Requests for money from various ostensibly charitable organizations. Never-to-be-repeated offers for charter subscriptions to three new magazines: a *Journal of Criminological Investigations* out of Stiles University; a monthly, *Real-Life Police Stories*, and something called *Balls*, a quarterly anthology of "the finest male poetry produced in the Northwest." "What is male poetry?" he wondered. Into the wastebasket. How the hell did they they get onto these mailing lists? I'll buy your list if you buy mine. Jesus! Hello. An envelope addressed to him. No stamp, so evidently hand-delivered. A note neatly scripted with fountain-pen by Rosamond Foxe!

> Dear Mr. McKay,
> Once again I'd like to thank you for the drawing you gave me last night at the Farringfords'. It's an excellent likeness, and I'm having it framed.
> As a token of my gratitude, please accept the enclosed two tickets to my concert with the Metropolitan Symphony on the evening of Thursday, March 12. Perhaps you have a friend who could use the second ticket?
> Also, there will be a reception for me following the concert—in the Gold Room on the top floor of Symphony Hall. I would be happy if you (and your friend) would come to the reception as my guests. I'm very glad to have made your acquaintance. 'Mr. McKay' seems so formal! May I call you Felix? If I may, you can call me—
> Rosamond.

Felix gave a whoop and canted back in the swivel chair. "You certainly *may* call me Felix!" he crowed. He grabbed the two tickets, pressed them to his lips, and noted that they designated much better seats than the tickets he'd purchased for himself and Carol two days ago. And—wonder of wonders—the reception, too! There, he'd have to clarify for Rosamond that the "friend" accompanying him was a colleague merely, nothing more—and then inquire if Rosamond would like to go out for dinner some evening when she was free.

He suddenly wanted to be out of the office, onto the street, and into his favorite bar. He quickly sorted through the rest of the mail. A letter addressed to Trntl from Mrs. Leopold G. Sternberg, marked 'PERSONAL'. He tossed it into Trntl's incoming box. Next, two bills and a catalog for survivalists—combat boots, camouflage clothing, telescopic sights, night-vision binoculars, walky-talkies, electronic bugs, assault weapons, rocket launchers. Jesus. Into the wastebasket.

Felix tidied Carol's desk and looked at his watch. Nearly midnight. Time for a couple of quick ones at Marshall's Pub before going home. He donned his coat, turned out the lights, went through the outer office and locked the door behind him. Apparently he was the last one out of the building; the hallway was dim and echoed hollowly to his footsteps.

The brightly lit sidewalk was crowded with strollers. Felix began walking briskly toward the pub five blocks away, observing with interest, as he always did, the night life flowing about him. Yet, as he walked, he was aware of something tapping away at the back of his mind—a nagging presence seeking admission to his conscious thoughts. When he was halfway to Marshall's Pub, it forced its way in. Yeah. Mrs. Leopold G. Sternberg. Surely— somehow—he'd encountered that name in connection with the Farringford Cadenza. Where, though? Try as he might, nothing came.

Down the steps into Marshall's, the finest basement bar in Manhattan. Crowded tonight. He nodded to several people he knew and went straight to the bar, where Albert made his special drink—Vodka Felix—with a dash of crème de menthe, a jigger of tonic water, the juice of half a lemon, and a maraschino cherry. "How ya doin' tonight?" Albert asked, as he set the glass before him.

"Better than last night," he answered. "I'd rather be here than in Baltimore."

Chapter 18

March 5   (Thursday)

It had not been a good day for Anton Farringford. Shortly after arriving at work, he'd learned that the external audit of the firm's trust accounts would begin on Monday, March 9—three days earlier than originally scheduled. During his coffee break in the employee canteen, he'd had the distinct impression that his co-workers were casually avoiding him. When he'd returned to his desk, he'd seen Tippett, head of the Trust Division, and Brownlow, chief of Internal Audit, casting cold and malevolent glances at him through the glass window of Tippett's outer office. A mounting wave of paranoia and despair had sent him to the men's room to vomit. His work went to hell; and just before noon, feeling as though his head were being crushed in a vise, he claimed illness and took the rest of the day off.

"You've had a terrible cold the last couple of days," Mrs. Woolley said as he signed out. "Be careful that it doesn't go down on you."

A sinister admonition. He wasn't sure what she meant: lungs? bowels? balls? The phrase echoed in his mind all the way to the train station. But during his journey to Queens, Tippett, Brownlow, and the External Auditors came to occupy his thoughts like an invading army. He heard drumrolls and the trampling of hobnailed boots, heinous charges barked out by the Senior Vice-President; saw before him a tribunal of grim, vindictive faces, a row of hands firmly poised with pens above his death-warrant. This was to be his lot: an executive broadside and ritual blood-letting before the matter moved beyond the walls, and he was flung out to be pulverized by the wheels of justice.

He'd have to hire a good lawyer (how? with what?). He'd lose his license, no doubt of that. Twila would leave him. The case would wind through the courts to conviction. And what would Mother say? Oh god, the disgrace. The scandal. He was streaming sweat when he left the train, his headache not one whit better—

staggering, shuffling blindly up the sidewalk, supporting himself on doorframes and fencerails.

There was no way he could pay back the money. And even if he could, that restitution wouldn't salvage his career if the embezzlement showed up in the audit. His only chance was to funnel back as much money as he could. But he had no means of doing it. He'd already restored about $7,000 to the various principals, but with the accrued interest the accounts would've earned over the last five years, that left almost $60,000 that he still owed.

Stumbling up the steps of his apartment building, he paused by habit to fish in his mailbox. A few items—but also, leaning against the wall at his feet, a large package wrapped in brown paper and addressed to him. From Baltimore.

Once inside his living room, he placed the package on the table and stared at it vacantly while he poured himself a stiff bourbon and gulped it down. Thank God Twila wasn't home from work yet. He couldn't face her now.

He went to his Workspace, sat at the computer, and checked his figures once again. Yes, computing the interest-earnings till Monday morning, the amount he owed was $58,209.37.

His math was accurate. It always was. Still staring at the figures, he finished his second whiskey and poured another. Foggily he tried to recall where he'd put his father's old straight razor. Twila would be home soon; he'd have to hurry. He knew it wasn't in the bathroom. Was it in the keepsake box in the record cabinet? His nose felt numb.

On his way to the cabinet, he again saw the package on the living room table. From *Baltimore?*

The package had been very securely taped. It took him a full two minutes to get the wrappings off. A brown briefcase. He read the note, stared at it blankly for a moment, read it again, and then grabbed the edge of the table for support.

"The cadenza!" he cried. Not in Baltimore. Not held for ransom! Here!

He tore at the leather flap, found that the case was locked. For another long moment he searched dazedly for the key—on and under the table, among the wrappings, in his trouser cuffs. With his hands he again scrabbled at the lock, and, after tearing a fingernail, ran to the kitchen to find something that would pry the metal apart. He came back with a screwdriver, a corkscrew, and a butcher knife. Surely one of them would work. But the screw-driver was too small to serve effectively as a chisel or pry; it simply scratched and battered the outside of the lock. The corkscrew was no help at all. The butcher knife was awkward and perverse; after it twice slipped and nearly sliced his hand, he became frightened and gave it up. But when he inverted the briefcase, or shook it from side to side, he could hear something sliding about against the leather. A stack of papers: his father's manuscript.

He reverently placed the brief case on the table. What luck! what joy! He should tell Mother the cadenza was safe; Dinch, that his long, anxious wait was over. Carrying his empty glass, he started unsteadily toward the telephone. He hadn't spoken to his mother since the bitter dispute two nights ago over her dimin-ished allowance. He hoped she wouldn't begin the quarrel all over again; he couldn't bear more wheedling and whining, insisting, demanding. She'd even threatened to sell Father's *piano!* He'd been as shocked and mortified at that as if she'd desecrated a holy shrine, or defiled a national monument.

He sat down heavily beside the phone, reached out to dial her number. And how gross of her to call the bastards who'd stolen the cadenza "the lucky ones" because "*they'd* be getting fifty thousand dollars!" "No, Mother," he muttered, "they won't be getting *any-thing*. The cadenza's safe now. *I* have it!" His finger froze above the dial.

Fifty thousand dollars. He pulled back his hand, clasped it tightly with the other, sat gripping them together in his crotch. He frowned and tried to focus his eyes.

No, he wouldn't call Dinch just yet, either. No hurry. He had to wait and think. Twila would be home soon. Oh god. He had to clear his head. He lurched up and shuffled to the bathroom, stuck his head into the shower stall, and doused himself with cold water. He should've eaten lunch; the whiskey had hit his stomach like a rock. He let the water play on the back of his neck. Had to have a clear head to work this out. Who'd sent him the caden-za? Trntl? No, she wouldn't have signed herself "A Friend". The people who'd been holding it for ransom—deciding, perhaps, that with two murders, it had become too hot a liability? Perhaps. Did it really matter?

Yes. Because it was important to know who was aware that the cadenza was now in *his* possession.

Had Peter Shipley Abbott sent it? He'd told Anton he was going to Baltimore to see how Trntl was doing. No, he'd have signed his own name, wanting credit for getting the cadenza back to the family. More likely yet, he'd have carried it back personally. Professor Pettigrew? No, he'd have signed his own name also, wanting it known that he'd finally rectified the disaster caused by his foolish press conference and his carelessness in allowing the cadenza to be stolen in the first place.

Anton seized a towel and scrubbed his head and neck while rushing back to the living room table. The note said, "Do with it as you will." The writer was clearly giving up all claim to it, shucking it off like a bad memory. All right. It was his now. What *did* he want to do with it?

Publish it, of course: complete Father's greatest work. Stupid question, Anton! why did you even ask it? Now that it's safe, of *course* it'll be published. Dinch and Morgan Latimer had been prepared to pay fifty thousand dollars to see it published. Latimer had been willing to pay ten times that amount to get it back. So rich he'd never miss it. And whatever Dinch paid would be written off as a business expense.

Since all this had been agreed to, the decision made, the ransom already set aside—in used, unmarked twenty-dollar bills— why, the transaction was, in effect, an established fact, a done deal. When the money was handed over, the cadenza would be delivered to Lunner & Dinch for publication. Dinch was simply waiting for the second call so the matter could be consummated.

And if Anton, in the next two days, could manage to obtain that cash, he might have a fighting chance to repay his Swinfurth Lightfoot borrowings before the auditors came. The computer programs were ready to go. Even if the External Auditors found evidence of his tinkering—surely his having returned the money *with interest* would mitigate his punishment. He'd been very clever in siphoning off his loans. If all the amounts were securely in place in the proper trust accounts—he just might be able to muddy the waters and obscure the trail sufficiently to keep the auditors from finding out precisely what he'd done. Then, even if they had suspicions, they wouldn't be able to *prove* anything. It had to be tried. Father would want him to.

Returning the cadenza would be easy. Obtaining the ransom money without being seen and identified would not. No longer having a car was a major problem. He returned to his Workspace, the towel draped around his shoulders. He needed paper, a pencil to write out what he'd say. New York was so crowded, with so little privacy! How, then, to arrange a drop-off of the briefcase and a pickup of the ransom without being seen—or running the risk of having someone else stumble onto the money by accident?

He tried to remember how these things were done in movies and detective novels. He thought of public lockers, museum checkrooms, confessional booths, elevators with sets of doors opening on opposite sides to parallel hallways, buildings with multiple exits, children's trains that wandered through amusement parks. No, all of them were too public, too chancy, too easily staked out. Since no one must ever know his involvement, he couldn't risk using a courier—not Twila, not Clara, not some hireling off the street.

A cemetery! The one nearest his apartment, where he'd often taken solitary walks. He knew its layout, its particularly striking monuments. It was private, filled with nooks for hiding and watching unobserved, easy to escape from undetected, and within walking distance from home. He quickly wrote out the message he would read to Silas Dinch on the telephone.

> If you want the Farringford Cadenza, the price has gone up. Put $58,300 in used, unmarked twenty-dollar bills in a black suitcase. Deliver it tomorrow, Friday, March 6, at 12 noon sharp as follows: go to Mount Myrtle Cemetery (Queens) and take the central road from the main gate till you come to the T-intersection with the tall DIGBY monument (square column with a red granite ball on top). Turn right at the T and continue till you come to the stone angel. Turn left and continue to the third right-branching road. Turn on it and proceed for about two hundred yards till you come to the HODGES tombstone (a large rectangular gray granite monument with stone urns on either side). Put the suitcase behind the stone so that it can't be seen from the road. Drive back to the main gate. If you follow these instructions, the cadenza will be returned to you. If you don't or if there's anything funny about the money, or if you bring anyone with you,

or inform the police, the deal is off. The cadenza
will be offered to your competitors and sold to the
highest bidder.

Anton read the note over, smiling with satisfaction at what
he'd written. He was especially pleased with the last sentence, the
ultimate threat that would guarantee Dinch's compliance. And his
choice of the HODGES plot was ideal; it was near a thick grove
of trees, and the stone was backed by a dense wall of evergreen
shrubbery—an effective cover from which he could reach out and
grab the money.

He went to the telephone and dialed the number of Lunner &
Dinch. Muffling his voice with a handkerchief, he informed the sec-
retary that he wanted to speak to Mr. Dinch about the Farringford
Cadenza. Dinch came on the line immediately.

"Listen carefully, mate"—(he pronounced it *myte*)—"This is
the message youse have been waitin' for. I ain't gonna repeat it, so
get it the foist toime." He read the script slowly, giving his vowels
what he thought was an Australian coloration.

"Fifty-eight thousand three hundred dollars?" said Dinch.

"The proice has gone up."

"Did you say Rogers or Hodges?" Dinch inquired curtly.

"Hodges," Anton said. "Twelve o'clock sharp." He hung up
and hugged himself in a rush of elation and relief. Before pouring
himself another drink, he hid the briefcase beneath the underwear
in his dresser drawer. When Twila arrived twenty minutes later,
tired and grumpy, he greeted her with a freshly poured drink of
her own and a pleasant surprise: "Wash up, Twila. Put on your
blue-sequined dress. We're going out to Chuck's for a steak dinner
and lemon meringue pie!"

Silas Dinch rewound the tape in his recorder and dialed the
number of N. F. Trntl Associates. Felix answered.

"Mr. McKay? Silas Dinch. We've just received the second ransom demand. I'm going to play you the tape to see what you make
of it." He pressed the play button.

"Now," he said, when the tape was finished, "do you think it's
serious, or someone playing a perverted joke?"

"We can't afford to regard it as a joke," said Felix. "It's certainly bizarre. The caller was trying to disguise his voice with a phony
Australian accent. If it was a local call, and he wants the money

dropped off in a cemetery in Queens, I think we should assume the cadenza is here in New York, and no longer in Baltimore. It's interesting that this call mentions your competitors and promises to hold an auction, whereas the first call simply threatened to destroy the manuscript if ransom wasn't paid."

"*You* may find it interesting," Dinch said heatedly. Felix had the sudden impression that Dinch would rather have the cadenza destroyed than have it fall into the hands of his competitors. He drew a circular frown-face on his pad, and turned his own mouth down to match it.

"To give such specific directions," said Felix, "the person also seems to know the cemetery well."

"A New Yorker?"

"Probably a resident of Queens." Or possibly, he thought, somebody who works in the cemetery—gravedigger? groundskeeper? mortician?

"This caller is not the same person who called earlier," said Dinch.

"You may be dealing with a gang. Or else the cadenza may simply have changed hands."

"If it's changed hands, how could the person know that fifty thousand was the original ransom?"

"Good question. Also, by saying that this is the call you've been waiting for, the person clearly knows of the first call, and that there's been no follow-up."

"What do you make of that?"

"I'm not sure. Perhaps an associate of Tony Scaevola's."

"Mentioning my competitors is an entirely new twist—one that I don't like."

"I don't know what that signifies. It's also interesting that the ransom has been raised by eighty-three hundred dollars."

"We'll pay it," said Dinch.

"The three hundred is the most interesting of all," said Felix. "It has a precision, a scrupulous refinement that borders on the burlesque."

"That's why I thought the call might be a joke. That and the Australian accent. At first I wondered if he might be drunk."

"Do you want me to be at the cemetery tomorrow?"

"He said I should come alone. I'm less concerned with who has the cadenza than that we get it back. I don't want anything to jeopardize the deal. No, I *don't* want you at the cemetery."

"As you wish."

"You should call Miss Trntl in Baltimore and tell her this new development."

"I'll do that. Thanks for keeping us posted." (Which means, thought Felix, that Dinch is preparing the way for terminating our services.) Dinch rang off. Before calling Baltimore, Felix sat thinking for a long while, tugging gently at his beard. So far, the investigation had provided them nothing to feel good about. Two murders. With Trntl's abduction, almost three. Frustration on all fronts. They had to get *some* satisfaction from the case; at the very least, to know who the ransom-caller was. Knowing *that* might lead to the recovery of the money. But here was Dinch intruding into their investigation and dictating limits on their professional responsibilities. They'd told him that kind of intrusion wouldn't be tolerated. Felix would damn well be at the cemetery long before twelve o'clock, to see for himself just what was there to see.

Having finished with Felix, Dinch called Morgan Latimer and played him the tape. The stockbroker's explosive excitement caused Dinch to recoil in distaste: Latimer harbored no doubts, had no skepticism, was not suspicious of a hoax. Did such credulous faith signal advancing senility? And his sheer unabashed joy, so effusive and puerile! Why, he sounded like a schoolboy who'd just discovered a peephole into the girls' locker room.

Finally Latimer calmed down enough to say "It does sound as though the cadenza's here, in New York. Thank God it's not been destroyed! The fifty thousand's in my safe. I'll get the rest and deliver it to you by ten tomorrow." There was a pause, and Dinch listened to him sucking on his dentures. Then: "Nevertheless, Silas, I don't like buying a pig in a poke. I wish to hell there were some way we could examine the manuscript to know for sure what we're getting."

"I agree," said Dinch, "but it's not an option."

"Call me as soon as you get it." When the line was clear, Latimer placed a call to Victor Zyzynski. As had been the case yesterday, the secretary informed him that Mr. Zyzynski was not available.

"Tell Mr. Zyzynski that Morgan Latimer has urgent news about the Farringford transaction. Have him call me back—he has my number."

He hung up, leaned back in his padded chair, and stared at the ceiling. His initial flush of excitement had dissipated. He should have been rejoicing at the prospect of recovering the cadenza, but instead he felt suddenly weighed down with doubts and misgivings. Was it simply fear that he might be disappointed yet again? He wasn't sure that he could survive another disappointment. After the expected second call hadn't come through yesterday morning, he hadn't slept, had hardly eaten—only a dish of cole slaw, one piece of toast, and a little weak tea. How many blows could he endure? His stamina was gone; and Bertha's, too, was faltering. Both of them together simply wasting away, like twin gold wedding bands having worn thin from sustaining the cumulative knocks and abrasions of sixty years.

It was that tape Dinch had played for him: the caller's voice, grotesque, like something out of a third-rate roadshow. Yet somehow disturbingly *familiar. Could* it be a hoax, after all? An evil joke? If so, he knew he wouldn't be able to bear it.

Zyzynski reached for the phone. He might as well get it over with; Latimer would keep trying till he got through. He sighed. Since the second ransom call hadn't been made, he'd assumed that Tony Scaevola's plan had collapsed, and that Tony had been taken off the scene. Chip claimed he'd disappeared without a trace. Latimer probably wanted to grieve that the ransom was off. Well, Zyzynski would talk to the old fart and let him get it off his chest. "Hello? Morgan Latimer, please." Click. "Morgan? Victor. You called?" He massaged a fresh cigar with the fingers of his free hand.

"Victor, I've got good news about the Farringford Cadenza. Dinch received the second ransom call this afternoon."

Zyzynski squeezed his eyes shut. Oh fuck, it wasn't over! Damn, damn, damn. "Good!" he said. "That's wonderful." Okay, he'd allow himself to be pulled in for ten thousand, but no more. He scowled at the broken cigar he'd been going to light.

"This was a different caller from the first one," Latimer said. "It was the voice of a drunk Australian with a bad head cold. He read a prepared script, and he raised the price from fifty to fifty-eight thousand three hundred."

"Do you think it's a legitimate call, Morgan? Or just someone trying to rip off the cash?"

"Dinch thinks it's the real thing. We can't risk assuming otherwise. I'm sending him the money tomorrow morning. Do you still wish to contribute to the ransom? I'll keep you anonymous, of course."

Clearly, there was no way out. "Fine. Yes. I'll put in ten thousand."

"That's very generous. Since we already have the fifty, I was going to suggest that you supply only the eight additional. But now, with ten from you, we can refund to Clara Farringford the two thousand she insisted on giving. She really doesn't have it to spare."

Zyzynski rolled his eyes upward, dropped the halves of his broken cigar into the wastebasket, and, with a broad finger, began patting the ink stains on his blotter. "Certainly, that sounds good. By all means, refund her money. I'll send you a check by messenger in the morning."

"Dinch is going to play it straight," Latimer continued. "He's supposed to take the money himself at noon tomorrow and leave it in a cemetery."

"Will he get the cadenza then?"

"That's not clear. The caller said that, if everything was in order, Dinch would receive the cadenza. It might be mailed, or delivered, or left somewhere for pickup."

"Which cemetery?"

"One of those in Queens. I'm afraid I don't remember which. There were two words in the name: something about a mountain."

Zyzynski scrambled in his desk drawer for a map. He spread Queens out before him. "Was it Mount Zion?" he asked. "Mount Olivet? Mount Carmel—"

"Olivet," said Latimer. "Yes, I think that's it. Mount Olivet."

"Not Mount Neboh or Mount Lebanon—"

"No, I'm sure it was Mount Olivet. It seems to me I once attended a burial there."

"At noon, you say?"

"Yes, twelve sharp."

"It's a rather large cemetery. Where's he supposed to leave the money?"

"That I don't know. The caller gave him detailed instructions, but I didn't take them down."

"It sounds like a scam to me," said Zyzynski. "I'll bet you whatever you like that Dinch will never see the cadenza."

"What else can we *do?*" Latimer cried. "I know it's a rotten situation."

"All right, all right, maybe I'm just borrowing trouble. You go on, get the money to him. Call me tomorrow just as soon as anything's resolved, either *for* us or *against* us."

Zyzynski was smiling tightly when Latimer ended the call. He had twenty minutes to get to the staff meeting to plan strategy for tomorrow's bout of merger negotiations. The trip to Baltimore had been disastrous. The absence of his guiding hand had caused today's negotiations to lurch off-track. He simply *had* to be at tomorrow's session. Before leaving for the staff meeting, he just had time to call Willett and Strunk.

He punched the buttons. "Willett? Zyzynski. Do you know how to get to Mount Olivet Cemetery? It's in Queens. Well, tomorrow at eleven . . ."

In view of the importance of Dinch's communication, Felix McKay decided not to wait till five-thirty when Trntl called in her nightly report. Besides, he wanted to get to Marshall's Pub for an early supper and "Jazz Combo Night"; he was taking his clarinet to sit in on the jam session that would follow the peak-time sets. He chose four-thirty to dial Trntl's room at the Cavendish Hotel.

Torvald Grimsson answered. "Trntl's not here. She and Carol went to a movie: Trntl really needed to decompress. I'm here with Peter Shipley Abbott." Felix caught the irony in his tone.

"Is Abbott still there? What's he doing?"

"Hovering," said Torvald. "Actually, he's in the bathroom now. He's *frequently* in the bathroom. But that's okay with me; it's the only time he's not underfoot."

"Can't you shake him?"

"No. He's a barnacle. Afraid he'll miss something. Seems to get a thrill out of playing detective. We think he's here to see that Dinch is getting his money's worth. Wup! the toilet just flushed. I think he'd sleep here if the women would let him."

Felix ate one of Torvald's chocolate cherries. "I take it nothing new has come up regarding the cadenza?"

"Nothing."

"Any further attempts on Trntl's life?"

"No, but she's lying low. Abbott's been telling me all about the piano music of Gershwin and Shostakovich."

"Learning anything?"

"You'd be surprised."

"Well, there's news here. Looks like the cadenza may be back in New York. Dinch got a second ransom demand about four this afternoon; the money's to be left at noon tomorrow in a cemetery in Queens. Dinch doesn't want me there to observe, but I'll be there anyway."

"Does that mean our work in Baltimore is finished?"

In the background, Felix heard Abbott cry out anxiously: "Who's on the phone?"

"Fill him in," said Felix.

Torvald relayed the ransom news to Abbott.

Abbott, close to the mouthpiece: "How much are they asking?"

"Fifty-eight thousand three hundred," said Felix.

Torvald: *"Three hundred?"*

"My reaction exactly," said Felix.

Abbott: "Are Dinch and Latimer going to pay it?"

"Yes."

"Any clues as to who it might be?" Torvald asked.

"Nope. It was a different voice from the first."

"Are we to leave Baltimore?" Torvald asked.

"Dinch didn't say anything about it. If the cadenza's here in New York, there's no reason to stay. If Scaevola's people are after Trntl, there's every reason to leave."

"When Trntl and Carol get back, I'll pass on your report."

Felix ended the call and locked up the office for the night.

In Room 917, as soon as the red light winked off, Marco tried to call Zyzynski in New York; but he couldn't raise the Chief at the "Confidential" private number. He then dialed the "Top Priority" recording machine and left his message there for Mr. Meggs. Chip was out following Trntl and her friend, giving Jerry a breather; and Jerry, down in 610, was presumably watching Trntl's door through his bubble. Should he ring the room and tell Jerry this latest news? Naw, plenty of time for that later. Marco went back to doing pushups.

In Trntl's room, Peter Shipley Abbott had made Torvald go through the few specifics Felix had provided regarding the ransom instructions. "Noon tomorrow," he repeated. "Which cemetery in Queens?"

"He didn't say," said Torvald.

"And you're staying here in Baltimore when the cadenza's in New York?" Abbott asked in disbelief.

"We'll have a conference and decide," said Torvald.

"Well, I'm going back to New York tonight," said Abbott. "I may be of more use there than here."

"That's true," said Torvald.

Abbott pulled the Amtrak schedule from his coat pocket and studied it rapidly. "Yes, there's a train that'll get me to Manhattan around midnight."

There was a brisk knock on the door. A man's voice said "Room service."

"I didn't order anything," said Torvald. "Did you?" Abbott shook his head and started for the door. "Don't open it!" Torvald whispered. "Look through the peephole."

Abbott craned his neck and peered out. "Just a man in a red jacket with a wheeled cart."

Another knock. "Room service." More insistent.

Through the door Torvald said loudly, "There must be a mistake. We didn't order anything."

"I have an order here for n—f—t—r—n—t—l in Room 609. Unless you sign my slip and state the order's an error, it'll be added to your bill."

"Crap," said Torvald, shooting back the bolt and releasing the chain lock. He opened the door, and immediately a man in a red jacket pushed a wheeled cart with covered dishes into the room.

Chapter 19

From across the hall, Jerry, peering through *his* peephole, saw much more than Abbott had. A second man in a red jacket stood beside Trntl's door with his back pressed to the wall. Hotel uniform notwithstanding, Jerry recognized him as Angelo Torelli. Trntl's door opened, and the man with the cart entered the room; Torelli quickly moved to stand behind him in the doorway, with his back to Jerry.

Torvald stepped back as the cart wheeled in. "Let's see your slip," he said.

A second man in red appeared in the doorway behind the first. The man with the cart was pushing it with his left hand. His right, resting on the top shelf beside the dishes, was completely covered by a towel folded lengthwise. The man looked swiftly around the room and raised his right hand. The towel, still draping it, came too. Even Abbott could see that, under the towel, he had a very long arm.

"N. F. Trntl?" said the man. A silencer poked from beneath the towel.

Torvald did several things almost simultaneously. With his right foot he kicked the cart into the man's groin; and while, with his left hand, he seized the gun barrel through the towel, twisting it upward, back, and to the man's right, with his right hand he chopped down on the man's wrist. The man screamed as his finger broke in the trigger guard; the gun fired—*pfsst!* (the bullet going *whunk* into the ceiling). Wrenching the pistol from the man's nerveless hand, Torvald kicked his right kneecap, and karate-chopped the base of his neck where it joined the left shoulder. The clavicle snapped like a rotten stick. The man dropped beside the cart with a great outrush of air, felled like a tree in just three seconds.

During which, Jerry had opened his door, stepped into the hall behind Torelli, and dropped and tightened a garrote cord around his neck. Leaning back solidly against the wall, firmly supported by his left leg, with his right knee in the middle of Torelli's back, he used both hands to pull the wooden toggles at the ends of the cord. Yanked backwards, Torelli clutched at his throat, then flailed his arms uselessly behind him and to the sides, became purple-faced, and never made a sound. Jerry had to restrain himself; it would've been so easy to finish the job, and it'd been such a long time! But he had no business killing Torelli; it wasn't his quarrel. When he observed with a practiced eye that Torelli's spasms and clutchings had become so feeble as to pose no threat, he released the garrote, spun Torelli around, and slammed his head resoundingly against the wall. He reached down, took Torelli's pistol from its shoulder holster, stepped back into his room and closed the door. A moment later, while Torvald was calling the hotel desk and Detective Adcock at police headquarters, Jerry emerged with his suitcase and darted down the hall to the stairs that would take him to the ninth floor.

Abbott, his face the color of a dish of grits, was bending down to examine the man who'd pushed the cart. "You made a mess of his finger," he choked in a squeaky voice. He felt a sharp twinge in the region of his prostate, and a wave of nausea so whelming he had to fight down the urge to puke. His own fingers, curling defensively, hid themselves deep in his coat pockets. Though horrified, he couldn't pull his eyes away. "And I think you broke his wrist!"

"Very likely," said Torvald. "What about the guy in the hall? I had the impression some stranger was dealing with him."

Abbott stepped around the man with the ruined finger and studied the body crumpled on the hall carpet. "He's unconscious, looks awful, and his breathing is kind of wheezy."

The house dick arrived, running up from the elevator, a trim and dapper man wearing a pin-stripe suit and pointed shoes with a mirror-bright polish. He looked at the casualties, heard Torvald's account of what had happened. "These are hotel employees," he said, noting the red jackets. "You say they tried to kill you? Uh, sir, why don't you give me that gun?"

"I'll give it to the police," said Torvald. "You'll find a bullet up there in the ceiling." At this point the manager arrived, a tall, morose man with broad shoulders and horn-rimmed glasses. He had to hear the recounting also, but when he'd examined the two men, he said: "These aren't hotel employees. They're just dressed up in our livery." To the house dick he said: "Find out where they got those jackets and that serving cart."

Police headquarters was not far away. Detective Adcock arrived with another man in plainclothes whom he introduced as Detective Price. Torvald handed Adcock the pistol, and he and Abbott gave their names. Adcock studied the silencer and looked at the bullet hole in the ceiling. As the police were listening to Torvald's story, Trntl and Carol returned from their movie.

"What did you *do* to these guys?" Adcock asked. Both were now sitting groggily against the wall. "And where's the other gun? That man's holster is empty."

"The stranger must have taken it," said Torvald. "He went back into that room across the hall."

Adcock rapped loudly on the door of 610. He turned to the manager, said "Open it," and the manager produced a passkey and let them in. "The room's empty," said Adcock. "Call down and see who's registered here."

The manager called the front desk and Trntl, having gotten a quick rundown from Torvald, announced to Adcock as he returned to her room, "The man with the bruised face is Angelo Torelli, as you may know. He and a man named Joe tried to kill me yesterday."

"We hadn't heard," Adcock said icily.

"I was hoping for a police presence when I went out last night pursuing the cadenza lead. But I never saw you or Price or anyone else. If you'd been there, you wouldn't have *had* to be told."

Adcock turned to Price and gave him a long stare. Price flushed and said, "When I got to the phone booth, she'd already gone."

"You should also know that Torelli knew I'd called your office," said Trntl. "He and Killer Joe both work for Giuseppe Scaevola."

Adcock did not respond to this. Torvald said, "I want these men charged. For starters, assault with a deadly weapon—with intent to inflict severe bodily harm."

"I want them charged too," Trntl said to Adcock. "You should do a ballistics check on this gun with the silencer. It might be the one used to kill Stephanie Simms."

Adcock turned to the two attackers where they lay gently holding and supporting various parts of themselves. "You're under arrest—"

"I want my lawyer," Torelli whispered, his voice a reedy croak.

The manager turned from the telephone. "Room 610 is registered to Mr. Ambrose Aarslof from Butte, Montana."

"He's the one who took care of Torelli," said Torvald.

"Hunt for him," Adcock said to the house dick. To the uniformed patrolmen now in the hallway, he said, "Take these two away. I'll follow you to book 'em. Price, get formal statements from Abbott and Grimsson. Miss Trntl, I wonder if you'd oblige me by coming down to headquarters. I'd like to talk to you some more."

"I was just a bystander," Abbott quickly said to Price. "Just visiting in this room when the attack occurred. My room's 603 down the hall;—look, here's my key. I'd appreciate it if you'd take *my* statement first. I've got to catch a train."

When, in short order, Lefty Scaevola heard about the arrests, he was in his study listening to *Rigoletto*. Theresa had gone to her sister's for the evening, his mother was off in her quarters watching television, and he had been anticipating some quiet time for himself. But, after hanging up the phone, he sat for a long time staring at the desktop while the ice melted in his drink and the opera ended. Initially his thoughts focused on his nephew Tony, whose free-lancing had set so much in motion. "*Cretino,*" he muttered, "*idiota!*" No brighter than his father. Then his thoughts shifted to the present difficulty. He picked up the phone, dialed his office manager: "Bernie, first thing in the morning: call Newark; have Johnny Speranza get back here as quick as he can. As for Angelo Torelli and George Fiocco—" He shook his head. "Bail 'em out—whatever it costs. Then take their names off the payroll."

It was almost ten-thirty when the limousine turned into the dark street and stopped at the side entrance of D. H. Van Voort's Gallery and Auction Rooms. With Strunk and Willett facing him on the jump-seats, Victor Zyzynski sat brooding with his hands clasped across his belly and a fat cigar projecting from the shelf of his lower lip. It had been an altogether unsettling day; the merger negotiations had bogged down, and Chip's call from Baltimore that morning had given him a nasty turn. "Yes, Chief, your ad's in today's paper. But there's another ad that's similar."

Zyzynski had felt a sudden throb in his lower gut. "Read it."

"'WANTED. Publisher desires original music manuscripts in composers' autographs—works of Stravinsky, Farringford, Amy Beach. Confidential.' There's a post-office box listed. This is the second day it's appeared."

"It was in *yesterday?*" Zyzynski's eyes filmed over with a red haze.

"Yep. When I saw it today while reading the classifieds, I checked the *Sun* for the last two days."

"Another collector," Zyzynski said tonelessly.

"Probably. But I even thought it might be Pettigrew, hoping to recover the cadenza anonymously."

"It's another collector," Zyzynski said.

And that jagged certainty had gnawed at him all day.

Adding to his discomfort as evening approached was his growing anxiety regarding the meeting he'd arranged at Van Voort's gallery. He was desperately curious to know what sort of rival was opposing him, and reason counseled that as long as anonymity was preserved, no harm would come from the encounter. But reason couldn't allay his nagging suspicion that insisting on the meeting had been a grave mistake. In the past he'd trusted his instincts, and they'd served him well. But in this case he was pursuing a course that denied them outright.

In view of the damnable murkiness of the situation in Baltimore, the inability of Marco, Jerry, and Chip to make any progress, and the new ransom demand Dinch had received this afternoon, he was becoming acutely nervous and jumpy.

At least tonight he'd be able to see what sort of threat this Other Collector posed. Van Voort's confidential clients (only God knew how many there were!)—like those of Yeager, Siefkis, Huyck, Fouchet, Kropotkin, and Patel—were rich, private, zealous in their pursuits, anything but amateur, and particularly interested in the exotic, the unique, and the legally unobtainable. To Mr. Meggs, Van Voort had let slip that this Unknown whom Zyzynski was meeting was a collector of his own rank and caliber: "Client 1-Primus-Triple-A has the assurance that he will be meeting with a collector of comparable stature."

Zyzynski had flushed purple on hearing this. Van Voort of course didn't know his true identity; if he had, he wouldn't have dared to say such a thing. In view of the inexhaustible extent of Zyzynski's resources, it was inconceivable that any other collector could be his equal. But Van Voort's ignorance of his true grasp and scope did not assuage Zyzynski's wrath; as the day wore on, he found the art dealer's glib statement a source of intense and growing irritation—like the fiery spread of poison ivy, or the itch of bleeding piles.

Already, sight unseen, this Other Collector had aroused in him a keen hostility. In the meeting, Zyzynski would have to assert his dominance at the outset, establish his primacy, and intimidate the Other into acknowledging it.

The limousine was standing at the curb. He could wait no longer. "Here, Willett, help me on with my mask." He felt damn silly putting on a latex mask that covered his whole head and neck. Masks! Van Voort had a bizarre sensibility. Yet, he grudgingly admitted, how else could anonymity be guaranteed in a face to face meeting? Turn out the lights, or put a sack over your head? Talk through a screen, as at confession? Bah. And turning out the lights in the presence of a man even remotely like himself had the appeal of walking alone down a South Bronx alleyway at night.

Mr. Meggs had at least picked out a mask that was tolerable. None of those stupid ones Zyzynski had seen in various novelty shops—the Cavemen, Apemen, Frankenstein's Monsters, Lucretia Borgias, Draculas, Mummies, Aliens, or Creatures from the Black Lagoon. It wasn't Goldilocks, any of the Bears, Dagwood Bumstead, Betty Boop, or the Big Bad Wolf. No, he rather liked it: the mask of a fierce craggy face—high-cheekboned, snub-nosed, bearded, framed with densely-flowing hair; the eyes deep-set, the lips twisted into a coldly cruel sneer. "The best of the lot," Mr. Meggs had assured him. "Attila the Hun."

When Willett had helped him get it on—and it was difficult, requiring much tugging and pinching—he found the mask a tight fit, stuffy and hot. Almost immediately he began to sweat; and of course the latex held the moisture in. But at least he could see through the eye-holes and breathe through the nostrils and mouth. He wanted to finish his cigar, but the mouth-hole between Attila's molded lips was too small to accommodate it. With a sigh, he stubbed it out.

Zyzynski left the car first; then Willett and Strunk in their wide-brimmed hats and black overcoats. The car pulled away. A swinging glass door opened, and D. H. Van Voort ushered them into a dimly-lighted hallway. "Client 1-Primus-Triple-A," Zyzynski announced, his voice slightly muffled by the mask. Van Voort was momentarily nonplused by the ferocious visage of the man before him. "I chose my own disguise," said Zyzynski.

"So I see," Van Voort replied with a nervous smile; his having been startled irked him, for he'd wanted to make a good impression on this excellent client whom he'd never met. He peered at the mask through an eyeglass suspended on a gold chain around his neck. "And it's a stunning choice!" he continued, trying to make back the ground he'd lost. "The face is so—so rugged and virile! Let me guess. Is it that of—Vlad the Impaler?"

The face stared at him for a long, frightening moment while the large body swelled even larger. "Attila the Hun!" Zyzynski thundered.

"Of course!" Van Voort cried, dropping his glass, clapping his hands together and bursting into a broad smile. "How stupid of me! An excellent choice! One of the most brilliant tacticians of all time!"

Van Voort was a short man, very slightly built, chic and svelte in his dark gray suit with velvet lapels. His skin gleamed in the dusk like ancient porcelain. Beneath his button nose a handlebar mustache like spun silver fringed his upper teeth; his iron-gray hair, worn longish, was combed smoothly back, parted on the right as though by a ruler, and exquisitely feathered into a frilled ridge above his left ear. He hastened to repair his *gaffe*. "I can't tell you how pleased I am to meet you at last, 1-Primus-Triple-A, after so many years of—ah, mutually beneficial transactions."

"When can we expect the other party?" Zyzynski asked impatiently.

"Oh, he's here already. He arrived about ten minutes ago, and is waiting for you in the private conference room. Allow me to escort you."

He led them across a large darkened salon filled with chairs arranged in neat rows, through an archway draped in blue velvet, and up a broad curved staircase to an upper hallway carpeted in dark burgundy. "I've arranged a suite of three rooms," Van Voort explained. "The conference room is in the center; you each enter from opposite sides. Your men can stay here in this antechamber. The other party also has two associates remaining in *his* antechamber. I've taken the liberty of providing several choice wines, a plate of modest cheeses, and a bowl of fresh fruit. Take as long as you need for your conference. When you're ready to leave, press the buzzer, and I'll escort you out separately through your respective anterooms." Dietrich Van Voort smiled graciously with a sweeping bow. "I'll leave you now. I hope that your conference is productive." He backed out of the room into the carpeted hall and gently closed the door.

While Strunk helped him off with his coat, Zyzynski said to them both: "Sit near the door. If I should need you, I'll simply press the button on this cigar case, and your beepers will go off." They nodded and moved chairs near the door. Zyzynski entered the inner room.

It was rectangular, fairly small; its walls were covered with rich ruby brocade, its floor with a thick blood-red carpet. It was as intimate as a pocket, and as remotely sealed away from the outside world as an underground bunker. In the center was a table—of dark burled wood, elaborately carved, its top inlaid with intricate designs in ivory, gold, and mother-of-pearl (eighteenth-century Italian, Zyzynski judged). Above the table, a small crystal chandelier provided the room's sole illumination.

There were two chairs at the table. In the one facing him as he entered, a short, thin man sat watching him, smoking a Russian cigarette in a long black holder. He rose as Zyzynski approached the table, but said nothing. He was elegantly attired in a tailored black tuxedo, pinched at the waist. The broad satin lapels gleamed in the overhead light, and his large black bowtie of watery silk was lustrous beneath his stiff wing collar. His mask was the sort Van Voort would have chosen: Italian, black as ebony, skull-like with its domed forehead, angular cheekbones, and deepset eyeholes—demonic, sinister, redolent of intrigue, and carnival, and Poe. Instead of a mouth, the mask possessed a large, triangular projection jutting wedge-like from beneath the pointed nose—a prow of an upper lip completely covering the wearer's mouth and chin. But, unlike Zyzynski's, it was a face-mask only; visible behind the curve of the forehead was a wave of glossy black hair. Zyzynski took the chair opposite, and the other immediately sat also. They did not shake hands.

"Tonight my name is Attila," said Zyzynski.

The Other acknowledged this with a brief, restrained bob of the head. "You may call me Abel," he said, "and refer to me as 'the Count.'" His voice was rich, deep, and resonant.

Zyzynski twitched in his chair and ground his teeth; he'd been so smugly pleased that *his* persona was in the A's. Moreover, in his blue business suit he felt at a disadvantage facing the crisp white shirt front of the Count and the glitter of his dazzling ruby studs. Damned if he would ever call him 'Abel'! He placed both hands firmly on the table and began to tap one finger rhythmically—a tactic which, on numerous occasions in the past, had proved effective in board rooms and negotiating sessions when it was important to intimidate the Enemy. Making a random stab, Zyzynski said, "It was kind of you to consent to this meeting." Tap, tap, tap . . .

"You should take it as a compliment that I did so," said the Count. "It's highly unusual for me to acknowledge my collecting to anyone. But I'll confess I was intrigued at the prospect of meeting a collector who was represented to me as having comparable stature." Then, indicating Zyzynski's tapping finger, he added: "There's no cause for you to be nervous. This is, I assume, a friendly meeting."

Zyzynski stopped tapping.

"As a matter of fact," the Count continued, "it's a distinct pleasure meeting you in person. In the course of my activities over the years, there are many times I feel I've sensed your presence."

"And I yours," said Zyzynski. "Perhaps, as we get acquainted, it will be possible for you to resolve some matters that have puzzled me for some time."

"Perhaps." The Count's gaze was intense through the eyeholes of the black mask.

Zyzynski forced himself to stare into the gaze. "The Star of Zambesi?" he asked.

The eyes twinkled as the Count gave a quick nod and blew a thin stream of smoke at the pendants of the chandelier. "Acquisitioned in 1968."

"My congratulations," said Zyzynski.

"Thank you," said the Count. "Perhaps you're in a position to settle some matters that have puzzled *me*."

"Perhaps," said Zyzynski.

The Count leaned slightly forward, and his voice betrayed his eagerness: "The Tears of St. Ursula?"

Zyzynski spread his hands. "All nine of them."

The Count leaned back. "Ah," he said with a gentle sigh. "My turn to congratulate *you*."

"Thank you," Zyzynski said. "The Book of Aldhelm?"

"Even so," said the Count. He tilted back his head, exposing his clean-shaven dimpled chin, and took a sip of wine beneath the prow of his mask. Then, with a sidelong glance: "The Manzini Altarpiece?"

"Far better protected than it was in Florence," said Zyzynski. He paused for a moment, thinking. "The Uxmal Sunstone?"

"Safely out of the sun."

It was Zyzynski's turn to sigh. "Well then," he muttered.

"The Celestial Throne?" asked the Count.

"With footstool," said Zyzynski. "Da Vinci's *Demeter*?"

"1973," said the Count. He tipped the ash off his cigarette and took a deep breath. "The Darjeeling Puzzle-Box?"

"A constant pleasure," said Zyzynski.

"A most difficult acquisition," the Count said. "For that you have my sincerest admiration." There was an unmistakable note of envy in his voice. Zyzynski smiled behind his mask. Then asked in turn: "Luther's Folly?"

"An amusing piece," said the Count. "I never tire of it.—The Plinth of Ptolemy?"

"Egypt's loss," said Zyzynski. And now a crucial item: "Bernini's *Sleeping Shepherdess?*"

"No," said the Count. He crushed out his cigarette, and both of them sat silent for a long moment, staring at the tabletop.

The Count was the first to look up. "And now before us is the matter of The Farringford Cadenza." But he did not immediately pursue the topic. First he reached for an open bottle and refilled his glass. "I can heartily recommend this wine," he said. "Chateau Beaupré Bonvieux 1938. May I pour you a glass?" Zyzynski nodded, and the Count filled the empty goblet. "It's remarkably good. I'm surprised that our host has it. I'd assumed the Nazis got it all."

"They probably did," said Zyzynski. Bastard! he thought. *Prick!* To have the Uxmal Sunstone, the Book of Aldhelm, *and* the Star of Zambesi! For just a second he caught himself staring at the small cheese-knife, wishing that their host had supplied them with a Renaissance stiletto. He tried to drink his wine, but the hole in the mask that served as Attila's mouth was too small for the rim of the glass—and, as he tipped the goblet, he found to his chagrin that the wine flowed along the lines of the rubber lips and spilled down Attila's chin. To form a large red stain on Zyzynski's shirt front.

"Dear me!" said the Count. "What a shame! Here, take this napkin." While Zyzynski wiped his shirt front, the Count fitted a fresh cigarette into his holder. While he patted and swabbed, Zyzynski silently uttered a string of curses. He desperately needed a cigar but knew he could never manage it with Attila's mouth; he found himself looking wistfully at the Count's open cigarette case. But damned if he was going to ask the bastard for a smoke. And on top of everything else, the mask was getting hellishly hot: sweat was trickling profusely down his face into his collar. He felt that his head was turning to soup.

Having lit his cigarette and leaned back comfortably in his chair, the Count said, "You asked for this meeting, my dear Attila. Perhaps you'd better explain why. Van Voort evidently informed you that I had made inquiries about the possible availability of the Farringford Cadenza. Initially I was quite angry with him for what I consider to be an inexcusable breach of confidentiality. However, as I said, I was intrigued to learn that there is another collector vigorously pursuing the same objective; and as I thought the matter over, my anger at Van Voort was somewhat tempered by my curiosity regarding the purpose of the meeting you request-ed. And thus it was that I consented to this irregular proceeding. You may be sure that such a meeting is unique in my experience." He paused, his eyes glittering in the sockets of the mask. "What, my dear Attila, is on your mind?"

"I was surprised to learn that Van Voort had received another query regarding the Farringford Cadenza," Zyzynski began cau-tiously, not knowing where the exchange would lead. "I found myself wanting to know the nature of this other collector's inter-est—what's motivating it."

The Count waved his hand gracefully. "The cadenza has leg-endary—almost mythic—stature. One of the world's great lost treasures now come to light. Isn't that motivation enough?"

"I wondered if perhaps you were one of the fortunate ones who heard Farringford perform it thirty-four years ago."

"Alas, no," said the Count. "I was only six when Farringford died. My ex-wife's aunt heard it, though, in the St. Louis concert. On her deathbed she said that her one great regret was that she had never been able to hear it again. She marked that concert as one of the high points of her life. Talked about it for years. I can see why that question might have come to your mind."

"I was also wondering if your interest might arise from your being a specialist in autograph manuscripts—from a desire to ac-quisition the rarity in Farringford's own hand."

The Count thought for a moment, framing his reply. "Since the cadenza exists in a unique manuscript in Farringford's holograph, acquiring the cadenza necessitates acquiring the manuscript. But—to answer your question—for me, whatever value resides in the manuscript is only incidental. The treasure—that which has the desirability and value—is the *music!*"

Zyzynski flinched; in reflex clutched the edge of the table. Now he knew where the Count stood. On the very same ground that he, Zyzynski, occupied! Through the veil of sweat stinging his eyes, Zyzynski stared with even greater loathing at the immobile demon-face before him.

"I take it then," Zyzynski said carefully, "that if you obtained the cadenza, you wouldn't publish it."

The Count gave a dry, hollow laugh—a series of rapid staccato chirps, like pebbles rattling down the inside of a drainpipe. "My dear Attila! Of course not! That would make it common property! If any honkytonk pianist could perform it, if any housewife or bookkeeper could buy a recording of it in their neighborhood shopping mall, what would be the point of possessing it?"

Zyzynski's position exactly. His bowels gave a deep queasy heave. Bile flowed into his mouth. The Count continued: "I have expressed myself candidly, as a gesture of good will. I'm going to ask that you reciprocate. What is *your* motivation for possessing the cadenza?"

Zyzynski had regained his equilibrium. It wasn't candor *or* good will that had brought him to the position of First and Foremost, at the top of the heap. Nor was it underestimating the Enemy. Instinct and habit together shouted *Caution!* What could be gained by letting the Count know that their aims and motivations were the same? What could be lost by revealing to this contemptible pipsqueak Zyzynski's conviction that the cadenza would heal his manhood and raise the dead? Confess his hopes, his single great infirmity? *No!*

He said, "I heard Farringford perform the cadenza in the Chicago concert."

"Ah," said the Count. "Then I can understand your wish to have it." He paused—then asked abruptly: "If you obtained it, would *you* have it published?"

The second lie was easier than the first. "Perhaps—after a suitable lapse of time."

"I see," said the Count.

"Perhaps you would answer another question for me," said Zyzynski. "Someone has run a classified ad in the Baltimore *Sun* angling for a lead on the cadenza. Did you, by any chance, run that ad?"

The Count gave his dry chuckle. "My dear Attila, you must be joking. Of course not! I have no need to run classified ads for my acquisitions!"

Prick! At a loss for anything else to say, Zyzynski concluded lamely, "Well, it indicates that someone else is trying to acquire the cadenza."

"Yes, that would seem to be a warranted inference," said the Count. Then, before Zyzynski could say anything further: "As soon as its discovery was announced, I assumed that numerous collectors would be interested in it. And particularly after it was stolen from the professor in Baltimore. Unlike most of the world's great treasures, it's not simply awaiting acquisition in some museum, archive, monastery, private home, or national repository—a fixed location universally known."

"No," said Zyzynski, "it's at large, floating—perhaps through various hands—"

"Which opens up the field to all contenders," said the Count, helping himself to some of the cheese. "It's a heady situation which pits all collectors against one another in a contest of wills, of skills, of intelligence, and resources. Refreshing! I detest boredom, my dear Attila. My life is a constant struggle to avoid being overcome by ennui. I'm in continuous search of novelty. The Farringford Cadenza's being at large, as you say—I like that term very much— presents a unique and stimulating challenge. I relish the titillation of the chase, the thrill of the hunt, the test of wits." He savored his cheese thoughtfully beneath the prow of his mask. "The mystery of its whereabouts, the sensational news coverage, the initial burglary of the professor's house, and—above all—the two murders add piquancy, do they not? Does not the Star of Zambesi gain luster from the fact that since 1894 at least twelve people have been killed for its possession?" He paused. "My dear fellow, you really must try some of this Camembert; our host has excellent taste."

Zyzynski would have liked to try the cheese; he knew, though, that the tiny mouth of Attila would not allow it. He settled for a grape. This, using one finger, he was able to push through the mouth-hole.

"The more contenders," the Count continued, "the more exciting the contest. And when one has won, the sweeter the victory!

In this 'floating' situation, as you call it, who can say how many contenders will compete? There's a publishing firm here in New York claiming that the cadenza's rightfully theirs—and I understand they've fielded operatives to recover it. But I don't think that serious and experienced contenders have anything to fear from Dunner & Lynch."

Oho! a misstep at last! Zyzynski leaped to correct him: "Linner & Dunch!" he said archly.

"Lynch, Dunch, what does it matter?" the Count said airily. "I've read their ridiculous claims in the newspapers of three continents. But they're not the only publishers interested in the whereabouts of the cadenza. Just two days ago in Paris I learned that L'Enfant Devereux has dispatched one of its vice-presidents to this country to monitor the situation."

"To Baltimore?" asked Zyzynski.

"That I don't know. And a friend of mine in Hamburg tells me that Otto Winkler of Humboldt-Hartmann Gesellschaft is deeply concerned with what's happening. I presume that firm, too, is entering the lists."

Normally, Zyzynski would have agreed that the more contenders, the sweeter the victory. "The Last Shall Be First, and the First Shall Be Last" required for its fulfillment that there be rivals to be bested, bypassed, pushed to the back of the line. In this case, though, the prospect of a contest did not excite him. There was just too much at stake.

While the Count was talking, Zyzynski had pushed his third and fourth grapes through the mouth-hole of his mask. If the Count had indeed acquired for his collection the things he'd claimed, it was obvious he had at his command an organization similar to Zyzynski's. His agents were probably in Baltimore at this very moment!

"I understand why you wanted this meeting," the Count was saying. "You wanted to size up the competition. That makes good strategic sense. I do it myself. And that's why I chose to come. All serious contenders must know the strengths, the determination, and the weaknesses of their opponents. I trust I've made it sufficiently clear that I am determined to have the cadenza."

"Yes," said Zyzynski, "you've made that quite clear." He reached out and punched the buzzer that would inform Van Voort that the conference was over. "There's nothing further for us to discuss." He rose, and the Count stood up also. While facing him Zyzynski backed to the door of his anteroom. "I've found this instructive," he said weightily, as a parting shot.

The Count clicked his heels and bowed. "I hope you found it as instructive as I do," he replied.

Zyzynski slipped into his anteroom and closed the door behind him. Taking up his overcoat, he said to Willett and Strunk, "Into the hall. Van Voort will show us out."

Strunk opened the door to the hallway, and there indeed was D. H. Van Voort emerging from behind a velvet drape. "Is the meeting over?" he said. "I hope it was profitable." He stopped, shocked at seeing the huge red stain on Zyzynski's shirt front.

Zyzynski ignored his stare. "Useful," he said. "We're ready to leave."

They hurried to the stairs with Van Voort in the lead and descended to the auction room. As they moved toward the outer door, Zyzynski said, "Mr. Van Voort, we've had some mutually beneficial transactions in the past. It would be nice if they could continue."

"Yes, very beneficial," Van Voort said nervously. "I'm afraid I don't catch the drift of your last statement, however . . ." He ended on a rising inflection that hung between them like a flag to test the direction of the wind.

"If you want our relationship to continue," said Zyzynski, "you will let me know immediately if you learn anything about the whereabouts of the Farringford Cadenza. Me and me alone."

Van Voort's face went a sickly yellow. "My dear 1-Primus-Triple-A! I value your patronage. But that's precisely what Client Abel told me just before the meeting!" His hands fluttered helplessly as Willett opened the outer door. "You're putting me into an impossible position!"

"Only if you choose to treat with the other party," said Zyzynski. The limousine drew up to the curb; and, still wearing the mask of Attila, he crossed the sidewalk and crawled into the dark interior.

Chapter 20

March 6   (Friday)

At nine the next morning, still smarting from his duel with the Count, Victor Zyzynski breakfasted in the sunroom, staring moodily down on Central Park. Tasteless grapefruit, a grilled perch fillet no better than yesterday's, hash-brown potatoes that left nothing to the imagination, bran muffins that left far too much. His valet Wilson brought him the telephone-recorder as he was finishing his coffee. "Last night's calls, sir; and I'd remind you of the staff meeting at ten-thirty."

Oh, damn the merger negotiations. "Tell Brim that I don't want perch for breakfast tomorrow; I'll have haddock instead. No muffins. Cornbread with currant jam."

The only message of interest was Marco's to Mr. Meggs, reporting a call to Trntl from Felix McKay which corroborated the information Zyzynski had gotten from Latimer. Except McKay hadn't named the cemetery. Well, Zyzynski was ahead of them there! At eleven, Willet and Strunk would be settling in at Mount Olivet to observe developments at noon. And, if it seemed appropriate, to *intervene.*

It was entirely possible they'd have the cadenza with them when they returned.

While selecting a cigar, Zyzynski allowed himself a sneer of triumph at the Count's expense. Not knowing about the cemetery drop placed his rival at a fatal disadvantage. With condescending arrogance, the Count prided himself on being the dominant "contender", smugly assured that his skill and determination would win him the race. Fool! In his ignorance he didn't know that he wasn't even in the running.

While Zyzynski was finishing his breakfast, Silas Dinch arrived at work tense and irritable after a fitful night. He snapped at his secretary when she gave him his incoming mail and barely mumbled a response to the cheery greeting of Ray Tuttle, who was standing by the coffeepot. He went into his private office, closed the door, and seated himself at his cluttered desk to play yet once again the tape recording of yesterday's ransom call. He carefully wrote down the instructions for dropping the money and slipped the paper into his coat pocket. The more he listened to the caller's attempt at Australian speech, the more convinced he became that the whole thing was a hoax. Damned if the man didn't sound intoxicated! Thank God it was mostly Latimer's money; Lunner & Dinch only had five thousand in the kitty. If it wasn't a hoax, and they did recover the cadenza, he'd write that off as a business expense—a commission, or a fee for contractual services. If they *didn't* recover the cadenza . . . But he didn't want to think about that possibility. Wait and see, that's all they could do.

The intercom buzzed, and, in a carefully neutral voice, his secretary said: "Peter Shipley Abbott to see you, sir. He doesn't have an appointment."

Abbott? What the hell— "Send him in."

And in he came, in fur-collared coat and natty black homburg, energetic and freshly-shaved—with only sallow skin and dark circles around his eyes to attest his late-evening train ride and two night's lack of sleep.

"Well, this is a pleasant surprise," said Dinch. "Have a seat. Do you want some coffee?"

"No coffee, thanks." Abbott began doing off his gloves, delicately, finger by finger. "I've been to Baltimore; came back last night. Things have gotten quite out of hand. Twice now someone has tried to kill Trntl—and last night, *I* was almost shot."

"Good God." Dinch leaned forward, elbows on the desk. "Who's doing this?"

Abbott removed his hat and coat and carefully laid them on a chair. The bright, bumpy red rash covering Dinch's face was repugnant to behold, yet interesting enough to merit close examination. He'd be having to shave off his mustache soon. Making a conscious effort to pull his eyes away, Abbott stared at the desktop. "Who, indeed? She's convinced it's one of the Scaevolas—either Tony or his uncle. I was present at both attempts. On the first occasion, she was abducted, and was rescued by two mysterious men—posing as police, but not police—who used efficient teamwork. She thinks they might be agents of one of your competitors. On the second occasion, we were attacked in her hotel room by two assassins with guns. We escaped only through the quick actions of her associate Torvald Grimsson and another mysterious man from across the hall—an Ambrose Aarslof from Butte, Montana—who subsequently disappeared. I never got a good look at him." He passed a hand over his brow. "Silas, I actually felt the bullet go past my head!"

Dinch rested his cheek against his palm and closed his eyes. "Aarslof—Aarslof. No. I can't place that name." He pushed a button on the base of the telephone. "Hello—Johnson? Check the dossiers for an Ambrose Aarslof who claims an address of Butte, Montana. No, I don't know how to spell it. Sounds Russian. Start with Humboldt-Hartmann Gesellschaft, than L'Enfant Devereux. Keep going till you find something or nothing." He hung up and turned back to Abbott. "Why does she think it may be a Scaevola who's trying to kill her?"

"She told the police she suspects Tony Scaevola of killing Stephanie Simms. She thinks the family wants to shut her up."

"Did she tell the police she's working for Lunner & Dinch?"

"I assume so. Anyway, the papers announced it—so everybody knows."

"I need some coffee," said Dinch. "No, on second thought . . ." He opened a desk drawer and pulled out a bottle of bourbon and a shot glass. Halfway through pouring, he looked up: "Would you like one?"

"No, thank you," said Abbott. "When I leave here, I've got to go home and do some practicing. I have a concert in Philadelphia the day after tomorrow."

Dinch tossed down his drink, then had another, then capped the bottle and put it back in the drawer. "It well may be the Scaevolas who are trying to kill her. I can't see why my competitors would be doing it; she hasn't come close to recovering the cadenza."—This with a note of bitterness.—"But I can't see why they'd try to save her, either."

"Last night when Felix McKay called us," Abbott continued, "he said that you'd received a second ransom demand. That made us wonder if the cadenza was no longer in Baltimore."

"Yes, we received a call yesterday afternoon. The caller wants to conclude the transaction today. At ten, Latimer will send me the money. I'm to make the drop at noon and wait for further instructions. Would you like to hear the tape?"

"Very much," Abbott said. Dinch pulled the recorder close and started the message again. Abbott listened closely.

"It's an odd voice," he said when the tape was finished. "I've never heard an accent quite like it—yet, you know, there's something strangely familiar about it. It doesn't seem possible, but I'm sure I've heard that voice before." He resumed his seat beside the pedestaled smoking stand and lit a cigarette. "And it's very strange that the price has gone up to fifty-eight thousand three hundred. Are you sure this is a serious demand—and not just a prank, or a scam to get the money?"

"No, but what choice do we have?" Dinch debated about having another drink, decided against it. He wiped his mustache with the back of one finger. "Frankly, I don't care who has the cadenza now—Tony Scaevola, or an unknown opportunist, or some pimply street-punk. I just want to get it back unharmed."

Abbott set down his cigarette. "Trntl learned that Tony's uncle doesn't want it—would destroy it, in fact, if he got his hands on it. It's clear that Tony made the first call, but Trntl thinks he's out of the picture now. At any rate—" taking out his checkbook and gold fountain pen "—I'd like to kick in some money for the ransom."

"That's good of you, Peter. But Lunner & Dinch has already contributed five thousand, and Latimer and his anonymous friend are providing the rest."

"I'd like to have *some* part in getting the cadenza back—"

"Put away your checkbook. You've done a lot already—given us all encouragement, been kind enough to catch me up on Trntl's investigation (for which I'm grateful). Been *shot* at, for Godsake!"

Abbott slowly pocketed his checkbook and pen. Resumed smoking. "Are you going to have someone watching the cemetery when you drop off the ransom?"

"No, I've decided to play it according to the caller's instructions: go alone, have no backup, send no spies. If the caller doesn't like the way I follow through, he'll put it up for auction."

"It's probably the best course of action," Abbott agreed. "You'll call me when you've received the cadenza, won't you? I'll verify the manuscript's authenticity so we'll know we haven't been conned."

"We're counting on your expertise," said Dinch. "You'll be at home?"

"All day today. Tomorrow I'll be in Philadelphia for rehearsal." He slipped into his coat and began the slow process of putting on his gloves.

"And what about Trntl and her associates?" Dinch asked. "Now there are *three* of them in Baltimore running up expenses. Should I tell 'em to come back?"

Abbott hesitated before answering. "I think you should hold off on that till you have the cadenza. If this ransom demand turns out to be a fraud, the cadenza might still be in Baltimore."

"I suppose you're right," Dinch grumbled. "I could deliver the money and never hear from the ransomers again." Screwing his face into an exasperated grimace, he began methodically cracking his knuckles. Abbott winced at this and, with a shudder, quickly turned away. "It's almost ten o'clock," said Abbott. "I've got to go. Good luck."

Dinch walked him to the door. "Thanks for dropping by. It was thoughtful of you to come all the way uptown to share what's been happening in Baltimore. I really do appreciate it." After the pianist had left, Dinch returned to his desk to sort through the mail.

The attempts to kill Trntl were puzzling; but the presence of the mysterious men who'd rescued her was downright disturbing. Who could they be? He paused, looking at but not seeing the large framed photograph of Jean Sibelius that faced his desk from the opposite wall. Was *that* why Abbott had come to see him? to report the presence of the unknown men? He decided that he would have that drink, after all. While he poured the bourbon, he reviewed his conversation with Abbott, isolating the specific things he'd said. Beyond relating Trntl's personal difficulties and his own peril in the hotel room, Abbott had said very little. Hardly worth a trip uptown; a phone call would have sufficed. Oh, of course! there it was: he'd heard about the second ransom call and wished to make a contribution to the fund. To do it in person. Well, it was a decent gesture, and maybe Dinch should've let him write the check. Oh, well. Abbott was a great pianist; but, like many artists, eccentric as hell. Satisfied, he turned his attention to the mail, and ten minutes later the secretary buzzed him. "Sir, Mr. Latimer is here to see you."

"Good," said Dinch. "Send him in."

At ten minutes till eleven, Peter Shipley Abbott drove through the main gate of Mount Myrtle Cemetery and began creeping along the central roadway into a bewildering maze of monuments.

Not only had he never been to this cemetery before, he generally avoided cemeteries altogether, since he found them dispiriting. This one, on this particular March day, was especially so. The sky was densely overcast; and a bleak, shadowless, lead-gray light lay on the tombstones, on the bare branches of the oak and maple trees standing above them, and the low ridges of the mole tunnels wandering among the graves. Except in a few sheltered places where green was showing, the turf was uniformly a frost-bleached yellow-brown, having the look of well-manicured straw. The evergreens—yew, juniper, hemlock, spruce—standing about singly or in somber groups served only to intensify the gloom.

As he drove, he continually rehearsed the directions he'd heard on Dinch's tape. Despite the terrors encountered in Baltimore, he found detective work exhilarating—the most glandular activity he'd known since his attempt, six years ago at a concert in Pittsburgh, to perform the Schumann concerto on a badly-out-of-tune grand. Today, however, the blend of excitement and feverish anxiety he felt had given him a headache. What if he couldn't find the HODGES monument in this forest of standing stones?

He reached a T-intersection, and sure enough, DIGBY stood right before him—a tall square column capped with a polished granite ball. He turned right, and saw—a hundred yards ahead—the stone angel. When he reached the angel—a mournful creature with drooping, half-folded wings and blank bulging eyes—he turned left and drove till he was able to turn onto the third right-branching road. After progressing very slowly for two hundred yards, scanning the monument names on both sides of the road, he saw on his left a large rectangular stone, perhaps five feet tall, with HODGES carved into the gray granite. At each end stood an ornamental stone urn. Close behind the monument grew a thick screen of yew bushes which the extortionist would undoubtedly use for his cover.

Elated at having so easily succeeded in his quest, Abbott drove past without changing speed. He turned again in a hundred yards, and kept driving until he was well out of sight of the HODGES plot. He parked behind a caretaker's shed designed to simulate a family mausoleum and began walking back the way he'd come. Well before HODGES, he left the road and started cross-lots, screening his progress whenever possible with shrubbery and the larger monuments.

Since Dinch had been instructed to leave the money behind the marker, Abbott had to find an observation post providing both concealment and an unobstructed view of the space between the stone and the yew bushes. His watch read 11:17.

His extreme caution made his progress very slow; and, on one occasion (having lost sight of the road), he nearly panicked, thinking he was heading in the wrong direction. But he regained his bearings, and finally saw, small in the distance, the HODGES monument.

He chose for his hiding place a low-lying clump of juniper between two large vertical stones: excellent cover, from which—lying on his belly—he could clearly see the back of the HODGES marker. 11:26. He settled in to wait.

Because of his excitement and the exertion required, Abbott hadn't felt particularly cold during his devious course through the graves. But only three minutes of lying motionless on the ground beneath the juniper was enough to chill him through.

To protect his ears from the sharp, searching wind, he turned up the fur collar and huddled deeply into it as far as he could. It didn't suffice. The ears gradually went numb. He then took his neck scarf, fitted it over the top of his head, covering the ears, and tied it beneath his chin. He was pleased to find that his black homburg still fit tolerably well over this makeshift babushka. But, even in their fur-lined gloves, his fingers ached and throbbed. Oh my God, he thought. *My joints!* And tomorrow he'd have to be in Philadelphia rehearsing. And, to make matters worse, because of the goddam trip to Baltimore, he hadn't practiced for three days!

Was the chance of observing the ransomer worth the risk of ruining his hands? Again he looked at his watch: 11:32. Even now the ransomer might be hiding in the yew bushes a hundred feet away! He decided to wait it out. To protect his fingers, he crossed his arms beneath him, elbows forward, and put his hands inside both overcoat and suitcoat, hugging them into his armpits. This helped his fingers but stressed his wrists and elbows.

On his side of the access road, and sixty feet beyond the HODGES plot, the ground had been prepared for a burial. Beside the freshly dug grave was a mound of earth covered with a green tarpaulin; above the grave, a green canvas canopy, its scalloped valance flapping stiffly in the breeze. Cold day for a funeral. He found himself focusing on the open grave, reflecting that it would probably be warmer down in the hole than here beneath the juniper bush. The shrub's aroma was making his stomach churn queasily and cramp: he'd always loathed the smell of evergreens—detested gin; hated the pine-scent his mother had used to clean the bathroom; despised the family Christmas trees. 11:51.

He was feeling thoroughly sorry for himself when a line of black cars swung into view, turning at the stone angel. A funeral procession. Oh hell! coming to the open grave. And Dinch would be arriving in nine minutes. The funeral could spoil everything! The hearse stopped at the gravesite, and still the cars kept coming.

He fought the urge to leap up shouting "No, no! Drive on!"—waving his hat and making faces—but of course that would reveal his presence to the watcher in the yew. No, there was absolutely nothing he could do to stop the funeral. In exquisite despair, he squeezed his hands into his armpits and watched resignedly.

Somebody GILBERT come at last to journey's end. Mourners stepping from their cars to gather under and about the canopy. The minister, white hair feathering in the breeze, opening his Bible; his mouth moving soundlessly. On supports above the hole, the casket gleaming gun-metal gray.

And—coming slowly past the funeral cars in search of HODGES—the Oldsmobile of Silas Dinch.

Some of the mourners looked up from their contemplation to stare as Dinch went oozing by. Abbott could see the ginger mustache sweeping right and left as Silas read the markers.

Dinch drove past HODGES. Stopped the car. Did not get out. Clearly was having a moment of indecision studying the funeral in his rear-view mirror. Then he stepped out carrying a black suitcase. Fully two-thirds of the mourners were watching him as Dinch strode resolutely to the HODGES monument. He casually set the suitcase on the ground behind it out of the mourners' view. Then he walked to the front of the stone and peered into both of the ornamental urns. Even the minister was watching him now.

Internally Abbott shrieked, Don't leave the money with so many people present! Surely Dinch wouldn't be so stupid. The publisher whipped out his handkerchief and began methodically wiping the granite clean—starting at the top and moving slowly down the face of the stone. Just as if he were a Hodge, Abbott thought admiringly.

It took Dinch all of three minutes to remove the bird drop-
pings. The mourners lost interest in him after a bit and turned
their attention back to the minister as he concluded the service.
When they broke into small groups and began moving away from
the grave, Dinch wadded up his handkerchief, stuffed it into one
of the stone urns, and went to his car. He had just got behind the
steering wheel when the first limousines started up and came
along the narrow road toward him. Dinch was blocking their way.
It wasn't feasible for him to do a U-turn into the grass and meet
the funeral cars head-on. There was nothing for it but to continue
down the road in the direction he was pointed. This he did, becoming the lead car in the procession as it left the cemetery.

Within four minutes, the funeral had departed, leaving behind three men to lower the casket and close the grave. Abbott lay
shivering, his gaze fixed on the suitcase. After two or three minutes more (it seemed an hour to Abbott), the yew bushes behind
the monument suddenly stirred, and a man scuttled out, humped
over in a stiff-kneed hobbling crouch as though dodging bullets.
He placed a flat brown object on the ground behind the stone,
snatched up the suitcase, and plunged back into the bushes.

Anton Farringford? Some shocks there are the mind can-
not encompass. It balks, goes blank, denies. As though a belt had
snapped, Abbott's brain spun madly like a flywheel disengaged.
He rolled over onto his back, panting for breath. *Anton?*—the
ransomer? Oh no. No. Not possible! But that's what his eyes had
shown him. *Oh...!*

Still disbelieving, he stiffly hauled himself up, resettled the
hat on his babushka, and darted across the road into the monuments on the other side. The men filling the grave did not see him.
Hunkered down behind HODGES, he seized the brown briefcase
with trembling hands, read with a jolt the name MORRIS WAITE
stamped on the leather. He clawed at the flap and found it locked.
Clutching the case to his chest with both arms, he ran raggedly
back to his car.

Numb with cold, still dazed with shock, he was a jumble of
rioting emotions: elation, dismay, relief, disgust, surprise, bewil-
derment, joy. And triumph. For finally! he—he alone!—was in possession of the Farringford Cadenza! Oh, lucky Peter! *Plucky* Peter,
to have succeeded where everyone else had failed! But:—*Anton*

Farringford the person holding it for ransom? How? *Why?* He'd think about that later. Now, there were far more important things to do.

In his car, he tried again to get the briefcase open. The thick leather flap was secure, resisting all his wrenching, twisting. He left the case on the seat beside him, gunned the engine, and, with a spurt of gravel, shot off along the road to the exit. Home to Brooklyn. Plenty of tools there.

Traffic was heavy; and by the time he pulled into the driveway of his modest brick house, his mind had somewhat settled, and he was thinking clearly again.

He ran up the walk, unlocked the door, and went straight to the living room where the grand piano was. As he burst in, his twice-a-week housekeeper, Mrs. Rosen, leaped up from the couch and hurriedly switched off the television set. "I didn't hear you drive in," she said. "I'd just finished the upstairs and was taking a break."

"That's fine, Edna." He put the briefcase on the music rack of the piano, shrugged out of his coat and flung it onto a chair, pulled off his gloves, and, still wearing his hat (he'd removed the scarf), knelt down at the fireplace to light a fire. "It's horribly cold out, and my hands are nearly frozen." Rolled newspapers stuffed beneath the ready logs. Two matches. Goose it with the gas jet. There! He smiled up at her. "Why don't you take the rest of the day off?"

"But I'm only half done with the cleaning."

"That's all right. I've got a great deal of practicing to do before leaving for Philadelphia this evening. I need to be alone to concentrate." He held his aching fingers before the fire. "You go on. I'll see you next Tuesday."

"Well, if you say so." She pouted a little to let him know it bothered her to be interrupted in the middle of her work; but he didn't notice—kneeling, eyes closed, hands outstretched to the blaze, flexing his fingers in the welcome heat, feeling the warmth penetrating deep into his frosted joints. In sequence, he gently massaged each of his ten fingers—slow, sensual stroking, from base to tip: Ah! so *good.* And, at the tip, the keening sensitivity of nerve-ends returning from the numb! Such joy in the subtle friction of ridge and whorl, in squeezing gently, rhythmically, the firm, resilient flesh, in exploring the curve of the bone, the elegant swelling of the joint.

Mrs. Rosen banged around for a bit, asserting herself by adjusting and rearranging things that didn't need it. Then, while she went to the back of the house to put away her dust cloths and mop, Abbott crossed to the writing desk to hunt for tools. Letter-knife, nail file, scissors. He needed something sturdier—hammer, chisel. Both were in the utility room behind the kitchen.

He brushed past Mrs. Rosen in the hall, went to his tool drawer and rummaged till he found what he wanted. When he returned to the living room, Mrs. Rosen was standing by the front door putting on her coat. Abbott swore inwardly: wasn't she gone *yet*?

"I didn't get the kitchen floor mopped," she told him.

"That's fine," he said impatiently, "it'll wait till Tuesday." From where he stood, he could see the briefcase standing on the music rack.

"You should also know that you've developed a drip in your bathroom faucet," she added. His grip tightened on the chisel. "Thanks, I'll see to it." He went past her into the living room, set the tools down on the hearth, put another log on the roaring fire.

"I'm going now," Mrs. Rosen said.

"Yes, you do that. Goodbye."

The front door opened and closed. Abbott glanced over his shoulder; gone at last. He ran to the record cabinet, found his own rendition of Farringford's Fifth as played with the Philadelphia Symphony, placed it on the turntable, and lowered the stylus onto the opening of the fourth movement.

First, the muted fanfare by the French horns; then the oboe's heart-breaking little song. Joined now by the clarinet in staggered duet—the piano making its entrance with soft staccato chords— God! what brilliant writing! And Abbott's own playing was exceptionally fine—undoubtedly the best recording of the Fifth he'd ever made. At the first full statement of the piano's theme, Abbott's eyes misted over. I'm so *good*, he thought. And soon would come the Abbott Cadenza—the two and a half minutes that represented the best that he could do to substitute for Farringford's six.

But Farringford's cadenza was here in his living room! He rushed to the piano, grabbed up the briefcase, carried it to the hearth. Gave the gas valve another turn. Seized hammer and chisel, struck again and again and again at the lock till it broke apart in fragments. Threw aside the tools. Whipped open the flap. And—with shaking hands—pulled the sheets of music manuscript into the light.

He looked inside the briefcase to be sure it was empty, then tossed it into the fire. Rose up to his full height, godlike in exultation.

Laughed aloud. Such giddy relief! For, having endured the past week's tension, the expense of energy, worry, and despair; the dismal trip to Baltimore; the danger; his sleepless nights; his fevered anxiety that Trntl would actually recover the manuscript and get it to Dinch, who then would *publish* it—he now had his reward: that he alone, of all humanity, would be privileged to know the Farringford Cadenza. He, whose *own* cadenza—replacing Farringford's so ably for nineteen years—would now *remain* the standard and *never* be relegated to oblivion!

But before he destroyed the manuscript, feeding it sheet by sheet into the flames, he must play the cadenza—must know what Farringford had written that merited such mythic stature.

He switched off the record player, went to the piano, placed the music sheets before him, pulled his reading glasses from their case, and poised himself to play.

The manuscript wasn't in Farringford's hand. Even more unsettling, the notes in their configurations looked dimly familiar. He dropped his hands onto the keys, squinting as he sight-read the spidery notation, began to play. Notes he had played before.

"Oh, hell!" he shrieked. *"It's Brahms!"*

And so it was. The *Intermezzo in A Major, Opus 118*. Abbott pawed through the other sheets. All in the same spidery hand. All of them Brahms. Bits and pieces of capriccios, intermezzos, rhapsodies. At the bottom of the tenth sheet, a penciled note in a rather childish hand, with circles dotting the i's: "Courage, Ted. *I* have faith in bridgework. Steph."

Two houses north, Abbott's neighbor looked up from vacuuming her carpet to ask her daughter, "Was that a scream?"

Had Mrs. Rosen still been standing in the hall, she would have fled aghast before the fury with which Abbott flung the papers into the fire.

Chapter 21

For Trntl and Torvald, Friday morning had been a series of disheartening frustrations. For several hours, they'd sat on hard chairs at police headquarters, talking at length with Detective Adcock and a young assistant prosecutor named Crandall Niepagen-Scholles.

In making her complaint the night before, Trntl had insisted that a charge of attempted murder be pressed against Angelo Torelli. But now, in discussing this with her, Mr. Niepagen-Scholles would only deal with the difficulties he foresaw in moving for an indictment and taking the case to trial.

It was particularly awkward, he said, there being no witnesses to the "alleged attempt" Torelli had made on her life in the Scaevola warehouse; and it was very unfortunate that Trntl couldn't identify the mysterious "Joe" who'd mixed the cement, or find his picture in the files of police photographs. As for the alleged second attempt on her life in the hotel room, Miss Trntl had not even been present. The likelihood of obtaining an indictment, much less a conviction, for attempted murder was greatly diminished because on that occasion Torelli had done nothing but stand in the hall wearing a hotel uniform; there wasn't even a gun in his holster when he was arrested. ("There's nothing in the law that would let us prosecute a man for wearing an empty shoulder holster, Miss Trntl.") With regard to the first attempt, in the absence of witnesses and hard evidence, it would boil down to her word against Torelli's. With regard to the second, it was one George Fiocco—and not Torelli—who'd come into her room and mentioned her name while flourishing a weapon.

('Flourishing'? thought Trntl. As he rattled on, she was struck by his resemblance to a self-satisfied pocket gopher with a walnut in each cheek-pouch.)

Now it was clear that Mr. Grimsson had a more substantial complaint in the hotel room incident, since the said George Fiocco *had* brandished a pistol and—when attacked by Mr. Grimsson in self-defense—*had* fired it. Thus, Fiocco *had* perpetrated an assault—but on Mr. Grimsson, *not* Miss Trntl. Even so, Fiocco hadn't fired at Mr. Grimsson: the gun had discharged only when Mr. Grimsson broke his wrist.

And it didn't help at all that Peter Shipley Abbott, equally in jeopardy, had refused to sign a complaint.

As for Miss Trntl's allegations regarding Torelli's supposed motive, or her conjecture that his employer, Mr. Giuseppe Scaevola, one of Baltimore's most prominent and respected citizens, had put him up to it—why, how far would that get with a grand jury, or with a trial jury, for that matter? Miss Trntl could possibly charge Torelli with an attempt at intimidation, perhaps; and Fiocco could certainly be charged with unlawful use of firearm in reckless disregard for public safety, and certainly there *was* a disturbing of the peace . . .

"I'd think you surely could charge Torelli with theft of hotel property and impersonating a waiter," said Trntl, stubbing out her ninth cigarette.

"Well, we might get somewhere with a theft charge. He did take the waiter's jacket from the locker room—" He paused, eyes narrowing, and turned down his mouth. "I take it you're playing a game, Miss Trntl."

She looked him squarely in the eye. "No more than you are."

Mr. Niepagen-Scholles gathered up his papers. "I was simply thinking aloud, Miss Trntl, trying to formulate the best approach to bringing a criminal action against Mr. Torelli and obtaining a conviction. Our job in the prosecutor's office is to obtain convictions. It's in the discretion of our office to decide what charges should be filed—"

"I think Torelli should be held on suspicion of murder," said Trntl. "While holding me captive, he as much as admitted that he was involved in the shooting of Stephanie Simms."

"Did he actually say he killed her?"

"I can't say that he actually pulled the trigger. But he strongly implied that he was involved."

"Again, no witnesses," said Mr. Niepagen-Scholles. "It's only hearsay you offer, Miss Trntl. Detective Adcock is aware of your allegations, and will take note of them during his investigation of the Simms murder. What we're concerned with here is *your* complaint, as an aggrieved party, against Mr. Torelli. And on that score, I've tried to tell you where we stand."

"Excuse me," said Torvald. "I'm an aggrieved party, too. I've signed a complaint against both George Fiocco and Torelli, and I want a vigorous prosecution. Fiocco did enter the room through misrepresentation, did say Miss Trntl's name and wave his gun about. He did fire a shot which could have caused severe bodily harm."

"Yes, that's true," said the assistant prosecutor. "The statement of Peter Shipley Abbott bears that out."

"And Torelli *was* wearing a hotel uniform and pretending to be an employee."

"So it would seem."

Trntl said, "I'm prepared to testify under oath that Torelli tried to kill me at the warehouse the previous night."

"And if Torelli testifies under oath that he didn't, where are we *then* without any evidence to refute him?" He closed his briefcase. "It's a pity that this Joe person you saw that night isn't in custody."

"He's probably in Wyoming by now," said Trntl.

"Yes, well." He started for the door. "Our office will formulate charges; the bond will be set later today." He put on his hat and left.

Detective Adcock leaned across his desk, preparing to light his pipe, and said with the hint of a smile, "Now you see what you're up against, Miss Trntl."

"Where did they find Crandall Niepagen-Scholles?"

"He's a hotshot from someplace up north; been assistant prosecutor for about three years. His friends call him Crandy."

"It figures," said Trntl. "What do his enemies call him?"

"Oh, a variety of things." He lit his pipe, puffed for a few seconds, and blew a smoke ring. "The coroner's inquest into the Simms death is scheduled for next Tuesday. You'll have to be here to testify."

"That," said Trntl, "is *very true.* I sincerely hope to be."

"What does that mean?"

"Just because Torelli's been arrested doesn't mean there won't be other attempts to kill me. What progress have you made in finding Tony Scaevola?"

"We have a search underway," said Adcock. "Quietly, of course. No one seems to be living in Tony's apartment. Every day someone comes and takes his mail."

"Takes it where?"

"Need I remind you, Miss Trntl, that this is *our* investigation—not yours?"

"Sorry." She smiled stiffly and rose to put on her coat. "Do you need us for anything else?"

"No, your statements are very complete. If you come across anything that could be useful in our homicide investigation, please let us know."

They left, walked a block to a short-order restaurant for a quick lunch, and then Trntl returned to the hotel, while Torvald went on to the courthouse to monitor developments there.

When Trntl reached her room, she kicked off her shoes and flopped full-length on the bed. Carol looked up from *The Wall Street Journal*: "Bad morning?"

"Adcock asked some good questions and let us talk. It's hard to know where he stands in all of this. He seems less unfriendly than he did, and he seemed really to be listening last night when I told him about the information source Scaevola has in the police department. But Torvald and I had a most irritating encounter with a gopher from the prosecutor's office. He futzed around for two hours trying to find reasons for not bringing felony charges against Torelli."

"What's the word on Tony Scaevola?"

"No word. Adcock claims to be hunting him for questioning."

"While I was sitting here by the telephone, I came across something interesting in the *Sun*." Carol handed her the classified ads, having carefully folded the sheets to highlight one column. "Two separate post office boxes requesting original music manuscripts by C. P. Farringford."

Trntl sat up and read the ads. "Well, well," she said. "A gleam in the murk."

"A publisher claims to have placed one ad, a musicologist the other. If we assume for a moment that both labels are accurate, could the 'publisher' be Lunner & Dinch covering all bases? Or one of Dinch's competitors, perhaps? Could the 'musicologist' be Professor Pettigrew, trying to redeem himself?"

Trntl shook her head. "If so, why would they list all these other composers? Pettigrew and Dinch only want the cadenza. Both could be straightforward about it, without having to throw out these other names as a smokescreen. Now, it's possible that the 'publisher' ad could've been placed by one of Dinch's competitors—and I could see why *they* would want to be circumspect and not reveal their true interest."

"And if the labels are phony?"

"Then your guess is as good as mine." She lay back on the bed. "And I'm too tired to do any more guessing at the moment. Let's put it to simmer on the back burner. I take it you haven't heard whether Dinch recovered the cadenza when he paid the ransom?"

"Nope. Felix said he'd call as soon as he learned anything."

"Well," Trntl said with a yawn, "maybe he'll report that Dinch recovered it, and we can all go home."

"And maybe," said Carol, "he won't."

At two-thirty, Felix called and they could tell at once from his voice that he was distraught. "Did Dinch get the cadenza?" Carol asked.

"There's a lot of strange shit coming down," said Felix. And that, of course, gave them their answer. "At noon Dinch left the money behind the proper tombstone, and he'd barely got back to his office when a call came through—in the same phony Australian accent—telling him to go back to the cemetery and pick up the cadenza where he'd left the money. The caller said it would be in a brown briefcase—" "Ah," said Trntl. "—so back he went to Queens, straight to the HODGES plot—and what do you think he found?"

"Nothing," said Trntl.

"Right you are! No briefcase, no cadenza. He searched thoroughly, then went back to his office and called Latimer, Mrs. Farringford, Anton, Abbott, and me. Dinch doesn't know what to think. Did somebody else find the cadenza before he returned? There weren't any other people in the cemetery when he got there. Did the caller leave the briefcase there at all? Dinch suspects that the whole thing was a scam to rip off fifty-eight thousand dollars— that the person who called never did have the cadenza. So he's convinced that it's probably still in Baltimore. And he's back to worrying about his competitors."

"Well, he may have reason to," said Trntl. And she told him about the classified ads. Then, as an afterthought: "Didn't you go to the cemetery to observe the money drop?"

"No, and that brings us to the other shit that's come down. I fully intended to be there, but when I went to the office this morning about ten, I found that somebody had broken in during the night." (He didn't think it necessary to say that, in SoHo the night before, he'd jammed with the Combo till three a.m., drunk far too much, and crashed at his friend Dirk's house, not getting home to hear the recorded Baltimore report until nine-thirty this morning.) "Nothing much was disturbed; it was a slick, professional job. They picked the locks, opened the dead-bolt. I stopped by to get the binoculars on my way to the cemetery; but when I saw what had happened, I thought I'd better try to figure out what they were after, and if they'd taken anything."

"The files?" asked Carol. "We've got lots of background on individual cases, much of it very sensitive."

"Everything neat and tidy. No folders seem to be missing; some may have been read or photographed. Particular items might've been taken from them."

"Exactly what did you see when you entered?" Trntl asked.

"The door was standing ajar; the wastebaskets were dumped out; the tape recorder had been used—the indicator read 084 instead of 000, where I always leave it; one cassette was missing from the new dozen I bought yesterday morning; and two of Torvald's chocolate covered cherries were gone. I knew exactly how many were in the box."

"Petty cash?" asked Carol.

"All there."

"Checkbook?"

"Checks all present, sequentially numbered."

"Not robbery then," said Trntl.

"Snooping," said Felix. "I suspect they found what they wanted in the files, read it onto a tape, and put the folder back."

"That would suggest they didn't have a camera," said Trntl.

"Anyway," said Felix, "that's why I wasn't at Mount Myrtle Cemetery."

"We've had lots of clients," said Trntl. "The break-in could be related to any of them. But it may well have been the Farringford file they were interested in. Look through it when you can, and see if anything at all seems to be missing or out of order."

"Will do. I wonder if you shouldn't answer those classified ads."

"We're going to. Carol is drafting a response right now."

In Room 917, Marco slapped his knee. "It took them long enough to see the ads," said Chip. "And now we know we've got at least one response coming!"

Felix gave a shy, almost embarrassed chuckle and cleared his throat before continuing. "About twenty minutes after I finished talking to Dinch, Rosamond Foxe called to inquire how the investigation's going. We had a nice talk. She sent me two tickets to her concert on the twelfth; and when she learned that Carol's going with me, she invited us both to the reception afterwards. Please pass the word along."

"Carol will be glad to know that," said Trntl. "I must say, you do work fast."

Felix gave a little laugh. "Well, this seems to be kind of a mutual thing. We're going out for dinner tomorrow night."

"I'm really impressed," said Trntl.

"Oh, one other thing," Felix continued. "Mrs. Farringford called, inviting me to her house at eight tonight. Says she has something important to discuss, but wouldn't say what."

"If you learn anything we should know, give us a call. We'll be up late."

Felix hung up. As soon as the red light winked out, Chip turned to the others. "The Chief will want to know the ransom scheme didn't pan out. And he'll be interested in the break-in at their office. Any thoughts before I call him?"

"Yeah," said Jerry, opening a fresh bag of jujubes. "When I was tailing Trntl back from the police station this noon, I noticed someone else following her, too."

"Tell us more," said Marco.

"A woman—blond, big-boned, about five-foot-ten. She was pretty good at it. Took me awhile to realize she was a shadow. I kept seeing her, and then realized I'd seen her yesterday, too. While Trntl and that Grimsson guy were eating lunch, the blonde browsed in a bookstore across the street watching them through the front windows."

"Where were you?" asked Marco.

"I went into the bookstore too, browsed the magazines, and got a good look at her. Then I went out and sat on a bench till Trntl finished her lunch and came back to the hotel. The blonde came with us, window shopping all the way."

"So who is she?" asked Marco.

Jerry shrugged. "She was well-dressed: Glendower overcoat, Gucci handbag and shoes."

"How old?" Chip asked.

"Somewhere between thirty-five and forty."

Marco helped himself to some jujubes. "Did she know *you* were following Trntl?"

"I imagine so. And she might recall having seen me yesterday. Though I did look a little different then."

"Do you want me to take over tomorrow?" Chip asked.

"Does that mean I have to sit by the phone?"

"Sure," said Chip. "I need a break."

"I could wear a heavy disguise," said Jerry.

"You sit by the phone," said Chip. "*I'll* wear a disguise." He crossed to the bag that contained the costumes and rummaged through it. "You've added some stuff. A pair of women's shoes—good sensible ones, with flat heels and crepe soles. Not Gucci, though. Another dress—but it's so big! And this new wig looks like a haystack. Couldn't you have found a nicer one?"

"Sure. But the point of that outfit isn't to create drag-queen-of-the-prom. It's to fashion a nice old lady of limited means, down on her luck. See, there's a shopping bag and scarf to go with it."

"And these horn-rimmed glasses—"

"Window glass."

"I'll wear those," said Chip, placing them on the bedside table. "And use some of this rinse to darken my mustache and hair."

"You could always shave the mustache," said Marco.

"Some things," said Chip, "aren't even to be joked about."

When Torvald returned at four-thirty, his news provided the dregs of a thoroughly depressing day. "Torelli and George Fiocco are both out on bail," he announced. "Torelli was charged with intimidation, petty theft, and criminal trespass; but Fiocco got assault with a deadly weapon and unlawful use of firearm."

"Ah, they've thrown George to the wolves," said Carol.

Trntl said, "How does the Scaevola machine get such quick results?"

"It pays to know the right people," said Torvald. "Things were nicely expedited. They appeared before a Judge McPhee who set minimum bond; they made bail, and are once again among us on the streets."

"Crandy Niepagen-Scholles has a bright future," said Trntl. "When I see such evidence of the working of our judicial system, I get all choked up inside. Lock the door."

Torvald fastened the guard chain. "I've also found us other rooms—two blocks west, at the Macready Hotel. I've reserved Room 523—in Carol's name—for the two of you, and one for myself two floors above. I think you and Carol should go there after supper. I'll stay here till midnight in case Felix calls, and then I'll check out and join you."

"We're pretty much packed already," said Carol. "We'll take the stairs down, and I'll get the car. The less Trntl's seen, the better."

Trntl handed Torvald the *Sun*. "What do you make of those circled classifieds?"

He read them twice over. "Placed by two parties who want the cadenza, and are as baffled as we are. Unless, of course, one of them has received it by now."

"How does this sound?" Carol handed him a sheet of paper. It was a very simple statement, addressed to two post office boxes:

> In response to the want ad in the *Sun*: I have in my possession the manuscript of a late composition by Charles Philip Farringford, in the composer's autograph. The composition dates from 1947 and has not been published. For sale if a suitable price can be negotiated. Strict confidence. If interested, contact me as soon as possible at the following number to discuss terms.

"We can put the telephone number of our new hotel room in the blank," Carol said.

"I have it here." Torvald jotted it down. "Now, what do you expect to accomplish with this little game?"

"If one or both of them take the bait," Carol said, "we can smoke out who else is after the cadenza. And we'll know for sure they don't have it yet."

"And if neither bites, you've proved nothing."

"Well, it's something to do," Trntl said irritably, peering down into the street. "Call it a necessary diversion. Necessary for *us*."

Torvald's and Carol's eyes met in brief communication; neither of them had ever seen Trntl so severely stressed. "Should we stake out the two post office boxes to see who comes for the mail?" Torvald asked.

"Boring, boring," said Trntl. "Who wants to stand in the post office all day?"

"I'd be willing to do it for awhile," said Carol. "It'd be more interesting than sitting in the hotel room by the phone."

Trntl left the window and sank into a chair beside the bed. She took off her glasses and rubbed her eyes wearily. "If only the logjam would break! I worry that we made a wrong turn somewhere."

"I think we've done what we could," said Carol. "It's not our fault that every avenue becomes a cul-de-sac."

Trntl put her glasses back on and picked up the copy of the letter Morris had written to Stephanie. "I'm really bothered by this message. Here's what he says: 'To play it safe I pulled the cadenza from the other music and hid it. The key is in our Special Place' (and he capitalizes that) '—the "Key Hole", get it? ... You better get it and send it to the publisher.' Now, he sent this letter *after* he told Stephanie that he'd locked the cadenza in his briefcase and hidden it in the stash-hole in his apartment. Therefore, the 'Special Place' is *not* the stash-hole, which was raided—presumably by Tony Scaevola. Though she never read this letter, she claimed in her note to have possession of the cadenza on the day she died. Yet Angelo Torelli claims that Stephanie didn't have the cadenza at the time of her murder, and her apartment was searched, presumably by Torelli and whoever else was along. I'm inclined to think that Stephanie never did have it."

"But she claimed she did," said Carol. "Wouldn't she know? She'd seen it before and could recognize it."

"She may have *thought* she had it. Try this for plausibility: Tony took the locked briefcase from Morris's apartment and made the first ransom call. Somehow Stephanie got the briefcase from him, assumed the cadenza was inside, but was never able to see for sure, because it was locked."

"So where's the briefcase now?"

"If the cadenza wasn't in it, it doesn't really matter," said Trntl.

"Then, by that hypothesis, Morris used the briefcase as a decoy to fool Tony?" Torvald asked.

"Possibly. And if that's what happened—since Stephanie never read Morris's letter—the cadenza is still where Morris hid it, waiting to be discovered."

"But what about the second ransom call?" said Carol.

"That's a hard one. Tony Scaevola makes the first ransom call, loses the briefcase, disappears. Stephanie's killed, but no cadenza's found. Torelli says that Tony's uncle doesn't have it, doesn't want it, would destroy it if he got his hands on it. Dinch gets the second call, pays the ransom, gets nothing—no cadenza, no briefcase. I'm guessing that the second call was simply a ploy to get the fifty-eight thousand, and the caller never had the cadenza."

"But where's the cadenza now?" asked Torvald.

Trntl shrugged. "I think we'll find it when we find the 'Special Place'."

"No," said Torvald, "Morris says the *key* is in the 'Special Place': *what* key?"

"It might be the key to the briefcase lock," said Carol.

"But if the cadenza wasn't in the briefcase," said Trntl, "why would he direct her to the briefcase key? No, I think it's a different key. Morris calls the 'Special Place' the 'Key Hole'—putting quotation marks around 'Key Hole' as though the term is the name of some location she's familiar with,—or as though he sees the term as some sort of metaphor, not referring to a real keyhole at all."

"Thinking that it might be the name of a specific place," Carol said to Torvald, "we checked the telephone directory's yellow pages to see if we could find an establishment named 'The Key Hole'. We went through taverns, bowling alleys, restaurants, locksmiths, bookstores, adult theaters, porn palaces, music stores, secondhand shops, and skating rinks—and found nothing so named."

"If it's a metaphor," said Torvald, "could Morris be using 'key' to mean 'answer' or 'solution'? His 'get it?' implies some sort of private joke or code he and Stephanie shared. Or he might be setting her a riddle."

Trntl emptied the ashtray into the wastebasket. "So what could it be that he and Stephanie called 'the Key Hole' but no one else did? Something that, with his 'get it?', he had to remind her of?"

Torvald raised his hands to stop the discussion. "Enough! We've got to get off this treadmill. Let's face it. Morris's references may have meanings only to him and Stephanie. Private, personal meanings that outsiders like us will never understand. Besides, all this talk is making me hungry. I suggest we write up our responses to the classified ads so we can drop 'em at the main post office on our way to eat. And then, Trntl, let's get you and Carol to the Macready Hotel. From there I'll call Rachel and tell her I'll be staying here for at least two more days. I'll have to miss her birthday party, though, and that'll take some explaining."

"You'll do fine," said Carol, smiling. "You've had so much practice."

Chapter 22

Mrs. Farringford greeted Felix warmly. "Come in, Mr. McKay. It's good to see you again. I'm glad you were free to come over on such short notice." She pointed across the dimly lighted entrance hall to an ornate coat-rack. "Hang your things there. We can sit in the parlor, where I have a nice fire going."

The fierce blaze crackling in the fireplace illuminated the tiled hearth, the plush chairs drawn up on either side, the decanter and glasses on the coffee table. A small shaded lamp some twenty feet away provided the only other light.

"Do sit down, Mr. McKay, and make yourself comfortable." He took one of the chairs beside the fireplace, and she sat facing him. "As you can see," she continued, patting her knee, "I'm no longer using that awful cane."

"I'm glad your injury's so much improved."

"Well, it *was* a nuisance. I've been warned repeatedly to be careful stepping off curbs. But you know how it is: I get to thinking about other things and moving fast. This time I'd just hailed a cab and wasn't watching where I put my foot."

Tonight she was wearing a loose-fitting white blouse, turquoise slacks, a gold bracelet on each bare arm, and a gold chain necklace with turquoise pendant. Her hair was more becomingly styled than the last time Felix had seen her; instead of being severely pulled back, it was drawn forward, loose and flowing, with bangs across her forehead. At the sides, the curled ends rested lightly on her shoulders. This arrangement softened the angularity of her prominent cheekbones and de-emphasized the slight droop in her left eyelid.

"And tonight," she continued, "for the first time in three weeks, I went out to dinner with friends. I got back only shortly before you arrived." Her crimson nails flickered in the firelight.

Felix smiled and nodded. Mrs. Farringford took a cigarette from a box on the table and deftly lit it with a match. After exhaling a thin stream of smoke from the side of her mouth, she leaned forward slightly and began speaking with restrained intensity.

"I asked you to come over because I need some answers I'm not getting anywhere else. At our first meeting, you impressed me as a sensitive man who could be trusted to speak openly and honestly."

"As one of our clients, you're entitled to whatever answers I have," said Felix.

"That's what I'd expect," she said. "But some of my fellow clients don't seem to be playing square with me." He started to speak, but she silenced him with a graceful wave of her hand. "I know that Silas Dinch called you today about his failure to recover the cadenza after paying the ransom. He called me too, and said that he'd spoken to Anton, Peter, and you. Mr. McKay, I'm beginning to despair of our ever getting it back. My great fear is that it no longer exists—that it's been destroyed. After hearing what Silas had to say, I was extremely upset and confused. I called Peter for his opinion as to what had happened in the cemetery. His reaction astounded me. He was very abrupt, downright rude. I know he's leaving for Philadelphia tonight and has a major concert day after tomorrow; I can understand his being edgy about *that*. But I've never heard him so short-tempered. And when I tried to talk to him about this ransom business, he—well, he developed the oddest *tone* and muttered something about its being a hoax—that the cadenza still existed, but was passing about from hand to hand. There was a—a *fishiness* about his answers that disturbed me greatly—not like Peter at all."

She paused to take a deep drag on her cigarette, and the gold bracelet flashed like a firefly. "Next I called Anton; he wasn't at work, but was home sick. He's had a terrible cold. The call from Silas had prostrated him—he was horribly distraught, almost incoherent. It took a full minute for him to calm down enough to talk sensibly. And that's not like Anton—he's usually so calm and in command of his feelings."

"What did he think had happened?"

"He's convinced that the cadenza's lost and gone forever, has no hope that it will ever be recovered. I would've talked to Clara, but she's involved in some sort of Arthur Foote celebration in Cambridge and wasn't available. I couldn't reach Rosamond Foxe. So in desperation I called you, not knowing where else to turn." She stopped and looked at him expectantly.

"What do you want to know?" he asked, feeling his way.

"I want you to tell me candidly whether you and Miss Trntl think the cadenza has been destroyed. If it still exists, do you think we have any chance of getting it back? And then, I want your thoughts on what this phony ransom attempt means."

Felix nodded. "After you called this afternoon, I talked to Trntl in Baltimore. We don't think the cadenza's been destroyed. We believe the ransom demand was a swindle by an opportunist who never did possess it."

She tamped out her cigarette and lit another. "In other words, someone who saw a chance for an easy fifty-eight thousand dollars."

"Right. And not the same person who made the first ransom call. We think *that* man was a petty hoodlum who's now off the scene."

"But if the cadenza hasn't been destroyed," she cried, "where *is* it? Passing about from hand to hand as Peter thinks?"

"Possibly. Or lying hidden waiting to be found. We think it's still in Baltimore."

"Then there's still a chance we can get it back?"

"Sure," said Felix, expressing more confidence than he felt.

She gave a great sigh and sank back in her chair. "You've relieved my mind considerably, Mr. McKay. I was afraid that you, too, would see the matter as hopeless. It's all very upsetting. I'm going to have a glass of Scotch." She leaned forward and unstoppered the decanter. "Please join me, Mr. McKay, I don't want to drink alone—and may I call you Felix? There's ice in this bucket—or, if you prefer, you can have it neat."

"I'd prefer ice, thanks."

She tonged ice cubes into two tall glasses and poured the whiskey. "Charles introduced me to the pleasures of Scotch," she said, as they settled back with their drinks. "I didn't drink at all before I met him. My father was a Methodist minister, a fiery-eyed teetotaler, and Prohibition was in force. After Charles and I were married in 1925, we lived in France for several years, and there I learned to appreciate wine. But Charles always drank Scotch—and always neat. He couldn't abide any sort of additive or dilutent. And after I tried Scotch, I found I liked it too—but I do want ice in mine."

She stared reflectively into the fire. "Charles had a rule of never drinking while he was working on a major composition. While writing his Sixth Symphony, he didn't touch a drop of alcohol for nearly three months. Then, when the symphony was finished, he polished off three fifths of Scotch in two days—all by himself."

Felix smiled. "He must have been a remarkable man."

"Oh, he was. I've never known a person who could match his capacity for work. It was almost an obsession with him. He was always practicing or composing. During the first twelve years of our marriage he kept up a full concert schedule, touring the United States, South America, Europe. And still he kept the compositions coming. After 1938, he limited himself to eight public concerts a year, sometimes with symphony orchestras, sometimes in solo performance—frequently premiering his new works."

"It's amazing how much he wrote to have died at forty-six," said Felix, recalling Torvald's notes.

"It *is* amazing," she agreed. "Eight hundred and twelve separate works, two hundred forty-eight opus numbers." Her voice was vibrant with pride. "Eleven symphonies, eighteen major concertos, one for cello; three for flute; two for violin; three for clarinet; one for saxophone; three for French horn; five for piano—"

"I have recordings of all the clarinet concertos," Felix said.

"—two orchestral suites, six serenades for strings and brass choir; twelve piano sonatas; four string trios; nine quartets; six piano quintets; the *Adirondack Interludes, Custer's Last Stand*, the Fantasy for violin, harp, and jazz trio; *Five Meditations on Melrose Abbey for Piano 4-Hands;* the "Natchez Trace" septet for winds; the *Elegy for Jane Addams*; *Mardi Gras*; *Harvest Home*; the *Walden Rhapsody*; the *Yankee Doodle* and *Shenandoah Variations*; *Years of Decision—*"

"I've always liked the *Shenandoah Variations*," said Felix.

"—nineteen violin sonatas, three ballades for oboe and harp, sixty-four songs, and literally hundreds of solo piano works—impromptus, eclogues, the *Urban Sketches*, nocturnes, fantasias, rhapsodies, epigrams." She clearly took great delight in rattling them off. With her head thrown back, her eyes closed, her fingers ticking off items in the air, the wattles of loose flesh swaying, jiggling beneath her upper arm, she seemed in a kind of rapture.

"Incredible," said Felix.

"Much of his composing was done here, in this house, which he inherited from his grandfather in 1932."

"How did you meet him?"

"He was just twenty-three, in the early stages of his concert career, but already with a list of published works. I was only twenty, living in Pittsburgh with my family. I heard Charles perform Chopin's Second Piano Concerto and was simply bowled over. He was so handsome and full of vitality, and played with such beauty, such authority and competence! Three weeks later, when I was visiting friends in Detroit, I heard him give a solo recital—and at that point I decided I had to meet him. A friend of mine was studying at the Hopewell Conservatory in Syracuse, where Charles was teaching theory and composition; she arranged an introduction, and Charles and I were married five months later."

Felix thought it was an interesting story and said so. Recalling Anton's long-winded narrative on the front steps, he added: "Didn't Charles also teach private students?"

"Only after we returned from France and moved in here," she replied. She tossed back the remainder of her drink and set the empty glass on the table. "A total of twenty-two students—some for less than a year. None of them went on to concert careers. Charles hoped that Anton would show musical talent, but he never did. This was a disappointment to him. He was pleased when Clara showed early musical aptitude, and he gave her much encouragement. He lived to see her doing quite well on the flute—but she was only thirteen when he died."

"How did he find time and energy to do so much?" Felix asked. People like Charles gave him a large pain.

"Well, he worked *constantly*. He didn't have any hobbies, wasn't interested in sports or literature. He read very little, as a matter of fact. We had a limited social life, and he didn't travel except to give concerts." (Felix thought, Correction: according to Anton, Charles *hadn't* worked constantly; and he'd had one very time- and energy-consuming hobby he'd pursued with zeal.)

"As you might imagine, his compulsion to work was hard on the rest of us," Mrs. Farringford continued. "We had to develop our own interests and social contacts. I traveled with the children to a few places, and took up bridge. Ironically, though, despite his working so hard, we were never financially well-off." Her tone took on a hint of hostility: "Charles wasn't a good businessman. Many of his early works, both here and in Europe, he simply sold outright for a flat fee—never receiving any royalties from them. Later, when he became a regular with Lunner & Dinch, I insisted on contracts that stipulated royalties. Mr. Lunner was very generous, and so was Silas's father, though less so. The royalties have provided us a continuous but modest income, and many of Charles's compositions have been used in film scores—which has helped considerably."

She took his empty glass and refilled it. "Don't misunderstand me, please. Charles was a good husband, attentive and considerate. A thoughtful, caring father. He always took an interest in the children's schoolwork, their triumphs, their childhood griefs. I've always considered it a rare privilege to have been married to such a great musical genius—a man looked up to and admired the world over. This house once saw a continual steam of international celebrities—composers, conductors, performers—visiting to talk shop or pay Charles homage."

"That must've been a good experience for the children," said Felix.

"Well, you know how children are. They took it in stride, the big names didn't mean anything to them. Anton went into accounting and worked up to a very responsible position in the trust division at Swinfurth Lightfoot. He lived here for ten years after Charles died, and was a great comfort to me in my loneliness, providing me company and a small monthly allowance for living expenses. I don't think a mother could wish for a son more loyal, devoted, and dutiful than Anton." She paused for a moment, smoking. "Clara, though, was more self-centered. She left home at eighteen to pursue her musical career. Went to the Hastings Institute and the Hopewell Conservatory, and settled in Boston. Now, I won't say that she's been an undutiful daughter; she's always been there when I needed her. But she's also maintained a determined distance. She almost got married when she was twenty-six—to a most unsuitable man, a newspaper reporter from Amherst. He would've stifled her career and kept her from developing her talent. Fortunately, she came to see what a mistake it would've been, broke off the relationship, kept the Farringford name, and went on with her career. And she's done quite well, all things considered." She lit another cigarette and leaned back swirling the ice in her glass. "Now tell me about yourself, Felix. Are you married?"

"Not any more," he answered, a little flustered by the abrupt turn in the conversation. He was finding the fire unpleasantly warm, and the whiskey was numbing his lips. "I was living in Wisconsin. My wife found she preferred a high school coach turned principal. He played a fast game of tennis."

"Oh dear. And you didn't play?"

"Only the clarinet, which was part of the problem. My wife felt I was neglecting her for nights in a jazz-band. And I suppose I was."

She lunged forward quickly, her cigarette swooping an orange arc. "Jazz clarinet! Oh, that *is* exciting, Felix. Charles introduced me to jazz when we were planning to be married, and showed me how to appreciate it."

"Playing in the band was a great pleasure," he said. "But I gave that up when I came to New York, and I find I miss it."

"Do you still play the clarinet?"

"For myself. Occasionally I jam with friends. I was pretty good in my heyday, I must admit."

She stood up suddenly. "Would you like to see Charles's studio? Not many people have had the opportunity in the last twenty years. But you have the sensitivity to appreciate seeing where he worked."

"I'd very much like to," said Felix. Once on his feet, he discovered that his balance was none too steady. And now his nose was numb, too.

"It's at the rear of the house," she said, starting for the hall. "In what was once a large back parlor. Clara used it for practicing while she lived here, but when she went to school, I arranged things the way Charles had left them and simply closed the door."

They were walking tipsily down the dim hallway past the stairs and the open door of a formal dining room. With a little giggle Mrs. Farringford leaned up against Felix and gripped his arm. "Scotch," she smiled, clinging to him for support. She smelled faintly of orange blossoms. "Clara accuses me of maintaining the studio like a shrine. But that's not true. It's really Anton who can't bear to have anything changed. He idolized his father, and I respect his wishes. Everything is just as it was."

They had reached a paneled door at the end of the hall. Mrs. Farringford turned the knob and ushered Felix into a dark room, quite cold, with stagnant air permeated by a faint musty odor. "I'm sorry about the chill," she said as she fumbled for the light switch. "Since this room's never used, I close off the heat registers."

Felix felt a thrill of excitement. After the buildup he wasn't quite sure what to expect; perhaps Charles Philip himself, embalmed or mummified, sitting at his piano—or, at the very least, as a portrait draped in black velvet. When the overhead light switched on, he felt a letdown. The studio was drab and ordinary: a large square room with three tall windows at the back and two on one side—all tightly shuttered against the night. A long plush sofa—The Couch of Anton's narrative?—ran along the windowless wall. It was flanked by shelves containing phonograph records— 78's for the most part, in their heavy cardboard albums, with some 45's. Opposite them, a console phonograph stood between the two side windows. The remaining available wall space was filled with shelves and cabinets containing complete editions of composers' works, stacks of sheet music, and reference books. In the center of the room, its lid down, its keyboard covered, a nine-foot grand piano squatted like a cenotaph. The harsh light revealed cobwebs in the corners of the room and a thin film of dust covering everything.

"I rarely come in here," said Mrs. Farringford. "I find it depressing. Charles used to have plants in hanging pots in front of all the windows. At night he always closed the shutters."

Felix approached the piano, touched it reverently, and raised the cover off the keys. "May I?"

"Of course." He struck a G-major chord and ran his fingers quickly up and down an octave scale. The sound was atrocious, and the F-sharp key wouldn't raise up after he'd pressed it.

"I'm afraid it's badly out of tune," said Mrs. Farringford. "I stopped having it tuned after Clara left. One of my necessary economies."

He closed the cover, rubbed the grit off his fingers.

"And over here," Mrs. Farringford continued, indicating a large cabinet on the rear wall, "are all of Charles's published works. And there, at the left end of the sofa, are all the recordings he made— Beethoven, Chopin, Hibbert, Bessemer, Brahms, Denby, Bartok, Granados, Ravel—and of course many of his own compositions. I suppose you've never heard any of his recordings—though a few have been reissued on LP during the last thirty years."

"I have his recording of Gershwin's *Concerto in F*," said Felix, "some Fauré, and a budget release of his performance of his Third Piano Concerto."

"Oh, good!" she said. "Then you know something of his playing. I'm glad." She was standing by the light switch, her hand poised. He took the cue and stepped quickly into the hall. She turned off the light, and, giving a deep sigh (either of grief or of resignation, Felix couldn't determine which), closed the door behind her. Felix waited for her to join him.

"It's been very lonely since the children moved out. It took me years to get over Charles's death; and though one has to make adjustments and go on, still the loss and emptiness are always present, and sometimes the pain of knowing what loneliness means goes through me like a skewer." She was lagging behind, wiping at her eyes with the back of her hand. "I'm sorry, Felix, to be going on like this. For some reason, I feel the loneliness very keenly just now. Going into the studio again, talking with you about the old times—they've just reminded me of what I've had to do without—"

Felix stopped and faced her in concern. "I'm sorry if my interest has caused you pain—"

"Oh, no! No, Felix. It's not your fault!" She reached out and gently seized his arm, giving it a reassuring squeeze, and pressing it to her. "I enjoy talking with you. It's not often I meet a man so serious-minded, so sensitive, so honest and straightforward, so—well, in a word—*exciting*." She smiled coyly and gave the back of his hand a playful pat. And again they were in the parlor, returning to their chairs. She reached for his glass to refill it, and he raised his hand in protest. "Don't you want a nightcap?" she asked.

"I've had enough, thanks," Felix said with a smile. "I'm feeling the effects."

"Ah, well then." She replaced the stopper in the decanter. "So am I. I suppose I should call it quits, too. Clara always says I don't know my limit."

Felix glanced at his watch. It was getting on to ten. "I really should be going. I have some work to do before meeting with another client in the morning." This wasn't true, but was plausible enough to get him gracefully out of the house. And he wanted out: his business with Mrs. Farringford was clearly concluded. He wasn't so sure about her business with him.

"Well, if you *must* go." Her voice indicated her disappointment. "I do thank you for coming. Talking with you has set my mind at ease that we still may recover Charles's cadenza. Please keep me informed of developments. And if Trntl & Associates does find the manuscript, I'd appreciate your calling me immediately. I'd prefer not to have to hear it from Silas Dinch—who irritated me greatly today with his patronizing tone. Will you promise to let me know?"

"Of course," said Felix, rising casually and edging toward the door. "Either Trntl or I will contact you immediately."

As he was putting on his coat, she said "Perhaps you'd play your clarinet for me sometime. I'd like that very much."

"Well, thank you. But I'm really out of practice." Which wasn't true either; but it served to get him out the door. She waved him down the steps and went inside.

Hurrying down the sidewalk, he systematically reviewed their conversation. He'd certainly learned some interesting things about Charles Farringford's personality and work habits. If Anton were correct in what he'd said, there were some things about her husband that Mrs. Farringford didn't know. She was undoubtedly strong-willed and possibly domineering in her relationship with Anton and Clara, and Clara's standoffishness was obviously painful to her. He really felt sorry for Mrs. Farringford. A lonely old woman rattling around in that big house, surrounded by reminders of a better time. With only her memories to keep her company, angry and hurt at the hands she'd been dealt since 1947.

A tough old bird, thought Felix—maybe *not* a kestrel; a cormorant, perhaps. Something of a romantic, but practical, trying hard to stay in the running. By God, he hoped they *did* get the cadenza back, if only to brighten her path at the end of a long and difficult journey. Was there anything in the conversation that Trntl needed to know tonight? No; the report could wait. He started his car and headed down to SoHo.

Abbott reached Philadelphia on the Metroliner at nine p.m., totally unstrung by the mind-blitz he'd suffered during the afternoon. Having checked into his hotel, he aimlessly wandered the streets staring blankly into shop windows. He hadn't eaten since breakfast; and a little after ten-thirty, suddenly weak with hunger, he stopped at a confectionery where he wolfed down a hot fudge sundae, two eclairs, and three large cream-puffs. Before leaving, he purchased a two-pound box of chocolate-covered caramels, half of which he devoured in his hotel room before turning out the light.

All night long, he squirrel-caged on his sweat-soaked bed struggling to comprehend the afternoon's grotesque turn of events. Again and again he cycled through the unanswerable questions. How had *Anton* come to be the one holding the cadenza for ransom? Anton was one of those who wanted it *back!* How had he obtained Morris Waite's briefcase? Surely *he* hadn't killed the Simms girl. Did Anton believe that the briefcase actually contained the cadenza? or had he known all along that it really held only a mischmasch of Brahms? *Brahms!* Each time he got to this point, Abbott would thrash and pound his pillow, giving vent to whimpers and hiccuping sobs.

The mind endures only so much of being whiplashed, and then it falters. Still stunned and reeling from the shock it had received in the cemetery, Abbott's had soared home on a gust of elation, exulting in victory, afire with anticipation at seeing, hearing the Farringford Cadenza before he destroyed the manuscript. And then—oh God! the second shock! Confronted with such trauma, the mind goes blank, can only twitch and gibber.

Reason and judgment paralyzed, the body explodes into physical frenzy. But when this is spent—the running back and forth across the room, the beating on walls, the smashing of Steuben glass, the consigning to flames of the detestable Brahms—and the mind tries to regroup its far-flung tatters, it butts up against the ultimate and irreducible question: *Where's the cadenza now?*

Unless, of course, there *was* no cadenza. Only that piss-ant Pettigrew had identified it. Maybe the whole thing *was* a fraud, a damnable lie got up by Pettigrew for his personal aggrandizement. Only three people claimed to have seen the manuscript, and two of them were dead. Had Pettigrew killed them to keep his secret? Anything seemed possible.

The final horror: there was no way Abbott could talk to anyone about any of this. To do so, he'd have to admit to knowledge that he'd had no legitimate way of acquiring, and reveal his true motive for wanting to recover the cadenza. Having burned both the briefcase and the Brahms, he couldn't go to Dinch and disclose Anton's betrayal—there'd be no proof; couldn't confront Anton or threaten him with exposure—he'd simply deny it; couldn't even let Trntl know what he'd learned.

But with the certainty that one knows the presence of an abscessed tooth—a red-hot coal confined and raging in the maxillary sinus—Abbott knew that the cadenza was *still out there*, waiting to be found. As dawn spread its dingy gray light through his room, he dragged himself from the tangled sheets, sat on the side of the bed in his drenched pajamas, and finished the box of chocolate-covered caramels.

All the while that Abbott was traveling to Philadelphia, wandering the streets, and groaning through his sleepless night, Anton Farringford was at his computer working frantically to balance the embezzled trust accounts. Under his feet, in Dinch's black suitcase, fifty-eight thousand three hundred dollars; at his fingertips, the means by which it would save him from the gallows.

Anton, too, had been emotionally drained by the day's events. The cemetery caper had exhausted him and done his cold no good. After leaving the briefcase at the HODGES monument, he'd come home and immediately called Dinch to tell him where the cadenza could be retrieved. He'd thought everything was settled then; that he could dismiss it from mind and get on with his financial restitution. But then Dinch had called to report that, though the money was gone, the cadenza had not been delivered. The news had knocked the stuffing out of him.

Someone else must've found the briefcase. One of those gravediggers? a caretaker? a Hodge?

Well then, it was gone forever. No one who got the briefcase open would have the faintest idea what they had in their possession. The capstone of his father's work would *just be thrown away!* Guilt and despair had combined to funk him nearly speechless; and when his mother had called to share *her* funk, he'd snapped and growled at her simply to get her off the line.

But now his own survival was a far more pressing matter. Fortunately he'd have all of Saturday and Sunday to work on it. By four o'clock he'd sternly resolved not to think about the cadenza until sometime Monday morning. He'd brewed a pot of coffee and gone to his computer; and there he was when Twila Bidwell came home from work chatty with gossip; and there he was again, after a ten-minute break for a supper of warmed-up leftovers. And all through the evening, while Twila chafed and pottered about the apartment, muttering under her breath, and later watched TV with the volume turned stridently loud.

At one-thirty, seeing that she'd gone to sleep in her chair, he turned off the TV, and there they'd sat, Anton grinding away with his figures, Twila snoring softly, until, at three, she'd roused herself and—making snide comments about his preferring arithmetic to sex—gone shambling off to bed.

Chapter 23

March 7 (Saturday)

Victor Zyzynski's breakfast was less than satisfying. Tasteless grapefruit, a grilled haddock no better than yesterday's perch, hash-brown potatoes with the consistency of glue, cornbread with currant jam that crumbled and went nasty-sticky in his hand. Wilson brought him the telephone-recorder as he was finishing his coffee. "Last night's calls, sir; and the written report from Willett and Strunk."

"Very good. Tell Brim that his haddock was undistinguished and that I'll have perch again tomorrow. Toast and honey. Cantaloupe instead of grapefruit." He punched the button on the phone-recorder, and Wilson left for the kitchen.

Of several calls, the only one of interest was Chip's from Baltimore. A dutiful report that Dinch had paid the ransom but, when summoned back to the cemetery to pick up the cadenza, had found no trace of it *or* the money. (No news there: Zyzynski had learned all of it yesterday afternoon, when Morgan Latimer had called him to say that his ten thousand was gone: "It must have been a hoax, Victor, a vicious trick to get the money. Silas returned to Mount Myrtle Cemetery as fast as he could, but found nothing."

"I thought you told me it was Mount Olivet," Zyzynski had said, far more casually than he'd felt.

"I believe I did," said Latimer. "A simple mistake. What difference does it make?"

The difference it made was that Willett and Strunk had spent two hours wandering around the wrong cemetery watching in vain for Dinch's arrival, scrutinizing with binoculars everyone who came to visit a loved one's grave. Strunk had even been pressed into service as an emergency pallbearer at an ill-attended funeral for a MARTINSON, who seemed to have no friends.

Old fool Latimer, Zyzynski had fumed, couldn't even keep his cemeteries straight. "We did what we could," he told the stock-broker. "The money's not the important thing. I stand ready to contribute again if there's another ransom demand." And that was that.)

Of much greater interest was Chip's statement that Trntl was planning to answer both classified ads in the *Sun*. And of greatest interest was the news that Trntl's New York office had been searched ("a smooth job"), and that Jerry had observed her being followed (skillfully) by a tall blond woman wearing expensive clothes.

This was highly disturbing information. He sat for a long time puffing his cigar and staring out the window. Okay, meeting the ransom demand had been a gamble that had cost him ten thousand dollars. A negligible amount; best to forget it. What concerned him now was finding out who'd searched Trntl's office, and who the blond woman was. Professionals. Like Marco, Jerry, and Chip. Trained agents. In all likelihood, the Count's.

Zyzynski still hadn't recovered from his interview with Client Abel two nights before. Disgusting little snot, with his superior ways, his name-dropping, his audacity in trying to bluff Zyzynski, to fake him out and give the impression that *he* was the one on top of things! Clearly, the Count was his chief adversary. And Zyzynski was determined to win. He placed a call to the Cavendish Hotel. "Marco? Got your message. Place a watch on that other post office box; see who picks up Trntl's response to the ad. Find out everything you can about the blond woman Jerry spotted. I think the item we're seeking is still in Baltimore."

Shortly after ten o'clock that morning, just after Marco and Jerry had finished a leisurely breakfast in their room and settled down to a game of cribbage, a hurried knock came: three—two—three. When Marco opened the door, Chip stuck his head in: "Nobody's left Trntl's room this morning. But a short middle-aged man just arrived with a small suitcase and let himself in with a key."

"A new player," said Marco. "Get back to six and watch that door." Chip hurried away.

"Is Trntl calling reinforcements?" Jerry grinned, as they returned to their game. "Another of her associates, I suppose. How many does she have, for crissake?"

"The Chief said three," Marco answered, staring at his cards.

Jerry lit a small cigar. "What a shitty assignment! Nothing to do but loaf around in hotel rooms, and shadow a skirt—"

"And keep her from getting killed," said Marco.

Jerry poured himself another cup of coffee. "Granted, we had to sit around in that strange hotel in Cairo for almost a month, and it took us a week and a half to dismantle the Assumption Window at Edelstein Abbey—but we were busy every day."

"Twelve days in Bangkok," said Marco. "Lots of sitting there."

"But *there* we were waiting for the opportune moment. *Here* we're just waiting."

"We've been in Baltimore a week," said Marco. "It seems like a month." He threw down his cards. "I'm sick of cribbage! A stupid game!"

Jerry continued sipping his coffee. "Do you want to go back to chess?"

"No, I'm sick of chess."

"Poker?"

"Boring with just two players."

"Strip poker?"

Marco wrinkled his nose. "We'd need more players to make it interesting. A few broads—"

"That's against the Chief's rules."

"But I know you too *well*, Jerry. There's no mystery or excitement left."

"Oh, come on."

Marco was inclined to pout. "Loser will have to—you know—into the coffee pot."

"You're disgusting," said Jerry, without removing the cigar from his mouth. "Okay. You're on. We'll use a fresh deck of cards."

Marco cleared the table while Jerry broke open and shuffled a new deck.

"Aren't we going to put on more clothes?" asked Marco. "It'll make the game last longer."

"You're right. Put on as many items as you like." They went through their suitcases and the disguise kit, piling on additional clothing: two pairs of socks, three shirts, an extra belt, the phony eyeglasses, the gray wig, a necktie each. One thing Jerry had learned in the Special Forces was to guard his flank; he wasn't about to be the loser. So while Marco was pulling on a second pair of pants, Jerry raided the closet and put on his own windbreaker, adding on Chip's topcoat, scarf, and porkpie hat. When they returned to the table, Marco was visibly shaken. "You're cheating."

"You could have gone to the closet," said Jerry, lighting a fresh cigar. "Shut up and deal."

They played the first hand, and Jerry removed the hat.

They were down to their skivvies when the red light flashed on the telephone. "Well, she's making a call at last," Jerry said, flipping on the tape recorder.

"Hello?" A woman's voice.

"Hi, honey." A man's voice they'd not heard before. "I thought I'd call to let you know where to reach me. I really lucked out and got a room at the Cavendish Hotel—where most of the convention meetings will be held. Room 609. The hotel is full-up, but somebody checked out late last night, and the room was available when I walked in this morning. I thought I'd have to commute in every day!"

Stony-eyed, Jerry puffed steadily at his cigar. Marco sat finger-combing the hairs on his chest. "How are things in Dayton?" the man asked. "You having the bridge club in today as you'd planned?"

"This afternoon," she said. "I've got brownies and cupcakes in the oven. Yesterday Henry had a runny nose, but I made him go to school anyway."

"I saw Barney Wolff down in the lobby. You remember him from graduate school?"

"Sure. The one with the twitch."

"Yeah. Well, he's nearly bald now. He's giving a paper tomorrow on Teddy Roosevelt's *real* feelings toward William Howard Taft. He says it'll be a bombshell."

"Are you going to hear it?"

"No, I'll be reading mine at the same time. Just think, Betty, I'm finally giving a paper at the Mid-Atlantic Historical Association!"

"I'm proud of you, Harry." And it went on this way for another two minutes till, with mutual I-miss-you's and lip-smackings, they hung up. Marco threw down his cards. "Harry and Betty?" He lurched to his feet and started for the door. "Trntl's gone! We've got to tell Chip!"

"Well, put your clothes on first," said Jerry, thrusting a leg into his pants. "People will think you're a pervert." While Marco got dressed, Jerry rewound the tape of the telephone call. So Trntl had eluded them. Her leaving could mean several things—one of them not at all pleasant to contemplate.

When Chip came in, he was flushed and defensive. "Marco says Trntl and her friends are gone—that there's a historian from Dayton in their room. Listen, I've been down there watching since before seven. None of 'em left the room."

"*You* listen." And Jerry played him the tape.

"Oh hell," said Chip.

"They must've gone late last night. *How* isn't as important as *why.*" They sat down at the table.

"Maybe they just changed rooms," Marco suggested.

They called the desk and asked for N. F. Trntl's current number. "Sorry, sir, that person is no longer a guest of the hotel."

"Did she leave a forwarding address?"

"We're not at liberty to say." They hung up.

"Well, we've lost her," Chip said. "Has she gone back to New York? Is she still in town but at another hotel?"

"There are four reasons why she'd go back to New York," said Jerry. "One is, that she's given up the search."

"Not likely," said Marco. "She's getting paid to stay on the job."

"Or, she's been scared off by the attempts to kill her—"

"Don't think so," said Chip.

"Or else," Jerry continued, "the cadenza's somehow gotten into Dinch's hands—like maybe the ransom thing worked out after all. Or else—" and here was the bad one "—Trntl's found the cadenza."

"If that's the case," said Chip, "the Chief will turn us into headcheese." He slammed his fist into his palm. "Godammit, we've never failed an assignment yet!"

"Don't panic," said Marco. "No calls have come through saying the cadenza has actually turned up in New York. And if she'd found it here, she'd have called Dinch or the Farringfords to let them know."

"At any rate," said Chip, "the Chief doesn't have to know about this till we learn more."

There was no disagreement on that.

"So what do we do now?" Jerry asked. "Shall we call all the hotels in town to see if Trntl's registered?"

"Or call her firm in New York to see if she's returned?" said Marco.

"Let's call the hotels first," said Jerry. "I'll start down the list." He opened the directory with a deep sigh.

"And I'll go check the post office box," said Chip.

As Marco and Jerry were starting their game of strip poker, three miles away in the private conference room at CIMACORP, Lefty Scaevola, in shirt sleeves and loosened tie, was having a serious talk with Giovanni Speranza, who had arrived from Newark on Friday afternoon. "Sorry to call you back on such short notice," Lefty was saying. "How's Tony doing?"

"Just fine," said Speranza, "his uncle's keeping him on a short leash."

"That's good," said Lefty, selecting a cigar and offering the box. "Vinnie knows how to raise a boy. And he knows he can count on me for a return favor." He lit Speranza's cigar and then his own. "You're my best trouble-shooter, Johnny; a person I can count on to do a job and do it right. I think you're due for a promotion."

He paused, and Speranza looked at him attentively. "A man should be rewarded for good service," Lefty went on. "Should be shown he's appreciated. Those who don't do their jobs, or fuck up their assignments, have to be retired. We've got a retirement, Johnny, and a vacancy that needs filling."

Speranza studied the short ash on the end of his cigar.

"Angelo Torelli is leaving us," said Lefty. "He and a guy named George Fiocco—you know George?—they bungled an assignment badly; failed in their mission and got arrested. Yesterday afternoon they both were bonded out, but it's not in anybody's interest that they should stand trial. As far as the court's concerned, they'll have jumped bail. What we need is someone to take 'em on a boat-ride—you get my drift. It'll have to be by tomorrow at the latest. And then someone will have to finish Angelo's assignment. Do you think you can manage all that?"

"I can handle it," said Speranza.

Lefty glanced at his watch: ten minutes till his meeting with the Congressman. "The assignment is a woman detective named N. F. Trntl—t-r-n-t-l—who's come to be a major pain. She told the police there's a connection between Tony and the death of that Morris guy. She's mentioned my name. She's trying to file felony charges against Angelo and George. On Tuesday, she's scheduled to testify at the inquest into the shooting of the Simms girl—Angelo's first fuckup. Now, this Trntl could say all sorts of troublesome things at the inquest. She mustn't get the chance. But she can't just disappear; it's too late for that—there'd be lots of questions. She's got to have an accident. It's gotta look so good there won't *be* any questions. Can you arrange it, Johnny?"

"Yes, I can. How can she be reached?"

"She's been staying at the Cavendish Hotel with one of her men friends; but we learned this morning from our Downtown Source that she checked out last night and moved over to the Macready, Room 523, where she's registered under the name of Carol Brown."

"What's her boyfriend like?"

"A tall blond guy named Torvald Grimsson, who knows karate. He broke George's wrist."

"Is this Trntl the one who's trying to find the music that got Tony in trouble?"

"Yeah. Angelo said she wants the music in the worst way. He used it as bait to hook her in. But somehow she turned the tables on him and got away. There's no way she coulda done it alone. That Grimsson guy musta helped. We had to pry Angelo out of a steel drum, and Joe Blanco, he'd been doused in wet cement and hung from the ceiling. All the guys are talking about it. Maybe you'll want Angelo to give you the details." He passed Speranza a piece of paper. "Trntl has a rented car; here's its description and license number."

"Which men can I use?"

"Benno's laid up with a fractured skull, and I've transferred Joe to Atlantic City. Alfredo's a possibility, and Frank. But you've got a free hand to choose your own people. Just let me know who." Scaevola patted his shoulder. "I've got an appointment. You leave by that door, I'll go out the front way. I want fast action on this, Johnny." He shrugged on his suitcoat, adjusted his tie, and left.

Smiling, Speranza lounged a minute savoring his cigar, then departed by the rear door with a springing step, rolling his shoulders like a basketball star who'd just scored a tie-breaker in the game's last second.

In Philadelphia, the sun was shining in a cloudless sky; but for Peter Shipley Abbott, the day was dark. To say that his rehearsal with the Symphony Orchestra was going badly would be a charitable understatement. It was a disaster.

Abbott knew Farringford's Fourth Concerto upside down and backwards, had performed it twelve times in concert with the finest orchestras; but today his mind kept wandering to Brahms. His stomach was sour, his timing off, his fingers traitorous. Gustav Niedermann, appearing with the orchestra for the first time as guest conductor, was appalled. He'd never seen Abbott play so ineptly; had, as a matter of fact, performed the same concerto with him in 1975 in Los Angeles—brilliantly. He wondered if Abbott was doing drugs.

Again and again they stumbled through the first movement, Abbott and the orchestra at sixes and sevens, Niedermann pausing frequently to exercise his celebrated diplomacy, smiling ever more tightly as his patience wore thin. My God, if Abbott didn't do better than this tomorrow night, he'd make them all look incompetent! He, Niedermann, a laughingstock in Philadelphia! "Ladies and gentlemen," he said finally, clutching the baton across his chest with both hands, almost as though it were a willow switch, "let's take a ten-minute break."

"No, no," said Abbott, wiping his forehead with a damp handkerchief. "Let's leave this and go on to the second movement."

"As you wish." Niedermann faced the orchestra. "The second movement, please." To the woodwinds: "Ladies and gentlemen, the clarinets must be *marcato*—and aggressive in the first twelve measures; in measures nine through twelve, the saxophones gradually emerge to dominate in thirteen." The movement began well, but at bar thirty-five, Abbott botched his entry. Niedermann flagged everybody down and distractedly ran a hand through his hair. The concert-master, a bearded chap named Osgood, sucked his mustache grimly.

"I'm sorry," said Abbott. "Let's try it again."

He tried to center his mind on the opposing chromatic runs that marked his entry, but instead found himself focusing once again on the pear-shaped figure of Anton Farringford scuttling from the yew bushes to place the briefcase behind the HODGES tombstone. Abbott managed to negotiate his entry, and this time they got to bar fifty-seven before Niedermann called a halt. The conductor was flushed a dusky purple, his eyes squeezed shut. Bathed in clammy sweat, Abbott sat stiffly, his fingers poised twitching above the keys. Osgood half-turned in his chair and glared at him ferociously down the length of his violin.

"Ladies and gentlemen, a thirty-minute break," Niedermann said evenly, not opening his eyes. "We shall do better when we're refreshed." He stepped down from the podium and hurried off the stage without once looking at Abbott. The harp and three cellos distinctly heard him mutter *"Scheisskopf!"*

When Felix McKay arrived at the office at ten-thirty, he'd begun a systematic inventory of the files to see whether anything was missing after the black bag search. He'd gotten halfway through the C's before he gave the job up as hopeless. He didn't know everything that had been in the folders; they weren't all his cases, and even in those cases the Associates had worked jointly, each of them would add new things to the files from time to time. Since Trntl had been particularly interested in the Farringford file, he hauled it out for scrutiny. It was already quite thick—what with Torvald's initial research on Farringford's death, transcriptions of the Baltimore reports, Torvald's and Trntl's investigation of Scaevola's operations, and sundry biographical and background jottings on the clients themselves.

As he looked through the papers, he mentally ticked off the things he remembered. He glanced through the accounts of Farringford's death and public funeral, re-read the biographical summary of Rosamond Foxe, and once again looked through the list of her recordings, making pencil checks beside six that he wanted to purchase. Then he leaned back in his swivel chair, propped his feet on the desk, and swung off into thoughts of fair Rosamond. Twenty minutes later he roused himself from his fantasies and hustled off to Brooklyn for a scheduled appointment with a client—a woman who'd engaged the firm to discover the whereabouts of her missing niece. They'd found the niece living in Scarsdale; she'd told them in no uncertain terms that she wished to remain missing, and had nothing to say to her meddling aunt. After making his report to the aunt—which proved a most discouraging and difficult task—Felix heartily empathized with the niece and wished her well.

After a quick lunch, he returned to the office. Still wearing his coat, he'd just tilted back in his chair for a nap, when the phone rang. The voice of an elderly woman asking for N. F. Trntl.

"She's not here, I'm afraid. I'm Felix McKay, one of her Associates. May I help you?"

"I'm Mrs. Leopold Sternberg. I wrote a letter to Miss Trntl several days ago. Do you know if she received it?"

Felix reached across his desk, glanced into Trntl's INCOMING box, where the letter lay three items down. "Yes, it arrived, Mrs. Sternberg. But Miss Trntl hasn't seen it yet. She's out of the city working on a case."

"I was hoping to have heard from her by now. The matter is very important to me. When will she be back?"

"I'm not trying to be evasive, Mrs. Sternberg, but that's very hard to say. She's in Baltimore working on an extremely complex case—"

"Trying to find the Farringford Cadenza," said Mrs. Sternberg. "I'm in close contact with Mr. Morgan Latimer, and through him I'm closely following developments. It's in regard to the Farringford Cadenza that I wish to speak with her."

"I see," said Felix, bouncing forward in his chair, snatching up a pen. "I'll be calling her later this afternoon; if you wish, I'll tell her that you want to talk to her. Or would you prefer to call her yourself? I have her number."

"She's probably busy. No, have her call me after six tonight at the following unlisted number." When she'd rung off, Felix studied her letter by holding it up to the sunlight. The envelope was an expensive laid paper, nicely textured. Her return address had been printed as part of a letterhead set. Trntl's address had been typewritten with a good carbon ribbon.

Mrs. Leopold G. Sternberg. It was a name he'd encountered somewhere fairly recently. Sternberg. Was it a name Rachel Weintraub had mentioned, when he and she and Torvald were at the play two weeks ago? No, he'd seen the name in print. He pulled over the Farringford file, flipped through it until he came to the news accounts of Farringford's funeral. He ran his finger down the columns until he found a lengthy list of notables in attendance. There they were—Mr. and Mrs. Leopold G. Sternberg—sandwiched in between Chesney Fleischauer, music critic, and Dimitri Mitropoulos, conductor. Felix reached for the phone and dialed Weintraub's Delicatessen on Lexington Avenue.

x x x

Chip entered the Post Office and started for the bank of mailboxes. He halted in mid-stride when he saw, about twenty feet away, a dark-haired woman leaning against the writing table holding an open magazine. Trntl's roommate: what was her name?—Carol. She was watching the mailboxes, too. Casually he approached a glass-fronted bulletin board and, while pretending to read notices, watched her reflection. Yep, she wasn't reading the magazine at all; was in fact alertly scrutinizing everyone who came through the lobby and went to the boxes. Chip ambled back the way he'd come until he reached a pay phone—and then he dialed the Cavendish Hotel. The line was busy on his first three tries, but he got through on the fourth. "Trntl's sidekick Carol is here in the Post Office," he told Jerry. "I'm going to hang around till she leaves and then follow her."

"Okay," said Jerry. "I'm halfway through the hotels with no success. Just starting the M's. I'll stop and let you handle it."

When Carol left the Post Office, she did not notice the brown-haired man with the dark brown mustache who followed her at a discreet distance to the Macready Hotel.

"We struck pay dirt," Carol announced, as Trntl and Torvald entered the hotel room. "One of the mailboxes was visited by a tall, blond woman, very nicely dressed—low heels and a leather trenchcoat. She got our message."

"Did she read the note?" Trntl asked.

"Yes, and then she slipped it into her handbag and left in a hurry."

"But no one came to the other box," said Torvald.

"No, and I stayed there till I thought it was safe to leave."

"Good work," Trntl said. "Standing a stake-out isn't fun."

"I'd just as soon not do it Monday," Carol said. "A lot of interesting people come into the Post Office, but after a while the excitement does fade."

"Torvald and I spent most of the day at the library," said Trntl. "He worked on the Ullman case, and having nothing better to do, I read microfilm of 1947 newspapers. I'm still intrigued by the initial disappearance of the cadenza at the time of Farringford's death."

"Did you learn anything new?"

"Not relating to the disappearance. But I got a sense of what was happening in the world at the time. As always, a lot was."

"It's almost five-thirty," said Torvald. "Time for Felix to call."

And at five-thirty, the phone rang. Felix gave a report on his meeting with Mrs. Farringford the night before; said that nothing further had occurred relating to the abortive ransom attempt; announced that he'd concluded the case of the missing niece—a two-week effort ("And our client is extremely pissed that the niece doesn't want to talk to her; we may have trouble getting our fee."); and—finally—told Trntl about the letter and call from Mrs. Leopold G. Sternberg. "She wants you to call her back at this unlisted number." He gave it to her. "Says it's very important and concerns the Farringford Cadenza."

"Who is Mrs. Leopold G. Sternberg?" Trntl asked.

"Rachel's dad was helpful on that," Felix answered. "Leopold was a prominent banker here in New York; he died in 1973. Mrs. Sternberg is a noted patron of the arts—she endowed a chair in Art History at City College as a memorial to her husband; created a writers' retreat and a raft of scholarships through the Sternberg Foundation, and over the last thirty years has provided funding for several music festivals and two massive sculpture projects. She serves on a number of boards: the Manhattan Arts Council, the Metropolitan Symphony, the Eubanks Museum, and others. And here's the kicker: she and her husband were listed in the papers among the VIPs who attended Farringford's funeral."

"Did she give any hint of what she wanted to talk to me about?"

"No. She said she's a friend of Morgan Latimer and is following our investigation through him."

"Okay, I'll give her a call. Anything else?"

"That's it. What about at your end?"

"Nothing whatever on the whereabouts of the cadenza. We all agree it hasn't been destroyed. But that's just a hunch—or maybe wishful thinking. I'm going to read you the letter Morris wrote to Stephanie just before he was killed. See if it suggests anything to you." And she carefully read Morris's letter aloud.

"I taped you," said Felix. "Just a second while I play it back."

She faintly heard her voice reading the message over again, and then Felix was back on the line: "From what Morris says, I don't think he hid the cadenza in his marijuana stash-hole. I think he put it in another location which he and Stephanie shared, possibly in private, as their 'special place'. Since Stephanie never read the letter, I think it's quite possible that the cadenza's still there. If that's the case, when Stephanie wrote you that she had the cadenza, she actually *didn't*—though she probably thought she did."

"So far you agree with our thinking," said Trntl.

"The way you read it on the phone, 'Key Hole' sounded like two words, not a single compound 'keyhole'. How is it written?"

"Two words, each capitalized."

"Then it's likely the phrase doesn't refer to a slot into which a key is inserted, but rather a hole in which a key is placed for concealment. If you find the hole, you'll find the key."

"But *which* key?" Trntl said. "The key to *what?*"

"To the briefcase? To the 'special place'? *I* don't know, Trntl."

"But Stephanie would've known."

"Sure. But I'd guess from the note that Morris couldn't assume she'd know immediately, or without some help. He follows 'Key Hole' with the phrase 'get it?'. He's telling her to think about it, to recall."

"We reached that conclusion, too."

"Look, you're trying to decipher the message as though it's some kind of code. It's a puzzle to you, but it wouldn't have been to Stephanie. Put yourself in Stephanie's place and try to read it as she would."

"We've tried that," said Trntl. "We lack the basic information she'd have had."

"Well, I'm sorry I can't be more helpful," Felix said. "At least I corroborate your thinking." He rang off, and Torvald, polishing his glasses, asked "Did he solve the riddle?"

"He said it's a riddle only to us; it wouldn't have been to Stephanie."

"So?"

"She would've known where the Hole was to find the Key."

"It's a pity Felix isn't here," said Torvald. "*He* could look for it."

It was just after six o'clock. Trntl quickly placed a call to Mrs. Sternberg.

"I've wanted to talk to you for some time," Mrs. Sternberg said. "I wrote you a letter several days ago, but apparently you never received it. I'm a good friend of Morgan Latimer, one of your clients in this cadenza business, and I've been following your progress through talking to him. He has great respect for you, Miss Trntl; not only for your skill as an investigator, but also for your integrity and trustworthiness. I've not told him that I've tried to reach you, and I would prefer that you keep that a private matter between us. I'm of course deeply concerned that the Farringford Cadenza be recovered. I heard Farringford perform it, and I know what it will mean for the world. I understand that since its discovery last week, the cadenza has been the cause of two deaths—"

"That's true," said Trntl. "And several serious assaults."

"I find that very sad," said Mrs. Sternberg. "It's incomprehensible that something so beautiful could be the cause of such violence. It should have brought joy and spiritual elevation, not grief and murder. I feel that we must have a conference, Miss Trntl—as soon as possible. I wish that I could travel to Baltimore—for I don't want to interrupt your investigation. But I'm seventy-six years old, and I'm simply not up to the trip. If you could come to see me I would be greatly obliged. I have some information that I think will be useful in your investigation, but I don't wish to discuss it over the telephone. Can you come? I'll defray your travel costs."

"I'll come," said Trntl. "My associates can stay to pursue the investigation. It's advantageous—for other reasons—that I leave Baltimore."

"Very good. Can I expect you tomorrow, then? Around four-thirty, for drinks with dinner to follow?"

"Fine," said Trntl. She took down the address Mrs. Sternberg provided and ended the call. When Trntl had recounted the conversation, Carol said, "Do you suppose she's a crank?"

"She didn't sound like one. Very straightforward and business-like. She and Latimer are evidently very old friends; and they have something very precious in common: they both heard Farringford play his cadenza."

"Ah," said Carol. "The stock-broker and the banker's widow."

"I think it could be a very interesting meeting," said Torvald. "Let's eat."

When they returned to Carol's room at 7:25, Trntl immediately began packing for her trip to New York. At 7:40 the telephone rang. Torvald answered, "Room 523."

"I received an answer to an ad I placed in the *Sun*." A man's voice, low-pitched and gravelly. "I was asked to call this number."

"Yes, I responded to the ad," said Torvald. "How may I help you?" He summoned the women with his free hand, and they came to the phone, putting their heads together over the receiver.

"I'm curious to know which piece of music it is that you have in Charles Farringford's manuscript."

"There's no title written on it."

"How do you know Farringford is the author?"

"I know his holograph, and his name is signed at the end."

"You said the work is for solo piano, that it hasn't been published—"

"That's correct."

"A late composition, you said."

"1947."

"I'd like to examine the manuscript. How shall we arrange for me to see it?"

"I've responded to two inquiries already," said Torvald. "As soon as possible would be to your advantage."

"Tonight?"

"Fine. A rather public place—"

"I'd prefer a private meeting."

"I'm afraid I must insist. Bracebeam's Lounge at ten o'clock. I'll be sitting toward the back, wearing a red neckscarf."

"I'll be there. Ten o'clock."

Torvald hung up. "You heard it?" They nodded. "Okay, when he wants to see the manuscript, how do we proceed?"

"I've been thinking about that," Trntl said, opening the briefcase which Dinch had given her in New York. "Here are photocopies of some of Farringford's manuscripts. Dinch thought I could use them to authenticate the cadenza when we found it. Let's take a few of these that don't have titles and let 'em serve as stand-ins. If your man knows immediately they're phonies, then he's awfully knowledgeable about Farringford's music, or else he's seen the cadenza already. If he thinks they *are* the cadenza, we'll know we aren't dealing with an expert."

"Sounds plausible." Torvald slid the papers into a brown manila envelope, and Trntl quickly finished her packing.

When they arrived at 9:30, Bracebeam's Lounge was less crowded than they'd expected for a Saturday night. Of the tables in the center of the room, only half were filled. Most people were in the red vinyl booths that lined the walls. All of the stools along the mirrored bar were occupied.

Torvald went straight to the back and sat at a small table by himself. He took off his astrakhan and overcoat but retained his scarf. Trntl and Carol chose a booth very near the front door so that they could observe, from behind, everyone who came in.

They ordered drinks and waited. A pianist on a circular dais in one corner was playing quiet cocktail music, skillfully modulating from one piece to another—show tunes, blues, jazz arrangements of old favorites. Torvald ordered a second drink.

People entered, people left. The bar stools continued to be filled. The pianist took a break. At three minutes till ten, the street door swung open, and two people entered: a tall blond woman in a fur coat, and a short dark-haired man wearing a gray windbreaker. He held the door open for her, but it wasn't at all clear from their demeanor that they were a couple. Carol nudged Trntl's foot and indicated the blond woman with her little finger.

The man in gray scanned the room, focused on Torvald, and took a step toward him. The woman reached out and jabbed his arm, and he stopped. Barely inclining her head toward his ear, she whispered something, then turned and quickly left by the swinging door. The man casually walked to the cigarette machine, fished in his pocket for coins, and bought a pack of Camels. Then he turned and went through the door also.

"It was the blonde from the Post Office," said Carol. "She recognized Torvald and buzzed an alarm."

"If she didn't recognize you at the Post Office, she might not now," said Trntl. "Why don't you go out and see what they're doing?"

Carol was up and out the door almost before Trntl had finished speaking. Torvald was looking toward her intently, trying to interpret what had happened. Trntl motioned him to stay seated. Then she became aware of other eyes watching her—a gaze level and cold in the mirror behind the bar. A big man, sitting on a stool, his back toward her, his reflected face flat, round, and expressionless, his neck as large as a bull's. Of course! *They'd* sent in an early-bird observer, too. And he'd seen Carol go rushing out. And herself signaling Torvald. Shit. She downed the last of her drink.

The pianist returned to the dais and did a little warm-up riff. Then she was off and running with *Smoke Gets In Your Eyes.*

The man at the bar was looking elsewhere now. Torvald was polishing his glasses. Trntl was on her sixth cigarette. She finished Carol's drink. It had been four minutes since Carol had left (it seemed like ten). Should she go out and see if Carol was all right?

The door swung open again, and the man in the gray windbreaker entered. He made his way to Torvald, spoke to him briefly, and sat down. But where was Carol?

"Do you have the music with you?" the man asked.

"I do," said Torvald, committing the man's face to memory: narrow, with rather ratlike features and a pointed chin, deepset dark brown eyes, bushy brows, a small wart or mole on the left side of his nose, thin lips, a chipped right incisor. "As you know," Torvald continued, "you're not alone in seeking this piece of music. Obtaining it cost me a great deal. I suppose you've been reading the newspapers?"

"Let me see the music."

Torvald produced the manila envelope and placed it unopened on the table, covering it with his spread hand. "The manuscript has great intrinsic value," he said. "Not to mention a high market value. What's it worth to *you?*"

"Let me examine the manuscript. I'll say nothing till I've seen it."

"Fair enough." Torvald opened the envelope and removed the sheets. The man pulled them across the table and squinted at them in the dim light.

"These are photocopies!" he said.

"You surely didn't think I'd bring the original," said Torvald. "A copy will suffice for identification."

The man leafed through the papers. A tall woman—obviously inebriated—left the bar and wobbled slowly past their table, teetering unsteadily on her high heels, heading for the washroom at the rear. She lost her balance and half-fell on the man with the gray windbreaker, who clutched the papers tightly and glared up at her. She gurgled "Sorry", and continued on her way.

"How many copies did you make?" the man asked Torvald.

"Why do you ask?"

"There must be no copies not accounted for. Purchase of the manuscript includes all copies." Though trying to hide it, the man was extremely agitated.

"I take it you're afraid that loose copies would make it possible for someone else to anticipate you in writing an article."

The chipped tooth flashed momentarily as he raised one eyebrow. "An article?"

"Didn't you say in your ad that you're a musicologist?"

"A musicol—" Then, with the hint of a smile. "That was the other ad."

"Oh, then you're the publisher," said Torvald. "You're afraid loose copies would make it possible for another publisher to beat you into print. That's an understandable concern. Rest assured: if you purchase the manuscript, the sale includes all copies."

"What price are you asking?"

"I'll repeat: what's it worth to you?"

A long pause. "I'll have to do some consultation before I can make an offer."

"All right," said Torvald. "Be advised the time is short. You know where to reach me."

He snatched the papers from the man's hand and began putting them back into the envelope. "Here!" the man said. "Let me take those to show—"

"And risk losing my investment?" said Torvald. "Have your employer come to me if further proof is required." He pushed back his chair and stood up, draped his coat over one arm, effectively covering the envelope, and moved rapidly toward the entrance.

The rat-faced man leaped up and stood undecided; he glanced to the man at the bar and caught his eye. The round-faced one slid off his stool and buttoned his coat. Trntl dropped a five-dollar bill onto the table and moved casually out through the swinging door ten feet ahead of Torvald. She was waiting for him in the vestibule. "He has a friend at the bar almost as tall as you are. Let's get to the street. Carol followed the blond woman out, and I don't know why she hasn't come back."

After the over-heated lounge, the night air was damp and chill. Several people were on the sidewalk, but Carol was nowhere in sight. "Now what?" said Torvald, putting on his coat.

"Surely she wouldn't have gone back to the hotel," said Trntl.

"Maybe she followed the blonde."

"She followed them both out, then *he* came back in."

"He'll be following *us* out," said Torvald. "And his friend at the bar, too. We can't just stand here."

A taxi pulled up to the curb. From the back window Carol beckoned for them to get in. They did.

Carol told the driver: "The Macready Hotel, please."

"Where have you been?" Trntl asked her.

"The blonde is around the corner in the lounge parking lot," she answered, "just sitting in a rental car waiting for her friend. They were having an argument when I followed them out. I pretended to be waiting for a cab and overheard just a little of it. She recognized Torvald immediately and linked him with Trntl & Associates. She smelled a set-up. The man said that, even so, it was possible that Torvald might have the cadenza and be willing to ditch the clients and sell it for a fat profit. He felt it was worth the chance and went back in. So, Torvald, if he talked to you, it was with full knowledge of who you are."

Torvald pursed his lips. "He talked to me. But he didn't seem to know the photocopies weren't the cadenza manuscript. I don't think he's very knowledgeable, and I assume he's serving as an agent for some principal. It's that principal who's willing to pay for the original. He wanted to take the copies to show his boss—but of course I didn't let him." He gave a thin smile. "So even if he knows I've been after the cadenza on behalf of Lunner & Dinch, he doesn't know whether I really have the original manuscript or not. He may think I have it, and that I'm willing to sell it. Likewise, for his boss there'll be an element of doubt. If so, they'll try to contact me again."

"He had a friend in there sitting at the bar," said Trntl, "who got a good look at all three of us. That may blow our game: they won't believe that we're *all* willing to betray our clients. And worse, the man at the bar will recognize us when he sees us again."

They arrived at their hotel, moved quickly across the lobby, took the elevator up, and unlocked the door of 523. Torvald went in first. They'd left the light on. "I should be gone only one day," Trntl was saying. "The meeting with Mrs. Sternberg won't take long. If there's anything you want me to bring you—"

"Stop," Torvald said, thrusting them back and dropping to a crouching posture. "Someone's been in the room."

They froze in the doorway while Torvald darted into the bathroom and pulled back the shower curtain. Next he peered into the clothes closet and under the beds. "Nothing," he said. "But look there."

They followed his pointing finger and saw a small, mashed object gleaming on the carpet. Cellophane. "It wasn't here when we left," said Torvald. He picked it up, smoothed it out, and sniffed it. "It's a candy wrapper. But none of us eats peppermint. I think it was stuck to the sole of someone's shoe."

"Another search?" asked Trntl. She opened and looked through her suitcase. "I can't see anything disturbed. You keep your satchel locked, Torvald; has it been tampered with?"

"Combination lock intact," he said.

"Mine's okay, too," said Carol, looking at her overnight case. "What about Dinch's briefcase?"

Trntl did a quick inventory. "Everything's here."

"If not a search," Torvald muttered, "*what?* If they didn't take anything, why enter? To check us out, go through our bags? Nah. To leave something! A bomb or a bug. Let's see what we can find."

They did a systematic search of the wastebasket, mattresses and bed frames, windowsills and drapes, lamps (shades and bases), the undersides of tables and chairs, drawers, closet shelves, and the backs of pictures. "Ah," Carol said. "A new scratch beside one of the screws on the telephone." With Trntl's Swiss Army knife, she quickly removed the screws from the telephone base. "Well," she grinned, "here's something that doesn't belong." She detached a small black disc and studied it. "Some sort of transmitter—manufactured by Arch-Apex Electronics. Attaches easily." They studied the device for a bit, and then Carol said, "This gives me an idea. I'll be back in a minute." She hurried out with the bug and the Swiss Army knife.

Ten minutes later she returned. "I put it in one of the house phones in the lobby," she said. "That should give them an earful."

After a fruitless half-hour searching through the photographs in Dinch's dossiers to see if they could identify any of the Bracebeam Three, they finally called a halt. Trntl said, "Well, so much for that. But we should take stock of what we've learned tonight. One of the newspaper ads has been accounted for: a woman and two men doing the legwork—"

"Probably for a boss or a client not on the scene," said Torvald. "They were having to make decisions on the spur of the moment, and weren't sure how to proceed. The fellow I talked to said he had to 'consult' before making an offer."

"Unless either the woman in the fur coat or the man at the bar was the boss," said Carol.

"I don't think so," said Torvald, "—though it's a possibility."

"The woman recognized Torvald," said Trntl, "but apparently not Carol. I'm sure that the man at the bar recognized me. Which means we've been under surveillance. They know exactly who we are and what we're doing. Are they detectives, too? One thing's sure: none of *those* three bugged our phone."

"And they're probably not the ones who searched our office in New York," said Carol.

"They aren't connected with Scaevola," said Trntl. "*These* people ran an ad."

Torvald yawned. "Tonight's contact was from the 'publisher' ad—not the one placed by 'musicologist', for whatever that's worth."

"Well, *are* they working for a publisher?" Trntl asked. "One of Dinch's competitors? If so, which?"

"And now they've got to decide whether we have the manuscript or not," said Carol, "and if we do, whether we're really trying to sell it."

"So who bugged our phone?" asked Torvald.

"Whoever it was, I'd like to know how they learned we'd moved to the Macready Hotel," said Carol. "We were pretty subtle about it. Except for Dinch and Felix, we only told Detective Adcock, so he'd be able to reach us."

"The room's registered in Carol's name," said Torvald, "not Trntl's. But if the buggers could find us, so can Torelli and George Fiocco."

"I'm glad to be leaving tomorrow," said Trntl. "I'll think of you while I'm gone."

Chapter 24

March 8   (Sunday)

Trntl took The Minute Man to New York, and Felix met her at Penn Station. "Good to be back," she said. "It's been a long six days."

"You don't look much worse than when you left," Felix grinned.

"You're too kind. Where can we get some Sunday brunch?"

They drove to Carmody's and ordered omelets.

Felix was enormously amused by Trntl's report of the confrontation at Bracebeam's and Carol's response to the attempt to bug the new hotel room. He agreed with Trntl's conclusion that whoever was doing the surveillance was hoping the Associates would lead them to the cadenza. "They're as baffled as we are." Spreading marmalade on a biscuit. "Maybe more so."

"If they think *we'll* lead 'em to the cadenza," said Trntl, "they're clutching at a very thin reed."

"When Dinch heard you were coming, he said he wanted to see you in his office tomorrow morning. He doesn't know you've come to visit Mrs. Sternberg."

"I suppose he's curious about the expenses we're running up," said Trntl.

"Well, there's always that. But I think what he really wants is a firsthand report from the front. I've kept him fully informed, but you're the one in the trenches. He's gotten very impatient."

"Miracles we didn't promise," said Trntl. "It's only been a week since the break-in at Pettigrew's."

"It's his injured pride. This ransom hoax, with the loss of money, is the final insult. He's convinced he's being made to look a fool."

"Blames his competitors, no doubt."

"Doesn't know who to blame. That's what really burns his ass."

"How are the other clients doing?"

"I haven't talked to any of them except Mrs. Farringford. Latimer's been taken ill."

"Well, it's mostly his money that got ripped off," Trntl said—then checked herself: "No, that's unkind. He may simply believe the game's over."

"Friday was a bad day, Trntl. After the ransom fiasco, everybody fell apart. Mrs. Farringford was terribly confused; when she tried to talk to Dinch, Anton, and Abbott, none of them had much to say. When she got to me, she was desperate for reassurance that we thought there was still a chance of recovering the cadenza."

"There's grounds for hope," said Trntl. "We at least know there's another group that wants it."

"Be sure to tell Dinch about those people at Bracebeam's," said Felix. "He might recognize 'em from your descriptions. Had any further thoughts on the 'Key Hole'?"

"Nothing that led anywhere. Thinking music might be a lead, I've considered 'piano key', 'key signature', 'key-note', 'keyboard', and the major and minor scales."

"Did either Morris or Stephanie play woodwinds?" Felix asked.

"Not to my knowledge. He played the dulcimer." She flagged down the waiter and ordered more toast.

The conversation drifted into other areas. Felix gave her a rundown on his activities of the last few days, recounting at some length the process by which he'd found the Brooklyn client's missing niece, and grumbling a bit about having to do everyone else's work while they were gone. Then, back at the office, Trntl looked through her mail, found Mrs. Sternberg's letter, which told her no more than the telephone conversation had.

"Do you want me to go with you to see Dinch?" Felix asked from his desk.

"If you're free. It's always good to have two present, in order to compare notes afterwards."

"Okay. I'll try to find time in my busy schedule."

"But you'd better *not* come with me to see Mrs. Sternberg. You weren't invited to dinner." She gathered up her things. "And I'd better get going. It's a long drive."

Almost in Connecticut, the Sternberg house was a slate-roofed brick with bay windows, high gables, and clustered chimneys. Set well back from the road in expansive grounds and surrounded by a low wall, it was approached through gateposts and up a curving drive. Recessed beneath a peaked Tudor arch, the paneled front door could have withstood a battering ram. Trntl's ring was answered by an attractive woman about her own age dressed in a maroon skirt and ruffled, long-sleeved blouse. "N. F. Trntl?" she said. "I'm Phyllis Lowery, Mrs. Sternberg's secretary. Come in, I'll take your coat. Mrs. Sternberg is in the library."

Heels clicking on the parquet floor, they crossed the entrance hall to the doorway of a spacious, high-ceilinged room bright with late afternoon sunlight that streamed through a tall mullioned window facing the west lawn. Bookshelves lined the walls, radiant with the luster of fine leather bindings.

At a large desk near the window, a white-haired woman sat engulfed by stacks of papers, reference books, and manila folders. As they entered, she glanced up, rose—pushing her glasses up onto her forehead—and came around the desk to shake Trntl's hand. She was about five-feet-three, slightly plump, casually dressy in a gray skirt and jacket and low-heeled shoes. Her hair was styled into an upswept mass of curls.

"I'm Naomi Sternberg." Her smile was friendly, her eyes bright with a level, penetrating gaze. "It was good of you to come all the way from Baltimore to see me. I know you're busy with your investigation and this must be an annoying distraction—"

"Progress is slow in Baltimore," Trntl said. "Almost nil, if you want the truth."

Mrs. Sternberg cocked her head to one side with a frown of concern. "I'm sorry to hear that." She gestured toward a liquor cabinet built into the wall. "I promised you a drink. What's your pleasure?"

"Scotch on the rocks, thanks."

"Phyllis, will you join us?"

"Happy to," said the secretary. "Shall we make our own?"

"Why not? There's ice in the bucket. I think I'll have a vodka tonic." She handed Trntl the Scotch and deftly opened a fresh bottle of vodka for herself. Phyllis poured a glass of sherry.

"Now let's sit down and get acquainted." Mrs. Sternberg led the way to the fireplace, where a pair of sofas faced each other across a low coffee table. "Sorry there's no fire," she continued as they made themselves comfortable. "It didn't seem cold enough to warrant one. I have an electric heater by my desk; it's far more efficient."

"The temperature's fine," said Trntl.

"My late husband didn't like being cold. When we built the house, he said 'Sixteenth-century architecture is fine, but we'll damn well have twentieth-century insulation!'"

"The windows are all double-paned, with lots of dead air space," said Phyllis.

"Your husband was a far-sighted man," said Trntl.

"In a great many ways," said Mrs. Sternberg. "Except in pacing himself, conserving his energy. He never developed a sense of humor sufficient to withstand the pressure of his existence; always took things too seriously. Wore himself out, and died at sixty-eight." She nodded slowly, agreeing with herself. "Nonetheless, he was kind and generous, and we had a good life together."

"That's his portrait over the fireplace," Phyllis said. Trntl had been assuming that it was. Leopold G. Sternberg had not been the J. P. Morgan Trntl had imagined him. In his late 40's or early 50's when the picture was painted, he'd been lean and ascetic in appearance, with large, prominent ears, a thin-lipped sensitive mouth, and mournful eyes.

"It was painted in 1949," said Mrs. Sternberg. "He was exhausted when he posed for it. For over ten years he'd been serving on international committees trying to get refugees out of Europe, then finding and relocating survivors of the Holocaust, and finally working to establish the State of Israel. He wasn't an ardent Zionist, never a zealot—and the turmoil surrounding the partitioning of Palestine took an enormous toll on him."

"His eyes seem very sad," said Trntl.

"He felt everything deeply." She pushed a ceramic ashtray across the table. "By all means, smoke if you wish, Miss Trntl." Trntl wasn't aware that she'd been fidgeting. "Phyllis smokes occasionally while we work. I used to smoke heavily, but gave it up years ago."

"Thank you," said Trntl, taking a cigarette from her handbag.

Phyllis leaned forward and held a lighter for her, then lit up a cigarette of her own.

"I'm sure you're wondering why I want to talk to you," Mrs. Sternberg said, removing her glasses and placing them on the table. (Yes, it would be well to get on with it, thought Trntl, her natural impatience chafing at the chitchat.) "Morgan Latimer and I are very old friends—currently we're serving together on the board of the Metropolitan Symphony. Knowing that I'd be interested, he told me that your firm had been hired to recover the Farringford Cadenza. You'd been highly recommended for the job by Henry Gittings, whose judgment we all respect. Morgan was very much impressed with you at the meeting you had with Mr. Dinch and the Farringfords. He's confident that you'll recover the cadenza if anyone can."

"I'm glad to have his confidence," said Trntl.

"Unfortunately, he's now convinced that the cadenza's been destroyed. The stress of the whole affair—the cadenza's theft on the heels of its discovery, the two murders, the attack on you, the bogus ransom demand—has sent him to the hospital with severe internal bleeding."

"I'm sorry to hear that," said Trntl.

"He feels a crushing sense of personal loss in the cadenza's disappearance; did in 1947, does again now. Doubly devastating. It's eating him alive. He has a passionate—almost frenzied—concern that it be found and shared by all. I feel the loss just as keenly as he does, and my concern for the cadenza's recovery is no less than his. Those of us who heard Farringford perform it are a select and shrinking company—very like a family—uniquely blest for having heard it, uniquely cursed for knowing what's been lost. Miss Trntl, I can't describe the happiness, the jubilation Morgan and I felt when we learned that the cadenza had been found. I was ecstatic, almost transported with joy—"

"That's putting it mildly," Phyllis said with a smile.

"And then, the very next day, when I heard it'd been stolen— why, it was as though part of me died. I couldn't function—"

"She stayed in bed the whole day," said Phyllis. "Wouldn't talk to anybody."

"On Monday, I called Morgan—to commiserate, I suppose— and he told me your firm had been hired, that you'd gone to Baltimore. I immediately sent you a letter, thinking it would be forwarded. When I got no response, and the murders appeared in the paper, and Morgan kept sharing those awful reports of what was happening—and then *collapsed*—I could wait no longer but called your office to see if you'd received my letter."

"What do you wish to tell me?" Trntl asked, her impatience getting the best of her.

But Mrs. Sternberg wasn't to be hurried. "I realize that officially I'm not one of your clients, and therefore have no right to inquire about your investigation. Yet my concerns are equal to those of

Morgan, Dinch, and the family. I'm hoping that you wouldn't feel it a violation of your professional ethics to give me your views on what's been happening—the theft, the murders, the attack on you, the ransom hoax." She paused and waited for a reply.

Trntl tapped the ash off her cigarette. "It's no breach of ethics to share what I know." And, in the space of six minutes, she outlined the circumstantial facts of the case. Mrs. Sternberg and Phyllis listened closely. "If this recent ransom demand *wasn't* a hoax," Trntl said in conclusion, "and the cadenza really *was* being traded for the fifty-eight thousand, then the cadenza's either been diverted or lost. If diverted, someone other than Dinch got it, whether by accident or design. If that's the case, it will be very hard to recover it. If lost, it may indeed be gone forever. However: if the ransom *was* a hoax (as we're inclined to think), there's a good possibility that the cadenza is still unattached in Baltimore. If that's the case, there's a good chance we'll get it back."

"But how will you know which hypothesis is correct?" Mrs. Sternberg asked.

"That's a good question. We're at a standstill until something breaks."

Mrs. Sternberg turned to her secretary. "Phyllis, please see if Mrs. Hale is ready with dinner." Phyllis nodded and left the room. "Phyllis will be leaving shortly; her husband gave up a movie he wanted to see this afternoon so that she could help me catch up on paperwork. Two fund-raising projects are approaching deadline." Her troubled frown was back. "I had no idea things were so complex regarding the cadenza. I've been hoping all week that there might be something I could do to—ah—facilitate its recovery. That's what I want to talk to you about. But in presenting my offer, I'm relying on your utmost discretion." She paused to take a sip of her drink, and Trntl watched her intently, not knowing what to expect. She was totally unprepared for what came.

"As I said to you on the phone, this meeting of ours must be kept confidential, a private matter between just the two of us. This is crucial. Morgan, Dinch, and the Farringfords must know nothing about it. You can regard me as an unofficial client, if you wish—a silent Friend of the Cadenza." She settled back and looked Trntl squarely in the eye. "Should you get the break you speak of, and find that you have access to the cadenza, please bear in mind that I have *considerable* financial resources that I'm willing to use to obtain it. Buying of information, bribes, outright purchase—

whatever it takes. Just give me the word, and you'll have all the money you need—however much. In cash." She turned away and finished her drink.

For a long moment Trntl stared at her in disbelief, sifting and weighing what she'd just heard. My God, was it possible? another one!—this time a likable old woman who'd had the luck of hearing Farringford perform his cadenza. But, my God!—no subtlety, no finesse, just a bald proposition: betray your clients; name your price; keep your mouth shut. Trntl slugged back the rest of her Scotch and said evenly: "That's very generous of you."

"Generosity has nothing to do with it," said Mrs. Sternberg. "I don't want the cadenza lost a second time." She stood up briskly. "Enough said. Would you like a refill?"

"No, thank you."

Mrs. Sternberg carried the empty glasses back to the liquor cabinet. "Leo and I began supporting the arts in a serious way back in 1938, and we became more and more involved as time went on. We never thought of ourselves as 'patrons', for that term implies a sort of condescension we wanted no part of. We saw our role as facilitators—simply helping to make things possible. Leo was particularly interested in visual arts and ballet, and in the early days I was concerned with music education and encouraging new talent—getting new music heard, young performers launched. After Leo died, I went on alone; and creation of the Sternberg Foundation in 1975 has made even more possible."

Phyllis returned wearing her overcoat. "Mrs. Hale says that dinner is ready."

"Thank you," said Mrs. Sternberg. "Before you go, please get the check we've written to reimburse Miss Trntl for her travel expenses." Phyllis brought it from the desk.

"How much is your round-trip cost?" Mrs. Sternberg asked, her pen poised to fill in the amount.

So, Trntl thought bitterly, a down-payment for services yet to be rendered. "It won't be necessary to reimburse me," she said smoothly. "I would've been coming to New York anyway. I had to confer with my associate Mr. McKay, and I'm to meet with Mr. Dinch tomorrow."

She put a heavily weighted inflection on this last phrase; but if Mrs. Sternberg noticed, she gave no indication. "As you wish," she said, and handed the check back to Phyllis, who returned it to the desk.

314

Phyllis said, "I must be going, Miss Trntl. It was good to meet you. I wish you success in finding the cadenza; and I hope you won't encounter any more personal danger."

"Time to eat," said Mrs. Sternberg, leading Trntl to the hall. She pointed to a doorway just beyond the stairs. "That's the music room. Why don't you go there and wait for just a second while I finish up a couple of business matters with Phyllis?"

Trntl nodded and crossed the broad hallway to the music room. Mrs. Sternberg turned back to Phyllis in the library and motioned her toward the desk. When she was sure that Trntl was well out of earshot, she whispered urgently: "Okay, Phyllis, what do you make of N. F. Trntl?"

Long, wide, graced with a huge crystal chandelier at each end, the music room was clearly designed for performances—string quartets, chamber orchestras. Down the far wall marched four tall windows hung with red velvet drapes. Toward the front, adjacent to one of the windows, was a concert grand piano; near it stood a covered harp. Antique musical instruments were mounted on the darkly paneled walls; beneath them, glass-topped display cases lined the room.

While waiting for Mrs. Sternberg, Trntl browsed these cases. As in a museum, everything was labeled. First editions of composers' published works. Plaster casts of both of Franz Liszt's hands. Personal letters written by a variety of important people. She scanned quickly down the long display, carefully (and with great interest) logging in whomever she could: Mozart, Wagner, Granados, Rameau, Debussy, Glazunov, Chaminade, Bloch, Elgar, Beethoven, Grieg, Paderewski, Rachmaninoff, Kreisler, Koussevitzky, Quantz, Mitropoulos, Lipatti, Dvorak, Ravel, and Carl Philipp Emanuel Bach.

Another case contained death masks of Muzio Clementi and Hector Berlioz. Verdi's day-book. Bartok's fountain pen. Chopin's gloves. Busoni's walking-stick. Melba's fan. Caruso's watch. And everywhere, a variety of original music scores in manuscript.

She was studying these when Mrs. Sternberg entered the room behind her. "I thought you might be interested in our collection. Leo and I spent many years putting it together. It was Leo's great joy; he scoured auction catalogs—and with his European contacts, got early word of the breaking up of major estates. As you can see, we have original manuscripts of—" pointing, with obvious delight "—Vivaldi, Haydn, Schubert, Weill, Stravinsky, Puccini, Beach, and Farringford. Since Leo's death I haven't pursued the collection as vigorously. Nowadays I'll purchase a manuscript only if it's an *outstanding* find—an exceptionally rare or historically important item."

"I understand," said Trntl. A clock somewhere chimed five times. Mrs. Sternberg motioned to the door. "We'd better get in to dinner. Mrs. Hale will be fierce if we let her food get cold."

After seeing the music room, Trntl expected a Tudor banquet hall with a table at least twenty feet long. But no, the dining room was small and intimate, its paneled walls tastefully hung with oil landscapes—two Constables for sure, and maybe a Corot. At a table that would have seated eight, two places facing each other were laid at one end.

They seated themselves, and from hot serving dishes filled their plates with sliced roast beef, small potatoes, and broccoli. "Do try one of Mrs. Hale's Vienna rolls," said Mrs. Sternberg. "The butter is unsalted. Would you like coffee? I thought so." She filled Trntl's cup from a silver urn. "My doctor tells me to reduce my coffee intake. But I told him I'll die first."

"That's the spirit," said Trntl.

The food was excellent, but Trntl couldn't fully enjoy it. She regarded the meal—something she couldn't gracefully get out of— as symbolically tantamount to sealing a bargain between them. The check she could refuse; but taking this gift of food already prepared struck her as disturbingly close to accepting a bribe. She felt ethically obliged to leave the house as quickly as she politely could.

To forestall any further overtures from Mrs. Sternberg, Trntl steered the conversation into neutral territory: "That's a fine piano in the music room."

"Yes, it is. Leo bought it for me on my forty-second birthday."

"Do you play a lot?"

"I used to, for my own enjoyment. Arrangements of show tunes and the simpler classical pieces. But not so much in recent years, as my fingers become less nimble."

"And the harp?"

"Oh no, that was my sister's."

Trntl refilled their coffee cups. "Tapioca pudding for dessert," Mrs. Sternberg said brightly.

A strange and complex woman, thought Trntl: 'Can you come see me?—I've something urgent to tell you.' And when I arrive, what do I get? Tapioca pudding and a confidential offer of money. 'To—facilitate—the cadenza's recovery.' Smooth Mrs. Sternberg, my 'unofficial client'. 'A silent Friend of the Cadenza'! Demanding that our meeting stay 'a private matter' between us! And here: 'Considerable resources' for 'buying of information, bribes, or outright purchase—you name it.' And then, the clincher: guiding me to the music room where I'd be sure to see the collection of original manuscripts. Beethoven, Amy Beach, and Farringford! Shrewd Mrs. Sternberg, doing an end run past Dinch, Latimer, and the family to grab the cadenza for herself. Roast beef and flattery! Cynical Mrs. Sternberg, presuming my greed. What gall! Stupid Mrs. Sternberg, to think I'd let myself be bought.

Trntl said, "Please tell Mrs. Hale that the meal was delicious."

"I will; I'm glad you enjoyed it." Mrs. Sternberg rose and moved swiftly to a swinging door in the rear wall. "I'll tell her we're finished. Go back to the music room; I'll join you there."

"Well, I really must be going—" Trntl said.

But Mrs. Sternberg was through the door. Trntl shrugged and left the table. Stepped into the hall and went to the music room doorway, lighting a cigarette. Okay, what now? Did Mrs. Sternberg have something more to say? Did she think, perhaps, that Trntl hadn't gotten the message?

There were no ashtrays in the music room. Trntl was just turning to fetch the one from the library when Mrs. Sternberg entered and handed her a saucer. "It occurred to me that you'd probably like to smoke after dinner, and I remembered there's nothing in this room to put ashes in."

"Thank you," said Trntl, taking the saucer, irked that her habit made her so predictable; doubly irked that Mrs. Sternberg, through foreguessing her need for an ashtray and supplying it unbidden, had scored another point in making Trntl beholden to her.

"Before you leave, I'd like to play a piece of music for you," said Mrs. Sternberg. "Have you ever heard the recording of Charles Farringford playing his *Adirondack Interludes?* It was the premiere recording of the work, back in 1940."

"No," said Trntl. "I've heard him performing other works on long-play reissues. My recordings of his piano works are fairly recent—played by Peter Shipley Abbott, Rosamond Foxe, and Ralph Edgeworth."

Mrs. Sternberg opened a door concealed in the paneled wall and exposed a built-in record-player and several shelves containing albums. "I don't much care for Edgeworth's interpretations," she said. "Abbott is very good, but Rosamond Foxe, in my opinion, has the best version of the *Interludes* after Farringford's. Her playing has an uncanny resemblance to his. By the way, did you know that she'll be appearing on Thursday with the Metropolitan Symphony? Playing Farringford's Second Concerto. As I said, I'm on the Board of Directors, and we feel fortunate to get Foxe—for, frankly, the Symphony is having serious financial difficulties."

"My associate Felix McKay will be attending the concert," said Trntl.

"Ah, but you'll probably be back in Baltimore, and will have to miss it. Unless," she added with a narrow smile, "you've managed to recover the cadenza by then." Mrs. Sternberg pulled an album off its shelf. "I don't know why they never reissued these on LP." She extracted one record from its paper sleeve and handed Trntl the album. "Would you mind holding this? I'll only be a second getting the record onto the turntable."

God, the 78's were heavy, Trntl thought. There were seven records left in the album. On the cover was a photograph of the composer, his eyes looking intensely into hers. Across his white collar was scrawled in black ink: "To my friends Leo and Naomi Sternberg, with my warmest regards. Charles Philip Farringford. 1940." She nearly dropped the album.

"I see that Farringford presented this to you," she said.

Mrs. Sternberg placed the stylus on the record and took the album from her hands, glancing casually at the inscription. "Yes, we became acquainted in 1937, just after his South American tour. He and Leo shared an interest in jazz. He gave us signed copies of all his recordings."

So of course, thought Trntl, you would want the cadenza too. In collecting, completeness is the guiding passion. Dammit, the longer she stayed, the more compromised she became. She'd leave just as soon as the record was finished.

She was so distracted by these reflections that she didn't attend to the opening of Farringford's first *Interlude*. But the com-

poser's playing quickly asserted itself, and in a moment she could
do nothing but listen. The music itself was exquisite (and familiar
because of its popularity—a standard rather like *Old Man River*,
The Battle Hymn of the Republic, or *Greensleeves* in the frequency
of its being played); but familiar as it was, Trntl had never heard it
as Farringford performed it. The authority of his address, the ex-
pressiveness of his touch—crisp and fluid—transcending the surface hiss of shellac and 1940's recording technology—caused her
to discern between the jig-like bass and the falling blues cadences
of the treble, a quiet middle voice—now plaintive, now sprightly—
that sang its own song, independent of the other two, in counterpoint with them, but going its own way to its own destination. All
too soon the music was over; but before Mrs. Sternberg could offer
to play more, Trntl said hastily: "That was wonderful. But now I
really must be going."

"No one can match his playing," Mrs. Sternberg said, turning off the machine. "I wanted you to hear that, Miss Trntl. But
beautiful as that music is, it comes nowhere close to the beauty of
the lost cadenza. After our talk tonight, I hope you're encouraged
to redouble your efforts. If you find the manuscript, please let me
know at once."

That did it. The smug assurance, the casual assumption that
money would buy anything—special privilege, loyalty, a person's
ethical commitment—pushed Trntl over the edge. She took three
long strides to the doorway and faced Mrs. Sternberg pale with
rage.

"I accepted your hospitality in good faith," she said coldly. "I
ate your dinner. But I must tell you that I resent your attempting
to subvert my relationship with my clients. I will not be regarded
as a whore. If I find the cadenza, rest assured you certainly will *not*
be the first to know."

Mrs. Sternberg stood thunderstruck, eyebrows raised, her
mouth fallen open.

"Good night," said Trntl, turning back to the doorway. "Where
did Mrs. Lowery put my coat?" She went into the hall.

"Wait!" It was an urgent appeal, in a voice both puzzled and
hurt. Trntl stopped and set her jaw. Mrs. Sternberg had swiftly
followed her into the hall.

"What you say astounds me, Miss Trntl. I can't help feeling
there's been some dreadful misunderstanding. I'm very upset—"

"Well, that makes two of us," said Trntl.

"You'll have to let me organize my thoughts," said Mrs. Sternberg, rubbing her forehead. Finally, she said: "What did you mean when you accused me of subverting your relationship with your clients?"

Trntl gave an impatient gesture. "Bringing me here for a private meeting. Offering me a wad of untraceable cash in order to facilitate the cadenza's recovery. My obligation, Mrs. Sternberg, is to Dinch, the Farringford family, and *your friend* Latimer. They're paying me to recover it for *them*, trusting me not to sell them out for a better offer."

Mrs. Sternberg had regained her composure. "There *has* been a misunderstanding. Please tell me precisely what you think it is that I want."

"I think you want the cadenza for yourself—for your precious collection. I think you've decided that I'm your best bet for recovering it, and you think I'd sell it to you for a large enough 'bonus'. I don't take bribes. I'm offended that you think I'm for sale."

Mrs. Sternberg shook her head sadly. "I must have presented myself very badly. No, Miss Trntl, you have it all wrong. And in fairness, you should let me show you why. Please step into the library again. I won't take much of your time."

Wanting to be fair, and moved by Mrs. Sternberg's extreme agitation, Trntl said "All right," and allowed herself to be led into the library. Mrs. Sternberg went straight to the liquor cabinet and poured herself a stiff shot of vodka. "Do you want anything?" she asked.

"No," said Trntl.

"Well, I'm having something." She knocked it back and replaced the glass. "Let's go to the sofa."

Seated, Trntl drew the ashtray toward her across the table and lit another cigarette. Mrs. Sternberg said, "Why do you think I want the cadenza for myself?"

Trntl said, "For your collection. You seem to have a lot of Farringford stuff already."

"I thought I'd made it clear that I wanted the cadenza recovered so that it could be published for the world."

"It wasn't clear to *me*."

Mrs. Sternberg shook her head again. "That's what Morgan Latimer wants. And Dinch, and the Farringford family. And it's what I want, too—" she met Trntl's gaze with an earnestness that couldn't be denied "—more than anything else in the world."

"I'd like to believe that," said Trntl.

Mrs. Sternberg gave her a long, appraising look. Trntl could almost see the balance-beam tilting behind her eyes. Then Mrs. Sternberg said, "Are you familiar with the circumstances of Charles Farringford's death?"

Surprised, Trntl replied, "I've read the newspaper accounts. The mystery surrounding the first loss of the cadenza intrigues me. I know that he died on a train en route from Cleveland to New York: that when the body, dressed in pajamas, arrived at Penn Station, Farringford's suitcase was missing and the cadenza with it. That there were two one-way tickets found in the compartment. That a woman had apparently been with him—Anton Farringford assumes it was a prostitute his father had picked up for the journey home. And that his death was ascribed to a heart attack—though Mrs. Farringford is convinced that Charles was murdered."

"At the time there was a great deal of speculation," said Mrs. Sternberg. "The scandal sheets had a field day. The more responsible newspapers confined themselves to the facts and tried to desensationalize things out of respect for Charles's memory and the family's feelings."

"It was an awkward way for him to die," said Trntl. "Though if the cadenza hadn't been missing, I'm sure the sensation wouldn't have amounted to much. The cadenza would have been published along with the concerto, and people would soon have forgotten the other loose ends."

"There hasn't been a day in thirty-four years I haven't thought about that," said Mrs. Sternberg. "And for thirty-four years I've been waiting, praying for the manuscript to turn up."

"Understandably," said Trntl. "You were one of those who heard Farringford perform it in concert."

"Ah, but I heard it *three* times, Miss Trntl. I was the woman on the train."

Chapter 25

Trntl sank back against the sofa cushions. One, two, buckle my shoe, she thought. Three, four, mop the floor. "Then you were with Charles Farringford when he died," she said.

"That's right," said Mrs. Sternberg. "You're the first person to know this, Miss Trntl, and I'm telling you in strictest confidence. In order for you to understand my actions on the night Charles died, you need to know the nature of our relationship.

"By 1947, Charles and I had been lovers for about eight years. Of necessity we had to be extremely careful in keeping our relationship secret. In our own ways, each of us was a public figure; and if word leaked out, the scandal-mongers would have been over us like ants. Leo was an important person in the banking community, and was already being vilified by Arab leaders over the partitioning of Palestine prior to the establishment of Israel. And I didn't want to cause him any pain, for I loved and respected him deeply. Charles had both his professional career and public image to safeguard, and the feelings of his wife and family to consider. Mrs. Farringford was a jealous and vengeful woman; had she known, she'd have expressed her fury either by suing him for divorce, naming me as co-respondent, or else privately making his life hell. To my knowledge, no one ever realized that Charles and I were lovers for those eight wonderful years. And I've never revealed it to anyone until this moment."

Trntl said, "You must have been *extremely* careful."

"Oh, we were. We were rarely seen together in public, and then only when other people were present. I was in his home only twice—on occasions when a large number of guests had been invited. When he visited us, he spent most of his time with Leo talking politics or jazz. Sometimes five or six weeks would go by without our being together. For a couple of years he had a rented room where we occasionally met; but most of our times together were out of town. I frequently traveled with him when he went on concert tours, or perhaps met him in a hotel in some distant city for a day and a couple of nights. Always under an assumed name, of course."

"Excuse me," said Trntl, "didn't your husband wonder about your absences?"

"As I've said, Leo was very busy, both as a banker during the war years, and with his international committee work. With my arts activities, I always had plausible excuses to be gone. Please don't think that I was dissatisfied with my married life; Leo and I had a very happy relationship. And I don't want you to think that my relationship with Charles was just a sordid affair. It was not. There was nothing about it temporary, or tawdry, or cheap. We were mature people who enjoyed each other, who found the relationship a source of joy and inspiration. An outlet for self-expression and sharing quite unlike anything we'd found with anyone else. My love for Leo was unaffected by my love for Charles. And I like to think that Charles felt affection for Mrs. Farringford too; I know he did for his children."

"If you don't mind," Trntl said, "I'd like to have that drink now." She went to the liquor cabinet, poured herself a Scotch, and returned to the sofa.

"Now: the cadenza," said Mrs. Sternberg. "While Charles was working on the Fifth Concerto during the summer of 1947, he was riding the crest of a creative surge greater than any he'd ever known. He shared in the general optimism that followed the conclusion of the war; his music was loved and played the world over; his stature as a major composer was established and secure; he had more money than ever before; his Eleventh Symphony (which had given him considerable difficulty) had been premiered in April and was well-received; his Sixth Piano Quintet and *Years of Decision* had met with critical acclaim; his daughter Clara was showing exceptional talent for the flute; and—yes—he and I had entered into a new phase of our relationship during the winter—a deeper, calmer, more liberating empathy. We were somehow newly attuned to the same wave-length—that's the only way I can describe it—and both of us grew through the experience over the spring and summer. We were able to spend more time together, since Leo was consumed with his activities and Mrs. Farringford had taken the children to England in July.

"The Fifth Concerto exploded forth while Charles was at the peak of his powers; almost day by day I watched it expand and develop under his hands. And the cadenza, which was the last thing to be written, summed up and expressed the happiness and fulfillment that Charles felt. He told me that I was the direct inspiration for it, and he played it for me repeatedly as it took shape. I'd make suggestions and give my reactions, and frequently he'd incorporate my thoughts in his reworking of the music. He called it 'our' cadenza—and said that without me it could not have been written.

"The rest of the score had been sent to the publisher, and galleys were ready for the three orchestras that would introduce the concerto to the public on his tour which was scheduled for October. He continued working on the cadenza right up to the time of the first performance in St. Louis. And I say this without bias, Miss Trntl—not because of the small and humble role I had in giving it final shape, but as a student of Farringford's musical achievement—the cadenza is the finest music he ever wrote: a six-minute distillation of his genius, affirming and surpassing everything that had gone before, and pointing new directions to the future.

"As the time of the concert tour approached, all through the month of September, the pressures on Leo got worse and worse. Leaders of various Arab groups were denouncing the partitioning of Palestine as an atrocity not unlike what Hitler had visited against the Jews in Europe. Leo, as I said earlier, was not an ardent Zionist, and the displacement of Palestinians from their homelands anguished him deeply. But he was nonetheless caught up in the efforts to create the State of Israel; and though he did what little he could to mitigate the upheavals, he was linked organizationally with the true zealots who didn't seem to care. He took personally the Arab allegations that New York Jewish bankers were establishing Israel out of personal greed; and the pain and frustration he felt that summer almost destroyed him emotionally. I tried to be supportive, but life in this house became simply unbearable. Leo was in an intense state of depression—angry, morose, short-tempered, and frequently absent. I could take no more; I simply had to get out of New York for breathing-space. So when Charles left for St. Louis, I went with him.

"The trip was a good one: in St. Louis, Chicago, and Cleveland, people were simply overwhelmed by the concerto. In full orchestral performance, it was all that I'd hoped, and far more than I'd dreamed. And the cadenza, in that context, was—sublime." She paused, finished her drink, and placed her glass on the coffee table. "Then, after the Cleveland concert, I waited for him at the hotel while he attended a post-concert reception. He returned just before we had to leave to catch the train back to New York. He didn't even have time to change out of his black tie and tails. We settled into our compartment for a joyous trip back, and began making plans for the future. He died about two-thirty in the midst of our celebration."

She stopped and passed a hand over her eyes. "The memory is still fresh after thirty-four years. As soon as I determined that he was dead, I had to force myself to decide quickly what had to be done. Can you imagine, Miss Trntl, in the face of shock, grief, and despair my confusion as I had to strategize how scandal was to be averted? I couldn't be with the body when it reached New York to face the press and answer questions for whatever investigations there might be. I had to get off the train. There was a scheduled stop at Bristow, Pennsylvania. I had about six minutes to get dressed, get Charles's body back into its pajamas, and make my escape. It dawned on me that I couldn't leave the precious cadenza manuscript to arrive unattended at Penn Station. To protect it, I'd have to take it with me. I knew it was in his suitcase, but I didn't have time to search for it; the train was already approaching Bristow station. So I simply took Charles's suitcase along with mine and left the train when it stopped."

"And then got back to New York on your own," said Trntl. (And didn't clean the ashtray or take your ticket, she thought.)

"Yes, in the station I transferred the cadenza to my suitcase, left Charles's in the women's washroom (having removed everything that would identify the owner), and took the next train that came through.

"When I got back to New York, I came straight home and hid the manuscript in the false bottom of my piano bench. I'd had the compartment made some time previously, and on occasion had kept versions of Charles's unpublished works there for safekeeping while I studied them. It seemed a logical place to hide the cadenza until the furor had calmed and I could get the manuscript anonymously to Lunner & Dinch to be published with the rest of the concerto. I planned to hold it for about three days and then find some way of sending it to Mr. Lunner. But then something happened that no one could have foreseen or planned for.

"The next day was my birthday; and when I came back from an afternoon committee meeting, Leo greeted me in the front hall and said he had a surprise for me. He said he knew he'd been hard to live with during the last several months, and he wanted to make it up to me through a very special birthday present. I'll never forget his words: 'You've complained about your old piano long enough; for over three years you've been wishing we could buy a new one. Look in the music room.'

"I rushed across the hall, and sure enough—my old piano and its bench were gone. In their place stood a brand-new concert grand. At that point, I'm afraid I behaved very badly. I raved, I shouted. Poor Leo! He must've thought I'd lost my mind. I demanded to know where my old piano was. He'd sold it, of course—to the people who'd delivered the new one. 'Who are they?' I shouted. 'I've got to call them!' 'Do you want the old piano back?' Leo asked, completely bewildered by my rejection of his gift. 'I want my music out of the piano bench,' I said. He smiled happily: 'We removed the music. It's here on the table.' And there it was, neatly stacked; but of course the cadenza manuscript wasn't with it. I called the people who'd bought the old piano; they no longer had it. That very afternoon a jobber had taken it away for resale elsewhere. I never was able to find out where it had gone.

"And that's why the cadenza was never delivered to Lunner & Dinch for publication. My best intentions were thwarted by the good intentions of a loving husband. For thirty-four years I've felt personally responsible for the loss of the cadenza. And that's why I was so relieved when Professor Pettigrew announced its discovery; so dismayed when it was stolen from his house; so determined that it be found again and published for the world. That's why I offered to provide whatever financial backup you need to aid in recovering it."

"You didn't feel comfortable coming forward with your offer to Lunner & Dinch?" asked Trntl.

"No. I don't wish to associate my name with the cadenza in any public way. Dinch is not the man his father was, and I don't want the Farringfords knowing about my interest."

Trntl was silent. She felt as though she'd just run a five-minute mile. "Thank you for telling me all this," she said finally. "It certainly clarifies a great many matters. I'm sorry I got the wrong impression of what you were telling me."

Mrs. Sternberg was showing the strain of her narrative; but she looked strangely relieved, too, as though she'd finally set down a heavy burden. "I would be grateful, then," she said with a cautious smile, "if you'd reconsider my offer."

"I'd be happy to have you as an official client," said Trntl. "Happy to know that, should the need arise, I'd have a pipeline of ready cash—how did you say it?—to facilitate the cadenza's recovery. It may be that I won't need to call on you for help; I hope not. But I certainly will if money's required."

"Excellent. Now, will you accept reimbursement for your travel expenses?"

"Yes," said Trntl, "I'd be glad to."

Chapter 26

After her talk with Mrs. Sternberg, and the long drive back into the city, Trntl found it pleasant to spend an evening relaxing in her own apartment. She aired the rooms, killed eleven cockroaches in the kitchen, inspected her plants which Mrs. Quillan from down the hall had been watering, went through her accumulated personal mail, showered, played with the cat, and—listening to her Miles Davis recordings—worked for awhile on the quilt she was making as a wedding present for her youngest niece. At ten-thirty, she had a 12-inch pizza delivered.

Then, in her plaid cotton bathrobe, she curled up in a corner of her couch with pizza, beer, cat, and a yellow legal pad. It was time to detail an inventory of precisely where the investigation stood. Dinch would want particulars in the morning, and she herself felt that she had to do a summative stocktaking.

On her pad she drew several headings. Under Tracking the Cadenza she wrote:

1. Morris tells Stephanie: cadenza locked in his briefcase. Then he sends Stephanie a letter saying that he's separated the cadenza from "the other music" and put it in their "Special Place."

2. Morris killed to obtain cadenza—probably by Tony Scaevola, whom he feared.

3. Dinch receives first ransom call ($50,000), probably from Tony, who has briefcase and/or cadenza. No follow-up to this call.

4. Stephanie claims to have cadenza (all she has for sure is the briefcase, obtained in Tony's apartment). Fails to get the briefcase to me or to Pettigrew.

5. Stephanie killed, her apartment searched. She did not read Morris's letter saying cadenza is in their "Special Place"—"the key is in the 'Key Hole'—get it?" (I HATE this riddle!)

6. Torelli tells me that when Stephanie was killed, she did not have the cadenza; nor did Torelli find it in her apartment. Moreover, G. Scaevola would destroy it if he could. CONCLUSION: She had what she thought was the cadenza (in the locked briefcase?) before she was killed.

7. Tony vanishes; staff at Hanrahan's and the police are given a cover story; his apartment is vacated. QUERY: did G. Scaevola find out about Tony's ransom attempt and stop it? Did he get him off the scene because of Morris's murder? Was Tony murdered too?

8. Dinch gets second ransom call from a different person than the first ($58,300). Dinch supplies money; no cadenza comes in exchange. (GUESS: caller did not have the cadenza to sell. Whole thing a scam. OR: caller does have cadenza, but kept it to sell to somebody else. But: whichever, the caller knew about the first call—that $50,000 had been asked, and that a second call would follow. Therefore: if not one of the Scaevolas—then (1) either a New York friend of Tony's, or else (2) an inside job: (a) one of the clients, or (b) someone a client had told about the first call, or (3) somebody else entirely. QUERY: Why did the caller raise the price to $58,300?

9. If the ransom-caller does not have the cadenza to sell, and if Stephanie had only the locked briefcase from Tony's apartment, and not the cadenza itself, THEN: it might still be in their "Special Place"—in Baltimore.

Under Players, she wrote:

1. Tony Scaevola—disappeared; probably out of it. Dead?

2. Torelli and George Fiocco—back on the streets (LOCK THE DOORS!)

3. Adcock and Price—clearly not trustworthy. Torelli implied that G. Scaevola enjoys a leak from police headquarters.

4. Two unknown men who rescued me from Torelli at Scaevola's warehouse. Who are they, and what was their stake in saving me? (I don't think they're Dinch's operatives. More likely working for one of the competitors, thinking I'll find the cadenza for them.)

5. The Bracebeam Trio who responded to our ad: Littlefellow, Bullneck, and Blondie (possibly working for a fourth person)

6. The man in the gray trenchcoat who followed me all over town.

7. The people who broke Finegold's arm (the Bracebeam trio? Some other group?)

Under a sub-heading, Who Wants the Cadenza? , she wrote:

8. Dinch, the Family, Abbott, Latimer, Foxe—want it published.

9. Mrs. Sternberg—ditto. Also, assuaging her guilt.

10. G. Scaevola—would destroy it.

11. Two parties (A and B) who've run ads in The Sun:

      A—unknown (the "musicologist")

      B—the Bracebeam Trio and whoever it is they're working for (the "publisher")

12. One or all of Dinch's competitors

Finally, under Questions to be Answered:

1. Where is "our Special Place"? What is the "Key Hole"?

2. Who are the Two Unknown Men who saved me at the warehouse?

3. Who was responsible for the 2nd & 3rd break-ins at Pettigrew's?

4. Who beat up Finegold? ANSWER: The Bracebeam Trio (minus Blondie, plus Another) is a possibility. One of them is named "Marco."

5. Who searched our New York office? What were they after?

6. Who is the "musicologist" who ran the ad? Pettigrew—trying to get it back? Humboldt-Hartmann Gesellschaft, etc. etc.?

7. Who called Dinch with the Second (phony) Ransom Demand? (SPECULATION: if one of Tony's friends, impossible to know who. Clearly a New Yorker who knew the layout of the cemetery. One of the clients? someone a client told about the First Call?) MOTIVE: the person wanted $58,300. Who?

Silas Dinch?—wouldn't make sense; it was his money.

Morgan Latimer?—no; he didn't need the money.

Mrs. Farringford?—no; how would she have obtained the cadenza? But: she could probably use the money.

Clara Farringford?—no.

Anton Farringford?—not likely. He has a good position at a major bank; and besides, he's too much of a wimp.

Peter Shipley Abbott?—hardly. He was in Baltimore when the call came through.

Rosamond Foxe?—no.

Trntl stopped writing and stared at the sheet. Who then? Somebody that one of these people had told. Or even more likely, somebody working at Lunner & Dinch, or at Morgan Latimer's brokerage firm, who'd got wind of the first demand. Aide? Secretary? Clerk?

Trntl decided to mention this possibility tomorrow, in case Dinch hadn't thought of it himself. She read through her notes

330

once again to see if she'd omitted anything important; and then, drowsy from her long day, the pizza, and two beers, she turned out the lights and went to bed. While composing herself for sleep, she reviewed once again the revelations of Mrs. Sternberg, relieved that the cadenza's initial disappearance from the train in 1947 finally was satisfactorily explained.

At his house in Brooklyn, Peter Shipley Abbott, having just returned from Philadelphia green with fatigue after four sleepless nights, knocked himself out with three stiff brandies and toppled into bed. If the first night, prior to his disastrous rehearsal, had been filled with bingeing on chocolate and frenzied speculations, last night, prior to the performance itself, had been crowded with terrifying hallucinations: he imagined being swallowed by a gigantic leather briefcase; crushed beneath a granite tombstone by a snarling Johannes Brahms; chased by Anton Farringford snip-snipping at his fingers with a pair of hedge clippers.

As abominably as the rehearsal had gone, the concert had gone infinitely worse. He and the orchestra could never get together. It was as though they were performing different concertos. Never in his career had Abbott played so badly: he missed his cues, continually struck wrong notes, omitted twelve bars of the first movement, lost his place in the second, and inadvertently repeated a section of the third while the orchestra went on to other things. From the corner of his eye he could see people leaving their seats and filing out long before the third movement was finished; and when the concerto finally stumbled to its end, there ensued: first, a long, embarrassed silence; then, a thin, reluctant patter of applause in widely scattered parts of the house; following that, a great deal of murmuring, whispering, tittering, and scraping of feet; and finally, a persistent hissing, as from a thousand steam-valves, that seemed to come from everywhere at once. The orchestra left the stage as quickly as possible. Never had Abbott seen such loathing as on the curled lip of Gustav Niedermann as he stepped from the podium—the sneer of absolute contempt, the glare of hatred flung at him like a spear of ice. There was no curtain call. As Abbott came backstage, Osgood the concert-master turned his back to him and farted.

While Trntl was relaxing in her apartment and progressing on her quilt, in Baltimore, at the CIMACORP Health Club, Giovanni Speranza was working diligently for his promotion. He'd spent Saturday afternoon and evening and some of Sunday morning gathering a staff to help him carry out his double assignment. To help with the planning and execution of Phase Two, he'd chosen as his lieutenants Alfredo Colonna and Davis "Fingers" Beauregard. For accomplishing Phase One, he'd selected, in addition, four muscle men to provide backup and physical strength, and a couple of scouts to serve as lookouts, or "ride shotgun" (as he called it). At four-thirty Sunday afternoon, Lefty Scaevola's private secretary had informed Angelo Torelli and George Fiocco that Lefty wanted them to meet with company lawyers that evening to discuss defense strategy for their upcoming trials. They would be picked up at their homes at eight o'clock and driven to the meeting.

At six, on orders from the front office, the Health Club had been closed, all employees sent home, the doors locked, and a sign posted on the front door: 'WEEKEND REPAIRS. OPEN MONDAY.' At seven-thirty, refreshed and fortified by an excellent dinner of roast beef and mashed potatoes, Speranza had set up shop in the club's second-floor conference room: a square table with four chairs, a bright overhead light, a tape recorder discreetly off to one side, a couple of ash trays.

Since N. F. Trntl was the target of Phase Two, and only Torelli and George had seen her, it was necessary that they should provide Speranza with her physical description before Phase One was concluded. He hoped that Torelli and George would supply the requisite information in a forthcoming and cooperative spirit. That would make things much tidier and more pleasant for everybody. If they didn't, the advantage of holding the interrogation at the Health Club was the proximity of the weight room and the swimming pool, where things could get much less tidy and far less pleasant.

When the car delivered him to the mostly-darkened Health Club, Angelo Torelli was mildly surprised—both at their destination, and by the club's being closed. On Sunday nights it was open and usually buzzing with activity until ten-thirty. As his driver Tiny Varro unlocked the front door, he saw the sign posted on the glass. Weekend repairs? A suspicious man by nature, Torelli felt the first twinge of serious misgivings—though he knew that Lefty Scaevola frequently preferred to do things in a secretive manner (particularly, as at present, when he was under Federal scrutiny). It was not out of keeping with his usual mode for Lefty to want a meeting with lawyers to take place as privately as possible. So he put his suspicions on hold as Tiny led him to the conference room.

George Fiocco was there already, his wrist in a cast, his arm in a sling. Standing beside the table were Giovanni Speranza, Fingers Beauregard, Alfie Colonna, and several others. But no lawyers.

"Ciao, Angelo," Speranza said, extending his hand.

"Johnny," said Torelli, shaking it. "When did you get back from Newark?"

"Friday afternoon. Tony's doing fine with his uncle, and Lefty wanted me back here."

"George and I were to meet with some of Lefty's lawyers. But I don't see 'em."

"They were delayed," said Speranza. He indicated the table. "Sit down, be comfortable. Careful of your arm, George." He seated himself facing the two men, pushed an ashtray to the center of the table, and began rolling a cigar between his fingers. "A lot's happened while I been in Newark. I get back and hear all these stories. Mainly about this female detective—Trntl's her name?—who's become a real pain. Shootin' her mouth off to whover'll listen, droppin' names right and left, tellin' the cops that Tony killed that Morris guy, mentionin' your name in connection with the Simms girl, plannin' to testify in the inquest on Tuesday." He lit the cigar, filled his mouth with smoke, and sent a cloud billowing about the overhead light. "So I understand you picked her up and took her to the warehouse. But jeez! she got away: Benno got bashed, Joe got coated in cement and hung on a hook, and you got dumped in a drum. I hear it took the boys almost ten minutes to pry you out."

His face bright scarlet, Torelli slapped his palm against the tabletop. "She had help! Three guys with guns ambushed us. Showed up at the last minute, claimed they were police to get the drop on us. They came close to *killing* us—" he stopped abruptly, and began fumbling in his shirt pocket for a pack of cigarettes. "We were outnumbered, and somehow they'd already nailed

Benno who was standing lookout, so we didn't get any warning."
With meticulous precision he extracted a cigarette from the pack,
tapped its end four times on the table, and slowly lit it with a great
show of calm.

George motioned with his sling. "Can you light me one too?"

Torelli stuck a cigarette in George's mouth and held a match
to it.

Speranza nudged his cigar ash into the tray. "And I understand there was a second attempt to take Trntl out—in her hotel
room. Only this time she wasn't even there. Just two guys were—
some karate whiz who broke George's arm, and a little wimp who
knocked *you* out, Angelo, and took your gun."

"No," said Torelli. "it wasn't the wimpy guy. It was somebody else—a third man in the hall. He got behind me—" Again he
paused, clamped his jaw, and focused on the smoke spiraling from
his cigarette.

"You make it sound like this Trntl has her own organization,"
said Speranza. "Three at the warehouse; three more at the hotel.
And efficient, too, when you look at what happened to Benno and
George, and the way you and Joe got clobbered."

Torelli was silent.

George said: "Johnny, I never saw nobody move as fast as that
blond guy did. Jeez, his hands were everywhere all at once. And
he's a mean bastard, too."

"Well, Trntl still has to be dealt with before Tuesday," Speranza
said. "She's at the Macready Hotel, registered under the name of
Carol Brown."

"It's the Cavendish," said Torelli.

"No, it's the Macready, Room 523. She moved after you and
George staged your attack, Angelo. She and that boyfriend of hers.
You're way behind the times. And since you two have been arrested and charged, you've become too public and visible to be involved in another go. Lefty wants you to keep a low profile and not
risk making things worse for yourselves. So he's decided to send
in a new team to finish the job. He called me back from Newark to
head it up."

Relief blossomed on George's face. "Hey, that's good news,
Johnny. This broken wrist has really slowed me down, and I think
the guy mighta gave me a hernia. I was kinda worried about havin'
to make another try. It's good to be off the hook."

Shut up, fool! Torelli thought. Nobody's off the hook. Keeping his face carefully blank, Torelli said, "You gotta hand it to Lefty; always lookin' to do whatever's for the best."

"That's right," said Speranza. "But we've got a problem. None of us knows what Trntl looks like. Benno's not able to talk; so it's only you, Angelo—and Joe, and George here, who've seen her. And Joe's in Atlantic City."

"I never got a real good look at her," George said. "She wasn't in the hotel room when we got there, and after her boyfriend did the karate bit on me, I was too hurt and groggy to pay much attention to all the folks who finally did come into the room. The cops I remember."

"Well, then, Angelo, I guess you're the only one who can give us a description of Trntl." Speranza turned on the tape recorder.

Torelli ground out his cigarette, rubbing the end back and forth in the bottom of the ashtray. "I only saw her on two occasions," he said. "And both times it was really dark. Once when she came to Hanrahan's with the Simms girl, and then in the car getting her to the warehouse. And it was dark at the warehouse, too." He felt tiny beads of sweat clustering at his hairline. Once they had his description of her, they'd have no further need of him. Clearly, whatever security he had was in *not* providing the description.

"Okay, okay, Angelo." Speranza's tone was registering impatience. "It was dark. So what *did* you see?"

Torelli lit another cigarette. Looked at his watch. "When are those lawyers gonna come? It's getting late."

Speranza turned off the tape recorder. "They aren't coming," he said. "Change of plan." He leaned forward across the table, eyes on a level with Torelli's. "Come on, Angelo. Give. How tall is she? What color's her hair?"

"What do you mean, the lawyers aren't coming?" Torelli asked. "*What* change of plan?"

"You need lawyers only if you plea-bargain or go to trial. You and George aren't going to do either, Angelo."

Sweat began trickling down Torelli's face. "Is Lefty sending us away? Are we going to jump bail?"

"That's right."

George nodded. "I done that before, up in Rochester in '72. Where's he gonna send us? Atlantic City? Harrisburg? I hope it's not Harrisburg. I got a cousin up there who thinks I owe him some money."

"He didn't tell *me*," said Speranza. "He probably wants it to be a surprise." He turned back to Torelli. "Okay, Angelo."

"I don't recall much of anything. She was kind of average looking."

Speranza sat back and motioned with two fingers. "Now."

Several men moved forward from the wall to stand behind George's and Torelli's chairs.

"Frisk 'em," said Speranza. And quick, sure hands patted them down, pulled open their coats, slid down their legs to their ankles. From Torelli, two guns were confiscated; from George, one gun and a knife sheathed under his sock. "That's all they have," said Alfie Colonna. "Okay," said Speranza. "Get George out of here. You know what to do." Two of them marched George out.

"Now, Angelo," said Speranza, blowing smoke in his face. "We'll get Trntl whether we have your description or not. Make it easy on yourself. Tell us what we want to know. If you don't, we'll take you into the weight room and apply some real pressure. Now: is she tall or short?" Again he started the tape recorder.

The sweat was streaming down Torelli's face. He didn't want to go to the weight room. He didn't want to be taken away like George. And he most certainly didn't want to make Speranza's job easier. He decided to describe a person who was just the opposite of Trntl in every respect—in hopes a false description would make Johnny fuck up, too. It might be the best he could accomplish by way of revenge.

"She was very short," he said. "About five-foot-four."

"Good," said Speranza. "Blond or brunette?"

"Dark hair," said Torelli. "Very dark brown; maybe black."

"Does she wear glasses?"

"No," said Torelli. "Unless contact lenses."

"Any distinguishing facial characteristics?"

"Wears her hair pretty long. Has kind of a small, turned-up nose."

"Age?"

"Under forty."

"Tits?"

"She was wearing a heavy coat."

"Rings or other distinctive jewelry?"

"I didn't notice."

"That's not really much for us to go on, Angelo. Could be almost anybody. Try harder. What else can you think of?"

Torelli pursed his lips and stared at the tabletop. "She was wearing some kind of strong perfume. Stunk up the car. I don't know what flavor it was." His brows bunched with the intensity of his thought. "Oh yeah, she had a high-pitched squeaky voice and a nervous giggle."

"And that's it, Angelo?"

"I can't think of anything else. It was *dark*, and you've gotta realize, Johnny, there wasn't any reason to make a point of re-membering what she looked like. Maybe more will come to me later."

Johnny turned off the tape recorder and stood up. "Okay, Angelo, you've been a help. Not much, but some. We're finished here. Fingers, Alfie, Booger, take Mr. Torelli out to the car. Rollo, you follow us and turn out the lights."

By one-thirty, after a brief journey toward the Eastern Shore, the company speedboat was once again mooring in its dock.

Chapter 27

March 9   (Monday)

All weekend Anton Farringford had worked feverishly to erase the evidence of his borrowing. On Monday morning when the external auditors arrived, all of his adjustments would have to be in place, every cent accounted for, all traces of tinkering removed, all irregularities so normalized that not even a breath of suspicion would be aroused. He had so much to do, and the exquisite detailing of the transactions required such concentration, that he had little difficulty putting aside his anxiety regarding the fate of the cadenza, and his puzzlement regarding what had happened at Mount Myrtle. He'd think about those matters later. But Saturday and all of Sunday until very early Monday morning had to be devoted to saving his skin.

It was far more difficult to put aside the insistent demands of Twila Bidwell, who craved attention and felt neglected. Left completely in the dark regarding his activity, she didn't understand his focused withdrawal, his refusal to leave his Workspace, his hunching there compulsively pecking, and scribbling, and sifting through papers. She'd nagged and nattered at him much of Saturday, wheedled and cajoled, faunched and fumed—to no avail. She'd thawed him a frozen dinner and gone to the movies. When she returned he didn't seem aware that she'd been gone. On Sunday morning she'd tried to distract him from his work for a "heart to heart" talk. He patted her hand and said "Another time; I'm working for our future." The day's trajectory was predictable from that point on (Twila, after all, was only human): anger in the afternoon, sullenness at suppertime, hostility and resignation in the evening. Leaving the television on, she'd haughtily drawn her robe about her, accused him of liking money more than sex, and marched off to bed.

Throughout the early morning hours (till four o'clock), he kept at his work; then, reasonably satisfied (he'd triple-checked everything), he locked his materials into Dinch's suitcase with the ransom money, and attached the key to his watch-chain.

While shaving, he was pleased to see his hand as steady as a nun's. At six-fifteen, he bustled through the front door of Swinfurth Lightfoot as though it were any other day. The guard greeted him with considerable surprise: "You're very early today, Mr. Farringford."

"Yes, I was sick on Friday and fell behind in some important work. Thought I'd get an early start today and catch up." The guard locked the door behind him and went back to his station.

Quickly Anton went up to his office, unplugged his telephone, then rushed to the main computer room, unlocked the door (thank God they hadn't changed the combination yet!), and let himself in. This morning he saw the real and practical advantage of having helped to design, program, and implement the system: his work was completed in seven and a half minutes. He locked the door behind him, went to the second floor and left $58,209.37 (cash) in the reserve vault, ran back to his office, and punched his personal computer into the mainframe.

He spent another six minutes feeding in commands, and then it was finished: fifty-eight thousand two hundred and nine dollars and thirty-seven cents electronically deposited in three dummy accounts established at widely dispersed branches in different parts of the city; that money, in the proper amounts, then transferred from the dummies to the thirteen plundered trust accounts; all of the transactions automatically, permanently deleted from the computer's memory of record, and the dummy accounts officially retired. If his programming worked as planned, there'd be no trace of any of this, and the only question that would arise for the auditors would be the unaccountable surplus of cash in the reserve vault.

Breathing more easily, Anton plugged in his office telephone, turned out his light, and with his hat and topcoat, went down the hall to the men's room. There he sat dozing in a toilet stall till the first arrivals of his co-workers unloading their breakfast coffee. Morning chatter; the shuffling of feet; loud flushings. "Morning, Anton. Heard you were sick Friday. How ya doin'?" "Much better today, thanks. When's your wife going in for her knee surgery?" "Hey, Anton, I understand the External Auditors will be here today. You got your department shipshape?" "We'll be ready for 'em." Washing his hands. "They've got their job to do, too." And back to his office where he greeted the secretaries. "Good morning, Mr. Farringford. Are you feeling better today?" "Much better, thanks. Shipshape." And so to work.

It was nine-thirty before he was again free to worry about what had become of the cadenza.

On Monday morning, when she and Felix were shown into Silas Dinch's inner office, Trntl was shocked to see the change that had come over the publisher since their last meeting. Thin, gaunt, his eyes sunken and deeply shadowed, he seemed to have shrunk in size; his shirt collar circled his neck at a quarter-inch distance from the flesh; his suitcoat hung from his shoulders like a tent. But most shocking, his face: from chin to forehead a fiery red rash had everywhere erupted, creating a hot, leathery mask, pebbled and lumpy, speckled with, and shedding, large flakes of dry skin. He had shaved off his mustache, revealing a short upper lip. From across the room, it looked as though his face had been scalded. His hands had developed a continuous tremor, and when he rose from behind his desk to greet them, Trntl got a waft of bourbon so strong it made her blink.

Dinch motioned them to chairs and got right to business. "Mr. McKay has kept me informed of your progress in Baltimore—if progress it could be called. I assume you're familiar with what's happened here. I want from you a firsthand report on the situation, an assessment of where we stand. In your opinion, what chance do we have of recovering the cadenza?"

Trntl gave him a succinct but full account of where the investigation stood. "It's possible the cadenza's been destroyed," she said, "but if it still exists, we suspect it's still in Baltimore, concealed by Morris and awaiting discovery. If we decipher the clues we think Morris left in his letter to Stephanie Simms, we can probably find the hiding place."

Dinch was fiddling with a paperweight. "Do you think the murders were committed by parties who were trying to get the cadenza?"

"The first was," she answered, "by someone who was responsible for your first ransom call. I think the second murder was simply to silence Stephanie, who knew too much about the first. I learned from one of the people involved that if the cadenza had been recovered at the time of her death, it would've been destroyed."

Dinch sighed resignedly. "Then there are the two attempts on your life. Despite what Mr. McKay's told me, I'd always assumed they were to prevent your recovering the cadenza for *us*."

Trntl couldn't restrain a humorless little smile. "I don't think I'm close enough to the cadenza that I need to be stopped. No, I think the attacks on me have nothing at all to do with the cadenza; they've occurred because of my knowledge about Stephanie's murder."

"But," said Dinch, "you've been followed and your office here's been searched. Surely *those* matters have something to do with the cadenza."

She nodded. "We know of at least two other groups who want the cadenza. Both have run veiled inquiries in the Baltimore paper. As a way of smoking them out, we answered the ads, claiming *we* had the cadenza and were offering it for sale. We've met with a representative of one of the groups."

Dinch spasmed excitedly and dropped the paperweight. "Who are they? Who do they represent?"

"That's not clear. It was an inconclusive meeting. There were three people on the other side; the man Mr. Grimsson spoke to said they'd have to consult their boss before making an offer. For all we know, there may be others as well."

Dinch pulled a pad from his desk drawer and poised his pen. "Can you describe these three people?"—and as she did, he took rapid notes.

"One was a short man, with close-cropped brown hair, about thirty-four years old. He had large nostrils and a chipped right front incisor. The second was a tall man, about six-three weighing—oh, two hundred and forty pounds, with a thick, heavy neck, and very long arms. The third is a blond woman, about thirty-five, of moderate height, with an extremely erect posture, thin lips, and generally attractive features. A rather square jaw. She uses make-up skillfully, and was nicely and expensively dressed."

Dinch's eyes rolled and glittered behind his glasses. "Did she have a small brown mole on her right cheek, just below the eye?"

"I never got close enough to see her that clearly," said Trntl.

Dinch chewed his lip while jotting on his pad. "It might be Ilse Sturm," he said. "Which would mean Humboldt-Hartmann Gesellschaft." He leaned back with an air of satisfaction. "I'll have the files checked to see if we can identify the others." He took a cigarette from a box on his desk and lit it. Trntl seized the opportunity to light one of her own. "I wish you could've seen whether or not she had a mole," said Dinch; then, moving on: "The second group that placed an ad hasn't contacted you?"

"Not yet."

"If they do, observe as many distinguishing features as possible. Anything at all that seems significant. You have our dossiers; you might be able to identify them from those." He smoked for a moment, pondering. "Do you think this group you've described is responsible for the second and third break-ins at Pettigrew's?"

"Don't know."

"Or for searching your office here?"

"Can't say."

"What's your opinion about the phony ransom demand? After dropping off the money, I was told to return to Mount Myrtle Cemetery to get the cadenza. But it wasn't there."

"We think that person never did have the cadenza, and just wanted the money. But about those ransom calls—Was the voice at all familiar? Was it a voice you knew?"

"A voice I *knew*?" Dinch stared at her in wonderment. "Of course not! It was a thick, mushy voice with a bad Australian accent. Do you want to hear it? I've got it on tape."

"Please," said Trntl.

He hauled out the tape recorder and two tapes. The first was the ransom call giving instructions. The second was very brief: "Oi got the money, myte, thanks very much. Go back to where you left it, and you'll foind the cadenza in a brown briefcyse behind the HODGES stone."

"But of course I didn't find it," said Dinch.

"The voice isn't one *I* know," said Trntl. "And yet there's something about it . . . in the phrasing, maybe? the breathing patterns?"

"Why do you ask if it's a familiar voice?" Dinch demanded.

"This caller knew about the first call; knew that it was to be followed up but wasn't; knew that the original ransom was $50,000. That information was known to only a few people; the caller had to be privy to it."

"One of *us*?" Dinch cried. "An inside job?"

"I don't think it's one of the clients—"

"Well, I should think not!"

"More likely someone in your office, or in Mr. Latimer's. Who did you tell about the first ransom demand?"

Dinch began massaging his brow with a thumb and forefinger. He took off his glasses and began rubbing his eyes. "Only Ray Tuttle, a trusted vice-president—and the comptroller—and my secretary—I'm sure that's all."

"What about Latimer?"

"I don't know who Latimer might've told. We all agreed on secrecy. You could ask him yourself if he wasn't so sick. He's in intensive care with a massive hemorrhage."

"I'd heard he was ill. I'm sorry."

"I'm afraid his prognosis isn't good."

"That's a real shame," said Felix.

"I'll call a staff meeting," Dinch muttered—"Ray, and Bob Quincy, and Mrs. Innes, and see if they told anybody."

"It might be wise," said Trntl.

"Do you think there'll be further attempts to kill you?" Dinch asked her bluntly.

"I can't safely assume otherwise," she said. "The men who tried are bailed out and running loose. Nevertheless, I've got to go back to Baltimore this evening; tomorrow I'm to testify at a coroner's inquest in the Simms murder."

"If you meet with the blond woman again, see if she has a little brown mole beneath her right eye."

"We'll do our best," said Trntl.

They left him on the phone to his secretary and took the elevator down to the street. Felix was smiling: "Well, at least you've given him some things to think about. He'll be busy all afternoon."

Trntl nodded. "I didn't want him to get around to asking how much we're running up on the expense account."

"That question will occur to him about four o'clock," said Felix.

They had an early lunch at a sandwich shop, then stopped by Trntl's apartment where she packed a small bag with a camera and two rolls of film, additional clothes, and assorted tape cassettes of music. Then, after she'd fed the cat, closed the apartment, and spoken briefly to Mrs. Quillan, they went to the office, where Trntl read through the Farringford file and caught up on her correspondence and Felix worked on three other cases. At seven they locked up and went to supper. And then, at eight-thirty, Felix drove Trntl to the train.

Gripping her shoulder in farewell, Felix said, "Be careful. Don't let the Scaevolas get you down. The firm needs you."

"I've learned not to sit in front of open windows," she said. "Remind Carol of Rosamond Foxe's concert and reception on the 12th. Tell her she'd better be back for it—or I'll find somebody else to take."

"Well, that gives us three days yet," said Trntl. "I'm sure we'll have the affair wrapped up by then."

Monday found Giovanni Speranza in high spirits. Phase One of his assignment was completed with no complications and minimal fuss. As for Phase Two, thanks to the description Torelli had provided them, getting a bead on their target was relatively simple: to find N. F. Trntl, they simply had to identify the guest at the Macready Hotel who called herself Carol Brown.

And—through a lucky occurrence—they'd already done that.

At six-thirty that morning, he and Tiny Varro had gone to the hotel to get a sense of the terrain. Having located the house telephones, they studied the physical layout of the lobby, noting with satisfaction that the side door giving access to the adjacent parking garage—while being situated near the two elevators—was not visible from the registration desk. They were also pleased to find no surveillance cameras or convex mirrors mounted on the walls. Finished in the lobby, they rode one of the elevators up to the top floor (the tenth), observing the arrangement of push buttons for the various stops, and the automatic door's mode of operation—how long it remained open, how long it took to open and close. They then took the stairs down to the fifth floor, where they established the location of Room 523 in relation to the elevators.

They were just on the point of hunting for the housekeeping supply room, when an elevator door slid open at the end of the hall, and a blond giant came ambling toward them. Speranza knew at once that it was Trntl's boyfriend Grimsson. He and Tiny turned away from the elevators and went on down the hall toward the 530's, as though they were guests proceeding to their own room.

At the door of 523, Grimsson knocked matter-of-factly, and when the door opened, they heard him say, "Good morning. Are you ready to go for breakfast?"

And a woman answered, "As soon as I turn off the television."

While Speranza stood watching intently (pretending to study his nails), Tiny was fiddling with his car key at the door lock of 542.

A woman came out of 523 and joined Grimsson, closing the door behind her; and together they walked down to the elevators, chatting quietly. A short woman, dwarfed beside her companion, probably five-foot-three or four at the most; long dark hair to her shoulders; no glasses. "Do you see her?" Speranza whispered. "Torelli told us true."

The man and woman got into the elevator and the door slid shut. Speranza could hardly believe his luck. "They've got separate rooms!"

Tiny pocketed his key. "Maybe one of 'em snores."

"The point is," Speranza said, "when he goes back to his room tonight, *she'll be alone!*"

"Okay, but how will we know when he goes to his room?" Tiny asked.

"That'll be *your* job. Find out his room number, so if you have to, you can check to see if he's in. But from five-o'clock on, I want you here, watching Room 523. They'll probably go out for dinner. But she'll have to come back at some point, and then he'll go to his own room. After dark, when she's here, and he's there, that's when we do it."

"You mean I have to stay here for five, maybe six hours?"

"You can sit on the couch in that little lounge area by the elevators. Bring something to read. Smoke your pipe."

"Why me?"

"Because you're smart, Tiny. You're the one I can trust to do the job right. You won't screw up like George and Torelli."

Tiny had been on the speedboat the previous night. He nodded and said, "I'll bring a book I've been meaning to read."

And with that, they'd left the hotel to go their separate ways.

At one-fifteen, in the cluttered office of Benno's Bodyshop—over a late lunch of ham sandwiches and potato salad—Giovanni Speranza was intensively planning Phase Two with Alfredo Colonna and Davis "Fingers" Beauregard. Now that he'd identified and located the target, and learned that her boyfriend wasn't always with her, all that remained was to work out the method for bringing her down.

Efficiency: that was the key! Careful planning. Stupid Torelli had fucked up because his first plan was too complicated—luring

Trntl out by pretending to have the cadenza, using phone booths and car-switches to get her to the warehouse, for crissakes. The whole Organization was laughing at Torelli, inventing dirty jokes about the fiasco at the warehouse. ("What was Torelli *doing* in the drum?" Two answers: "As little as possible!" or, "Piss little!" And at least two jokes were making the rounds about the large curved hook pronging out of Blanco's fly: something about "pulley, pulley on my chain", and "Keep it in your pants, Joe; you'll scare the cleanup crew.") But Torelli's second plan—the hotel-room hit—was *really* stupid. Risky, too public, too vulnerable to unforeseen and unpredictable circumstance. He should've known better. When others learned of Torelli's bad judgment, they were astounded and could explain it only by assuming that his warehouse humiliation had so crazed him with rage that he'd spun wildly out of control.

Well, Johnny Speranza wouldn't make those blunders. It would be clean, simple, swift. No wasted motion. No surprises. No slip-ups through over-elaboration. But time was short: they only had tonight.

Having to make it look like an accident was a real pain. It ruled out familiar and conventional methods: guns of all types, poison, strangulation, car bombs, knives. Even a fatal mugging would be too suspicious in the circumstances. Since Trntl had already mentioned Scaevola's name to the police, and since they knew she planned to testify at the inquest, nothing could even *suggest* foul play. And she couldn't just disappear: too many questions would come Scaevola's way. As an "accident", even asphyxiation in a closed car would be too dangerous. Suicide? Impossible. An auto crash? Difficult. Being run over by a speeding car? Maybe. Electrocution? Falling from a window? Drowning? Incineration?

It was fortunate that he had on his team the specialist Fingers Beauregard, who—of the people he had available—was by far the most experienced in "taking out the garbage." Mouth full of ham, he said to Fingers: "You know our problem. What's worked in the past?"

Fingers was a squat, burly man with large ears, ponderous jowls road-mapped with crimson capillaries, and restless belly-button eyes. Before answering, he lifted his upper lip and licked a film of potato salad off his white plastic spoon. When he spoke, it was in a thin piping voice: "Accidents are a pain, Johnny. I like things more straightforward. Disappearances are best. When you go on trips, do you ever think about how many bodies are buried under the Interstate Highways?—all those folks you might be driving over? Hey, I know of two on the way to Frederick, and three more between here and Washington alone. But accidents? We've had several involving cars. Doctoring brakes is tricky, and you can't always control where the accident will happen. It's really easier to simulate a fatal car accident than cause one. And hey: unless we can get this broad out of the hotel, and into her car, and then control her movements, forget it."

"What else besides cars?"

"Industrial accidents. I recall an explosion at a chemical plant in Wilmington eight years ago. Took out five, six people besides the target. So it wasn't clear he *was* the target. And there was a very effective removal in '72, with a guy turned into sausage by a worm-auger. And when we were building that stretch of highway out toward Glen Burnie, there was the union organizer who got flattened by the earth-mover—"

"None of those are helpful in this case," Speranza said impatiently.

Fingers dug his spoon into a fresh carton of potato salad. "Well, remember that political banquet back in '78?—the commissioner who was done in by botulism in his clam chowder?"

"Yeah," said Alfie with an excited nod. "Him and twenty-nine others. All Democrats."

Fingers focused on his eating. "Closed the restaurant, too. And, like in Wilmington, with such a large take-out, nobody guessed that Hawkins was the target. Those are the really elegant ones."

"We don't have control over Trntl's food," said Speranza.

"Well, there was that thing in Jersey where the carnival ride went crazy. Real spectacular. Tony 'The Cat' Tolumbo liked to ride a gizmo called the Swirl-a-Swoop, and this one night—I wasn't there, but I heard about it from a guy who was—the ride started going faster and faster and finally flew apart, and Tony took a long nose-dive over the treetops into the middle of somebody's barbecue. Damn, I wish they wouldn't put chunks of celery in this potato salad. The little green threads get caught in my teeth." He paused to dig at his left uppers with a fingernail. "And hey—you remember Franco 'Worms' Faggotti, who was going to testify before the Senate subcommittee back in '75? The Doctor followed him to Washington, and Worms never got the chance. Died of cardiac arrest on the Metro between Farragut West and Foggy Bottom."

"Yeah, but now The Doctor's gone too," Speranza said. "And a stopped heart is more appropriate for a man of sixty-nine like Worms than for a woman in her thirties like Trntl."

"Well, you never know," said Fingers.

Speranza shook his head in exasperation. "We've got to think of something else—and it's got to be quick, simple, sure."

"Okay, okay," said Fingers. "The first thing we've got to decide is whether the accident happens inside the hotel, or outside."

"Outside," Speranza said. He'd been mulling this question for hours. The opportunities and means for engineering an accident inside the hotel were limited at best. Since Trntl would be on her guard after Torelli's attempt at the Cavendish, it would be difficult to gain access to her room—in order to have her fall out of a window, say, or slip and crack her skull in the shower. And anything else they might try in the building itself—such as tinkering with the elevators—would be awkward to pull off, liable to discovery, and hard to disguise as an accident.

"Okay," said Fingers. "Then we've got to find a way to get her out of the hotel without suspecting anything and into a prearranged situation we can control."

"She'll have to leave sometime," said Alfie. "If we follow her, maybe we can surround her on the sidewalk and push her in front of a car."

"Not so good," said Fingers. "She might only be injured." He finished the potato salad and flipped the carton into a wastebasket. "Seriously, it might be easier to simulate an accident after the fact than to actually make one happen."

"What about the boyfriend who knows karate?" Alfie asked. "Does he have an accident too?"

"We want to keep this simple," said Speranza. "Better deal with her alone. When Tiny and I were scouting the hotel this morning, we learned that he has his own room. Let's leave him there."

Fingers nodded. "Yep, better deal with her alone." He opened a bakery box of jelly doughnuts, selected one with blueberry filling, and then another, with pineapple custard, before handing the box to Alfie.

During the next twenty minutes they considered and rejected a variety of plans. But, by the time the doughnuts were gone, they'd finally arrived at one that promised all that Speranza wished by way of simplicity and efficiency. After dark they would use one of Benno's closed panel trucks to take Trntl from the hotel to a quiet residential area northwest of downtown; there they'd stun her with a tap on the head, lay her on the pavement, and drive the truck over her.

Fingers would immediately start pounding on doors to rouse the residents, saying there'd been a hit-and-run accident, urging people to call an ambulance and the police. ("It's all a matter of illusion," Speranza said. "If we tell 'em there's been an accident—that it was a green Pontiac that ran her down, driven by long-haired teen-age kids, they'll believe it, and that's what they'll tell the police. Some of 'em will even think they saw it happen.") Once a crowd was milling on the street, Fingers would walk one block over to the waiting truck, and they'd all return to Benno's, where the tires would be removed, washed, and stacked with other used treads to be eventually shipped away. Events would follow each other almost mechanically—one, two, three—in stepwise fashion, with none of Torelli's junior-G-man complications. Simple, swift, clean—the way these things ought to be.

Only a few preparations were needed. The panel truck had solid walls with a double door at the rear, and inside, two benches along the walls facing each other. While Alfie emptied the interior by removing a huge tool chest, oxygen and acetylene tanks, cutting torches, and various sealed cardboard boxes, Fingers busied himself in the backroom printshop. First, he created two large rectangular placards reading FANCY'S FLOWERS, just the proper size to mask the BENNO'S BODYSHOP signs which were painted on both sides of the truck. Next, sixteen neatly-lettered cardboard signs for the hotel elevators:

OUT OF ORDER
PLEASE USE THE STAIRS
WE APOLOGIZE FOR THE INCONVENIENCE.

While Fingers and Alfie were busy at work, Speranza, using a map of Baltimore, charted the shortest, most efficient route from the Macready Hotel to the site of the accident (avoiding as many stoplights as possible). Then, already feeling the thrill of the hunt, he settled back with a Havana cigar of Lefty's brand, and—in accord with what he thought his promotion required of him—continued cautiously learning how to inhale.

When Tiny Varro called at six-thirty to report that Trntl and Grimsson had gone to dinner, the three of them piled into the truck and left for the hotel. Alfie, who'd been chosen to drive, found a parking place in the hotel garage and settled in to wait. The others, carrying the sixteen OUT OF ORDER signs in a large briefcase, entered the lobby and rode the elevator up to five. There, in a small lounge beside the elevators, they found Tiny settled into a vinyl couch reading a book.

"They're still gone," Tiny said.

"Did you learn which room the boyfriend's in?" Speranza asked.

"748."

"Okay. Fingers and I will go down to the lounge on four. After they come back, and Trntl's in 523 and Grimsson's gone up to seven, come down to four and let us know." He opened the briefcase and showed Tiny the cardboard signs. "Then you'll take ten of these and go up to the tenth floor, and work your way down, putting an OUT OF ORDER sign on each elevator door. Fingers will do the same for the fourth, third, and second floors, which will leave only the fifth floor without signs. Then Fingers will go to the house phone and call Trntl down to the lobby. I'll be waiting here on five by the elevators and ride down with her. It doesn't matter if people come up from the lobby, but we don't want anyone except Trntl and me going *down*. Once Trntl and I reach the lobby, Fingers will join us, and we'll all go to the parking garage. Tiny, it'll be your job to remove all the OUT OF ORDER signs. Then you're to go to Benno's and wait for us. You got any questions?"

"Nope," said Tiny. "Everything's clear."

Speranza gave him an approving thumbs-up; then he and Fingers took the elevator down to four.

It was already quite dark when Carol and Torvald returned from dinner at ten after eight. They settled down by the phone to play chess on Torvald's traveling-board. Since, for two days, they'd heard nothing from the "publisher's" agents they'd met at Bracebeam's, they were not expecting a call tonight. "Something scared them off," Carol said, capturing Torvald's queen's bishop. "The deal appeared too fishy, and they suspected either a swindle or a hoax."

"Maybe they obtained the manuscript from some *other* source," said Torvald, "and they've departed happy. Or maybe they simply haven't been able to consult with their boss. I think we'll hear from them."

At nine-thirty he said good night and left for his room. Carol settled back in an easy chair and opened her copy of Orwell's *Burmese Days* to where she'd left off on page 68; but, after reading three more pages, she thought better of it, put the book aside and turned on the television. At seven minutes till ten the telephone rang. "Well, they've called at last," she said, reaching for the receiver. "Hello?"

A man's voice, stressed and urgent. "Is this Carol Brown in Room 523?"

"Yes, it is."

"This is the night manager at the Registration Desk, calling at the request of Mr. Grimsson. He's here in the lobby; I'm afraid he's had an accident—"

"Mr. Grimsson?" Carol said. "What sort of accident?"

"A fairly bad one, I'm afraid. He fell at the entrance to the gift shop, seriously injured his leg and cut himself on the broken plate glass. He wants you to come down to the lobby at once, before the paramedics arrive."

"I'll be right there." She slammed down the receiver, grabbed up her purse, and hurried into the hall. A man standing at the elevators pushed the DOWN button as she reached them. Torvald! she was thinking. Paramedics! The elevator arrived; she quickly got on; the man followed her into the car, and the door slid shut.

The descent to the lobby seemed endless. But at last the elevator eased to a stop, and the door slid open—to reveal a heavily-built man facing her. As she stepped out into the lobby, the man roughly grabbed her arm and turned her to the right. The man who'd ridden down with her grabbed her other arm, and said: "Okay, walk straight ahead through that door. I've got a gun here so don't try anything funny."

"What's going on?" Carol demanded, stopping dead in her tracks. The snout of the pistol jabbed her ribs. "Shut up. Keep walking. Believe me, we'll shoot you right here."

She believed him. Still protesting, she kept walking and was shoved through the door into the parking garage. A panel truck parked against the far wall started its engine and came toward them.

"Who are you people?" Carol asked. "What do you want with me? Where's Mr. Grimsson?"

"Mr. Grimsson's up in his room," said the man with the gun. "Who we are doesn't matter. We've got you, that's all we want."

The truck stopped beside them. The heavy man opened the rear door of the truck and motioned her to climb in. She did not budge.

"Hurry up, Miss Trntl," said the man with the gun. "You've got a date with an accident."

"Trntl?" said Carol. "I'm not Trntl. You've got the wrong person. I'm Carol Brown."

"Save it," said the Gun. "We know all about that. You must think we're pretty stupid. Now get in the truck." The muzzle prodded her viciously. She hoisted herself into the truck. "Fingers, you ride in back with her. I'll sit up front with Alfie and show him where we're going. It she causes any trouble, kill her." The man called Fingers nodded and produced his own gun—a long-barreled .38 equipped with a silencer. He climbed in after Carol, and the door was closed behind them. A moment later, with a grinding of gears, the truck lurched forward and rolled toward the exit and the quiet street.

Chapter 28

Carol and the man called 'Fingers' sat facing each other on narrow wooden benches, their knees almost touching. He kept his silencer pointed at her stomach. A small electric bulb in the center of the roof provided dim light. The compartment was separated from the front seat by a wall containing a small rectangular window covered with wire mesh. The small windows in both of the rear doors were covered on the inside with brown paper.

"Hey," Carol said, "I'm not the person you want. I'm Carol Brown. Trntl's in New York." She studied the man's face to see if this evoked any response. His tiny eyes stared at her without blinking. Centrifugal pull told her that the truck had turned a couple of corners in quick succession. They stopped for a long moment, then started up again. Presumably a stoplight.

The man's cold eyes were disturbing. "I want to talk to Mr. Torelli," Carol said. A stab in the dark.

"Can't," said Fingers. "He's gone."

So this *was* a Scaevola hit. "If you don't believe I'm not Trntl," she continued, "look at my driver's license. It's in my purse."

"Open the catch, then hand it here."

Moving slowly, she slipped off the shoulder strap, thumbed the gold clasp, and held out the bag. "It's in my billfold." He took the bag with his left hand, and—the gun never wavering—opened it and fumbled around inside till he had her billfold, which he flipped open to her driver's license. He frowned when he saw it, then sucked on his teeth, dropped the billfold back into the bag, which he put on the bench beside him.

"See? What did I tell you?" she said. The truck had stopped again. As it started up, he said, "Nice try. It's a pretty good job; but hey, my brother's been forging documents for twenty years—driver's licenses, passports, Social Security cards, work permits—so I'm not that impressed, Miss Trntl. I've seen the best." His eyes never leaving her face, with his left hand he continued fishing around inside the bag where it sat beside him on the bench. "What else you got in here? No gun, that's good. Comb, keys, lipstick, hanky, cigarettes—" (Cigarettes? Ah, the open pack that Trntl had left on the table at the hotel coffee shop the last time they'd been there) "—lighter, tampons, ballpoint pen—" (lighter? I don't have a lighter in there, Carol thought; oh! the tube of pepper spray! Well.)

"Where are you taking me?" she asked.

"You're going to have an accident."

"What sort of accident?"

"You won't feel nothin'."

"But why me?"

"Because you decided to make yourself a problem for a lot of people. You messed around in things that didn't concern you, and started blabbin' names."

"Well, could I at least smoke a last cigarette?"

"Go ahead," he said, handing her the bag.

She carefully removed a cigarette from the pack, dropped the pack into the purse, and reached in for the small cylindrical canister that contained her pepper spray.

"Hey, what's that you've got?" he inquired, leaning forward tensely.

"My lighter. You said I could smoke." She put the cigarette in her mouth, hefted the bag to her right side and slipped the strap over her shoulder. Wouldn't they ever come to another stoplight? With her right hand she held the pepper spray cylinder at the end of the cigarette. "Do you like to look through women's purses?"

"Sometimes it's interesting," he said.

At last! the truck was slowing to a stop. "It's really not polite," she said. And taking and holding a deep breath as the truck braked to a full stop, she lowered her thumb and sprayed pepper directly into Fingers's eyes. Simultaneously she twisted to her right, and with her left hand, shoved the gun barrel downward.

The bullet whunked into the truck floor. With her left foot she stomped his arm just above the wrist, and the gun clattered free. Fingers recoiled against the wall, choking and paralyzed. Still holding her breath, her eyes smarting, Carol threw herself at the back doors, twisted one handle, and leaped out onto the street. Her legs buckled when she hit the pavement, and she fell to her knees. She was feeling the effects of the spray herself. But half scuttling, half crawling, she reached the curb. Around her, bright lights blinked and glared. The street was lined on both sides with pornography shops and peepshows. She'd seen this block before on her walks about the downtown, and had a general sense of how the land lay. Behind her, shouts and curses.

She hoisted herself to her feet and began running unsteadily down the sidewalk past the paint-blanked windows and blinking lights. A glance over her shoulder revealed the driver looking into the back of the truck, and the third man pursuing her on foot. Two doors ahead she saw a sudden puff of cement dust, and a white pock appeared in the masonry. If they were shooting, she'd never make it to the end of the block. Nothing for it, then, but to get off the street. She flung herself sideways into the open doorway of a shop.

She was crossing a square room brightly lit with overhead fluorescent tubes; the walls were lined with book and magazine racks, where maybe eight to a dozen men were leafing and browsing. To one side stood a large glass case filled with dildoes, cock rings, and other toys. Suspended in one corner, as though from a yardarm, a lifesize plastic inflatable woman stared down with round blue eyes and a scarlet O-shaped mouth. At a high counter beside the doorway—far behind her now—a man leaned around the cash register and shouted: "Hey, there's a fifty-cent browsing fee!"

An archway at the rear led into a dim hallway lined on both sides with wooden doors of peepshow booths. Five or six men were pacing the corridor or lounging against the walls. They looked at her startled as she dashed into their midst. "Hey, doll, what's your hurry?" one asked as she brushed past him. She reached the end of the hallway, turned to her right, then right again, and found herself in another hallway, identical to the first, but running back toward the front of the shop. Again, the double row of wooden doors, some standing slightly ajar, others tightly closed, with red lights—"In Use"—above them. Too late she realized that the metal door with the push-bar she'd passed in the center of the back wall was a rear exit from the shop—probably into an alley. But as she spun around to head for it, she heard the thud of running feet on the hardwood floor in the adjacent hallway. Very close. Angry shouts from the front room.

Carol stepped into an open viewing booth and closed the door behind her, locking it with a hook that fit into a metal eyelet screwed into the doorframe. For her pursuers' eyes, the booth had to be "In Use." She scrabbled in her bag, found a quarter, and dropped it into the coin slot.

The booth was hot and cramped, permeated by a nasty stale odor compounded of cigarette smoke, amyl nitrite, and semen. Her shoe soles stuck to the floor. On the splotchy, streaked wall before her, a scratchy film unwound its writhing bodies. She could hear doors banging open along the corridor; more running feet; a general commotion and hubbub. A man shouting: "He's got a gun!" The screen went dark, and Carol dropped another quarter in. A large breast covered the wall.

The hubbub and commotion were in the other hallway now, gradually moving toward the front of the shop, a scuffling, thumping shuffle, as of many feet. The front wall of her booth creaked as a heavy weight slammed into it from the other side. Again the screen went dark. But before she put in another quarter, Carol listened hard, trying to fathom what was happening. The ruckus seemed to be localized at the front of the shop. She unhooked the door, eased it open, and peered out cautiously. The hallway was empty.

Quickly she retraced her steps to the rear door, pushed the horizontal bar, and felt the cold night air strike her face. Before she went out into the alley, she glanced back toward the front of the shop. The display room was crowded with people—most of them policemen in uniform. She slipped out into the alley and began the five-block trek back to the hotel.

When the police arrived in force (and it didn't take long, since there was normally an official watch on The Block), they found the following: bottling up traffic at an intersection, one brown panel truck marked BENNO'S BODYSHOP beneath temporary signs that read FANCY'S FLOWERS; in the back of the truck, one Davis Beauregard sitting stunned and weepy, nursing a broken arm, with a silencer-equipped revolver at his feet; at the Exotica Book & Filmstore, a bullet-shattered front window and one Alfredo Colonna, bruised and sullen, tightly held by two burly managers from upstairs. And, unconscious, with blood congealing from a gash on the back of his head, one Giovanni Speranza—alas, poor Johnny!—sprawled face-down, his body strewn with books for racy reading: "High School Orgy", "Bitch Goddess", "Coach Takes the Team", "Rear Deliveries", and "Daddy's Little Girl".

356

"You're damn right we want to press charges," one of the managers was telling the investigating officers. "These two jerks came in here and wrecked the place. That one"—Speranza—"had the gun you're holding. Jim"—the clerk—"conked him with a Coke bottle. Before he went down, he put two bullets through my plate glass window."

"If *you* didn't want to press charges," said the patrolman with Speranza's pistol, "*we* would."

When Torvald responded to the frantic knocking on his door, Carol came limping into his room, covered with grime, her knees skinned and raw. "My God," he said, "what's happened to you?"

She slung her bag onto the bed. "I've just escaped from three of Scaevola's goons. They tried to kill me thinking I was Trntl. Trntl masquerading under the name of *Carol Brown!* Think about *that* for a bit and let me know what you come up with. I want to take a shower, Torvald; I feel dirty all over. Afterwards, I'll tell you the whole story."

While she was in the bathroom, Torvald made her a cup of instant coffee and sat staring at the floor. Only the police—specifically Detectives Adcock and Price—had known that Trntl was at the Macready in a room registered to Carol Brown.

Returned from her shower wearing Torvald's huge terrycloth robe, Carol sampled her coffee and agreed with his conclusion. While drying her hair, she told him where she'd been. When she was finished, he asked "How are your knees?"

"Sore," she answered. "But I soaped 'em good and put on some disinfectant I bought at a drugstore on the way home."

"What happened to Fingers and the other two?" he asked.

"I don't know. There were lots of police on the scene."

"If they weren't arrested, they may try again."

"I think of little else," she said. "Trntl's due back just after midnight. To be on the safe side, you'd better come down to my room till she gets here."

"Come to your room!" he said in mock horror. "And you already wearing my bathrobe. What will Rachel say?"

"Nothing," said Carol. "She knows you too well."

At eleven twenty-five, the telephone buzzing beside his pillow jolted Lefty Scaevola awake. In the dark, the red button of the secure line was blinking at him. He lifted the receiver and punched the button. "Yeah?"—his voice thick with sleep—"Who is it?"

A man's voice, high-pitched with suppressed excitement. "Lefty? This is Nick. Nick Dellanotte. I got bad news. About Johnny, Fingers, and Alfie. They've all been arrested—on a buncha charges."

It took a second to register. Then Lefty cried "Oh hell!"

His wife stirred in the bed beside him, half-turned her face. "What's wrong, Giuseppe?"

"Nothing," he snapped. "It's just business. Go to sleep, Theresa." Then, into the mouthpiece: "Hang on, Nick. I'm going to another phone." He punched the HOLD button viciously, hauled himself out of bed and, in his bare feet, padded down the hall to the little room he called his study. He flopped into a chair at the desk, reached into a drawer for the secure phone, and activated it. "Okay, Nick. Tell me."

"About an hour ago they were arrested on The Block. Johnny and Alfie had started a fight in a porno bookstore—just a second— here it is: the Exotica Book & Filmstore—"

"Is it one of ours?"

"Yeah, it's one of the group run by Star-Spangled Amusements. Well, anyway, they wrecked the place, and Johnny shot out the front window."

"What the hell happened?"

"Well, they were chasing some woman, and she ran into the store, and they followed her in—"

"What became of the woman?"

"She got away. Nobody could find a trace of her. Musta got out the back door."

Lefty began rubbing his forehead as a dull throbbing began just above his eyes. "They really trashed the place," Nick continued. "Then Johnny got bonked with a Coke bottle, and the managers took Alfie. And then the cops found Fingers in the back of one of Benno's trucks—Benno's name as big as life on the sides. Fingers was just sitting there—*crying*, if you can believe it. And the cops got his gun—the Special with the silencer. It was the *wrong* gun for them to get, if you know what I mean." Lefty said nothing, trying to cope with the horrific pain that had begun stabbing him in the stomach. "You remember," Nick hastened on, "that problem last year that took out Superintendent—"

"I get your drift," Lefty gasped at him through clenched teeth. He fumbled open the desk drawer, uncapped a bottle and began chewing a handful of antacid tablets. Day by day the pains were getting worse. Lefty took a pipe from a rack on the desk and began biting on the stem. "And the woman got away?"

"Yeah. She evidently was in the truck and jumped out. God knows what all she did to Fingers. Broke his arm, that's for sure."

"Tell the manager of Exotica Bookstore not to file a complaint," said Lefty.

"He already has," said Nick. "And the police have a string of their own charges, too."

Lefty leaned back in his chair, his eyes squeezed shut. The pain had subsided, but only barely. "When they go to court," he said, "bail them out, whatever it takes. Don't let 'em stay in jail." He paused for a long moment, gnawing the pipestem. "And come see me in the office tomorrow. About ten. Nick, you been with the Organization a long time. And you've been a good worker. I think you're overdue for a promotion."

When Trntl arrived at the Macready Hotel shortly before one in the morning, Torvald let her into her room. Carol was sitting on the bed nursing her skinned knees.

"Welcome back," said Carol. "Some people have all the luck. You missed another attempt on your life while you were gone."

"Trntl didn't have *all* the luck," Torvald said to Carol. "You had your share." To Trntl he said, "Scaevola's people nearly succeeded in killing N. F. Trntl under the name of Carol Brown."

"How could that happen? Torelli *knows* me!"

"It wasn't Torelli," Carol said. "It wasn't George. It was Fingers and two of his friends." She told her story in great detail. "They wanted it to look like an accident," she concluded. "A simple hit would've been much more efficient. And here," she added, handing Trntl an open pack of cigarettes, "these are yours. I never thought I'd see the day I'd be glad you smoked—but they came in very handy." She took one cigarette from the pack and lodged it behind her ear. "I'll keep one for a souvenir, put it with my keepsakes."

"Maybe I should carry pepper spray," Trntl said. She lit one of the cigarettes. "Of course, Detective Adcock was the only person who knew that I was staying at this hotel in a room registered to you. Fingers and his friends had to get their information somewhere."

"Somebody tried to bug this phone," Carol reminded her. "And *they* knew we'd changed hotels."

"Adcock again," said Trntl. "Not that he bugged us, necessarily. But that he *knew*."

"Unless we were bugged at the Cavendish also," Torvald said. "And *that's* how they knew we'd moved."

"But why did they want it to look like an accident?" Trntl mused. "The first time, they'd have been satisfied with a disappearance. The second time, they went for a conventional hit. Ah! of course. They're afraid of what I might say at the inquest tomorrow. Name-dropping and theory-spinning." She gave a wry chuckle. "I'll see what I can do to realize their worst fears."

"As for the cadenza," said Torvald, "since we haven't heard from the 'publisher's' people who approached us at Bracebeam's, we don't know if they're still interested. But late this afternoon we got a call from the *second* party who advertised in the *Sun*—the 'musicologist.' He wanted to meet with us immediately, but since I thought you ought to be present, I put him off till eight-thirty tonight."

"Oho," said Trntl. "Bracebeam's again?"

"No, a Chinese restaurant this time: the House of Wang."

At two o'clock that Monday afternoon, in accord with Zyzynski's instructions, Mr. Meggs had flown into Baltimore in one of the private jets, and Marco had driven him to the Macready Hotel. In the seclusion of their room, Chip and Jerry had briefed him on the appearance, habits, and investigative style of Trntl and her associates. They showed him the ad they'd placed in the *Sun*; they showed him the response Trntl had sent to their post office box. They cautioned him that the entire gambit might be a hoax designed simply to see who else wanted the cadenza. In his dry, featureless voice, Mr. Meggs explained to *them* that Mr. Zyzynski was aware of that possibility; but since Trntl had already met with another group who'd placed an ad, the assumption of a hoax could not be risked. "It may be that they have found the cadenza, and are willing to sell it to the highest bidder."

"We don't think they've found it yet," Chip said.

"Perhaps not," said Mr. Meggs. "But if they have—? And if the other group should obtain it—?" He stared at each of them, in turn, his eyes lidless and blank behind his rimless glasses. "Jerry, I understand that you monitored the meeting they had with the other group. Describe our rivals, please."

"There were two of them," said Jerry. "I was in disguise. The one who actually talked to Trntl's associate Grimsson was five-foot-six, about thirty-five, with brown hair, cut short. He had a chipped front tooth. The other was a tall blond woman about the same age who didn't stay for the conversation. She's the one who's been following Trntl: she wears designer clothes and carries Gucci handbags."

"Chipped tooth," said Mr. Meggs. "You must have got quite close to him."

"I pretended to be a drunk and stumbled against him while he was looking at photocopies of the manuscript. Though I had only a brief glimpse, it looked like the real thing to me."

Mr. Meggs twice clicked his tongue. "Photocopies: *not good.* Mr. Zyzynski can't tolerate there being copies."

"Particularly when we don't know how many sets there may be," said Chip.

Mr. Meggs folded his hands on the tabletop. "Any agreement we reach must include the purchase of the original and *all* copies. I don't like this at all; it's getting very messy."

"It's been messy from the start," said Jerry, then held his tongue as he saw Marco and Chip frowning at him, shaking their heads.

"I am here," said Mr. Meggs, "to be the contact person. They don't know me, and they'll never see me again. They might recognize one of you since you've been following them for so long. Also, you may be having to deal with them in the future. Give me the number; I'll make the call. If they don't wish to meet with me, we'll know that they may have decided to treat with the other group. In which case, you'll have to come up with an alternative plan."

When he answered the call, Torvald had assumed that the Bracebeam respondent was making a second approach following consultation. Then, with a shock, he'd realized that this was a different respondent altogether.

"Yes, I'll be happy to meet with you to discuss the Farringford manuscript in my possession," Torvald said. "You're the second party to express interest."

"Can we meet tonight?"

"Let's meet at eight-thirty *tomorrow* night—Tuesday—at the House of Wang, a Chinese restaurant two blocks east of the Macready Hotel. I'll be seated at a table or a booth wearing a white scarf and an astrakhan."

"Eight-thirty," said the other. "I shall be wearing a tweed overcoat and a cloth cap."

After hanging up, Mr. Meggs had briefed Marco, Jerry, and Chip on what had been said. Then, retiring to a chair by the window, he'd spent a few minutes looking out at the city before methodically trimming and filing his nails.

Chapter 29

Tuesday morning found Trntl edgy and out of sorts. She skipped breakfast, consenting only to a cup of black coffee; the plate of Danish pastries Torvald brought to the table gazed at her like hostile eyes—which she found, to her discomfort, she couldn't stare down. If another attempt were to be made on her life, it would undoubtedly come before her testimony at today's inquest. "Maybe when it's over, I'll feel like having a big lunch," she told herself.

Carol agreed to stay in the hotel room by the phone, and Torvald accompanied Trntl to the inquest. He drove her right to the courthouse door; she darted from the car across the sidewalk into the building and hugged the wall till she reached the coroner's suite.

There weren't many people present to witness the proceedings. A group of police officers, including Detective Adcock; several men in business suits whom she didn't know; Crandall Niepagen-Scholles, cheek-pouches full, pointedly ignoring her. A man and woman looking quite distraught, who (she later learned) were Stephanie's parents. Mr. Eggleston, ill at ease in a brown pin-striped suit; Mrs. Gresham, rouged and powdered, decked out in her Sunday best.

The findings of the inquest were predictable. Stephanie had died from two gunshot wounds from a single weapon inflicted by an unknown assailant during an invasion of her home. Officers testified that the door had been forced and the room searched. That the victim had apparently just returned from the outside, since she was wearing overcoat and earmuffs and was surrounded by unopened mail. Mrs. Gresham testified that there had been commotion and running up the stairs. Mr. Eggleston helped to establish the time the shooting occurred (and became quite emotional when describing the discovery of Stephanie's body).

Trntl took the stand, corroborated Eggleston's account, and—determined to express her views—asserted that, in her

opinion, the shooting was definitely linked to the theft of the
Farringford Cadenza from Morris Waite's apartment, his murder, and Stephanie's discovery of what she at least *thought* was
the cadenza subsequent to Morris's death. Her presentation was
hurried and more muddled than she liked, but she did manage to
get out the names Tony Scaevola and Angelo Torelli before the
coroner stopped her. "Miss Trntl," he said, "this proceeding is not
a criminal trial; it's an inquiry into the circumstances and cause
of a particular death. We are concerned with findings of fact, not
conjecture. If you have information or evidence that will assist the
police in their criminal investigation, please give it to them. I must
rule against the airing of your theories and speculations here."

A routine inquiry; open and shut. And thus was Stephanie
consigned to the category of business-as-usual. Angry, Trntl concluded her testimony and stood down. Throughout, she observed
that two men in the back row were scrutinizing her intently with
immobile faces. Both were in overcoats. One had a fly-away shock
of jet-black hair and a small mustache. The other was tall, thin,
and extremely wiry, with a square-chiseled jaw, cold gray eyes,
and the right side of his mouth drawn up in a perpetual half-smile.
Crandy Niepagen-Scholles was whispering to a suave gray-haired
man who had the appearance of an attorney. (Probably Giuseppe
Scaevola's, Trntl thought.)

After parking the car, Torvald had come in and made a point
of scrutinizing *everybody*.

The inquest over, people began gathering up their things
and preparing to leave. Without rising from his chair, Detective
Adcock beckoned Trntl over. She leaned down, and he said very
quietly: "It might interest you to know that, as the result of an
internal investigation, Detective Price has been suspended—with
pay. A hearing will follow later this month. This is confidential
information, and my sharing it with you could cost my job if you
aren't discreet. I'm telling you only because I have a strong feeling
that you think I've been a rotten apple all along, and I don't wish
to be thought of that way."

"Yes, it does interest me—very much."

"It might further interest you to know that, as far as we can
determine, both Angelo Torelli and George Fiocco have disappeared."

"Wyoming seems to be popular this time of year," said Trntl.
"I understand the fish are biting."

"Yes," said Adcock, "they well may be."

"Now," Trntl continued, "if you could give me one more bit of information, I'd be much beholden." He raised his eyebrows. "Who are those two men in overcoats in the back row?"

Adcock turned his head and casually surveyed them as they moved along the wall toward the door. "The dark-haired one with the mustache is Nick Dellanotte; he manages a local lumber yard and sits on the Citizens' Advisory Committee for Urban Renewal. The other one I don't know."

"Nick o' the Night, eh?" said Trntl. "If I should happen to have a fatal accident, do check him out. He's been memorizing my face, and his pal's been taking notes. And who's that gray-haired man talking to Crandy Niepagen-Scholles? Scaevola's lawyer?"

Adcock craned his head to look where her eyes pointed. All it took was a glance; he gave a little laugh. "Goodness, no, Miss Trntl. That's Judge McPhee."

"He has beady little eyes," said Trntl. She began buttoning her coat. "Thanks for the information."

"Scaevola's lawyer," said Adcock, "is the fat man with the maroon tie sitting by the window."

"Goodbye," said Trntl. She started for the door where Torvald was waiting, but Mrs. Gresham stopped her with a little wave. "Miss Trntl, I'd like for you to meet Stephanie's parents, Mr. and Mrs. Simms from Scranton. This is Miss Trntl, a friend of Stephanie's, and a friend of mine."

There was no way out of it. Trntl shook hands with each of them, murmuring condolences.

They were glad to meet Stephanie's friends; they didn't know a great deal about her life in Baltimore; she'd been a private person. Their daughter's death had devastated them, and the mystery surrounding it had nearly driven them crazy. Trntl was a private detective hired to find the Farringford Cadenza, wasn't that right? It seemed clear that the cadenza had something to do with her death. Trntl's testimony had aroused their curiosity: did she know something about Stephanie's murder that she didn't get to say?

"I think she simply knew too much about the original theft," said Trntl, "and the forces at work felt they had to silence her." Stephanie's mother reached for her handkerchief, and her father continued talking: the on-site investigation was completed, and the police had unsealed Stephanie's apartment; he and Mrs.

Simms were now responsible for cleaning out Stephanie's things, deciding what to keep, and packing those things up for transport to Scranton. An appalling task: they didn't really know where to begin, but would start this afternoon, right after lunch.

Trntl seized upon this as an opportunity to satisfy herself that the cadenza was not in fact still hidden away in Stephanie's apartment—a possibility that had been nagging at her since the murder. "Would you mind if I visited Stephanie's room?" she asked. "I'd only look around to see if I could find the Farringford Cadenza or any trace of it."

"Well, I don't know," the father said. "We understand the cadenza's importance—"

"What do you think, Mrs. Gresham?" Stephanie's mother asked.

Mrs. Gresham smiled. "It's what Stephanie would have wanted. Miss Trntl is entirely trustworthy, and was a true friend of your daughter. And *I* can vouch for her too; it says good things of people if they appreciate Nelson Eddy."

Mr. and Mrs. Simms exchanged a thoughtful look. "We have no objection," the father said. "We'll be there about two o'clock," the mother said.

"Thank you," said Trntl. "I won't disturb anything. But as you know from today's testimony by the police, the apartment was thoroughly searched by the intruders."

It would be far better, Trntl decided, to conduct *her* search alone, before the parents were underfoot and watching. If all went well, she'd be through long before they arrived. She turned to Mrs. Gresham: "Do you and Mr. Eggleston have a ride home? We'd be happy to give you a lift."

"Oh, that would be nice," said Mrs. Gresham. "We took a cab to get to the inquest. I'll be happy to make you both a sandwich if you'd like some lunch."

"I'd appreciate that," said Trntl. "You're very kind."

"Do you want me to come with you to Stephanie's apartment?" Torvald asked. "In case—you know."

Trntl thought for a moment. "I don't think it's necessary; we agreed that the real danger was before my testimony at the inquest. I've done what damage I could—which wasn't much. It's broad daylight; I'll be locked inside the apartment house. Why don't I take the car and come straight to the hotel when I've finished?"

Thus it was that, ten minutes later, Trntl had dropped Torvald at the hotel and was driving the superintendent and Mrs. Gresham back to the apartment building. Mr. Eggleston was morose and silent, chin sunk on his chest as he slumped in the car seat. Mrs. Gresham had the need to talk.

"I've never been to an inquest before, and I didn't know what to expect. I found it very depressing, Miss Trntl. Stephanie was such a lovely person, so warm and full of high spirits—and none of that seemed to matter to anybody. Everything was so cold and scientific! Unfeeling, as though Stephanie wasn't a person with wonderful qualities, but just a problem to be solved."

"An inquest is a fact-finding procedure," Trntl said, her irritation with the procedure welling up yet once again, "concerned only with establishing cause and circumstances of death. The dead person's qualities are beside the point."

"It must've been awful for Stephanie's parents," Mrs. Gresham went on. "They were traveling in Europe when she was shot, and were called back. They're so bewildered and angry, and they've got the funeral to plan, and her belongings to sort through." They were moving north on Charles toward the Washington Monument and Mount Vernon Place.

Mrs. Gresham pulled a handkerchief from her purse and began wiping her eyes. "It's so *unfair!* She was kind and generous, a good student. Every day after her classes, she'd walk home from the Institute through these little parks. She loved the pool, the statues. She'd talk to people sitting on the benches. And she loved the Monument there—" it towered above them as they circled round its base "—with its winding stair inside. She wanted me to go up with her, but I never would."

"I went up once," Mr. Eggleston said. "All the way to the top. Two hundred and twenty-eight marble steps. My leg muscles ached for a week."

Having crossed Monument Street, Trntl turned right onto the continuation of Charles. There were no parking spaces near the apartment building, so Trntl let the two of them out and went round the block.

On Monument Street, she parked facing west just past the intersection with Charles. She only had a long block to walk, and the parks that formed the boulevard were empty of people. Nevertheless, with a watchfulness that had become habit during the past week, she moved quickly, all senses alert, twice glancing over her shoulder, and surveying the interior of each parked car long before she reached it. No Angelo Torellis or Nick Dellanottes emerged from doorways to accost her.

She hurried up the steps of Stephanie's apartment building and pressed Mr. Eggleston's buzzer. The inner door buzzed back at her, and as she entered the foyer, the superintendent stepped into the hall. "Come on in. I'll give you the key to Stephanie's apartment."

When she walked into his living room the blue and yellow parrot was gnawing with his beak on the wires of his cage; immediately he cocked his eye at her, then reared back and, in what Trntl took to be a distinctly insulting tone, croaked "Hiya honey."

"Shut up, Rossetti," Mr. Eggleston said. "She ain't interested in your kind." While he crossed to a wallboard that contained keys hanging on hooks, he noticed her observing the room's clutter, the Sunday newspaper scrambled on the couch, the scrolls of dust feathered beneath the coffee table, the smeared remains of at least two meals on blue plastic plates—and, as he handed her the key, he said, "Sorry about the mess in here. I just haven't had the heart to tidy up since—the trouble last week. Well, you know how to find Stephanie's apartment. I hope you don't care if I don't go up with you. Prefer to stay here, maybe get some cleaning done."

"That's fine," said Trntl. "I don't much like going up there myself. I'll bring the key back." (Thank goodness; she didn't want *him* underfoot either.)

After knocking gently at Mrs. Gresham's door Trntl had to wait for a long moment—listening to scurrying sounds from inside—before the door opened and her hostess, a bright flowered apron covering her Sunday dress, invited her in. Mrs. Gresham was flushed and short of breath. "I've made some tuna salad," she said, taking Trntl's coat. "I hope you don't mind it with chopped celery and hard-boiled eggs."

"Oh no, that's fine," said Trntl.

"Make yourself comfortable. I'll just pop some bread into the toaster." She bustled back out to the kitchen. "I've got some water boiling. Would you prefer tea or instant coffee?"

"Tea," said Trntl. "Is there anything I can do to help?"

"No, you just sit down and relax."

Mrs. Gresham's apartment, unlike the superintendent's, was meticulously clean and well-ordered. Trntl sat on the plush sofa and began leafing through an issue of *The Christian Missionary*.

She'd just made the transition from a school in Nigeria to a hospital in Paraguay when Mrs. Gresham beckoned her from the kitchen door, and Trntl found a further transition—from tuberculosis to tuna salad—most welcome.

"I've been thinking about what you said the other day," Mrs. Gresham said, when they were seated at the little table in the kitchen. "As to whom Stephanie might have given the cadenza for safekeeping. If she wasn't able to get it to you or her professor friend, and she didn't get it to me, then I can't think of *anyone* else she knew well enough."

The speech had begun on such a promising note that Trntl felt a bit let down at the finish. Still— "That's what I suspected," she said. "I have reason to think her killer didn't find it in her apartment. In her note to me, she said the cadenza was locked in Morris's briefcase. If she somehow got it out of the briefcase, it might still be concealed in her apartment, in a place difficult to find, or else—like Poe's purloined letter—in a place so obvious no one would expect to find it there. We're told the manuscript is several sheets of music paper. It could be mixed in with other musical scores, or feasibly ditched in a wastebasket like trash. It could be sealed in an envelope, or rolled up tightly into a thin tube or cylinder."

"And if Stephanie's parents came across it while cleaning out her things, they wouldn't know it for what it is," said Mrs. Gresham.

"I'm afraid you're right," said Trntl.

"I hope you find it," said Mrs. Gresham.

Chapter 30

When Trntl opened Stephanie's door, she was met by stale air and a profound emptiness. Someone had pulled the blind of the single window, and the room was dim. Needing all the light she could get, Trntl switched on the bulbs in the Victorian chandelier, and the sickly gleam that came through the morning-glory (or tulip) shades revealed even worse disarray than she remembered. Crossing to the kitchenette to raise the window blind, she was jolted by the irregular chalk mark on the floor outlining the position of Stephanie's body. "How gross of the police," she thought, "to leave that for the parents to find." She skirted the outline and raised the blind. Stephanie's unopened mail lay neatly stacked on the kitchen counter. Trntl opened the window a couple of inches to air the room.

During the next half hour she made a thorough search, beginning with the wastebaskets, the refrigerator and freezer, and the kitchen cabinets. Someone had removed the garbage from the pail beside the stove. Milk and cottage cheese were going sour in the fridge, a loaf of bread in the cupboard was blue with mold. She looked in the oven, behind the stove, on the undersides of table, chairs, and drawers. She looked in all the storage canisters, and the tall boxes of detergent on the off-chance that the manuscript had been rolled up and shoved into the powered soap. After looking under the large throw rug, she opened up the sofa bed and linen closet and examined them closely. Nothing under the bed sheets or between the stacked towels. Taking the throw rug to the kitchenette, she spread it neatly to hide the chalked outline; if Stephanie's parents didn't look under it, they'd never know.

Next she turned her attention to the heaps of sheet music, magazines, and record jackets lying about. Stephanie's treasures from her foraging in secondhand shops; the Victrola, the old piano rolls; the old hymnals and yellowing editions of sentimental songs from 1910. Ethelbert Nevin and Amy Beach, Victor Herbert and John Philip Sousa. The thick albums of phonograph records—all 78's: Koussevitsky, Caruso, Brewster, John McCormack, Nellie Melba, Fritz Kreisler, and Haydn's *Creation*. No cadenza stashed between the cardboard covers or folded into the paper sleeves. Spiral notebooks full of classroom jottings, a portfolio of Stephanie's own exercises in theory and composition. Stacks of old periodicals: *The Etude*; *The Piano Teacher*; *Music, Maestro! Magazine*. What a jumble, and clearly rummaged through previously by someone else. Most of the books had been tumbled from the built-in shelves onto the floor, but a few short rows remained standing in place. Trntl ran her hand behind these, found only spider webs—except on the third shelf down, toward the end of the case. There, behind a run of paperback volumes of ghost and horror stories, she found a small thickish book lying on its side, up against the wall. No cobwebs, either. She pulled it out: Stephanie's diary.

"Jackpot!" thought Trntl. She should have guessed that Stephanie would keep a diary. Would it supply the "key"?

She opened it from the back, thumbed through the blank pages till she found an entry dated almost a week before Stephanie's death.

> FEBRUARY 25. Tonight Morris and I went to the film series and saw Casablanca. It cd of been such a wonderful evening, but M spoiled it by bitching about my relationship with Ted. It got really nasty. He used to be so much fun, but now all he does is grumble and whine. Honestly, he's just like a child! But Ted is so mature! If he knew I was still seeing M, <u>he</u> wouldn't be jealous. I know he wdn't. And he needs me. He needs someone to talk to, to share his hopes with, someone who appreciates the work he's doing on Brahms. Mrs. P can't talk to him about the things nearest his heart. She doesnt understand the real importance of his work and doesnt care. Ted's so lonely. I'm glad I can comfort him and make him feel good about himself. He calls me his "little Miss Fix-it". I just wish he had as much energy as M. But I guess that's not so important when you consider all the other things he has to offer. Besides, if I can get M off this jealousy thing, I'll still have <u>him</u> on week-ends!

Trntl forced herself to go on reading. The final entries recounted Stephanie's discovery of the cadenza at Finegold's Flea-Market, and her shock and dismay on hearing of the burglary at Pettigrew's house. Skimming quickly entry by entry to the front of the book, Trntl found that, for the most part, the diary recorded the ongoing drama of Stephanie's love life; there was a great deal about squabbles and reconciliations, flights of the tattooed bluebird, tennis games on autumn afternoons, the insensitivity and base cruelties of Mrs. P, laid-back summer picnics with Morris at Patapsco Park, the feverish thrills of the New Haven Convention where she and Ted had "real nifty adjoining rooms." A marvelous memento, Trntl thought, for Stephanie's parents to find as they cleaned out her apartment. Stephanie told it all.

Well, Trntl would take the diary with her when she left, would go through it carefully, at leisure, hunting for some hint, some clue that would identify the "Special Place" and illuminate "the Key Hole—get it?" And then she'd discreetly destroy the diary so that it wouldn't be available to embarrass *anybody*. Trntl slipped the book into the pocket of her coat and quickly finished her search of the apartment. When she locked the door behind her and went downstairs to return the key to Mr. Eggleston, she was satisfied that the cadenza was not in Stephanie's apartment, and that it probably never had been.

Trntl was especially pleased with Torvald's choice of meeting-place. She staved off her hunger with a candy bar and bag of potato chips, and prepared herself for a luscious Chinese meal at Dinch's expense. They arrived at the House of Wang at ten till eight, Torvald entering first and selecting a booth halfway to the rear. Trntl and Carol entered three minutes later and chose a table near the door—a spot conveniently separated from the main body of tables by an open-work carved screen. For a Tuesday night, the place was fairly crowded; from their vantage point, they could survey the entire room through the screen without being greatly visible themselves. Ideal. Trntl ordered a large bowl of hot and sour soup for the two of them and then studied everyone in the restaurant.

"See anyone you know?" Carol asked. "I don't."

"Bullneck isn't here," she answered—"and I don't see Blondie or Littlefellow."

Carol said, "Down at the far end there's another screen like ours—with people behind it."

While waiting for their food, they continued to observe the people who came and went and the white-jacketed waiters criss-crossing among the tables. During the soup, five couples entered, and three left. For their entreés, Trntl ordered pork, Carol shrimp. Across the room, Torvald sat wielding his chopsticks with great relish over a large mound of something-or-other.

"The shrimp's good," said Carol.

"So's the pork," said Trntl. "Want to share?" They shared.

Two Roman Catholic priests came in—the taller, a strapping fellow with a bush of white hair and a rolling gait, the shorter—pushing before him a rotund belly—a bit on the dumpy side, gray-haired and using a cane. Engaged in earnest discourse, they took a table some twenty feet from the women and ordered egg-drop soup.

At eight-twenty-five, when Carol and Trntl had nearly finished eating, the door opened and a small, portly man in a tweed over-coat and cloth cap stepped in. He looked around sharply, saw Torvald in his white scarf and astrakhan sipping tea, and crossed to him immediately.

Torvald looked up casually as the man joined him in the booth, facing him across the fortune cookie on its white saucer.

"Good evening," said Torvald. "Are you the man I talked to on the phone?"

"That's right. I understand you possess a Farringford man-uscript. A late work, you said in your response to my advertise-ment."

"And never published. I take it you're a publisher?"

"No. I'm representing a noted musicologist—or, to be more precise—a consortium of musicologists. I have been authorized to make inquiries as to precisely what it is you have to sell, and if terms are agreeable, to purchase it from you for cash."

Torvald made mental notes of the man's appearance. He was a wizened gnome, extremely short, with an exceedingly thin and pointed nose, the skin of his face cross-hatched with deep lines and creases. Behind rimless lenses, steel-blue eyes stared un-blinking; the sphincter of his mouth was a tight pucker. On the table before him, his hands rested plump and pawlike, corrugated with prominent blue veins and freckled with age-spots. His nails glistened as though painted with clear lacquer.

"As I said on the phone," Torvald continued, "I've already been contacted by another party who wishes to buy the manuscript."

"If the item is the lost cadenza to the Fifth Piano Concerto, I'm prepared to top their offer."

"It is."

"Do you have it with you for me to examine?"

Torvald produced the brown manila envelope. "I have a photocopy; the original is not something I choose to carry about the streets."

"Any purchase would include *all* sets of photocopies," said the other. "What guarantees would we have that no other copies exist?"

"You'd have my word on it," said Torvald. "But surely the value of the purchase resides in the original manuscript."

The other was silent for a long moment. "Let me see what you have."

Torvald took the sheets from the envelope and passed them across the table. The gnome studied them carefully with a magnifying glass. Torvald poured himself another cup of tea. A waiter approached the table and stood expectantly beside the sharp-nosed man, who had not removed his coat and cap. "Here's a menu, sir. Would you like something from the bar?"

The gnome waved the menu away without looking at the waiter. "I won't be staying." The waiter shrugged and left.

"What's your price?" the man asked Torvald.

Torvald had pondered long how he'd answer this question. "I've been offered one hundred thousand dollars. If you'd care to go above that, I'd feel obligated to tell the other party your offer to see if he would wish to make a higher bid."

The steel-blue eyes regarded him. The sphincter contracted, working, then pushed out three words: "Two hundred thousand."

"Very well," said Torvald. "I'll tell the other party of your offer and let you know his decision. How may I reach you?"

"I will call you at four o'clock tomorrow afternoon." The gnome handed the papers back to Torvald, rose from his chair, and walked to the door without looking back.

Two tables from Trntl and Carol, the tall, white-haired priest rose from his half-finished meal, whispered something to his

plump colleague, and followed after the tweed overcoat. The remaining priest extracted a roll of bills from his coat pocket, laid a
twenty on the table, and heaved himself up. Leaning heavily on his
cane, he rapidly made his way across the room to Torvald's table.
He slid into the booth, hooking his cane over the table edge.

Torvald set down his teacup. "Yes, Father, may I be of service
to you?"

The priest took off his glasses and leaned forward urgently. As
he spoke, Torvald noticed his chipped right front incisor. "When
we talked three nights ago, I said that I had to consult with my
employer. I have done so."

"You've gained some weight since then," said Torvald, "and
gotten grayer."

"A necessary precaution," said the priest.

"I'm glad you contacted me," Torvald said. "I was wondering
how I'd get in touch with you before tomorrow afternoon. I'd begun to think you weren't interested in my offer."

"My employer is interested," said the priest, "provided that
your price is reasonable."

"I've received a firm offer from another party," said Torvald,
"and I'm prepared to let you know what it is, to see if your publishing friend would care to better it."

"The amount—?"

"Two hundred thousand dollars."

"I'm authorized to say that my employer will go—two hundred
and fifty thousand."

"A quarter of a million," said Torvald. "I'm obligated to let the
other party know what you've said. Call me tomorrow at four-thirty."

While this exchange was taking place, Trntl observed it closely, trying to read the priest's lips. Carol was more interested in
the couple—a tallish man with a dark brown mustache, and a
rather plain red-haired woman in extremely high heels—who had
emerged from behind the screen at the far end of the room and
were following the white-haired priest out of the restaurant. As
they passed the cash register by the door, the mustached man laid
his check and what looked to be a fifty-dollar bill on the counter
and told the proprietor. "Good meal. Keep the change."

They'd been gone no more than a minute when the plump
priest left Torvald's table and went stumping out with his cane.

Torvald finished his tea in a leisurely manner, flagged down the waiter and asked for his check. Trntl and Carol broke open their fortune cookies and unrolled the slips of paper they contained. Carol's read: *"A stranger will soon bring adventure to you."* "Oh good," she said, "my life has been so dull." Trntl's read: *"You have strong opinions, but you're not always right."* She gave a disgusted grunt. "One doesn't need to be be told that by a fortune cookie."

Carol said, "Better a fortune cookie than to hear it from your friends."

They joined Torvald on the sidewalk. "If we actually had the cadenza," he said, "we'd be rich. The price is up to a quarter of a million."

"Did you recognize the man in the tweed overcoat?" Carol asked. "And who was the priest?"

"No, I'd never seen Tweed Overcoat before," said Torvald. "He offered two hundred thousand. The priest was our old friend Littlefellow wearing a wig and lots of padding. He upped the first offer by fifty thousand. Overcoat will call me tomorrow at four, and I'll tell him Littlefellow's offer. Littlefellow will call at four-thirty. Shall we see how high the price will go?"

"Why not?" said Carol. "But who'd be willing to spend that kind of money for a piece of music?"

"Morgan Latimer would," said Trntl.

"Perhaps people *like* him?" said Torvald. "Other rich folks who heard it performed thirty-four years ago?" There well might be some of those, Trntl mused, thinking of Mrs. Sternberg.

"Let's look at it from their point of view," said Carol. *"They're* the ones who advertised. We just responded. We've not presented ourselves as holding it for ransom. Littlefellow, Bullneck, and Blondie know who we are and why we're here. They must assume we're betraying our clients. Tweedcoat may not know that we're detectives. But both groups worded their ads to obscure the fact that it's the cadenza they want. What sorts of people would be willing to spend that much money yet be concerned with keeping their identities secret?"

"Collectors," said Trntl. "Whatever intrinsic value the manuscript may have as a historical document—ink on paper in Farringford's hand—it's nonetheless just a vehicle for conveying the music. In the manuscript, the music's symbolically encoded, or locked away, present only as *potential* in the notes written on paper. To be actualized, it has to be *performed*. The music itself isn't like a painting or postage stamp or rare book that can be hidden away and enjoyed for its own sake. To be appreciated, it has to be *heard*. Mark Twain has a story—I think it's "The Canvasser's Tale"—about a man who collected echoes; to acquire them, he had to buy the mountains that produced them. But it wasn't the mountains he wanted, it was the *echoes*. Given the amount of money these people are willing to pay, I don't think it's the manuscript they want; I think it's the *music*."

At twenty-two minutes after nine, in his shirt sleeves, with a glass of mineral water before him, Mr. Meggs placed a call from the Macready Hotel to Victor Zyzynski in New York.

"What did you find out?" Zyzynski asked. Since the previous evening when he'd learned of the meeting at the House of Wang, he'd been unable to concentrate on his work, spending too much time pacing restlessly about his rooms, smoking too many cigars and drinking far too many whiskey sours.

"Per your instructions," said Mr. Meggs, "I met with Trntl and Associates—one of them, actually—and saw a photocopy of a manuscript for solo piano indisputably in Farringford's hand."

"A photocopy!" Abysmal sinkings of heart. "How many copies *are* there, Mr. Meggs? We must have the original and *all* copies."

"I told him that. However, another interested party—the person who placed the other ad, I presume—has already offered them a hundred thousand for the cadenza."

A hundred thousand! "It must be another Collector," said Zyzynski. Oh god! *The Count!*

"I offered two hundred thousand," said Mr. Meggs.

"And—?"

"They'll tell the other party what I've offered, and I'm to call back again at four o'clock tomorrow. I'm convinced they're going to milk this for all they can get."

"Are you absolutely sure they actually *have* the cadenza?"

"It certainly looks like it."

"The Count must *not* get it. Go as high as necessary. Bid in large jumps; we'll force him out of the running."

"Very well. You should know," Mr. Meggs added, "that when I left the meeting, I was followed by a white-haired Catholic priest.

On the street he was joined by a dark-haired woman in a fur coat."

"Trntl's people?"

"No. Trntl herself and her two associates were in the restaurant. These people may be connected with the Other Collector. However, Marco was waiting for me in the parking lot at the end of the block, and we gave them the slip. Chip and Jerry followed the woman."

"Not so fast!" Jerry whispered. "Running is hell in these spike heels!"

Chip said nothing, but dragged him along. Ahead, they saw the brown car with Marco and Mr. Meggs leaving the parking lot. The white-haired priest and the woman in the fur coat stood conferring animatedly on the sidewalk. Then, apparently having reached a decision, the priest stepped into the street to hail a passing cab. One pulled over, the priest climbed in, and the cab roared off on the tail of the brown car.

"What now?" said Chip.

"Marco will look out for Mr. Meggs," said Jerry. "Quick, the fur coat's coming this way."

They turned and stood looking into a shop window at a display of summer lawn furniture, the very picture of a loving couple out for an evening stroll, Jerry leaning happily on Chip's arm, both of them smiling and whispering and pointing at the folding lawn chairs, the padded chaise lounge, the small round table with the green-and-yellow umbrella perched jauntily above it. In the window glass they watched the reflection of the woman in the fur coat as she walked past them in the direction of the restaurant—tall, self-assured, unsmiling, gold earrings gleaming beneath her short brown hair.

"Last time we saw her, she was blond," Jerry whispered.

"Last time she saw you, you weren't a red-head," said Chip.

She was nearly at the restaurant doorway when the other priest came out onto the sidewalk, walking fast, adjusting his hat, the cane tucked under his arm. They fell into step and started in the direction of the Cavendish Hotel. Moving chattily from window to window, Chip and Jerry followed.

In the lobby of the Cavendish, they watched the elevator dial as the car took the cane and gold earrings nonstop to the eighth floor. Then they sat on a sofa and waited. In about ten minutes, the tall white-haired priest entered suddenly from the street and marched angrily to the elevators. Jerry and Chip rose casually and followed him into the car, rode up with him to the eighth floor, and got off as though on their way to a honeymoon. The priest paid them no heed, but hurried to a cross corridor and vanished. They reached the intersection in time to see him enter Room 822.

Then back down to the lobby. The desk clerk was a young man, about 24, whom they hadn't seen while they'd been staying at the Cavendish. "Should we?" said Chip. Why not. They approached the counter, and Chip caught the young man's attention with a twenty-dollar bill.

"Yes sir?" said the clerk.

With one finger, Chip casually pushed the bill over the edge of the counter. It fell onto the papers on the desk top. "I wonder if you could check to be sure that our friends, Mr. and Mrs. Willie Philpotts, are staying in Room 822. My wife and I just flew in from Dallas, and we want to surprise them."

The clerk's hand covered the twenty. "Yessir, I'll find out." He moved to the end of the counter and fingered through a card file. "I'm sorry, sir; there's no Willie Philpotts registered for that room."

"That's very strange," said Chip. "I *know* he said it was 822. Are you absolutely *sure* he's not there?" Another twenty slid across the counter and dropped onto the papers.

"I'm sorry, sir. That room is occupied by a Mr. Juniper Gale."

"Well, that's certainly a disappointment. I do thank you for your help." They turned from the counter. "And of course," Chip added with a smile, "you needn't tell Mr. Gale that we thought someone else was registered for his room."

"Of course not," the clerk said, neatly stacking the papers.

"Juniper Gale?" said Zyzynski. "No, the name means nothing to me."

"I'll call again tomorrow evening," said Mr. Meggs, "with a report on the next round of bidding."

Zyzynski cradled the receiver, went to the bar and mixed himself another drink. God*dam* the complications! It *had* to be the Count. Loathsome, arrogant twit—with his ruby studs and Russian cigarettes and smooth presumption of superiority! "My dear Attila," he'd said, "*I* don't have to advertise." Liar, hypocrite! If only the Count knew who he was up against, he'd quail and do a doubletime retreat from the field. No one can outbid *me*, Zyzynski thought grimly. Which was undoubtedly true, given his personal net worth.

Why, then, this anxiety—and yes (to himself he could admit it)—this terror he felt that the Count would get the cadenza first? Even the successful conclusion of the merger negotiations couldn't offset his anger and frustration at being thwarted in Baltimore. He walked to the window overlooking Central Park and viciously yanked the cord that closed the drapes. And how long *had* Trntl and her gang possessed the cadenza? Had it been from the beginning?—deceiving not only Lunner & Dinch and the Farringfords, but also Marco, Jerry, and Chip? Playing everyone for fools? Bastards! He paced, he simmered. He growled and muttered as he sipped and smoked.

It must have been the Count who'd burgled Trntl's office. Had it actually been the Count's people—and not Scaevola's, as Trntl thought—who'd killed Stephanie Simms? And who the hell had pulled the fraudulent ransom scheme? He threw himself into the leather chair at his desk, pulled a fresh cigar from the humidor, and fished in his vest pocket for the gold guillotine. The thing he hated most was not being in control of the situation, of feeling himself hostage to the unpredictable machinery of events. Having *someone else* call the shots. *Snick!* The blade nipped off the end of Havana's finest.

His eyes came to rest on the gold-plated desk calendar. Thursday, March 12, circled in red. Just two more days till Rosamond Foxe's concert! The one bright gleam in all this shitty mess. And following the performance, at the reception and buffet supper in the Gold Room, he would assert himself as never before to gain her attention, ignite her interest, get her all to himself, and then—*prevail*. He could visualize the scene quite vividly: the usual supper fare at these events—smoked oysters and champagne, a variety of cheeses, olives, curried eggs, chocolate mousse, Bavarian cheesecake, assorted fruits and nuts. And the usual people, fluttering about and cadging free food—the critics and reviewers; the parasites and hangers-on; the bronzed and leathery society matrons; other musical celebrities who happened to be in town; the Board members, seducing wealthy invited guests to become Symphony benefactors; the gossip columnists and prissy intellectuals.

But *this* time, he would separate Rosamond from the herd, engineer a private tête à tête, and have her—however briefly—*all to himself.* If Peter Shipley Abbott was there—and he undoubtedly would be, sniffing and fawning about, clinging to Rosamond in his proprietary way—*touching* her, for God's sake! as though he had special claims on her—well, this time Zyzynski would cut him out, would neutralize and *crush* him!—would, if necessary, arrange a phone call to summon him from the room, an urgent call, informing him that his house was on fire. And then, with the bastard gone, he, Zyzynski would have the opportunity to touch her arm! Inhale her fragrance! Look deep into her smiling eyes!

Breathing heavily, Zyzynski leaned back in his chair and unzipped his pants. He scratched his belly where the elastic of his shorts had dug into the fat. Ah, Rosamond! With her eyes, her smile before him, he felt a surge of hope. O yes, tonight the spirit was *more* than willing! But the flesh—?

As the minutes dragged by, Rosamond faded from view, to be replaced by a parade of all the women he had known, archly eloquent in their silent contempt, poking fun at his vain endeavors. He gave it up, hoisted his pants, and shuffled off to bed.

Chapter 31

March 11 (Wednesday)

Trntl and Carol slept late on Wednesday morning. They both
were feeling exhaustion and a sense of letdown; New York and
the inquest had taken a large bite out of Trntl, and Carol was
still recovering from her truck ride and visit to the Exotica Book
& Filmstore. Besides, they were at an impasse in their investigation; they could think of nothing more to do until the buyers' calls
came through at four and four-thirty. And *that* had devolved into
merely a game; a rather pointless put-on.

Torvald, more dispirited than they'd ever seen him, had told
them last night he wouldn't be coming to their room until one-
thirty—since he wanted to see the B & O Transportation Museum
and visit Fort McHenry. And after an early solitary breakfast, off
he'd gone in his rental car to do it. Carol, who would be leaving for
New York on the evening train to attend Rosamond's concert the
following night, had decided to do a little shopping before Torvald
returned. Trntl, left alone, would dutifully sit by the phone and
read through Stephanie's diary—an exceedingly dismal and disheartening task which she dreaded quite as much as going to the
dentist for a root canal.

Up finally, and having dawdled through their morning showers, they dressed in casual street clothes and, just before ten
o'clock, went down to breakfast. Carol left from the restaurant to
do her shopping, and Trntl went back to 523 to do her chores.

Though certainly not an intellectual challenge, reading
Stephanie's diary was tedious and tiring. After thirty pages, Trntl
felt as though she had been slogging through thick, resistant gum-
bo on a journey to nowhere. Despite the endless and excruciating
detail with which Stephanie recounted her eating and sleeping and
habits of hygiene, her grumbles against Mrs. P, her joy in picnics
and tennis and walks in the woods, her passion for prospecting in
secondhand stores, nowhere had Trntl found anything remotely
useful in defining "keyhole" and "Special Place". But finally—in an
entry for the previous August—she read:

"A wonderful day! M and I went up the Washington Monument to celebrate my birthday. We had it all to ourselves, played hide-and-seek on the winding stair, chased each other up and down the steps. Such fun! And then in the little room at the top we looked through the windows out over the city, and M asked me to marry him! Well, I was just floored! I had no idea he was thinking about settling down. He's so sweet—just like him to wait till we were in our special place to pop the question. But I told him I needed some time to think about it before I gave him my answer. I'm not sure I'm ready to think about marriage yet. It seems so final somehow. And I dont think Ted would like it if I married Morris. It might spoil everything!

I wonder if M just wants to tie me down? I know he tends to be jealous. But I didn't want to put him off, either. So I said that I appreciated his offer, and I'd let him know when I made up my mind. He was very disappointed, I could tell. He took off his class ring and put it in the keyhole; said he'd leave it there, and when I was ready to say yes, to get it and give it back to him. Otherwise it could stay there forever. I said you don't want to leave it there. What if some electrical maintenance man found it? So I took it out and said I'd keep it, and when I was ready to let him know, I'd give it back to him. He said okay, he hoped it would be soon, and we went down to the harbor and had lunch."

Trntl slammed the diary shut. In a surge of excitement she scribbled on the telephone note pad "Have gone to the SPECIAL PLACE—the Washington Monument—in search of the KEY. Maybe, just maybe, this is IT." She shrugged into her coat, slipped the diary into her pocket, and left the room, hoping fervently that the key in question wasn't just the key to Morris's locked brief-case.

On the south side of Monument Street, facing west, Jerry and Marco sat in the gray car watching Trntl's car through the bare shrubs of the park. Between them on the front seat were the re-mains of their lunch—the last half-eaten hamburger, the tall cups that had contained their milkshakes, the fragments of a jumbo or-der of fries.

Chip had stayed at the hotel to keep an eye on things there. Mr. Meggs had gone to the Transportation Museum to look at trains.

Because Trntl had discovered the bug they'd put on her phone, they'd been forced to disconnect their listening device (the strange spaghetti hodge-podge of calls they'd been listening to had nearly driven them crazy), and as a result—although they were rooming only two floors above her—they were feeling very much excluded. Surveillance now required more sight-of-eye and shoe leather. And there were still questions they couldn't answer. Who were the two priests representing—holed up at the Cavendish Hotel under the name of Juniper Gale? and who was the woman who did the blonde/brunette switch? Since none of them had been following Trntl after the meeting at the House of Wang, they were apparently convinced that Trntl had found and was trying to sell the cadenza.

Mr. Meggs, too, believed that Trntl and her associates were in possession of the cadenza; but Marco, Jerry, and Chip didn't share his conviction. (Trntl was still wandering about too purposefully. Why, after the inquest, had she gone back to Stephanie Simms's apartment? Why had she now left the hotel in such a toot and made fast tracks to the Washington Monument?)

Far worse than their keen humiliation at being unable to complete their assignment was their knowledge that the Chief no longer believed in their infallibility. The calling-in of Mr. Meggs was proof that Zyzynski no longer trusted them to do the job. But Trntl's actions implied the game wasn't over; and damned if they weren't going to stay the course—not only out of pride, but to prevail, and thus redeem themselves in the Chief's eyes for possibilities of future employment.

Jerry was pensive and restless. They'd parked their car just after Trntl had parked hers. They'd thought she was returning to Stephanie Simms's apartment. But no, after leaving her car, she'd gone straight to the monument. Almost at a trot she'd rushed through the gate in the high ornamental fence that circled the base and run up the steps to the entrance. "Something's doing," Jerry said. "She don't look like a sightseer."

"Should we go in too?" asked Marco. "She'd recognize *me* for sure."

"She'll have to come out again," said Jerry, not sure what to do.

So, they'd sat, and Marco, behind the wheel, had begun to work a crossword puzzle. "What's a seven-letter word for 'a setback or defeat in meeting one's hopes or goals'?"

"FAILURE," said Jerry. But it could just as well have been CADENZA. He was sewing a button on one of the costumes from the disguise kit, which lay open on the back seat.

"Yeah, that works," said Marco. "What about this one? A four-letter word beginning with C. 'Something a person is said to eat when humiliated or proved wrong.'"

"CRAP," said Jerry.

"No," Marco said, "that doesn't work. The P spoils it."

Jerry said, "Hey, look there." On the far side of the street, from a gray Plymouth parked half a block behind Trntl's car and partially hidden from their view by the bulk of the monument, two men in overcoats came striding rapidly toward the fence, clearly as full of purpose as Trntl had been. Their heels clicking loudly on the cobbled pavement, they came round the fence to the gate, entered the enclosure, and started for the monument's doorway.

"We haven't seen them before," said Marco. "They look like hoods."

"They don't look like cops," said Jerry, tossing the costume into the back seat.

"Well, that settles it." Marco reached under his seat and pulled out a thick leather blackjack with a wrist strap. From under his, Jerry pulled the long stocking with the billiard ball tied in the toe. They got out of the car, locked their doors, and started for the gate.

In the rectangular entrance hall, an attendant was sitting at a small desk. Trntl said, "I'd like to go to the top of the monument, please."

The attendant cocked his thumb. "Sure thing. The stairs are through that door."

Passing through the doorway, she entered the base of the tower proper, a small circular space, the walls of which were gray-painted brick. Immediately in front of her, a flight of worn white marble steps ascended clockwise in a tight spiral around a central column. Two hundred and twenty-eight steps, Mr. Eggleston had said. Oh boy. She started up at a brisk clip.

Round and round, always turning tightly to her right. Always the gray bricks curving at her side, the white steps mounting underfoot, cold white pie-wedges diminishing upward to disappear at shoulder-height. Narrow at the central column, each step fanning wider toward the outer wall. Easiest to hug the outer wall where the wedges provided footing and a railing was fastened to the bricks; close to the center, there was no footing at all. Up and ever up she climbed; but her surroundings never changed. Since she'd forgotten to count steps, it was impossible to tell how far she'd come, how near to the top she was. Her calf and thigh muscles began to ache, and she paused for a second, turned and looked down the staircase. Steep counterclockwise spiral; from the wall she could see only eight to ten steps down, and only parts of the lower ones. She started up again, this time going faster and taking the steps two at a time. *It was easier somehow, aiming for every other step.*

When Marco and Jerry ambled into the entrance hall, the very picture of tourists from Dubuque, only one of the overcoated men was present. Standing by the desk listening to the attendant recount the history of the monument, he studied them as they entered—eyes opaque as milk-blue marbles. The right side of his slit-like mouth was elevated in a frozen mirthless smile. Jerry crossed to the desk and stood attentively while the attendant continued his spiel; Marco turned aside and went through the doorway into the base of the tower.

Marble-Eyes gave a shout. "Hey wait! There's already people up there!"

"That's okay," the attendant said. "There's plenty of room." Marco, leaping up the steps two at a time, had disappeared.

Marble-Eyes started for the doorway. Jerry said, "Excuse me, mister. Is that your gray Plymouth parked on Monument Street over by the church? I think the police are towing it away."

The man stopped in mid-stride, spun around and stared at him, his mouth slightly open, then rushed out the front door and down the steps. Jerry followed him. But whereas Marble-Eyes turned right to circle the monument for a look at the place he'd parked his car, Jerry turned to the left, to stand out of sight behind the corner of the building that housed the entrance hall.

A moment later the man came running back and went storming up the steps into the building; Jerry darted to the outside of the entrance to hear what was being said inside. "Did that guy go upstairs?" Marble-Eyes was shouting. "No," said the attendant—"he followed you outside." With a muttered curse, the man went into the tower and started up the stairs.

Jerry re-entered, shaking his head apologetically, and said to the attendant: "It wasn't his car after all. Too bad I gave him a scare. Well, time's short." He laid a ten-dollar bill on the desk. "Here's something for upkeep. How many steps to the top?"

The attendant told him, putting the money into a metal box. And Jerry, too, began the ascent—keeping count of steps, and taking from his coat pocket the billiard ball and sock. An awkward trick to play on Marble-Eyes to gain Marco more time to do his thing; but hell, one has to be flexible in the face of circumstance. And it worked out very nicely that, on this climb, *he* was behind old Marble-Eyes—and not the other way around.

The steps were narrowing in width as Trntl approached the top of the monument. She was discovering muscles in her legs she didn't know she had—and was far from overjoyed at finding them.

Bright sunlight flooded the gray brick wall above her, and she rounded the last curve and stepped up into a very small room at the top of the tower. Three glassed windows looked out in three directions over Baltimore. Overhead the gray bricks formed a shallow dome; electrical cables looped around this and extended down the wall. All right, she thought; this is the Special Place. Now where's the Key Hole? There was nothing in the walls, the window frames, or the floor that could have served. On one side there was a locked door that led onto an exterior railinged walkway around the summit of the tower; but it was bolted, and the concept "Key Hole" didn't seem appropriate to it.

She pulled Stephanie's diary from her coat pocket and scanned the turned-down page: Morris had offered to put his class ring into the Key Hole, but Stephanie had been afraid that an electrical maintenance man would find it. Trntl followed the electrical cables, saw what appeared to be a couple of metal terminal boxes. In the one positioned highest on the wall, a square hole near the bottom invited exploration. With due caution she inserted a finger and began feeling around. The hole opened onto a sizable interior space. Wadded chewing gum wrappers had been stuffed into the bottom of the cavity. As Trntl's finger explored the inner wall adjacent to the hole, she found, at the top, above the opening, a hard object fastened with adhesive tape. With her nail she pried it loose, then pulled it into the light. It was a key folded into a small piece of paper. A large tabbed key; and scrawled on the paper, in Morris's hand: "Greyhound Bus Station."

There in the cramped stuffy room high above Baltimore, she wanted to let out a war-whoop and do a victory dance. But behind her, someone was coming up the stairs. She slipped the key and note into her coat pocket with the diary and turned to see first the head, then the shoulders of a man in a dark overcoat rising into view. A black-haired man with a black mustache. In his right hand was a pistol equipped with one of Scaevola's silencers—pointing straight at her navel. The man halted four steps down, looking a bit more flushed and winded than he had at the inquest.

"Well," said Trntl, "if it isn't Nick Dellanotte. I was wondering when I'd see you next."

His face tightened, and his whole body went rigid with surprise. "How dya know my name?"

"Not just me, Nick. The police. You're a marked man."

"Shut up. You talk too much." His face had gone slack; pallor drained away the flush and left his face a mottled pink. Why doesn't he just go ahead and shoot me? Trntl wondered.

"Well, what do you want to see me about?" she asked.

He hesitated; then, "You've gotta take a fall."

"Well, you've certainly got the advantage," said Trntl. "Kind of like shooting fish in a barrel, isn't it?" Why was he stalling?

"You're gonna fall and break your neck on these stairs," he said. He hadn't come up the final steps, had not moved closer. There was no way for him to join her in the tiny room without coming dangerously close to her. But she had her answer. "It's got to look like an accident, huh? Well, I don't think I *want* to break my neck on those stairs."

The gun barrel moved up to point at her face. "I'll shoot you if I have to."

"And disobey orders? Very dangerous, Nick. Remember what happened to Angelo Torelli." (She herself didn't know; Fingers had merely told Carol that he was "gone." She was hoping Dellanotte knew at least as much as Fingers.)

Nick had become quite pale now. "Shut up. Move back against that wall. But slow."

"No," she said. "I won't." If he was to make her fall, he'd have to be above her on the steps; therefore, he would have to come up

388

to the chamber, trade places with her, and make her go to the head
of the stairs. There was no way for them to pass without his opening himself up to attack.

"Okay then," he said, and came one step higher. Trntl shifted
her body as though to move backward, but instead leaped forward
and kicked him as hard as she could in the center of his face. The
toe of her shoe hit him between the eyes, and the heel flattened his
nose. With a burbling shriek Nick Dellanotte pitched backward,
somersaulting downward around the curve and out of sight. When
kicked, he'd fired the gun; and Trntl heard the bullet whiz past her
face and thud into the dome. Brick dust showered her hair.

She immediately followed her assailant, listening with satisfaction to the bumps and slithers preceding her down the steps
between the narrow walls. The white marble steps were here and
there smeared and spattered with blood.

Trntl found the pistol lying against the outer wall on the wide
portion of one step; she stooped and pocketed it on her way past.
Finally, about thirty steps down, she found Nick wedged diagonally across the stairs. At first, she surmised, he must have bounded from wall to wall during his descent—then, gravitating to the
central column, slid more or less vertically over the narrowest
points of the steps. He was unconscious, breathing shallowly; she
stepped over him and continued downward—faster now, thinking
that he might've had a confederate with him, such as the chilly
fellow who'd been sitting with him at the inquest. The sooner she
could get out of this corkscrew trap the better.

She began leaping down the stairs two at a time—but found it
was harder to do than taking two at a time while going up; there
was a tendency to hesitate, and a sense of vertigo. She went back
to taking the steps singly—but still running as fast as she could.
Round and round to the left, her hand sliding down the railing
fastened to the outer wall.

Suddenly, in front of her, she heard heavy footsteps rapidly
ascending. She couldn't tell how close the person was. Either she
could stop, and wait in ambush for the person to reach her, or continue her running descent. She chose the latter and maintained her
speed, moving to the outermost, widest part of the steps, plunging
down and around at the person who was dashing up toward her.

She turning left, he turning right, they rushed together; and
Trntl, arms stiffly out before her, shoved him with all her strength.
He lurched away and down, his head meeting the bricks of the

outer wall with a resounding crack, then slid and tumbled out of sight. Thrown off balance by the impact, Trntl fell sideways, caught the railing, and slid several steps on her tail-bone. She clenched her teeth, hauled herself up, and continued her rapid descent.

Three complete revolutions below she found the man she'd shoved. He was lying across the stairs, apparently unconscious, his head and shoulders propped against the outer wall. She looked him over carefully as she passed: a burly dark-haired man she'd seen before—yes! the fellow in the trenchcoat who'd been following her around town. The guy she'd taken to the zoo and lost in the tangled streets north of Druid Hill Park. Well, good riddance.

Two more turns, and she saw below her the ascending head of Dellanotte's friend from the inquest. Even as she stopped her forward plunge and flung her weight backward, turning on her heel, she saw the silencer at the end of his hand. *Pfsst!* Behind and below her shoulder, one of the bricks in the outer wall exploded in dust and fragments.

Round and round, now to the right, up and up she leaped, taking the steps two at a time. She couldn't look behind her; her pursuer was more than ten steps below and invisible. As she leapt over Trenchcoat's body, she was struggling to pull Nick's gun from her coat pocket. All right, if it came to a shootout, they'd be on an equal footing: if she had the disadvantage of having no way out, he had the disadvantage of being below her and having to stand on the narrowest part of the steps.

Since she didn't really want to see Nick again, with his bloody face and squishy nose, she decided to stop and make a stand. If she hugged the central column, she could use it for a shield. But that would limit the scope of her fire, and there the thinness of the step treads would make standing difficult. To the outer wall, then, where (though more exposed) she'd have a broader field of control, and could see further down the staircase. She aimed the pistol just past the central column and as far down the stairs as possible. Fire, she thought, when you see the whites of his eyes.

A head came into view. Trntl fired. A red gouge appeared in the gray paint of the outer wall. The head vanished as though jerked down by a string. Trntl moved to the middle of the step, reducing her opponent's field of fire. He would move closer to the central column also, would possibly creep around the column gun barrel first. She waited, straining her eyes to see the slightest hint of movement.

There was a short, sharp sound, not loud, somewhere between *thunk* and *thwack*, with something of *skush* as well. Not a shot, though. It sounded more like an egg breaking. An ostrich egg.

Then silence. The minutes ticked by; Trntl became impatient. How long should she crouch here aiming at the gray bricks? She had a key in her pocket that had to find a lock.

The attendant looked up from the magazine he was reading and pulled his feet off the desk as two men descended the last of the marble steps and came into the entrance hall. The taller of the two was supporting his friend, one arm around his waist, the other holding the shorter man's arm over his shoulder. The shorter man was dragging his feet, managing to walk only with great difficulty.

"It's all right," Jerry said. "My friend's just discovered that heights bother him; the monument was more than he'd bargained for."

"He doesn't look very good," the attendant said.

"He'll be all right once we get outside into the fresh air." The two of them bumbled out into the sunlight, the shorter leaning heavily on the taller. The attendant put his feet up on the desk again and opened his magazine. He could sympathize with the poor guy; he didn't like heights either, and always dreaded climbing those miserable stairs.

Jerry helped Marco into the passenger seat and poured him a cup of coffee from the Thermos they always kept in the back seat. "How are you feeling?" he asked.

"Better. A headache you wouldn't believe. I hardly know what happened. Trntl came barreling down those stairs and gave me a shove. Next thing I know you're slapping my face and making me sniff ammonia."

"At first I thought you'd been shot," Jerry said. "The guy I followed up took a shot at Trntl, and then I find you all crumpled up against the wall. After I made sure you were alive, I kept going up the stairs—using Ranger Stealth—and there he was, hunkered down with his gun out like he was waiting in ambush. I crept up behind him, used the billiard ball, and came back down to wake you up. Here's his piece; it's got a nice silencer." He held it up for Marco to see. "Trntl's still up there, very much alive."

Marco swished the coffee in his mouth. "Who are they, and why are they after her?"

"Who knows? They may be after the cadenza too. They may be related to those turkeys who tried to deep-six her at the warehouse. Look, if you're feeling okay, I've got to get back in there and see what's happening. Trntl came here for a purpose, and she may have found what she wanted." He left Marco in the car and went back into the entrance hall.

The attendant put down his feet. "How's your friend?"

"Oh, he's feeling much better, thanks. He's a little embarrassed about getting sick, so while he recovers himself, I thought I'd come back here. Say, you could do me a favor, if you would."

"Be happy to, if it's something I can."

"Well, we're from out of town, and I wonder if you could tell me what there's to do in Baltimore. Places to go, sights to see." He'd give Trntl five minutes to come down; and if she didn't, he'd go up to see what had become of her.

"Well, there's lots," the attendant was saying. "You like trains? There's the B & O Transportation Museum—"

Chapter 32

Trntl inched her way downward, pausing long on each step, muscles tensed, ready to spring backward at the first suspicious sound or movement. She kept the gun steady, not even wanting to blink her eyes. Her nerves were jangled, and her tail-bone hurt. She found herself thinking that this was a hell of a way to earn a living.

Suddenly she saw something dark at the juncture of the central column and the lowest step within her sight-range. It took her a moment to identify it: the top and back of a man's head. Then, the upper body, arms flung outward, hands empty. She moved closer. It was the gunman, all right, stretched face-down across the edges of the steps, looking as though someone had dropped him there from a great height.

"My god," she thought, "did I shoot him after all? I could've sworn the bullet missed." And where was his gun? Had it bounded down the stairs? No, on closer inspection, he didn't appear to have been shot. There was no blood. Just a large bump on the back of his head. She felt for a pulse, found one, then straightened up from her squatting position and—the gun still poised—continued down the stairs, but going faster, far less concerned that she'd be walking into an ambush. Corkscrew-sandwiched between stairs above-and-below, she wanted to get out of the confining walls, out into the sunlight. The endless counterclockwise motion, down and down, was making her dizzy. Just when she was thinking the stairs would never end, she was on the solid floor again walking out into the entrance hall. The attendant was at his desk lecturing to a tourist. She strode to the desk. "Excuse me, how do I get to the Greyhound Bus Station from here?"

The attendant looked at her with a slightly puzzled expression. "Down Monument Street," he said. "Two blocks west, one block south."

"Thank you." She hurried out.

The attendant turned back to resume his lecture. "And then there's Fort McHenry—" But Jerry was already moving toward the door.

"Yeah, I think I'll go see the trains," Jerry said. "Thanks for your help."

The attendant shrugged and looked at his watch. Just two more to come down, and then he could close up for the afternoon. He opened his magazine and yawned.

When Jerry arrived at the car, he saw across the park that Trntl had just reached hers. "Marco," he whispered, "she's goin' to the bus station. Are you able to drive? She saw me in there, and would recognize me again."

"I can drive," said Marco, sliding over to sit behind the wheel. "The coffee helped."

"Two blocks west, one block south," Jerry said. "Stick with her; I think it's important."

Trntl pulled into a parking space along the curb, and, feeling a great sense of fatigue, hurried into the bus station. She pulled Morris's key from her pocket and searched for the storage lockers. She found the locker whose number was on the key tab, then saw to her dismay that there was already a key in the lock. The door opened on an empty compartment.

"Oh hell," she thought. There was a note taped to the inside of the door. An official printed form: "The contents of this locker have been removed as of March 3. They will be held at the ticket desk until March 18 and then disposed of. Renter may claim contents by presenting locker key and making payment for overtime storage." Trntl breathed a groan of relief. Today was only the Eleventh.

The waiting room was full of people—most of them sitting with their luggage, several standing in line at the counter. Exhausted and impatient, she went to the ticket desk and joined the queue. After what seemed like ten minutes, but was actually five, it was her turn. She presented the key, and the clerk left for a moment, a sour expression stamped on his face. When he returned he was carrying a large manila envelope sealed with Scotch tape. Across the front Morris had printed FOR STEPHANIE SIMMS.

"Yes, that's it," Trntl said.

"There's a storage fee to pay," said the clerk.

"Yes, yes," Trntl said, hauling out her handbag from her coat pocket and scrambling in it for her billfold. "Whatever it takes."

He computed for a moment, named his price, and Trntl forked over the money. He made change before he handed her the envelope. "Next," he said.

Trntl stepped away from the desk clutching the envelope with both hands. At last! And in a week it would have been "disposed of"! She stepped out of the thick of the crowd, went to a quiet place near the wall, and gently unsealed the envelope. Inside were a number of sheets—ten, twelve?—of the thin, tough paper that Farringford habitually used. She edged the top sheet one inch out. Ah! in Farringford's precise, meticulous hand, neatly inked, tiny but bold, the notes of a piano solo. She slid the paper back into place, closed the flap, and hurried out of the bus station and back to her car.

She scanned the street. There was nobody near except an old woman standing on the curb preparing to cross. Clutching the envelope to her chest, Trntl was inserting her key in the lock of the car door when the old woman darted up behind her and sapped her with a blackjack above the right ear. Trntl fell against the car and slid down the door onto the pavement. The old woman snatched the envelope and ran to the gray Chevrolet that was driving forward to meet her.

"We got it!" Jerry cried, leaping into the passenger seat. "The bastards had it all the time, stashed in a Greyhound locker!" He waved the envelope like a flag.

Marco said, "Better get that costume off. I don't think Mr. Meggs would approve." With a grin, he pulled into traffic and started for the hotel.

Flailing up through swirling black fog spreckled with bright flashes, Trntl for a moment could only focus on the spots swarming before her eyes, the diffused pain thudding in her skull. Through her mind, *Oh shit!* kept running like a tape on endless loop.

Scuffling about on her hands and knees she searched on the pavement for the envelope, but only found her keys. Fighting back waves of nausea, she climbed to her feet, leaning against the car door for support. *She'd had the cadenza in her hands!* Jesus! How could she explain this to the clients? To Mrs. Sternberg? What would Carol and Torvald and Felix think? *Stupid, stupid!* She'd forgotten the investigator's first principle: be aware of the total environment and watch your back. She ought to resign from the firm and open a pretzel stand.

Mr. Meggs was back from the Transportation Museum when they arrived. Seeing the cadenza safely in hand, he announced, "Well, I'm no longer needed here; I'm off to Denver," packed his bag, and left.

"And we should leave, too," said Chip. "I'll call Winslow to ready the jet."

"I'll check us out of the hotel," said Jerry.

"And I'll scour the room," said Marco. "Should we call the Chief?"

"Let's surprise him," Jerry smiled. He patted the brown envelope into the bottom of his suitcase, deep down, underneath his shirts.

Torvald Grimsson shrugged and spread his hands. "Don't hate yourself, Trntl. It could've happened to anybody. You got away from Scaevola's people in the Monument. And you did crack Morris's code."

Trntl lay full-length on the bed; the cold compress and double Scotch had only barely mellowed her out. "Yeah, but it happened to *me*. I feel I've let us all down. I don't even know who hit me."

"He may be one of the men who beat up Finegold," said Carol. "But is he connected to the two groups of bidders?"

"Group Two will be calling us at four, Group One at four-thirty," said Torvald. "If one of them doesn't bother, we'll have our answer."

Four o'clock came, and four-twenty-five. The phone did not ring. "Well," Torvald said, "Group Two may have the cadenza."

"Tweed Overcoat," said Trntl.

At four-thirty, a call came through. Torvald recognized the voice of the man called Littlefellow. Impatient, cold: "Where does the bidding stand?"

"The music is no longer for sale."

"I see." The phone went dead.

"In all likelihood," said Carol, "Group Two *does* have the cadenza."

"Whoever they are," said Trntl. She'd recovered much of her steam and was now pacing angrily about the room. "We've got to make some decisions. Should we stay in Baltimore and try to find them, or throw it up and go home? If I've blown it, I don't see how we can justify running up expenses for Silas Dinch."

Carol said, "If Group Two isn't local, but came in like we did to get the cadenza, they're probably gone by now. I'd say, let's return to New York."

Torvald nodded agreement. "Yah, I think we should call it quits. We have no leads whatever."

Trntl sighed in resignation. "Okay." She indicated Stephanie's diary, which was lying beside her on the bed. "I want to dispose of this, too, so that it'll never be read. Maybe I should take it back to New York and ditch it there. Carol, we'll go with you on the train. And now let's get something to eat. But *not* at the House of Wang."

When they returned from eating, they found that, once again, their room had been entered and thoroughly searched.

At ten-fifteen that night, in his apartment overlooking Central Park, Victor Zyzynski received with exultant and exquisite pleasure his Baltimore surprise: the Farringford Cadenza, hand-delivered by Marco, Jerry, and Chip. "Ah, well!" he said, pouring drinks all round. "Once again you justify the confidence I place in you. For awhile there, I was wondering if you were going to let me down."

"It was a difficult assignment," Chip said. "But we knew it was just a matter of time."

"What about photocopies?" Zyzynski asked. "Mr. Meggs said that he saw a set when he met with Grimsson."

"There was just that one set," said Jerry. "We have them here." He handed over a second envelope. Zyzynski opened it and compared the sheets it contained with those of the original manuscript, then released a grunt of palpable relief. "You men are thorough," he said. "I give you that." He selected a cigar from a mahogany humidor. "That's what I expect, and what I pay for." He snipped the cigar-end with his vest-pocket guillotine, lit up with a jeweled lighter, and voluptuously inhaled. "But now let's drink a toast to this successful acquisition: gentlemen, The Farringford Cadenza!"

"The Farringford Cadenza!" they echoed dutifully, and tossed back their drinks.

"Now," Zyzynski said, indicating the tray where they were to deposit their glasses, "you've earned a rest. Report to Strunk tomorrow at nine, and you'll get sealed orders for your next assignment. It will take you to Thailand, and then to Singapore. That should especially please *you*, Jerry."

"Sounds good, Chief."

"Yes, well good night, gentlemen." He pressed a button on his desk; the door opened, and Wilson arrived to usher them out.

Zyzynski took the twelve sheets of manuscript from the envelope and saw that Farringford had numbered them in sequence. Penned at the bottom of the last page were the initials "C.P.F." With trembling hands he spread the pages in the proper order across the desktop, then stood back and regarded them with a proprietary smirk. "He *hah!*" he bellowed. *His!* And his *alone!* Exhilaration gusted with a rush that nearly blew off the top of his head. He gave a shimmy, squirmed, and hugged himself, and danced around the room. Each time he acquired an item for his Collection, he felt this flush of relief, this rapturous spasm of self-congratulatory glee. But only twice before had his joy even approached the ecstasy he felt now: first, when he'd watched *The Temptation of Saint Anthony* being lowered by helicopter into his Santa Barbara vault; and a year and a half later, on St. Croix, when he'd witnessed The Manzini Altarpiece safely sealed into its humidity- and temperature-controlled glass casket.

With a fresh whiskey sour, he circled round and round the desk admiring the sheets filled with Farringford's intricate notation—now and then gently caressing with his fingertips the paper's texture. For a long time, gloating, he puffed happily on his cigar. Then he expansively pulled up his leather chair, and ponderously lowered himself into a cloud of smoke to undertake, with hand-held lens and jeweler's loupe, a close examination of Farringford's notes. My god, what a tiny, paper-saving script! Almost as small as Zyzynski's own. Nothing sloppy about it; Farringford was obsessive in his neatness and precision. Even when, on rare occasions, he'd changed his mind and canceled something he'd written, the original was neatly cross-hatched through, a near obliteration. Since Zyzynski could not read music, he had no way of knowing what the written notes signified, could not discern a melody. The piece appeared to be quite lengthy, yet by all accounts it was supposed to take only six minutes' playing-time. Incredible.

He pulled from their envelope the photocopies Jerry had provided. It was reasonable that Trntl would have made photocopies if she'd had the manuscript all along; *he* would have, in her position. Yet Jerry had said that these were the only set. Obviously, then, this was the set that Mr. Meggs had seen. Page by page he checked them against the originals. Yes, they were identical. But now there was no further need for them. And *every* reason for them to be gone.

He reached to a bank of buttons on his desk and pushed a red one. One end of the desk opened like a door, revealing the maw of a paper-shredder. He was proud of this machine, manufactured by Out-Front Security Systems, a subsidiary of Arch-Apex Electronics. He fed the photocopies one by one into the shredder. After the long teeth had tasseled the papers into shoestring strips, the patented chopping action turned the strips into confetti. Suitable for throwing at a party, or for mulch.

He went to the stereo and placed Rosamond Foxe's recording of Farringford's Fifth Concerto on the turntable. Ah, the trumpets and kettledrums! He again seated himself before Farringford's manuscript to stare at the meaningless thicket of decisive, densely-penned, never-smeared strokes. But owning the manuscript was only a necessary first step to possessing the cadenza. On paper, the notes were merely a mute encoding of Farringford's music. Only when the music was *heard* would his acquisition be complete. And to be heard, it would have to be performed by a consummate artist in the most private and secret circumstances. By a pianist who would never afterwards reveal Zyzynski's possession of the manuscript or admit to having played the cadenza. The final step would require the performance to be recorded on the best equipment available; and this recording to be merged with a recording of the complete concerto, so that he could experience the music whenever he wished and be able to assert his full manhood with the flick of a switch.

Since his hatred of Morgan Latimer for having experienced the cadenza and enjoyed its powers had cost Zyzynski more than one night's sleep, it was with great pleasure that he'd read of the old fossil's death in the paper this morning. He was always gratified to see his rivals eat dirt. With intense satisfaction, he'd clipped Latimer's obituary to mount in his album with all the others.

But now his attention returned to the concerto. The piano had made its entry, and, as always, the incomparable Rosamond's fleet fingers soothed and beckoned him. Clearly, it would have to be Rosamond who performed the cadenza. Her rendition of it spliced into this recording of the concerto, replacing the feeble substitute written by Peter Shitface Abbott. Yes! It *would* be Rosamond! And when he heard her play it, and he rose again to his Number One position, there she'd be, his for the taking. A sweet seduction, with candlelight, and oysters, and champagne. And she would melt, and yield, and give herself completely; and then Abbott would be finally dismissed, sent forever to the back of the line; and, at long last, *he*—not Abbott—would possess her.

Theirs would be a long relationship. As for her keeping the existence, and his ownership, of the cadenza a secret, surely that would seem to her a small price to pay for access to his sixty billion dollars. He'd tell her that she was committed to the secret only as long as he was alive—he was 65, after all, she only 26; and, after he was gone, she'd be able to announce the rediscovery of the cadenza and use her exclusive possession of it to her own advantage. It was a proposition not to be refused. He smiled and rubbed his hands together. He'd never before contemplated such an arrangement. But Rosamond was a very special woman, requiring special generosity.

But where would she learn and practice it? Record it? Where was there sufficient privacy? The recording studios at Top Notch Records were too busy, too public. It had to be someplace where he could be in constant sharing with Rosamond as she mastered the cadenza. Somewhere altogether remote and inaccessible. *St. Croix.* Of course. The house there was certainly isolated from its neighbors; it had a top-of-the-line security system and several large sound-proofed rooms. One of them could be equipped as a recording studio. But there was no piano at the villa. Well, that was a small matter.

Tomorrow night Rosamond would be performing with the Metropolitan Symphony. He'd have to move quickly. He'd approach her at the reception following her concert, get her to consent to go with him to St. Croix—and once they were there, everything would follow naturally. But the way had to be prepared;

there couldn't be any hitches. He pulled out a note pad and did some rapid jotting. Then reached for the phone.

"Stephens, call the staff at St. Croix right now—tonight— and have them prepare for my arrival tomorrow evening. Call Macintosh and have him take a team down there tomorrow with the very best sound-recording equipment and fit out the West Guest Room as a professional recording studio. State-of-the-art. I want the job finished by sundown. Is that understood?"

"Yessir."

"You have the duty-roster there. Call Rademacher in Purchasing—tonight—and have him buy two concert grand pianos—the best available—and have them flown to St. Croix by tomorrow afternoon at the latest. He can use the Double-A-1 Cargo Jet—"

"What if he's unable to find two concert grands on such short notice? There may be a waiting list for new ones."

"I don't care if they're brand new or already in use. If new, and there's some sort of advance ordering necessary, or a waiting list for availability, *money is of no concern*. Have Rademacher make that clear to the manufacturers, and simply spend whatever's required to buy the pianos. If there aren't any new ones available, pianos currently being used will do as long as they're in tip-top shape. Stephens, *I've* never bought a piano! Let Rademacher figure it out. It's his responsibility. Tomorrow afternoon at the latest!"

"Yessir."

"When the pianos are in St. Croix, one is to go in the West Guest Room, and the other in the Large Den. Have them professionally tuned, and put the tuner into the Guest Cottage for an indefinite stay. I'm sure we have tuners on staff; check the computer and get the best one. Tell Winslow to expect a night flight to St. Croix on Thursday evening, the 12th, in the Personal Jet. Is that clear?"

"Yessir."

"And I want thirty pounds of fresh oysters and six cases of champagne—you know my brand—on the plane tomorrow night. And three dozen of frozen filet mignon from Leonardo's. Cigars are already down there in the walk-in humidor."

"Yessir. And powdered rhinoceros horn?"

"Not this time." He glanced at his notes. "One more thing, Stephens. Call Strunk tonight and tell him that when Marco, Jerry, and Chip come to see him tomorrow morning, their assignment is changed. They're coming with me to St. Croix."

Zyzynski hung up, leaned back and listened to Rosamond threading her way through the labyrinth of Farringford's second movement. He still had to formulate a plan for getting her onto the plane for the trip to St. Croix. It was crucial that she should *want* to come; everything depended on that. She knew him only as an acquaintance, a board member of the Metropolitan Symphony. How might he reveal to her that he had the cadenza and enjoin her to secrecy so there'd be no risk of her telling anyone else? and how could he get her onto the plane of her own free will? He'd have to sleep on it.

He gathered up the sheets of Farringford's manuscript, slid them back into their envelope, and went to the door of what appeared to be a closet. Behind the panels stood a blue-black safe as tall as the doorframe. He worked the combination and swung open the heavy steel door. The safe was filled—not only with file folders, notebooks, and bundles of papers neatly stacked, but also with numerous treasures awaiting transfer to his collection-vaults. Bending down, he shifted slightly the silver-gilt reliquary (laced with Byzantine filigree, studded with gems) which contained all that was left of the Arm of Saint Eustace, and stood the envelope carefully on edge between Boudica's Helmet and the pigeon's-blood sparkle of the Irrawaddy Fist.

Lefty Scaevola's day had begun well. After arriving at work, he'd received a report that last night's fire in the Hagerstown paint factory had gone according to plan. At lunch, he'd heard that Hippo ("The Greek") Aristides of Newark, his brother Vinnie's chief competitor in the supply and servicing of vending machines, had been hospitalized with a heart attack. At two, he'd been informed by his personal attorney that N. F. Trntl had said nothing damaging at the inquest. At home tonight, at nine-thirty, he'd be meeting with the Highway Commissioner to discuss the sealed bids on the new freeway construction. And it was his wife's birthday; in his pocket he carried the gift of a small wristwatch which he would present at dinner.

But at four-thirty, the ground had suddenly shifted, and a bottomless abyss had yawned beneath his feet. On the secure phone, a frantic call from one of his lawyers in Washington informed him that he'd been indicted on twenty-seven counts of violating Federal law—racketeering, extortion, conspiracy to defraud the Federal Government, wire and mail fraud, kidnapping, perjury . . . "Drug trafficking," the lawyer had bleated at him, "theft of government property, suborning of perjury, violation of civil rights (read 'murder'), and income tax evasion. We're talking heavy-duty, Lefty, long-term. Get all your attorneys and accountants together. If you're convicted on *half* these charges, you're facing thirty to forty years in prison."

When Lefty had arrived home at six forty-five after alerting his legal advisors to the coming crisis, his stomach was aheave with sour twinges and rumblings, his mind teeming with confused, half-formed thoughts and chaotic, razor-sharp terrors, jumbled and spinning. His mother was drinking wine in the living room. (Why did she insist on wearing floor-length dresses in funereal black?) "Giuseppe," she said, as he tried to get past her into the hallway, "a man's been calling you every fifteen minutes since five o'clock."

He turned anxiously to face her. Something to do with the indictments? The Commissioner, canceling tonight's meeting? "Did he leave a name?"

"No, but he said he'd keep trying. Theresa said he sounded urgent."

Lefty hurried toward the kitchen. Oh no, he thought: Trntl. He hoped that Nick had managed to make it look like an accident.

Theresa was pulling a dish from the microwave. "You look tired," she said.

"Mother said a man's been calling. Do you know who?"

"He didn't give his name—but I thought he sounded excited and nervous. He'll call back." She wiped her hands on her apron. "Don't you want to know what we're having for dinner?"

"What?"

"Pot roast and creamed cabbage."

He frowned. "Theresa, you know that cabbage gives me gas."

"Well, that's what you say. But I like it, and it's *my* birthday. If you don't want it, you can have a baked potato."

"I'm not sure I want a baked potato either." He raised one eyebrow and stared hard at the pot roast. "Did you put onions in with the meat?"

"No, you say they give you heartburn."

"They do." He pulled a stick of raw carrot from the relish tray. "I'll be in my study waiting for the phone call." He felt weak and nauseous.

Munching the carrot stick was not at all satisfying. In his study, he dropped the remnant into his wastebasket, sat down at the desk, and filled and lit his pipe. That was better. He opened the wall safe and took out the envelope thick with hundred-dollar bills—the Commissioner's commission if the meeting went successfully. No, this pipe wasn't doing it. God, it needed cleaning. The stem slurped and burbled as he drew on it; he gagged as he sucked a thin stream of tarry tobacco juice into his mouth.

The phone rang. He grabbed up the receiver, scrubbing his tongue with a Kleenex. "Yeah?"

"Lefty? This is Pete Martello. I got some bad news."

"Say it."

"Nick Dellanotte and Sammy Green are in the hospital. Nick's face is busted up something awful. Sammy's got a concussion."

Lefty sagged against the edge of the desk, his fingers clutching at the blotter. "What happened? An accident?"

"No accident. They told the police they were mugged in the Washington Monument. The guard found 'em unconscious on the stairs and called the cops."

"Why were they in the Washington Monument?"

"Nick told me they were on assignment and got ambushed."

"Was a woman there?"

"Yeah, but she got away. And something else: their guns are gone. Maybe the police took 'em."

"Are there any charges filed against Nick and Sammy?"

"No, the police logged it in as a mugging."

"Thanks for calling me, Pete. Don't call the house again." Scaevola slammed the receiver down and slewed around in his chair. The stomach cramps were unbearable. Gasping for breath, he began ticking off his casualties: Angelo, and George Fiocco, Benno, Johnny Speranza, Alfie, Fingers Beauregard. Now Nick and Sammy Green. Damn! Even Detective Price was suspended from duty. In just one week Trntl had wrecked his Organization.

He was bent double hugging his belly when his mother came to the doorway sipping her Marsala. "Giuseppe," she called, "dinner's ready." She stood staring at his gray face, his upturned eyes. "Hey, you don't look so good. You want some of my wine?"

Lefty Scaevola squeezed shut his eyes, gagged, and heaved—a mighty retch. His mother began screaming. "Theresa—*Theresa*, come quick! *Hurry!* And bring a bucket and a coupla mops!"

Chapter 33

March 12   (Thursday)

Trntl had been dreading Silas Dinch's reaction when she told him that—having found and then lost the cadenza—she was resigning the case. She fantasized shouting, curses, an apoplectic fit—or worse yet, disdain and cold contempt. ("Well, what else could one expect, with a female detective in charge?")

She was therefore pleasantly surprised, and more than a little grateful, when, hearing the sorry news on Thursday morning, Dinch did nothing but rub the back of his neck and blink his eyes. It was as though he, too, had acknowledged the need for resignation. "So," she concluded gamely, "having no further leads to follow, we feel there's no reason for you to incur further costs. It isn't easy to admit defeat." She placed a stack of manila folders on his desk. "Here are the dossiers on your competitors, and the other materials you gave me."

Torvald, who'd come with Trntl for moral support, handed Dinch a thin sheaf of papers. "And here's an itemized list of our fees and expenses." He was already anticipating his departure that afternoon for a long weekend on Cape Cod with Rachel Weintraub.

Dinch barely glanced at the papers. "You'll be paid out of the fund which Morgan Latimer placed at our disposal. As you may know, Mr. Latimer passed away two nights ago following surgery."

"I'm very sorry to hear it," said Trntl.

Dinch rose and went to the liquor cabinet. He poured bourbon into three glasses, gave a glass to each of them. "He was a close friend of my father's, and I knew him almost all my life. An honorable man." He raised his glass. "To Morgan Latimer." They drank to the man who'd heard Farringford perform the cadenza.

Dinch reached for the bottle as if to pour himself another, then checked himself, closed the cabinet, and collected their glasses. "Mr. McKay kept me fully informed, almost on a daily basis, about what was happening in Baltimore. Still, I'll admit that I'm terribly confused by nearly everything that's occurred—the false ransom demands, the three attempts on your life. And you're *sure* those attacks weren't the work of one of our competitors?"

"I'm sure they were all ordered by Giuseppe Scaevola, a local gangster who simply wanted to keep me from telling what I knew about the Simms murder."

"You've said that he didn't want the cadenza for himself."

"No; I was told he'd destroy it if he obtained it."

"Then who has it now?" Dinch cried. "Sombody who'd slug you on the street, that's who! Both L'Enfant Devereux and Cameron Stewart would be capable of it. Well, they *all* would. Did you double-check the dossiers?"

"Carol Brown did," Trntl said patiently. "Found nothing. It's possible the man's connected with one of your competitors. But I think it's unlikely. We have reason to believe he's working with one of the two groups who were bidding for the manuscript."

"And you're sure—"

"Mr. Dinch, one group was willing to pay two hundred thousand dollars. For a manuscript *known* to be stolen. The other, a quarter of a million—without batting an eye. Does that sound like two competing music publishers?"

"Well, frankly, no," he said. "But who *are* they, then?"

"We arrived at only two hypotheses that make any sense," said Trntl. "Either the two sets of negotiators represent private collectors who are vying for a unique work of art; or else they represent art dealers who are trying to pick up a choice investment item for clandestine resale. We were conducting an *auction*, for heavens' sakes."

"Then it may never be published," said Dinch.

"That's quite possible."

Dinch leaned back in his chair and closed his eyes. After a long moment he said exhaustedly, "It seems we're fated not to have the cadenza. Thank you for your help. I'm sure you did all you could. I'll phone Mrs. Farringford and Peter Shipley Abbott and tell them your decision."

And I, thought Trntl, will phone Mrs. Sternberg.

Mrs. Sternberg heard Trntl out, allowing her to talk without interruption. Then, responding to the undertone of defeat that came across clearly, she said: "I appreciate your calling me and being so forthright about losing the cadenza. Please believe that I can empathize with what you're feeling. I went through something similar back in 1947 and felt equally responsible. Do you have *any* idea who took it from you?"

"None at all."

"But you suspect it might be in the hands of a collector now, or a dealer in stolen art." She thought for a moment. "Of all the collectors I know of in the music field, not *one* would do such a thing as attack you on a public street. I don't know a great many dealers; and outside of my own transactions with them, I don't know their practices at all. Some of *them* might."

"If the cadenza does wind up in private hands, it may be inaccessible to the public for the foreseeable future," said Trntl. "I feel I've let everybody down through my carelessness and stupidity. Thanks for being so understanding."

"To change the subject," said Mrs. Sternberg. "As you may know, Rosamond Foxe is performing tonight at Symphony Hall. You may not feel up to going; but if you'd like to, you'll find a ticket in your name at the box office. And I'd like you to be my guest at the reception following the concert."

"My associates Felix McKay and Carol Brown are going to the concert," Trntl said. "And Miss Foxe invited them to the reception. I may very well take you up on the offer. Thanks."

"I hope to see you there. We try to keep our receptions from becoming too awful."

Having worked diligently for three days on the Swinfurth Lightfoot trust accounts, on Thursday the External Auditors called together the appropriate executives and department heads for a high-level briefing at noon. When he arrived at work at eight, Anton Farringford was ordered to the meeting by Tippett, head of the Trust Division; and at ten-thirty, Brownlow, chief of Internal Audit, stopped by to remind him not to be late. This plunged Anton into a bog of despair. Oh my god, they'd found him out. He must have slipped up somewhere. But there had been so many avenues to travel, so many lanes and footpaths and back alleys—always having to be sure to cover his tracks. It was just as he'd feared: some trivial oversight had tripped him up and brought him down. And he'd been so careful. He'd cooperated fully with the External Auditors—supplied them information; brought them documents;

explained procedures; anticipated their needs and requests. But this was it. The end of the road. Swinfurth Lightfoot would seal his office, change the locks, turn him over to the authorities.

Fearing he might not again have the chance, he decided to clean out his desk, removing his personal things. He opened his attache case and began putting items in. From the desktop, photographs of his father, mother, and sister; his matching pen and pencil set; the iron pyrite paperweight which was a souvenir of a childhood trip to Colorado. From the back of the bottom drawer, the thin stack of well-thumbed girlie magazines in their taped brown paper bag; an overnight shaving kit; a necktie and two extra pairs of socks. From the top drawer, the book given to him as a student by his favorite accounting professor: *Your Money Talks, but Can You Make it Walk?* His monogrammed coffee cup; old racing forms from two years ago which he'd forgotten about; a fingernail file, a comb, and his toenail clipper. From the wall, his framed diplomas, commendations, and certificates. Into the wastebasket went the bag of stale jelly beans and the executive puzzle-toy he'd been given by his staff (but had never been able to solve).

Just before the meeting, he went hot-footing to the men's room; and when he emerged ten minutes later, tie straightened, glasses polished, hair freshly combed, he marched down the corridor to the conference room as ready as he'd ever be.

Nearly everyone was there when he arrived. He seated himself in an empty chair positioned half-way down the boat-shaped table, stood his attache case on the floor beside him, and began fiddling with his ballpoint pen. Coffee, water carafes, and cups were on the table, sugar and cream. Several people were eating sandwiches from brown paper bags. Anton wasn't the least bit hungry.

The president cleared his throat. "Are we all here? We'd better begin. As you know, auditors from the firm of Benton Murray Mayfield have been working here for three full days. They've been examining our books and procedures, investigating the irregularities which Mr. Tippett and others have perceived to exist in our Trust Division. With us from Benton Murray Mayfield are Mr. Ogden, Mr. Hazelton, and Mrs. Hix. They wish to brief you on what they've found so far." He sat down and the auditors took over.

"After intense scrutiny," said Mrs. Hix, "we've found evidence to confirm that Mr. Tippett's suspicions are justified. There are losses in the Trust Division that are not the result of procedural glitches or human error. We have evidence of a systematic and long-term embezzlement of monies from specific named accounts. We are well along in our investigation and wish to consult with you on how to proceed."

Oh God, thought Anton. Here it comes. Shall I deny it? brazen it out? confess? throw myself on their mercy? My mother needed $500 a month, Twila . . . the horses . . . oh God.

Mr. Ogden rose to continue the presentation. He had a long aluminum pointer in his hand which he kept slapping into his opposing palm. "Evidence we have; and though evidence does not, per se, constitute incontrovertible proof of a suspect's culpability, we have enough information to establish a prima facie assumption of conscious and premeditated malfeasance."

Anton was sweating profusely. No, throwing himself on their mercy clearly would be of no use.

Mr. Ogden continued, "The embezzlement was accomplished by a clever—perhaps I should say ingenious—misdirection." He paused and scanned the expectant faces before concluding: "The creation and juggling of dummy accounts."

But I returned it all! Anton shouted silently. With interest!

"So far, we have established a discrepancy of nine thousand four hundred and twenty-six dollars," said Ogden. "And our investigation is continuing."

You've got a long way to go, Anton thought ruefully, to get to fifty-eight thousand two hundred and nine dollars and thirty-seven cents.

"The embezzlements have occurred in two very large trust accounts," said Ogden. "Nugent and Pickering."

Nugent? *Pickering?* Anton had never had anything at all to do with *those* accounts.

"Nugent and Pickering," said Tippett. "Why those are managed by Bill Adams. He's been with us for twelve years."

Ogden shrugged. "Do you want to see the charts?" He turned with his pointer to an easel with graphs on cardboard and began pointing.

Bill Adams! thought Anton. *Quiet* Bill? who kept to himself, brown-bagged his lunch, greeted you with a pleasant smile and vanished into his work; who avoided office politics and brought his mousy wife to the Christmas parties; who drank Pepsi and ginger ale, and kept his socializing to a minimum? Adams borrowing from the Nugent and Pickering accounts? (And how many *others* in his purview?) My god, thought Anton, and all of nine thousand four hundred and twenty-six dollars! So *far!* He poured himself a cup of coffee while Ogden blathered on, flipping through his charts, tap tapping with his pointer. Well, then, what did this portend for Anton's future? Probably too early to say for sure, but could it possibly mean that he was out of the woods? Overlooked in favor of a more obvious and graspable prey? The president's voice, tense with controlled anger, brought Anton back to the present reality: "Thank you, Mr. Ogden. What you've shown us leaves little doubt that Bill Adams is embezzling the Nugent and Pickering accounts—"

"Evidence is not incontrovertible proof—"

"Yes, yes. But we certainly have enough to proceed. We'll need to know how much further his pilferings extend, see to what extent this information resolves the irregularities that have come to our attention. Tippett, continue working closely with the Benton Murray Mayfield team; build an airtight case so that when we confront Adams he'll see there's no way out. Farringford, you've been very helpful to the team so far—"

"Very helpful," said Mrs. Hix.

"—and you know more than anyone else about the internal configurations of all our accounts. Continue to work closely with the team and provide them with whatever information they need. You're doing a good job."

"Thank you, sir," said Anton.

"I'm shocked," said Tippett, "that Adams has betrayed the trust and confidence which Swinfurth Lightfoot placed in him. Anton, we'll rely on you to help us build an airtight case."

"I'll do my best," said Anton.

At home in Hempstead, Long Island, Rosamond Foxe was following the routine she always followed on days she was to give a concert. Having returned from her hairdresser, she'd eaten a light lunch and settled down for a couple of hours of practicing. The grand piano occupied nearly half the living room of her modest house; and the room itself was cheerful and well-lighted by floor-to-ceiling windows that overlooked her back yard and small garden. The white plaster walls set off to good advantage her framed lithographic prints; two walls were entirely devoted to music cabinets and bookshelves.

Tonight she would be playing Farringford's Second Piano Concerto. Since rehearsal had gone well, she did not play it now. Instead she limbered up with preludes and fugues of J. S. Bach, a Mozart sonata, and Tenery's *Spanish Caprice*. Then she settled into the main work of the afternoon—Marchaunt's *Scherzo Diabolique* and the finale of Lemnitzer's *Concerto #7*.

Well along in the Lemnitzer, she'd just paused to make some pencil notations on the score, when the phone rang. "Crap!" She got up and went to answer it. Should've unplugged it earlier. "Hello?"

"Rosamond Foxe, please." A gruff, masculine voice. Tight and a little asthmatic.

"This is she."

"Miss Foxe, this is Victor Zyzynski. I'm sorry to bother you at home."

"Oh, yes. Mr. Zyzynski. That's all right, I was just working at the piano." Why would the billionaire be calling her? She remembered him as an obscenely fat man in his sixties, with bushy eyebrows, beady little eyes, and a prominent potato nose. Beneath this (she remembered with a shudder) was a spongy shelf of lower lip like a skinned chicken thigh. "What may I do for you?"

There was a long pause, punctuated by the rasp of heavy breathing; then—"Perhaps you remember sitting near me at the last Beaux Arts Banquet? I believe we spoke briefly on that occasion."

"Yes, of course. I remember it well."

"I'm looking forward to hearing your concert tonight, Miss Foxe."

"Thank you; I hope you're not disappointed."

"Perhaps you recall that I'm on the Board of Directors of the Metropolitan Symphony—"

"Yes, I'm aware of that." Good grief, was this a fund-raising call? A request for her to do a benefit for the financially-ailing Metropolitan?

"At the reception following your concert, I would like—that is, I hope it will be possible—if it's acceptable to you—to have a few words with you in private. Just the two of us. On a matter of extreme importance."

She frowned in puzzlement and studied her nails. "Concerning the Symphony?"

"No—uh—something—uh—*very unusual* has come into my possession, and I need your expert advice. I would prefer to wait until tonight to say more."

"Certainly. I'll arrange to see you at the reception."

"Thank you, thank you so much. Uh—well—goodbye."

She continued to frown as she cradled the receiver and returned to the piano. How very *strange*, she thought, taking up her pencil.

After showering, Felix McKay trimmed his beard, touched himself here and there with fragrant musk oil, and laid out his black tuxedo on the bed. He hadn't worn the tuxedo since he'd stopped playing clarinet in the Racine Jazz Band almost three years ago. When he stripped it out of the plastic sheath that had cocooned it since its last dry-cleaning, he was pleased to see it looking quite presentable. He hummed a little tune as he rummaged in his dresser drawer for suspenders, onyx studs, and black bowtie. The shirt with the pleated and slightly ruffled front still fit him fairly well; but in trying to close the high-waisted trousers across his middle, he encountered a major obstacle. No matter how much he pulled and stretched the pants and sucked his stomach in, the top edges of his fly refused to meet. He finally conceded defeat: which translated into leaving a gap at the top of his fly, the edges stabilized and held together by a large safety pin. The black satin cummerbund would effectively cover up his improvisation. Finally—to his intense dismay—the coat seemed to have shrunk: was far too tight across the shoulders, with a binding under the arms. He hoped no one would notice.

At seven-thirty, as arranged, he met Carol Brown at the office, and together they rode in a cab to Symphony Hall. She was wearing an attractive ensemble in avocado green, with a knee-length skirt and jacket with black piping; her longish hair was pulled back into a chignon, just short of a pony tail, which set off to advantage her dangling ear-rings, gold with inset garnets. In the cab, Felix said "You look very nice tonight."

"Thanks," Carol said. "You're wearing musk oil." Felix grinned. "Black tie and studs," she added. "I've never seen you in a tux, Felix. You're quite dashing."

"It's a very special occasion," he said. "The reception and all."

"Especially 'and all'," said Carol. "I'm sure she'll be swept off her feet."

"I hope so," said Felix. "I haven't worn this suit since Wisconsin."

"It does look a little tight," she said. "It's all those pizzas and Rachel's father's blintzes. Which reminds me—how was your dinner date with Rosamond last Saturday?"

Felix smiled happily. "Very enjoyable. We talked about a variety of things. Parents, for one—her father's a history professor, and her mother used to run an air charter service before she became a syndicated columnist doing political commentary. And music, of course, and growing up in Eau Claire and Richmond, cooking with garlic, life in the conservatory, detective work, Eleanor Roosevelt, baseball, books, and Ronald Reagan."

"Goodness," said Carol, "it must have been quite an evening."

"We'll be doing it again," said Felix. "And—she likes Benny Goodman as much as I do!"

When they arrived at ten till eight, only a few of the people who filled the lobby were wearing evening clothes like Felix. Most of the men wore dark business suits; most of the women, longish skirts—though some were in pantsuits. Many of the younger people, both men and women, wore blue jeans or corduroys.

They found their seats in the first balcony and studied their programs. Mendelssohn's *Overture: Calm Sea and Prosperous Voyage*; Mozart's *Maurerische Trauermusik*; three of Brahms' *Hungarian Dances*; and, following intermission, Farringford's *Piano Concerto #2 in D Minor, Opus 83*.

The members of the orchestra filed onto the stage and took their places. The lights gradually dimmed as the tuning-up began. The crowd muttered and rustled and whispered itself into expectant silence. Then, to enthusiastic applause, the conductor, Gregory Mitchell, strode to the podium, where he faced the audience and held up his hands until the crowd became quiet. "Ladies and gentlemen," he said in a soft voice that barely carried to the back of the hall, "we mourn the passing this week of a major patron of the arts—Morgan Latimer, long a benefactor of the Metropolitan Symphony and for many years a member of its Board of Directors. We wish to dedicate this evening's performance, the last of the current season, to his memory." He turned, raised his baton, and the orchestra launched into the Mendelssohn.

In his gilded box, stage left, Victor Zyzynski, sweating like a cheese in his white tie and tails, settled back with a dry chuckle and a smirk of satisfaction. Nineteenth-century Romanticism! Morgan would have hated it.

During intermission, Carol and Felix discovered Trntl on the mezzanine. "We weren't sure you'd decide to come," said Carol. "How is center front?"

"I'd rather be in the balcony. As for coming tonight, I decided that if Mrs. Sternberg reserved a ticket for me and invited me to the reception, I really ought to. My God, Felix, where did you find that tux?"

"In my closet," said Felix. "It dates from my former life."

"Well, your cummerbund is creeping up, and your safety-pin is showing."

Felix blushed and began tugging at the cummerbund. "Mrs. Farringford is here," Trntl said, "and her daughter Clara. They're sitting two rows in front of me."

"And here comes Peter Shipley Abbott," Carol whispered. The pianist had seen them, and was eagerly making his way toward them through the crowd.

"Oh God," said Trntl, "he wants to talk." The three of them moved as quickly as possible toward the stairs. The lights dimmed briefly, and a chime sounded. "Saved by the bell," said Felix.

Of her father's works, the D-minor concerto was Clara Farringford's favorite. She'd been seven years old when he was composing it, and she recalled with the clarity of yesterday his inviting her into the studio at the back of the house, placing her beside him on the piano bench, and saying, "Hey, punkin, what do you think of this?" And he'd played for her the piano part of the second movement—a glorious andante, sweetly melancholy with falling cadences in the treble over a rippling bass. It had made her cry—not with sadness, but with joy in its sheer beauty, its repeated questions and never quite satisfactory answers, its disturbing dissonances and affirmative resolutions. She'd sat there beside him, her feet not quite touching the floor, gripping her upper arms, with the tears streaming down her cheeks. When he'd finished playing, he'd looked at her quizzically, surprised at her tears. "Oh, Daddy," she'd whispered, "it's wonderful"; and, hugging her, he'd said, "Well, punkin, it's for you. It'll always be our special piece— just yours and mine." This was a delicious secret they shared—for when it was published, the concerto was officially dedicated to her mother. And hearing Rosamond Foxe creating the andante now— with a manner and inflection so similar to her father's—Clara gripped the arms of her seat and again felt the tears welling in her eyes. Her mother, sitting beside her, offered her a handkerchief; and later, when the lights had gone up and people were rising to leave, Mrs. Farringford said to her with more than a trace of pride—while tapping the program notes significantly—"Yes, your father was a genius. And *that* music, at least, is dedicated to *me!*"

When Carol and Felix arrived at the reception on the top floor of Symphony Hall, the Gold Room was already filled with people. A long table laden with food ran along one wall. Platters of cheese and olive canapes, deviled eggs, pickled herring and a rich pâté. A punchbowl full of shrimp. Slices of glazed ham and cherry cheesecake. Two white-coated caterers busied themselves with champagne—one opening bottles, the other filling long-stemmed plastic goblets. Here there was a higher proportion of formal dress; but still the majority of the men were in business suits. And not a single pair of blue jeans in sight.

A quick scan, and Felix found Rosamond Foxe on the far side of the room, her back to the wall, boxed in by a clutch of admirers. He muttered his irritation under his breath: no chance of getting close to her with a crowd like that. He'd wait; they'd thin out after a bit. Meanwhile, there was the food. Carol had already started for the table.

Taking a glass of champagne, Felix saw that Trntl had arrived, in the company of Mrs. Farringford and Clara. She was talking animatedly to the two clients, filling them in, no doubt, on the details of the fiasco in Baltimore. "Poor Trntl," he thought. But he kept away from them, having decided long ago that, after the strange night in her parlor, there was nothing more *he* wanted to say to Mrs. Farringford.

"The herring is good," Carol said beside him, "but avoid the pâté."

"I always do," said Felix. He helped himself to a cracker with cheese and olive. Rosamond was still hemmed in, and new people kept joining the crowd. A plump woman in a mauve dress handed Rosamond her program to autograph. Felix saw that Rosamond's glass was empty; on impulse, he took a fresh goblet with—champagne? no, mineral water!—and carried it to her across the room. Standing three people back in the tight phalanx, he caught her eye, winked, and handed her the glass over shoulders and heads. She took it with a nod and gave him a grateful smile. He made her a gallant bow and felt his safety-pin give way. With both hands he jerked down his cummerbund, and, holding it firmly in place, went stiff-legging back to the serving table.

"Carol!" he whispered. "Where's the men's room?"

"Out in the foyer; we passed it coming in." She observed his hands at their tugging. "Oh, a problem. Do you want some help?"

"I'm hoping I didn't lose the safety-pin."

"Let's go out and see what's to be done," said Carol, taking one last bite of herring and setting down her plate. She led him into the foyer. "The rest-rooms are out," she said: "I can't go into yours; you can't go into mine. So let's see what it's like behind this potted fig."

He raised his cummerbund. She leaned forward to peer at the top of his fly. "No, the pin's still there, still fastened. The cloth ripped out. Here, I think I can re-pin it." She undid the pin, used both hands to pull the edges of the fly together, said sharply, "Here, you'll have to help." He helped, looking nervously over his shoulder in dread of curious passers-by who, observing the intense activity behind the fig-tree, would no doubt assume the worst. After Rosamond, the person he most dreaded to see walking by was Mrs. Farringford on her way to the john. But the only persons to pass were three women and two men going into the reception from the elevators, and their backs were to the fig-tree for most of the distance.

"There! It's fixed," said Carol. "Now, remember to stand tall, breathe shallow, and go easy on the food. And for heaven's sake, don't sit down."

"I appreciate your help," said Felix. "Have some cheesecake for me."

Chapter 34

Mrs. Farringford lit one of her Turkish cigarettes, inhaled, blew the smoke through her nostrils. "Needless to say," she said to Trntl, "your failure to recover the cadenza is extremely upsetting. Without it, there won't *be* a second edition of the concerto. Silas kept me apprised of what you were encountering, the dangers you faced. The cadenza has already caused three deaths, if you include Morgan Latimer's. Four, with my husband's—if, as I think, he was murdered for it."

"I understand your being upset," said Trntl. "I'm upset, too; not only with losing the manuscript when I had it hand, but also with the fact of my own incompetence."

Mrs. Farringford glanced at her briefly, then looked away. "I'm sure you did everything that you could have." Her tone carried the finality of dismissal and imparted a palpable chill. She turned her back on Trntl and moved off toward the champagne. Clara Farringford touched Trntl's arm: "Mother was *terribly* upset when Mr. Dinch told her what had happened. She hasn't gotten over the shock of losing the cadenza for a second time. When I arrived this afternoon, she was still quite agitated—and angry, I'm afraid. Please forgive an old woman's disappointment."

"Her disappointment's no greater than mine," said Trntl. "Thanks for your comments."

"It's almost as though the cadenza carries a curse," said Clara. "Whoever has it now may be in for a rough time."

"I certainly hope so," Trntl said fervently.

Mrs. Sternberg joined them, bringing with her a slim, handsome man in impeccably tailored black evening clothes. "Ah, Miss Trntl, I'm so glad you decided to come. Clara, here's an admirer who'd like to meet you." The stranger stepped forward smiling as Mrs. Sternberg introduced him: "Clara Farringford, N. F. Trntl, allow me to present Friedrich Haeckler von Schaffhausen—also known, in banking circles, as Friedrich von Schaffhausen."

He clicked his heels, bowed crisply to each of them, then smiled anew, and gave a discreet little wink. "And also known, to my friends, as Freddy Haeckler." He turned to Clara. "I have long admired your flute playing, Miss Farringford—have heard you twice in concert. Once in Boston, once in Vienna. You have a considerable reputation in Europe."

"Why, thank you," said Clara. "How kind of you to say so. Vienna was eight years ago. Are you from Austria, then?"

"No, I'm Swiss." His smile broadened to show perfectly even, unnaturally white teeth. Capped, thought Trntl; and this caused her to scrutinize the rest of him more closely. He was of moderate height, with black curly hair showing just a faint spattering of gray at the temples; his dark brown, deep-set eyes sparked with intelligence. Though Trntl placed him in his mid-forties, the skin of his face was as tight as a thirty-year-old's. Face-lift, she decided. His ruffled shirt front sported bright ruby studs.

Aware of her examination, he turned his intense eyes on her. "N. F. Trntl," he said, as though searching his memory. "Are you the private investigator the papers talk of who's seeking the lost Farringford Cadenza?"

"I confess to it," she answered.

"How is your search progressing? I'm sure we all would have learned of it had you discovered the cadenza."

"The investigation's at a standstill, I'm sorry to say."

"I regret to hear that. We Farringford enthusiasts are *quite* anxious that it be found. And made available."

"It's lucky that Mr. Haeckler was in New York tonight," Mrs. Sternberg interjected. "He just flew in from Bogotá this afternoon."

Trntl nodded. "You're in banking, I believe Mrs. Sternberg said?" She took a cigarette and a book of matches from her bag.

"Banking is one of my interests. I have others: chocolate, pharmaceuticals, precision instruments." He reached out and lit her cigarette with a platinum lighter. "Fortunately, I enjoy traveling." From a platinum case he selected a cigarette of his own—rather short, with a stiff paper tube for mouthpiece—and fitted it carefully into a long black holder. "Business took me to Bogotá. Business brought me to New York. While here, I couldn't miss the opportunity of hearing Miss Foxe perform Farringford's Second. It's a superb concerto; though, for me, not as exciting as the Fifth—even when the Fifth is played with Peter Shipley Abbott's pretentious little cadenza."

"Abbott did his best," said Clara, "but I agree, it does seem to lack something. I prefer hearing the concerto with no cadenza at all."

Friedrich von Schaffhausen smiled at Trntl, meeting her eyes. "Those of us who love the Fifth Concerto will owe Miss Trntl *a great deal* if she can supply us with Farringford's cadenza."

Something went *click!* inside Trntl's head. Continuing to look into his eyes, she exhaled smoke slowly.

"Speaking of Abbott," said Mrs. Sternberg, "he's just arrived—apparently with a bouquet of roses for Rosamond."

"He'll probably want to talk to me about what happened in Baltimore," Trntl said. "I'd prefer not to."

"We can try to divert him," Clara said, "—and get him talking to Mother."

"And if you'd allow me, Miss Trntl," said Friedrich von Schaffhausen, "I'd be happy to walk with you out on the terrace. I would relish more of your company."

"That would be interesting, Mr. Haeckler," Trntl said.

"Oh, call me Freddy," he urged.

Felix McKay beat a hasty retreat when he saw Mrs. Farringford coming toward the champagne bottles. He tugged Carol's arm and they brushed past three journalist-types who'd never left the punchbowl (and who'd earnestly depleted the shrimp). He hustled her in the general direction of Rosamond Foxe.

"Who's the elegant stick talking to Trntl?" Carol asked.

"Hard to say," Felix muttered. "Probably a friend of the Farringfords."

Biding his time till Rosamond was free, Victor Zyzynski had been standing near the far wall chatting abstractedly with three other board members. He too had observed the elegant chap standing next to Mrs. Sternberg. Though he'd never met the man, he knew who he was: Friedrich von Schaffhausen, one of his many rivals in international finance and specialized manufacturing. He scanned his memory: banking, of course; chemicals; electronics; pharmaceuticals. Chocolate. Precision lenses, gun- and bomb-sights, earth-moving equipment. And a global trade in illicit drugs and sophisticated weaponry (supplied wherever it was wanted).

But von Schaffhausen wasn't worth more than twelve billion at the outside. Pooh! a piker, a flit. A Swiss bonbon.

Zyzynski's attention shunted to Peter Shipley Abbott, who'd just entered with a large bouquet of red roses. The little turd was heading straight for Rosamond! Oh, no, not tonight! No, tonight was Zyzynski's, Godammit! But there he was, intruding his arrogance as always: worming in, dewy-eyed, insinuating himself between Zyzynski and Rosamond, with that superior smirk on his prissy lips! Zyzynski longed to plant a fist on Abbott's upturned nose; scrub off the shitty smirk against the flagstone floor. He abruptly excused himself from the board members and propelled himself across the room.

From the fringes of the group surrounding Rosamond, Felix and Carol had worked their way through to the inner circle. Rosamond—finally freeing herself from the chatter of a music critic who was infinitely more taken with what he was saying than with her performance—turned her head and saw Felix standing three feet away. She gave him a broad smile and extended her hand. "Mr. McKay! I'm so glad to see you!"

Felix shook her hand while using his left to hold down his cummerbund. "I very much enjoyed your performance, Miss Foxe. I'd like for you to meet my fellow-investigator, Mrs. Carol Brown."

"I'm pleased to meet you," said Rosamond, shaking Carol's hand. Carol had to give Felix credit: he hadn't exaggerated Rosamond's beauty. But before she could respond to the greeting, a huge bunch of roses was thrust between her and Rosamond, and Peter Shipley Abbott was crowing: "Magnificent performance! My dear, you've outdone yourself!" He placed the green waxed-paper bundle into the crook of her outstretched arm, leaned forward, and decorously kissed her cheek.

Bastard! Blocked by Carol's back, Victor Zyzynski gnashed and fumed. Defiler of Rosamond's purity! marking with his filthy lips a claim that wasn't his! If they'd been alone, and he'd had a suitable weapon, Zyzynski would happily have killed him.

Rosamond blushed, adjusting the roses in her embrace. "Oh, Peter, you shouldn't have."

Abbott beamed. "A small gesture of appreciation."

To himself Zyzynski muttered, Fool! It will gain you nothing. *I* have the trump card!

x x x

As she and Freddy Haeckler stepped onto the roofed and windowed terrace, Trntl's warning systems were flashing *caution*. Perhaps she was feeling residual paranoia from her experiences in Baltimore, perhaps simply responding to her long-standing distrust of middle-aged men who flaunted face-lifts and excessively white teeth. She thought it very odd that a man who'd claimed to be so eager to meet Clara Farringford had—once he was given that opportunity—blown her off so quickly. It was now apparent to Trntl that Haeckler had wanted to talk to *her*.

They crossed to the windows and looked down at the tops of passing taxicabs. Haeckler said, "Since you're not wearing a wedding band, should I assume you're not married?"

"That's correct." Surely he wasn't going to ask her for a date.

A pause. Haeckler stubbed his cigarette into an ashtray on the marble sill. "Mrs. Sternberg is a charming woman," he commented. "So active in supporting the arts! One of my associates serves on the board of the Sternberg Foundation, so I have some knowledge of her activities. Music seems to be her chief love; she's helped to advance the careers of many young musicians and composers. Established scholarships, subsidized festivals, commissioned new works. And she's also a serious collector of things musical—antique instruments, memorabilia, manuscripts."

"Yes, I've seen her collection."

"Well! then you know what I mean." Another pause. "Perhaps you're a collector yourself, Miss Trntl?"

Where was this conversation going? "No," she said, "I don't have the money to collect things in a serious way. And I'd much rather *make* things than *acquire* things. I've been working on a quilt for nearly a year—"

"Ah, a quilter! Quilts are not a main focus of mine, but I do find them interesting, and know a little about them. Are you using a traditional design? or creating one of your own, perhaps?"

"Traditional *motifs*," she answered, "but certainly my own design. I'm combining double distelfink and the aster variation of the Dresden plate."

"Charming," he said, with a nod. "Now I myself am a *collector*. And though I have many interests—classic automobiles, jade carvings, paintings, postage stamps, Roman coins—acquiring unique manuscripts of famous musical works in the composer's holograph is almost an *obsession* with me."

"It must be frustrating when there's an item you desire that you aren't able to obtain."

"Oh, indeed." His teeth gleamed in a quick smile. "But I usually manage to get what I want."

"That must sometimes become rather expensive."

"My dear Miss Trntl, please believe me: when I wish to acquire an item, the price is of no concern to me whatsoever. I will pay whatever it takes." Again he smiled, but this time did not show his teeth.

"You're fortunate to be in such a position," she said. "With an obsession, and all. Do you collect Farringford manuscripts, by any chance?"

His eyes locked on hers. "My *specialty*," he said. "That's why I was so glad to meet you tonight. You've been pursuing, and have had intimate acquaintance with, one of the great finds of the twentieth century." He paused for the space of a long breath. "But I was extremely concerned when you mentioned a few moments ago that the search has come to a standstill."

He left it hanging as an implied question. Trntl decided to respond to it. "I've told my clients, who commissioned me to recover the cadenza, that all my leads have petered out: I can't provide them with the manuscript."

"Indeed. Well, that is *extremely* interesting." He again looked down on the taxicabs. "For, my dear Miss Trntl, rumors are circulating that you've *already* recovered it."

"Oh, really? Not in the press, surely."

"No, not in the press."

"Where then?"

"Oh, here and there. In Europe. In collecting circles."

"Then," she said, "probably even in Baltimore." She lit up another cigarette. "I knew there was interest in Europe. Certain publishers. Humboldt-Hartmann Gesellschaft—"

"Humboldt-Hartmann—!" He jerked his head around in surprise.

"You probably own that," she said.

"No, as a matter of fact, I don't. One of my associates serves on the board of directors, however."

"L'Enfant Devereux of Paris, Cameron Stewart, Ltd. of Edinburgh; they've all expressed interest."

His face became grim, all lines pulling downward. She saw him actually gripping the window sill. "You astonish me, Miss Trntl. Publishing firms all have *limited resources.*"

"None of Lunner & Dinch's competitors have made me an offer," she said.

He recovered his poise and slipped his hand into his coat pocket. "Then the rumors are accurate?" he said. "You *have* recovered the cadenza?"

"If I had, what would be the point of my telling you?"

"I am the soul of discretion, Miss Trntl. You say you've not delivered it to your clients—"

"That's right."

"Have you disposed of it in any other way?"

"No."

"Then do you currently have it in your possession?"

"Well, no," said Trntl. "I did recover the cadenza. In Baltimore, two parties tried to buy it from me by bidding against each other. It is no longer in my possession. I'm convinced it's now in the hands of yet another collector."

"So you *did* sell it to the other party!" Haeckler blurted out.

"No, sir, I did not. Just after I found it in a bus station locker, the manuscript was stolen from me by an agent of the unknown collector, who mugged me in the street."

Haeckler arched back with a frown and looked down his nose at her. Then he threw back his head and laughed—a cascade of staccato barking cheeps, sounding for all the world like a quartet of wide-beaked sparrow nestlings waiting to be fed. He recovered his breath and locked eyes once again. "Surely you don't expect me to believe *that*, Miss Trntl!"

"I don't care whether you do or not. It's the truth. And I've resigned the case."

He studied her without smiling. "When did this happen?"

"Yesterday afternoon, in Baltimore."

"But the photocopies—where are they?"

"There are no photocopies. There never were any. What Rumor saw were copies of *other* Farringford works."

Freddy stood for a long moment, tapping a fresh cigarette against his thumbnail. *"O mein Gott!"* he said at last. "It *was* the ridiculous Attila! Oh! Hun Victorious!" He laughed again, and fitted the cigarette into his holder. "Well, there are many other plums to pick. Good night, Miss Trntl." And he strode away.

Trntl followed at her leisure. When she re-entered the Gold Room, she saw Haeckler passing through the foyer toward the elevators. She joined Carol at the serving table and helped herself to a roll of pickled herring.

"Felix is still trying to get a private word with Rosamond," Carol said. "Where've you been?"

"Out on the terrace talking to one of the Baltimore buyers."

"Good grief! Are you sure? Who was it?"

"Friedrich von Schaffhausen. A Swiss banker and chocolate-mogul. But he's not the one who got the cadenza."

"Who then?"

"If I'm not mistaken, it's Attila the Hun."

The crowd around Rosamond Foxe had considerably thinned. Peter Shipley Abbott, seeing Trntl across the room, had gone to interrogate her about losing the cadenza. That left Felix, two women journalists, Clara Farringford, and Victor Zyzynski.

After congratulating Rosamond on her performance, Zyzynski had lapsed into silence, awaiting his promised private talk. Felix, too, was waiting until he could get Rosamond alone. But the chit-chat pleasantries seemed never to end. Felix was feeling the imperative call to empty his bladder. Finally, unable to wait longer, he excused himself and quick-stepped to the doorway, where Peter Shipley Abbott was talking at Trntl. As she saw Felix approaching, Trntl quickly disengaged herself from the one-way discourse to join him in the foyer. "Thank goodness you came along," she said. "I told Abbott I wanted to talk to you. Which I have now done. So—have fun; I'll see you at the office tomorrow morning." And she retreated hastily down the stairs.

Felix went to the men's room and, as he pushed open the door, saw to his dismay that Peter Shipley Abbott was following him. Felix went to a urinal, hoping that Abbott wouldn't join him. But the pianist stopped short in the middle of the tiled floor and said urgently: "For God's sake, McKay, I've got to know! Who's Attila the Hun?"

Felix nearly soaked his pant leg. "What are you talking about?"

"Trntl says that Attila the Hun has the Farringford Cadenza. Who *is* he?"

It took a moment for Felix to process this; then, buttoning up, he said, "She was probably using a figure of speech. She doesn't know—none of us do—who has the cadenza. She's resigned the case." He went to the sink.

Abbott shook his head. "She knows. It wasn't just a figure of speech."

"This is the first I've heard of Attila," Felix said, drying his hands on a paper towel. "Now if you'll excuse me—"

"She thinks he's a collector of musical rarities. If that's the case, isn't it possible that the cadenza will *never* see light?"

"Quite possible. Now, if you're going to stand between me and the door, would you please open it?"

Abbott took a quick step to the side. "I never touch door handles in public restrooms."

Felix pulled the door open and hurried out; Abbott wedged the door open with his foot and elbowed his way through after him.

Fatigued from standing in one spot and smiling politely, Rosamond Foxe was relieved when the last chatty congratulator called it quits and departed. That left her alone with Victor Zyzynski, who'd been hovering silently at her side, clearly impatient to speak his private piece. She faced him, and, with a supreme effort, mustered up her best smile. "When you called this afternoon, you said you wished to speak to me in private. Would you mind if I sat down? I'm quite tired."

"Of course," he said. "Why don't we go to one of those tables on the terrace?"

Felix entered the room behind them and saw them going together through the doorway. Oh shit, he muttered. Well, dammit, he'd wait. He went to Carol Brown who was conversing with a short elderly woman at the serving table. "Hello, Felix. Done with Rosamond?" He shook his head, but she was going on: "Trntl introduced me to Mrs. Sternberg, a friend of Charles Philip Farringford's. Mrs. Sternberg, this is Felix McKay, one of our Associates."

"Oh, yes, we've spoken on the phone," Felix said. "I'm pleased to meet you."

"And I you," she answered. "Miss Trntl has said many good things about you; and I'm equally pleased to make the acquaintance of Mrs. Brown. I understand you're waiting to speak with Rosamond; she's just gone off with Victor Zyzynski, who's on the Symphony's board of directors."

"Mrs. Sternberg was one of those who heard Farringford perform the cadenza," Carol said.

Felix regarded her with new interest. "Ah, you and Morgan Latimer."

"It was one of the things we shared. As you may surmise, having the cadenza published is very important to me. But I'm beginning to doubt that it will be recovered in our lifetimes."

At this moment, Peter Shipley Abbott joined them, and the conversation quickly went downhill.

Rosamond seated herself at a wrought-iron table and waited while Zyzynski lowered his broad bottom onto a chair that seemed absurdly small. She couldn't move her eyes from the white waistcoat stretched across his belly, and the taut bulge of his stiff white shirt front with its arc of matched star sapphire studs. Momentarily, she expected something to pop.

Zyzynski pulled a cigar from his inside coat pocket, snicked off the end with his gold guillotine, then paused to ask: "Do you mind if I smoke? It's the finest Havana."

"As you like," said Rosamond. "Cigars don't bother me."

Better and better, he thought, moistening the end by rolling the cigar back and forth on his lower lip. He lit up and blew a dense blue cloud toward the windows.

"When you called this afternoon, you said it was a matter of extreme importance," she reminded him.

"Yes, yes it is." He had rehearsed his speech all afternoon, formulating what he would say that would convince her to drop everything and fly with him to St. Croix. But now he found himself breathless and tongue-tied, sweat puddling under his arms.

"Miss Foxe—" he began, "I have followed your career since you won the Farringford Competition. I hope I've made it clear how much I respect your—your artistry and competence. To me you're one of the world's finest pianists—certainly the finest interpreter of the works of Charles Philip Farringford—"

"Oh, come, Mr. Zyzynski, you flatter me. I'm only twenty-six. There are many vastly more experienced pianists. And as for interpreting Farringford's music, I think that Peter Shipley Abbott—"

"No!" he snapped. "Not Abbott. *You* are the finest." This wasn't going at all the way he'd planned. He paused to get his bearings. "Your modesty is becoming, Miss Foxe, but you underrate yourself. I—may I call you Rosamond?"

"Certainly."

"Rosamond," he continued, savoring the feel of it in his mouth. "I know your interest in the lost Farringford Cadenza, your desire that it be found."

Her attention perked at this. He noticed, and took heart. "What I'm going to tell you is in the strictest confidence. You must tell no one." He leaned forward earnestly across the table, lowering his voice almost to a whisper. "Rosamond, a most astounding thing has happened. I can hardly believe it myself. A person I know has come into possession of what purports to be the Farringford Cadenza. How he came by it he won't say; but I have every reason to believe it's the authentic manuscript—twelve pages, signed 'C.P.F.' at the end. He's offered to sell it to me but has given me only twenty-four hours to make the purchase. If I don't buy it, he will offer it to other contacts he has—collectors, mostly. If one of *them* should get it, it will disappear forever!"

"Good heavens!" was all she could say.

"You understand the importance of acquiring it now, while it's available. He's asking a great deal of money, which I'm willing to pay to keep the cadenza from falling into the wrong hands. I have until three o'clock tomorrow to let him know my decision."

"This takes my breath away," she said. "But why are you telling *me*?"

"Because I need you, Rosamond, and you alone—the person I trust as the foremost Farringford authority and expert—to verify that what's being offered is truly the lost cadenza. I don't wish to be defrauded by a counterfeit out of simple ignorance and my inability to recognize the real thing. No one knows the score's appearance; but you know the concerto intimately. You'll know if the music is authentic. If it is—and I'm ninety per cent sure it is—you will be the first pianist to see and play it!"

"But surely we should tell Mr. Dinch."

"Absolutely not! No one must know about it until the music is certified as the Farringford Cadenza. There have been too many false hopes, too many disappointments in this sorry business. They finally killed Morgan Latimer. We have to be absolutely sure before any announcement is made."

She nodded. "Yes, that makes sense. Of course I want to help however I can. Where's the manuscript?"

Here it was, the ultimate leap. "St. Croix."

"The Virgin Islands?" Startled; but he'd expected that.

"That's right. Near Christiansted. Have you been there?"

"No; to St. Thomas only—on a cruise."

"Splendid. My private jet is fueled and ready to go. If you're willing to perform this service, we'll have to leave tonight."

Flustered, she rose from the table. "A night flight to St. Croix?"

"Yes. A quick trip. We'll be back tomorrow night." They wouldn't, of course; but what was a small lie in accomplishing such a monumental objective? He smiled inwardly, feeling a surge of power, knowing that once again he was in command.

"I'll miss my ten o'clock dental appointment," she said. "And dinner with the Talbots. I'd want to stop at my house and pick up a few things. I live in Hempstead."

"Right on our way," said Zyzynski. "Do you have your car here?"

"Yes, it's in the garage down the block."

"I'll follow you home, and we'll ride together from there. I must make some telephone calls before we go."

"My coat's down in the dressing-room. And I should call the Talbots, late as it is, and cancel tomorrow's dinner engagement."

"You can do that here, in the staff offices downstairs, before we leave. But *don't* tell them you're going to St. Croix—we've got to keep this trip absolutely secret."

They re-entered the Gold Room, which now was nearly cleared of people. She pulled away from him. "And I must really thank Mrs. Sternberg for arranging the reception. Oh, and I promised Mr. McKay I'd speak to him before I left."

Zyzynski chewed the end of his cigar impatiently while Rosamond spoke briefly to Mrs. Sternberg. The caterers were cleaning off the serving table and packing things up. He heard Rosamond say to the bearded man in the too-tight tux: "I'm sorry I can't talk tonight, Felix; something important has come up, and I've got to leave. I'll call you at home Saturday afternoon."

No you won't, Zyzynski thought. It pleased him to see the look of disappointment that crossed the bearded man's face. He looked like some sort of struggling artist; not hungry certainly, but haunted, and somewhat desperate—a writer, perhaps, or maybe a third-rate musician—viola (probably), but possibly oboe or French horn. Zyzynski glanced at his watch. And thus he didn't see Rosamond highsign Carol Brown with a quick nod toward the door. Zyzynski cleared his throat significantly. Rosamond excused herself from the group, and went with him into the hall.

"I have to use the restroom," she told him. "Too much champagne."

"All right. I'll go to the executive director's office and use the phone." They went opposite directions down the corridor; and Rosamond entered the women's powder room, where a moment later Carol joined her.

"I need to talk to you," Rosamond said urgently. "Victor Zyzynski, the man I was with on the terrace, tells me that someone has offered to sell him the Farringford Cadenza. He wants me to verify its authenticity, and to tell no one about it till we're sure it's the real thing. We're going to fly to St. Croix tonight in his private plane—"

Carol gasped. "St. Croix?"

"That's where the cadenza is. I thought you should know, so your firm can stop searching for it."

"Hadn't you heard? Trntl found it in Baltimore, and actually had it in her hands. And then someone hit her on the head and stole it. She blames herself and feels that continuing on is hopeless."

"No, I knew nothing of this. It must've been stolen by the man who's now trying to sell it to Zyzynski."

"Trntl was afraid that a collector had gotten his hands on it."

"To keep for himself?" Rosamond went pale. She turned, ran water in the sink, and bathed her temples. "It's just incredible that anyone would want the music all to himself and deny it to the rest of the world! It's so *selfish*, so un-civilized!" She patted her face dry with a paper towel. "Frankly, I feel uneasy about flying to St. Croix with Mr. Zyzynski. He's so urgent, so intense. I've no reason to distrust his motives; he's a well-known and well-respected man. And he's promised to get me home tomorrow. But he insists on absolute secrecy. No one is to know where we've gone or why. His insistence made me feel I had to tell *somebody* where I'd be. Do you understand?"

"Indeed I do," said Carol. "Of course, it may be entirely legitimate. I do wonder why whoever stole the cadenza chose *him* to sell it to."

"He's very rich."

Carol gave a shrug. "Do you know where in St. Croix you're going?"

"He said the cadenza's near Christiansted."

"That's toward the eastern end of the island. Why don't you give our office a call when you get back? So we'll know that you *did*."

"All right. I've got to go now." She patted Carol's shoulder and went into the hall. After waiting for a bit until she thought that Zyzynski and Rosamond would be safely gone, Carol quickly went back to the reception-hall. Felix, Mrs. Sternberg, and Peter Shipley Abbott were waiting for her.

"What's up?" Felix asked.

She told them everything that Rosamond had said. Felix exploded: "This whole thing's as weird as bat shit!" He quickly glanced at Mrs. Sternberg. "Sorry."

"Oh, I think so too," said Mrs. Sternberg.

Peter Shipley Abbott had pursed his lips and sucked in his cheeks like a morose and thoughtful carp. He stared first at Carol, then at Felix, and then at Mrs. Sternberg, who, slowly shaking her head back and forth, said: "I've known Victor Zyzynski for fifteen years. I've watched how he operates on this board of directors. I know that he has a house of some sort near Christiansted. Finally, I know for a fact that he's been a collector in the past. Back in the mid-1960's he was outbidding me in public auctions for various musical items."

That did it for Felix. "I don't like it one bit. I'm going to St. Croix."

Mrs. Sternberg said, "The Foundation has a private jet which I'll put at your disposal. We'll call the trip Foundation business. I'll make the necessary calls right now; the pilot is a special friend of mine. You should be able to leave tonight."

"I'm going too," said Abbott.

"That won't be necessary," Felix said quickly.

"It might be good if there *were* two of you," Mrs. Sternberg said.

Felix, desperate: "Carol?"

"Can't. Trntl and I have to conduct the seminar at the New School tomorrow."

Torvald? No, he and Rachel had run off to Provincetown for the weekend.

"I'll pack my bag," said Abbott. "Call me tonight, Mrs. Sternberg, as soon as the arrangements are made."

At 12:55 on the morning of Friday, March 13, Zyzynski and Rosamond Foxe boarded his sleek private jet. Rosamond had never seen a plane so luxuriously fitted out. Behind the galley (like a suburban kitchen, cabinets and counters of mahogany and teak), the main cabin—with leather chairs, a sofa, bookcases, magazine rack, game table, gilt-framed paintings, and deeply carpeted floor—reminded her of a hotel lobby. Curtains were drawn over all the windows. "There's an office behind this cabin," Zyzynski told her, "then four sleeping compartments. This is Marco, who will see to your needs." (In white jacket, he bowed and smiled.) "At the bar we've got whatever you want; and we've plenty of food. Let me introduce two consultants who'll travel with us: Jerry and Chip. Gentlemen, Miss Rosamond Foxe."

They too smiled and bowed. "Is the cargo stowed?" Zyzynski asked. Jerry nodded. "Good; then I'll speak to the pilot, and we'll be on our way. Make yourself comfortable, Rosamond. I'll be back in a moment." He hurried toward the cockpit.

Rosamond felt increasingly disoriented by the airplane that didn't seem to be an airplane. By the drawn curtains, excluding the world. By the three smiling men so solicitous yet so distant. She selected a chair and sat down. The man called Marco said, "Have you been to St. Croix, Miss Foxe?"

"No. I've been to St. Thomas. And to Puerto Rico twice."

The man called Chip seated himself across from her. "The Caribbean will be a pleasant change from March in New York City."

The man called Jerry said, "I'll put your bag in Cabin 4." He set a large dish of candies on the table before her. "And if you'd like jujubes, help yourself. *I* think the lemon-flavored ones are best."

Chapter 35

March 13   (Friday)

Through massed banks of dusty green foliage and stretches of open parkland, the silver limousine with smoked windows speeds eastward from the airport into the sun. In the rear compartment, Rosamond and Victor Zyzynski sit side by side facing the inbuilt bar and tape deck—and Jerry and Chip, who are perched on jump seats. Marco rides in front with the chauffeur.

"I could've had the helicopter meet us," Zyzynski says, "but thought you'd find this more comfortable. Would you like a drink? some music?"

"No, thank you. I'm enjoying the scenery. It's drier than I expected."

"The eastern end of the island is almost desert. Arid soil, cactus. We won't be going that far. My house is just east of Christiansted, on the coast."

Conversation flags. Rosamond has slept fitfully on the flight down, and the suddenness of the trip and the unfamiliarity of the surroundings have made her irritable. Zyzynski seems preoccupied, his chins sunk upon his chest. A left turn takes them into the city. The buildings are fairly low with stucco walls; many have shingles on the upper stories. Shuttered windows. Peaked roofs, some galvanized and corrugated, brown with rust.

They pass a large open-air market, an imposing church, and ever more elegant buildings. Here the exterior walls are frequently painted in bright pastels; and many buildings extend their second stories out over the sidewalks to make covered arcades as shelter from sun and rain. These galleries open through broad arches directly onto the streets. "Many of these buildings near the harbor are Danish colonial," Zyzynski volunteers, "with lots of fancy shops for the tourists."

And tourists are everywhere, with their straw hats and cameras, their sunglasses, pale, puffy bodies, and bags of duty-free loot. The street ends at a broad esplanade and grassy park facing the Caribbean. Zyzynski points: "That's the old Danish fort."

A not very formidable building. At the waterfront many boats are moored; and a large cabin cruiser is disgorging passengers, some of them darkly tanned, some badly sunburned. "A ferry?" Rosamond inquires.

"No, commercial sight-seeing. People pay to be taken out to Buck Island to go snorkeling over the coral reefs." The driver turns east, away from the fort. Zyzynski adds, "When I'm in residence, I don't often go into town. There's plenty to do at the house."

He leans forward to activate the tape player. Debussy's *La Mer* engulfs them. And so they ride, paralleling the coast, till suddenly the car turns north off the main road, past a string of bungalows neatly situated in lawns and gardens. Then east again. The sea's to their left, brilliant sapphire under the late-morning sun; large, impressive houses with swimming pools and hedges dot the slope leading down to the water.

"What sorts of neighbors do you have?" Rosamond asks, more to make conversation than because she cares.

"I know who they are, of course—a retired movie star, a real estate speculator from Pennsylvania, a former golf champion. But I don't associate with them. Ah, we're coming to my place now."

They've been following a high stuccoed wall topped with steel spikes and shards of jagged glass. Abruptly, between two square posts, a gate of steel bars and ornamental scrollwork halts them. Marco gets out and punches some buttons mounted on a panel on one of the posts; the gate slowly swings open, the car rolls through, passing a small guardhouse just inside the wall. Rosamond observes that, on the inside, the wall is banked at ground level with coils of razor-edged concertina wire. The gate closes, and the car continues down the hill toward a large group of white buildings.

Until this moment Zyzynski has been apprehensive that something would somehow intervene to upset his plan; that Rosamond (at the airport; on the journey; in Christiansted) would suddenly decide not to go on with the project and announce her desire to leave. An irrational fear, of course; he can see that. Ah, but only when he has her within the walls, is again on his own turf, the gate locked behind them, does he feel the deep electric tingle of once more being totally in control. This buoys him to almost laugh aloud.

They pass several large outbuildings before they come to the house.

"It's an impressive establishment," Rosamond says.

Zyzynski enjoys pointing things out: "We keep the helicopter in that shed. And that's the barracks for the security staff. That building there houses our electrical generator; we have to have our own backup in case the power fails. The entire estate's protected with an electronic alarm system—top of the line. Believe me, no one gets in here who isn't invited."

The house is surrounded by a second wall, with another gate that has to be electronically opened. This wall is protected with broken glass at the top, but not with concertina wire. Rosamond can't help saying, "Good heavens! It's like a fortress."

Zyzynski waves his hand in deprecation. "The house contains many valuable objects. Though I'm in residence only three or four times a year, the property has to be protected year-round. There's a permanent staff—along with the five guards, a housekeeper, groundskeeper, and cook—because sometimes I arrive unexpectedly, or on very short notice, and things have to be in readiness. At night the house is completely secured; we deactivate the alarms at eight in the morning."

The car stops before a large paneled door deeply recessed in a windowless wall. Access to the door is blocked by an ornamental steel screen. Again Marco performs the pushbutton ritual, then opens the grill and the door behind it. Zyzynski ushers Rosamond into a specious entrance hall, from which side corridors branch left and right. In the wall opposite the door, an arch opens into a roofless atrium which contains a garden courtyard with jetting fountain, neatly tended beds of bright flowers, and stately fan palms. Marco, Jerry, and Chip enter behind them and immediately hurry down the left-hand corridor and out of sight.

Zyzynski says, "They're going to the west wing: staff bedrooms and lounge, gymnasium, photographic lab, and a fully-equipped, state-of-the-art recording studio. Ah, I thought that would surprise you. The east wing contains guest bedrooms, the master suite, and a business office. The general purpose and dayrooms are on the far side of the courtyard facing the sea. Come, I'll show you. And then I'll have to meet my contact regarding the cadenza."

She walks with him down the right-hand corridor on a polished travertine floor. Cool white walls, adorned now and then with an oil painting, a gilt-framed mirror, a small carved table with a statuette or porcelain vase. "When I bought the property in 1952," he says, "I immediately saw its potential. Over the years,

I've added to the house in various ways. It's the biggest private home on the island."

After passing four additional arches opening onto the courtyard, the corridor turns left; sixty feet more brings them to another hallway branching right. "Here's the east wing," Zyzynski says, guiding her around the corner. He pauses at the first doorway. "My office." He opens the door and stands aside while she enters. High-ceilinged, without windows, the room contains a mahogany desk, large leather swivel chair, two filing cabinets, shelves filled with fat reference books, and a work table with stationery, brown manila envelopes, stapler, tape, and rubber stamps. A steel door with two combination locks and the ever-present pushbuttons stands in the center of the north wall.

"Safe?" she asks.

"Yes indeed," he answers. He goes to it and inspects the temperature and humidity gauges. Never would she know—no matter how long she lived with him—that behind the steel door a flight of concrete steps descends to a deep basement containing yet another office, smaller than this one, and another locked steel door leading to the St. Croix portion of his Collection.

After the office, Rosamond gets a brief tour of the guest bedrooms. She's a bit dazed after seeing all eight of them. "And that," Zyzynski says, pointing to a massive paneled door, "is the master suite." Discreetly he does not open the door. (Plenty of time for that later; far better now to tantalize her by withholding knowledge; letting her wonder what lies behind the door will surely inflame her curiosity; and when the desire to know has peaked and become unbearable, then the timely revelation will not only resolve the mystery, but also provide a consummation and a satisfied fulfillment.)

Leaving the east wing, Zyzynski and Rosamond continue north around the courtyard till the hallway turns left and brings them to a large, richly-carpeted room lined on three sides with bookshelves and, on the fourth, with broad windows overlooking the ocean. "This is the study," Zyzynski says. "The record and tape collections are here, and the playback equipment; but the sound is piped all through the house." Moving her on: "Next, the conference room." Dominated by a boat-shaped table and stern high-backed, leather-upholstered chairs. "Now and then I have business meetings here of international import." He gestures to the central courtyard behind them. "Would you like to walk in the garden?"

"No, thanks; I can see it fine as we walk along."

"Very well. This next door's the lavatory—or the Necessary Room, as I call it. And next, the Large Den. Then the dining room, kitchen, and the hall to the west wing." Turning right, they go down three steps into a room that seems to Rosamond half the size of a football field. It's furnished with tables, easy chairs, and a long leather sofa that would seat one of the teams entire, in their uniforms, without crowding. A concert grand piano stands near the windows. Adorning the walls, two huge Flemish tapestries and many oil paintings—all by French Impressionists. "Your house is a regular art museum," she says, admiring a group of bronzes by Rodin, Remington, and Russell.

He smiles and eloquently shrugs. "These are just a few of the lesser lights, all of them early acquisitions. What do you think of the piano?"

She goes to it and touches its glossy surface. "It's beautiful."

"There's another just like it in the recording studio. Why don't you play something to see if it's still in tune?"

She seats herself and plays the first Chopin Prelude. "It sounds fine."

"Excellent. Well, if you'll excuse me, I'll meet with the person who's selling the cadenza." He takes a cigar from his pocket case, and climbs the steps to the hallway.

Snick!

Remaining at the piano, Rosamond stares out at the azure Caribbean glittering under a cloudless sky. Briefly she indulges a pleasant fantasy, imagining what it would be like to live here all the time. But the grillwork outside the windows—even though it's scrolled into graceful botanic shapes—gives her the feeling that she's in a cage. For a shuddery moment, she has the notion that she's imprisoned in this grand villa, isolated from the outside world by security alarms, walls, and concertina wire. Quickly she turns back to the keyboard. Is playing Shostakovich when Zyzynski returns with a black leather briefcase.

"That's very nice." He comes to the piano. "Here's the manuscript. See what you think." He pulls the sheets from the case and hands them to her.

She studies the pages for several minutes, but knows at once the manuscript is genuine. She's seen many of Farringford's manuscripts, knows his hand. "There's no doubt about it," she declares. "It's the cadenza." Placing the manuscript on the music rack to sight-read, she feels suddenly weak, her breathing shallow and tight.

Beside her, Zyzynski beams and squirms. "Then I'll buy it! If you'll excuse me again."

While he's gone, Rosamond can't resist sight-reading the score. She hums the orchestral theme leading up to the point of majestic pause in the fourth movement where—for thirty-four years—the piano was to have begun its solo: and begins to play. Yes!—her fingers feeling the way—my God! Farringford was beginning the cadenza with a simple inversion of the *first* movement's second theme! And, in the left hand, counterpoint, an echo of the accompaniment supporting the violas in the *second* movement! Fascinating! Whoever could've guessed it?

Oh, why, why did Farringford have to write with such a crabbed, parsimonious hand? She stops playing and puts on her reading glasses. Better. But it's still difficult making her way down the first page. The harmonies—disquieting. Why a subdominant at that point? And does that tiny squiggle indicate a sharp or a natural? Ah. It has to be a sharp. Diminished seventh . . . my God, *brilliant!* And the poignancy of that particular chordal progression at that particular spot—! Tears well up in her eyes and begin coursing down her cheeks.

She stops to wipe her eyes; and, having caught her breath, goes back to the beginning and tries the first page again. Smoother now, faster, noting things she'd overlooked the first time, correcting mistakes she'd made. She stops again. Works out the fingering for a particularly complex right-hand tumbling cascade. Engrossed, loses track of time.

When she's worked her way to the bottom of page three, she realizes what Farringford's done: with consummate wit, economy, and skill, he's summed up, epitomized, and commented upon the entire concerto up to the point in the fourth movement where the cadenza begins. And, knowing as she does the entire concerto, Rosamond sees that these first three pages also foretell what's to come in the rest of the fourth movement. She suspects that, in the cadenza's recapitulations and summarizing, Farringford has brought the various elements of the whole concerto into such interesting, unexpected, and utterly novel relationships of contrast and juxtaposition that henceforth *all* the concerto's structures will have to be seen in a new light. Unbelievable! And now, on page four, something entirely new: a lyrical melody so pure, so exquisitely simple and straightforward that she finds herself melting before its beauty and power. But, while it unfolds, what's that happening in the bass? And why that ominous D-minor chord? . . .

Halfway through the fourth page, she must stop to recover herself. She's exhausted, amazed, emotionally drained by engaging with Farringford's genius as it emerges moment by moment, note by note, from the compacted page. It's as though he's speaking to her personally, communing with her deepest self, reaching out to pull her lovingly into his vision:—she simply has to rest.

She took off her glasses, wiped her eyes, rose from the bench, and was startled to see Zyzynski watching her from the sofa.

"I'm sorry," she said, as flustered as though she'd been caught doing something personal and very private. "I didn't know you'd returned. I'm afraid I lost all sense of time. I feel so privileged to be the first pianist to see and play this music since the composer. I'm just overwhelmed."

"What I was able to hear—even with your study breaks and false starts—was quite wonderful," Zyzynski said. "And tantalizing. What's the rest of it like? How would it sound in a smooth, polished performance? And integrated with the rest of the concerto?"

"I'm only in the middle of the fourth page," she replied. "There are twelve altogether, and a couple of indicated repeats. Farringford supposedly took six minutes to play it. But his tempo markings are all in place. It's a very clean manuscript, ready for the publisher: no unreadable passages, no blottings, very few cross-outs. There are even some indications of fingering. Though I haven't played it through, I'm sure the whole cadenza is going to be just what everyone who's heard it claims it to be: stunning, exquisite—and all the other hopelessly empty and inadequate terms people use to describe the indescribable. I wish I could have an expanded copy to work from, with larger notes and more space for my own scribbles. Farringford's notation is very hard to read."

"It would take a rather long time to copy it out," said Zyzynski. "But you should probably do that so you can practice it comfortably. By the way, it's almost two o'clock. Would you like some lunch?"

"Oh, that would be nice. I didn't realize how hungry I am."

"Come to the dining room. I've had the cook prepare something for us."

Gratefully she followed him to the table; and in a moment the cook served them with soup and green salad, French bread, and a large platter of oysters on the half shell.

"I take it you've purchased the cadenza?" she asked as she spread a napkin on her lap.

"Oh, yes, it's mine now."

"Such a relief to have it safe! Mrs. Farringford, Clara, Mr. Dinch—they'll be so happy to hear it. And so grateful to you for having saved it from oblivion."

Zyzynski smiled modestly, waved his hand dismissingly, and continued sucking up oysters.

"Did the seller say how he'd obtained it?"

"He didn't say. I didn't ask."

They ate for awhile in silence. Then Rosamond said, "I suppose, to be safe, we should make photocopies of the manuscript."

Hardly, thought Zyzynski. Aloud, he said, "I've done that already. In my office—before I brought it to you." Another lie, but again in a good cause. And besides, what was a small lie between friends? "Won't you have some of these oysters? They're wonderfully fresh."

"No, thank you. I don't much care for oysters. When will we be leaving for the airport? If there's time, I'd very much like to study the cadenza a bit longer—if I may—while having access to your fine piano."

Zyzynski looked up at her with wide eyes, the soup spoon pausing halfway to his mouth. "My dear, of *course* you may. And as for leaving, why, as far as I'm concerned, there's no hurry. There's nothing I'd like more than for you to familiarize yourself with the music. It's already approaching three o'clock. Why not take the rest of the afternoon to study the cadenza? I have my own work to do. You're welcome to spend the night. Leave tomorrow. Or Sunday, for that matter. I'll have Dolores prepare one of the guest rooms for you."

"Well—" But it was only a brief hesitation. "That's very kind of you. All right. I really am eager to work on the cadenza. Maybe after a short nap; I'm very tired."

"Splendid!" He wiped his mouth with his napkin. "I'll leave you alone with the music all afternoon. Won't disturb you. Since we've had a late lunch, let's meet for dinner at eight o'clock. And tonight we'll have a real feast—with champagne—to celebrate our good fortune."

Having made the overnight arrangements and shown Rosamond to her room for a nap, Zyzynski went to his office in the east wing. Passing the desk, he crossed to the steel door, checked the temperature and humidity gauges, twirled the combination locks and pushed his buttons. When the door had swung open, he hurried down a flight of carpeted concrete steps to a lower hallway. There, having used an electronic code to pass through a second door, he entered his lower office, flipped on the lights, and threw himself into the padded chair beside the marble-topped desk. This room, sound-proofed and kept at constant temperature and humidity, was bare-walled except for the framed motto opposite the entrance: THE LAST SHALL BE FIRST, AND THE FIRST SHALL BE LAST. Zyzynski reached into the desk drawer, brought forth a bottle, and poured himself a generous snifter of cognac.

Getting Rosamond to stay had been far easier than he'd expected. That had been the one sticky part of his plan. If she'd insisted on returning to New York today, he'd have been forced to use his strongest powers of persuasion. And that could have been disastrous: for a single wrong note, the slightest hint of coercion or imposition of will, could disrupt the harmony of their relationship and blight its fruition. But glory of glories! she'd *volunteered* to stay and learn the cadenza! Would tonight be too soon to profess his love? To propose a longterm partnership?

He'd left her alone with the music not only because he wanted her to be able to apply her full concentration to mastering it, but also—and more importantly—because he feared that if he first heard the cadenza in bits and snatches while she was learning it, with re-workings, re-thinkings, and the repetitions required by her practicing to get it right, the impact of the whole might be diluted—diminished or lost altogether. So much depended on his hearing it as near to perfection as possible! He was convinced that, like Morgan Latimer, he'd have to hear it performed complete, in polished form, and once again as part of the whole concerto for it to have the effectiveness he so desired.

Before meeting Rosamond again at eight, he'd have time to shower and shave, relax with his Collection, and further plan his strategy. Feeling bloated and queasy after so many oysters, he sank into the soft leather chair and pulled a fat cigar from his pocket.

In this room he could smoke; once he'd passed through the green door facing him and entered the Collection, he could not. He'd have a quick cigar and then go in and reacquaint himself with his old friends—the mammoth red granite head of Amenhotep III (twice the size of the one in the Berlin Egyptian Museum); Rembrandt's large painting *The Death of Socrates* ("vanished" in Napoleon's first Austrian campaign, lost to the world for almost two hundred years); the Komiroff Sapphire; the manuscript containing sixty-eight sonnets and nine dirty ballads written by Queen Elizabeth I, in her own hand; the ancient cloth, pressed flat between sheets of glass, which Zyzynski knows is the *real* Shroud of Turin. All forty-two years of Thomas Jefferson's secret diaries; all nine years of Hamilton's, with their shocking revelations as to the true authorship of *The Federalist Papers*. The Dresden Baptismal Font; the Smiling Buddha of Bangkok; the Manzini Altarpiece; the twelve love letters written by Shakespeare to the young Welshman living in Stratford—unknown to scholars—for whom the Sonnets were composed.

Old friends, too, were the empty spaces reserved for, and awaiting the arrival of, the *Mona Lisa*, King Tut's burial mask, Michelangelo's *Pietà* of St. Peter's, the Head of Nefertiti, the Great Bull of Damascus, the Lindisfarne Gospels, and the Book of Kells.

But first his cigar. On a marble footing beside his desk stood a gold guillotine six feet two inches tall from base to top. The solid steel blade was eight inches wide, gilded, with a razor edge. Zyzynski placed the end of his cigar in the round notch in the base where a victim's head would go, and tripped a lever to release the blade. Down it flashed—eight and a half pounds in free fall—and with a resounding *thunk!* sliced off the end of the cigar with a clean shear. Zyzynski smiled as he examined the end of the cigar. Not one shred of tobacco left hanging. The scale model guillotine had been made to his specifications by Leclair of Limoges in 1968. It gave Zyzynski no end of pleasure.

Peter Shipley Abbott and Felix McKay got into a nasty squabble at the airport. Abbott was determined that they should rent a single car and go to Christiansted together. Felix, knowing that he could do much better alone, and having had his dislike of Abbott blossom into loathing on the flight down, said that Abbott could do as he liked, but that he, Felix, would rent his own car and get his own hotel room.

"My concern is to make sure Rosamond is safe," he said, "and to do that, I've got to find her. I don't know who this Zyzynski person is, or whether he has the cadenza or not. And frankly, that's the least of my concerns."

Abbott had puffed himself up. "Of course, I'm concerned about Rosamond too. But we must find out if Zyzynski really does have the cadenza. He's a very rich and powerful man. If he does have it, we've got to know if he means to publish it or keep it out of public view forever."

"Well, you hunt Zyzynski. I'll hunt Rosamond."

"Please!" said Abbott. "I'll pay the whole cost of the car rental!" He waved a credit card under Felix's nose.

Felix marched to the rental counter. "I'd like to rent a car, please."

"You're in luck sir," the attendant said. "We have one car available. It's a busy weekend, with St. Patrick's Day and all."

Oh hell. "He'll pay for it," Felix said, indicating Abbott, who was hovering beside him.

"Okay. How long will you be using it?"

Felix turned questioningly to the pilot from the Sternberg Foundation who was standing nearby.

"Our instructions were to bring you down and to stay till you're ready to leave," the pilot said. "The Foundation will pay our hotel expenses."

"Hopefully, no more than two days," Felix said to the attendant. Out came the rental forms, and Abbott plunked his credit card onto the counter.

As a consequence of their late start from New York, it was getting on toward evening when they reached Christiansted. The transition from daylight to dark was so rapid there was almost no twilight. Tourists crowded the downtown, shopping in the elegant boutiques, sauntering on the waterfront and beneath the galleries of the old buildings. The hotels were full. "Busy weekend," they were told. "You should've made reservations." Finally, the pilot and co-pilot got a room together in a small hotel several blocks from the waterfront, and Felix and Abbott got a room in a large hotel on the esplanade that faced the water—but only because of a guest's cancellation. Abbott was well pleased with the arrangement. Felix immediately went to the telephone directory.

To his surprise, Victor Zyzynski was listed. The address meant nothing to him. But a helpful bartender in the hotel restaurant took the map Felix had picked up at the airport and drew an elliptical swatch on the north coast east of Christiansted. "It's one of those big houses along there," he said—and smiled as Felix slipped him a dollar.

Felix wanted to leave at once to reconnoiter, but Abbott wanted to eat first: "I always eat dinner about this time. Tonight I'm in the mood for a tasty fruit salad, perhaps some lime chicken. We'll have to find a decent restaurant, clean and popular with tourists. Here in the tropics, you can't be too careful about your food."

"Well, you eat. Give me the car keys, and I'll go exploring by myself."

"No, I *won't* relinquish the keys. The car's in my name, remember, and I'm responsible for it."

Felix exploded. "Abbott, you're a real pain in the ass!"

Abbott shrugged. "When I hear such things as that, Mr. McKay—and I've heard such things for years—my standard answer is 'Sticks and stones may break my bones—' "

"Then I'll be hunting for a large stick," said Felix.

Abbott sniffed and turned away. "I will ignore that remark—because I'm very hungry. Are you, or are you not, coming with me to find some lime chicken?"

Felix thought it over. "I'll come with you," he said at last, "because that way it'll go faster. But I'll settle for a pizza, or a burger and fries."

Chapter 36

At Pinnacle House, dinner was lavish. Zyzynski began the meal with a champagne toast: "To the Farringford Cadenza! disproving once and for all that Friday the 13th is an unlucky day!" After the toast, Marco refilled their glasses.

In the ambience provided by mellow candlelight and a Mozart wind serenade, Rosamond enjoyed a savory clam consommé, filet mignon with mushrooms and artichoke hearts, ripe olives and gingered yams, brandied peaches with nutmeg garnish, and pineapple rum-whip. She even ate three oysters when Zyzynski urged the heaping platter upon her. It wasn't pleasant, but she made a game job of it. Zyzynski ate the rest.

And the champagne! She knew that several bottles had been brought to the table, but she had no idea how much she'd actually drunk (the food *was* rather salty)—for whenever she looked down, her glass (thanks to Marco) was always full.

She'd changed into shirt and slacks and a lightweight long-sleeved sweater. Zyzynski's preparations for dinner had been far less casual. After his long and searching shower, he'd dusted himself with musk-scented talcum powder, applied liberal doses of *Feramone 3* to his armpits and behind his ears (guaranteed, his dealer had assured him, to drive women wild), and smeared oil of peppermint under his scrotum. Then, as befit his plan, he'd slipped into a loose-fitting flowered shirt and baggy Bermuda shorts (sans underwear).

At eight, when they were seating themselves at the table, he'd asked Rosamond how the cadenza was progressing.

"Oh very well," she answered happily. "I've been all the way through it several times. And it's true, Mr. Zyzynski—"

"Please call me Victor."

"Very well, Victor. The cadenza is fully as wonderful as legend claims. Some of the very finest music Farringford wrote. Frequently, during certain passages, I've simply had to stop playing and get up and walk around the room—and this happens *every time* I encounter those passages! As a cadenza, it fits perfectly with the rest of the concerto, but as music in its own right, it transcends the concerto, if you know what I mean. No, you can't know what I mean. You'll have to hear it as it occurs in the context of the whole."

"Yes," said Zyzynski. "Oh yes."

Her eyes were moist and sparkling, her face flushed with the memory of it. His own breathing was becoming rapid just listening to her. "I feel so honored, so privileged to be playing it," she said softly. "It's as though Farringford himself is reaching out to touch me: a direct communication—not only with my body, but with my intellectual faculties, and the secret innermost depths of my being."

A twinge of jealousy caused Zyzynski's lower lip to twitch. Feeling the swell of a rising anger, with great effort he forced it down. Farringford was *dead*, dammit—in no way a rival for Rosamond's affections. Not a rival of flesh and blood at any rate. There was no way in hell that Zyzynski was going to compete with a ghost. Besides, if the cadenza *did* have the powers everyone who'd heard it attested, it was unavoidable that Rosamond, too, would have her own sexual response in experiencing it. His turn would come. And *he* would be the first (and *only*) person to hear it performed by *Foxe!*

All he'd said was, "It's time we celebrate!", reaching out his arms to give her a discreet and amiable hug—which, though carefully casual, had nonetheless set his pulse pounding and glazed his face with a film of sweat. And then, with the china and crystal gleaming in the candlelight, the cook had emerged from the kitchen to serve the clam consommé.

When they'd finished the pineapple rum-whip, the cook appeared and began removing their plates. "Champagne—we'd like three more bottles on ice," Zyzynski told her, "and two more platters of oysters on the half shell. And then you're free to go, Mrs. Jones. Free to *go*."

Rosamond said, "It was a delicious meal, Mrs. Jones." The cook smiled and took out the plates.

Zyzynski beamed. "She's the best cook on the island." Again he filled his glass with champagne. "And contracted exclusively to me." He slurped down the last oyster, stifled a belch with his napkin, looked up at her sideways from under his bushy brows. Gave her a little wink. "Shall we go to the Den?"

When she rose from the table, Rosamond reeled with a wave of dizziness, and staggered a bit as she followed Zyzynski into the hall. She felt as though she were walking on fat cushions; there was a buzzing in her ears; and when she spoke, she heard her voice faintly, as though it were coming from very far away. "I don't know when I've drunk so much champagne. I'm afraid I'm feeling the effects. It does sneak up on you." Yeah, she thought, and then it's like a sledge hammer to the back of the head.

"We have more bottles to go," Zyzynski said, setting down the ice bucket on the coffee table opposite the long leather sofa. He went back to the dining room to get the fresh platters of oysters. Rosamond rubberlegged across the carpet and plopped herself down on the yielding leather. She closed her eyes, immediately discovered *that* to be a mistake, and snapped them open again.

Zyzynski returned, swaying a little from side to side, holding the mountainous oyster platters before him like a ritual offering. He carefully placed them on the table next to the ice bucket and, with a sigh, lowered himself onto the cushions beside her. Beads of clammy sweat glistened on his forehead. "Ah, Rosamond— Rosamond," he said. And then was silent.

He was sitting awfully close to her, she felt. And he had such a peculiar odor—peppermint, and something else she couldn't iden- tify that made her want to retch. She scooted farther away from him, still not trusting her legs to hold her if she stood.

"I was hoping you'd play the Farringford Cadenza for me after we ate," Zyzynski said.

"I don't know it well enough yet to do it justice."

"You had all afternoon to practice." He slid closer to her.

"Yes, and I have a real sense of what Farringford was trying to do. But I haven't mastered it. I could play portions of it for you if I weren't so tipsy. But actually, Victor, I'm too drunk right now. My fingers wouldn't find the right keys."

"I guess I don't understand how you musicians work," he said. "I assumed you'd be further along."

"It would take several days of intensive work to become proficient. Learning a piece of music is one thing; becoming tech- nically proficient is another; but *finishing* a piece, getting inside it and rendering its musical essence, its *soul*, is still another. It might take months, even years of living with it, to achieve mastery of something as complex as this cadenza." The buzzing in her ears was louder now, and she'd begun hiccuping.

Zyzynski nodded his head slowly. What she was saying made a kind of sense to him. "Like taking over an ailing corporation," he said, working at opening another bottle of champagne. "Getting rid of the deadwood, putting in a new management team, cutting costs. Making necessary adjustments to force the business to show a profit." The cork popped, and froth spewed out onto his leg and into his shoe. Shakily he filled her glass and his own, spilling a little, then replaced the bottle in the ice bucket and leaned back with another great sigh, exploiting the movement to inch his thigh closer to hers.

The compact Ford crept along the narrow road, its headlights showing, on the righthand side, bushes and dry grass climbing a steep slope to disappear in utter darkness. To the left, the ground fell away gently toward the sea. "Stop," said Felix, pointing to the left. "Another driveway." Peter Shipley Abbott braked abruptly and Felix hopped out, using his flashlight to sweep the gateposts. "No, this doesn't seem to be it either. The name on the sign is McFarland." He got back in the car, and Abbott released the brake.

Abbott was becoming testy. Unable to find lime chicken, he'd had to settle for pork chops and rice. He *had* been able to find his fruit salad. But something in the meal hadn't agreed with him, and now he was feeling ominous cramps in his gut. He wished fervently that he was back at the hotel. "Wouldn't it be easier to do this in daylight?" he growled.

Felix didn't answer him. He'd had his hamburger and fries and was doing fine. *His* discomfort was born of discouragement. They'd come a long way down this road, stopping at every driveway for a look-see, and he was beginning to wonder if they were on the wrong road. "There's another one," he said, and Abbott hit the brake.

The flashlight beam revealed an elaborate grilled gate barring the driveway. A bronze plaque on one of the posts read PINNACLE HOUSE. "This is it," said Felix. "It's a wide drive; turn around in it and put out the lights."

Abbott parked the car facing back toward Christiansted, doused the lights, and turned off the ignition. "Now what?"

"How far have we come from town?" Felix asked.

"I don't know. Too far."

"I thought you looked at the odometer."

"I forgot."

"Jesus, Abbott."

The pianist slipped the car key into his pocket. He pulled his leather gloves tighter and climbed out of the car. The sky, luminous black, was suffused with a dust-explosion of stars. "My God," said Felix. "The Big Dipper is almost down on the horizon."

Abbott was more interested in mundane matters. "There's no way through that gate. And look at the wall. No way over."

"What are you doing here?" A man's voice from the darkness.

A spotlight blinded them. Felix heard the click of a pistol being cocked. And another voice, as though speaking into a radio: "Two prowlers at the front gate."

"What are you doing here?" the first voice repeated.

"Just taking a leak," said Felix, shielding his eyes from the spotlight.

"Well, do it somewhere else. This is private property; you're trespassing."

Abbott scuttled back to the car, slid into the driver's seat, and locked his door. Felix followed more slowly, with a shrug of his shoulders, maintaining as best he could an air of affronted dignity. He'd barely climbed into the car, when Abbott started them off down the road. The beam of the spotlight followed them. "They're taking down our license number," Felix muttered. "Damn! I should've known there'd be guards. We'll have to wait till daylight. But I'm sure Rosamond and Zyzynski are still here and haven't gone back to New York. Abbott, we're past the boundary of the estate. Stop here. I want to see how far the wall extends toward the water."

Abbott did not stop the car. Felix stared at him. "I said to stop. What's wrong with you?"

Through clenched teeth, and with an angry sidewise glance, Abbott hissed, "I've got to get back to the hotel."

Felix understood. He sank back in resignation against the door, his elbow out the window. "If you had stopped," he said, "we each could've done our own thing. Killed two birds with one stone." Abbott snorted and stepped on the gas.

On his last trip to the Necessary Room, Victor Zyzynski had turned down the rheostat to dim the lights. He was pleased with the result. Cozy. Intimate. Just right, he thought, through his alcohol fog, for the next stage of his conquest. Seating himself close to Rosamond, he gobbled several more oysters and again filled both glasses with champagne. Rosamond was sitting scrunched up in the corner of the sofa against the arm, unable to scoot farther.

"Rosamond, I've admired you for a very long time." Pause for the slurping of another oyster. "I have a scrapbook containing notices of your performances and clippings of your interviews. Young as you are, I feel that you're the finest classical pianist in the world."

"Mr. Zy—Victor, I appreciate your feelings. But you're given to overstatement. There are *many* talented—"

"I've gone to all of your New York concerts—even the benefits you did for the Vietnamese refugees and the crippled children, and—and all those other charities you support. You're my ideal of what a concert artist should be. You do not—*could* not—have a more devoted fan than I." He lowered his head as though in humble obeisance, and from under bushy brows fixed his eyes on her breasts tightly stretching the fabric of her shirt. He imagined undoing the buttons one by one, with a subtle squeeze here and a gentle poke there, till, opening the shirt like parting a veil, he could reach in to fondle, knead, and stroke the taut warm flesh, tweak and pinch with thumb and finger the dainty nipples, rolling them back and forth like fresh plump raisins . . .

"I had no idea you were so interested in my career," said Rosamond. "I'm quite flattered." While he turned away to search out fresh oysters among the empty shells, she quickly poured her champagne into a potted cactus at the end of the sofa.

"Time to start the second platter," he said, finishing up the first. "You're twenty-six, born near Richmond, Virginia on May 9, 1955. Studied at the Hopewell Conservatory under Max Hueber and Georgina Travis. Received First Prize in the Farringford Competition in 1977. You've traveled widely: Salzburg, Caracas, Nice, Tanglewood—and taught master classes at Hotchkiss and the University of Michigan. Your grandfather Foxe was one of the founders of Blueridge Frozen Foods; your father is Downing Professor of Medieval History at Thorpe University; your mother was a pilot in her own charter air service following the Second World War; then, after her marriage, she became a news reporter in the '50's and—finally—writing under her maiden name—Mildred Angstrom—a syndicated columnist distributed to at least sixty newspapers nationwide. You have an older brother and a younger sister. Ruth Chamberlain composed a piano sonata for you—"

"Goodness! You amaze me—" (She also found the recital extremely disquieting.)

"I said I'd followed you closely." He swallowed another oyster and refilled his glass. "I'm surprised that you're not married by now." He belched. "A lovely girl like you."

"Oh, I've had a couple of offers," she said. "But, really, music is the most important thing in my life, and I've been so busy with my career, I just never concerned myself with developing serious relationships. Too self-centered, I guess." She gave a little laugh.

"No boyfriends?"

"Well, one. A very nice guy I knew at the conservatory. I liked him a lot, and think I could've contemplated marriage. But he decided he was gay—was upfront about it, for which I respect him—and entered into a longterm relationship with a pro football player. The three of us are very close friends."

Zyzynski slapped his knee in a transport of relief. She was still a virgin! This issue had been a matter of desperate anxiety for him, but now he knew for certain . . . *the last shall be first!* It called for an additional celebration.

He opened another bottle of champagne, noting that there was only one bottle left. Well, he'd get some more on his next trip to the Necessary. He refilled her glass, and then his own, and wolfed down six more oysters. But then a dark thought gripped him.

"What about Peter Shipley Abbott?" he asked. "I'd always assumed that he had a thing going with you."

"Peter?" Again she laughed. "If he has, it's all on *his* side. As far as I'm concerned, he's just a close friend. Our relationship is purely professional."

On your side, maybe, Zyzynski thought. But he'd seen Abbott too many times hanging around her as though she were a bitch in heat. Possessively clutching her arm. Preening himself, doing his dance! Lusting like a weasel.

As the silence lengthened, Rosamond decided she could trust her balance to walk to the bathroom. It was a decision forced on her not only by a full bladder, but also by a nauseous hot flash that popped a chilly dew of sweat onto her forehead, and a lurching pressure in her stomach that said in no uncertain terms that something wanted out.

But before she could haul herself upright, Zyzynski suddenly slid his beefy arm along the sofa back to encircle her shoulders; leaning close, he said in a husky voice: "I want you to know I find you very attractive, Rosamond." His other hand dropped to her thigh, six inches above her knee, and squeezed gently.

She blinked in astonishment, then turned her face away to escape his wine-sour oyster breath. Clutching the arm of the sofa, she hoisted herself to her feet. "Excuse me, please, I have to go to the bathroom."

She was walking more steadily now, hardly dizzy at all. But her brain felt numb, unable to clearly process what had just happened; and she had other imperatives: her heaving stomach, the sharp metallic taste and flood of saliva in her mouth. She lurched into the Necessary and flung herself toward the toilet, arriving just in time.

While she was gone, Zyzynski reveled in the exhilaration of having, at long last, made his initial move, professing both his admiration of Rosamond and his attraction to her. Yet he was disturbed by her sudden departure, and more than a little apprehensive that perhaps he was crowding her somewhat with an approach too amorous.

Out of this welter of thoughts, it came to him that now would be the time to get more champagne. He dragged himself off the sofa, set the remaining full bottle on the coffee table, and, holding the ice bucket upright in both hands to avoid spilling the melt, began a long, wobbly journey to the kitchen.

Maybe he should back off a bit, and not push Rosamond too far too fast. He'd waited so long to express his feelings! But really, there was no hurry. He shouldn't take advantage of her naiveté, overwhelm her innocence with his masculine force and broad sweep of worldly experience. It was natural that the very fact of who and what he was would be intimidating to her. But to frighten her could have extremely detrimental consequences for later. Dear girl, so pure and innocent! She hadn't even understood the lustful designs of Abbott! Well, that danger was behind her now. *He'd* protect her. But how to proceed? It would be hard to take up where they'd left off when she went to the bathroom. No, for now, it was sufficient for him to have *said* it: now, at last, she knew his feelings.

Therefore, he'd best change the subject: tell her something about himself. She had a right to know. It would be hard, though, since he wasn't accustomed to revealing anything of himself to others. Nonetheless, he would have to now, in order to demonstrate that he too was desirable. Rich, powerful, always the winner! First and foremost. Not only in wealth, but in *everything*. Yes. That was it: he must convince her that she could never do better. Where was the kitchen? Ah. And in the kitchen, where had Mrs. Jones left the champagne? An empty case near the refrigerator. Of course.

He set down the ice bucket, opened the refrigerator door. There were four more bottles. He closed the door and emptied the water from the bucket into the sink. Went to the ice-maker, filled the bucket with tiny cubes. Back to the refrigerator. How many should he take? Two? Three. They wouldn't fit in the bucket, which was full of ice. He wedged one down into the cubes, tucked one under his arm, and carried the third in his free hand. Nearly fell when he closed the refrigerator door with a swing of his hip. And now—hell!—with both hands engaged, he couldn't switch off the lights. Craning his neck, he flipped the switch with his topmost chin.

Now back to the Den. His feet schluffing on the travertine floor. Yes. That was it: he'd take it slower with Rosamond. Tell her something about himself. If only he didn't have this throbbing headache, and didn't keep guiding into the wall.

In the Necessary, Rosamond was coming to her own conclusions. Dealing with the demands of the champagne had taken a long time; but after flushing the toilet, rinsing her mouth, and bathing her face with cold water, she found that her thinking was much clearer, and she could focus on the implications of Zyzynski's last statement—and his graceless squeezing of her thigh.

It was hard to believe that Zyzynski was putting the make on her. Why, he was old enough to be her grandfather! It had to be the alcohol; his judgment sufficiently impaired to cause him to step outside his normal inhibitions.

Still, she didn't want to go back to a continuation of that activity. How to avoid it? Should she yawn and say she was tired and needed to go to bed? No way. If he was putting the make on her, he might take that as an invitation. Pretend to doze off while sitting on the sofa? *Not* a good idea. In no way should she encourage him with the appearance of being vulnerable.

She'd already been in the bathroom a long while. She'd make it longer. Maybe he'd be asleep when she got back. If not, maybe she should distance herself by playing the piano. Not the Farringford Cadenza. Something she knew by heart. Schumann's *Kinderscenen*, Satie, Bartok's *For Children*—something quiet and not very demanding. Something that might put him to sleep.

She extended her stay till ten minutes had passed and decided that when she returned, she wouldn't sit on the sofa, but in the armchair opposite, putting the coffee table between them. However, when she reached the Den, Zyzynski was sitting in that chair—which left the sofa for her. And far from being asleep, Zyzynski had finished the second bottle of champagne from the first batch, and opened the third. With acute dismay she saw the ice bucket and the three fresh bottles ready to go. Zyzynski had just lighted a cigar.

"There you are," he said, when she came into the room. "I've poured you a fresh drink. Sit down, Rosamond, there's something important that I want to say about the Farringford Cadenza."

With reluctance, she seated herself in the exact middle of the sofa, on the very edge of the cushion. The glass of champagne stood before her on the coffee table, but she couldn't bring herself to even look at it.

"A few minutes ago you seemed surprised to learn how much I know about you. How closely I've followed your career." His voice was thick, his speech slurred. "If you knew me better, you'd see there's nothing surprising about it. I've always admired perfection—whatever's at the top of its class. I'm an excellent judge, with much experience. My judgment places you, Rosamond—as a concert pianist—at the top of your class. And, in addition,"—he spread his arms expansively—"you are very beautiful. The most beautiful woman I know."

She stammered, "I don't know what to say."

He slowly shook his head. "No need to say anything." His cigar had gone out. He set it in an ashtray and began rummaging through his pockets. "Wherza lighter?"

"You left it on the table."

He leaned forward, spilling half his drink, and retrieved the gold lighter. On the second flick, he got a flame which he held shakily to the ashy end of the cigar. When satisfied with the draw, he replaced the lighter on the table with exaggerated care and continued slowly, as though having trouble finding the words: "I'm gonna tell you things I never told anybody else—"

Terrified, she blurted: "Please don't feel you have to!"

"No, you don't unnerstand." The cigar was waving back and forth between them. "I want to tell you. 'Cause you're number one in your field. I don't play the piano. But I'm number one in everything that *I* do. Thass what I set out to be. Thass what I am. The richest man in the world. You knew that, didn't you? The richest man. Shake it all down, I'm worth over sixty-three billion dollars. Sixty-three *billion*, Ros'mond. An' growin' every minute. Most people can't even imagine what that means. It means *power*, Ros'mond. Means I'm the most powerful man in the world!"

This brought him to his feet, and for a moment he towered over her like a huge balloon tethered to the floor, weaving and bobbing from side to side. For one breathless moment she thought he was going to fall flat on his face across the coffee table and into her lap. But he maintained his balance and began pacing about unsteadily, cigar in one hand, glass in the other.

"How'd I get to be Number One? By bein' smarter an' quicker, an' more 'mag'native, an' more darin', an' more ruthless than my rivals. I hadda be willin' ta take chances, an' change my mind, an' do dirty tricks—'cause if I wasn't—if I didn't—some of *them* would be, an' they'd do those things to *me*, and squeeze me out. I know you unnerstand this. Didn't you set out to be the best pianist in the world?"

"No," said Rosamond. "I truthfully can't say that I did. I don't know what that would mean. I wanted to make beautiful music; I had talent I wanted to develop; I've worked hard to become the best musician that I can."

Zyzynski suddenly flopped down onto the sofa, at the far end. He drained his glass and set it on the table. There were seven oysters left. He ate four of them before responding. "Well, you're an F. You're pretty well-placed. You have no idea what it's like to be a Z. You didn't come at the end of the alphabet. You didn't get the dirty end of things. No one called you 'Tail' for always bein' at the rear. I begged my father to change our name. In those days it was spelled Z-z-z-y-z—"

"Three Z's?" said Rosamond, alarmed at how angry and congested his face had become.

"Some shithead immigration officer played a stinkin' trick on my grandfather when he got off the boat. My father refused to change it, said we should be proud of our American name. I wanted to drop the first two Z's, but he laughed and said I'd still be at the end of the alphabet. God, I hated him. But when I was twenty-one, I *did* drop the Z's. And I *wasn't* at the end of the alphabet. There was a man named Zzasz I knew of, a steel-worker in Pittsburgh. But he died three years later." While talking, he'd been fumbling with the cork of a new champagne bottle, getting nowhere. Now he held out the bottle to her. "Would you open it, Ros'mond?"

She said, "Do you really think we need it? I'm done."

"Afraid of the pop, huh?" He kept working away, all thumbs. "And those people who'd always come before me—I swore I'd push *them* to the end of the line. The Andersons and Ardmores—" grunting with his exertions "—the Burtons, Finneys, Goodwins, Halls." Ah, the cork was moving. "The Morriseys, Nordstroms, Olivers, Susskinds, Tylers, Wingates, Youngs—" With a whoosh the bottle blew, and a long jet of white foam shot out in a high arc across the room. Seeing the long trail it splattered on the carpet, Zyzynski roared with laughter. "Pop goes the weasel!" He poured a fresh glass for himself, saw that hers was still standing full. "Better drink up, it'll go flat. Got to celebrate." He drank his and poured another. "I decided that when I wanted somethin', *nothin'* would stand in my way. I'd *have* it. Take the Farrin'ford Cadenza. That Trntl woman thought *she'd* get it, then Silas Dinch, then the whole world! Oh no. And the Count, who wanted it for *his* collection. Well, I showed 'em all! I always get what I want. The one-of-a-kind at the top of its class."

He leaned toward her. "Oh, Ros'mond! I've wanted you for so long! But you were always out of reach. Surrounded by hangers-on. By piss-ants like Peter Shipley Abbott. This is the very first time we've been able to be together in the right kinda circumstances." He moved closer. She leaped up and darted around the table to the chair he'd vacated.

"What are you saying?" she cried. "You talk as though the cadenza's your personal possession, as though you intend to keep it for yourself!"

"Thass right." He closed his eyes, slumped over, and lay full-length on the sofa.

"But you told me you'd bought it to share with the world!"

He settled deeper into the cushions, still holding his empty glass and the dead cigar. "Didn't buy it. Took it away from Trntl. It's mine now."

Rosamond said, "I want to leave for New York the first thing in the morning!"

"Can't," he said. His eyes flickered open. "You haven't played the cadenza for me yet. You said it'd take several days to get ready. And then you've gotta record it in my studio—"

"You can't keep the cadenza for yourself!"

"Yes I can. And nobody'll ever know. Issa secret. Jus' you and me. I'll make you happy, Ros'mond. You'll have all the money you want. We don't hafta get married. Jus' be very very close friends." He shook his head slowly from side to side. "You won't even have to give up your career." His eyes had closed again. "The cadenza's for my Collection. Some of it's here. In the basement. Mine. The Manzini Altarpiece." The cigar dropped from his fingers and rolled away across the carpet. "Jefferson diaries. Ashoka's Eye. Shroud of Turin . . ." He rolled over on his side to face the coffee table, stared briefly with one eye at the shells heaped on the two platters, said "Don't *want* more oysters," took a deep breath, and fell fast asleep.

For nearly three minutes Rosamond sat frozen in her chair, mind racing, staring at the great mountain of flesh which was snoring loudly, a trickle of saliva drooling from the corner of its mouth. Several things emerged clearly from the jumble of information she'd just received. (1) Zyzynski had stolen the cadenza manuscript from Trntl to keep for himself; (2) would have it disappear into his private collection along with the world-famous Manzini Altarpiece and the Eye of Ashoka (stolen in 1977 from the Danish Museum while she was in Copenhagen giving a concert); (3) he was going to use her to play and record the cadenza for his private delight, and (4) insure her secrecy by making her his concubine!

Damned if he was! She had to get away now, tonight, and take the cadenza with her. *How?*

She leaped up and went to the windows. Studied the bars. The wall that coursed downhill to the sea. She thought of the electronic alarm system in force till eight in the morning. The security guards outside. Marco, Jerry, Chip down in the west wing. The road to the airport. The long way home.

But first, the cadenza. She went to the piano, gathered up the twelve pages of manuscript, tiptoed past the sofa and into the hall, instinctively looking right and left, then quickly headed for the east wing and the bedroom she'd been assigned.

Chapter 37

March 13   (Friday night)
March 14   (Saturday morning)

Rosamond Foxe was not easily daunted by the demanding and difficult; she'd always taken pleasure in challenging herself. At ten, she'd systematically tackled all twenty-seven of Chopin's *Etudes* because she liked the way they sounded when Brailowsky played them. At twelve, Bach's *Well Tempered Clavier*, because a particularly insensitive teacher had said she was too young for it. At thirteen, Prokofiev's Third Piano Concerto. At fourteen, Brahms' First, and Rachmaninoff's Second. At seventeen, she'd taken up scuba diving; at nineteen, climbed Mount Rainier; at twenty, learned parachuting—but gave it up, for, as she explained to puzzled friends, she liked sky-diving even less than playing Liszt. Now, trapped in Zyzynski's house on an unfamiliar island and faced with the need for immediate escape, she shifted into problem-solving mode and became calmly analytical.

On her way to her room, she stopped off in Zyzynski's office to see if anything there might be of use to her. A fairly sparse room. Ah, but on one wall was a floor-plan of the house; not an architect's drawing, but Zyzynski's own preliminary sketch (his name was scrawled at the bottom). This she studied carefully for several minutes.

Since she didn't relish carrying the pages of the cadenza loose and exposed to whatever perils she'd be passing through, she looked for something to protect them. On the work table were piles of manila envelopes of various sizes. She selected one of just the right size. Then having folded the cadenza pages neatly in half, she slid them into the envelope, which she sealed with spit and tape. Suitable for mailing. Well, why not?

She seated herself at the desk, found a supply of ball-point pens in the top drawer. Since she didn't know Dinch's address, or Trntl's, she carefully penned the address of Mrs. Charles Philip Farringford, in New York City. In case there might be a delivery problem, she put her own home address in the upper left-hand corner to insure a return to Hempstead—whether she herself returned or not. She wrote AIR MAIL in large letters and went through the desk drawers until she found several sheets of postage stamps. Taking the highest denominations she could find, she pasted down blocks and strips to a total of just over sixteen dollars. Now all she needed was a mailbox. Hopefully, the cadenza would get to New York even if she didn't.

Done in the office, she went on to the guest room she'd been given. The bed sheet was neatly laid back, the pillows plumped. She put the cadenza envelope into her shoulder bag, packed her traveling clothes of the night before, and—as an afterthought—checked the bedroom window. Barred. She turned out the lights and retraced her steps.

Following her memory of the house plan she'd studied, she turned left and took the hallway round past the front door—in order to stay as far away as possible from Zyzynski sleeping in the Den. Turning right, then left again, she found herself in the corridor leading to the west wing. Careful now. At the end of the corridor was the transverse hall that led past the staff bedrooms. But, before that, there was a door that, according to the diagram, should open onto the gardener's patio. She reached it and found that it wasn't locked. Opening it cautiously, she held her breath; but no alarms went off that she could hear. She stepped out and closed the door behind her.

It took a long moment for her eyes to become accustomed to the dark; but when they had, she was surprised to see how much illumination the brilliant stars provided, their light reflecting from the white-painted walls.

The patio was exactly as she'd expected. Rectangular, paved, enclosed on three sides by walls of the house, open on the fourth to a narrow patch of lawn, it contained large piles of white chat—gravel or crushed shells; a tool shed; a wheelbarrow; a large coil of garden hose. Beyond the strip of lawn was the defensive wall that surrounded the house; and in it, directly before her, there was a high padlocked gate of ornamental scrollwork. Between the ground and the horizontal bar that formed the bottom of the gate was a space of about four inches.

The tool shed was unlocked. Inside she found hoes, rakes, a riding lawn mower, bags of fertilizer, a large can of gasoline, and a ten-foot ladder. Well now!

The wall was about eight feet tall, lined at the top with shards of broken glass and, in all probability, an alarm tripwire. She detached the ladder from the brackets which held it on the shed wall, and half-dragged, half-carried it onto the lawn. Heavy mother. Then she paused, thinking hard. She was sure that she could use the ladder to get over this first wall; but there was another wall at the perimeter of the estate, also about eight feet tall, that she'd have to get over as well. Once the ladder got her over this first wall, how could she get it to the other side in order to use it again to get over the second? She would have neither the strength nor the mechanical advantage to haul it up and over while balancing on the summit. If, after climbing the ladder, she could knock it down somehow, and, from the other side of the wall, drag it over to the gate—

And there was the answer, right before her. She pushed one end of the garden hose under the gate to a distance of five or six feet. Using knots she'd learned in mountaineering, she tied the other end securely around one leg of the ladder and what shortly would become the bottom rung, all the while humming softly under her breath the main theme of the second movement of Tchaikovsky's First Piano Concerto. Then she lifted the ladder into an upright position and leaned it steeply against the wall.

Everything in readiness, Rosamond slung the bag over her shoulder by its strap and climbed the ladder. Sure enough, a narrow band of wire mesh ran along the top of the wall, meandering about among the vicious shards of glass. There was no way she could stand on the wall, or hang from it to drop to the ground on the other side. Nothing to do but jump from the top of the ladder. She tossed the bag down into a clump of bushes. The ground looked far away. Above all things, she had to protect her wrists and hands. Having a choice between landing in gravel or grass, she chose the grass.

The ladder projected over the top of the wall, the top rung just clearing the edge. She used this rung to launch herself, and leaped, balancing herself with her arms to land feet first. She dispersed the shock of hitting the ground by going into a roll. She came out of this a little winded, knowing that later she would find scuffs and bruises. But the impact hadn't been any worse than some of her rougher parachute landings. She sat for a moment to collect herself, then retrieved the bag and went to the garden hose projecting from under the gate.

Keeping the hose against the ground so that it wouldn't rub against the underside of the gate and perhaps trigger an alarm, she began slowly pulling it; and after a minute or so, she felt it go taut. Placing her foot on the hose so that it wouldn't rise up with the resistance, she continued to tug. A gradual yielding, a scraping as the ladder angled and slid sideways along the edge of the wall. Finally with a hollow resounding crunch and clatter, the ladder toppled full length at the base of the wall. After that, it was simply the tedious business of pulling it over the ground.

When she had the end of the ladder in view, she reached under the gate and manually moved it through the opening to the distance of the bottom rung. Then, using the corner of the near gatepost as a fulcrum and applying sheer brute strength, she slowly forced the ladder to rotate until it was perpendicular to the opening. From then on it was easy pulling the entire ladder out of the enclosure into the yard.

She untied the garden hose, found the mid-point of the ladder, and hoisted it for carrying. Since she'd have to avoid the main gate with its guardhouse, she'd already decided that the best place to go over the estate wall was the section that lay behind the clustered outbuildings. Though there might be more danger of encountering security guards near the generator building and helicopter shed, there would also be more cover for her movements. Her watch told her it was almost three o'clock: she had no idea when dawn came this far south, but she was sure she could hear roosters crowing in the far distance.

Keeping to the cover of shrubs and shadows as much as possible, she made her journey to the dark outbuildings, pausing four times to rest. She encountered no one, and soon was at the boundary wall. Banked concertina wire lined the base of the wall, snug up against the masonry in waist-high weeds. Damned if she could tell whether, with his elaborate precautions, Zyzynski was trying to keep intruders out, or house guests in. She doubted that the concertina wire would be connected to the alarm system, or even electrified. But what the hell, her choices were limited. She crept as close to the wire as possible, and wrestled the ladder into an upright position, walking it into the concertina loops. The razor-sharp edges snagged her clothing, scratched and sliced her skin. But finally the ladder was leaning against the wall, its top barely projecting above the upper edge.

With her bag on her shoulder, up she climbed. This wall was slightly wider at the top than the other; but here too wire mesh ran through the broken glass; and, in addition, there was a row of steel spikes on the far side of the broken glass. Below her were bushes and, about fifty feet away, a thicket of small trees. There was just room to crouch sideways on the near side of the broken glass. Reaching down, she gave the ladder a sideways shove, and had the immense satisfaction of watching it slide down the wall, jounce on the concertina wire, and disappear from sight into the weeds. Then, balancing carefully, she shifted around to face frontwards, still crouching, her weight on her toes. She sprang, aiming herself at a particularly dense clump of bushes. In the dark she couldn't tell what sort of plants they were; she hoped they wouldn't be cactus or agave.

This landing was worse than her first; for although the bushes did cushion the impact, she wasn't able to roll, and consequently (with one arm up to shield her face) crashed forward onto her knees and stomach. The bushes weren't cactus or agave; but, as her weight crushed them down, she nonetheless was plunged into a tangled thicket of sharp twigs and spiky stubble that did her damage.

She wasn't sure how long she lay there breathing heavily and getting used to her pains. In the distance she definitely heard roosters crowing and dogs barking, and the sky was lightening in the east. Time to move on, to get as far from the estate as possible before the sun came up. If her bearings were right, and she'd made her exit over the eastern wall, the main road back to Christiansted and the airport lay to her right. The first road she would encounter was the access road that ran right by Zyzynski's front gate; the main road would lie farther on parallel to it.

She hauled herself stiffly to her feet, sore in more spots than she would have believed possible. Shouldering her bag, she moved some three hundred yards from the wall, then followed it back to the access road. Crossing this, she continued up the slope into a dense thicket of trees. The sky was rapidly brightening. She could see other houses, some large, some modest, all apparently asleep.

Since she evidently hadn't triggered any alarms in her departure, she would not be missed until Zyzynski had awakened and searched the house. She took vengeful pleasure in imagining his anger and puzzlement; the room by room hunt, her bag and the cadenza gone, the doors and gates still locked; the panicky combing of the grounds and outbuildings; the interrogation of the security guards; Zyzynski's doubt and distrust of his own staff. But what could she expect to come after that? The search to widen: at least one car on the roads; use of the helicopter. Someone dispatched to the airport to prevent her leaving by that route. Someone to watch the waterfront.

And where could she turn for help? The police? How could she be sure that Zyzynski, with his sixty-three billion dollars, didn't have a special relationship with them? She could hear the telephone conversation already: "We got her, boss. Holding her in a cell down at the station. Do you want to come get her, or shall we deliver her to your door?"

Well, the most important thing was to find a mailbox and post the cadenza. Then to lie low and not be found. No, the airport wasn't a possibility. Even getting to it was a problem. Hell, it lay at the other end of the island. Frederiksted, which lay even farther west, was a town she knew nothing about. It wouldn't offer any more safety than Christiansted.

For some time now, she'd been hiking through people's back yards. Would one of these families give her shelter or take her into town? Zyzynski had said he didn't associate with his neighbors. Yet why should they help a tramp coming out of the woods? Ah, she'd reached the main road. To the left lay the eastern end of the island; Zyzynski had called it a desert with cactuses. Probably lonely. Not good. Go right, then. Toward Puerto Rico. A nice long swim.

When Chip found him, Victor Zyzynski was standing in Rosamond's bedroom mightily hungover, his cheeks bristling with gray stubble, his great belly thrusting out over the waistband of his Bermuda shorts. "She's not in the house, Chief," Chip said from the doorway. "We've been over every inch of it."

Zyzynski spun around furiously. "She's taken the cadenza, too!"

"She can't have left the grounds," Chip said. "The guards noticed nothing, and all the alarm systems are working. She *has* to be here."

Marco appeared in the hallway behind him. "Chief, we've searched the grounds. There's not a trace of her anywhere."

"Impossible!" Zyzynski cried.

"The only odd thing we found was a length of garden hose out in the front yard."

"Did you search all the outbuildings?"

"Every one of 'em."

Flecks of saliva frothed at the corners of Zyzynski's mouth. "She *must* have gotten off the property. She'll head for the airport. Have Edmunds and Kelly get over there and watch for her. Get Nichols and Pruitt to watch the waterfront. Chip, I want you and Vernon to take the helicopter up, search the roads, the beaches, Christiansted. Marco, you and Jerry take the small car and scour the countryside to Christiansted, then do the town. I'll wait here for your reports. If you find her, bring her back. And be double damn sure she has the cadenza with her. That's *mine!*"

They left, and Zyzynski stormed back to the Den. There he was confronted once again by the littered remnants of last night's celebration. He recalled being awakened on the sofa by Mrs. Jones, who'd inquired if he and the lady would be wanting breakfast. Embarrassed, and damning the champagne, he'd gone to Rosamond's room and knocked softly on her door. "Rosamond, wake up. Do you want breakfast?" Worrying how he could adequately apologize for having conked out the night before. But when, receiving no answer, he'd opened her door and found the room empty, the bed not slept in, he'd felt a chill of apprehension. He'd wandered back to the dayrooms and looked into the garden; and then, finding no evidence of Rosamond, he'd gone wild and roused the staff for a thorough search. Now they were telling him she'd simply vanished. He glared at the bottles lying about, the platters of heaped oyster shells, the three slimy gray oysters remaining. He rushed to the intercom and buzzed the cook's living quarters. "Mrs. Jones, get to the Den and clear away the mess on the coffee table. What do you think I'm paying you for?"

With the sun well above the horizon, the early morning cool was rapidly dissipating. Rosamond had been walking along the margin of the main road for a considerable distance. Limping with pain in her right foot, she was going slower and slower, continually shifting the bag from one shoulder to the other. At the sound of a car approaching from behind, she turned quickly, crouching as though to run. It was an old, paint-faded pickup truck, driven by a young islander wearing a straw hat and a green shirt. Beside him in the front seat was an attractive woman in a green dress. And in the bed of the truck, four children—two girls, two boys—stair-stepped in age, and all wearing green.

The driver pulled over and leaned out the window. "You goin' to Christiansted for the St. Patrick's parade?" he asked. "Give you a ride."

"I'd be much obliged," Rosamond said. She went around to the passenger side; the woman opened the door for her, and Rosamond gratefully climbed in. In the daylight she could see how dirty her clothes were, how snagged and torn, how grimy her arms and hands, how scored with bloody scratches. She was aware that the woman was noticing too. But the woman could also see that, though the clothes were soiled and ripped, they were of good quality and had been rather expensive.

"You've got a knapsack," the woman said. "You been camping out on the beach?"

"No, I was hiking and got lost in the woods."

"You from the mainland?" the man asked.

"Yes."

"You talk like my cousin," he said. "He went to live in Virginia."

Rosamond smiled. "I was born there. I live in New York now."

There was some kind of rumpus going on in the bed of the truck. "Ron," the woman said to the driver, "tell those kids to stop it." The man leaned out his window and yelled, "Quit horsin' around back there! You're gonna fall off."

"We decided to get an early start," the woman said, turning to Rosamond. "Have breakfast with my sister in Christiansted, and then find a good place to watch the parade. You been to a St. Patrick's Day celebration before?"

"No. It sounds like a big event."

"Every year," the woman smiled. "A big parade, with all the schools' royalty going by in flashy convertibles. Music. Stilt-walkers."

"Free beer and hot dogs," Ron said. "Streets jammed with people. And by mid-afternoon, the streets are knee-deep in empty beer cans. It's a gas!"

Rosamond took heart. "Big crowds, you say?"

"City's full. Everybody partyin', goin' to the bars. Lotsa music."

"Maybe there'll be some place I can wash up," Rosamond said. She became aware of a loud chattering noise overhead—then focused on it. "Is that a helicopter?" she asked.

Ron craned out the window. "Yeah. Headin' for Christiansted. Hey listen, you say you want to wash up. Why not come with us to Sophie's sister's house? Have breakfast with us, go to the parade." He turned to the woman. "That sound all right, Sophie? Tanya won't mind; and we got all those eggs to give her."

"It's fine," she said.

"You'll come with us?" he asked Rosamond.

"Thank you very much," she said. "I'd be happy to."

Felix McKay was up and dressed long before Peter Shipley Abbott. The pianist finally responded to his roommate's impatient prodding and hauled himself out of bed and trotted to the bathroom. Abbott had not had an easy night; he'd been up to the toilet three times, for a long stay on each occasion.

"You know Zyzynski," Felix called into the bathroom. "We'll go out there and knock on the gate and simply ask to see him. If he's there, it's dollars to doughnuts Rosamond is too."

"I don't know him very well," Abbott moaned. "He's always been standoffish around me, if not downright unfriendly. I think he's a snob."

"Well, ask to see Rosamond, then. That'll tell Zyzynski somebody knows she's here."

"I need to stop at a drugstore and get something for my stomach."

"There's one right down the street. I'm going for breakfast. Meet me in the dining room when you're ready to go."

Abbott groaned. Felix went downstairs and ordered waffles and eggs.

When Abbott finally joined him at a quarter to nine, Felix had finished his third cup of coffee and was at the point of going upstairs to rattle him loose. Though Abbott was nattily dressed in a well-tailored charcoal suit, pale mauve shirt with enormous gold cufflinks, and black tie, he looked altogether unwell—his face cream yellow, his mouth pinched into a pale rosebud, his walk tight-cheeked and very cautious.

"It's about time," said Felix. "Did you get your medicine?"

"Yes. Now let's go; I don't want to be away too long."

Felix paid his bill, and they went to the car. Neither of them said much on the way to Zyzynski's. At the gate, Abbott pulled over and said, "Are you sure you don't want to do the talking?"

"You're the one who knows him. Out."

Abbott led the way to the gatepost, found the buzzer and pushed it. After a long wait he pushed it again. A man in a gray uniform suddenly appeared from around a screen of shrubbery. "What do you want?"

"I'm Peter Shipley Abbott. I want to see Mr. Zyzynski."

"Is he expecting you?"

"No, but he knows who I am."

"Just a minute." The guard disappeared behind the foliage.

"*Abbott!*" Zyzynski screamed into the phone. "What the fuck's he doing here? No I don't want to see him. Tell him to go screw himself."

"Mr. Zyzynski doesn't want to see you," the guard told Abbott through the gate. "He told me to tell you to go screw yourself."

Abbott took two steps backward, his mouth agape, and began fingering his tie. Felix came forward.

"Tell Mr. Zyzynski that Felix McKay of N. F. Trntl Associates wants to speak with Rosamond Foxe. Immediately."

"McKay?" said Zyzynski. "N. F. Trntl Associates? O my God. Asking for Rosamond Foxe? How the hell did he know she was here?" Zyzynski thoughtfully chewed his lip. "Tell him I don't know him. And tell him I'd like to speak to Rosamond Foxe myself."

When he received this message, Felix hitched up his pants and started for the gate. "Watch it!" the guard said. "It's electrified. Nobody here wants to see you. Buzz off." He unsnapped the holster on his hip.

Felix cussed and muttered all the way back to Christiansted. "Would it be possible to rent a boat," he wondered, "and come in by sea?"

"And do *what?*" Abbott cried. "Rescue Rosamond and swim out to the boat? What about the cadenza? Zyzynski has all the fire power. I'm certainly not going to trespass on that property. And *you're* not a one-man commando team."

"I wish Torvald were here," said Felix.

x x x

Tanya Martin was a harried mother of three who accepted Rosamond without question as her sister's guest and set another place at the table. "You go right in and wash up, honey," she said, jerking her thumb at the bathroom door. "Rafael, you hurry up in there!" She expressed only mild curiosity about Rosamond's disheveled state—the scratches, bruises, tangled hair, and torn slacks. All she said was, "Looks like you had a rough night, honey"; but Rosamond suspected that Tanya thought she'd probably been mugged or raped. Her husband Charles, dressed in green pants and shirt that looked very much like a surgery scrub outfit, merely smiled at her, revealing a handsome gold tooth, and continued laying out the kids' clothes on the bed.

Rosamond took her bag into the bathroom; and after she'd thoroughly washed, she changed into the clothes she'd worn on the plane. When she emerged, she felt much refreshed and looked far better. The two families were just sitting down to breakfast, and she joined them. Eggs, fresh-baked biscuits, milk for the kids, and fruit juice for the adults. Sophie said, "I've seen your picture somewhere. Maybe in *Time* or *Newsweek*, one of those magazines they have at the doctor's office. Yeah—you play the piano, don't you?"

Rosamond smiled. "That's right. Last month there was an article in *View* on concert pianists under the age of thirty. My picture was there among lots of others."

"Well, what do you know," said Ron. "A real celebrity. Lemme have some more of that grape jelly, Charles."

"We've been thinking about giving Lavonna piano lessons," Tanya said, indicating her eldest daughter, about twelve years old, who was sitting beside Rosamond. At being picked out for special notice, Lavonna shyly looked down at her plate and began mopping up egg yolk with a piece of biscuit. "Charlie there,"—indicating her eldest son, about sixteen with his hair bushed out in a moderate Afro—"he plays lead guitar with a group of boys who've formed a band." Charlie gave Rosamond a quick glance out of the corner of his eye and then hid behind his glass of milk.

"That's good to hear," said Rosamond. "I saw your piano when I came in." An old upright against the front room wall, its keys yellowed, its finish checked and scarred.

"It's not much of a piano," said Tanya. "It was given to my mother by some people she worked for when they packed up and went back to Texas. They used it in their recreation room, and used it hard."

"Maybe you could play us something?" Sophie asked hesitantly, but with a thinly masked eagerness.

"I'd be happy to," Rosamond said. "As my thanks for a wonderful breakfast." She got up from the table and went to the piano, fearing the worst. "In honor of St. Patrick's Day, some Irish music." She sat on the unsteady bench and ran some rapid scales up and down the keyboard. The piano was horribly out of tune; two keys didn't sound, and middle E-flat remained depressed and wouldn't spring back again. She mentally transposed into the key of D-major to avoid as much as possible the sticky E-flat, and launched into *When Irish Eyes are Smiling*. She followed that with *The Irish Washerwoman* and *The Rakes of Mallow*. It was not easy going, and the aberrations of pitch jangled her to the core. Her listeners loved it. "You're awfully good," Tanya said. "Thanks so much. Wasn't that good, Lavonna? wouldn't you like to be able to play like that?"

Lavonna wasn't about to commit herself to anything; but she was watching Rosamond with wide and shining eyes. Rosamond decided then and there that if she got out of the mess she was in, she'd see to it that this family got a decent piano. While the final preparations were made for going to the parade, she wrote down the family's address and put the paper into her billfold.

"You don't have anything green to wear," Tanya said. "Here, we'll fix you up." She went to her sewing table, found a length of green ribbon which she tied, with a fancy bow, around Rosamond's waist.

Ron and Charles were already on the front stoop. "Hurry up, it's almost ten o'clock," Charles called. "We got six blocks to go. There won't be any good spots left to watch the parade."

A loud chattering sounded overhead. "Damn!" said Ron. "There's that 'copter again. Down awful low, too."

The mothers herded the children out the front door, and the two families, with Rosamond in their midst, began walking along the street toward the main business district. As they progressed, more and more people filled the sidewalks. The sun was very hot, and as the crush of bodies increased, tourists mingling with residents, progress became difficult and slow. Already Rosamond had lost sight of Sophie and Ron in the crowd, and the children around her were only Charles's and Tanya's. "I need to find the post office," she told Tanya.

"It's down on Church Street," Tanya answered, pointing along the block.

Somewhere nearby there was a marching band, the persistent street beat of the drums echoing off the buildings. The sidewalks had become ceilinged galleries beneath projecting upper stories; spectators jammed the broad arches opening onto the street, where auto traffic had ceased, and people were continually crossing from side to side, jostling and elbowing past those who had already taken curbside positions for watching the parade.

Tanya stopped to talk with a friend; Charles hurried the kids across to the other side of the street. Seeing that Tanya was engaged, Rosamond went on to the corner and turned it.

Currents of excitement rippled the crowd; laughter, babble, shouts and cries. Rosamond was getting a headache from the heat, the press of bodies, and the endless rhythmic pounding of the drums.

Where was the post office? The next cross-street was even more crowded than the one she'd just left. What a jam of people! black, brown, white; young, old, and in-between; now and then a uniformed policeman.

Thirty feet in front of her, looking her way, she saw one of Zyzynski's men. The one called Jerry who'd flown with them to St. Croix.

He saw her at the same time she saw him. Between them was a large group of school children. Rosamond darted back around the corner and dashed through the entrance of a shop filled with tourists. At the rear wall, she dodged behind a rack of hanging dresses and sunsuits and peered out through the garments at the plate glass window.

Almost immediately she saw Jerry rush past. When he found she'd vanished, there was every likelihood that he'd come back and systematically search the shops he'd passed. But he'd seen her wearing the same outfit she'd worn on the plane—a distinctive matching skirt and jacket in brown and muted orange plaid. She studied the clothes racks around her and called to a clerk who was just finishing with a customer. "Oh, Miss, I wonder if you could help me find something?" The clerk came over. Rosamond provided her size-measurements and asked if she could see a selection of slacks and blouses. "Something in green, if you have it." In just ninety seconds, she was safely closed into a small fitting room with four pairs of slacks and three blouses. If Jerry came back, it would be very soon; if he looked into the shops, he'd be in a hurry and give them only a cursory inspection. She managed to stay in the fitting room for ten minutes.

When she emerged—cautiously, cracking the door and peering about before she showed herself—she was wearing a white blouse and bluish-green slacks, similar in color to the clothing of hundreds of people on the streets outside. "Oh, you look very nice in that outfit," the clerk said. "Thank you," said Rosamond. "I'm also interested in a straw hat with a wide brim. I see you have a large selection. And I'd like a large bag with a shoulder strap—"

"Yes, we have many. Do you want leather?"

"Plastic will do; or fiber. It has be to large." She pointed to a display near the window. "That white one there to the left is fine. Could you bring it to me, and also a selection of hats? Wide brim. Thank you." She went back into the fitting room and closed the door.

In a moment the clerk tapped on the panel. Rosamond opened the door, took the shoulder bag in, and stood looking at the hats the clerk had brought. She selected one and tried it on. Good fit. "This is fine, thank you. Here, these are the clothes I *don't* want." She handed the clerk the rejected and slacks and blouses. "I'll be out in just a moment." She closed the door, transferred the contents of her old bag into the new plastic one, stuffing her plaid outfit to the bottom and placing the envelope containing the cadenza manuscript on top. Then she emerged and beckoned to the clerk. "You've been very helpful. I'll take these items I'm wearing. Here's my credit card. Could you write me up a ticket?"

"You're going to wear them?" the clerk asked.

"Oh, yes. And do you have dark sunglasses, too?

"In the other room."

"Fine, I'd like to see them."

Rosamond put on her dark glasses, and, walking softly, like a cat, stepped out onto the street to hunt for the post office.

Chapter 38

March 14   (Saturday)

Felix McKay despaired of penetrating Zyzynski's private do-main. He'd seriously considered renting a boat and invading from the beach, but not knowing the layout of Zyzynski's compound, he knew he'd be at a fatal disadvantage. He *wasn't* a one-man assault team; he wasn't armed; and he wanted neither to be shot by one of Zyzynski's guards nor arrested for trespass and immobilized by the police.

Abbott was more a hindrance than a help, for while he was willing to grant that Rosamond probably *was* in Zyzynski's house, he thought it probable that she was there by her own choice—as a guest, not as a prisoner. It was unlikely that a man of Zyzynski's position and reputation would resort to something as heinous and risky as kidnapping. Abbott felt that if Zyzynski *had* acquired the cadenza for his private possession, then it was gone forever. And if he'd bought it (from whatever source), then it was *rightfully* his property (since it wasn't clear that it was legally anyone else's). Had he taken it from Trntl at the Bus Station?—well, perhaps. But how to prove it? And even if he *had*, it wouldn't be theft in a tech-nical sense, because it hadn't been *her* property, either.

Felix had shouted at him, "If that's the way you feel, then why the hell did you come?"

Abbott was sitting on the edge of the bed in their hotel room methodically filing and buffing his fingernails. "The difference be-tween us is that I think Rosamond knows what she's doing and is capable of making her own choices. You seem to think she's un-able to look out for herself, and is ripe to be victimized. Her ap-prehension at coming down was a normal reaction to the shock of learning that Zyzynski had been offered the cadenza. I came down not out of fear for Rosamond's safety, but to do what I could to insure the *cadenza's* safety—if it truly *was* here, and somehow started floating again. To monitor the situation, and to be *par-*

ticularly vigilant if you, representing Trntl and Associates, should somehow get *your* hands on it—"

"I resent that!" Bristling with rage, Felix had almost hit him.

"You asked why I came." Abbott slipped his nail file into a small leather pocket case. "If the cadenza starts moving about again, I will do what I can to keep it from harm. Frankly, I don't think there's much chance of its getting loose."

At that point Felix had stormed out of the room. He attempted to call Trntl and Carol in New York but got no answer at any of the numbers he tried. And Torvald was still in Provincetown with Rachel. He spent half an hour in the bar brooding over a ginger ale. If he went to the police with his wild accusations, complaining that Zyzynski wouldn't let him onto his property, the police would laugh at him, ask him what evidence he had that Rosamond Foxe was being held against her will. Suggest that it was a man's right to keep cranks and loonies off his property. Imply that he Felix was a trouble-maker whose best interest lay in returning to the mainland as soon as possible.

When he tired of staring at his empty glass, Felix left the hotel and went to the little park along the waterfront. There he sat on a bench near the old Danish fort and watched the boats coming in.

Peter Shipley Abbott, his bowels much calmer since his medication, left the hotel to watch the parade.

Large crowds, with their random movement and chaotic noise, did not appeal to Abbott. To the extent possible, he avoided the congested streets and stayed in the covered arcades as the parade got underway. Several flatbed trucks with local bands went slowly by. Though his musical sensibilities were deeply offended by some of what he heard, Abbott considered the location and the occasion and chose to be charitable.

Of more interest were a group of men and women stilt-walkers, who towered twelve to fifteen feet above the heads of the crowd. They were uniformly dressed in blue-green shirts and trousers. The pants—covering the stilts all the way to the ground—created a flawless illusion of very long legs. Some stilt-walkers had straw hats, but the majority wore green plastic visors as eye-shades. Abbott found he couldn't take his eyes off them as they walked about waving and calling to people who were leaning over balcony railings and out of second-story windows. How do they keep their balance? he wondered. And then the crowd parted for the first of a seemingly endless sequence of convertibles, each with a school-girl queen, resplendent in St. Patrick's finery, smiling and waving to the folks lining the route.

He was wishing desperately for a vodka tonic when he heard his name being called from the crowd on his right. "Peter!" A woman in dark glasses, her face shadowed by the wide brim of a hat, was working her way toward him.

"Rosamond!" he said as she reached him. "We thought you were at Zyzynski's house." He'd *known* McKay was full of shit thinking she was a prisoner.

"I was," she said. "I escaped last night. Why are you here?"

"I came down with Felix McKay to find you and protect the cadenza," he said.

"Is Felix here too? Where?"

"I don't know. He may have gone back to Zyzynski's hunting for you. We tried twice to get in, but they chased us off."

Rosamond said, "Zyzynski was going to hold me prisoner indefinitely—until I learned the cadenza and played it for him. And then—well, he wanted to possess *me*, too."

Abbott frowned. "So he *does* have the cadenza, then?"

"He *did* have it. He's the one who snatched it from Trntl in Baltimore. To have for his private pleasure. He has a huge secret collection of things he's stolen: Jefferson's diaries, the Shroud of Turin, the Eye of Ashoka, the Manzini Altarpiece—"

"The Eye of Ashoka! Good God!"

"That's right. And the cadenza was to join them. But I took it when I escaped, and have it here." She patted her shoulder bag.

"Let me see it!" His urgency startled her.

"It's sealed in an envelope to be mailed to Mrs. Farringford. I'm not going to open it. It's the cadenza, all right. And every bit as wonderful as people have claimed."

"You've *played* it?"

"Yes. All yesterday afternoon."

For a moment Abbott was unable to speak, his jaw clench-ing spasmodically, the whole left side of his face dancing with a jittery tic. Rosamond was deeply moved by his strong emotional response. She continued, "So, for the moment, at least, I've saved it. But I've got to find a mailbox and get it posted. Zyzynski has men hunting me. It's his helicopter that keeps passing overhead."

"What will happen if they catch you?"

"I'm sure they'll take me back to Zyzynski. He thinks the cadenza's rightfully his. And then—? Since I know about his private collection, I don't think he can afford to let me go."

"I have a hotel room, if you want to hide there. Come on, let's go back right now."

"That sounds good," she said. "But first I want to mail the cadenza."

"I haven't seen any mailboxes."

"The post office, then. It's supposed to be close by."

It was very near, as a matter of fact. Abbott had passed it on his way to this vantage point for watching the parade. "Okay," he said, "let's find it." And taking her arm, he guided her in the direction he'd been heading—away from the post office. The globules of sweat which had popped out on his face were not due to the heat. For a week he'd been haunted by the recurring nightmare vision of Anton Farringford creeping from the cemetery shrubs to deposit a briefcase containing not the Farringford Cadenza, but handwritten copies of assorted works by Brahms. *But here was the real thing*—now—in Rosamond's white shoulder bag, *four inches from his fingertips.* Its proximity, coupled with his inability to have it, nearly drove him wild. For he couldn't quite bring himself to snatch her bag and run.

But it must not be mailed to Mrs. Farringford, who'd immediately give it to Silas Dinch for publication. If Abbott couldn't manage to get the manuscript away from Rosamond and destroy it himself, then the next best solution would be to have Zyzynski bury it forever in his collection.

The crowd blocked them for a bit, and Rosamond said over her shoulder: "Zyzynski wanted me to become his mistress and play the cadenza just for him."

Abbott chortled with disbelief. "That old tub of lard? Why, that's ludicrous!"

"Be that as it may," said Rosamond. Suddenly her muscles tensed. "That man across the street, taking our picture with the Polaroid camera. That's one of Zyzynski's men—the one called Marco. Let's get out of here. Fast."

She began elbowing her way through the crowd, pulling Abbott along in her wake. He caught only a glimpse of the man with the camera. Short, dark-haired, barrel-chested—vaguely familiar. Where had he seen him before? The man was paralleling them across the street, struggling through his own obstacles. When there was a lull in the parade, a space between the convertibles, Abbott knew the man would dart across the street to narrow the gap. Sure enough, they'd only gone a few yards farther, when the man wormed through the crowd at curbside and angled toward them across the pavement.

"Run!" cried Rosamond. There was a slight opening in the bodies, a narrow passageway at the back of the gallery. By hugging the building wall, she was able to sprint to the corner. Abbott yelled, "He's running in the street!" Rosamond turned the corner without breaking stride, dragging Abbott along by the arm.

Glancing back, Abbott saw that the mob at the intersection had stymied their pursuer. Marco was engaged in a shoving match with a burly man who clearly had buddies to back him up.

The crowd was thinner again. "Where's the damn post office?" Rosamond panted, starting off at a trot. Huffing along beside her, Abbott said, "Listen, they're chasing *you*—not *me*. They don't even know who I am. Why not give *me* the cadenza? I'm going right back to New York. I'll hand deliver it to Mrs. Farringford. It'll be safer that way."

She shook her head in silence and kept running.

"You don't know what'll happen to it in the mail!" Abbott shouted. "Let me have it, Rosamond. I'll take good care of it." He began grabbing at her shoulder bag as they ran.

"Peter, I appreciate your concern," Rosamond gasped. "But if you had the cadenza, *you* wouldn't be safe. Zyzynski will stop at nothing to get it back. I can't put you in that danger." Suddenly: right in front of them stood a large mailbox. She stopped, popped open the shoulder bag and fished for the envelope.

"Well, let me *see* it at least," cried Abbott. "Please!"

She held the envelope before his eyes. "It's in here," she said, "sealed and ready to go." Open-mouthed, he watched as she dropped it in the mail slot.

"Well, that's that," she said. "Now what? Your hotel room?"

Abbott had leaned up against the mailbox, both arms draped over the top. "I'm exhausted," he said. The diarrhea was back again. Running had jarred things loose, and now he was afraid to walk. "I've got to rest a minute."

"We don't have a minute," Rosamond said, as a loud chattering drowned out the noise of the celebration. "Zyzynski's helicopter is back. Keep your head down." And the helicopter passed over them, low above the building roofs. Head down, with his hand covering his face, Abbott saw a man walk past them in the direction they'd just come from. He knew he'd seen *him* before—at the Cavendish Hotel: that scar on the left side of his face . . . "That's the one called Jerry," Rosamond whispered. "He was chasing me earlier, but I was dressed differently. Oh oh." A block away, Marco had just turned the corner, recognized Jerry, and waved to him. "We've got to move. Can you walk at all?"

Abbott dragged himself off the mailbox and followed her diagonally across the street, stiff-legged and setting his heels. On the opposite corner she'd seen a second-story tavern reached by a stairway leading from the sidewalk to a covered balcony. "We've got to get off the street," she said, starting up the steps.

"I think they've seen us," Abbott said. "Marco was showing him the photograph. They're coming this way."

From the top of the stairs, looking over the balcony balustrade, she saw that Marco and Jerry were about half-way to the corner and coming strong. "Hey, doll," said a lounger with a bushy blond mustache, "can I buy you a drink?"

"I'm with somebody," she said, indicating Abbott, who'd finally made it to the top of the stairs.

Mustache gave a sneer. "That tight-ass? Doll, you can do better than that."

"Can it, Jack," she said, moving into the dim interior. "Hurry up, Peter."

The saloon was a single square, high-ceilinged room with a bar across one side, tables and chairs scattered about, a pool table in the center, and two large ceiling fans revolving slowly. To her dismay, Rosamond saw that the only door out was at the far end of the same wall she'd entered by; and it simply gave onto the balcony farther along. Oh, shit. "Peter," she whispered, taking off her dark glasses. "I'm going to the ladies' room; they can't follow me there." And she left him, crossing to the door marked HENS.

A huge woman in a crisp apron was standing at the end of the bar wiping glasses. Rosamond said urgently, "A man is after me, and he knows I came in here. Is it okay if I hide in the women's room? and is there another way out besides the front door?"

The woman gave her a slow once-over with cool eyes. "Boyfriend trouble, huh? I've had to deal with that myself. You go right in there, honey. You'll be safe. And there's a window that opens onto the roof. From there you can get to the fire escape at the rear." Rosamond went in and shut the door.

Peter Shipley Abbott, with his own agenda, hurried to the door marked COCKS, whipping out his handkerchief to cover the doorknob before turning it. The door was locked. He rapped loudly.

"Busy," said a voice from inside. "You'll have to wait. I've got a ways to go."

Over his shoulder, he saw Jerry standing in the doorway, with Marco taking up a stationary position at the head of the stairs. Abbott quickly joined the men playing pool and pretended an intense interest in their game. Looking carefully around the room, Jerry passed right by Abbott, found none of the few women present to be Rosamond Foxe, then focused on the door marked HENS. Crossing quickly to it, he found his way suddenly blocked by a large woman in an apron.

"Hold it, sonny boy, you ain't goin' into the ladies' room. Just find somethin' else to do. Nobody gets by Big Verna."

Jerry stood poised on the balls of his feet, trying to decide what to do. "I'm looking for a woman who came in here," he said finally.

"Well, you ain't gonna find her in there."

"Hey, Verna," called a man from a table near the door. "You need some help over there?" He stood up; six or seven other men stood up, and two came from the pool table cradling their cues.

"Nothin' I can't handle, boys. Thanks." To Jerry, "Now, mister, you better leave. I don't want your trade."

Again Jerry stood undecided. The men in the place were all standing now, and slowly converging on the scene of action. Marco had stepped in from the balcony to help out if needed. Peter Shipley Abbott seized this as an opportunity to creep along the wall and sidle quickly out—fully aware that Marco had recognized him and was watching him go.

Oh my god, the parade had turned and was coming up *this* street now! Fighting the cramps, holding off the imminent explosion, Abbott minced down the stairs as fast as he could. Four steps down he passed a face no more than an arm's length away watching him from the street side over the concrete bannister. The oddity of this did not register with him.

And that's why, when he reached the bottom of the stairs and lurched around the buttress onto the sidewalk, he ran smack! into the legs of a very solid pair of green trousers nine feet tall. "Hey watch it, man!" A male shout from high overhead. "You just about knocked me over!"

Abbott recoiled and looked upward. The stilt-walker, tipped backwards and clinging with one arm to the bannister, was cursing loudly while struggling to regain his balanace. Two others came striding up to help him, glaring down at Abbott, who hurried on as fast as he dared.

And now *these* sidewalks were jammed with people; and here came the convertibles with the school-girl queens. Abbott had to twist and worm his way among the packed bodies for much of the route back to his hotel; and as the crowd became thinner and he could move more easily, he found that his steps were keeping pace with the thudding beat of a distant bass drum. Preoccupied with getting back to his room, he did not notice Jerry and Marco following him at the distance of half a block.

So eager was Abbott to get to the toilet that he didn't bother to lock the room door behind him. And thus it was that, sitting on the commode, he was suddenly aware of his two pursuers staring down at him from the bathroom doorway. Marco grinned. "Looks like we caught you with your pants down."

"We're a long way from Baltimore," Jerry said. "You seem to get around as much as we do."

"Get out of my room!" Abbott shouted, trying with one hand to pull his pants up to his knees.

"Naw, we'll wait till she comes back," said Jerry.

"Till *who* comes back?" Abbott sputtered.

"Miss Foxe. We saw you with her on the street. We couldn't stay at the bar, and rather than wait outside for her to show, we decided to follow *you*. What's he got to drink, Marco?"

From the bedroom Marco answered: "Just Pepto-Bismol and mineral water."

Abbott said, "Miss Foxe doesn't know where my room is. She won't be coming here."

Marco returned and stood beside Jerry in the doorway. "You trying to tell us you just happened to run into her on the street by accident?" He began methodically cracking his knuckles.

"That's exactly what happened," Abbott said. "Stop doing that; I can't stand it."

Marco continued through all his knuckles, one by one, and then Jerry started on his. "We'll wait awhile," Marco said. "And if she doesn't come, we still have *you*."

Rosamond climbed through the restroom window onto the gently sloping roof. The fire escape was a ladder affixed to the wall at the far end of the building; it let her down into a small alcove which opened onto the street.

Peter would have to fend for himself. She wished he'd said which hotel he was staying at. She simply had to get out of sight. Perhaps she'd be safer among the tourist boutiques at the waterfront. Maybe there she could find a secluded restaurant or bar where she could efface herself and have a sandwich and cup of coffee. Maybe even find a hotel room and get some sleep. Fatigue was overtaking her. After her adrenalin surges of the last hour, she needed to raise her blood sugar; she felt punch-drunk and was beginning to doubt the reliability of her judgment. At least—thank God—the cadenza was in the hands of the U. S. Postal Service. She made her way quickly and cautiously toward the waterfront.

In two hotels she was told there were no vacancies. Discouraged, she went into the restaurant of the second and had a sandwich and two cups of coffee. Then she walked along the quay to the parking lot, and through that to the esplanade that led to the old Danish fort. Boats were moored side by side in a little marina, many of them occupied by people sunbathing or chatting in deck chairs over drinks. For anonymity, Rosamond wished she could climb aboard and join them. Moving east toward the fort, she saw a black-bearded man sitting on a bench.

"Felix!" she cried.

McKay looked up startled and then leaped to meet her. "You're all right!" he said, clutching her hand. He gave her a big hug. "I was worried that Zyzynski was holding you against your will."

"He'd like to be," she said. "His men are after me now. Can we go someplace private, out of sight? I'll tell you all about it."

"Abbott and I have a hotel room. Only a block away. Let's go there."

"I'm exhausted and need to rest. But the cadenza's safe; I mailed it to New York. Zyzynski's the one who stole it from Trntl in Baltimore—to put in his private collection. We've got to get off the island, Felix."

"We have our own plane from the Sternberg Foundation waiting at the airport," Felix said. "The pilot and co-pilot are staying in a different hotel from ours. And we have a rental car—you can see it over there in the parking lot—that red Ford next to the two green ones. Right now it's locked, and Abbott has the keys." They'd reached the hotel entrance.

"I'm sure Zyzynski has someone watching the airport," she said.

"Let's get inside. Then tell me all about it."

They crossed through the lobby to the outside stairs at the rear, which, in two stages, took them to a balcony lined with louvered doors. Below this was a courtyard with fan palms and a fish pond. Felix's room was four doors along the balcony. He said, "That's odd, the door's ajar."

He opened it slowly and stuck his head in. "Come on," he said, and Rosamond entered. Looking into the bathroom, Felix said, "Abbott's not here. He *has* been, though, and forgot to flush the toilet." Felix flushed it. Then, coming back to the center of the bedroom, he took careful inventory. "Abbott's suitcase is here, but his medicine's gone. He's probably just stepped out." While Felix locked the door, Rosamond went to sit on the bed.

"I've talked to Peter," she said. "I ran into him on the street just before Zyzynski's men showed up. He said you were here."

"Were Zyzynski's men after him too?"

"I don't think so; they chased him only because he was sticking with me."

"But you *were* being held against your will on the estate? I want the whole story."

She told him, omitting nothing of substance. When she'd finished, he said, "It must have been his people that searched our office in New York."

"He was desperate to hear the music," said Rosamond. "It's some sort of obsession with him."

"But the manuscript will stay in his collection with all the other treasures he's stolen." He went to the window, looked along the balcony as far as he could see, and down into the courtyard, then closed the Venetian blinds. "The cadenza's out of his reach while it's in transit. And he doesn't know you've mailed it, or where you sent it. Don't think about it anymore. The important thing is to get you out of St. Croix."

She had lain down full-length on the bed. "I'm very tired, and need a nap. Will you stay here with me?"

As if he needed to be asked.

Chapter 39

By mid-afternoon, Zyzynski had worked himself into a frenzy. His early chagrin and befuddlement had given way to rage and a naked hate so virulent and terrifying that Mrs. Jones had retreated to her room and locked the door.

At nine-thirty, while the search of the house and grounds was winding down, and Zyzynski, freshly awake, was trying to function through the haze created by a crushing headache, it had been an unwelcome and nasty jolt to hear that Peter Shipley Abbott and one of the detectives from Trntl's firm were at the gate. *Asking for Rosamond!* What the hell—? Somehow she must've gotten word to them before leaving New York. Since they knew she was here, they also knew that *he* had the cadenza! And how many other people might *they* have told?

Shortly before noon he'd taken a shower—both to cool his fevered brain, and to wash off the oil of peppermint, which was causing a ferocious itch. Shaving, he'd gouged a deep nick on his chin and sliced a half-inch gash under his nose. Both bled profusely, and after sponging his face with a damp Turkish towel, he'd plastered bits of toilet paper onto the wounds, and then lit a bitter cigar that gave him as much satisfaction as smoking a piece of rope.

By one-forty, the erotic warmth he'd felt for Rosamond the night before had long been obliterated by his vengeful fury. Rosamond was now the Enemy, had always been the Enemy, would *always* be. She'd deceived and betrayed him, violated his trust, thwarted his plans, spurned his affections, rejected his companionship, scorned his riches, robbed him of the Farringford Cadenza, and played him for a fool. And, to put the final spit-shine on his humiliation, she'd evaded his top-of-the-line Out-Front Security System and escaped scot-free, leaving no clues as to how she'd done it.

If the bitch got back to the mainland, she'd publish the cadenza, exploit his profession of love for cocktail party titters, and brag to all the world about how she'd bested him. *A woman!* He'd be a laughing-stock. His reputation for invincibility, for winning, would dwindle to a joke; his power to intimidate and terrify and vanquish rivals would be nullified. Never again would it occur to *anyone* to regard him as Number One.

And, since he'd told her of his Collection, she would broadcast *its* existence, too, arousing the interest and speculations of former owners, insurance companies, and police agencies the world over—*Of EVERYBODY who'd ever had ANYTHING stolen!* Investigations and legal proceedings would be launched to locate and repossess the Manzini Altarpiece, the Komiroff Sapphire, and all his other treasures. Why, he'd be suspected of stealing things he *hadn't*—things that were in *other* people's Collections! The FBI, Interpol, and the KGB—not to mention twenty other security forces and special tactics squads—from Israel, Turkey, the Vatican, Brazil, Iran, China, Indonesia, France—would hound his steps, surveillance his movements, disrupt his business, and come to visit! He might have to destroy his treasures to avoid discovery and prosecution.

Clearly, before she could leave the island, Rosamond would have to be captured and silenced. The cadenza would have to be recovered; another pianist would have to be found to record it (he'd even *hire* one, if it came to that). And as for having a woman with whom he could enjoy the cadenza's powers, why *that* could be arranged easily enough.

As he dressed, he selected his clothing with the same care he'd have used in preparing for an important business luncheon: pondering long, choosing this, rejecting that, organizing an ensemble that would denote authority and power. The pale cream shirt—not the white or blue; the vested charcoal pin-stripe, not the Glencairn plaid or the chocolate check. With the cream shirt and charcoal suit, he should probably wear—yes! the burgundy tie. And black pearl cufflinks, not the platinum or gold. Clocked socks, or plain? Clocked, with garters. And the lambskin shoes. How comforting, how reassuring to be engaged in activity where once again he clearly was in command! To be making crisp, definitive decisions with his customary dispatch! He stood before the full-length mirror to comb his matted hair. By God, he *did* look good! Cream and burgundy went well with his complexion. He plucked the toilet paper from his face and studied his coagulated shaving wounds. Hell, there certainly would be scabs—but probably no scars.

Once he'd finished dressing, he had nothing left to do but brood and fidget. Both of these he did in earnest. As he felt his fury mounting once again, he mixed himself a whiskey sour. Damned if he'd be defeated! He would *not* give up First Place. But why didn't his men report from the field? Where was Rosamond hiding? Finally he went to the basement to find comfort in his Collection.

But there was no solace in it. The jewels were dimmed in their luster; the Shroud of Turin looked downright dingy; *The Death of Socrates* was too depressing to contemplate; and both the Smiling Buddha and the broad granite face of Amenhotep III (with its blank staring eyes and gently sneering lips) seemed to be mocking him.

It was these last that pushed him over the edge. With a hoarse croak, he fled the Pharaoh's gaze and the Buddha's superior smirk, thudded up the stairs into the upper office, slammed shut the steel door, flung himself into the swivel chair, and laid his head upon the desk.

And there he was at two-forty-five—a distended vein throbbing in his temple, his eyes bulged out like a frog's—when the call came from the gatehouse that Marco and Jerry had returned.

And did they have Rosamond Foxe with them? "No, we've got Peter Shipley Abbott."

"Abbott!" he screamed. "You were to get Foxe!"

"Abbott was *with* Foxe," Marco said hastily. "We almost had her, but she got away. We think he can lead us to her."

"He was *with* Foxe?" So: as he'd known all along, it was a conspiracy! a scummy plot hatched up between them—and maybe Trntl, too—to steal the cadenza and bring him down. "Go find Foxe!" he thundered.

"But what about Peter Abbott?"

Oh, hell, Abbott knew too much! Godammit— "Bring him to the office."

He slammed down the receiver, took a deep, expansive breath, and rose up invigorated. Calmer too, now that he was obviously—at least in some measure—regaining control of the situation. Zyzynski, *still* to be the Victor: undiminished, augmented, thirsting for revenge. And punishment.

He mixed himself another whiskey sour: rolled it on his tongue, savored its tang. Conniving Abbott had over-reached himself. No one puts a fool's cap on Zyzynski! And Rosamond, with her fake-innocent smile, had told him a bold-faced lie when she'd simpered, "Oh no, he's just a close friend." *Very* close, and not at all "professional"! His instincts had told him they'd been lovers. Why hadn't he listened? Well, Abbott was about to learn how dearly this conspiracy would cost him.

When Marco and Jerry brought Abbott in, the pianist was far from being his usual natty self. He was rumpled and dusty, with the appearance of having lain for some time on the floor of a car; his clothing was an ill-assorted combination of blue suitcoat, casual tan slacks, tieless yellow shirt wrongly buttoned, and a limp-brimmed Panama hat which looked as though it had been wadded into a pocket.

"How dare you kidnap me from my hotel?" Though his voice quavered a bit, Abbott addressed Zyzynski coldly, in the same tone he'd have used in correcting a mistake made by a particularly dense piano student in one of his master-classes. "I demand to be released at once. The FBI shall hear of this."

"Shut up," Zyzynski said.

Marco showed him the Polaroid photograph. "See, here's the picture I took of 'em together."

Zyzynski held it to the light. Yes, there was Abbott talking earnestly to a smallish woman whose face was hidden by a floppy hat. "You're sure this is Rosamond Foxe?"

"That's right, Chief. She and Abbott were head to head, and they ran when they saw me coming. Jerry and I lost her in a crowded bar, but we followed Abbott back to his hotel."

The photograph clinched it. God, they'd played him for a fool.

"Where's Rosamond?" he asked Abbott.

"As I told your men, I haven't the faintest idea."

"Where's the Farringford Cadenza?"

Just the slightest pause. "How should I know? I assumed you had it."

"Oh, you did? Now why would you assume that?"

A longer pause. "Well, Rosamond said you did."

"Rosamond *stole* it from me," Zyzynski snorted. "As you very well know. She gave it to *you*, didn't she, Abbott?"

"She didn't give it to *me*," said Abbott.

To Marco and Jerry: "Did you search his room?"

"Every inch," replied Jerry.

"Have you searched *him?*"

"We watched him change clothes," said Marco. "He doesn't have it."

"What's that in his pocket?"

"A bottle of Pepto-Bismol. He's got the trots."

Zyzynski set down his empty glass. "You're being less than candid with me, Abbott." Now was the time to terrify him into submission. Zyzynski drew down his bushy brows, bulged his eyes to their most ferocious glare, and stood directly before the pianist. "Look me in the face, Abbott. What do you see?"

Abbott flared his nostrils haughtily: "I see that you've cut yourself while shaving. If that's the best you can do, you ought to go electric, or grow a beard."

Zyzynski bared his teeth. He wanted to shriek *No, no, you shit! You should've seen that I'm an implacable foe who always gets what he wants, who will crush you if you resist!* But it didn't seem appropriate, somehow. Instead, he said, "You think you're so god-damned smart. You'll have a chance to show how smart you are. What's the name of that person from Trntl's detective agency who came with you to my house this morning?"

This time, no hesitation at all. "Felix McKay."

"Where is this McKay now?"

"I don't know. I haven't seen him for hours."

"He came to St. Croix to help you and Rosamond steal the cadenza, didn't he?"

"I don't know what you're talking about. I had no intention of stealing the cadenza. I've never even seen it."

"Did Rosamond give it to *him?*"

"I don't see how. They haven't been together that I know of."

The telephone rang, and Zyzynski answered it himself. "Chip, Chief, reporting in. We haven't seen her. And she hasn't been to the airport. Do you want us to keep looking?"

"Damn right. Marco and Jerry saw her in Christiansted, so do your looking there."

"It's hard, Chief. The town's full of people, and there's a big party going on in the streets."

"Then get out of the helicopter and mingle with the crowd. I want her here by sundown." He dropped the receiver into its cradle.

"By now she may have linked up with McKay," Jerry said. "And none of us knows what he looks like."

Zyzynski said, "Describe him, Abbott."

"No," said Abbott. "You've kidnapped me; you're holding me against my will. Why should I cooperate with you? why help you kidnap someone else?"

"Because," said Zyzynski, "it's the only chance you have of mitigating your punishment."

"Punishment? For what?"

"Time is short. Describe him, Abbott."

"He doesn't *have* the cadenza! Rosamond mailed it back to New York!"

"Bullshit, Abbott. Surely you don't expect me to believe that! This is your last chance. *Give us a description of McKay.*"

All right, Abbott decided: it might placate Zyzynski and deflect him from his altogether disquieting focus on "punishment"—but the description would be so vague and general as to be no help at all in finding Felix. Abbott said, "He's of moderate height, with a neatly trimmed black beard. He was wearing dark slacks and a white or pale brown shirt when I saw him last. No hat."

"Jerry, get on the phone, alert the people at the airport and the waterfront. When they find McKay, have him brought here. He's to be searched to see if he has the cadenza." Jerry went to the telephone, talked rapidly, then returned to the others. Zyzynski was staring hotly at Abbott, who was standing downcast and sullen against the far wall.

"All done, Chief. Anderson is handling it."

"Good," said Zyzynski. "But Abbott here needs squeezing dry. He's not telling us all he knows. Take him down to the basement. We don't want to disturb Mrs. Jones."

Though he protested loudly, struggled, and set his heels, Abbott was half dragged, half carried across the room to the steel door, where Zyzynski spun the tumblers and poked the buttons. Marco and Jerry forced Abbott down the stairs with Zyzynski following, and pushed him through a second door into the lower office.

Shaken, and now feeling true panic, Abbott quickly took in his surroundings—the featureless walls, the single filing cabinet and swivel chair. The marble-topped desk and the huge gold guillotine standing beside it. At the sight of the guillotine, Abbott had to clench and hold tight to his bowels.

Zyzynski opened a closet and brought out a straight-backed chair which he placed next to the desk facing the guillotine. "Sit," he commanded. "The room is completely soundproofed, Abbott, so spare us any outbursts. Marco—Jerry—stand just behind his chair, one on either side. That's right." Zyzynski seated himself behind the desk and leaned back, his hands folded over his belly.

"Now, Abbott, there are several things I want you to tell me. First: how many people know that you and McKay have come to St. Croix to seek me out?"

"Lots of people."

"Who?"

"Everybody in Trntl's firm. Mrs. Sternberg. Everyone they may have told. And the pilot and co-pilot."

"Mrs. Sternberg?" A disturbing new wrinkle. "What's her connection with your plot?"

"There *is* no plot—"

"How does Mrs. Sternberg know you're here?"

"She let us fly down in a Foundation airplane."

Ah, so that's how they got here so fast. "How did she get involved?"

"When she learned you had the cadenza, and that Rosamond was coming down to authenticate it, and that McKay was worried about Rosamond's safety, she gave us use of the plane."

"Did *she* have doubts about Rosamond's safety?"

"She said she didn't trust you."

Zyzynski chewed this one over. Mrs. Sternberg was coming to possess the same quality of surprise as a fighter plane attacking out of the sun. "How did she learn that I had the cadenza?"

"Rosamond told one of Trntl's friends before she left the reception."

The lying bitch! He'd sworn her to secrecy, and she'd gone and spread the word at the earliest opportunity. He should've known better than to trust her out of his sight. He'd expected loyalty, discretion, truthfulness at the very least. The more fool he! Loyalty was nothing but a two-bit whore; truthfulness, a tin can strumpet. "You claim that McKay came down because he was worried about Rosamond," he continued. "He really came down to help her steal the cadenza. Like *you* did, Abbott."

"No! I came down to see if you really *had* the cadenza. And if you did, to see if you planned to publish it—and if so, to see if I could be an intermediary in such a project. On the other hand, if you *didn't* wish to publish it, if you wanted to keep it for your private collection, that would be *your* business."

"What collection is *that*?" said Zyzynski

"Rosamond said that you wanted to put the cadenza in your collection with the other things—Jefferson's diaries, the Eye of Ashoka, the Manzini Altarpiece, the Shroud of Turin—" Abbott's voice took on a pleading tone: "Look, I don't care if you keep the cadenza for yourself. I didn't come here to steal it from you. That was Rosamond's idea."

Zyzynski scratched the end of his nose and communed with himself. See, Victor, it's beginning already. No sooner does she escape than Abbott knows about the Collection. And McKay, too, no doubt. If she gets back to New York, Mrs. Sternberg will know, and the police, and the newspapers, and the KGB, and Interpol—

Too bad. Oh, too bad, too bad.

He said, "I'm tired of your bullshit, Abbott. Pretending you aren't part of the conspiracy. Trying to evade the consequences. Does McKay have the cadenza?"

"No!"

"Twist his arm, Marco."

Abbott shrieked with pain.

"Does he?"

"No! I told you Rosamond mailed it to New York! Please stop! You're ruining my arm!"

"Bad for a piano player," said Zyzynski. "Come on, Abbott, do you seriously expect me to believe she'd entrust something so precious to the mails?"

"It's the truth, whether you believe it or not."

"Marco."

Abbott screamed "Wait! She *did*. She put it in a mailbox in Christiansted. Said she wanted to get it off the island."

"Well, if she *did* mail it—and I'm not granting that for one second—who did she send it to? Mrs. Sternberg? Trntl? Dinch?"

"Mrs. Farringford."

Zyzynski sighed tiredly. "Surely you can do better than that."

"Look," Abbott said, his voice trembling on the edge of hysteria. "I've told you the truth. Why are you doing this to me?"

Truth. A broken-down trollop lifting her skirt for the streetcorner johns. Zyzynski shook his head. "Why, you ask? *Why?* Because you've conspired to rob me of my property. Because you've always stood between me and Rosamond, and finally you've succeeded in poisoning her mind against me so that she was willing to betray my generosity. Because you've always been a pain in the ass with your airs of arrogant superiority, your cocksure preening for public view, your smug certainty that you're better than everybody else. You're a pompous toad, Abbott, a self-important sniveling twit. You haven't satisfied me with your answers. I think it's time for stronger measures." He took a cigar from his inner coat pocket. "Do you see this guillotine, Abbott? A handsome piece of work, wouldn't you say? Crafted for me by a master. It's six feet two inches high; the blade is eight and a half pounds of gold-plated solid steel. When it drops, it generates a force of thirty thousand pounds per square foot—all of it concentrated on that thin razor edge. Allow me to demonstrate." He put the end of his cigar in the head-notch at the base and tripped the lever. *Thunk!* And the cleanly-severed cigar tip dropped onto the platform before Abbott's nose.

"Now," said Zyzynski, lighting the cigar, "imagine what that would do to a *finger.*"

Abbott's face went curdled milk. He hurriedly stuffed both hands into his coat pockets. Zyzynski pointed to the framed motto on the wall. "What do you make of that?"

Abbott craned his neck around and read it: "'. . . and the first shall be last.' Sounds Biblical. Is it from Deuteronomy?"

"It's from *Judges!*" said Zyzynski. "Oh, how I despise you, Abbott. I've *always* despised you. *You've* always known what it means to be first. *You've* had the nicest crayons, the best seat in the bus!"

"What are you talking about?" Abbott cried, cringing back in terror.

"Your name, asshole. You come at the first of the alphabet: A-B-B! *You've* never known what it's like to be Z-Y-Z! But now you *will* know what it means for the first to be last!"

Abbott's eyes were wild and frantic. "Wait!" he said eagerly. "I'm *not* at the first of the alphabet! There's lots of folks ahead of me—like—uh—well, like Aaron Aaronson, the violinist. Have you thought of *him?*"

Zyzynski leaned forward and put his elbows on the desk. "He didn't try to make a fool of me, Abbott. *He* doesn't know about my Collection."

Omigod, that too. "I promise—I *swear* I'll never tell anyone about your collection! As far as I'm concerned, it's a private matter, nobody else's business."

"Very private," said Zyzynski. "And I can't rely on you to keep the knowledge to yourself." He sent a cloud of smoke to the ceiling. "This is your last chance, Abbott. *Where's the cadenza?*"

"I told you! Rosamond mailed it to Mrs. Farringford!"

Zyzynski said, "Marco, Jerry, bring me his hands."

"No!" Abbot shouted as they grabbed him on both sides and tried to pull his hands out of his pockets. Abbott flailed his elbows, struggling mightily; on Marco's side the pocket ripped; on Jerry's the hand came out swinging the bottle of Pepto-Bismol like a stone. But Abbott was no match for the two of them; the bottle crashed onto the floor, and, pinioned and screaming, Abbott was hauled forward to the desk, one arm twisted behind his back, the other extended toward the guillotine. Zyzynski rose up over the desk, seized the hand, which Abbott had clenched into a fist. Pried the middle finger loose, separated it from its fellows, positioned it in the head-notch of the guillotine, reached for the trip-lever. Abbott's eyes bulged; and though his mouth had stretched impossibly open, no sound came out.

"You know, Chief," Jerry said, exerting all his force to hold Abbott steady. "I think he may have been telling the truth."

"Yes," said Zyzynski, "so do I."

Thunk!

When Rosamond woke in the late afternoon, she found Felix sitting by the bed regarding her tenderly. "Goodness," she said, smiling to hide her faint embarrassment. "I really needed that sleep. Thanks for standing watch."

"My pleasure," Felix said, giving back the smile. "Incidentally, there's been no sign of Abbott, or of anybody hunting for you. But I think we'd better get away from St. Croix as quick as we can. This is what I propose: let me go to the other hotel and ask the Sternberg pilots if we can leave tonight. I don't think you should risk being seen on the street, and I don't think you should stay alone in this room. I'm not sure Zyzynski's men weren't here earlier; they might come back. Why don't you go down to the bar and hole up in the ladies' room. When I get back, I'll rap your name on the door: BUMP-bu-bu-BUMP for ROS-a-mond-FOXE. What do you think?"

"How long will you be gone?"

"Hopefully, no more than ten to fifteen minutes."

"Okay," she smiled, "the ladies' room it is."

Felix was gone just over twenty minutes. When he rapped on the restroom door, Rosamond opened it a crack to identify him, then stepped out, disturbed at his distraught expression. "What's wrong?" she asked.

"Both of them greatly enjoyed St. Patrick's Day. The pilot hasn't come back to the hotel room, and the co-pilot's had so much beer he wouldn't be able to *find* the plane, much less fly it. When I woke him up, he said he last saw the pilot going off with a woman he'd met at a tavern called The Trade Winds."

"So what are we going to do?" said Rosamond.

"Think," said Felix. They went to a small table in a secluded corner of the bar. "Abbott doesn't seem to have come back to the room. The rental car's still locked up in the parking lot. If we had the keys, we could drive out to the country for the night."

"Look!" she whispered suddenly. "Coming in at the main door: the two men who chased me!"

"Down," he said. "Get behind the menu. They're going on through the lobby toward the back stairs. They're on their way to the room."

The waiter came up. "Are you ready to order?"

Felix got up and motioned Rosamond to follow. "We've changed our minds, thanks. Nothing now." They quickly went out the side door onto a broad boardwalk that led to the quay. "The streets are fairly empty now," Felix said. "The crowds have trundled home to digest their beer and hot dogs; crews are cleaning up the litter. We'll be very noticeable if we stay on the streets."

"See all the boats moored along here," Rosamond said. "Do you suppose we could get someone to ferry us over to St. Thomas? It's about forty miles, I think."

"A good idea," he said, looking nervously first over one shoulder, then the other. "We can ask."

Many of the boats were apparently empty, but some had people on deck. Felix and Rosamond avoided those that clearly had parties in progress, and those where people were stowing things away for the night. On one, though, a man of about fifty was smoking a pipe in the stern, cocked back in a folding chair watching people walk by. Rosamond approached to the edge of the wharf and said, "Excuse me. It's extremely important that we get to St. Thomas tonight. Would it be possible to hire you to take us?"

He regarded her for a long while in silence, puffing slowly, the smoke rising in the still air to form a nimbus above his head. He looked Felix over, too, with considerably less interest (or with interest of a markedly different kind). "I don't run a ferry service," he said at last. "Just take people fishin'. You might try that fellow there—the fourth boat down. He does a regular run out to Buck Island to let tourists snorkel over the coral reef."

"Thank you," said Rosamond. They moved down the quay, Felix continuing to scan the streets and building fronts on their right. The hotel was a fairly long distance behind them now, and he began to breathe more easily.

The boat was a large cabin cruiser moored behind a sign which advertised snorkeling tours. In the stern were lockers where a man with a clipboard was taking inventory of snorkeling gear and life preservers.

Rosamond said "Hello," and the man straightened up and looked at her attentively. "Hello yourself," he said. He was in his mid-forties, with a craggy, sun- and wind-burned face and pale crusty patches on the tops of his ears. He wore a mustache and a blond-grizzled beard, through which his teeth, crooked and to-bacco-stained, showed in a broad smile. "A man up the way said you might be able to help us," Rosamond continued.

"If you want to see the reefs, you'll have to wait till tomorrow to buy tickets," he said.

She shook her head. "It's urgent that we get to Charlotte Amalie tonight. We hope you'll take us across. We can pay you two hundred dollars." They'd counted their money in the hotel room, and they had two hundred and forty-three dollars between them.

"Make it two twenty-five," he said, "And I'll provide rum swizzles on the way."

"Wonderful! How soon can we leave?"

"The sooner the better, unless you want to travel after dark." He was appraising Felix shrewdly.

"If you need to know why we have to get to St. Thomas—" she began.

"I don't make a point of askin' questions." He helped her into the boat, and then gave a hand to Felix. He indicated Rosamond's shoulder bag: "Is that all the luggage you got?"

"That's it."

"Okay, then. You can call me Cap'n Jed. Do you want to stay on deck, or would you rather go into the cabin till we're out of the harbor?"

"The cabin, I think," said Rosamond.

"I'll stay on deck," said Felix. The better to watch the water-front.

"Let me see your money," said the captain. Felix showed him. Cap'n Jed clapped a mate's cap on Felix's head and made ready to start. Felix saw the two men who'd been chasing Rosamond exit the hotel, confer a moment by the front door, and then start walking toward them along the quay. "How soon can we leave?" he asked.

The captain squinted in the direction Felix was looking, took in the two men rapidly approaching, and said "Right now."

They cast off, and with a throb of engine, the boat moved away from its dock. The two men on the quay stopped and watched the boat leaving; one even trained binoculars on Felix, who pointedly turned his back to shore. Then the binoculars were put away, and the men walked on toward the fort.

Felix let out a great sigh of relief and went to the cabin door. "I think we made it," he told Rosamond.

"Keep your eyes peeled for a green and white helicopter," she said.

"How many men does Zyzynski have?"

"I don't know. A lot." She came out on deck.

"When we reach St. Thomas," said Felix, "we've got to make some telephone calls. Trntl, Mrs. Sternberg—"

"And Mrs. Farringford," said Rosamond, "to alert her that the cadenza's coming. Then the FBI."

The sun was very low, and the breeze had turned chilly. Cap'n Jed gave them each a rum swizzle and presented them with a large blanket. This they pulled around them in the lee of the wheelhouse and huddled together sipping their drinks. Rosamond said, "Now that we've made it off the island, I'm getting the shakes. Feel my hands; they're like ice."

Hey, it was snug cuddled under the blanket; Felix thought it was the best boat ride he'd ever had. And he did his very best to keep her warm.

Chapter 40

March 15-17   (Sunday, Monday, Tuesday)

Midnight found Zyzynski faced with a hard decision. If indeed (as Abbott claimed) Rosamond had sent the cadenza to Mrs. Farringford, he'd have to intercept the mailing before it fell into the hands of Dinch. Yet he couldn't leave St. Croix till Rosamond was captured or otherwise accounted for. If she were allowed to run loose blabbing what she'd learned about him and his activities—what he'd *revealed* to her, through the effects of champagne, in his misguided moment of trust and intimacy—and about his Collection, she could cause him damage far beyond her comprehension and wildest imaginings.

All day Saturday his men had scoured the island to find her. Those at the airport swore she'd not flown out. Those who'd stayed at the waterfront till four-thirty, when most of the boats were in and things were closing down, swore she'd not left by water. Till noon the helicopter had swept the eastern end of the island, the coasts and beaches, inland golf courses, and other tourist attractions. After noon, it had gone west, scanning the road to the airport, the botanical gardens, and Frederiksted. In the late afternoon and early evening, Marco, Jerry, and Chip had systematically combed through Christiansted's bars and restaurants, and even a couple of churches—and reported back no trace of Rosamond or Felix McKay.

So where the hell *were* they? Shacked up in a hotel room? Hiding in a ruined sugar mill? Camping in the woods?

Through hefty bribes, the men at the airport had obtained the description of Peter Shipley Abbott's rental car and learned that the Sternberg Foundation's plane was parked with the crew absent. The car was found locked in the lot near Abbott's hotel. Using the keys from Abbott's pocket, Marco and Jerry had searched it thoroughly in the late afternoon, finding no trace of the cadenza manuscript. A second search of Abbott's hotel room had turned up nothing new—except that the bed had been rumpled, and someone had flushed the toilet.

Torn between the necessity of returning to New York to intercept the manuscript and the necessity of staying in Christiansted to silence Rosamond, Zyzynski finally decided that he would remain long enough to search during the day on Sunday, and then, on Sunday night, leave in time to beat Mrs. Farringford's Monday mail delivery. After announcing his decision to Marco, Jerry, and Chip, he added, "Before you go to bed, take Abbott back to town. We can't keep him in the vault."

Shortly after midnight, with Marco driving, Chip riding shotgun, and Jerry sitting in the back with Abbott, the limousine returned to Christiansted. The empty and silent streets were so tidy, the gutters so clean, that one would never have guessed that hundreds of people had partied all afternoon. Abbott's hotel swung into view; Marco angled into the parking lot and stopped with the engine idling.

"My God," he said, "where's Abbott's car?"

"Oh crap," said Jerry. "I left the keys in the lock when we searched the trunk."

"Not bright," said Chip. "It's probably in Frederiksted by now."

"Then what are we going to *do?*" Marco asked. They'd been counting on that empty trunk.

But their resourcefulness as a team saved them. And four minutes later the limousine was leaving the waterfront, taking them to Pinnacle House and bed.

A little after one o'clock, a lone figure comes striding along King Street toward the waterfront; a young man, thin, four inches over six feet tall, dressed in loose shirt and ragged blue jeans, his long hair twisted and plastered into dusty dreadlocks. Behind him trails an acrid whiff of marijuana. A Rastafarian with his ganja.

He makes a slow circuit of the fort and then moves west along the quay, finally selecting a bench and flopping down at one end of it. He stretches his long legs out before him, digs in his heels, and smokes. The stars, unwinking eyes, stare from a bottomless blue-black bowl. He sits there for a long time staring back at them.

And then he becomes aware of a man sitting at the far end of the bench. How long has he been there? When did he sneak up to silently join him on the bench? Some tourist faggot tryin' to put the make on him? Well, this Rastaman don't take shit off honky faggots. Without turning his head, he continues to smoke, watching the creep out of the corner of his eye. Waiting for him to make a move. But shit, the guy don't even *look* at him. Hasn't looked at him *once*. Well, okay, maybe he's got some spare change, anyway. Won't hurt to ask. But he don't ever blink his eyes, either. The Rasta turns and looks at him squarely. No, he hasn't blinked once.

"Hey, mon," he says in a soft husky voice, "you don't look so good." He leans closer. "Hey, you look *bad*. You wanna toke?" And then: "Oh shit, mon! *Where's your fingers?*"

But Peter Shipley Abbott makes no answer. Just sits there, unblinking, staring across the water in the general direction of Newfoundland, Greenland, and the Big Dipper.

The telephone jangled Trntl out of sleep a little after nine on Sunday morning. She fumbled for her glasses on the night table, grabbed up the receiver, and croaked "N. F. Trntl Associates."

A crisp, wide-awake voice, faint but efficient: "A collect call from St. Thomas, the Virgin Islands. Will you accept?" Of course.

Then, cheerily: "Good morning, Trntl—it's Felix calling from Charlotte Amalie. You awake?"

"Almost," she answered. Cradling the phone between chin and shoulder, she worked on lighting a cigarette. "You sound perky, downright euphoric. Been having a good time?"

"You could say that. Yes, you could. Rosamond and I are holed up in a quaint little hotel surrounded by bougainvillea. On her credit card."

"I take it this call is a report," Trntl said drily, "and not a greeting to say 'wish-you-were-here'."

"I can't truthfully say I wish you were here," said Felix. "Though you'd have been more than welcome in St. Croix yesterday. Here's a run-down. Zyzynski did have the cadenza, but he hadn't purchased it from a third party. It was one of his goons who stole it from you in Baltimore. Zyzynski wanted Rosamond to verify its authenticity, and then learn to play it and record it for him. He was going to keep the manuscript for his private collection, and keep *her*, too."

"For his collection?" Trntl asked.

"As his mistress. Zyzynski tried to seduce her on Friday night, but crapped out with too much champagne. Rosamond escaped, taking the cadenza with her. On Saturday she mailed the manuscript to Mrs. Farringford; it'll probably get there Monday or Tuesday. You're to call Mrs. Farringford to let her know the cadenza's coming. Also, Mrs. Sternberg to let her know her airplane will be home shortly. I've already contacted the pilot in Christiansted and told him to fly over and pick us up tomorrow."

"Tomorrow," said Trntl.

"Should be home by suppertime."

"I'll tell Mrs. Sternberg. Is Abbott with you?"

"We haven't seen Abbott since yesterday afternoon. If the pilot can't find him in Christiansted, Abbott will have to make his own way home."

"Why aren't *you* in Christiansted?

"Zyzynski sent his men to find Rosamond and take her back to his estate. So we hired a boat to take us to St. Thomas. Rosamond is contacting the FBI."

"Does Zyzynski know the cadenza was mailed to Mrs. Farringford?"

"No. Or, put it this way: I don't see how he could. Rosamond pitched it into the first mailbox she saw."

"I'm glad things are going so well," Trntl said. "Mini-vacation, and all."

"See you tomorrow."

"Right." She hung up, put coffee on to perk, went to the bathroom, and, after a quick shower, padded back to the kitchen in her bathrobe to boil an egg for breakfast.

After eating, she dialed the Farringford house. Clara answered. "I decided to stay for the weekend," she said. "Mother's at church. Shall I have her call you back?"

"Shouldn't be necessary," Trntl said. "You'll be glad to know that Rosamond Foxe has recovered the cadenza and mailed it to your mother from St. Croix. It should arrive tomorrow or Tuesday. Victor Zyzynski had planned to keep it for himself, but Rosamond got it away from him. Evidently Zyzynski doesn't know that Rosamond mailed the cadenza, but he wants it back for his private collection. When it arrives, it's crucial that you get it to Lunner & Dinch at once."

Clara said, "This is wonderful news! But how did Mr. Zyzynski obtain the manuscript?"

"It was one of his men who stole it from me at the bus station."

"Good Lord! Well then, is Rosamond all right?"

"Yes, she's in St. Thomas with Felix McKay. They'll be return- ing tomorrow."

"I'll tell Mother as soon as she comes in. She'll be so pleased!"

Next Trntl called Mrs. Sternberg. "And the Foundation plane will return tomorrow evening," she concluded, "—with a detour to St. Thomas to pick up Rosamond and Mr. McKay."

"I'm relieved that Rosamond's safe," said Mrs. Sternberg. "Is she going to charge Zyzynski with kidnapping?"

"She's contacting the FBI."

"Good. But I won't feel easy till the cadenza's in Dinch's hands."

"Nor I," said Trntl.

"Send me a bill for any expenses your firm has incurred," said Mrs. Sternberg. "I insist."

"You're very generous," Trntl said.

"It's *my* fault we've had this problem at all," Mrs. Sternberg countered. "It's one way of making restitution."

Her calls completed, Trntl quickly read several sections of the *Sunday Times,* washed the breakfast dishes, then put on a record- ing of Buffy Sainte-Marie and settled down to work on her quilt.

As was nearly always the case when she returned from church, Mrs. Farringford was in a foul mood. When she paid the cab-driv- er (not bothering to tip him) and started up the steps to her front door, she was still stewing about the sermon, which today she'd found especially irritating. For thirty minutes she'd been forced to fidget in her pew while the Reverend Dr. Stroop self-righteously inveighed against the worldliness of his congregation. Today he'd used the prophet Isaiah as a club to beat them with: old Isaiah, railing against the women of Jerusalem, their haughtiness and finery; denouncing their ornaments and expensive dresses, their feminine charms and alluring ways; warning them that God would replace their fragrance with stink, their nicely-coiffed hair with scabby baldness, their gorgeous fabrics with sackcloth, their beau- ty with burning.

And she, fresh from the hairdresser's with a perm and tint, sitting there in her lovely new suit with matching accessories purchased just last week at Bloomingdale's! Why, it was as though the Rev. Dr. Stroop had been aiming his barbs directly at her. He might as well have pointed his finger. She didn't know why she persisted in subjecting herself to this weekly trauma. Well, next Sunday she wouldn't go. If there were enough empty seats and a corresponding emptiness in the collection plate, Dr. Stroop would get the message and be forced to clean up his act.

When Clara heard her mother's key in the lock, she ran to meet her; and while Mrs. Farringford pulled off her gloves and hung up her coat, Clara repeated the whole of Trntl's news. "And the cadenza will be coming in the mail tomorrow or Tuesday! She says we should get it to Silas Dinch immediately."

Mrs. Farringford shook her head in amazement. "You mean to tell me after all this time—after the fruitless searching, the thefts and violence, the murders—after we'd assumed the cadenza was gone forever—that here, at last, it's being delivered to our very doorstep? Clara, I'll believe it only when I see it." Yet she was moving about excitedly, clasping and unclasping her hands, touching the surfaces of tables and chairs, pausing before a gilt-framed mirror to fluff her hair. "Your father would be astounded if he could know all the grief he set in motion by writing the cadenza. Astounded—and quietly pleased."

"*Pleased*, Mother?"

"Yes, I think so. For all his genius—and who knows, perhaps as an inescapable part of it—your father could be extremely insensitive and cruel. He wrote the cadenza here, in the studio, but never played it while I was in the house. In September, 1947, when he was finishing the concerto, he told me the cadenza was the finest music he'd ever written. I begged him to play it for me—but he refused. He said that, to be fully understood and appreciated, it would have to be heard as part of the complete concerto, with full orchestra—and of course that wouldn't be possible till his concert tour. I offered to go with him on the tour, but he said, No, he wanted to go alone. He always went alone. Not once after 1937 did I get to hear him play an out-of-town concert. This time, he insisted that I stay with you and Anton. I offered to call Aunt Wilma, to have her stay with you. He wouldn't hear of it. Said he was negotiating a New York performance for January, and I could hear it then. But of course it never happened. I hated him for that. And I've always envied those who got to hear him perform it, always re-

senting their privilege and good fortune—denied to me. The lucky
ones. The favored ones." Her tone had become so bitter that Clara
was alarmed.

"At least you'll get to hear the music now," she said quickly.
"Rosamond or Peter will be happy to premiere it."

"Yes, we can be thankful for that," said Mrs. Farringford. "But
it won't be the same."

"I've already called Anton," said Clara. "He was delighted with
the news. He'll come by tomorrow after work to see if the cadenza's arrived. And oh yes, Miss Trntl said that we should call Mr.
Dinch."

"I'll call his office the first thing tomorrow morning," said
Mrs. Farringford. "Well, Clara, this turn of events requires a ma-
jor celebration. Would you like to go out for brunch? How about
Carmody's? It'll be my treat."

Monday, March 16

Intent on his sorting, the mail carrier moved slowly up the
street unaware of the five pairs of eyes measuring his progress.
Watching through heavy brocade drapes from the bay window
of the large brownstone two doors farther on: the eyes of Mrs.
Farringford and Clara. Peering through smoked windows of the
gray car parked across the street: those of Marco, Jerry, and
Chip.

Having cased the house quite early that morning, they now
sat in their car with box lunches and an ice chest filled with cans
of soda pop. They'd surveyed the approaches to the house—alley,
back door, basement areaway—determined the location of the telephone wires, and observed that, rather than a mailbox, the house
possessed an old-fashioned mail-slot in the solid front door. If
Abbott had been telling the truth, if the cadenza had indeed been
mailed to this address, it probably would arrive today or tomorrow. Since Zyzynski didn't want to risk knocking over the mail carrier and going through his bag, they'd have to wait until the mail
was delivered and then determine whether or not the cadenza was
in the batch. With an outside mailbox, it would've been easy. The
mail-slot meant they'd have to get into the house to know if the

manuscript had come. To accomplish this, they'd devised a simple plan requiring only a small box of tools and three gray uniforms.

As soon as the mail carrier slid the mail through the slot and descended the steps, the three men piled out of the car. Jerry disappeared down the narrow areaway between the Farringford house and its neighbor to the west, hurrying straight to the rear, where he cut the telephone wires. In their dull gray uniforms Marco and Chip marched together up the front steps and knocked on the door.

Mrs. Farringford opened it and stared at them inquisitively.

"Sorry to bother you, ma'am," Chip said, with a business-like, apologetic smile. "We're from the telephone company. A key transformer has blown in the substation servicing this neighborhood, and many phones are dead. We're trying to determine the extent of the shutdown. May we please come in to see if yours is working?"

"Yes, come in. It was working earlier today."

She pointed them to the telephone on a table halfway down the hall; Marco went to it, picked up the receiver with his back to them, and fiddled a bit. Chip hung back near the doorway, where a younger woman was shuffling through the newly-arrived mail. Small envelopes, many of them with business logos, some sort of book-sale catalog, and a glossy magazine. "It's all fairly routine, Mother," the younger woman said. "Junk mail mostly, and a letter from Aunt Wilma."

"Let me have the letter," the older woman said.

"I'm afraid your phone is out of order," Marco announced, rejoining them. "Sorry about the inconvenience. We'll continue to monitor the situation and will check back with you tomorrow about the same time."

"Well, it *is* an inconvenience," the older woman said. She closed the door after them.

"Maybe it will come tomorrow," said Clara. "I was planning to go back to Boston in the morning, but I don't have to be back till Wednesday. I'll wait and go tomorrow evening."

Shortly before five o'clock, Anton Farringford arrived. "I tried to call, but nobody answered the phone." He stood with buttoned overcoat just inside the door. From the studio, Clara's flute flooded the hallway with a cascade of Baroque jigging.

His mother lit a cigarette. "The phone's not working; we never heard it ring. It's a problem with the company. They sent some repairmen out to check things."

"Did the cadenza come?"

"No."

"Then I'll be back tomorrow." He reached for the doorknob.

"Wait," Mrs. Farringford said quickly. "Have you reconsidered your hasty decision regarding my monthly income?"

Anton made a wry face. "No, Mother, I haven't. It was not a hasty decision. It was a long time coming, and long overdue."

She struggled to find a rejoinder, but nothing came. Finally she said plaintively, "I feel I don't know you anymore, Anton. You've—you've *changed* somehow."

"Mother, you've *never* known me," Anton said patiently. "Not as I really am. And yes, I've probably changed from what you *thought* you knew. I'm more like Father than you've ever guessed or realized. And I'm *not* going to change my mind regarding the money."

She inhaled deeply, then jetted smoke from her nostrils. "I'd always thought you a dutiful son—a bit secretive and standoffish, but loyal and worthy of trust—certainly not duplicitous. Now I learn that for years you've deceived me, dissembled your true nature, masked your selfishness, lived a lie, and set me up for this final betrayal! How trusting, how foolish I must've seemed! Why didn't I see through your vicious masquerade? Was it the blindness of mother love? a need to assume the best, out of fear of discovering the worst? falling prey to loneliness and desperate hope? And now I have to wonder what *else* you've been hiding from me!" She laughed mirthlessly. "Thank you—thank you, Anton, for finally opening my eyes. Yes, you're *very* like your father—indeed you are."

Anton found and clutched the doorknob. "For almost thirty years I've provided you a substantial allowance," he said. "Month by month, tick tock like a metronome—even though I knew Grandpa had left you and Aunt Wilma sizable annuities. And Clara—out of her teaching salary and concert fees—has never given you less than two hundred a month. You've had it pretty good. And you'll keep having it pretty good—especially if you keep on saving your aluminum foil and string." This last barb was quite uncalled for, and he felt a twinge of annoyance after flinging it; but *god*, she pissed him off.

Mrs. Farringford sniffed haughtily, extended her free hand in a graceful rolling motion, and snapped her fingers two inches from his nose. He recoiled from the flash of her scarlet nails. "Leave Clara out of this!" she said. "She's always done everything she could; I've no complaints on that score. She's been dutiful, and loyal, affectionate, and concerned with my welfare. None of this duplicity, this sneaking around wearing a false face, hiding from me things I've every right to know. *She's* not a hypocrite!"

They became aware that the music had ceased; that Clara, cradling her flute, was coming toward them down the hall. She took charge of the sudden silence: "Shame on you both. Nattering at each other like spoiled fifth-graders! I'm trying to practice, and all I hear is yip! yip! yip! What's *with* you two? Seems like there's a fight every time you get together."

"It's not *my* wish," said Anton. "Not *my* doing."

"Don't put the blame on *me!*" his mother cried. "You've got someplace to escape to—your apartment in Queens, and that Bidwell woman you've been living with for over a year. Oh, yes! you're surprised I knew that, aren't you? Hah! I know more about you than you think, Anton! That woman is more important to you than I am. *That's* clear. But *I* have no escape. I'm stuck here in this gloomy house with taxes going up, strange people begging for handouts at every corner, and week by week the garbage piling deeper on the sidewalks. I'm trapped, with barely enough to live on. *I* can't move to Queens!"

Crimson with embarrassment that his mother had breached his wall of secrecy, mortified by her deigning to let him bask in delusional security by archly not telling him she knew of Twila, Anton snatched open the door and stormed out onto the stoop. This was worse—*far* worse—than her finding his condoms when he was sixteen. Going down the steps, he shouted, "For all I care, you can rent out the upstairs rooms!"

Mrs. Farringford slammed the door behind him. "You see," she said to Clara, "that's what I've had to put up with. First he slashed my monthly allowance by forty per cent. Now he's cut me off completely. For all my economies—and you know how hard I work at saving money—I can hardly get by. What am I going to do, Clara? I can't take in roomers. You've been generous over the years, and for that I'm grateful. But now I feel I'm at the brink. I suppose I could auction off your father's manuscripts and memorabilia. Maybe sell his piano. It's old, but it should bring something." She dabbed at her eyes with a Kleenex and stubbed out the nub of her cigarette.

Clara patted her arm soothingly. "Don't be hasty in making decisions, Mother, and don't give way to despair. I'll talk to Anton and see what's possible. Have you thought about selling this house and moving into a retirement apartment—something smaller, more efficient, cheaper to maintain? Maybe it's time to consider that option. I don't really think Father's piano would bring much money. It's in pretty bad shape."

"I don't want to move into a retirement apartment!" said Mrs. Farringford. "This is my home."

"Anton and I will talk, Mother. We'll study all possibilities. Now, I'd like to get back to practicing. Give me another half hour, and then I'll make tuna sandwiches for supper."

Twice during the afternoon and once in the early evening Trntl had called the Farringford residence to learn if the cadenza had arrived. The telephone rang and rang but nobody answered. Finally she called Anton Farringford, who informed her that the cadenza had not arrived. Frustrated, she did her laundry and her exercises, watched TV, and went to bed.

Tuesday, March 17

At ten o'clock on Tuesday morning, she called again. Again the phone rang and rang with no answer. Concerned for the Farringfords' safety, Trntl decided to visit the brownstone. She pulled Torvald from behind a stack of reference books and together they drove uptown.

Mrs. Farringford opened the front door as they climbed the steps. "I saw you coming from the parlor window," she said.

"I've been trying to call you," said Trntl. "But no one's ever here."

"Oh, Clara and I have been here. Our phone's on the blink; we can't hear it ring, and we can't call out. The phone company's working on it."

"Your son told me the cadenza didn't come yesterday," Trntl said.

"No, we're hoping it'll come today. The mail delivery's due any time now."

"Perhaps you'd let us wait?" Trntl said.

"Of course. Come in." Entering, they were greeted by a languorous flute melody which Trntl recognized from one of her recordings at home. Fauré? Debussy? Boehm? "Clara's practicing in the studio," said Mrs. Farringford. "Let me get her." She hurried to the back of the house.

Torvald went to the telephone, picked up the receiver, listened, dialed. "Couldn't be deader."

"Yet the person calling in hears the phone ringing," said Trntl. "I wonder if we should check the wires coming into the house." Mrs. Farringford and Clara were coming down the hall toward them. "Later," said Torvald.

It had been a bad three days for Victor Zyzynski. When he'd boarded his jet on Sunday night for the trip to New York, he'd been seething with frustration and fury. Rosamond had not been found. She and McKay had vanished utterly. Thwarted, bitter, grouchy from lack of sleep, he'd wanted ferociously to kick ass. But after settling his score with Abbott on Saturday night, there'd been no ass to kick. Now, completely baffled in his hopes and forced by circumstance to quit the field, he'd felt his hostilities balloon beyond endurance, building like a head of steam that had no means of outlet or release.

Zyzynski had spent the whole of his adult life acquiring the resources and devising the means to insure that he would never know frustration, humiliation, or defeat; would never find himself in someone else's power, or be perceived by others as less than omnipotent. But now, in the space of a few hours, he'd been maneuvered into a state of collapse on all these fronts by a conniving little tart who'd managed to worm through his defenses, sniff out his secrets, trick him with lies, wound him severely, and simply walk away.

The keen humiliation he now felt was but a pale foretaste of what undoubtedly would come his way when her story circulated. In a single stroke, she had demolished the structure he'd so carefully and skillfully erected with fifty years' unremitting labor and had rendered him helpless to control his own destiny. Events and circumstances were now proceeding inexorably under their own power, and at their own pace, toward guessable but unthinkable conclusions; and he was left powerless to forestall, or even mitigate, whatever might occur.

Well, at least he'd retrieve the cadenza. It was rightfully his, and he was damn well going to have it back. Unable to sit inactive, swelled up with anger and the need to exact revenge and punishment, he'd decided to take the initiative and come himself to intercept the mail. Since the cadenza hadn't arrived on Monday, it would probably come the day after. Consequently, Tuesday found him hunkered down in his limousine across from the Farringford house, like a spider waiting for its prey. Unshaved since slicing himself on Saturday, unbathed since Sunday night, he now sat sweaty and ripe in the rumpled clothes he'd worn since Monday morning. Determined to begin his vigil early, and so angry, agitated, and depressed that he felt no hunger, Zyzynski had skipped breakfast. But at nine thirty, hunger struck, and Chip was sent to find a grocery store and bring back food.

Thus, Zyzynski's breakfast was an improvised (and messy) affair: two bananas, four tins of sardines—two in oil and two in mustard sauce—a carton of soda crackers, and coffee from a vending machine. Marco, Jerry, and Chip ate doughnuts, beef jerky, and yogurt, a combination which Zyzynski found loathsome. Finally, having eaten, Zyzynski was just fixing himself a whiskey sour from the inbuilt bar when Jerry whispered "Look! It's Trntl and that Grimsson guy coming to the house."

They watched as Mrs. Farringford talked to her visitors and then invited them in. "Okay," said Marco. "How does this change things?"

"It means we can't go inside after the mail's delivered," said Jerry. "The old lady would've been a pushover, but that Torvald guy, he's mean."

"And Trntl knows me," said Marco. "Even the phone company uniform wouldn't fool her."

"Then we've got to knock over the postman before he gets to the mail slot," said Chip. Jerry began fingering his billiard ball and sock.

"On the street?" said Zyzynski. "With all these people? You're being stupid. Even if we got the cadenza, somebody would take down our license number as we drove away. And that would bring on the Feds in ways I can't afford right now. No, you *have* to go in."

Chip said, "I don't think Trntl would recognize *me*. What if I go in the front, and Marco and Jerry go in the back?"

"A pincer movement," said Jerry. "Yeah, I like that."

"Look," said Marco. "Here comes the mailman. Right on time."

Chapter 41

March 17, 1981   (Tuesday)

"While we're waiting," said Clara, "would you like to see Father's studio?"

"Love to," said Trntl, and she and Torvald followed Clara down the long hall. The room was bright with reflected sunlight streaming through the windows. Clara pointed with her flute: "There on the back wall are all the editions of his works . . ."

In the parlor, Mrs. Farringford stood in the bay window watching for the mailman. Yes, there he was, three doors down. She hurried back to the front hall and waited at the mail slot.

In their gray uniforms, Marco, Jerry, and Chip emerged from the limousine; and while the mailman climbed the Farringford steps, Jerry and Marco casually crossed the street to the areaway that led to the back of the house. Following the mailman, Chip saw him push the delivery through the slot, and nodded pleasantly to him as he passed back down the steps to the sidewalk.

Holding her breath, Mrs. Farringford gathered up each item of mail as it came sliding through the slot. Yes! a large brown envelope postmarked Christiansted! She rushed into the parlor and closed the door.

Clara was saying, "And these are recordings of Father's works by various artists. Most of the albums are signed by the performers. Feel free to look at them. It's quite a collection of autographs." Loud knocking at the front door. "It's all right," she said. "Mother will get it. Here, you see: George Gershwin, and Edith Bascomb, Fritz Kreisler, and Arturo Toscanini, Rachmaninoff, and Sybil Greene—" She paused. "No, Mother's *not* answering the door. Excuse me." She hurried out, leaving Trntl and Torvald frantically trying to reshelve the heavy record albums into their proper spaces. "Look!" said Torvald, pointing out the rear window. Trntl peered out and down. Directly below, the tops of two visored gray caps were bobbing toward the back door.

"We'd better see what they're up to," said Trntl. Re-entering the hall, they saw a young man in a gray uniform and visored cap speaking with Clara just inside the front door. He was clearly looking past her, impatiently scanning the room as she talked. "I'll see what's doing at the back of the house," Trntl said to Torvald. "You deal with this one."

"We think we've solved the problem," Chip was saying, "but I need to check your phone." Where the hell was the *mail?* He'd seen the postman just now slide at least eight items through the slot, one of them a brown manila envelope. Stepping toward the phone, he saw Trntl duck through a doorway behind the stairs. Well, he'd simply have to stall till Marco and Jerry joined him. Shit, why wasn't the Viking going with Trntl? Chip picked up the phone, listened, then worked the dial.

"Well?" said Clara.

"Still dead, I'm afraid."

The Viking said, "Let me try it." Chip handed him the receiver. Torvald listened. "It's not working. Are you a repair man?"

"That's right."

"Where are your tools?"

Chip grinned nervously. "Out in the truck."

"Better get 'em," said Torvald. "You've got some repairing to do. I'll go with you." He strode past Chip and opened the outer door for him.

Having no choice, Chip moved toward it. Damn! Where were Marco and Jerry?

On the stoop, Torvald closed the door behind them and looked up and down the street. "Well, where's the truck?"

"Just down the block," said Chip.

Torvald said, "I'll wait for you here."

Chip trotted down the steps and started west along the sidewalk, not glancing at the limousine parked across the street. He didn't even want to guess what Zyzynski must be thinking.

Clara opened the parlor door. "Oh there you are, Mother. The repairman says the phone's *still* not working." Mrs. Farringford was standing near the fireplace, where leaping flames licked hungrily at the logs. On the floor beside her, a pile of envelopes. "Oh! the mail's here. Did the cadenza come?"

Tossing aside a brown envelope ripped lengthwise open, her mother dropped a thin stack of papers into the fire. As they fell, Clara glimpsed music sheets dark with densely inked notes.

Then—unaware of crossing the room—Clara was kneeling on the hearth, bare hands scrabbling at the blazing logs to save the music, her mother clutching her shoulders to yank her backwards, and failing that, throwing her full body weight to slam her sideways; but—still frantically plucking sheets from the flames—Clara twisted her body and shoved back with her shoulder, maintaining her ground, her Mother grasping to pinion her arms, scarlet nails digging in like talons, but Clara, successfully fighting her off, kept grabbing and snatching till—finally—ah! all of the papers were safely out, with only five barely singed at the edges.

Clutching them to her chest and heaving a bottomless sigh, Clara struggled upright, backed quickly away from the fire, her fingers painfully scorched, and stared down at the figure collapsed on the hearth.

"Oh, Mother, how *could* you? Why would you want to burn Father's cadenza?"

Mrs. Farringford hauled herself to her feet, breathless, greatly shaken, her body tensed as though she still intended to wrest the papers from her daughter's grasp. But, seeing Clara's tight mouth and ferocious eyes, she gave it up and sank onto the sofa. Her face, crumpled in upon itself, was half hidden by hanging strands of hair. Through clenched teeth, she hissed "Why? Why do you *think?* To pay him back!" And then, her bitterness spilling forth as from an overturned basin: "He thought he was so clever! That I was blind and stupid. Would he ever play the cadenza for *me?*—oh no! he reserved it for *her!* He didn't think I knew what was going on for all those years. Well, I had eyes and ears. I had friends."

"What are you talking about?" Clara cried.

Mrs. Farringford's eyes sparked and glittered in the firelight. "That Sternberg bitch! *She* was the favored one. *She* got all your father's attention. All the overflow of his creative energy—everything that should've been mine. The cadenza was *hers!* He wrote it for *her! with* her! Can't you see them?—he playing it for her, leering and smirking, and she, breathless with ecstasy, stroking him, making suggestions—*taking my place!* God, how I hated them *and* their goddam love-child!

"And how I *rejoiced* when it disappeared! Yet for twenty years—*twenty!*—I lived in terror that it would come to light and be published—be *played!*—and the whole world would get to enjoy the fruits of your father's betrayal, and applaud my humiliation! But as the years went by, the fear gradually faded, and, like a fool, I came to assume the threat was past. When the manuscript turned up in Baltimore, the shock nearly killed me.

"Then, when it was stolen from Pettigrew, I prayed that the thieves would destroy it. When it was offered for ransom, I prayed that Dinch would never get it back. And then, a miracle! It's delivered to me in the mail!" She looked at her daughter over the back of the couch. "Give it to me, Clara. Now. It's mine. I have a *right* to burn it." Her nails stretched upward, groping.

Utterly dumbfounded, Clara backed away. "Mother, you horrify me!" She seized her flute and ran from the room. In the hall, she heard a thundering crash from the kitchen.

Trusting her instincts to bring her to the back of the house, Trntl had dashed from the rear of the hallway through a small sunroom, past a narrow flight of back stairs rising up into darkness, and into the kitchen. Through the window in the back door she recognized one of the two men coming up the steps: her old friend from Baltimore—Trenchcoat, whom she'd taken to Poe's grave and Druid Hill Park. She shot the deadbolt and wedged a small serving table beneath the knob. But, simultaneously recognizing *her*, the men charged, their combined weight exploding the bolt from the frame, and the door inward.

Knowing that Trntl and Torvald were in the house, they'd come prepared for a fight—Marco with a long, flexible blackjack encased in leather and strapped to his wrist; Jerry with his billiard ball tied into the toe of a long black stocking. In the brief but nasty skirmish that ensued, Trntl had to make do with whatever came to hand. First, a canister of flour, the contents flung into Marco's face. Next, a breadbox and a peppermill aimed at Jerry's head. He ducked them with ease and continued stalking her, smoothly, eyes fixed like a panther's, swinging his stocking in snapping swift circles.

He lunged. Trntl leaped backward, the toe of the sock whizzing past her nose. She snatched up a broom that stood against the wall; and, holding it before her like a quarterstaff, edged toward the sunroom door. White with flour, half-blinded, still coughing and choking, Marco lurched into her path, blocking her exit, and she found herself suddenly cornered beside a tall glass-fronted china cabinet.

Again Jerry swung the sock. Trntl raised the broomstick to meet it—and the weighted stocking wrapped around it in a tight coil. Abruptly, she was face to face with Jerry, who grabbed at her throat with his free hand. She doubled him up with a knee to the groin; and with the broom between them, they both swung around and slammed hard against the front of the china cabinet—which, with a shattering of glass, rocked back against the wall and then bounced forward.

Lengthwise it fell across the kitchen, buckling at the midpoint as the top smashed into the opposite wall; the doors popped open, and a huge dinner service of bone-white china cascaded onto the hardwood floor. Twisting away from the path of the fall, Marco wrenched his knee; Jerry, closer in, was struck in the face by a soup tureen; and Trntl fell painfully against a corner of the large butcher's block that stood in the center of the room. The crash left them stunned. *Trntl scrambled past Marco and stumbled across the sunroom into the hall. Clara was staring at her from the front entryway.*

"They're after the cadenza!" Trntl shouted. "Get the police!" Marco's fingers raked her shoulder. She spun around, kicked him in the kneecap, and darted up the narrow backstairs immediately to her right. As she reached the top, footsteps were thudding up behind her in hot pursuit.

Clara made a quick decision. She stepped back into the parlor and closed the door. Where could she hide the cadenza? Her mother was slumped on the sofa staring into the fire. Not this room, clearly. Ah, of course! She set down her flute, took the twelve sheets of manuscript and stacked them neatly. Then, doing her best to ignore the pain in her singed fingers, she rolled the papers into a tight cylinder which she slid into the flute, pushing them as far into the tube, and as far away from the end, as possible. Satisfied that they were effectively hidden, she opened the door and stepped into the entrance hall to get her coat. From upstairs she could hear running footsteps and slamming doors.

She hurried onto the stoop and called to Torvald who was standing on the sidewalk: "Miss Trntl's on the second floor and needs help. Someone's chasing her—she says they're after the cadenza. I'm going for the police."

Torvald bolted up the steps and into the house. Clara ran down to the sidewalk and—holding the flute in the crook of her arm—began jogging west, toward Central Park. She'd gone less than a hundred feet when she saw running toward her the telephone man whom Torvald had escorted from the house. One of Them! She shunted into the areaway between two buildings, ran to the back alley, and followed it east to the end of the block. No one seemed to be chasing her. At the cross-street she turned south, and, half walking, half trotting, covered another block, then turned east once again. She slowed now to a rapid walk, continually looking over her shoulder for signs of pursuit. She'd seen no police at all.

At curbside, garbage lined the sidewalks—bulging plastic bags, cardboard boxes filled to overflowing, great ever-present heaps of refuse, day in, day out awaiting pickup. And sure enough, occasionally at cross-streets she could see in the distance garbage trucks doing their job—great yawning mouths into which, at each stop, trash was hoisted and shoveled—halting only long enough to engorge their loads, then, grinding their gears and spewing noxious fumes, moving on to the next stop. The people she passed—young women in slacks and car-coats, panhandlers, well-dressed matrons with shopping bags, winos lurking in doorways, young men in three-piece suits with briefcases, teenagers sporting bizarre hairdos—all of them intent on their own lives—gave her hardly a glance.

By now she was tired; though the pain in her fingers had abated somewhat, her brain felt numb; she needed coffee. But she'd left the house without money. Well, she'd walk to the apartment of her friend Melinda, less than a mile now, and call the police from there.

Pursued up the backstairs to the second floor, Trntl had raced toward the front of the house to descend by the front staircase. But Marco, swinging his blackjack, was coming up those steps, his dark hair matted white with flour, his eyes as steady as a cobra's. With Jerry on her heels, Trntl ducked into a side room, rushed through a communicating door to the room behind, even as Jerry came barging through the hall door she'd entered by. She slammed this connecting door, turned the key in the lock, and left the room through *its* door opening onto the hall. Marco, having just reached the top of the stairs, shouted "Get her, Jerry. She has the cadenza!"

As Trntl descended the backstairs, she could hear Jerry right behind her. From the sunroom she saw Marco running toward her along the downstairs hall. In a matter of seconds, Jerry would exit the backstairs behind her. To avoid being sandwiched between the two of them, Trntl leaped into the kitchen, thinking to escape by the back door. Finding her way blocked by the fallen china cabinet and the mound of broken dishes, she turned in desperation, saw another door in the side wall, opened it, and rushed through.

Oh shit. It was a closed pantry dimly lit by one small window high on the outside wall. It contained shelves along the walls and a single naked lightbulb activated with a pull chain. She'd slammed the door behind her to hinder pursuit. Through the thick panels, she heard Jerry shout "Gotcha!", and the click of a key tumbling the lock. She turned on the light. There was no way out. The shelves were filled with canned goods, detergents, floor wax, piles of neatly folded grocery bags, tall stacks and bundles of wrinkly aluminum foil, and seven great balls of string.

"Now," said Jerry through the door. "Where's the cadenza?"

"How should I know?" Trntl snapped. "*I* don't have it. You guys took it from me in Baltimore. Don't you remember?"

"Marco says you have it."

"Marco's wrong."

"We can always unlock the door and see if you do."

"That would be a mistake," said Trntl. "I have weapons in here you wouldn't believe."

"You're bluffing," said Jerry. But he didn't unlock the door.

Torvald, hearing the thump of running feet in the upstairs hallway, had charged up the front staircase to aid Trntl. Six steps from the top, he met Marco plunging down. With precise aim, Marco struck with the blackjack, bashing Torvald on the top of the head as he rushed past him. Torvald gave a groan and went kabumping down the stairs.

Trntl was deciding what her weapons would be if Jerry *did* unlock the door. There was a mop she could use as she had the broom. She could always throw canned goods, and there was a squirt bottle of ammonia-based glass cleaner. Then—

Marco's voice: "I just knocked out that Grimsson guy. Hey, Chip just came in."

Jerry: "Chip, stay at the front of the house and hunt for the mail."

Marco: "Didn't you get the cadenza from Trntl?"

Jerry: "She's locked in the closet. Says she doesn't have it."

Marco: "Well, we can't just stand here. The Chief's waiting."

Chip, having found no evidence of the mail delivery in the front hall, entered the parlor, where he found a cozy blaze in the fireplace, old lady Farringford flopped on the sofa, and a pile of envelopes on the floor. One of them was large and postmarked the Virgin Islands. But the envelope was torn and empty. He turned to the woman and roughly jostled her shoulder. "Where's the cadenza?"

She didn't look at him, seemed almost unaware of his presence. "Clara took it."

Clara: the middle-aged woman he'd talked to earlier—who'd come onto the sidewalk carrying a flute. Who'd ducked between two buildings and disappeared as he was coming back to help Marco and Jerry.

Chip ran from the room and shouted down the hall to the kitchen, "Come on, guys! The cadenza's getting away!"

Trntl heard the key pulled from the lock. Then running footsteps toward the front of the house. A door slamming. Then nothing. She began making her own noise.

Torvald, coming to his senses at the foot of the front stairs, gingerly touched the spongy lump on the crown of his head and grimaced with pain. He gradually became aware of someone pounding on a door. A muffled voice—Trntl's—raised in angry impatience: "Help! Get me out of here!" Out of *where?* He climbed to his feet and tottered into the kitchen. My god, what a mess of broken china! And there: the door behind which Trntl was yelling. Locked, of course. "They seem to be gone, Trntl," he said through the panels. "There's no key on this side."

"Well, there isn't one on *this* side, either, as you may have guessed."

"I'll find Mrs. Farringford and see if there's a spare."

"I take it the cadenza *did* come in the mail?" Trntl said testily. "*I* certainly haven't seen it."

"I don't know. I've been confused since we came."

"Get me out of here," said Trntl, "and we can be confused together."

When Marco, Jerry, and Chip piled into the limousine, Zyzynski cried: "Did you get it? What the hell was going on in there? Why did Clara Farringford come out?"

"*She* has the cadenza!" Chip said.

"Clara? Drive, Marco! we've got to find her!"

"Which way did she go?" Marco asked.

"Between those buildings," said Chip.

"There's an alley at the rear," Jerry said.

Marco had already started down the street.

"She was dressed in navy blue slacks and a light-blue sweater," Chip told him. "She has kinda reddish hair."

They'd turned the corner. Zyzynski opened a compartment and drew out two pairs of binoculars, handing one to Jerry, one to Chip. North. South. Nothing. "Go east," said Zyzynski, and Marco turned into the cross-street. The search continued, east and south.

While waiting in the car, Zyzynski had unbuttoned his vest, loosened his tie, and removed his shoes. His thick neck and whiskery chins had rubbed a greasy yellow ring all round his collar. His fingernails were bitten short, and he was quite unaware of the dribbled fish oil on his vest, the mustard smears on his right sleeve and left lapel, the urine stains around his fly. The ashtray was filled with half-smoked cigars whose stench was overpowering. "May I?" said Chip, and, without waiting for a reply, emptied the ashtray out the window. Zyzynski seemed not to notice; with his mouth dropped open, he was scanning the sidewalks with the concentration of a hunting ferret.

"Which way?" said Marco. "North or south?"

"South," said Zyzynski

Crisscross. East, West. Scan. Scan. "Goddamned one-way streets!" Zyzynski hissed.

"There!" shouted Jerry, directing Chip's binoculars. "Yep," said Chip. "That's her."

"All right then," said Zyzynski. "Take her."

Despite the cool air, Clara had worked up a sweat. She'd just transferred her flute to her right hand when, with a screech of brakes, a long dark car pulled up beside her. The doors swung open and two men in gray jumped out, leaped through and over the garbage piled at the curb and seized her even as she flexed to run. As they muscled her across the sidewalk toward the car, Clara screamed "Help! Murder!", kicking at them, thrashing with her arms. Her foot, locking behind the taller man's ankle, tripped him, and all three of them went down onto the fat garbage bags, the rotten fruit, damp cardboard, and broken crates. Though Clara fought valiantly, the two men finally wrestled her to her feet and tumbled her into the back seat of the limousine. They slammed the doors, and the car swiftly moved off into traffic. Six, seven people had watched the snatch with varying degrees of curiosity and interest, but when the car had gone and there was nothing more to see, they went on about their business.

Zyzynski looked down at Clara on the floor of the car. "Give me the cadenza," he commanded.

"I don't have it," Clara said, struggling to regain her breath.

"Your mother said you took it. Now give it here. It's mine. I want it now!"

"I tell you, I don't have it!"

"Pull over, Marco. Jerry, come back and join us." The car pulled over, Jerry got into the back, and the car resumed its aimless cruising.

"This is your last chance," Zyzynski said. "I'm not a patient man. Give me the cadenza, and we'll let you out."

Clara was trying to adjust her glasses to sit comfortably on her nose. The frames had been bent in the struggle, but at least she still had both lenses. "For the last time," she said tiredly, "I don't have it."

Zyzynski sighed, took out a fresh cigar. "Jerry, Chip, take off her clothes."

Jerry held her arms; Chip began unbuttoning her sweater. "No!" Clara cried, trying to twist away from his fingers. "I had the cadenza when I left the house, but I don't anymore! It's rolled up in my flute!"

Zyzynski dropped his cigar. "And where's the flute?" Eyes wide with terror.

"I dropped it when your bully boys grabbed me."

"Oh my god!" Zyzynski shrieked. "Marco! Turn around, get back to where we picked her up!"

Around the block they went, the traffic lights against them. There were agonizing waits. Zyzynski sat rigid, staring out the window, clutching his knees and making little grunting sounds. Jerry and Chip continued holding Clara to the floor.

Finally, the car slowed against the curb and came to a stop. "This is where we caught her," Marco said. "Out, Chip," said Zyzynski. "Find the flute."

After a diligent search, Chip leaned in to report. "No flute, Chief. Sidewalk's clean. They've even picked up the garbage."

For five seconds, dead silence: then Zyzynski yelled "Find the garbage truck!" Chip barely had time to scramble in before the car leaped away from the curb.

Marco followed the cleaned sidewalk for three blocks. They saw no truck ahead of them. Scanning down a cross-street, Zyzynski cried, "There it is!" The car skidded to a halt. Two blocks away, a truck was starting up after a stop, its gaping maw filled with re-fuse, a strip of newsprint protruding like a tongue. Zyzynski cried "After it!", as the truck stopped again.

"Chief, I think that one's on a different route," said Jerry. "It hasn't been on this street. There's lots of routes."

"Lots of *trucks*," said Chip.

"Well, Godammit, one of them has the flute!" said Zyzynski. "And we're damn well going to find it! Drive, Marco."

"Wait!" Clara cried from the floor. "You don't need me any-more. Please let me out."

"Shut up," said Zyzynski.

The car continued as before, paralleling the cleaned curb. But abruptly in the middle of a block, garbage again lay heaped and piled. "What happened?" Zyzynski cried.

"The truck's full," said Marco. "They've prob'ly gone off to dump it."

Jerry trained his binoculars on the street. "There's a truck four blocks ahead moving with the flow."

"That's the one!" cried Zyzynski. "Catch it, Marco."

But traffic was getting heavier, and Marco found it difficult to maintain speed. "Faster!" Zyzynski said. "It's up there! I see it!"

Jerry said, "It's going to cross the bridge,".

"Then *we* cross the bridge," said Zyzynski.

Lots of vehicles crossed the bridge—including three additional garbage trucks that had converged at the bridge access. Jerry was able to keep the truck they were pursuing in view; but during a momentary slowdown in their lane, two of the other trucks passed them—nearly identical in appearance to the one they followed. Chewing an unlit cigar, Zyzynski was making an awkward fumble of putting on his shoes.

Traffic was only a little less hectic in Queens. As their lane slowed again, the third truck passed them. But finally Jerry said, "*Our* truck's turning off!"

So were the others. The limousine followed them into a side road which, skirting water through scrubby industrial wasteland, led them onto a huge landfill that reared like a barren headland above the bay. Here, undulating hills of garbage, heaped mountains of trash were being worked and moved about, compacted and smoothed by great earth-moving machines. Here and there columns of smoke rose smudge-like from the smoldering refuse. Clouds of seagulls wheeled and dipped with raucous cries.

The truck they'd been following and five more besides were moving out onto the headland to disgorge their loads. Four empty trucks were leaving, and still others were freshly arriving from the city.

"Stop the car!" Zyzynski flung open his door and lurched onto the road. As he ran toward the truck they'd been following, he bellowed over his shoulder, "Hurry, hurry!" Jerry and Chip followed him onto the landfill. Marco set the brake, and without even a glance at Clara, dashed after them.

Running was difficult. The landfill surface was uneven, deceptive. Sometimes soft and spongy; sometimes slippery with puckered slime; sometimes thinly crusted, concealing things that collapsed or rolled sideways underfoot. Coiled bedsprings clutched at their ankles. Streamers of shredded office work wrapped about their legs. And all the while, newspapers and bread wrappers, whipping in the breeze, danced toward them across the desolation. The smoke plumes rising about them were like fumeroles venting from the plugged throat of a quiescent but wakening volcano. And everywhere, hundreds, thousands of gulls flapped and soared, circled and dived, screamed and nattered.

At the truck Jerry had identified as "theirs", Zyzynski scrambled up to the cab just as the driver was starting his dump: "Wait!

Stop!" he shouted. The driver looked down in surprise. "We're hunting a flute! It's in your truck!"

The driver stared at him incredulously. "What the hell—! A *flute?* You've got to be kidding!"

Jerry asked, "Weren't you collecting on the East Side?"

The driver laughed. "Naw. I been in Times Square."

"Then which of these trucks was on the East Side?" Zyzynski shouted.

"Beats me," said the driver, and proceeded to dump.

Zyzynski dashed to the back of the truck, dropped to his knees, and began digging through the garbage. "Hurry, hurry!" he cried to Marco and Chip, and they too knelt to rummage through the trash. Jerry ran to the next nearest truck to inquire where *it* had been collecting . . .

Clara Farringford crept from the limousine, and keeping the car between her abductors and herself, bent low and ran back along the road to the landfill entrance. Here she flagged a departing truck. To the driver she said, "Those men in the car tried to kidnap me. Do you have a radio? Can you call the police?" The driver looked her up and down; then, staring past the distant limousine, studied the four men who were scrambling over and wading knee-deep through heaps of garbage.

"What are they doing?" he asked.

"They're hunting a flute. Please, can you call the police?"

"Sure," he said. "And hey, I'm heading back to Manhattan. Do you want a ride?"

In the smoke and stench, hands raw from digging, Zyzynski runs from truck to truck, from heap to heap, pawing through wads of insulation, cat-pan litter, grapefruit rinds, gnawed pork chop bones; dropping on his knees to scrutinize a length of pipe or peer beneath a toilet seat; fighting off the snags of tangled baling wire; plunging ankle-deep in boggy squish.

Trucks depart, new trucks arrive. Nearby, a bulldozer moves methodically back and forth, shifting the mounds and leveling the surface. Zyzynski shouts to the driver, "Stop doing that! You're covering things up!" The engine roars, the blade keeps pushing. Zyzynski shakes his fist: "You've got to stop!"

The driver gives him the finger. Shouts back: "Get the hell outta here! You're in my way."

"Who owns this landfill?" Zyzynski yells. "I'll buy it!" The gulls shriek back at him. "Do you hear me? I've got the money! I'll buy the whole dump!"

Let's step back a bit in time. Clara Farringford has just been pulled into Zyzynski's car. Garbage still lines the street. Not two minutes after the limousine has driven off, a white-haired man with threadbare clothes comes shuffling along the curb, taking stock of things before the garbage truck arrives. It's only half a block behind him. Today has not been fruitful, but he knows from long experience that patience is rewarded. What's that? Between two plastic bags, a silver gleam. O my! Well, well. A flute!

In good shape, too. Just one small dent. He brushes it off, and, clutching it close, goes quickly to a pawnshop that he knows three blocks away.

"It belonged to my Uncle Max," he tells the broker. "It means a lot to me."

The broker looks it over. "Where's the case?"

"There ain't no case. There's just the flute."

"No case, a good-sized dent. Three dollars."

"Can't you make it four? It's not that big a dent. My Uncle Max—"

"Three. It's not worth four."

And three it is. Carefully the seller folds the money into his shoe and hits the street.

The pawnbroker takes the flute to the front of the shop and puts it in his window with the other five—all of which have cases.

To order Robert D. Sutherland's novel

STICKLEWORT AND FEVERFEW

(355 pp.; 74 illustrations by the author, and a map)
fill out the following and send with check or money order
(credit cards not accepted) to

The PIKESTAFF PRESS
P.O. Box 127
Normal, Illinois 61761 USA

Name_____

Street address _____

City _____

State _____ ZIP _____

Please send me the following:

_____ copies of *Sticklewort and Feverfew* at $9.00 each.
        ISBN (10-digit): 0-936044-01-2
        ISBN (13-digit): 978-0-936044-01-9

Total for books ordered-------------------------- _____

Shipping:

$3 for first book; $2 for each additional   _____

Illinois addresses, add 7.25% sales tax per copy_____

TOTAL ENCLOSED: _____

The Pikestaff Press is an imprint of Pikestaff Publica-
tions, Inc. The press may be contacted by telephone at
(309) 452-4831 and e-mail at *staff@pikestaffpress.com*.

To order additional copies of

THE FARRINGFORD CADENZA

fill out the following and send with check or money order
(credit cards not accepted) to

The PIKESTAFF PRESS
P.O. BOX 127
Normal, Illinois 61761 USA

Name _____

Street address _____

City _____

State _____ ZIP _____

Please send me the following:

_____ copies of *The Farringford Cadenza* at *$14.95* each.
        ISBN: 978-0-936044-08-8

Total for books ordered   ------------------------- _____
Shipping:
$3 for first book; $2 for each additional   _____
Illinois addresses, add 7.25% sales tax per copy _____

TOTAL ENCLOSED: _____

The Pikestaff Press is an imprint of Pikestaff Publica-
tions, Inc. The press may be contacted by telephone at
(309) 452-4831 and e-mail at *staff@pikestaffpress.com*.